RIDDLES IN TIME

Tom McCloud

Volume One

Library of Congress Control Number (LCCN): 2009902234

Riddles In Time: a novel / by Tom McCloud — 1st ed.

Summary: When sixteen-year-old Melinda and her friends agree to find a lost professor during a summer archaeology contest, they unintentionally embark on a heroic quest. Passing through ancient time portals, they confront primeval creatures, historic pirates, and a secret connection to the world's biggest archaeological mysteries.

ISBN-13: 978-1-439-23209-5 / ISBN-10: 1-439-23209-1 (Paperback)

[1. Action & Adventure—Fiction. 2. Museums—Fiction. 3. Contests—Fiction. 4. Global Star-Aviation—Fiction. 5. Texas (State)—Fiction. 6. Houston (City)—Fiction. 7. Enchanted Rock State Park—Fiction.] 1. Title.

Printed in the United States of America

For Michael and Amanda,
My Reason and Motivation.
《》

Chapter One

CHANGE OF PLANS

SLAM!

Melinda Taylor dropped her book bag like a useless scarf onto the foyer's exquisitely handcrafted wood table placed below a vast chandelier. Eager to embark on her long-awaited summer plans, the slender 16-year old glanced upward from underneath the massive twelve-foot wide chandelier. It overflowed with row upon row of dazzling hand-cut crystals; reminding her of an enormous wedding cake narrowing into smaller sections as it ascended to the lofty ceiling.

"It's bigger than a suburban," she recollected her friend Allen's remark.

Comparing the weight of the lighting structure to the huge SUV, caused Melinda to speculate if the significant load had stripped the connection bolts throughout the years, and if so, she imagined it crashing down on visitors. She visualized it shattering amongst the mayhem of screaming gown-clad women, husbands, and white-coated servers during one of her mother's celebrated black tie parties.

To detach herself of the gloomy thought, Melinda stared affectionately at thousands of multicolored prism shapes dancing in tempo high above her. Filtered sunshine passed through the beveled cut crystals, producing sparkling reflections on the rounded walls above a magnificent elliptical mahogany railed staircase.

Relaxed in her familiar home surroundings, she strolled noisily in Louis Vuitton shoes across the vast polished marble floors, until she hesitated briefly to study her likeness within an ornate wall mirror. Pleased with how her lustrous dark hair, eyes, and long eyelashes naturally accentuated her high cheekbones, she was generally happy with her facial appearance and how her cinnamon tinted skin made her white teeth shine. Contented her new forehead blemish was not too noticeable; Melinda passed through an impressive molded archway, which separated the entry from a tennis court-sized family room. Skillfully navigating stylish furnishings, she approached a chef compliant dream kitchen, and cheerfully smelled the wonderful aroma of brownies baking.

Echoes quickly reverberated throughout the large kitchen from her hard-soled shoes on the wood flooring, inlaid with imported Italian limestone. Louisa, leaning into the combination steam and convection oven, spun suddenly at hearing the clamorous footsteps. The apple-shaped cook rapidly placed her hand to her chest and inhaled deeply to catch her breath.

"OHH MELINDA — you scare me," she gasped in a halting Argentine accent, emphasizing the creased worry lines in her age worn appearance.

"I bake your favorite brownies before you come home, but ran out of mix and hurry to buy more at store," she said faintly, still winded in her constricting black and white staff uniform. "There no enough time to bake them before you come home from school. Sorry dear; they not ready yet. Sit — I get you a drink until they done," the pleasant cook offered as she closed the oven door.

Melinda smiled caringly at the older woman, and threw her arms around the shorter woman's plump neck.

"Louisa, you're always taking such sweet care of me. Why don't you sit while I get you something to drink?" Melinda offered her, while she pointed at a decorative island counter seat.

"No, no honey, how it appear if you wait on hired help — *especially* on last day of school year?" Louisa exclaimed with a twinkle in her eye.

"It would look like I care about someone who cares even more about me. Now you sit, while I worry about what we're going to drink," Melinda replied saucily, and stepped close to one of the two Sub-Zero refrigerators.

Just as Melinda anticipated upon opening the door, she found a glass pitcher filled with strawberry lemonade, inclusive with both lemon and strawberry slices, reflecting her image in the rounded sides. She grasped the cold handle, and with a slight twist, set the tart lemonade onto the granite counter. Next, she removed two Waterford glasses from an elegant French style cabinet and positioned each below the icemaker's shoot. Falling ice produced tinkling sounds from bouncing inside the leaded crystal before she poured the lemonade.

Melinda offered a brimming glass of ruby-pink lemonade to Louisa, and extracted one of the hinged chairs to sit next to her at the island counter before drinking. Observing her ice-cubes roll and settle, Melinda noticed her glass begin to frost with condensation from the chilled drink, outlining her still warm fingerprints. Watching the color soften to a melon pink from the melting ice, she enjoyed a lengthy swallow.

"Louisa, I believe this is your finest lemonade yet!" Melinda exclaimed as she placed a slim russet hand on the cook's sloped and rounded back.

"Melinda, for *you*, I make only best," Louisa boasted in a meaningful way.

"Ah, you're going to spoil me with that kind of talk," Melinda giggled, familiar with sharing her feelings with the mature woman.

"Truly Melinda, I wish my daughters be more like you! They started liking boys, and seemed to turn into someone else's kids," she paused as if remembering something distressing from the past, and then she added with a new smile, "When you get a serious boy fever, I hope you don't change on me," Louisa said hopefully.

"I hope you never change either, when I get the boy fever. I love you just the way you are too," Melinda said in a serious tone as she leaned forward to hug Louisa.

At that exact moment, Melinda's mother frantically entered the kitchen, dressed in an elegant custom-made business suit, looking as if she were ready to preside over a major corporation boardroom meeting.

"Melinda — I see you're home! I hope your last day as a sophomore was pleasant."

Not waiting for Melinda's reply, Mrs. Taylor faced Louisa to inform the older cook, "Mr. and Mrs. McNickle will join us for supper next Wednesday, and I promised them a dazzling casual meal. I am thinking of something simple like Cornish game hens. Will you finish a menu for me? Oh and please have the meal served without delay, at 8:00 pm sharp!"

Melinda's mother turned abruptly to her daughter and concluded, "Mr. McNickle is the Chief Executive Officer of a very large insurance company, and your father and I would appreciate getting to know him better — at least well enough for his company to use our airline for their business travel..."

Without looking at either Melinda or Louisa, Mrs. Taylor redirected herself, "Oh dear — I just realized I need Adrianne to do some personal shopping for that evening."

With those words, she spun around, and promptly exited from the kitchen.

Melinda and Louisa stared at each other, startled by Mrs. Taylor's hasty disappearance, and then both broke into amused laughter.

Melinda loved her mother, but realized for her to be the socially accomplished wife of a major airline president; the effort demanded *all* of her mother's attention. Melinda never doubted that her parents treasured her as their only child; but she had learned from watching them that in a mounting world of air travel competition, her parents focused carefully on what they considered right to build her father's career.

Nearly twelve years earlier, the division executive vice president over her father was Hispanic. Her parents desiring to do what they perceived as the *"right"* thing, feverishly looked for a Hispanic child to adopt. Since they were unable to have children of their own, but worked for the opportunity, in their opinion, a calculated decision would envelop both areas simultaneously.

Both of her parents pompously exhibited numerous photographs of their new Hispanic-looking daughter at the following corporate assembly, commenting to everyone how blessed they were to adopt beautiful Melinda.

Although her father, Mr. Andrew J. Taylor III, was an exceptionally bright and capable Vice President at the time, he shortly received a promotion to the title of Sr. Vice President.

Her mom and dad leveraged this career promotion formula ever since that job advancement.

Without warning, her mother returned saying, "One additional item dear — with school out this year, your father and I have discussed the suitable way for you to spend your summer. We decided on a *wonderful* idea during last night's clubhouse dinner party, I am happy to say.

"We discovered that an energy company's Chief Financial Officer is a considerable financial benefactor to a highly regarded Museum's student program located in Houston, Texas. The curriculum introduces young people to cultures from around the world and throughout history. To help us lobby for their company's use of Global Star-Aviation, your father and I feel it would be wise for you to attend the course this summer."

Mrs. Taylor fanned the air about her face with her hand before she continued, "Not only will you benefit from a wonderful education dear, but just imagine how it will resonate with the CFO when we share the news that our very own daughter will personally attend his cherished program. He'll be so delighted — Oh, I can already see the look on his face!"

"WHAT?" cried Melinda, feeling the foundation of her exciting summer plans quickly crumbling away.

"Mother, you're not serious! You know Bethany and I planned a trip to Hawaii in three weeks with her parents," Melinda said with unwavering urgency. "You promised I could go! I don't want to attend some Museum program, especially over my summer break. I'm receiving excellent grades, and you promised that as a reward, I could spend the summer with my friends. This will ruin everything," she persisted.

"MELINDA!" her mother said piercingly, "This is very important! If your father acquires this account, it will establish him as the foremost candidate for the airline's Chief Executive Officer Position next year. Really, dear, you have the rest of your life to go to Hawaii, but your father only has a few years to really make something of himself." Pausing to regain her composure, Mrs. Taylor explained, "Named as the CEO of a major airline is making himself something! When you complete the Museum program, then you can go to Hawaii."

"Mom, can't you just tell them I'm thinking about the program, so you can still bring up the subject?" Melinda whined. Without noticing a change in her mother's expression, but hoping she would soften, Melinda continued, "I'm sure he'll tell you both all about it! I don't need to actually go."

Her mother broke her unyielding silence by tapping her perfect fingernails on the counter, and prodded her daughter with guilt, "Now dear, you don't want to neglect this important occasion to help your father do you?"

"I guess not," Melinda grumbled, losing her resolve.

"*Do* you? Her mother insisted.

"No," she said in a dutiful tone.

"Brilliant! Then we have it settled," touted her mother. "You will leave tomorrow morning," she sang delightedly, leaving the kitchen.

Melinda and Louisa stared at each other in complete shock, and then Louisa sighed, "Things change fast here, we go upstairs and get you packed, before there no time to plan what you wear."

Chapter Two

RESCUED

Ten months earlier, eleven year-old Jennifer Nelxon was the girl-next-door type, who enjoyed helping everyone in every way, especially wayward or lost animals. Constantly bringing home stray cats and dogs, she reasoned that without her aid, none of the poor destitute creatures would survive.

Her parents often pleaded with her to refrain from adopting every perceived misplaced animal by explaining that she may actually prevent many of them from naturally finding their own homes, if they were not lost.

Jennifer considered the possibility this might be true in some cases; however, she believed they all deserved her help, considering how their careless owners had allowed their escape.

As Jennifer rode her bicycle on the cracked pavement behind the strip mall, she avoided the dangerous commotion of multi-directional cars and trucks driving in the storefronts' parking lot. Near the end of the long building, she noticed a young thin auburn haired girl, sobbing next to a large commercial-sized garbage dumpster.

Years of exposure to the elements and garbage truck scrapes changed the once-solid Kelly green dumpster into an aged and camouflaged pattern.

Jennifer's instincts drove her to help the crying girl.

"What's wrong?" she asked the girl, "Where's your family?"

The smaller girl replied, "I waited for my dad in our car, until I saw something pop up inside this dumpster. When I got here, I heard scratching noises inside. I think an animal is trapped inside."

Jennifer's eyes smiled in excitement, while asking in a hopeful tone,

"Really? What kind?"

"I don't know. When I climbed up to find out, I slipped and scraped my elbow," the girl replied while dramatically thrusting out her hurt elbow at Jennifer to view.

Jennifer's emotions took control of the situation. Before she could help the smaller girl find her family, she first determined to ascertain the potential need of the animal. The first part of her plan intact, Jennifer used the concrete curb to raise her foot up to the dumpster's lowest side ladder rung, and then she climbed to the top of the dumpster. Peering over the top edge, the odor from months of decomposing trash instantly assaulted her nose. Alone on a crumpled cardboard pizza box, a black dog stared curiously up at her, sporting a rotten banana peel over its left shoulder. Jennifer thought to herself, *"How long have you been in here breathing this rotten air?"*

The dog watched Jennifer warily, to determine her motive rather than jumping excessively without reason, as other dogs might do to escape. Staring at the black dog for a moment longer, she noticed the upturned corners of its mouth and wondered, *"Is that dog smiling?"*

"Are you lost?" she asked the dog in a soft caring voice.

Immediately, it lifted off its hindmost legs and stretched up its lengthy front limbs, as if reaching for Jennifer. Excited with the challenge to free the dog from the smelly jail, Jennifer swung her leg over the top edge of the dumpster.

"OUCH!" she hollered, burning the exposed part of her leg below her shorts on the sun-heated metal.

Jumping hastily into the huge dumpster, Jennifer's foot squashed through a sun-faded green container of moldy tomatoes.

The rotten food clung to her shoe, and she whined, "Gross!"

Looking up from her shoe and at the dog, its size seemed to dwarf her. A refined and chiseled head rose nearly to her adolescent chin. Cropped tapered ears framed its striking features, while its crinkled forehead skin suggested it was inquisitive.

Immediately, its large wet nose reached down to nuzzle Jennifer's hand, as if thanking her for coming to its rescue. Excited by the dog's friendly reaction, she petted its sleek head and searched for cuts or other visible injuries. Without seeing anything revealing, Jennifer reassured the dog using a high-pitched baby voice.

"Don't worry big doggy; I'm going to get you out of this old nasty dumpster."

"What is it?" the little girl called impatiently to Jennifer from outside.

"It's a big dog!"

Jennifer now required a plan to get the huge dog up and out of the garbage container, and carefully analyzed their surroundings to use anything of value.

Beneath two large bloated plastic trash bags, Jennifer noticed several unfolded cardboard boxes, and decided they might be useful packed together to allow the dog to leap up, and hopefully out of, the dumpster. Jennifer gingerly stepped over rotting lettuce heads and avoided a busted package of moldy mushrooms to reach the boxes.

While she evaluated how best to stack the cardboard boxes, Jennifer had the odd notion the dog somehow understood her intentions. As it watched her in silence, she unfolded each cardboard box, and then stacked one above the other in a stair-type fashion. A mumble of approval passed from Jennifer's lips as she observed her work. Using her own weight to test the strength of the cardboard, she stood on the bottom box. Suddenly, it crashed inward, causing her to lose her balance. Unsure how the big dog moved so quickly, it flashed towards her and blocked her path from falling onto the disgusting floor.

After the unsuccessful test, Jennifer realized the boxes needed interior support, and she reinforced them by filling each with rubbish from within the dumpster. Due to the large size of the dog, she hoped her efforts would sustain it to make a single good jump. Prepared to find out, Jennifer raised her foot onto the lowest internal bracket.

Bouncing upward, Jennifer gripped the internal railing and pulled herself up; until she positioned her feet along the inside corners of the brace. When she looked up at the top edge, Jennifer sadly noticed a large space remained between her head and the top of the dumpster. She looked hopelessly at the dog, and squatted slowly to say, "It's too high..."

Without aid from the boxes, the Great Dane sized dog sprang upward to place heavy paws on her bent knees like a first step. Next, using Jennifer's shoulders for the second step, it leapt up and out of the dumpster. Underneath the sudden unexpected burden placed on her shoulders, Jennifer lost her stability, and reached behind her for support. Her situation worsened when she grasped only air. Even with flailing arms like bird wings, Jennifer pitched face-first onto the rancid floor.

"Ahhhhhh!" she screamed falling.

Instantly Jennifer felt a warm sensation on her cheek. She jerked up onto her hands and knees, and wiped moist sticky oatmeal off her face. Unfortunately, she realized too late that she had added a putrid, dull colored paste clinging to her finger onto her nose.

"DISGUSTING!" she screamed louder.

With her ruined clothes currently the focus of her attention, Jennifer shortly forgot about the dog, until she heard the smaller girl squealing with delight. Anxious to know if the dog was hurt from the large leap to the ground, Jennifer hurriedly climbed to the dumpster's top, and hastily swung her right leg over the top edge of the garbage container. Her now greasy fingers slipped, which in turn caught her right shoe on the metal edging and pulling it off, she heard it tumble to the outside ground. With a big effort, Jennifer cleared herself over the hot metal of the top rim.

From her high vantage point, Jennifer watched the small girl hug the big dog's neck. Comparatively to the younger girl, the dog seemed to be the size of a Shetland pony. Afraid the dog would soon leave without her; Jennifer jumped down from off the garbage container, and instantly felt a raw sting on her shoeless foot when it struck the hard pavement. Jennifer quickly squatted to rub her foot gingerly, and after a few seconds, replaced her absent shoe.

"SUSAN" a man bellowed, "what's going on here? I told you to wait inside the car!"

The father of the smaller girl stormed towards them with angry eyes, ignoring both Jennifer and the dog.

"People are *searching* for you *right now*! What's going on back here?" he demanded.

Shocked, yet excited, Susan begged, "Daddy, I found this dog in the trash, can I keep him? Can I keep him pleaassse?"

Susan's father glared first at the dog, and then at Jennifer. Distressed by the little girl's desire to reap her hard-earned reward from rescuing the trapped dog, she readied to counter Susan's claim.

Beat out by Susan's father dragging his daughter's hand behind him, Susan extended her other hand towards the dog, as if emotionally willing it to tag along beside her.

Tears streaming down her face, the younger girl cried, "I want that big puppy!"

Her father glanced crossly one last time back to Jennifer and the dog, yet saw neither while he scolded his daughter. Thrilled the dog was now exclusively her project, Jennifer turned to observe it loping away.

Alarmed, Jennifer chased it while coaxing, "Here doggie, come back here!"

Nevertheless, within seconds, the black dog bounded from her sight. Frustrated with zero results, ruined clothes, and smelling like rotten vegetables, Jennifer scornfully snapped up her bike and spun it around to ride home.

Chapter Three

THE MUSEUM

Melinda searched overhead for airport signs that pointed towards the Houston Baggage Claim Area after she disembarked from her plane. Although experienced at airliner travel from vacationing with her parents, this was her first trip alone. Confident, but a little uneasy with the new surroundings, Melinda reached the airline's luggage carousels by following other people she recognized from her flight. Scanning the area, she read her name on a driver's white sign.

"I'm Melinda," she announced, reaching the man holding her name.

Global Star-Aviation provided Melinda with luxury transportation as the daughter of the company's president. Smiling, the tall driver stood attentive in his pressed dark slacks and a matching single-breasted jacket. Below his white starched collar, the man's gray and white striped tie hung slightly offset to the left of center.

When the driver removed his hat to introduce himself, Melinda noticed he had more silver hair than his remaining dark hair.

"Good Morning!" he said in a rich resonant Scottish accent. "Pleasure te meet ye; I'm yer driver today, Carl Dunbar."

Still smiling, the man pointed at a door across the room behind Melinda that read:

EMPLOYEES ONLY

Melinda stepped through the door, and noticed how sparsely furnished the room was. The most prominent attribute was a Global Star-Aviation motivational sign that read:

THE PASSENGER IS OUR GUEST

Three outdated dark brown metal vending machines covered most of the room's rear wall. Collected first off the plane from flying first class, Melinda's luggage carried special VIP tags, which notified baggage handlers to pre-load her luggage into the trunk of an assigned limousine.

Carl led her out of the waiting area, and then to the side of their long black limousine. Once he opened the door for Melinda to enter the passenger area, he closed it with a heavy unyielding sound. Placing his seat belt on while sitting in the drivers screened-off cabin area, the man started the car's engine, and then lowered the privacy partition to the passenger section.

"Is there anywhere ye wish te go before we drive te the Museum?" he asked, viewing Melinda through the rear view mirror. Melinda thought for a moment, and then shook her head no. As he began to raise the privacy screen, Melinda spoke up, "Carl, wait a second, could we stop and get a frozen slushy?"

"No worries" he said smiling, "there are several places along the way,"

The easygoing driver gave gas to the big V-8 motor, and merged the stretch car easily into the traffic, leaving the Airport. Twenty minutes later, Melinda sat deeply in one of the puffy leather seats and enjoyed sipping her flavored icy drink.

Melinda wondered if she should text a friend during the ride to the museum or watch a DVD, until she glanced through the darkly tinted windows. Noticing the immediate difference between dry arid Phoenix and lush green Houston, she became interested in learning more about the city. So instead, she searched for internet articles on her cell phone, while they traveled south on I-45 towards downtown Houston. The first one read:

"Houston is the largest city in Texas and one of the largest in North America. Despite being the heart of the country's Oil and Energy industry, the town's nickname is actually 'Space City' reflecting the fact that NASA has launched huge rockets and space shuttles for decades."

After reading the article's introduction, Melinda viewed the blue skies with wispy clouds outside the window, and thought about space travel. She soon returned from her daydream and thought, "*I wonder if I can see the Hospital District.*"

Excitedly, her mother had raved to her before her flight about Houston's famous hospital district by saying, "I know you will be well taken care of should something happen, because Houston has the largest group of specialized hospitals in the world."

After peering into the distance, she spotted multiple clumps of tall buildings, and decided one group was larger than the others were. She figured it must be the famous skyscraper district. The sun's rays reflected brightly off of an 80-story glass building, and reminded her of a lake's twinkling surface.

Interested in reading about the Museum to make sure she understood why she had to give up going to Hawaii, Melinda searched the web again and found an article. She scrolled partway down and read:

"...prior to the turn of the 20th century, Elliot Harper, a wealthy industrial giant who employed thousands of workers in his mills and factories, moved his young family from Philadelphia to the booming island of Galveston. Considered in those days to be one of the richest cities in the nation, Galveston was the first city in Texas to have electricity and to use the telegraph. Railroad connections brought many of the country's prominent banks to the area, that later created the nickname Wall Street of the South.

During 1900, a hurricane hit the island, killing thousands. Away on business, Elliott Harper lost his wife and their two children when the storm's surge destroyed their island home. Distraught, and wanting to escape the vicinity of such intense personal tragedy, he was reluctant to leave the gravesites of his beloved family. Instead, he compromised internally, and relocated fifty miles north to the outskirts of Houston.

It was rumored he spent a fortune building an imposing stone home, rivaled by none other in the region. Some whispered he built the immense home to surmount his grieving loss, while others speculated it was a monument to his cherished departed family.

After completing the monolithic home, he lived isolated, rarely seen by the townspeople. Years later, Elliott Harper sold his companies to conserve his declining strength until he passed away in 1924. Although few truly knew the man late in his life, most were surprised when he bequeathed his home, cash, and stocks to the neighboring school district.

Using Mr. Harper's vast resources, the main house turned into a school, and later added two supplementary building wings. The prodigious school's reputation led to steady growth, and attracted premium teachers from across the country until the great depression of 1929. The wealth transitioned to the school succumbed with the crash of the once great stock market.

Years later, older electrical wiring and maintenance repairs forced the school to request financial aid. Local philanthropists raised money; however, the funding depleted by the end of World War II. Later boarded up by city council members, they proposed the building's demolition, but due to its enormous size and the quality of its construction, the project surpassed the city's tight economic resources. The city petitioned citizens for aid, and with their help, nearly sixty percent of the mandatory funds were collected when an eccentric counter proposition surfaced.

Ross Jacobson, the solitary heir of an oil-wildcatting tycoon, proposed matching the money raised to preserve the building. Aghast, council members quickly seconded a motion to terminate its advancement. Shrewd Mr. Jacobson ingeniously planned to make a fortune with the city's partnership. Later meeting with wealthy influential city leaders, he described his plan to create a well-known tourist attraction that would generate many new jobs, expand extensive down line distribution, and finally bolster the local economy.

He collaborated with elite leaders to use their considerable wealth to refurbish the immense structure into a Museum, which would free him to use his own vast assets in another way.

His plan was uncomplicated, yet brilliant. With the future Museum amid its renovation transformation, he would traverse the globe to acquire exceptional works of art. The city would retain both the land and the Museum, while his wealthy associates achieved income tax benefits and society acknowledgment. Yet, he alone would possess the fine art entirely, with a free secure location to house his planned collection.

He studied the markets, and anticipated that inflation was in the near future, in which case, collected works of fine art would appreciate tremendously. He offered to exchange upfront revenue, sharing in the Museum's admittance fees to view his collection, with the promise he would bestow a sizable portion of the tremendous collection to the Museum upon his death.

Armed with influential leadership support, he re-presented his proposal. Rather than spend stretched city resources to demolish the landmark, council members quickly voted unanimously for his application to expand their economy.

The mansion, once turned school, now underwent momentous restoration to become a museum, while Mr. Jacobson acquired notable works of art. Inflation came earlier than he expected, and although he was wealthy, works by great artists became too costly for a solo collector. He decided to refine his strategy and leverage his capital by traveling to second and third world countries to purchase sensibly priced treasures. As an alternative to a Museum of fine arts, it transitioned into a Museum of antiquities.

Mr. Jacobson's exploits soon became visible around the globe. Remarkable artifacts outside of his original planned scope quickly filled the Museum. Enjoying the bartering process so thoroughly, he never passed on the concluding 'won' acquisition sum. He felt the actions of bartering provided the psychological image of two superb warriors, brandishing long sharp tipped spears at each other. Victory required each warrior to move sufficiently close to inflict possible lethal injury, without falling prey to the opponent's razor-sharp tip.

Filled with identifiable Greek, Roman, Asian, Egyptian, and Mesoamerican artifacts, true to his word, he donated one of the most illustrious private collections to a lone Museum..."

Engrossed with her thoughts, a speed bump shook Melinda unexpectedly as the limousine drove up a long driveway. Riding past manicured grounds, she turned her phone off and slid to the other side of the limousine to view the Museum. Catching her breath, she marveled at the magnificent structure.

Elaborate granite and mineral window casings balanced massive rectangle stone blocks. Blue-green glazed slate tiles covered the roof. After they drove into the main unloading circle, her gaze rapidly turned to an immense cascading water fountain. Momentarily lost in the flowing streams and sparkles, she jumped in her seat when Carl suddenly opened her door. When she exited the car, her focus drifted to colossal carved columns that supported an enormous oval-shaped front portico, reminding her of fantastical sentries.

Lulled like a moth to a fire, Melinda felt drawn into the Museum's ambiance and grandeur. Loaded with her luggage, together she and Carl passed the beautiful gardens that lined the walkways leading to huge front doors. Pigeons and sparrows fluttered beneath their passing feet as Melinda thought, "*It's just like you see in the movies.*"

Prior to leaving her home, Melinda had other desires, but they faded as she breathed in the glamour of the majestic structure. For the first time since learning of the program, Melinda now looked forward to spending her summer at the Museum.

Chapter Four

INJURED

After evading the oversized dumpster, the new environment shocked the edgy black dog. Astounded by new sights, smells, and thoughts, the dog felt bombarded with a multitude of undecipherable meanings all at once. Unsure if the sudden strange surroundings created her confusion, she was unable to remember anything about her life before awakening in the dumpster.

Virtually treeless, a dark gray plaster had replaced soil she knew well. Confounded by many foreign colors and sounds, her mind wondered at the irritable beasts of unrelated shapes. Unexpectedly, a large green beast, with round legs and white globes for eyes, awoke. Startled, she whirled as another black beast backed up in her direction. A sudden blaring directly behind her assailed her ears, and scared her easily with the combined sound of screeching tires. She leapt without thinking, more than twelve feet sideways due to her athletic capability, in order to get away from the unexplainable situation. She turned to see the snout of a large red creature bobbing its head from the fast stop where she had stood only a moment before.

As she sidestepped onto the sidewalk to avoid a bulky blue creature that whirled quickly in her direction, a man wearing a hat inside the car yelled to her, "Get out of the way dog!"

Distracted by the rude man, she unintentionally blocked the pathway of a young mother walking with her two small children. Unexpectedly, from the corner of her eye, she spotted another dog, identical-looking to herself. Energized to see a recognizable face in the midst of her new confusion, she leapt powerfully towards it. The grin on its face expressed the eagerness she felt too.

She moved left in a correct greeting pose, however, the new dog flew unswervingly at where she should stand. The unexpected change in greeting protocol made her leap high hoping to soar over the new dog, when it leapt upward too. She realized that the sudden collision course provided little opportunity to shift her position in time. Moments prior to their impact, the amnesia-afflicted black dog dropped her head low, hoping the other new dog's mass would slide easily over her back to avoid a head-on collision.

Unpredictably, the new dog had the same thought and lowered its head too, exactly in the same manner. Hastily reacting to the new situation, the black dog jerked her head up out of the way, when instantly the new dog reflected the movement. The big black dog closed her eyes tight and braced for the imminent crash.

Pain rippled throughout her head and neck from the ruthless stop against a concrete wall, fully covered with chromed metal shiny enough to resemble a mirror. Nearly knocked unconscious from the unforgiving crash, she slumped to the ground. Shaken, she gradually stood. Dazed and in a stupor, the black dog glanced at the new dog and saw the pain in its eyes, without grasping her own condition. In her mind, it seemed to her that the other dog groggily staggered away.

The ground immediately whirled beneath her paws, which made her tip headfirst into the path of an oncoming speeding vehicle. As if in a fuzzy hallucination now gone terribly wrong, the previous events quickly transformed into screeching that sounded far away in the distance, when a new gold colored beast suddenly appeared with menacing silvery teeth and slammed directly into her.

Floating through the air, her thoughts swirled into nothingness.

***

Jennifer rode her bike home across the far end of the strip mall's parking lot to change her ruined clothes, when she heard a car's screeching tires on the hot asphalt. Startled, the sound made her forget about the stain covering the front of her shirt. Reflexively, she twisted her handlebars in the direction of the growing crowd.

"IS THERE A VET HERE?" a woman yelled as Jennifer rode nearer to the gathered people.

Anxious at hearing the word 'vet', she dropped her bike to press her way into the group's inner wavering circle. In dark sunglasses and lime green shorts, a middle-aged woman wearing a white blouse shouted, "Does anyone know who owns this dog?"

Jennifer recognized it immediately, and noticed its broad back slumped alongside the sidewalk. Afraid of her worst fears after spotting its broken leg, and instinctively dropping to her knees beside the dog, a tall and slightly balding, thin man also squatted beside her. Eyes welling with tears, Jennifer felt responsible for the situation.

The kind man noticed her tears and calmly said, "She has a broken leg. Otherwise, she seems initially ok; however, I want to be sure. Are your parents close by?" he asked.

"No," she whispered through her tears.

The thin man considered the circumstances, and then said, "Stay here. I'll be right back."

In agreement, Jennifer petted the lifeless shoulder. Vulnerable with grief, she looked pleadingly at the gathered people for help. She made cloudy eye contact with several of the onlookers, however, each one darted their eyes to avoid becoming involved.

Moments later, a silver SUV drove up next to the dog. The tall thin man exited the vehicle, and said to no one in particular, "I'm going to open the rear door."

He opened the rear door of his vehicle, and retracted a folded table. With a snap of his wrists, in a quick motion the table expanded into a gurney.

Shortly, he returned pushing the gurney to where Jennifer waited, when he directed, "You hold the dog's hips while I lift her head and shoulders."

Jennifer nodded, and squatted over the rear legs of the giant dog.

"On the count of three, we'll lift her at the same time," he said expectantly.

Jennifer said, "OK," and placed her small hands under its thick hips.

"One — two — three — lift!"

Under the heavy weight, Jennifer floundered until a sporty woman in sweats realized her small size and assisted them. Thankfully, with the friendly woman's help, all three hoisted the big dog onto the gurney. At the rear door of his automobile, the tall man pushed the gurney against the bumper. The front legs folded quickly on contact, and slid the secured dog easily into the rear compartment. After surveying the interior walls of the vehicle, Melinda noticed it displayed various sized rolls of tape, gauze bandages, ropes, and splints.

With the gurney fitted in place, the thin man twirled and asked Jennifer, "Do you want to ride in back with the dog, or up in front?"

Suddenly suspicious as he was a stranger offering her a ride in his car, Jennifer retreated with a puzzled expression.

"Where are you taking the dog?" the fit woman asked.

"My office is about a mile in that direction," he replied while nodding his head the way he pointed, "I need to splint the leg, and to be safe, I'd like to check for internal hemorrhaging."

"Honey, my car is over there," the woman said hesitantly to Jennifer, while she peered closely at the tall veterinarian.

"We'll follow you to your office," the woman said loudly, and began walking in the direction of her parked car.

Not waiting for the man's response, the kind woman motioned for Jennifer to follow her. Torn because the woman was a stranger too, she knew not to ride with this woman either; but her caring instincts constrained her to stay with the injured dog.

Jennifer read the SUV door that displayed the words *NORTH SIDE PET HOSPITAL*, and bit her lip pondering her new dilemma. Nervous about the decision, she began to fidget and glanced back and forth between the two vehicles.

"Honey, it's ok, we'll call your parents on the way in my car," the lady called to Jennifer.

Resigned to doing what she thought best, Jennifer jogged to where the woman stood beside her car.

Once inside, the woman started her engine and spoke calmly, "Hi, I'm Michelle, what's your name?"

"Jennifer Nelxon."

"How old are you Jennifer?" Michelle asked, while she backed out of the parking stall.

"11."

"What's your home phone number?" she asked, pulling up her purse flap to retrieve an older model cell phone.

Michelle slowly dialed Jennifer's home number with difficulty during the course of a red light, with freshly manicured, raspberry painted acrylic nails. They followed the vet's SUV, until it turned left into the parking lot of a small building displaying an overhead painted sign that read:

North Side Pet Hospital

"Hello," Michelle said to a woman's voice over the cell phone, "Is this Jennifer's mom?"

The concerned voice hesitated, and then replied, "Yes, who is this?"

Michelle quickly handed her cell phone to Jennifer, who explained the situation while sobbing the recent events to her mother. In the parking lot, the vet bounded out of the SUV to unlock the clinic's front door, and then after propping the door open with a kickstand, returned to unload and move the dog inside his office. Jennifer returned the cell phone to Michelle, who gave the vet's address to Jennifer's mom.

When she hung up, Michelle said, "Ok, let's go in and wait for your mom to arrive," as they exited the car and entered into the pet hospital.

Chapter Five

ROOMATES

Instantly struck by the overpowering opulence of the Museum's main hall, Melinda was breathless. Her parent's home drew admiration from many who entered; however, when compared to the majesty of Elliott Harper's former house, she could only stare wide-eyed in fond appreciation.

Melinda first noticed the huge limestone blocks that made up most of the walls, displaying intricate alabaster base moldings more than two feet tall. Next, her eyes traveled across the marble floor patterns, which seemed to blanket the floor. High above her head, rich mahogany wooden beams supported a grand expansive coffered ceiling, all of which supported a gigantic glass dome in the center.

Carl smiled cheerfully at Melinda when he saw her enamored expression. While almost reading her thoughts he said to her, "Ye know, I felt the same way the first time I saw this place too. It's hard te imagine this was someone's home."

Melinda remained speechless, and could only nod in stunned agreement. Carl pointed across the room towards the information desk, and then led her to the end of the already formed line.

"Stand here by yer bags while I learn where we need te go next," he instructed her.

Plum velvet ropes topped with polished brass caps outlined Carl's path over to the employees behind the counter, helping other Museum patrons. As he proceeded in the line, Melinda looked beyond the information desk at the intricate ironwork stair railings that flowed across the rear wall.

Beautiful hand-carved alabaster benches offered visitors luxuriant rest at the base of each stair entrance. Melinda's eyes rose up the converging stairs to see that they coupled in the middle and fashioned into a large rounded alcove. Above the alcove, magnificent granite columns, chiseled with precision, transformed from simple smooth surfaces at their bases into giant Roman clad figures of men and women that supported both the second and third floor balconies.

Melinda lowered her eyes to the main floor where she spied a long, opulently carved hallway, running perpendicular under the main stairs to lead into a large rock and glass atrium.

Carl soon returned displaying a navy blue plastic card, with a gold "S" printed on both sides.

"We are supposed te take this pass down te the security desk, which is through them doors behind ye. Once yer registered with the guard station, someone will escort ye te the rear o' the property where the student center is located."

Carl handed the plastic card to Melinda and helped her gather her luggage before leading her to the security office. After passing by the gift shop beyond an arched doorway, Melinda noticed a security sign attached to the wall that pointed down the stairwell. At the bottom floor, they came face to face with a glass encased security office.

The security man sitting behind the desk had a wide square face that sloped into a ruggedly shaped chin. When he noticed the navy blue pass, he seemed pleased to welcome Melinda as they entered through the large glass doors. His warm smile and grinning green eyes gave her confidence to approach him. He pushed his chair back to stand up, up, and up and Melinda needed to step back a few paces in order to see the full size of the man.

Unlike Carl's thin frame, this man seemed as wide as he was tall. Each time he moved, his loose-fitting shirt waved with undulating movements underneath, to suggest the man had gigantic muscles on top of gigantic muscles.

"Hello there missy, my name's Albert Manning, but most people call me Al," he said, in a husky booming voice. Shaking her hand with a sunny smile, he added, "and I'm the head of J-MA's security."

"J-MA?" she repeated quizzically.

"Oh, that's right; I sometimes forget new Museum guests might not always know the inside lingo. Jacobson Museum of Antiquities can be a mouthful if you're not used to saying it, so we just call it J-MA for short," the enormous man said with a wink.

Melinda stared from the man's well-kept highlighted hair to his massive hand as it engulfed hers, thinking, *"He's the biggest person I've ever seen!"*

Nearly forgetting herself, she replied, "I'm Melinda Taylor. I'm here with the Jacobson Muse... a...I mean," while she blinked bashfully, "J-MA student summer program."

While she peered upward at Al, she hoped to receive a friendly demeanor to her response, as she would not want to be around him to find out otherwise during a bad mood.

Al crossed his Atlas-sized arms across his chest and cracked a smile, and to Melinda's relief, half chuckled.

"See, you're going to fit right in around here."

"Well, you already know who I am. I'm presuming you're both together?" Al said to Carl.

Nodding his head yes, the driver replied, "My name is Carl Dunbar sir, and I'm Miss Taylor's driver."

"Very well," Al said.

"Would the two of you wait here a moment, so I can make sure the desk is covered while I escort you back to the student area?"

Melinda nodded her acceptance.

As soon as Al barked a few prompt orders over a walkie-talkie, another stoutly built middle-aged guard approached the desk with his uniform hat cocked to the side and wearing the same taupe slacks and shirt under his burgundy jacket. Melinda noticed the man was lightly gray around the temples, and walked with a slight swagger like in old western movies.

Al introduced them to the guard, "Melinda — Carl, this is Brock Dennison. He's part of our elite staff. In fact, he's an ex-Navy Seal, so try not to spook him in a dark hallway at night around here," he said with a sly grin.

Brock extended his hand to Carl and then to Melinda, giving her a better view of his dark hazel eyes, when the man said in a rough weathered voice,

"Melinda, Carl, it's nice to meet you both. Don't let him mislead you; I'm the good natured type around here, compared to this big brute," to which the group laughed together.

Melinda suddenly found herself at ease with both tough-looking security men.

Al offered, "Let me help you with these bags."

The enormous muscle man tucked each bag easily under his great arms, and then he directed, "This way folks; it's a bit of a walk from here, but at least you'll get a feel for the Museum along the way."

With Al leading the way, it seemed a bit comical from behind to see one person carrying so much luggage, but he just kept going unconscious of the fact as if he were simply holding pillows.

When they passed through the adjoining doorway, Melinda heard Al mention, "You're probably thinking we're in the basement, but in fact, we're still on the first floor!"

Carl spoke up from behind the huge man, "I was wondering, considering the water table is high in Houston."

Melinda asked, "What do you mean when you say the water table is high?"

Al answered her, "Houston is part of the Gulf Coast. The city is not built on mountainous rock, like those that you have somewhere back east. At sea level, the ground is fully saturated with moisture."

Puzzled, Melinda was still not sure what this meant, and hurried up to his side. To keep in stride with him wasn't as easy as she had anticipated, and she wished she had worn different shoes.

"You mean because the ground is too wet, it can't soak up the excess water?"

"You got it little lady. So if someone tried to build a basement like they do in other places, within a few feet the hole fills with water."

Carl added, "Some builders tried te waterproof the basement walls, but with small success."

Melinda noticed the passageway and saw it was bright and clean. She considered the previous comments, and as she tried to listen and still seem graceful keeping up the pace, she decided she had better just grip her toes and bear it. She asked, "So, how are we in a basement with everything you just told us?"

Al chuckled at the question and then he said, "I wondered the same thing when I first arrived. Later, I learned old man Harper came from where they have basements. The fact that he lived in Houston was not going to change his accustomed lifestyle, so he chose this property because it had a slight natural incline. Instead of constructing a basement beneath the ground, he built the first floor as normal, and then surrounded it with a mountain of boulders and dirt. He took advantage of the inherent slope of the property, and gradually excavated around the foundation of the house until it was not noticeable. The beautiful part was how the architect tricked the eye by building the water moat out in front of the house.

"Elliott raised the foundation to enhance the gradual descent, and to drain rainwater away from the house into the moat. Therefore, you're not actually walking in a basement, but in fact, you're on the first floor. No one notices because of the massive size of the place."

Al stopped walking, but continued giving the Museum's history review, "This passage we're in now was used by the early staff to migrate from the main house to the memorial in the back, where your group will stay."

"What do you mean memorial? I'm going to be staying in a graveyard?" Melinda's eyes suddenly bugged out in panic.

"No, no — that's just what we call it. Mr. Harper built it after the original house was completed. In the beginning, the staff lived in the central house, however, later in his life; Elliot built the staff house we're going to now after he became more of a social recluse. He extended this tunnel between the buildings, so that on hot summer or rainy days, the staff could access the main house without going outside to get wet or track in mud."

Together they continued the walk for a few minutes more, while Melinda noticed they passed several connecting hallways, which flowed away under the paneled ceiling and lights. When they later approached the base of a separate turret of stairs, Melinda noticed that beautifully framed pictures hung on the walls. They followed Al up to the next level and at the second-floor exit; Melinda discovered they had entered a smaller, but well-appointed lobby.

She admired the immense elegant rugs and the heavily built furniture, as Al crossed to a window and greeted a woman in her late sixties who staffed another information desk. Her dark chocolate hair color revealed little of her naturally white hair. Because of plucking out her actual eyebrows, the older woman had painted them on her face in high, dark brown arches.

Al boomed, "Mrs. Neely, I've got some new friends for you to meet."

Calmly, the older woman looked up from a stack of papers and smiled when she saw the monstrous security man.

"This is Melinda Taylor. She's one of our new summer students, and this is Carl Dunbar," he said loudly.

"Oh, it's so nice to meet you both," the elderly woman said.

Without much eye contact and with a preoccupied but friendly attitude, Mrs. Neely rattled off, "I've been expecting you today. Let me see…I know I have your paperwork here somewhere on my desk. A few of you are here already. Let me get up, and then come with me into the lecture hall," she said, as she disappeared from the window.

Moments later, Mrs. Neely exited from the office door.

"Follow me this way dear," Mrs. Neely said, grasping Melinda's hand.

Slowly they shuffled towards an open set of double doors, while Carl and Al silently followed. As they neared the open doors, Melinda viewed what looked like walnut colored pews.

When Melinda passed through the open doorway, the other students who had arrived earlier stopped chatting. She watched as Al placed her luggage beside a mound of the other student's suitcases.

The big man stood, and when he faced the other students, he said, "As promised, I told you guys I would see more of you this summer, and so here I am once again," Al said, smiling.

Some of them smiled at his remarks, but the rest were busy evaluating the new girl. Melinda's eyes quickly canvassed her surroundings. It was a much larger room than it had appeared from outside the double doors.

A considerable podium filled the center of a stage that seemed large enough for several people to speak from at once. Melinda turned towards the other students, and noticed they all sat around a large round table filled with sandwiches, salads, and an assortment of drinks.

Melinda realized she was famished after seeing the enticing food and spun around when Al stated, "This is the end of the line for me today. Carl, how about if you and I swing by the Museum's cafeteria on the way out to eat a bite of lunch before you leave?"

Surprised by the invitation, Carl happily said, "That sounds like too good of an offer te pass up!"

With his large hands resting on his hips, Al said to all of the kids in the room, "I'm looking forward to learning more about each of you this year, however, right now I've got to get back to the office and help other students find their way to this area. I'm leaving you in Mrs. Neely's capable hands, so be good to her now, and I'll see y'all later." And with a wave and a turn, he approached Carl.

On cue, Carl and Melinda squared off with each other. Although Melinda had only met Carl earlier in the day, it seemed as though they were already friends.

Melinda said calmly, in the way her parents had coached her etiquette, "Carl, thank you so much for driving me here today. I really have enjoyed meeting you," she finished by shaking his hand, and then added, "I hope I get the chance to see you again before I leave Houston."

Carl replied with a cheery smile, "It's been my pleasure. Hopefully, when yer time here is complete, I'll be yer driver on yer trip home."

Each noticed the genuineness in the other's eyes.

Al looked at his watch, and then belted out in a booming voice to the student group, "Feel free to eat your fill; it's going to be a while before dinner."

The big man grinned at Carl and asked, "Are you ready?"

Carl nodded in agreement, and together they left the auditorium.

Mrs. Neely directed Melinda, "Get to know the other students dear, and wait here until I come back. Once all of the students arrive, I'll pass out the room assignments so you kids can unpack."

Warmly, the older woman smiled at everyone, and then slowly exited from the large room.

Suddenly the focus of everyone's attention, Melinda met his or her questioning eyes.

"Hi, I'm Melinda Taylor. I'm from Scottsdale, Arizona. What are your names?" she asked confidently, as taught by her mother.

The thin boy closest to her with piercing ice-blue eyes and wispy light brown hair, quickly stuffed the rest of his sandwich into his mouth with a skittish movement, and then stared shyly at his feet when Melinda looked at him.

An older-looking and muscular boy with brown hair sat next to the thin boy. He reminded Melinda of a cute senior wrestler at her school with his well-built easy movements. He noticed Melinda's surprised expression when the thin boy stuffed his sandwich in his mouth and said, "You'll have to forgive my brother; he's deaf. He reads lips really well, but as you can see, he can be shy sometimes when he meets new people. I'm Trent Davis, and this is Ted, but we all call him Tab!"

Without meaning to, Melinda wrinkled her face in disbelief, uncertain if Trent was teasing her.

Knowing this, a down-to-earth looking, but very pretty girl with gold-spun hair sitting across from Trent supported him, "It's true; Trent told us that ever since they were little, their mom had Trent and their older sister keep tabs on him so much, he ended up being called Tab."

The blonde girl then stood, and introduced herself to Melinda, "Hi, I'm Leslie Lyons from Oregon. This is my first time to Houston, so everything here is completely different to me. My family and I live in a little place called Five Rivers, where my dad is trying to become a screenwriter. We moved to Oregon when I was a freshman from San Diego, so he could have more time to develop his writing skills."

Melinda shook Leslie's hand, and from the corner of her eye, caught movement and noticed the deaf boy staring at her. She looked back at Tab.

He nervously smiled at her, so she waved casually at him, which caused the boy to duck his head again.

Melinda turned back to ask Leslie, "Has your father written anything I would know about?"

"No, he's written a few smaller scripts, and he's worked for the local paper for about a year, but now he's writing his first novel. It's some sort of a spy story set during the Revolutionary War. We're not sure how it will do, but when he gets a new twist in his head, he can disappear into his office for days at a time."

"Is there anything good to eat?" Melinda asked her, looking closely at the food.

Leslie answered, "I liked the BLT wraps."

Melinda agreed by placing one on her stoneware plate. She added a few corn chips on the side, and then studied the chicken sandwiches and a vegetable salad, but kept her eyes on the brownies. With a four-pronged fork, she stabbed the largest piece she could find on the tray, and then approached the other kids. Melinda sat down to eat her lunch.

After Melinda took a bite from her wrap, Trent explained, "Just so you guys know, Tab is really, *really* smart. Although he's hearing impaired, don't let that mislead you. He spends most of his time reading and studying. Even though he's my younger brother, he helps me with my homework. Once you get to know him, and he forgets to be shy, watch out! He can be a real practical joker."

After pausing for another mouthful of his food, Trent continued, "In addition, as a fair warning, he touches everything! Because he's unable to hear, he compensates by being visual and tactile with his hands. His doctors told us it helps him gather information by being able to feel different types of textures, and studying things up close. So don't worry if you see him pick up something of yours; I promise he's not trying to take it, or ruin it. It's probably something new that he wants to better understand."

Melinda swallowed her chip to ask Trent a question when Mrs. Neely re-entered the room.

"I don't know where the others are today; I suppose they're running late…must be a problem at the airport." With an aged and cracked voice, she added, "Anyway, here are the room assignments," waving a piece of paper in the air from the stack, she held in the crook of her elbow.

Slowly, she shuffled across the room and instructed, "When you're through eating, follow the signs for your room numbers. The girl's rooms are to the right of the hallway, and the boy's rooms are to the left."

After holding the papers far from her eyes, she blinked and then handed them to Leslie.

"Dear, I left my glasses at my desk — could you please read the names and then hand these packets out to the other students?"

After the earlier introduction to the boys, Leslie was excited for the task, as it would give her an idea of where everyone would stay. She smiled and studied the names on the packets.

She handed two of the packets to Trent saying, "It looks like you and Tab are in the same room. And here's yours Melinda...ah, this one's mine," Leslie said with her curiosity satisfied.

"Does everyone have their room numbers?" Mrs. Neely asked.

All nodded in agreement.

"Ok, when you're ready, find your rooms, and then unpack. Dinner is promptly at 7:00pm. If you need help, maps and other types of information are in your quarters to answer most of your questions. Should you require anything else, find me, and I'll see what I can do."

Mrs. Neely stepped close to the food, and bending over the table, took a chocolate chip cookie. As she enjoyed a quick bite, she slowly departed again.

Leslie said to Melinda, "When you're ready, do you want to find our rooms together?"

Melinda finished chewing a mouthful of her brownie for a few seconds more, and then said, "I was just about to ask you the same thing. Let me finish this, and then I'll be ready."

The two girls suddenly noticed Trent signing to Tab with a flurry of hand movements. Tab stopped texting on his cell phone to respond in the same manner, and the girls froze as their eyes moved back and forth, like watching a tennis match between the brothers.

Both boys stood simultaneously with Trent telling them, "We're off to find our room. I suppose we'll see you guys later at dinner." Then they headed for the pile of luggage.

"I'm ready too," Melinda offered to Leslie, and then she whispered loud enough for only the blonde girl to hear — "Do you think that's all they really said to each other?

Leslie smiled an impish look, and together, they walked side-by-side, each giggling, until they gathered their luggage. With a final glance at one another, both girls went to find their rooms.

***

Melinda surveyed her summer dorm room as she rested on the edge of one of two beds. Older, but with slight wear, it was clear the furnishings were evidently purchased while Mr. Harper was alive. Like everything else in the Museum she had seen, it was fit for monarchs.

"Whatever Mr. Harper was, he was not the type of person to hold back the best of everything — including to his staff," she said aloud.

Two four-poster queen beds filled the spaces between three separate nightstands. One nightstand stood in the middle of the wall under the window between both beds; while the other two framed each bed's outer edge like bookends. A crystal and brass lamp with a dated ivory shade resided on top of the middle nightstand. Two matching dressers faced each other across from the middle of the room.

As Melinda walked towards the two built-in wooden desks near the door, she slid off her second favorite pair of shoes, the leather Anne Klein mules. Sitting at the desk on her chosen side of the room, she realized that the quality of the desks did not match with the rest of the furnishings, yet she decided it was more than adequate for two teenage girls. Beautiful woven silk rugs covered the floor, and two paintings of water scenes hung on the walls above each dresser. One portrayed an inviting stone gazebo located high on a hill, surrounded by colorful wild flowers, and overlooking a coastal U-shaped harbor.

She crossed the floor to the second picture and noticed similar movements in the brush strokes. After a few moments, she decided it was a zoomed in view of the same U-shaped waterfront on the other wall, and that the same artist had signed both paintings. The identical sailboats with large white billowy sails sped across the summery blue waters.

Melinda felt there was something odd about how the once golden wood frames now faded into a copper hue. She moved closer to touch the frame, just as the door suddenly burst open. A tall girl about Melinda's age, with short-cropped dark

- 32 -

brown hair and tight-fitting clothes filled the doorway. She folded her arms and wrinkled her nose in discontent. No one spoke. They stared, each sizing the other up.

Melinda offered her hand first, "Hi, I'm Melinda."

The tall girl ignored Melinda's extended hand, and brushed by her to throw her luggage onto the bed that Melinda had chosen first, only moments before.

The tall girl spun to face Melinda asking, "Do you mind if I take this bed? I sleep better on my right side. If I take the other bed, it means I will stare at the wall all night."

Melinda hesitated for a moment and then replied, "Sure, I guess that's not going to be a problem."

The impolite girl plopped onto the bed and rolled over onto her stomach.

In an agitated voice, the new girl blurted, "Can you believe this stodgy old place? This is going to be a boring summer," she said, complaining dreadfully and rolling her squinty, freckle-surrounded eyes.

"You like to have fun?" the unhappy girl queried Melinda, while scrunching back up onto her knees and messing up the bedding.

Smiling, Melinda nodded her head yes, while neatly sitting on the side of the other bed.

"You don't talk much do you?" the tall girl said, jumping off her sequestered bed.

After marching past Melinda, she switched on the ceiling light, and studied their room.

With her hand held at the side of her head, she dramatically gasped, "This place is unbelievable!" and frowned.

Puzzled, Melinda's eyes followed the hard-to-read girl, and asked, "What do you mean?"

The tall girl scoffed at her, "You mean you haven't noticed? Look around in here, the furniture is contemptible, and did you see that old white marble in the girl's bathroom? It's alarming and incredibly, they have plastic shower curtains, instead of using real glass doors! Wait until my parents hear how their money only buys hand-me-down desks and beds. They will be shocked when I tell them about this place."

The thin girl breezed past Melinda as if she were non-existent, flopped onto her acquisitioned bed again, and hung her large feet off the side, instantly striking a sideways pose. Melinda felt like a spinning top with the constant buzz and movement of this new roommate.

Finally, Melinda asked, "What's your name?"

The tall girl smiled self-righteously and projected, "Mea! Mea Ross — of the Florida Ross's — you have no doubt heard of my family. My great-grandfather formerly owned a great deal of the land around the Fort Meyer area — we're old money!"

Mea sighed aloud to give one more gesture of her disapproval of the room, and stood up. She glanced around one last time, and then she headed towards the room's door saying, "I'm going to check this place out, and see if there's anything worth doing."

Before Melinda could reply, she was gone. Surveying the room again, it suddenly took on a different tone. Unpacking her belongings, Melinda now considered that this might be a lengthy summer after all.

Chapter Six

ANTICIPATION

Melinda was disappointed to awake from her nap and notice the real evidence of Mea's existence — the girl was not a dream, but she could be a living nightmare if she chose to be. Determined to avoid the tall girl as much as possible, Melinda dressed for the evening, and using the in-room directions, closed her room door behind her and proceeded through the empty hall leading towards the student lobby's front desk.

Glancing around the large deserted area, she felt a chill run up her spine at the eerie silence of the shadowy place. Statues and people in paintings stared back at her, as if she were the only person alive. Anxious to leave, she entered the same stairwell where she, Carl, and Al had climbed earlier from the bottom floor up to this level, and looked further up the tall winding granite staircase. Troubled when her shoe heels echoed in the hollow sounding staircase, Melinda immediately stepped on the balls of her feet. The clunking sound stopped, allowing her to feel better as she was now able to hear if anyone was nearby.

Indecisive with her directions, she thought, "*Am I climbing up to the second floor, or the third floor? This water table thing is making an easy concept more difficult than it needs to be.*" At the top corridor, Melinda re-checked her instructions one more time.

"Turn right and proceed down the hallway," she read aloud.

She walked unaccompanied down the long passage, lined with pictures of distinguished people on both walls. She looked briefly from one to another and noticed that black and white pictures hung near the stairwell, while further away towards the end of the corridor, modern colored styles illustrated the passing decades.

Around a corner, she viewed open double doors at the end of the hallway. Melinda passed through them, and immediately felt transported into one of her father's company banquets. Round dinner tables set with complete dinnerware settings, glasses, and breadbaskets met her gaze. The corner stage included a simple podium, unlike the enormous podium in the main lecture auditorium.

Unable to recognize the kids sitting at the first table, she advanced to introduce herself, when she heard a voice yell, "Melinda!"

She scanned the room, and saw Trent motioning her to join his table near the back of the room by waving his hands above his head in the air. Melinda responded with a short wave back and walked towards him. As she neared the table where the older brother sat, she stared at Tab sitting at his side. The thin teen attentively watched her cross the room, but when their eyes met up close, he quickly peered down at the plate in front of him. At the table, Trent motioned for Melinda to sit with them, and pointed towards an empty chair. When she stepped closer to take the seat, Melinda noticed an unfamiliar boy sitting next to it.

His shaggy white-blonde hair accurately fit his surfer-type style. A white shelled necklace vividly stood out in extreme contrast to his darkly tanned face and neck. When Melinda met his stare, his hazel eyes lit up his face in a big smile, displaying his perfect white teeth.

She introduced herself to the new boy saying, "Hi, I'm Melinda Taylor."

He waved his right hand as his response, and simply said, "Brian Markham."

Melinda left an empty chair between her and Brian. Not sure why, she quickly unfolded the napkin on her plate and placed it in her lap.

"Did you have any trouble finding this dining room?" Trent asked her.

"No, I followed the directions, and it seemed easy enough. What about you?" Melinda queried.

"Like everything else around this place, Tab memorized the map, so I just followed him."

Tab, having read their lips, blushed.

Melinda met Brian's stare by asking the California looking teen, "Brian, where are you from?"

"Santa Barbara! It's about an hour north of Los Angeles. It's such a sweet place and the girls are so nectar."

"How did you get such a great tan?" she asked.

"My friends and I spend a lot of time boarding at the beach, but don't worry, I won't show you my tan lines," he said jokingly.

Everyone smiled at the bad joke, and then Melinda re-directed the weak conversation. "I'm from Arizona, and when the temperature gets over 118 degrees during the day, everyone runs indoors to stay out of the sun."

"Woo, are you serious? It really gets that stoking?" Brian asked, as his face morphed from his normal carefree expression to astonishment.

Melinda nodded.

"Believe it or not, it gets hot where we're from too, but it's mostly because of the humidity," Trent said.

Brian asked him, "Where do you live again?"

"Chaska Minnesota," Trent replied.

"I heard it's seriously brutal in the winter."

"Brian, you can't ask for a nicer place to live during the spring, summer, and fall; but in the winter, it can get well below zero with the wind chill factor."

"No way dude, does your blood freeze in your veins?" Again, he could not hide his amazement at the opposite temperature any more than an elephant could hide its size.

"Actually, you're not far off. When people start their cars during the winter, they wait outside of them because it is usually warmer than inside their cars. That's why you don't want to stay in your car if you break down in the cold without burning a candle to stay warm, or if you don't have an emergency pack."

Melinda asked Trent, "How can people drive like that, I mean, in all that snow?"

"It doesn't always snow, but when it does, it can stick around until spring."

"What do people do for fun in the winter if you can't go outside because of the cold?" Brian asked.

"You'd be surprised; people really love the winter in my state. My brother and I live next to a small lake. After it snows, we sweep it clean with brooms and play hockey with our friends. A lot of people fish too."

"Yea, that's right; I saw something like that on TV," Brian agreed, "people sat in these funny little shacks on frozen lakes."

"I know it sounds crazy, but it's really fun. Most people have heaters, TV's, stoves, and chairs. It's almost like home, except you catch walleye through the ice floor," Trent explained.

"Walleye?" repeated Melinda squeamishly, "Sounds weird."

"It's a game fish," Trent added.

"So it's not as cold as it sounds?" Brian asked.

"Really it is! But people have learned how to go weeks without braving the outside cold temperatures."

"What do you mean, how can you not go outside?" Brian asked with skepticism.

"OK, think about it in this way. In the morning, people drive from their home's heated garage to a heated garage at work. At noon, most of the professionals head to the second floor of their office building for lunch."

"Why the second floor?" asked Melinda.

"All of the downtown Minneapolis buildings are connected to each other on all four sides with heated walkways. That floor has restaurants, stores, dry cleaners, tailors, and banks — everything normally needed during the week. After work, they drive home to their heated garage."

"What about gas stations or food stores?" Brian asked in wonder.

"It's a yes and no answer. As expensive as gas can be, some gas-stations offer full service pumps, but it's super expensive."

"Full service pumps. What's the big deal there?"

"It simply means they have warmly dressed people come outside to pump the gas, while the drivers stay inside their warm cars. Some Minnesotans are willing to pay quite a bit extra for the service."

"Wow!" Brian said, amused.

"But what about the grocery stores in your city? Don't people leave their cars to shop inside the stores to buy food?" Melinda asked, trying to trip up Trent in his explanation.

Unfazed by the question, Trent said, "Well, for example, my dad drops my mom off at the entrance of her favorite store to avoid having her walk outside. He then waits in the car with the heater on while she shops. When she's done, the cashier hands her a numbered plastic card. She calls my dad on his cell phone, and he picks her up at the front of the store. Next, they drive around to the store's side, while their numbered groceries come off a conveyor belt in a covered area. When the grocery numbers match, the store employees load our food into my dad's trunk. Although my mom might be in the cold air for a few seconds, my dad might never be for weeks. They have it all worked out," Trent finished.

"I couldn't live there dude, it sounds too brutal for me!" Brian exclaimed.

Melinda suddenly heard metal tapping on glass, and turned towards the chiming, where she was stunned to see a full dining room. She noticed a distinguished looking speaker with silver hair who seemed to have a cloud of superiority about him. Melinda thought, *"That guy's head is tilted back just enough to stare down his nose at everyone."*

The silver haired speaker began — "My name is Dr. Swinford, and I *am* the Curator of the Museum. It is *my* pleasure to welcome you to this year's student summer program. We are delighted to host such a fine group of young men and women, and hope that each of you may magnify the qualities necessary to contribute in our Museum exchange program. Your individual efforts will encourage an enormous amount of reciprocal goodwill...not only with your fellow peers in this room, but from those yet to meet around the world in similar programs."

Pausing for emphasis, the man then continued, "Through the support of our Board of Trustees consisting of local professionals and educational leaders, the Museum's student center strives to combine uninhibited students perspectives with those of our veteran professors. United as one, your efforts and that of your assigned professors can make consequential links into understanding how ancient cultures lived, worked, and later developed into sophisticated societies. This is not a simple review of theory, but a working curriculum, designed to intertwine learning between both the students and their instructors.

"Moreover, and without further ado, I would like to introduce this year's program coordinator — our associate curator, Dr. Stephen Turcasso. Please help me welcome him," Dr. Swinford stated as he stepped back and clapped his hands.

A younger man in his mid-thirties quickly approached the stage wearing wire spectacles beneath his jet-black wavy hair. In contrast to Dr. Swinford, his navy blue suit nicely balanced his unassuming air. Melinda noticed the fine tailored fit of his jacket.

He positioned a sheet of notes on the podium, and promptly began his speech, "While there is much we can learn from ongoing archeological excavation sites, for every answer we unveil, further questions are raised regarding the very same discovery.

"The minutia of research details can and does create contrasting theories between many of today's leading experts, almost immediately after announcing each new victory to the public. Through our courses here in the Museum, we have determined that the uncluttered view of young students, without predisposition, many times can glimpse past the arguable details, and recognize truths that can lead into new hypotheses.

"Archeology is more than the science of digging up and unburying historic cultures. When we classify new clues, we provide small missing puzzle pieces, with the weight to direct our work into novel uncharted areas. We can analyze new conclusions against the known evidence, and if determined to be a promising fit, our work can help us outline the basis of new research possibilities. Archeology is the art of discovering truths about the way ancient people perceived the world around them in their everyday lives."

Melinda thought at first his presentation would be boring, but soon she felt drawn into the message, and listened with interest to his descriptive concepts.

He continued, "Even the tiniest artifact can tell us a story. With enough artifacts, we can diagram the puzzle pieces in such a manner as to construct a picture of a particular era. As in our time, how we think translates into how we live. The mapping of these similarities is where we perceive much of our information about dissimilar parts of the world.

"For instance, we might look at the massive labors vital to construct the great Pyramids of Egypt, and marvel how early Egyptians performed feats that would be tremendously complicated, even if attempted with today's contemporary machines.

"Across the globe, we see comparable pyramids in Central America and Mexico. Yes, each region developed its own style, yet the related foundational character raises the question — did both civilizations develop similar construction methods independent of each other, or was there a correspondence sharing a best construction practice with each other?

"This is an exhilarating time to be part of this research program. The world is growing larger instead of smaller, when you understand that three quarters of the Earth's exterior is beneath water. In addition, man's exploration of the ocean bottom amounts to only a few percentage points when compared to the total size.

"For all we know, the Polar Regions may well contain far more information than we ever dreamed probable, simply waiting below the snow for detection much like the 40,000 year-old baby mammoth found in Siberia. Each calendar day we gain new knowledge of events not yet answered by science.

For example, even today, science is unable to establish the basis for ghost sightings, unexplainable healings, agree on the total number of plant and animal species, and of course everyone's favorite — UFO's."

Everyone chuckled at the UFO comment.

Dr. Turcasso went on, "At the core of majestic ancient civilizations, or the remnants of an earliest small rural community, one thread is widespread amongst our work. Those who built them often declined or disappeared without a decisive or verified explanation, which is where our work becomes invaluable.

"Were enormous successful cultures later unable to feed such an immense populace, or did illness swiftly bring their disappearance? Did enemies conquer them, or could they merely have declined into obscurity slowly over time? Explanations range from one extreme to another. Occasionally hard work in the field proves a serious scientific discovery, and at others, it presents us with a larger baffling mystery. Stories and mythology proliferate throughout history. Are you aware the recorded annihilation of Atlantis as written by Plato happened nearly

12,000 years ago? Or that Ancient Egyptians alleged after being mummified and buried with their affluence, servants, horses, and important daily items that they then passed from this life into another to carry on the continuance of their former preceding lives.

"They understood the relocation of their spirit to be a corporeal evolution through a veil, rather than merely a spiritual passing into an elevated energy plane. Did you know that in Alaska, there are native tribes that believe in a supernatural dimension they claim the Otter People control? Legends describe that some tribe members simply disappear; as a burst of lights accompanied the episode. When the friends or family arrive to where the missing person stood, moments after viewing the event, nothing remains to indicate the person ever stood there, excluding footsteps in the snow, which seem to stop in mid-stride. The missing people, along with their possessions, vanish. As fantastic as this claim is to our scientific minds, our job is to sift throughout layers of details, and organize them in assorted combinations to decipher prospective pictures to sustain the evidence.

"Finally, we can then map a new theory against other known archeological discoveries. Equivalent to a finding a key fitting into a specific lock, once we comprise a match, we can then advance through new doors to document the findings and maintain our work. This is where you fit into the program. Over the next few days, you will gain knowledge about the Museum during your orientation. We as the program leaders can select random teams to work together, or permit you to choose your teammates.

"Either way, each team must consist of five members. When a team does not comprise of the full five members, one of our two proxy associate students will supplement that team. When I call their names, will they please stand? Scott Swinford and Dale Bradan!"

Both stood as requested. Scott Swinford stood at a table closest to the podium. From a distance, he appeared petite, with sandy colored hair combed with the latest style. It was apparent that like his gray-haired father, he dressed in the newest fashion trends. He displayed a smirk of superiority, and promptly sat down. Melinda felt there was something under the surface about Scott that she should be cautious of, similar to a sliced onion in plastic wrap that appears well on the surface, until unwrapped to release the potent contents, which could bring a person to tears.

Dissimilarly, Dale Bradan appeared ordinary in his clothing, manner, and had slightly tousled hair; however, Melinda determined he looked to be about fourteen-years old and lacked the same self-assurance as the older Scott. Standing at a center table, Dale hesitated in knowing when to sit down. Self-conscious of the fact, his features turned crimson by the time he did.

Dr. Turcasso continued, "Within your first few weeks in the program, each of you will be exposed to classical civilizations through a lecture style format. The subsequent weeks will consist of each team choosing a project hypothesis, and begin preliminary field research right here in the Museum, learning from our dynamic artifacts.

"Each team will be assigned a research lab room for the remainder of your stay, to discuss, test, and validate your theories with your project instructors."

After a pause, Dr. Turcasso spoke, using an elevated tone of voice that was noticeably louder, "This is very significant for you to comprehend. There are stages that each team must win to advance in the program. If you develop your project outline, identify strong supportive evidence, and remain ethical in your work and your behavior towards the other teams, a panel of judges will appraise and select those teams whose concepts have the most merit to continue. These will be our first stage winners. Regrettably, those teams not chosen will have concluded their participation in the program, and must soon return home."

Melinda glanced about the room during the sudden hush to gauge the students' reactions at hearing some of them would leave the Museum. Like herself, concern became evident on many faces. All attention turned again toward the podium, especially from the few pocket protector types, fearing that kind of doom.

After clearing his throat, Dr. Turcasso excitedly said, "Due to the generous sponsors of our program, the first stage winning teams will each have one fully funded field trip to the area of their study anywhere in the world."

Wide-eyed students filled with surprised enthusiasm, which quickly replaced the preceding concerns. The volume of their zealous voices crowded the room from talking to neighbors about possible trips to thrilling foreign countries.

Dr. Turcasso raised his hands into the air.

"Excuse me, will everyone please remain quiet! There is a catch!"

Instantly, the room became eerily quiet.

"If you conduct yourselves as anything less than true ambassadors of the Museum, be it only one, or two individual team members, the entire team will be disqualified to return home."

Fearful expressions surfaced on many faces as they scanned the room, wondering who would be suitable and trustworthy team members.

"However," his voice rose a few degrees, "I shall expect we will not have those troubles from anyone in this group. The competition will continue until there is one winning team! The final winning team will have submitted the most unique and exciting supposition, pooled with supportive facts gathered from their field trip. Now for the electrifying news! The competition's winning team will receive an additional second all-expense paid, first class trip to unveil their work at a Museum of their choice anywhere in the world. The first-place team members will be photographed, and have their conclusions published in leading industry journals and magazines."

Several students rose from their seats, clapping with further anticipation.

"Finally, as if this were not enough, our program victors can accept a full grant to return to their field site, to expand their leading edge research the following summer, if they choose."

Whistles and cheers erupted from the entire room, everyone filled with excitement and emotion. No one had predicted the program would be so important. Most visualized in their minds the program was nothing more than a sugar coated cover up for a teenage summer camp. Conversely, to choose any topic of research and journey into any associated foreign country leading to publish their work into prestigious Museum circles seemed over-the-top for most of the students.

Melinda's eyes panned the room seeing some students giving each other high five slaps.

Trying to regain control of the eager students, Dr. Turcasso called out, "Two more items...students...two more items!"

The room quieted down more slowly. "Once you select your teammates, if you wish to substitute the current roommate arrangements in order to spend added time discussing your projects, please see Mrs. Neely in the next few days. Second, there will be no cell phone use or texting allowed during the lectures to disrupt others in class. Make sure you leave them in your room or turn them off during each assembly. Please save those activities for your own time. As for tonight, I strongly suggest you meet new people, make new friends, and tomorrow, get ready to embark on one of the most challenging and stimulating adventures of your life! Welcome again, and have a great dinner. Thank you!" he concluded.

At that, Melinda thought, "W*ow, hope at last! If I can find a great teammate, perhaps I can move in with her, and then Mea will be history for me.*"

A thrilling charge overflowed the air about them. Melinda and Brian did a high five, while Trent and Tab excitedly signed to each other. Melinda felt it could definitely be a remarkable summer.

Prepared to leave, Melinda gathered her purse when the blonde girl she met earlier, Leslie Lyons, approached her from behind and tapped her on the shoulder asking, "Are you leaving before you eat dinner?"

Melinda stared vacantly at her for a second, and then in a rush, remembered they were here to eat their supper and choose teams.

Embarrassed, Melinda's face and neck altered color to a brilliant pink, "I was so wound up; I forgot we're supposed to eat."

"I know — did you imagine it would be this cool?" Leslie asked.

"My parents never said a word about the travel," Melinda responded with a puzzled expression, "I wonder if they knew?"

Without another word, Melinda pointed at the chair next to her and both girls sat down laughing together at their table.

Once introductions were completed between Leslie and Brian, Trent took the discussion lead, "We could go around meeting every other student in the room tonight, but I have a feeling they may not be as good as the group right here.

"With the exception of Brian, we were the first four to arrive at the Museum. I am hoping that means something good. Plus, ending up together at the same table with Brian gives us a team of five…"

"It must be a good thing," Leslie finished his sentence.

"What do you guys say? Are you in?" Trent prodded.

Melinda observed the group's positive acceptance. With the exception of

Tab and herself, everyone shook their heads in agreement.

Facing Trent, Melinda asked, "How does Tab feel about us being a team?"

"Hold on," he said, and after signing to each other, Tab raised his eyebrows, and smiled while Trent offered on his brother's behalf, "he likes the idea."

Curious, but not wanting to seem rude, Melinda asked, "Will it be difficult for us to work together with Tab, I mean; I don't know any sign language. Will either of us feel left out?"

Empathetic to her concern, Brian and Leslie stared questioningly at Trent.

"I promise it won't be an issue. After only a few days, he'll seem just like one of the guys. He may be a little shy at first, but seriously, he can read lips like you wouldn't believe."

"What about sign language — will he be able to keep up with the classes and discussions?"

"Absolutely Leslie," Trent acknowledged, "Tab uses ASL or American Sign Language. The name is a misnomer, so let me provide some background to explain what I mean. In the early eighteen hundreds, a wealthy New England man hired a tutor to help his deaf daughter learn to converse with their local townspeople. The tutor traveled to Paris to locate an institute known for helping deaf people sound words and use hand signals to speak with each other, and then he returned with one of their hearing-impaired teachers.

"Within a few years, the mix of French and American Sign Language spread into what we have today. The reason I am telling you this, is that sign language does not use words like "the," "and," "an," and so forth. Without those smaller filler words, it increases the communication speed of signing."

Just then, waiters interrupted the conversation.

Offered an entree choice of chicken with rice and vegetables, or prime rib with a baked potato, Trent paused in his explanation for the team to place their orders. Melinda and Leslie chose the chicken meal, while the brothers and Brian ordered the prime rib. Melinda felt starving from smelling the food, and silently grew more impatient as her stomach grumbled until hers arrived.

Trent continued as he sliced through his prime rib, "A hand sign is like a picture or a concept. You know the saying that a picture is worth a 1,000 words.

Instead of signing just words, we're communicating those same concepts"

Leslie caught on, "So what you mean is that Tab could process information faster than the average person, by assimilating all of those pictures at one time?"

"Exactly," Trent smiled.

"Overall, fewer deaf people read lips, because they never learned to sound words in a sentence, however, Tab spoke more than ten years ago before he was hit by a car at five years of age. The accident hurt the part of his brain used for hearing, which prevents him from sounding words well, but it doesn't affect his ability to read your lips and the lecturers too. He won't miss a thing."

"I never thought about it that way, but it makes sense to me," Brian added.

Tab knew he was the topic of conversation, and that his brother loved to brag about him, even though he usually tried to ignore Trent's charming theatrics.

Melinda raised her hand close to her face saying, "I'm in."

"Me too," Leslie confirmed.

Everyone peered at Brian. Feeling the weight of their stares, he said smiling, "I'm in — I'm in."

All eyes returned to stare at Tab.

From reading their lips, instead of looking at his plate in shyness, he was smiling at the acceptance.

"Me too," he said out of tone, causing the group to smile and wink at him.

Servers removed the main meal plates, and quickly replaced them with dessert plates containing a slice of Raspberry cheesecake.

Leslie giggled and then said, "This thin line of chocolate zigzagging across the plate makes me think the dessert chef is a food artist and his job is way too easy."

With the conclusion of dessert, the entire group of students departed from the dining area, clumped into new teams.

Reaching the girl's hall, Leslie and Melinda said, "Good night guys — see you for breakfast?"

"Sounds good," Trent responded, while Tab nodded before turning into their room's hallway.

Chapter Seven

MUMMIES

Having missed breakfast because of oversleeping, Melinda shuffled into the auditorium for the first student lecture. She noticed a man in his mid-fifty's, dressed as if he recently stepped out of the Hippy part of the 1960s. White wiry hairs notably spotted his full brown beard, and he had unruly matching hair circulating his head to cover the balding spot.

When Melinda noticed his plain brown shoes, she had a funny visualization of him wearing sandals. Often speaking about the older software engineers at the airline, her father affectionately used the phrase, "Beard and Sandal folks."

The instructor greeted everyone cheerfully, and urged them, "Take your seats everyone — hurry now, there's a lot of material to cover today."

The instructor hesitated a few moments before he began his lecture, "My name is Dr. Clyde Koffin. I'm one of the Museum's resident professors. My area of research is in Egyptology. In fact, I'm sure most of you know more of the subject then you may be aware."

Scanning the room, he asked a very tall, gangly boy, "What is your name?"

"Colby De Vaney, sir."

"Thank you for the sir, however, in the future, Clyde or Dr. Koffin will suffice."

"Now — what can you tell me about Egypt?" he asked the now surprised boy.

Embarrassed by the first question of the first lecture, Colby stammered, "I'm from a smaller city in Canada and the closest I've been to anything Egyptian was in the movies and on TV, does that count?" he asked bashfully.

The other students busted into laughter. Colby's face flushed a vivid red, believing the students were laughing at him, until he realized they thought his comment was funny. He then sat up straighter in his chair with a shy smile.

"Ok — ok — you bring up a good point! We can *all* know something about Egypt; however, most of us in this room know very little about the culture, history, or even many of the rulers. The expanse of knowledge is so vast, it is literally overwhelming; no one can really know everything."

An athletic girl in blue sweats abruptly raised her hand.

"Yes and your name?" Dr. Koffin sputtered.

"Uh — my name is Joyce. I really don't know much about ancient Egypt, because I spend most of my time practicing to play sports. So — what was it about Egypt that made you devote all of your time in that one area?"

Mentally disheveled by the unusual question, Dr. Koffin paused to collect his thoughts before proceeding.

"Well, that's a bit of a long story...but let me see if I can explain it quickly," he said more to himself than to Joyce.

When he faced the sidewall, his eyes seemed to drop in personal embarrassment.

"Years ago when I was a senior in high school, I was selected to participate in the People-to-People Student Ambassador Program. Is anyone familiar with the program?"

He spotted their blank stares, and added, "The People-to-People program was established by President Eisenhower. You guys *do* know who President Eisenhower was?"

A well-dressed African American boy answered, "Wasn't he the President of the United States after World War II?"

"Your name is?"

"Jerome Whitfield."

"Correct, Jerome," stated Dr. Koffin.

"After touring the European countries, he was surrounded by wreckage after the war, and he believed that people needed hope if they were going to re-build their lives and communities."

The professor continued, "Riding around in military jeeps through dozens of towns riddled by warfare, he felt impressed by the children. No matter how bad the situation had become, they could always smile back at him. This gave him an idea.

"If students from around the world could meet and make lasting friendships, he hoped they could break down their traditional cultural differences to share new ideas. Several cities around the globe still participate in the program today. Each summer, nominated students traveled to assigned cities to stay with a host family. With me, my family could not afford the travel portion, which was the personal responsibility of each family. I was completely dejected when I learned I could not go. Making matters worse, I later discovered I would have stayed with a family in Egypt as my assignment. Many of my school classmates knew I had been nominated, however, no one knew I couldn't afford to go when I dropped out of the program."

Dr. Koffin held his hand in front of him as if in a defensive posture, and continued, "Even though I knew it was wrong, a sneaky thought formed in my silly young mind. I decided if I learned everything about Egypt on my own over the summer break, perhaps by the time school resumed in the fall I could pass myself off as having been to Egypt as part of the program."

Mark Lister, a blonde boy, made a stunned blinking stare at the instructor, while a petite Japanese girl, named Kim Otani, glanced at another girl with a look of concern.

"I know what you're thinking, but you need to understand — my not being able to attend this seemingly once in a lifetime opportunity really hurt my parents too. Even by working two jobs, my father was unable to support the trip financially. Unlike many kids in my school, my family had to make sacrifices.

"I needed more self-assurance in those days, because I often felt like a second-class citizen. We were unable to afford stylish school clothes for me, and I never received a new car when I turned 16. For some reason, at the time I felt I had little excitement to offer to my friends when they gathered to talk about their exciting spring break vacations. I remember listening to them with envy, wishing I had any story to share.

"After school let out, I watched movies about Egypt, read library books about the pyramids, and studied the culture during the entire summer. As wrong as it was, it seemed to me the only way to tell my own stories, even if they were mostly pretend. Before I knew it, for someone my age, I was sort of an expert on reciting Egyptian facts, legends, and well, to be more accurate, as much as someone who never actually went to Egypt."

Lost to his own thoughts while the class stared at him in silence, and realizing his refrain, Dr. Koffin noticed the bewildered looks on the student's faces. He quickly faced the chalkboard.

"So, I discovered I was hooked on the topic. The more I learned, the more I wanted to learn, and eventually travel there someday. The good news is that the experience motivated me to study as hard as I could, until I graduated with a Ph.D. in Archeology. And — finally I might add, I spent a great deal of time in Egypt," he proudly stated.

"Moreover," he went on, "I learned to have more self-assurance, and realized finally, that no matter whom you are as a person, certain percentages always seem to ring true with regard to fitting in socially. The moral of my understanding goes like this — approximately 25 percent of the people you go to school with will like you for the right reasons. Another 25 percent of them will like you for the wrong reasons. Conversely, 25 percent will dislike you for the right reasons, and finally, 25 percent will dislike you for the wrong reasons no matter whom you are or as I explained about me in my story, pretend to be. Using music as an illustration, regardless if western music, hip-hop, rock, or classical music fits you best; enjoy listening to it, and be who you are as a person, as the percentages always average out. A similar number of people will like you or dislike you no matter who you choose to be, or what you listen to, so it's best to just be yourself!"

The ice was broken while the students digested the good advice. Several students had raised their hands when Dr. Koffin said, "All in good time, all in good time."

He returned to the front of the lecture auditorium continuing, "We still have much to cover today."

Professor Koffin collected his thoughts, and while holding a piece of white chalk, drew a large triangle on the board behind him, and then began his lecture. "When most people think of Egypt, they immediately visualize mummies in underground tombs, buried beneath the great Pyramids or in the Valley of the Kings; however, there is a great deal of excitement to study beyond those two subjects. For instance, does anyone know what the Sphinx is, or its purpose?" the professor asked, glancing at the wall clock.

With the atypical introduction, many in the room now felt at ease with the professor. Lost in their thoughts about his comments, several of the students reflected about how the advice could help them deal with their own peer pressures, or reasons for impressing their friends at school, and perhaps even the Museum program. The fact this was a new program year, with new kids, meant none of the students wanted to be the first to look foolish by answering a question wrongly. On cue, as if their instructor had flipped a gravity switch to the 'On' position, most of the teen's heads and chins dropped to break eye contact with Clyde, and stare blankly at their desks or feet, reluctant to be engaged in another question.

As if failing to notice the sudden class affliction, Dr. Koffin pulled a hanging string, connected to a light-colored rolling window-type shade. Lowered completely, it revealed a large picture of the infamous Sphinx. Emotion fading from his face, his tone transitioned from that of a teacher who was being personal, to a lecturer presenting a well-rehearsed script.

"As we start at the top and work our way down, we see the head of the Sphinx. Some local authorities claim it to be the head of a god; however, it is much smaller in proportion to the enormous lion-shaped body. While this suggests that later stonemasons re-chiseled the current appearance from out of something larger, the head is still nearly fourteen feet wide and almost thirty feet tall. This may sound huge to you, until you realize the entire length of the body is more than two hundred feet long.

"Carved from the immediate bedrock, the stone is quite porous. After surviving rushing winds, pelting sands, and draining rainwaters, most authorities believe the head eroded at a different rate than the body, in part because sand covered the body for thousands of years. Nevertheless, while newer erosion and celestial mapping theories suggest it could be 12,500 years-old, many traditional experts believe its construction occurred during the fourth Dynasty, somewhere around 2550 BC.

"No one is sure of its exact history or purpose, except that to the Egyptians, the Great Sphinx symbolizes strength and wisdom. We know of at least two times the Sphinx has been fully uncovered throughout history, though the real mystery is why the Egyptians buried it. The mystery continued after the Stella was uncovered in the early 1900's, between its great paws."

Luke Hammer, a young man dressed in wrangler jeans and cowboy boots, raised his hand.

"Yes," said Dr. Koffin.

"Did you say a Stella? What's that?"

"Look at this area," Professor Koffin said, pointing a red laser beam into the space between the giant paws. "This is where a tablet call 'the Stella' resided and told an etched story, which was dated much later than the actual building of the Great Sphinx. I'm paraphrasing of course, but during the eighteenth Dynasty a young prince named, Thutmosis IV was said to have fallen asleep on the sand beneath the Sphinx."

Dr. Koffin stepped off the stage, and walked towards the center of the room.

"In his dream, the Sphinx told him if he completely unburied it from the sand trapping it's body, he would be the next ruler of Egypt."

"Did he become king?" a redheaded girl blurted from her wheelchair.

Smiling at her, the professor said, "Great question, but we will have to wait for that lecture on another day."

After he returned to the stage and stepped back in front of the podium, he briefly reviewed his notes and proceeded with the lecture.

"Because of the Sphinx's position in relationship with the great Pyramid, no one knows for sure, however, some archeological experts believe it was commissioned and built by the Pharaoh Khafre, who ruled Egypt from 2520 to 2494 BC. Still other Egyptologists believe Khafre's father built the Sphinx, whom you may not know, is credited as the builder of the Great Pyramid. In addition, many believe that at one time, the Sphinx was brightly colored with paint when it was later found on one of the ears. We don't have much information about its significance, or its purpose, yet considering it represents strength…"

"Doctor," Matt Faraday, a heavyset boy interrupted in a rasping voice, "is it true the Sphinx has a tunnel inside it? I saw a documentary one time, about some kind of chamber or passages underneath it."

Dr. Koffin cleared the uncertainty, "Yes, a chamber, and a secret passage were…"

Suddenly, the Museum fire alarm blared!

Chapter Eight

BIZARRE BEHAVIOR

Mrs. Nelxon yelled up stairs to Jennifer, "After you clean your room, feed the dogs and clean out the guinea pig cage! I'm running your brother to soccer practice."

Waiting for a response, her mom yelled louder, "Jennifer!"

Behind the wall at the top of the stairs, Jennifer removed her loud earphones. With a tiresome groan, she was too familiar with the tedious tasks her mother asked of her, and acted as though she did not hear the request by her mother.

"What did you say?" Jennifer hollered.

Her mom repeated herself and added, "I'll be back in two hours, and I want your room spotless, the dogs fed, and no going out until Squeaker's cage is cleaned! I'm going to check those items when I get home!"

Jennifer winced and yelled, "Ok!" and disappeared behind the wall to replace her earphones.

Re-entering her messy room, it was clear that various types of clothes had been tried on but not worn, and littered the floor around her unmade bed. A week-old stack of folded clothes rested on the floor at the foot of her bed. After folding the family's laundry, her mother put her brother's and her clothes on the bottom step of the staircase that led up to their rooms. Both siblings were required to carry a pile up to their rooms each time they went upstairs, but usually only one in three trips resulted in the clothing finding their rooms.

Jennifer decided to choose the path of least resistance and started putting the folded clothes into her dresser drawers. She paused in her cleaning activity, and before reaching for the next pile of clothing, she reflected on the ordeal she had created concerning the big dog, and decided in the end, she got off easy when her dad grounded her for only a month. He scolded her, "Your mother and I understand you're an animal rescue junkie. And we're usually tolerant of your helping lost dogs and cats in the neighborhood; but when your mother got a call that you were riding in a complete stranger's car, to an unknown vet's office, because of a strange dog, this is a serious problem young lady!"

Mrs. Nelxon had blown an angry gasket after arriving at the vet's office to discover that Jennifer had somehow implied responsibility for the black dog. The vet implied that they both owed $478.63 for the emergency office visit, x-rays, antibiotics, and the neon green oversized cast completely encasing the dog's powerful front leg.

It became worse. Jennifer later remembered that she had left her bike at the strip mall before driving in Michelle's car to the vet's office. They discovered it stolen from the parking lot when they returned to recover it, and her mom was furious with her at the loss. Not deserving of a brand new bike after creating the enormous financial mess, her working parents could not chauffer Jennifer around at her whims during the summer time, which meant she would still need another bike.

Between the vet bills, the new bike, the follow-up vet visit, and the extra dog food the big dog ate; Jennifer eagerly took her dad's proposal to work off the bill in exchange for not getting her allowance.

After cleaning her room, Jennifer headed downstairs into the kitchen. She removed a stem of celery from out of the refrigerator, and sat down on the tile floor next to the guinea pig cage. Upon hearing her, Squeaker, her solid black Guinea pig, except for a white stripe on his nose and a white top knot of spiked fur, smelled the celery in her hand, and whistled in excitement.

"Hi Squeaker, how's my little skunk look-alike? Oh, you're a cutie," she said, hearing him coo, sounding like a small purring cat. When she gave the adorable pet the treat, he demonstrated his enjoyment by springing up and down, popcorning happily. Jennifer finished cleaning his cage and put in new wood chip shavings, refilled his water bottle with enough water and vitamin C solution, and then picked up two white and gray dog food bowls from off the floor. Using a large plastic scoop her mother kept in the dog food bag, she piled the extra food into the new dog's bowl.

Butch was her two-year-old golden retriever. It was love at first sight when Jennifer had spotted Butch in a box with other golden retriever puppies' years ago. At first, she watched them roll and wrestle with each other, and then she gave in after the sign read:

Free Puppies!

Jennifer thought, *"How could my parents say no if he's free?"*

Later after the excitement settled down, her father explained, "Honey, free is only free to the person giving away the puppies."

Surprised at her dad's comment, he told her, "These puppies have not received their shots, which can cost between $35.00 to $50.00 and more for each one. Plus, now we need to buy a dog tag and a dog license."

She might have lived it down if the cost stopped there; however, little Butch soon trampled their neighbor's flower garden while chasing a small chameleon lizard. Neither Mrs. Murphy nor her husband ever forgave him. Teething for months during his growing puppy stage, Butch had also chewed her mom's formal dining room table leg. Jennifer could not watch TV for two weeks when the furniture repairman charged her mom over $150.00.

"No," she told herself, "free is not free after all."

She placed both bowls on the kitchen floor and called the dogs, jumping back suddenly at seeing the big dog sitting unnoticed behind her. Startled by its unexpected appearance to eat, she watched it limp over to its food bowl.

Jennifer had told her friend Mary at school, "She looks like a pirate dog with a peg leg walking in her cast."

Longer than the dog's leg, each step of the cast lifted up the dog's same side a full inch. To make eating easier, Jennifer set the food bowl on a box so the dog would not have to struggle to bend down with the cast.

After making her weekly vet payment, the veterinarian explained to Jennifer, "She's doing great! I expect the cast should come off in a few days."

Jennifer thought he was nice enough, especially for accepting her allowance payment plan for the new dogs vet bills; however, she was not sure if he was one of the best in city.

She would usually ask him during the check up visits, "What type of dog is she?"

Unsure of the breed, the thin man would usually say, "Well, she seems to me to be a cross between several types of dogs. Let me look into it," was his standard answer.

"Butch…come and eat!" Jennifer yelled through the kitchen window into the back yard.

Like a fuzzy golden flash, Butch rushed inside the room and gulped down the food. While Jennifer stood behind both dogs as they ate, she pondered how dissimilar they were from each other. Butch required constant guidance from her family, while the big dog seemed one-step ahead of them.

Jennifer enjoyed playing a game with the new black dog. After first spotting her sleeping in the family room or lying in the sun outside, Jennifer would sneak silently on her tiptoes into the laundry room to get dog food for them. Jennifer was always disappointed to see the big dog waiting patiently for her to exit the laundry room with food. In contrast to her, Butch seemed content to be clueless of the feeding activity until officially notified.

Many consider Golden Retrievers to be large dogs, yet when compared to the big dog, Butch resembled a puppy. Their new vet had pointed out that the top of Butch's shoulders were level to the lowest point of the big dog's chest. Although the black dog was much taller than Butch, their hips were almost equal in width, nonetheless, this ended the comparison between them. Butch's shoulders noticeably widened from his hips when watching him from behind, but it was different with the black dog. Immense deltoid muscles rippled underneath her short shiny flat fur. She reminded Jennifer of a blending between the long sleek head of a hieroglyphic Egyptian Jackal, and a nearly tail-less, extremely muscular Great Dane.

For a male, Butch looked like the typical "ninety-eight pound weakling." There were other differences between the dogs too. The poor big dog noticeably flinched at normal kitchen sounds of pots and pans coming out from beneath the cabinets from the moment she arrived, and Jennifer's family laughed wildly at her behavior when they discovered their big screen TV drove the new dog crazy.

Two weeks earlier while Jennifer and her family watched the Discovery channel, upon hearing a male lion roar at another nomadic male lion encroaching on the first one's territory, the black dog rose to her feet. She rumbled a long, low, and loud menacing emanation from deep inside her chest, reminding Jennifer of the sound alligators make when vibrating to form bubbles in the water.

Nervous by her hasty behavior change, Jennifer's parents worried for their children's safety until her mother soon realized the big dog had placed herself between them and the television set, making it apparent to all that she was shielding the family from the would-be danger.

Shortly before her arrival into Jennifer's home, her dad had built a new rock pond in their back yard. In its center, a fountain peacefully cascaded water into the air from an electric pump hidden below the waterline, and the pond presented Butch with a full time temptation to swim into the deeper end.

While barbequing chicken and hamburgers on his grill in their backyard, Mr. Nelxon happened to see Butch standing in chest deep pond water, chewing on the fountain pump's electric wires. Stung with fear of Butch's electrocution in less than another moment, Jennifer's dad instantly screamed, "BUTCH, GET OUT OF THERE NOW!"

Frightened by the unexpected shriek of his name, Butch wilted from the sound of the angry voice and leapt out of the water. Jennifer and her brother dashed outside of their house and into the backyard after hearing their dad yell so thunderously. Focused on Butch's well being, no one saw the big dog burst into a run towards Butch until it was too late. In spite of wearing an immobile cast, her incredible speed knocked the golden retriever off his paws to fall flat onto his back. Worried the big dog would hurt Butch; Mr. Nelxon rushed forward to protect him. Lying submissively on his back to the new dog, they all heard her issue a strange snarl while peering deeply into his eyes.

Jennifer's dad noticed something unidentifiable, and prevented her and her brother from interfering. The black dog quickly released Butch from her dominant pose. Her demeanor did not appear angry, yet each person felt she was satisfied with the results of the encounter. After trying everything to prevent Butch from swimming in the pond, from this point forward, he never again entered the pond. In addition, each time a family member scolded Butch for *any* reason, the big dog repeated the same type of lesson. The results were always predictable — Butch never duplicated any unwanted act under the watchful eyes of the big dog. She groomed their family dog in a way they could not fathom.

In the beginning, while posting pictures of the big dog around their neighborhood, Jennifer's family joked often that its former owners, aware of her eccentric behaviors, knew a good thing when she escaped. Conversely, because of her later unique actions, after the first few weeks, each time the phone rang in their house, the family evolved into trading nervous glances, fearing her owners had called to claim her back.

The more they witnessed the big dog's hard-to-explain antics, the more Jennifer's family struggled to hit upon the right name to call her. They simply referred to her as 'the dog' yet Jennifer wanted to name her Tausha, or maybe Athena.

Three months later, Jennifer's grandmother exposed a bizarre new talent of the beautiful dog. Mr. Nelxon, a software sales manager, returned home at random times each day, as dictated by the number of sales calls he attended with his sales reps. When Jennifer's grandmother believed the big dog wanted to go outside, she opened the back door, but it would not exit, and only sat and waited. Mr. Nelxon soon arrived 10 minutes later, and the big dog happily greeted him.

Unannounced, Jennifer's grandmother observed the amazing dog during the week, and documented that it was one hundred percent accurate in predicting when Jennifer's father would come home from work, by waiting at the back door.

All were amazed when Jennifer's grandmother shared her experiment with the rest of the family.

Chapter Nine

DANGER

Bewildered by the unanticipated ringing fire alarm, students in the lecture auditorium glanced around wildly for the nearest exit.

Over the blast of the buzzing alarm, Dr. Koffin yelled, "Follow me everyone — hurry, this way — single file please!"

Melinda and the other students rushed towards the lecture room's rear double doors, and madly pushed against each other, until they all burst out into the hallway like the contents from a spilled box of cereal. Melinda scanned both directions of the hallway for smoke and flames, when the Asian Studies instructor Dr. Edwin Wong called to Dr. Koffin, "What is happening?"

"I've no idea;" Dr. Koffin replied, "we were in the middle of our lecture when the alarm rang."

Suddenly, the dreadful buzzing muted slightly when the entire museum heard an authoritative voice over the museum speaker system, "Please, may I have your attention. Will everyone exit from the Museum through the front entrance doors into the west parking lot? Again, please remain calm, and meet your party in the west parking area. Thank you."

"This way everybody — stay close behind me," Dr. Wong cried out above the noise to take charge of the immediate state of affairs.

Dr. Koffin watched as the students trailed behind Dr. Wong down the hallway, and counted the heads of the students in his lecture as they followed, "One, two, three, four...."

The shorter Dr. Wong quickly reversed his expected direction, yet the students could easily track his arm, held high above his head dangling a silver medical alert bracelet. Herding the teenagers through another set of double swinging doors, he turned right, and then quickly left. Shortly lost from view around a corner, he appeared, now hurrying side-by-side with Dale Bradan, and led the students to the main hall's stairs.

Melinda bounded down the stair steps and from her elevated position, she spied museum patrons gawking frantically about them for the danger, and clogging the main entrance doors leading to the outside portico. For a moment, she felt flushed and visualized angry masked warriors pressing urgently against the escaping mob's madness. In front of her, Dale suddenly disappeared inside a crowd swell, and lost his place until he scrambled free to follow behind Melinda across the marble hallway towards the front doors. Without warning, a frightened patron shoved Dale from behind and he slammed heavily into Melinda's back.

Melinda swiftly caught herself on the entry stair railing near the main doors, when another panicked museum visitor accidentally sideswiped her, breaking her grip loose from the polished brass. Melinda fell precariously to the floor amongst hundreds of running and kicking feet, when suddenly strong and sure hands aided her. As a fading daydream, her eyes lifted to see a strange figure hovering above her, when the warrior altered in front of her eyes to become a firefighter. Protected in a helmet and face shield, he had surged through the swarming crowd carrying a long-handled axe.

With little effort, the capable man pulled Melinda up from the floor, and swung her over his shoulder in a firefighter hold, while consecutively grasping Dale under the arm and hauling him to his feet. Using long, fast strides, they were soon outside beyond the enormous car portico, where the firefighter lowered Melinda securely to her feet. Unsteady from the unpredicted event, she stared blindly up at the rescuing man with a stunned expression.

The man lifted his facemask to comfort her saying, "You're going to be okay."

Persuasively, he advised Dale and Melinda, "Move to the railing overlooking the water until directed otherwise, OK? I need to get back inside to help the others." Then he looked down at Dale and added, "You need to slow down, kid.

You almost turned your friend into a human doormat."

With a blank face, Dale nodded trance-like in agreement to the lofty man, when the firefighter repositioned his face shield and jogged away from them towards the Museum. Melinda grabbed Dale's elbow, and pulled him, still watching the fireman, to where the man had just pointed.

Dale hesitated before staring at the building's exterior and said, "Wait a minute — I don't see any smoke in the air, do you, Melinda?"

She gazed upward to observe the building's roof and agreed with him, "No!"

"Dale, Dale!" A man's voice called from behind.

Melinda turned back to stare in the direction of the voice, when Dr. Wong urgently waved for both of them to move toward him. Then he pointed at more students Melinda recognized from Dr. Koffin's lecture, standing behind him against the wood beam railing overlooking swans floating gracefully on the mote.

"You two come back here! We don't want to take any chances."

Dale approached the professor and asked, "Dr. Wong, what's going on?"

The educator shook his head sadly, and replied, "I don't know what is happening, but I hope it's nothing serious. There has not been a fire here before, and if ever there were, I'm afraid to think of the monumental loss."

Still pondering about what Dale asked her, Melinda questioned the girl taking pictures of the museum with her phone camera directly behind her, "Did you see any fire or smoke?"

"No — nothing," the girl replied.

***

An hour and forty minutes later, a small group of firefighters now in unfastened jackets that revealed their red suspenders, slowly retreated from the Museum's entrance. Some carried their helmets in their hands and strolled leisurely to their fire trucks.

Melinda's former rescuer broke away from the others while he removed his helmet, and returned to where she stood next to Dr. Wong to provide an update, "It's safe to return inside the building."

With a shrug of his narrow shoulders, the Asian teacher lifted his hands in a questioning manner and asked, "What was the problem?"

Melinda suddenly felt self-conscious about her appearance around the tall and handsome firefighter. She tried to pull her bangs to the side without arousing any notice of the movement, while she stood straighter. Without his helmet, the firefighter's intense brown eyes flashed warmly between Dr. Wong, Dale, and Melinda, beneath his now-tussled hair. Flushed from staring intently at him, Melinda became nervous he would notice her dreamy gaze, when the fireman answered, "Seems that two of the exhibit display crew men claim a tiger got inside the museum and growled at them where they were working. In fear for the public's safety, they pulled the fire alarm handle in the room, hoping everyone would quickly exit the building."

"You're kidding?" Dr. Wong asked in disbelief.

"I wish I were, but that's their story. I'd hate to be those two when the head guy in there gets through with them. He's yelling at them now," the man explained, smiling at the small student group. He continued, "Well, that about does it for now. Nothing personal, but I hope I don't have to see you guys anytime *too* soon."

With a quick wave good-by, the firefighter walked slowly to a large diesel fire engine as it roared to life. Melinda watched intently as the handsome man placed one boot onto the lowest step and bounced up with a short hop inside the passenger cabin.

Dale pressed backwards into Melinda as the students near them gave way to make room as the giant rescue truck swung past them and rolled away down the long driveway.

"The party's over! Everyone back inside," Dr. Wong directed.

Melinda merged with the other students and Museum personnel through the main entry that lead into the grand hallway, when she heard a familiar angry voice shouting, "...GOODNESS SAKES MAN, DON'T YOU UNDERSTAND WHAT NEGATIVE PUBLICITY CAN DO TO SLOW DOWN OUR ADMISSION REVENUE?"

Chad, the Exposition Manager, stood next to Dr. Swinford while the Curator listened to the larger of the two display builders, who explained their dramatic actions.

The pear-shaped man in blue-jean overalls said, "We truthfully thought we did right to rush people out of the building as quickly as possible."

The second, thinner worker chimed in, "If you'd seen the way it stared at us, you would have done the same..."

Dr. Swinford cut him off in mid-sentence, "What tiger, you idiot? Why would — no! How could a tiger get in here?" he raged at them throwing his arms wide. "Next thing you know, you'll be telling us pink elephants are flying around in the building!"

Dr. Swinford spun to face Chad and yelled wrathfully at the youthful slender man, "THIS IS YOUR PROBLEM! YOU HIRED THEM; YOU DEAL WITH IT APPROPRIATLY!"

The Curator smoldered inside and stared angrily at the two workers. He clenched his fists at his sides, and tensely turned away from the men to stomp upstairs towards his office. Fortunately, for both exhibit builders, the unmerciful shouting had ended. Instantly, the two display workers pressed verbally in on Chad, which prevented him from speaking first.

"Really, you've got to believe us; it's true we saw something up there! Why would we risk our jobs just to pull a silly stunt?" the larger man complained.

"We honest-to-goodness saw a tiger in the exhibit room," the small man added.

Chad sighed, as he wavered with indecision, and then told them, "Come on guys, I've got to figure this one out."

Chad led both employees slowly through the long stone passageway, muttering visibly to himself under his breath. Trent and Tab passed Chad and the departing workers through the alabaster passageway from the opposite direction. Melinda and Dale spotted the brothers and hurried in their direction.

Trent held up his hand to stall the approaching friends, while he watched his brother signing to him. He said, "Wait a second guys — Tab read the workers' lips, and he's telling me what they said."

Trent translated to their group of friends what Tab signed to him about the conversation between Chad and both of the workers, "...Sorry, but he expects me to fire someone over this if I want to keep my own job."

"Why won't anyone believe us?" the bigger man asked disapprovingly.

In support of his co-worker, the smaller carpenter persisted sarcastically, "We tried doing the right thing, and now it comes back to bite us. Well now, isn't that just fair?"

With his hands lowered, Tab stopped signing to Trent.

"What's going on? What were they talking about?" Trent queried Melinda and Dale.

Melinda glanced between Tab and Trent before answering, "Evidently, they claim a tiger snarled at them while they were building a new exhibit display."

"A tiger?" Trent whispered, "Are they crazy? How could a tiger be in a Museum?"

Tab signed to Trent, and then he said, "Tab says today's newspaper never mentioned anything about a missing tiger from the zoo, or from anywhere else in the city."

"This doesn't make any sense; they were so insistent to Chad and they seemed very genuine," Melinda offered, "I believe them."

She looked around the main hall, and reminded everyone not to stare in the direction of the departed workers to avoid being conspicuous about what they were discussing.

"Wonder what they really saw in that exhibit area? Dale, do you know where they were working?" she asked, staring down at the rust-and-cream colored marble floor patterns.

"Sure, I know. They're building cabinets to display the new artifacts."

Trent asked, "When will it arrive at the Museum?"

"It's already here!" Dale answered knowingly.

"The exhibit space is nearly done. They were putting up some of the last display cases."

Melinda asked, "Can we see the exhibit?"

"No problem, as part of the student program, you can get into any of the exhibits for free."

"No, I mean, can we go see it now?"

With this comment, Tab's body language changed, and he grinned with large eager eyes as the potential excitement to investigate the area dawned on him.

"I don't know," Dale said in a worried tone, and then suspiciously asked, "Why do you want to see it?"

At this response, Tab's shoulders slumped, and he began to shift his feet impatiently.

"Think about it, Dale," Melinda said, "They believe they saw something important enough to pull the fire alarm at the risk of losing their jobs. Whatever it is, I'm not sure I want to run around this place without knowing," she explained.

"Hmm, good point," Dale muttered.

Suddenly, Tab nudged Melinda with his elbow, and rolled his eyes in the direction of the discussed workers as they bumbled past them with their heads down, and sloughed out the front doors. Each instantly knew by the workers' body language and demeanor that Dr. Swinford had forced Chad to fire both men.

As the friends stared at each other, feeling bad for the two jobless carpenters, Trent tried to redirect the conversation away from the sad men by saying, "How about this, right before dinner, let's investigate the exhibit area. While everyone else is eating, we should go unnoticed if we happen to run a few minutes late. Dale, is that area locked?"

"Now that the artifacts are located inside the exhibit area, it's usually locked with its own separate security system."

With dejected faces, they all felt they had reached a dead end.

Tab signed to Trent who then explained, "Tab thinks with all of the fuss with the alarm, and the firemen clearing out everyone from the building, and now that the two workmen have left the building, the exhibit area is probably unlocked. He wants us to go there NOW!"

"But what about attending the rest of our lecture today? We're supposed to be somewhere right now," Melinda reminded him.

Trent grinned playfully, "Normally, you'd be right about the schedule, but I overheard Dr. Koffin telling some other students that he would resume his lecture tomorrow, as our minds would not be on the material because of today's excitement. That's why we came this way; we wanted to find out what happened."

Dale appeared edgy.

Trent asked him, "What's wrong, don't you want to go?"

"It's not that. I do, but if we're caught, you guys will only get your hands slapped being new to the Museum, but I can get into serious trouble. Dr. Swinford will take it out on my father. They seldom get along, but he keeps my dad around here because of his good work. It's just that I don't want to put my dad's job at risk."

"Well, we better not get caught then," Trent, said brightly. "Let's hurry while we can." He started towards the main stairs. After a few steps, he stopped, and seemed puzzled for a second, then asked, "Dale, which way is it?"

"The entrance is up there," Dale said woefully, pointing towards the top right of the main stairs.

Scanning the area, Melinda observed, "With all of these new patrons around, we can't just walk up there in plain sight. It's not going to work."

Dale quickly piped up, "You're right, we better not go," hoping to derail more thoughts towards crossing any uncomfortable boundaries and breaking possible Museum rules.

Relieved at not having to take the risk of getting caught from leading the group into the restricted exhibit area, Dale turned around, hoping to lead them away from the potential trouble, only to find more panic welling up within him. Dale's nerves tingled once more, and he tensed in fearful anticipation at seeing Tab sign to Trent. Dale bit his nails in nervous annoyance, as he thought, *"Oh, no — what are they planning now? These two are just like a bunch of monkeys. Why don't they leave well enough alone?"* Fully perturbed, he waited for the translation.

"Tab's positive there's a fire escape door at the rear of the exhibit room. How do we get to that door, Dale?"

Startled, Dale stared at Tab, moaning, "How does he know that?"

"Guys, I told you, Tab knows everything," he said proudly, and in an almost reminding tone, "While we're talking, he's usually reading or studying. He probably memorized the floor plans in the brochures," Trent suggested.

"Floor plans are one thing, but the doors into all of the rooms are another!" Dale exclaimed.

"That's my Tab," Trent beamed, putting his arm around his brother's shoulder, feeling amused at Dale's exasperation.

Tab acted bashful, and turned away to hide his rosy face.

"So — which way do we go from here?" Melinda questioned Dale.

Dale paused in silence, deciding if he should stand up to the peer pressure pushing him away from his conscience, or cave in to preserve his status with the group, while he let out a long sigh.

Taking advantage of Dale's hesitation, Trent shared his plan, "It's ok, Dale. Tab will lead us to the back of the exhibit room, so you can honestly say you had nothing to do with taking us there. It would be our own doing."

"Sure, and when we all get caught, what do I say then?" Dale asked sarcastically.

"That you truthfully saw us go into the exhibit area, and told us not to be in the room, which is exactly what you're doing right now. You can't get in trouble for telling us not to be in the room, right?"

"Maybe…"

Seconds ticked by before Dale gave in to the pressure, when he finally asked Tab, "Can you get us there?"

As soon as he read the assistant student's lips, the brilliant boy grinned and signaled for all to follow him. He guided the group though the stone hallway to the middle of the building.

After several minutes of passing through a labyrinth of back corridors and museum chamber rooms, Tab halted abruptly outside of a large metal door.

Trent asked Dale "Is this it?"

Dale studied the door carefully, and after he nervously glanced around them, finally said, "I've been coming to the Museum for two years now, and I needed to double-check myself, coming the way we did to get here. Tab's only been here for two days, and brought us here without a single mistake." Feeling his confidence growing, having made it this far, Dale said with authority while holding up his hands in front of the team, "You guys should not be in this area, it's off limits."

Trent smiled waywardly and teased him "Like I always say, truthfulness is the best policy."

Tab turned the handle and pulled opened the door. Cold air swirled around them from inside the dimly lit room. Melinda rubbed her bare arms to keep warm and asked, "Why is it so cold in here?"

"This area has its own thermostat. Carpenters usually turn down the temperature when they're in here working." Dale answered.

Melinda followed the three boys into the room and stared around the oversized space, suddenly forgetting the chilliness. Glass, wood, and metal cases were visible everywhere, and many contained ancient pottery, gold hammered jewelry, pearls, gems, crystals, copper ornaments, clay figures, skin manuscripts, and stone statues. Weapons, animal hides, and native art covered the walls.

Melinda gasped all of a sudden, making the others jump too.

"Sorry," she whispered after placing her hand on her stomach, "I thought they were real from the corner of my eye."

Trent looked beyond her, and remarked in a hushed tone, "Wow, they do look real."

Dale caught his breath too; relieved to find the people were only wax figures. A huge royal palace dining room exhibit displayed life-size wax models of beautiful Indonesian women, clad in extravagant colorful ceremonial dress and dancing assumedly in front of their king and his court. The realness of the models was creepy, and made everyone uncomfortable and eager to continue.

When they passed the convincing display in a single file, Trent wandered around sweeping the oversized room with sharp eyes, until he stumbled upon work tools, lying on the floor beside an un-assembled wood and glass case.

"Look! I bet they dropped their gear when they thought they saw the tiger," Trent said excitedly.

"You don't think they really saw something scary in here, do you?" Melinda shuddered unconsciously.

"Of course not, this place is secure. Don't you think *someone* would have noticed a six-hundred pound tiger, stroll through the front doors?" Dale chuckled loudly.

"Well — I think they saw *something* that spooked them," Melinda countered.

Trent methodically suggested, "Come over here; let's stand where they were working at the time. See if we can notice some sort of reflection in one of the other glass cases to explain what happened."

Positioned to look in multiple directions at once with their backs to the discovered display case, Dale stuttered, "I — I don't see anything scary."

"Me either," Melinda added with relief.

Trent validated them by bobbing his head back and forth as well as up and down to ensure he saw everything in his line of sight, and then said, "I'm not seeing anything odd myself. Maybe they *were* just fooling around and felt they were getting even with the Museum for some reason. At this point, it seems this is just a wild goose chase," Trent sighed disappointedly.

Truly hating to be disproved, but trying to look as if it were his idea, he then voiced unhappily, "We better do as Dale told us and leave the exhibit now."

Retracing their steps back to the rear fire escape door, Trent, by habit, double-checked over his shoulder to ensure Tab was still behind him, but this time, he could not locate his brother.

Concerned about the sudden absence, he said, "Wait a minute you guys; Tab must not have seen us leaving. I'll run back to get him."

After Trent returned to where the unassembled case stood, he spotted Tab down on one knee beside another nearby display case. Trent approached his brother from behind, when Tab suddenly stood up and spun around. At seeing Trent, he signed quickly.

Trent spoke aloud while signing back to Tab, "Slow down, and repeat what you said."

Instead, Tab pulled him by the arm behind the display case for him to see.

With a quizzical look, Trent noticed Tab had an un-easy look, and looked where his younger brother pointed towards the floor on the opposite side of the case. To see what Tab was pointing at, Trent lowered his eyes to look at the floor, when his blood instantly ran cold. Frozen, he could only stare aghast at Tab.

***

Waiting for both Trent and Tab to return, Melinda pulled on Dale's sleeve for his help to find them. Surprised not to see either next to the unassembled case, Melinda decided they must have passed by without seeing each other.

"Dale, let's head back the way we came — wait — is that them?" she asked.

They both approached the brothers, when Trent shot them a quick glance. Immediately Dale and Melinda knew something was wrong from his expression. Without saying a single word to either of the advancing friends, Trent simply pointed down at the floor. Moving to his other side, Melinda saw nothing except for the litter of sawdust that blanketed the floor, made from the construction of the case by the two display workers. Then she saw it in plain sight. She gasped for her breath, but only fear rose inside her, making every nerve in her body tingle. She urgently scanned the area, and gripped Trent and Dale's arms when they all heard a noise.

Chapter Ten

ENEMIES

Capable in most daring situations from his former military training as a Navy Seal, Brock Dennison enjoyed a confidence that he was a gifted individual. Retired with a respectable pension after spending twenty years in the Navy, he felt too physically active to spend all of his time playing golf. Instead, he chose to continue working full time, not only to remain mentally and physically fit, but also to receive a regular paycheck alongside of a pension check for engaging in an activity he enjoyed.

Not expecting any actual danger at the Museum, still, his Armed Forces education prepared him to fight for the right things, especially for those who could not on their own. He imagined with rare and precious artifacts to tempt potential thieves, it gave him a good opportunity to apply his prior training into his new work. By thinking like a burglar, he decided to work only the late afternoon — early evening shift, knowing museum security teams remained on high alert throughout the late-night shifts. He felt the perfect time to strike at the Museum was smack in the middle of his shift.

Brock believed that no one knew, not even Security Chief Al, what he stashed in various strategic locations throughout the Museum. He chose clever hiding spots just beyond their security camera's views to stash radios, food, guns, and additional ammo in small or restricted spaces like a fire hose cabinet, or atop easy-to-reach exhibits. Brock planned for his readiness during a possible surprise raid anywhere within the Museum. Every day he checked and re-checked each secret item's location during his afternoon security rounds to assure him they were in their assigned places.

Unable to separate his personal life from his work, Brock furthermore placed similar objects including pepper spray, pocketknives, and money in different tactical areas around his home and neighborhood. Eager to impart his emergency preparedness with his new wife, he shared the location site of each hidden article with her. Initially, she believed his extra effort to guarantee their wellness was cute, and encouraged him to proceed during their first year of marriage. Shortly thereafter, she realized it was more than just a cute form of affection. It was his obsessive compulsion.

She noticed Brock's attitude darkened when he missed going on daily walks to check on his concealed items. It became worse the longer it continued, especially during his no-sleep phase. Brock read about a clan of ancient Ninjas who had trained themselves to function at higher levels of awareness without sleep. He wanted to learn their secret, to remain in an advanced security mode twenty-four hours a day. Brock easily accepted the fact that a person's aging process increased during their sleep, and if he could sleep less, he felt it would slow the degeneration progression. Week by week, Brock weaned himself of ten minutes less sleep.

All seemed well in the beginning of the sleep deprivation, but the disruption did affect his attentiveness and caused him to doze during work meetings. Awakened when the alarm clock rang earlier each week, his wife was unable to fall back asleep, which affected her job performance. When she received a negative performance review at work, she gave Brock an ultimatum. She demanded he stop interfering with their sleep, or he would need to find a new wife.

Brock used his former Military combat skills to adapt and overcome the situation by analyzing the circumstances. The answer was easy; he would replace his neighborhood nightly walks with daily security rounds inside the Museum. Halfway through the day, Brock decided that he felt sorry for the two exhibit workers fired earlier in the day, and paused to wonder if anyone had secured the exhibit hall after screaming about a tiger. On a hunch, he retraced his former steps to the main exhibit doors, and when he pulled the door handle, it swung open easily.

"What if I had not checked the doors?" he spoke proudly to himself.

Waiting patiently for his eyes to adjust to the interior darkness of the expansive chamber, Brock easily navigated through multiple displays on his way to check the rear fire door. He passed the carpentry tools, which still remained on the floor, and soon reached and pressed against the fire door. Satisfied when it would not open, the former Navy Seal leisurely resumed his return back towards the front entrance, when he stopped suddenly, gripped by a premonition.

He held out his good left ear to listen for the faintest sound, yet nothing appeared unusual to his eyes as he surveyed the room's contents. Yet something troubled his senses. A few safe strides carried him cautiously through more of the room, as he constantly scanned in all directions, until his leather gun holster scraped the sharp edge of a display case.

Humiliated for the rookie mistake, Brock hesitated, and then hurried past more displays to leave the room and arm the security system. Upon keying the activation code into the electronic pad, the system provided thirty seconds for the person to leave before the area doors sealed.

As Brock waited and listened for the magnetic click to inform him the room was secure, he leaned over the third floor railing, and stared down at the great hall's marble floor. "*Man, that Harper spent a fortune on this place,*" he thought. While he expected the impending click of the locking mechanism, he started down the steps until he noticed a small smudge on the otherwise sparkling brass railing. When he extracted his small brown notebook from his front shirt pocket, Brock reminded himself to inform the cleaning people when suddenly, the alarm SCREAMED!

The shriek from the speakers behind him startled him completely. Unsure of the cause for the high-pitched blare, he peered back at the exhibit center. Emergency lights blinked wildly as he raced up the steps. Brock entered the override access code into the electronic panel, and the magnetic locks clicked loudly when the door opened. In one motion, Brock thrust both front doors wide open, and then he zipped through the doors in a roll across the floor, to crouch at the right side of the entrance.

He hoped his quick access might cause a prowler to lose him in the sudden brightness of the open doorway, and give him an extra moment's edge on the situation. Unable to see or hear any movement, Brock dropped to one knee, eager to identify potential visible feet or legs throughout the gallery. Only hearing the sound of pounding footsteps approaching up the stairs outside the exhibit room, Brock knew by their heavy and quick tempo, that they belonged to the Security Chief.

Seconds before Al blazed through the doorway, Brock alerted the big man, "I have the door covered!"

Moments later, the entire doorway went dim when Al's three hundred and twenty pounds of iron-strong muscles filled the opening with his semi-automatic gun drawn. Brock expected Al to mimic his actions while the smaller guard stared trance-like at the open gallery, wishing he could see the tiniest flicker, while whoever was in the room focused their full attention on the giant man.

Except for the soft footsteps made by both of the Museum's security men, silence remained in the area. With amazing stealth for such an enormous man, Al quietly canvassed the room, looking for any signs of intrusion while Brock covered the area behind them. When they reached the exhibit room's rear fire door, a thin blade of the exterior hallway light poured into the room from between the edge of the door and its doorjamb.

Stopped in mid-stride by the reason for the alarm, Al asked Brock, "Did you check the door before setting the alarm?"

"Affirmative," Brock replied promptly, and then added earnestly, "I made sure it was locked."

When he pointed at the door, the former Navy Seal exclaimed excitedly, "That's not right!" and turned back the way they had just come. Walking around displays throughout the room, Brock remained closest to the left wall. Al mirrored his movements on the right side. Suddenly, the Navy Seal remembered that his earlier intuition had flamed alive near a display of exquisite silk weavings. He peered closely at a wax figure weaving a blanket, to ensure it was not a real person.

Together, they secured the room and found no intruders. They both began to look for clues. When Brock stepped behind the hanging silk blanket near the rear wall, he pointed his pistol in a quick three-point movement within the enclosed space. He noticed Al heading towards him, as his brain assimilated what his peripheral vision saw inside the empty storage area.

"Al!"

Work dust covered the floor behind the blankets. Nearly visible in the powder was the edge of a shoe pattern. Both officers bent down on one knee to analyze the print's type and size, when they suddenly spun around towards the bellow in the room's doorway.

The left door forcefully thudded into the interior walls, when they next heard, "FIRST A FIRE ALARM, AND NOW SECURITY ALARMS! I demand an explanation immediately!" Dr. Swinford yelled furiously.

"Man, this guy's always blowing his top," Brock thought irritably, *"I wish he'd flap his jaw somewhere else, and let us finish our work without his slowing down the process!"*

"We had an intruder," Al informed him.

"WHAT DO YOU MEAN?" the Curator hollered crossly at the disclosure.

"Over here," Al said intently, "let me show you."

The big man pointed at the shoe print recently found in the dust, when he explained, "Brock secured the room earlier, but after the alarm, we found this print. Someone's been here."

Dr. Swinford bent at the waist, but did not see the shoe pattern. He scowled as he stood up; when he then noticed the perfect curve in the dust.

"Whose shoe print is that?" he asked Al, angrily.

"It's too soon to tell, but I'm positive it's not from the workers" Al replied with certainty.

"How do you know?" Dr. Swinford quizzed him heatedly.

"Workers are required to wear steel-toed boots. That boot type leaves a waffled pattern unlike this print," Al explained.

His boss looked at him without recognition of his explanation.

"If you come over here, I believe I saw some sawdust. If we're lucky, we might see the steel toe pattern," Al hoped to show him.

When the three Museum men strolled to the unassembled case, Al quickly perceived the disturbed sawdust had erased any clear prints.

Al felt foolish for the false effort, as he looked down at the much smaller Dr. Swinford saying, "Too bad; it's not as clear as I hoped for you to see the difference."

Brock yelled, "OVER HERE!"

Together, the two senior employees hurried past the half-finished display case towards a completed case where Brock stood. It was apparent sawdust remained scattered around it on the floor. To one side, a footprint was visible.

Al pointed at it saying, "See, this is what the work boot prints look like Dr. Swinford. They're absolutely different from the other print."

After following the trail around the case to identify if there were any other prints on the floor, Al froze motionless.

Dr. Swinford knew he would never see past the big man, and whined, "I can't see what you're looking at."

Al stepped easily to the side, allowing Dr. Swinford a full view of the floor in front of them. None of the three men knew what to say to each other, except to watch the blood drain from each other's faces. Without a word, all three dashed to the exhibit entrance. With a rush, Al slammed the thick doors shut so hard behind him, the heavy reinforced hinges rattled.

After turning to face Brock, Al ordered his staff member, "Get on the phone, and get a specialist over here to validate if that's real."

He turned to Dr. Swinford, and stated, "Sir, law enforcement will be responding to the alarm. You had better advise them of the situation while I hurry to evacuate the students and staff from the building until they arrive."

Not waiting for a response, all three scrambled to fulfill their assignments.

Chapter Eleven

WARNINGS

Trent grabbed Tab's arm, and quickly raised his own index finger to his lips to signal for his hearing-impaired brother to remain quiet. Quietly, the older boy ducked, and slowly pulled Tab and Melinda behind another display. Unaware of the sound's source, but fearing its connection to what they saw on the floor, each student held their breath, feeling the throbbing of their own hearts deep within their chests.

Fearful her heavy breathing would make subtle movements in the delicate silk blanket they hid behind; Melinda was too frightened to move. Suddenly, they each heard a close scraping noise!

Melinda pressed her back hard against the wall behind them. As each student stood still like statues, they tensely watched a dark shadow move gradually past the other side of the silk blanket. Melinda's heart raced faster when she shifted her feet to improve her balance, and the silhouette they watched immediately stopped in the room's center. With her lungs burning for a mouthful of fresh air, Melinda was unable to contain her painful breath another moment, and she squeezed her hand over her mouth to restrain her exhale before alerting the shape of their presence.

Exploding carbon dioxide rushed up her windpipe, giving her a woozy feeling, just as the indistinguishable outline moved away. She strained with all of her might to exhale gradually through her nose, until she almost passed out from not gasping for air.

Dale hissed, "Ohhh, were in serious trouble now — the security alarm has been armed," upon hearing the front doors close, soon followed by six distinct electronic beeps.

"We're trapped until tomorrow with whatever else is in here," Dale whined.

"Not if we hurry," Trent cried aloud, as he suddenly raced towards the rear fire door, closely followed by Dale, Melinda, and Tab.

Dale warned, "Hurry, it might be coming!"

The frightening thought made Melinda run faster.

As soon as he reached the rear fire door, still running too fast, Trent missed the push bar with his open hands. He scrambled to open it, when Dale uncontrollably slammed into him from behind, pushing Trent's waist into the bar, and springing them both out into the open hallway with a crash.

Only a second behind the two boys, Melinda spotted Tab turning back, as if to re-enter the darkened exhibit room.

She skidded to a stop, and called, "Stop!" instantly realizing he could not hear her warning. Instinct made her dart forward to grab his shirtsleeve before the door slammed shut, however, at the last second, Tab moved beyond her reach and jabbed his arm between the closing fire door and its doorframe.

With a rush, the deaf boy pulled open the door, and quickly wiped both the door and its push bar clean of their fingerprints with his sleeve. Melinda then jerked Tab backwards, allowing the exit door to slam shut, exactly as the security alarm rang.

Filled with pumping adrenalin, Melinda dragged Tab backwards too forcefully, accidentally causing him to lose his balance, and knock both of them to the floor, where he landed on top of her legs. Unable to hear the panic alarm sound echoing up and down the vacant and sterile hallway, Tab moved unhurriedly in contrast to Melinda, who hastily scrambled to escape from underneath him. They scarcely moved as their non-rhythmic movements negated each other's effort.

Instantly, Trent hauled Tab to his feet, while Dale helped Melinda to her knees. Once she was up, the four friends rushed down the hallway towards the far exit door. After passing through the doorway leading into another corridor, they stopped to catch their breath.

Gasping, Dale yelled at Trent, "I TOLD YOU...WE WERE...GOING TO GET...INTO TROUBLE!"

Ignoring the jumpy teen's comment, Trent exclaimed cheerfully, "That was too close!"

"I thought for sure I was going to pee my pants when Tab and I couldn't get up back there," Melinda said, winded.

"You! What happened back there?" Trent asked.

Tab signed how they could not move on the ground.

Trent laughed at the slapstick events and said, "I'll bet you guys thought it was the end for a minute, didn't you?"

"Yeah, I thought we were busted for sure," Dale chimed in.

Trent placed a hand on Dale's shoulder and boasted to the shorter boy, "See, I told you we'd be ok."

"What?" cried Dale, "You call that ok? Forget about the alarm, did you see what I saw in there?" Dale yelped in fear.

Melinda waded into the conversation, "I know, I thought we were dinner as soon as I heard that scraping noise."

Trent immediately took on a serious tone, "If I didn't see that tiger print with my own eyes, I would still think the exhibit guys were mental cases."

Dale asked, "Do you guys think that was a real paw print?"

Tab signed to Trent while he translated for his younger brother, "Tab believes the exhibit guys were sincere about seeing a tiger. If they were only joking, he doesn't think they would have caused that much commotion and expected they would have come clean."

Melinda added with a strained face, "If they didn't put the tiger paw print on the floor, then who did? I mean, there couldn't be a real tiger in the Museum — right?"

"You guys have seen this place; it's like Fort Knox. There's no way a tiger could be in the building," Dale claimed.

"One thing is certain, now that the alarm has been sounded, that tiger print will soon be discovered. If it's a joke, we'll hear about it soon enough, and if it's for real, the program leaders won't risk any of the students getting hurt," Trent consoled the group. "We would be bused out of here tonight if they thought we were in any real danger."

"You're probably right," Melinda agreed with him.

"We better hurry back for dinner, or they'll wonder what happened to us," Dale suggested.

Turning to Tab, Trent asked him, "What's the quickest way to reach the student area from here? We need to get there quick — and look like we're coming up to dinner from the student game area, as if nothing happened."

Tab glanced around to validate their present location, and waved his dependent friends to follow him into the Arms and Armor room. Melinda admired the extraordinary armor. She gazed romantically at the full size horse replicas displaying bright, shining protective gear, imagining formidable knights riding upon their steeds destined for battle, or riding from a castle on a chivalry mission.

After they moved from the Arms and Armor room into the Medieval room, Melinda recognized a distinct European flavor from a trip with her parents to the British Museum in London. The chamber displayed many of King Henry VIII's court flags, family crests, shields, and beautiful royal robes.

As they moved through the gallery, the team soon entered the Religion Hall, which was full of Christian, Jewish, Eastern, Middle East, and Islamic types of antiquities. An intricately carved corridor bridged this room into the Asian hall. When Melinda passed by a large, smiling gold Buddha statue, she reached up her hand with a sudden urge to rub its great belly, but resisted, remembering their previous narrow escape with the exhibit's security alarm.

Tab located a turret staircase, and they descended the steps.

"It's amazing how Tab can take us anywhere," Melinda said aloud to no one in particular.

Melinda tracked their movements through the vast rooms and chambers with little success. She gaped through the open archways that lead into the South Asian room as they passed it on their way to the first floor. When they exited into one of the lower tunnels, Melinda was unsure where to go next, until she observed Tab pull open a door marked **LAUNDRY**.

Surprised the Museum provided students with washers and dryers, she looked around the area and noticed several stacks of fresh white bed linens. They reached the far side of the narrow space in haste and silence, until Tab peeked through the opposite door, which led into the student's game area. Without seeing anyone, he opened the door for the group to exit, but was unable to hear the approaching footsteps.

Trent whistled, "Wow, safe at last!"

Melinda agreed, offering, "This is the first time I'm happy to see…"

Mea entered the room with the well-dressed boy Melinda had seen during the orientation dinner.

"Don't stop talking on our account," Melinda's roommate sneered at her.

"Sorry, you're right, where are my manners? These are my friends. This is Trent and his brother Tab. And this is…"

"DALE BRADAN!" exclaimed the short boy before Melinda could finish her introductions.

The way the boy spit out Dale's name confirmed they knew each other — and were enemies.

"We know who you are Scott," Dale said loudly during his turn to face Melinda. "His father is the Curator of the Museum."

Melinda brightened up, and politely offered, "Oh, I bet its enjoyable being in the Museum all the time. I really like it here."

Scott ignored Melinda and her comment, but stared angrily at Dale as he distastefully condemned, "Not everything around here is worth liking if you know what I mean."

Dale was about to retort back, when Mea sneeringly offered to Trent, "Sorry, my roomie failed to properly introduce us; I'm part of the program too."

Melinda realized the earlier halt in her introductions, and apologized, "Sorry, you're right, we need to get to your introduction."

"Get to my introduction — without my reminder, we still wouldn't know who I am!" she said scornfully to Melinda.

Melinda bit her lip to hold back her annoyance, but politely continued, "All, this is my roommate."

"What? Now I'm nameless! Well, like they always say, if you want something done right, you must do it yourself."

The tall girl gave a forced half-smile to the boys, and said, "My name is Mea. I'll leave it up to my socially unskilled roommate to inform you with my details."

Much taller than Scott, Mea looked down at him, and urged, "We're out of here. You were right to warn me about *them*."

Without making eye contact with anyone, Mea strode towards the girl's wing, with Scott tagging toddler-like directly behind her.

"What just happened? Did you guys get into some type of a fight already?" Trent rattled to Melinda.

Unsure what to say, Melinda shrugged her shoulders, "If we did have an argument, I'm not sure I remember what it was about. I think she's bent that way all the time."

"You're kidding!" Trent uttered in amazement.

"No, actually, I met her that first day we all arrived, and this is the first time I've seen her since that time. She's acted the same way both times."

Deep in his thoughts, Dale frowned and informed the small group, "If she's friends with Scott, she's not someone to let your guard down around. They sound like two of a kind."

Trent asked the professor's son with a chuckle, "Is anybody friends around here? Or do we have some serious damage control to work on?"

"Let's forget about it and get some food," Melinda offered to change the mood.

Trent smiled, and agreed with her by leading the group up the steps where they soon entered into the student dining room.

Chapter Twelve

BRAWL

Dr. Swinford stomped down the main central steps with a sense of urgency, to explain to the Houston Police the need for them to dispatch a request for an expert from the Houston Zoo to join them at the Museum. Surprised by the Curator's difficult-to-believe story, the two lead officers separated themselves to re-group and define a tactical plan. Officer Benson, a strong African American man, was the top ranking lieutenant on the scene. As he spoke with Officer Gomez, matching him in size and one year less in seniority, both were puzzled.

"Where do these people come up with these imaginative stories?" he smiled, shaking his head in disbelief.

Officer Gomez chuckled, "I thought I'd heard it all, however — a tiger — in a museum! How do you suppose something like that could happen?"

Officer Benson replied, "The strange thing is — I'm no tiger expert, but the paw print looked real to me. If we're wrong on this one, and a tiger *is* running loose around this place, it's our job to find and remove it. If it's a joke, we had better find the source. I'm for continuing this investigation cautiously until we know more."

Officer Gomez, considering his plan to campaign for a future public office agreed, "This is too strange! We need to run this by the book. I'll have someone contact the Zoo to verify if this is a joke. In the meantime, you'd better have your people do a full sweep of the Museum and grounds."

"Right," Officer Benson mumbled as they parted.

When he approached his waiting officers, Officer Benson bellowed, "Pete...have your men give me a double sweep inside, and make sure everyone's out of the building. Jack, post your people outside the perimeter of the building, and look for anything — and I mean anything."

Lieutenant Gomez called to a waiting female officer and ordered, "Culley, come over here!"

Officer Culley, a tough middle-aged sergeant with a two-by-four build, trotted to where he stood. "Sir," she attentively stated as her light brown hair poked out from under her police hat.

"Look Culley, this is going to sound peculiar, however, I need it done ten minutes ago. Get on the horn with the Houston Zoo and get a large cat specialty team over here now! The museum security team found a large paw print in the vicinity where the alarm was tripped. We're not certain if it's real, but we can't take any chances at this point in the investigation."

Officer Culley paused to say something sarcastic, but noticing the deep creases in his forehead made her decide otherwise.

"Aye sir, I'm on it."

She walked back to the men she had previously stood with only moments before. She issued her orders, and the men promptly engaged in their activities.

***

Inside, Al hustled through the Museum hallways and chambers, looking for anyone to alert of the potential big cat menace. Comfortable with his own immense capabilities as a foremost athlete in college, where he was poised for great success, he worried about the other people still inside the building.

Naturally large-boned and blessed with minimal body fat, reporters and photographers had stalked him in college, eager to film his remarkable hulking chest and arms during his football days. A middle linebacker, he was curiously fast for such a large and powerful man. Topping the scales at three hundred and forty pounds during his prime, he looked like an enormous gladiator, even more so when dressed in his football shoulder pads. Most strong men have square wrists when they are in great physical shape, but because of his massively built arms, the muscles in his forearm formed thick, round wrists.

An incident in his past had changed him irrevocably and he had decided to use his strength and abilities to help others. While on a date with his girlfriend Carmel during his university years, four rough men from a rival college entered the same restaurant, and instantly identified Al. Unable to badger him into a brawl, the four rivals left and extracted baseball bats from their car's trunk.

Waiting for Al and his girlfriend to finish their meal, they hid in a murky alleyway. When Al stepped next to his car and opened the door for his date to enter, two of the men attacked him from behind. The first impact would have hospitalized a normal man, and absolutely on the second, but equally, both bats ricocheted off Al's rippling shoulders.

Surprised at the sudden assault, Al turned in time to evade a third bat by jumping backwards. The gravitational force of missing Al's body sucked the baseball bat from the smaller man's hands and it flew through the air to connect accidentally with the face of his date. Instantly she collapsed to the ground, and her head rolled sideways like a rag doll. As the attackers continued to circle and assault Al, concern motivated him to take action and defeat the rivals so he could then rush to assist his lifeless girlfriend. Finally squatting beside her unconscious body, he encouraged her, "Carmel, are you all right? Please wake up!" when an officer behind him yelled "FREEZE!"

Apprehensive for the girl's safety, Al quietly froze in place, hoping to end the bizarre encounter and thereby allow medical personnel to care for Carmel's injuries. Once an ambulance arrived, they rushed her to the local emergency room for treatment.

At the hospital, Carmel fought for her life in a coma. Devoid of her testimony, the smaller men claimed that Al had started the fight leading to her injury. With their visible injuries, it seemed believable, and the officers released them. Al alone remained in police detention.

Months later during the trail, it appeared the former athlete would go to prison until Carmel recovered from her coma. Armed with her testimony of the events, a reporter investigated the alleyway near where the fight occurred, and noticed a tiny video camera at the rear of a small business, sloped towards the conflict area. The saved tape footage revealed two of the adversaries pacing the alleyway and carrying baseball bats, before the battle started. The tape was the missing evidence needed.

Acquitted of all charges after the harrowing experience, Al struggled to find his normal life again, but it was not the same as the one previously lost. Too far behind in his studies to catch up in all of his classes, Al focused his energy on football. Teammates accepted his return, but Al felt awkward without knowing many of the new plays. Although proven innocent, for many, he somehow remained different in their eyes.

He reacted to the un-justness of his situation, and refused to be in the lime light again. Al later completed his university education and received his degree, but he never again stepped foot inside a team locker room as a player. While Al searched for a new outlook on life, he hoped no one else would ever have to endure his experience.

The huge man decided to use his abilities to protect people, and the FBI, CIA, and NSA vigorously courted Al to enlist. He declined their spotlight too, causing him to enter the lower visibility of private security. After refusing higher profile positions, he felt comfortable joining the Museum's security team. Successfully proving himself, the Museum promoted Al to lead the security force after only a few years on the job. His world seemed right, and he felt at peace again.

Al shook his head to get the former flashbacks from his mind, and focused on his ability to hunt the deadly tiger! His gun drawn, and covering the safety pin with his thumb, the large man held a bright flashlight in a crossover position beneath his pistol. Secure in his powerful abilities, he worried about the tiger finding a vulnerable program student. Apprehensive they might unknowingly stumble onto the ten-foot long killer, Al searched quickly through the Museum. When Al arrived at the student quarters, he escorted all of them rapidly through the rear entrance, where police waited to protect the students outside the building.

Satisfied all of the employees and students were safe, he quickly rejoined the search for the predator with the other police officers. Six hours later, with the area checked and rechecked multiple times, there was absolutely no sign of the supposed animal. Zoo personnel confirmed the print perfectly resembled that of a tiger's, but were at a loss to explain why they found it in the secured exhibit room. Without additional evidence, the log recorded the incident as a practical joke.

With a partial human footprint discovered near the tiger print in the same area as the triggered alarm, it seemed the only feasible explanation. Al wished they had not removed their outdated Museum security cameras yet, expecting to install the new high-tech models that same day.

Unfortunately, a light-rail train in another city collided with the delivery truck carrying the cameras in an intersection accident, and damaged the camera boxes. Concerned some units may fail from the jarred incident; they refused the delivery, and quickly re-ordered more.

Al's position as the Museum's Security Chief required him to report this as a practical joke to Dr. Swinford. He respected the man's business shrewdness and knew this would not go well for him as he personally persuaded Dr. Swinford to replace the obsolete and antiquated cameras.

Still in the dark about the alleged tiger paw event, without the aid of cameras to record the activity in the room, Al frowned when he looked at his watch and the time showed 2:18am.

Al rapped on the office door, and Dr. Swinford yelled, "COME!"

Chapter Thirteen

ANTIQUARIAN

Melinda hastily slid past Dr. Bradan through the side theater door, right before he shut it to begin his lecture. Last inside the room, she stared suddenly at the students facing her. Feeling uncomfortable, she desperately looked for an open seat, hoping to stop being the center of their attention.

Waving her hand in the rear of the room, Leslie called, "Melinda!"

Thankfully, Melinda melted into the saved seat behind the tall boy Colby.

Leslie leaned over to whisper, "So, is it done?"

Nodding her agreement, Melinda added, "Between sleeping in from last night's tiger hunt, and Mrs. Neely's slow motion speed, I was almost late today."

"When are you supposed to move out of your room?" Leslie asked her.

"As soon as your roommate moves out, I can move into *our* room."

"I'll bet you're glad not to room with her majesty Mea."

"You know it," Melinda smiled, "I haven't seen her yet today to tell her I'm moving in with you, as my new teammate."

Leslie questioned her, "Do you think she will be happy or upset?"

"Good question; it could go either way. We'll know soon enough."

"Ms. Lyons, perhaps you would be good enough to answer the question!"

Leslie's eyes flashed up at the instructor Dr. Bradan. Embarrassed at being caught not paying attention to the lecture, she turned progressively darker shades of crimson.

"Sorry, what was the question again?" Leslie asked timidly.

"Ms. Lyons, the question was what an Antiquarian is?"

After a long pause, Leslie replied, "I think it has something to do with studying old things — right?"

"Vague, however, close enough," Dr. Bradan said a bit sarcastically.

"I am an Antiquarian, meaning I make my living by studying the ancient world. The profession originated some time ago in Europe as an academic discipline, but the formal field of study did not take root in this country until much later. In fact, besides the War of 1812, can anyone deduce what else happened?"

The long pause went unanswered.

"The Antiquarian Society was established. My specialty is Mesoamerica. I focus on civilizations primarily found in Mexico and Central America. Would anyone care to share with us the names of several of the more dominate cultures in that region?"

Brian raised his hand.

Dr. Bradan motioned for him to answer.

Sitting up straighter, Brian answered, "One would be the Incas, and I think another might be the Mayans."

"Nice job, you're correct. Those were two of the more prominent empires. Can anyone help him remember some others?"

Silence responded.

"It depends," he continued, "on the time line, but the Aztec, Toltec, and the mysterious Olmec also fall into this category. For those of you not familiar with the Olmec people, they are considered now to be the first major advanced civilization in that region of the world, becoming the forefathers of the Mayans, and impacting all later area cultures.

"Generally when we think about these vast empires and their subcultures, we most commonly refer to the sun pyramids and human sacrifices," he said, hoping to increase their attention.

"Sacrifices," Alicia Bailer, a junior beauty pageant queen objectionably repeated, "Human sacrifices?"

"Yes, human sacrifices. These poor souls were many times the unlucky victims of invaders. Unlike today's modern legal systems, most did not receive fair and impartial trials or treatment."

Smiling at the students, he said happily, "I'm starting to like this group. Keep this up and perhaps we'll conclude our discussion a little sooner today."

"Yee hah!" hooted Luke Hammer, the cowboy, as he leaned back in his seat.

"Okay, let's not get excited too quickly. Its estimated people lived in Central and South America for more than thirteen thousand years. Chances are slim that we will filter though their entire history in the next few hours."

"Shucks," the cowboy drawled, dropping his head.

"Or, if we focus our time productively, devoid of too many needless interruptions, we can proceed by only covering the highlights today. How does that sound?"

No one cheered, but several students smiled and nodded in approval.

"Moving along, these were some of the most remarkable people in history. Prior to Europe's progression into the later dark ages, these nations performed proficient head surgery, produced shipping lanes, became great merchants, and built cities equally as great as London, Paris, and Rome for their day."

Pointing to a chart of Central America, Dr. Bradan proceeded, "Throughout this area around the Yucatan, the ground consists mainly of limestone, vines, and substantial jungles. Constructing magnificent cities, they later networked them cooperatively with long straight roads, comparable to the way we link our cities together with modern highways.

"Further to the North in Mexico, a single pyramid, prior to its being destroyed by the Spaniards, was larger than the biggest pyramids in Egypt. Existing thousands of years ago does not mean these groups lived in the Stone Ages. In fact, these same people influenced and fashioned part of our modern humanity with a very intricate innovation we use every day. With that obvious hint, will someone tell us what development I'm referring to?"

He used a significant pause to stress the importance of the topic.

"Each of you attended today's lecture for a reason. Moreover, how did you know to be here today at this time? Because we organize our actions around an annual calendar, similar to what these people first developed, demonstrates that nations in Central America were extremely proficient in uniting their mathematic talents with astronomy. One of the early cultures in the world to develop the concept of zero, they also built observatories to diagram the planets and stars.

"Using their distinctive symbol system, authors compiled knowledge and communicated most of it throughout the kingdoms. This sharing of information permitted farmers in vast rural areas to gain an elevated understanding of their soil and agriculture. In addition, their achievements led to trading food, pottery, artisanship, gold, and jade. Accounts signify they interacted with realms as far-off as the Vikings."

Colby, who was still sitting in front of Melinda, raised his hand.

"Yes, Colby?"

"If they were so great, what happened to them? I mean, where did they go?"

"That's the million dollar question," Dr. Bradan stated. "It's not an easy question to answer. A great deal of speculation by many experts suggests they simply outgrew their capability to cultivate and grow sufficient food for their needs. Some of the foremost research suggests that environmental changes over time made it gradually more difficult to produce comparable amounts of food in later years.

"Nonetheless, other theories tell that as a peaceful people, they were invaded and conquered. This later proved factual considering the conquistadors defeated the Aztecs, partially from the Aztecs desire to hail these men as the prophesied return of a great white God.

"Early civilizations in this region alleged a great personage had visited them. Nearly all of the evidence indicates the indigenous people were beardless, shorter, and had a deep rich brown skin. In contrast, their historical description was of an extraordinarily tall light-skinned God, described to have a full beard not typical of the region, suggesting it would be difficult for so many to fabricate, or doubt the event. Perhaps some of you have heard of his name…Quetzalcoatl.

"Prior to his departure, those in this region recorded that this stranger miraculously healed their sick, shared advanced knowledge with them, and established many of their foundational laws that governed and influenced later civilizations."

Continuing, Dr. Bradan emphasized, "Many worshipped him for bringing peace and order. Parting from the people, Quetzalcoatl promised to revisit them. It's easy to understand when the conquistadors arrived in what must have been amazing and grand sailing ships from the East; they believed this event to be his return. Sadly, the Spanish conquistadors exposed the local people to the plagues of Medieval Europe, and devastated them due to their pursuit of gold in the New World.

"Whatever the causes of their disappearances, or the abandonment of their fields, they were there, and now they are gone. Should your team choose a project in this discipline of study, I will enhance your understanding of how these enormous civilizations lived, worked, and prospered. We will also evaluate clues as to how they may have failed in the end. It is clear that climatic changes affected their way of life from studying soil layers in the area, which may account for some of the loss of people, but does not provide a definitive answer as to why they disappeared without a trace.

"Nevertheless, new breakthroughs are occurring every day in the field. Each latest discovery offers us further details to consider with what is already known." Grinning brightly, Dr. Bradan said, "It's my hope that very soon, many of these questions will soon be answered."

***

Following the Mesoamerican lecture, Melinda and Leslie hauled Melinda's belongings into Leslie's room. Although it was annoying to pack and unpack twice, Melinda felt pleased that they permitted the shifting of roommates. Spending less time with Mea was an obvious benefit, but having added time to work mutually on their project would save homework time later.

"Now that we've been to half of the introduction lectures, what should we do for our project?" Melinda asked Leslie.

"I don't know," Leslie replied, "after the Egyptian lectures, I was sure I wanted to work in that field — you know, maybe get the curse of the mummy," she said with a spooky cackle. "But now, I'm curious about what we learned today. I'm interested to hear about the Central American people in tomorrow's session."

"Me too," Melinda agreed, "For some reason, I've always been drawn to that area of the world. I remember as a little girl, I sometimes dreamt about living in a place like one of those old cities."

"Really? I didn't know about them until only a few years ago. What did you dream about?" Leslie asked, puzzled.

"I don't dream about it anymore. I remember it more as a feeling, than anything in particular. When I was about three of four years old, some people found me wandering the streets. When no one claimed me, the authorities had no choice but to place me into an orphanage. I only had the clothes I was wearing at the time — oh, and my necklace. No one is sure exactly how old I am."

"Orphanage?" Leslie questioned her friend.

"I was adopted. I don't know my birth parents; only my parents who legally adopted me. They've been great ever since."

"Wow, I had no idea. Was it hard on you?" Leslie wondered.

"It must have been, because I remember being scared a lot from the time I was small. For a long time, I had no idea what people were saying, but I finally learned to speak the language."

"Well, look at it this way, your adopted parents may not be your original birth parents, but you still have both of them today. That's more than many kids can claim. Even my parents have been quarrelling more than usual. That's why I'm here this summer. They were afraid I would get too emotional staying home while they sort out their issues. It's just as well when I think about making new friends and going on a big field trip. I'm sure I'll have more fun here."

"Me too," Melinda agreed.

Chapter Fourteen

INFLUENCE

An irregularity to all she met, the majority struggled to describe Dr. Yvonne Kirkchappel as only a charismatic personality, a refined academic, a genuine friend, or simply an embodiment of incredible beauty. Remarkable woman exhibit two, or possibly three of those qualities, but seldom does such a diverse blend harmonize so equally within a solitary person. Prioritizing her exterior beauty far below her celebration for inner attractiveness, which she considered a continuous process, Dr. Kirkchappel carried sporty eye-catching curves on a sleek five foot nine frame. Exquisite golden hair was styled in bold flaxen curls. This contrasted with her serious, professional glasses that she wore throughout the day.

Male employees nicknamed her 'Claudia' due to a familiar resemblance of the supermodel Claudia Schiffer. Instant physical responses were present everywhere she appeared in the Museum. Men admired her striking features, while she was the prime target of women. Quickly appraised as unrivaled competition, her appealing figure and fashionably chic outfits remained modestly covered underneath her pressed white lab coat.

Enormously friendly and uncomplicated to approach, Dr. Kirkchappel exuded a keen intellect in a wrapper of flair and allure once she began speaking. Countless found it difficult to remain focused on her eloquent vocabulary while peering into her incredible sapphire colored eyes. Unable to attend the student orientation banquet, her introduction trailed into today's lecture. Entering the assembly room, students noticed her reading a museum trade journal. Immediately creating a drone without effort on her part, they debated her reason to be in the room.

The bell signaled the start of the lecture. Punctually dismissing the industry publication to a side chair, the splendid instructor stood gracefully in front of the auditorium.

Smiling brightly at the students, she began, "Welcome! My name is Dr. Kirkchappel. We shall begin today's discourse by framing religious and political governance as a key to understanding the daily lives of ancient civilizations."

As she paused for the group's mental absorption of the topic, Joyce, the athletic teen, raised her hand.

"Yes, Joyce?" Dr. Kirkchappel asked.

Amazed that Dr. Kirkchappel knew her personally by name, having never met the professor, Joyce hesitated, and then asked, "I'm not sure I follow what you just said, but what do you mean by governance? How does religion relate to artifacts in a Museum?"

"Your inquiry is the basis of our discussion. Yet, I would ask you to hold those questions until later, as our agenda will explore the answers. If later you feel they need more clarification, please let me know. Is that fair?"

"Sure," Joyce responded.

Organizing her thoughts, Dr. Kirkchappel proceeded.

"Museums display the physical traces of religious and political motivation within ancient civilizations. Multitudes of people throughout the past have measured their religious conviction as a personal, life-altering journey. Yet, each individual's views become the bedrock for what shapes a communal society. Can anybody shed light on the connotation of this statement?"

A hand rose in the middle of the room.

"Thank you, Dino!"

Surprised that she knew his name as well, the young man threw a delighted look at the girl next to him.

"I may not have all of my facts correct, but I read somewhere that there is something like eighteen hundred different religions around the world. If that number is true, how does it fit with what you said?" Dino asked.

"I appreciate the question; it's appropriate as divergent religions have progressed throughout the emergence of many past civilizations. Many ancient cultures formed using the following analogous formula. More than four thousand years ago, simple families bred domestic animals. Often raided by bordering antagonistic tribes over water and pastures, notable growth later erupted when irrigation and farming knowledge benefited these groups.

"During the next two millenniums, empires evolved and fell. Beyond their eminence and collapse in history, another common premise surfaced throughout many places in the world.

"Places of worship or temples were constructed by governing leaders to worship their gods and resided usually at the uppermost point within each smaller town. Daily activities occurred openly in their vicinity. They bought, sold, or traded food for other valuables such as blankets, pottery, and clothing.

"Local ideology became associated with each god, and the citizens provided strict guidelines of behavior, shaping how each individual needed to satisfy the deity. The more prosperous a city, the more followers it attracted to its political infrastructure believing in the power of the overarching god. Expanding these religious segments strengthened governments and their rulers with followers and taxes.

"Some kingdoms passed down from father to son, while others are divided into two empire types. The first were compassionate for their citizens, while the second yearned to increase their power. Regrettably, the latter type invaded bordering cultures. Conquering and annexing their beaten opponent's lands and wealth, they forced the trodden people to adopt the victors' gods and laws — where the defiance of those political laws many times resulted in death.

"Societies evolved during such vast and radical changes. These early religious and political values later melted into the citizens' philosophy, culture, writing, architecture, and art. Consequently, numerous archeology artifacts many times have a religious or political context. To decipher the implication of the item's meaning can provide us with noteworthy facts regarding the people's choices in their everyday lives.

"I apologize for the lengthy monologue. Yet, to cover thousands of years of any geographical region is challenging. Does anyone have a question before we move forward?"

The small redheaded girl sitting in a wheelchair hesitated, but asked, "I can see how ancient beliefs may have inspired people in the past to behave in certain ways, but compared to the amount of social and scientific information we have today, do you feel there are still pockets of people that can shape our modern times?"

Smiling warmly, Dr. Kirkchappel said, "Very insightful question."

Expecting to hear her name too, the red headed girl was disappointed until Dr. Kirkchappel offered, "I'll answer your question this way, Ruth Ann. We should expect a considerable knowledge gap amid our modern science and the knowledge of ancient civilizations. Yet, recognize that those kingdoms who existed five hundred years ago also felt supremely superior to the inhabitants of other kingdoms existing more than a thousand years prior to them. This is analogous to our mind-set regarding today's hygiene; comparatively to the people living during the Dark Ages."

Noticing Ruth Ann's confused face, Dr. Kirkchappel added, "Perhaps this will help. Let's use an imaginary object lesson and congruently integrate Dino's earlier question. Imagine if we belonged to a neighborhood or social club where other members share many of our political or religious beliefs. Collecting our shared beliefs and mingling our unique philosophy with supportive rules or regulations on how to act among ourselves could be the germination for a new formalized religious or political group. The key point is many ancient cities grew from similar individual combined beliefs or direction.

"Let us consider a modern example. In your mind, visualize the development of a new rural population. During its initial growth, we know the civil infrastructure must expand in proportion to the civil requirements of the community. The relevance is best observable during the process of a public or district election. Drawing out this example further, our responsibility as members of this community should be to vote for the candidate representing our individual values and concerns.

"Should the majority of townspeople share a conviction, the candidate on behalf of them will be elected, and therefore, will directly influence not only the creation of new laws, but also the punishments sustaining them. Therefore, it's feasible to trace large scale morality or political behavior to its foundation, generally predicated on grouping individual decency beliefs."

"Does that help you Ruth Ann?"

"It does. Thanks," she replied, impressed.

"Does anyone else have other questions or comments?" Dr. Kirkchappel asked.

No one raised his or her hand. Stepping from the stage, Dr. Kirkchappel said, "Answering Joyce's earlier question too, by understanding and linking the ancient local religions and politics to discovered Museum artifacts, integrates how and why ancient convictions became entwined into their daily lives. Many Museum art artifacts exhibit localized examples of then widely held religious and political attitudes. In Italy, Michelangelo's fresco painting on the Sistine Chapel ceiling completed in the year 1512 inspired many. In contrast, other artifacts by many other artists exemplify passionate conflicts during the medieval religious crusades.

"Religious and political conflicts were very often the groundwork of monumental changes in ancient history. I am not referring to a person joining one political party vs. another, or replacing one religious belief for another as seen from missionary work, but of the power that a cluster of individuals wields on a whole society, and its governing laws."

Dr. Kirkchappel took a breath and continued, "Again, we're covering material swiftly; nevertheless, at this point, are there any questions?"

During a long pause, no one moved, and then a British boy lifted his arm.

"Go ahead, Andy."

Unsurprised at hearing his name, he asked with an English accent, "My family used to live in the United Kingdom, so I understand about the crusade wars in Europe, but what about significant behavioral changes within a single country without warfare?"

"Well defined," replied Dr. Kirkchappel. "During the 1950's, many rural townspeople around the world supported laws aligned with similar values predicated on their family, political and religious area rearing. In summary, during the 50's, a majority of the people supported behavior that was generally considered to be right or in the best interest of all. This led to minimal friction between people moving collectively in similar directions within their own communities.

"In contrast, to summarize current societies, a great amount of people have shifted to what they consider is right for them as individuals. Today, people move in different directions simultaneously depending on self-interest, and that has a tendency to create increased opportunities for friction. This intense focus on only self-interest could fractionate a community or society. We may benefit from numerous positive choices in careers, movies, radio stations, restaurants, or purchasing shoes at the mall," she said with a guilty smile, "yet we also have scores of negative choices such as buying or selling drugs, dropping out of school, abandoning children, or worse."

Studying the group, Dr. Kirkchappel asked, "Does having more religious, political, or personal choices hurt or help a society?"

No one raised their hand, yet their expressions validated a preoccupation with the question.

Continuing, Dr. Kirkchappel said, "Going back to our earlier question, as the number of choices increase, there may be several areas to explore a correlation.

"Last year, researched evidence suggests an elevated number of imprisoned criminals around the globe, when comparing the same type of citizens-to-crime ratio percentages during the 1950's. This could suggest that the growing number of choices or shifting loyalties may not be the only overarching answer. What about the converse?"

Again, they only stared blankly.

She continued, "Let me assure you these questions and problems are not exclusive to any country or time, but is the very keystone for today's lecture. We are not alone in the history of the world. The majority of cultures throughout the ages grappled with similar questions and decisions. This lecture's intention is to hint at the motivations used by ancient people to make choices and study them in the artifacts we discover, not in relation to what we should or should not do as individuals.

"Joyce, this is the relationship between religion and Museums. In this Museum, our department performs research using archeological investigations to learn how ancient religion affected localized politics, which shaped civilizations. Direct application informs us why Egyptians built magnificent pyramids to assist their mummified rulers into their next life, because of religion. The Mayan governments dedicated vast resources to build observatories to exemplify their religious view of the stars. Greek and Roman leaders built numerous historic shrines filled with statues of their gods. Buddhism and Confucianism parallel legislative laws to guide their believers to live in harmony with others and their environment. Sadly, nations have and continue to war over differences in religious and political perceptions.

"If we hope to improve our tomorrow, we must recognize how ancient civilizations chose to deal successfully or unsuccessfully with similar issues, by reviewing historical examples to see possible trends."

Allowing the students to digest her lecture, Dr. Kirkchappel flipped a switch on the wall to lower a large projection screen from the ceiling. She remained with her back to the students until the screen came to a complete stop.

Facing the students, she said, "You will now watch a film documenting societal impacts within a diverse number of ancient time periods. At the termination of the film, you should have a broader viewpoint of human deeds through the past four thousand years."

An electronic display panel automatically dimmed the lights as early film credits flashed on the screen.

Dr. Kirkchappel finished, "After the documentary has ended, the lights will automatically turn on, and the projector will shut off by itself. At that point, you are free to leave for lunch. Thank you for your time," she said, as she slipped out of sight through the side door.

***

Forty minutes after the documentary's end, Melinda finished a phone call with her friend in Hawaii, and then joined Leslie to search for Trent and Tab in the student dining room. Unable to find them within the room, Melinda noticed Mea sitting with Scott, Mark, Andy, and Dino. Heading towards the back of the room, she nudged Leslie to follow her.

Huddled over a table listening to Scott, they seemed guarded in their manner, and spoke with lowered voices. With their approached unnoticed, Melinda and Leslie stood back to give them privacy for their conversation.

Mea spotted them first, and then held up her hand to those sitting at her table hissing, "It's obvious you two have hideous manners!"

Dishing it right back, Leslie replied, "Compared to the tone of your voice, it's obvious you don't have any!"

Mea's eyes glared while her mouth curled in anger.

Melinda, seeing the conversation had started on the wrong foot, offered, "Mea, I only came to tell you that I enjoyed being your roommate, and as I will be moving into Leslie's room so we can have more time to work on our project together, I wanted to wish you well on yours."

Mea's condescending eyes flashed back to Melinda when she spewed out, "Looks more like you're trying to eavesdrop on us for project ideas."

"That's completely untrue Mea! We couldn't hear what you were saying."

"Sorry to disappoint you!" Mea spat with feigned concern.

Melinda rebutted, "We have a different project than whatever you're doing…"

Cutting Melinda off, Scott demanded, "Ok, what's your project then?"

Leslie defended them saying, "Wait a minute, we haven't finished all of the lectures; we're still keeping our options open."

Dino piped up, "Sounds to me like you're open to our options," which immediately caused snickering around the table.

Ignoring Dino's comments, Melinda, being the bigger person stated, "Mea, I want to remain friends, and wish you well. Now that I've done that, Leslie and I will be on our way."

"We were never friends, so it's all the same to me whether you're my roommate, or that sports jock Joyce," Mea sneered in a bored voice.

Leslie, who was ready to blow her composure, controlled herself when Melinda pinched her elbow saying, "Fine — good luck!" while turning to leave.

Boiling in anger, Leslie followed Melinda to their table. Both girls steamed inside as Mea and her table laughed aloud.

Chapter Fifteen

CHEATING

Another week behind them, Melinda and her student team of friends were returning to their project workroom after finishing lunch, which was located directly across the hall from a large oval shaped office. *"I'm glad our assigned work room is close to the stairs, the dining room, and my dorm room,"* Melinda thought as they approached the area.

Assigned by specific topics, their team's chosen project related to Mesoamerica, which inserted the team into one of Dr. Bradan's workrooms. Dr. Bradan and the other professors were sincerely motivated to engage with the apprentice projects for several reasons. When photographed as the winning project's mentoring Professor in the top industry journals, this became a huge benefit to their Museum instructor careers. As it was also mandatory to lecture on the student team's project, advancement further elevated each educator with additional industry visibility. However, the home field gain was to have the Museum's Oval Room as their personal work office.

Each year, the winning student team's professor occupies the Oval Room, designated as their private office for the rest of the year. Three times larger than the standard faculty offices, both the front and rear room walls curved to create an oval shape, giving it the prestigious connotation.

Rivaled only by Dr. Swinford's personal office in furnishings; floor-to-ceiling windows constituted the largest part of the back wall, offering an indisputably premium view of the Museum's interior courtyard.

Photographed in the prominent Oval Room generally ensured the winning faculty member with considerable vocation prestige as conducting important work, along with many new employment opportunities. Dr. Steele, last year's faculty winner, resigned from the Museum with a better offer to supervise a four-year, wholly funded excavation in China. As his early departure left the room available, Scott Swinford, as the Curator's son, had appropriated the room for his team. Approaching their workroom, Brian glanced across the hallway and noticed the door to the Oval Room was wide open.

He asked Melinda and the others, "Have any of you seen the inside of the Oval Room or the view from the windows?"

No one had.

Brian informed them, "I heard Carrie Keepsake in the gift shop telling a new employee that it has a most excellent view of the Museum courtyard. Let's take a quick glance out the windows before Scott and Mea come back from the lunch room."

Leslie laughed out loud saying, "The way she makes everyone tip-toe around her, she must think she's royalty. Where's the French guillotine for her majesty Mea when you need one?"

"LESLIE! You're terrible!" Melinda exclaimed, and then thought to herself, *"It was funny though."*

Passing through the unlocked door, Brian exclaimed immediately, "WOW! This is awesome! You guys — this is *way* nice!"

Raised window blinds exposed the marvelous courtyard's breathtaking scene of the manicured grounds, statues, water fountains, and intricate marble relief work along the Museum's inner walls.

Trent echoed Brian, "THIS IS AWESOME!"

"The view is so...beautiful," Melinda finally found the right word to support him, as she stood near the center of the room.

Stillness packed the room for virtually two minutes while they gazed at the spectacular courtyard view.

Leslie warmly said, "Can you imagine staring at that view all day? No wonder each of the faculty wants to win this office. I would love to work here too."

Melinda agreed, "I wouldn't mind..."

"HEY! Look at this!" Leslie pointed to a large white board covering most of the front wall, hanging on the left side of the office door. It was covered with a large rectangular chart drawn with a blue marker and was filled with hand written writing.

Is the Goseck ring the first human clock or calendar?

Description	Theories	Supporting Evidence
The Goseck circle is the best preserved of many similar structures in Germany. It consists of several concentric circles (a dirt mound that is surrounded by a ditch and two wooden pole fences) with three gate openings placed strategically to allow the sunrise to enter through them from the southeast, southwest, and northern directions.	Possibly the oldest European astronomical sun observatory.	Used the sunrise to determine the Winter Solstice through the southwest and southeast gates.
Archaeologists validated the concept by reconstructing a circular wooden fence design.	Earliest known European lunar clock.	Accurately coordinates times of the Winter/Summer Solstice.
Two southern openings map to beginning of Summer/Winter Solstice.	Original solar calendar?	Measurements align to calendar dates using modern GPS methods.
Referenced in Germany as a possible Stonehenge.	???	No discovered earth bank.
Pre-Bronze Age – 3,500BC	Mid-Neolithic structure.	Pottery shards suggest it dates to nearly 5,000 BC.
Built by:	???	???

Melinda's face furrowed, "Is that Scott and Mea's team project? What is a Goseck *ring*?"

Trent added, "It must be what they're doing for their assignment."

Brian echoed, "It seems strange to search for a clock."

With a cringing look in her expression, Leslie said, "Guys, I wish we hadn't seen this white board — we'd better go before they come back!"

Anxious to leave, the team hustled towards the door, when abruptly Mea and Scott blocked the entrance, causing their friend Dino to collide into Mea from behind.

Realizing Melinda's full team was in their private workroom infuriated Scott, who shouted, "HEY, THIS IS OUR PRIVATE WORK AREA! GET OUT

NOW!"

Framed by the doorjamb, together the two made a comedic pair. Five foot, six inch tall Scott resembled being a little tag along brother, in direct contrast to taller five foot, eleven inch Mea, who wore brown two-inch heels.

"I never thought much of you Melinda, however, this stunt is worse than I would have expected, even from *you*," Mea said with venom.

Scott glanced at the white board, and quickly realized it was not possible for the invading students to miss or ignore the essence of their team's project.

He accused them, "This is cheating! You can't snoop into our work! You guys are out of here when my father hears about this!"

"It's not like that at all," Melinda squeaked.

Dino grunted with smugness, "I told you so; they *were* open to our option. This proves they were eavesdropping on us in the dining room..."

Trent interrupted, "No way you guys, we're not trying to see your stuff!"

Mea threw up her hand saying, "I don't want someone like you to waste *my* time. You can tell it to Dr. Swinford and the program leaders. Scott, go call your father now!"

Scott hesitated with indecision.

"Hurry up, Scott!" Mea bossed, "I don't want to stand here looking at them all day."

"OK...I'll be right back!" Scott said.

He pushed past Dino and Chris and then ran from the room.

***

In Dr. Swinford's office, Melinda knew that they were finished with the student program. She, along with her friends, sat sweating on one side of the room, dreading the coming exchange of dialogue, while Dr. Kirkchappel and Dr. Koffin sat against the opposite wall.

Ominous behind his imposing walnut desk in the middle of the room, Dr. Swinford gruffly said to the two faculty members, "This is alarming!"

"Spying on the other students' work is intolerable! Frankly, I'm ready to pull the plug on this team immediately for cheating," the Curator said with a gesture of displeasure.

Tab stared at his shoes in his silent world, and refrained from reading the Curator's lips, oblivious of the accusation the Museum's leader cast at them.

Clearly distressed by the ridiculousness of the situation, Leslie rolled her eyes in disapproval at his unjust comments.

Brian, who felt personally responsible for the current state of affairs, leaned forward in his chair and held his head in both hands, while his stomach ached.

Trent, as the team's oldest member, tried to shield them from the allegation, "Sir, we were only looking out the room's windows at the courtyard grounds — the door was left wide open. When we entered the room, we had no idea their project was on the wall behind us. We only saw it as we were leaving the office!"

"Mr. Davis, I might advocate something similar if I were in your situation. However, *your* word *is* in question, which is why we are wasting precious time here today to deal with your predicament, instead of addressing matters of positive substance," Dr. Swinford retorted.

Dr. Koffin attempted to mediate the discussion, "They may be telling us the truth. It's well known that those windows have the best view in the Museum."

Dr. Swinford frowned at the comment, aware that he only had two small windows behind him in his otherwise dignified office. Dr. Koffin felt guilty for his last remark when he read the expression on his boss's face, and quickly tried to distance himself from the unexpected comment's reaction by offering, "I may have a simple way to address this quickly."

The bearded professor looked at Dr. Swinford and Dr. Kirkchappel and instructed them, "Follow me into the hallway, and I'll explain."

Outside of Dr. Swinford's office, Dr. Koffin whispered to his advocates, "If they were spying on the other students to get ideas, it would mean they probably don't yet have a project of their own. I believe if we query them about the particulars of their supposed project, we'll soon know if they're guilty of the charges."

Dr. Swinford thought for a long moment and then said, "Ok — I don't want to squander a lot of time here, but your suggestion may cut through the 'he said — she said' routine."

The Curator stared sternly at Dr. Koffin as he snapped, "When we go back inside my office, I want you to lead the questioning."

Dr. Swinford held the door for Dr. Kirkchappel, and closed it after Dr. Koffin entered the room. As he rounded his desk to sit down, Dr. Koffin asked the students as he sat in his own chair, "If you were not in the Oval Room to get project ideas from the other team, then you must be engaged in a project. Can you share details about it with us?"

Together, Melinda and her team looked nervously at each other, and then Trent said, "Sure, that's easy."

Bubbly as usual, Leslie jumped at the chance to describe the team's topic, "Our project is to investigate if Columbus really was the first person to discover America."

Melinda helped Leslie since she was part of the reason for the chosen topic, "Everyone assumes that Columbus was the first person to discover America, primarily since he has the earliest known record for such an event. Yet, nearly five hundred years before Columbus sailed with his ships, the Vikings had moved west after raiding most of Europe."

Unsure of the connection, and looking at Brian next, Dr. Koffin ordered, "Continue please."

Brian looked hesitantly between Dr.'s Koffin and Kirkchappel for a moment before he began again, "Supposedly, after his defeat, Erik the Red was booted out from the main Viking settlement, and with nowhere else to go, sailed to Iceland. From there, he and his rowdy son Leif Erickson migrated to Greenland — at least they called it Greenland, hoping the name would tempt other Vikings living in Iceland to tag along behind them and bring needed supplies.

"Around this point in time, the story gets a little sketchy, but word has it that Leif Erickson later sailed west again, and landed in..." he trailed off, while looking at Trent for help.

Trent whispered to Brian, "Newfoundland."

"Thanks...Newfoundland, which they named...well, simply because they found it."

Dr. Koffin nodded saying, "I'm following you so far. I have heard of this claim, however, it is somewhat controversial. Please help me understand how you make the correlation to the Vikings discovering America?"

"Easy," Brian stated, "because Newfoundland is practically a skateboard leap over the hill from the state of Maine."

Dr. Koffin blinked at the surfer boy, expecting the tan teen to offer more in his explanation. Melinda sensed the declining lack of engagement between Brian and the Egyptian professor, so she quickly jumped in.

"It all connected when I told my team about a vacation trip to the Yucatan my parents took me on last year. When we visited the ancient Mayan city of Chitzen Itiza, our half-Mayan tour guide showed us some hieroglyphics of Vikings on a stone block. He told us the region was quite sophisticated in its advancement, and that the native people had traded with many countries."

Trent added, "When Melinda told us about her trip, my brother Tab signed us the story about Leif Erickson, and about how Viking artifacts were recorded to have been discovered in Newfoundland. He then told us if you draw a straight line between Newfoundland and the Yucatan, it crosses directly through America. So the main question is how can Vikings be in the hieroglyphics, if they did not land anywhere along the American coast line?"

Dr. Koffin glanced at Dr. Kirkchappel with a questioning face when he asked her, "Have you heard of this association before today?"

Shaking her head no, the attractive instructor moistened her lips and replied, "I'm familiar with the Vikings discovering Newfoundland, although the portion about them sailing to or along the Americas to the Yucatan, well, I'm not familiar with any substantiation to the theory."

Turning to Dr. Swinford, the balding professor asked his boss, "How about you, Swinford?"

Again supporting his chin with his thumb and forefinger, Dr. Swinford stared at his desk as if he were in a trance, before answering the question, "Same as Yvonne — I don't recollect the straight line theory to the Yucatan. Nothing comes to mind."

After a short silence fell upon the room, Dr. Koffin stood up and said, "Excuse us for a moment again."

He reached for the door handle and opened the door. He closed it behind

Dr. Swinford and Dr. Kirkchappel after they entered the hallway.

"I have to admit, I can't fathom why these kids would try to get ideas from Scott's team with a prospective project like they just described," Dr. Koffin announced.

Dr. Kirkchappel agreed with her peer, "I'm with Clyde. The way they each carried the story line makes it obvious they've been working on it as a group. As reckless as the decision was to enter another team's room, I believe they were only looking through the Oval Room windows at the courtyard.

Dr. Swinford stared blankly at the hall baseboards before he spoke, "It does seem plausible. Therefore, if you two agree, we'll let them off with a warning. However, I want to reinforce that if one more action seems suspect, the whole team will be disqualified from the competition."

The others agreed.

Once the program leaders had returned into the Curator's office, each of the five troubled students stared wide-eyed at the three leaders, hoping to determine something of their fate within their expressions.

Sitting down in his chair behind his desk, Dr. Swinford began, "We have reviewed your project hypothesis and concluded you have a sound project."

This time, Melinda and Leslie smiled at each other with relief.

"However," he said, causing the girls to sit up straight, "the rules are quite clear. If only one member of the team steps out of line, we are required to expel the entire team. I'm not expecting to have any of you in my office again — am I right?"

Relieved to hear what Dr. Swinford said, and in full agreement with his comments, Melinda and her friends quickly filed through the office door.

After the students in question had departed, Dr. Swinford said, "Good Suggestion Clyde. We can carry on now..."

Dr. Kirkchappel interrupted her boss by clearing her throat to raise another issue, "I'm not sure we're finished with the overall situation. I am somewhat apprehensive about the nature of Scott's team project. It seems too controversial for the program, and may bring unnecessary bitterness from our friends in the archeological community."

Taken back, Dr. Swinford studied her features before saying, "Yvonne, of all people, I thought you'd see this as a worthwhile and very challenging project to formulate a concluding opinion about why it was built. There's a lot of world history about why ancient man built rings like Stonehenge, however, considering the energetic mystery it and others have played in times past, I'm not sure if this question has truly been answered before."

"Sir — with all due respect, the topic sounds too close to the excavation work being conducted right now at Goseck, and I'm not sure this is the type of work I personally feel comfortable sustaining. There are considerable options; they could select a better project," Yvonne stated confidently.

Dr. Swinford looked hard at Clyde, "What are your thoughts in this matter?"

Before answering, Dr. Koffin brooded the question and its ramifications until he replied, "I'm somewhere in the middle of you two. From my personal standpoint, I must admit that I'm not thrilled with our program coming under examination for potentially leveraging other peers' good works. Yet, I'm grappling internally with my professional opinion. As you know, I believe we should question everything and see where the evidence leads us and maybe our group could possibly uncover something new."

Dr. Kirkchappel began to speak until Dr. Swinford raised his hand and said, "One moment you two, we're not trying to bring any tainted press to our program, so we should proceed cautiously with this hypothesis. I'm in agreement with you Clyde; I believe we should investigate and expect one of two things to happen. One, Scott's team will prove the value in their premise, or two, without any evidence support, the hypothesis will have a short runway, and will halt as a wrong conclusion. Either way, our job is to support research, and they would essentially be studying an exciting discovery to determine either option. I know Scott could benefit from learning more about the region and topic!"

Dr. Kirkchappel suddenly interjected, "Yes, but even the project titles oozes possible plagiarism and political ramifications...."

"Yvonne, if you're troubled by the possible perception of the title, then change it! Try calling it something like...*A Comparison of Modern versus Historic Timekeeping*, or maybe, *Today's Broad Interpretations of Ancient Calendars,* or anything else you like. It's all the same to me."

Before either of the professors could respond to counter their leader's direction of the project topic, he walked into his office saying, "Keep me informed of their progress…," and shut the door.

Both knew in one efficient motion that they were overridden and excused. With a look of abject disappointment on her face, Dr. Kirkchappel whispered to Dr. Koffin when they left the administrative office area, "Each year that goes by, I worry we deviate further from the program's primary charter and purpose, and this time it feels to me to be too far out of scope and decency. I can't support this project the way it's been positioned."

Dr. Koffin grunted his depressed agreement saying, "Let's schedule some time to work on it together. Perhaps we can shift the premise in a more appropriate direction. You can count on my support!"

Chapter Sixteen

STRANGE SIGHTINGS

"I'm so bummed we missed the first Asian lecture! I really wanted to attend it. The Far East seems like such a mystical place to me," Leslie said romantically.

After returning to their student team workroom, Brian echoed, "Same for me. I spent most of last summer surfing in Hawaii, and now I have tons of friends there who are Asian. I was hoping to learn more about their cultures."

Trent and Tab signed to each other with an outbreak of hand signals.

"Tab says Matt Faraday mentioned something about the Asian lecture being rescheduled until tomorrow, because there were students that couldn't make the lecture in time. I think that means us?"

"Really?" Melinda interjected and then eagerly asked, "When did he say it will be rescheduled?"

"Wait, let me ask," Trent replied, and signed with Tab.

"Tab didn't catch that part; he said Matt was eating at the time, and he couldn't read his lips."

"No wonder that guy is so big. If I ate half as much as he does, I'd never ride a surfboard, and if I did, man it would wipe me out," Brian chuckled.

No one acknowledged his comment, and sensing he had been rude, said, "Then again, I'll bet he can do lots of things I can't. He could be a bodyguard if he wanted…"

This time, his friends gave approval nods when Melinda added, "That's better Brian, because for all we know, Matt may have a medical problem, and can't drop the pounds. He's probably unhappy about the way he looks, and feels even worse when people point or laugh at him. I don't know what it's like for him, but it doesn't help us to make it harder on him. We all need help sometimes to feel better, instead of putting down others just to make us feel good. You know, he's probably a great guy — you aren't giving him a chance. No one's perfect."

Brian lowered his head with the realization of Melinda's meaning, and said, "You're right. I somewhat understand how he feels. I have a large pink birthmark on my shoulder, and that's why I have such a dark tan to hide it, because I used to be called *'raspberry patch'* when I was a kid."

The room remained uncomfortably silent until Tab tapped Trent on the arm, and signed to him in order to lift their spirits and change the mood.

"With the Asian lecture cancelled, Tab says it will probably be rescheduled, and if we want to find out when, the program leaders placed an agenda schedule in the rear of the lecture room today. It may be updated by now," Trent interpreted for his brother.

"Agenda, I had no idea there was an agenda in there, did you?" Leslie asked Melinda.

"Actually — no," she replied.

"You guys wanna go scope it out?" Brian cheerfully suggested, hoping to forget about his recent comments.

Trent laughed, "I don't know about checking anything out with you again; you almost got us tossed out of here today, buddy."

Brian instantly went red in the face.

"I'm sorry guys; I only wanted us to see the view from the windows."

Tab put his hand on Brian's shoulder, and smiled. Leslie nudged him and then put her arm though his at the elbow saying, "We'll let it go this time, but next time — don't count on your good fortune holding up."

Melinda added, "We're not doing much right now, so let's 'scope it out', as Brian would say," she finished, winking at him.

With the decision made, they proceeded together to the lecture hall. Inside it, Melinda noticed two other students. Jerome Whitfield, the African American boy, was reading what she thought might be the new agenda, and Kim Otani, the tiny

Japanese girl, was taking a picture of something posted on the wall with her phone camera. She knew both were on the same student team.

Leslie walked across the area towards Jerome, followed by Trent and Brian, when Jerome looked up in surprise to be surrounded by the new students, and insecure of their intentions, asked, "What's up?"

Leslie questioned him, "We heard the Asian lecture was rescheduled, and we were curious to know when?"

"Oh, well — here it is," Jerome pointed at the agenda, "it says tomorrow at 9:30 am."

"Excellent!" Brian exclaimed, knowing they could make the class.

Melinda, who was unable to see the agenda through her bunched together teammates, glanced at Kim, who was writing something on the wall with a marker. Inquisitive, she went near the black-haired girl to read what she wrote.

"What are you writing?" she asked Kim, standing next to her.

"We're supposed to list our team's project on this poster paper."

Melinda looked at the large sheet and read:

Student Team Projects

Team (1) How the first Pharaohs rose to power in Egypt?

Team (2) Who built the first human clock in Europe?

Team (3) Why is there a worldwide reference to dragons?

Team (4)

Noticing her team did not have a project listed in a blank space; Melinda picked up the black marker, and added next to Team 4 - *Vikings Discover America*, as her friends joined her.

Trent chuckled when he tapped his forefinger on the page, "We're team number four," and glanced at Brian to tease him, "See, you put us in fourth place already," bumping the embarrassed surfer boy on the shoulder.

Brian's face blushed again.

Kim explained, "We haven't heard tomorrow's lecture yet, however, we came up with a project title anyway. If we decide on something better after all of the lectures are completed, the rules say we can change it."

"Where does it say you can change the projects?" Melinda asked her.

"Down here. They just posted these rules today," Kim said, pointing to her right.

Melinda stepped over to a poster pinned onto a corkboard and read:

<u>Project Rules</u>

Each team will record their Project Title beside an open slot number. Once a project has an assigned number, that number will reference each team for the entirety of the program.

Teams may change their project title only once during the program. The deadline to choose another project title will be at the conclusion of each team's field trip.

Once a team's field trip is complete, that team must proceed with a chosen project topic (presumably the topic with the greatest supportive evidence).

Attention: Once a team field trip is completed, there will not be a second trip.

Leslie joked, "Well, I guess we better be sure about where we go on our field trip. If we end up in the wrong place, we're hosed," she said.

Trent paused, and sided with Leslie, "That's a good point! Do we know where to go on our research trip?"

No one offered any suggestions, so Trent advised, "Well, we're not going to figure it out here, so we might as well go somewhere else for now."

With Trent leading, they departed the lecture room. Once in the lobby area, the older brother's step hesitated while he decided where to go next in the Museum.

Her mind still twirling on the previous trip location topic, Melinda bubbled, "I know! We can go to the Yucatan!" When her friends stopped to listen, she added, "I know the Viking reference is located there, so maybe there are other examples of their trip nearby to check." With deflating enthusiasm, she then added, "But from what I remember, there seems to be very little information about it, or if our tour guide said they found other similar hieroglyphics."

Leslie sighed, "If we're trying to link the Vikings to America, then maybe we should travel east to Maine, or somewhere like that."

"That's the problem," Trent explained, folding his arms across his chest, "There's no known evidence back east, which is why no one is very familiar with the concept. So where would we look? It would be like finding a needle in a haystack kind of thing, only worse if there isn't actually a needle."

"I know, I've been thinking the same thing," Brian agreed, but quickly changed his expression at the rumble that escaped his stomach, leading his mind towards a new topic, "Hey, how about this — since we have some time until dinner, who wants to come with me to the museum's main cafeteria? We can get a snack and talk more about it."

Melinda shook her head, "I'm not that hungry, but I do want to visit the Gift Shop. I'll walk with you until we get to the lobby."

"Ok," Brian smiled in return.

"Works for me too," Leslie, added.

"Maybe while we're in the Gift Shop, we can buy stuffed tigers in there," Melinda said teasingly to Leslie.

"I know, can you believe it — my little brother heard about the big tiger scare from his friends, and now my parents are worried sick I'm going to get eaten by it," Leslie snickered at the absurd thought.

"You're kidding. I thought it was nothing but a dumb hoax!" Brian exclaimed.

"Ha, just goes to prove, one person's nothing is someone else's something," Trent laughed, failing in the attempt to be funny.

Without a smile or giggle from the others, Trent felt embarrassed and announced, "Brian, I'm a little on the tired side. I haven't slept well here at the Museum. I'm going to my room to catch some shut eye, but Tab said he'll go with you to eat."

Tab looked at Brian and rubbed his stomach. Brian smiled approvingly, and patted his stomach in return. Together they laughed.

"Coming girls?" Brian asked. "Man, I'm hungry!"

"Be right there," Leslie mentioned cheerfully, "I need to make a quick stop at the washroom first."

"What is it with girls? Every time you need to get somewhere fast, they've got to hit the bathroom first," Brian whined. "And you take forever too! Is there some secret day spa or makeover stand in there?"

Leslie smiled at Brian in a deliberate way, but refused to respond as she left him waiting.

***

Minutes later, which seemed an eternity to the anxious teen boys, Ruth Ann, the redhead girl who sat in a wheelchair, exited the girl's bathroom with Leslie, who was explaining, "…are going to eat, and we're going to the Gift Shop," as she pointed to Melinda.

Ruth Ann smiled while she glided easily by Leslie's side. She exuded a bright and amiable personality as she validated her acceptance, "Hi everyone, I hope you don't mind if Leslie invited me to roll along."

"Glad to have one more sensible girl around for company. These guys only think about food, cars, sports, food, you know," Melinda joked as she playfully smiled at Tab and Brian.

Brian tried to hurry the group along, and walked from the area asking, "Ruth Ann, where are you from?"

"New Mexico," she answered promptly pushing herself to remain at his long-legged side.

"Have you always lived there?"

"No, we used to live in Lake Tahoe before we moved to Albuquerque."

Leslie asked her, "Did you move because of your dad's job?"

"No, it was my accident."

"I'm so sorry — I didn't know," Leslie said apologetically.

"Oh, don't worry about it. I am used to it now. At first, I felt miserable all the time about my accident, and kept asking 'why me'? Then I met someone else in a wheelchair, who is now one of my best friends in the whole world. He can do anything he wants, which helped me to realize that I can too if I try."

"What happened...I mean the accident?" Brian asked nervously, unsure of the etiquette required to ask the sensitive question.

"I was snowboarding. My girlfriend Kelly's parents took us. We went together all the time, so no one imagined anything would ever happen. Kelly and I were shredding down a run when a man just learning to ski lost control, and hit us from behind.

"He and Kelly crashed to a stop together, while I was pushed over the edge of a roped-off area. I tumbled down a steep ravine into some trees, and two days later, I woke up from a coma in the hospital. My family already knew my spine was injured."

"Wow, I can't even imagine how I would deal with something like that," Leslie muttered at the thought.

"For me, when I found out, I was crushed, and then I became angry. Now I'm ok with it."

"Whoa, that sounds rough," Brian said, and smiled at her courage.

Ruth Ann continued, "It was so hard for me at first. I mean, the physical part was tough, don't get me wrong, but the emotional aspect was much worse. My parents blamed themselves for letting me go that day to the point, they sold our house, and we moved to a very different climate, to avoid seeing the slopes every day. As I said, it gets better for me with each new day. Now I'm able to do lots of stuff I never imagined possible in a wheelchair. About the only tricky area for me is stairs. I have to ride the elevator, so sometimes I run late from waiting for one."

Near the elevators, they saw a balding man with poor posture wearing gray slacks and a blue striped shirt push the down button in the waiting area. Within seconds, the elevator bell rang, and both stainless steel doors slid open. The man disregarded Ruth Ann and entered before her, but upon noticing the glare in Brian's eyes, reached down to push the 'door open' button allowing Ruth Ann and the team to find their place within the floating metal room. Her wheelchair rolled slightly backwards when the pulleys slowed the elevator during its descent. At the main floor, the bell signaled their arrival. Everyone exited into the central hallway and parted ways.

Tab and Brian navigated through the swarming crowd towards the cafeteria as Leslie, Melinda, and Ruth Ann turned right and entered the Gift Shop.

The shop employee welcomed them and said, "Hello — ah, with student badges, you get an additional fifteen percent off everything in the store."

Leslie said, pointing to each of the girls as she said their names, "Hi, this is Ruth Ann, this is Melinda, and I'm Leslie. Extra discounts — now you're speaking my language."

Smiling at the three students, the woman said, "I'm Carrie Keepsake; if you have any questions, please let me know."

***

Tab and Brian waited in line to order their food behind a married Hispanic couple, who were correcting their two young boys in Spanish to stop them from running around noisily.

Absorbed in the excitement of the small family, Brian realized they both forgot to pick up a tray at the front entrance, and instantly held up one finger to Tab before informing the deaf boy, "I'll be right back, " as Tab nodded.

Returning to where Tab stood, Brian nudged him with his tray. The younger brother took the brown plastic tray, and stared forward, as neither was quite within reach of the buffet style food. As Brian drew closer, he saw an offering of stuffed baked potatoes covered with chopped brisket, cheese enchiladas, and freshly baked pizzas. Brian chose his main entree, and then guided his tray along the metal shelf towards the fruit salad segment as Tab selected his meal.

"What would you like to drink?" the cashier asked them.

Brian replied, "Soda for me," and Tab nodded for one too.

Her nametag displayed **Karalee Cook**

Karalee handed the teens their sodas as Brian introduced them both while gesturing, "I'm Brian, and his name is Tab. Also, he's deaf."

Karalee smiled brightly hearing about Tab, and cheerfully said so he could read her lips, "My grandfather was unable to hear too, so I know sign language."

Tab smiled excitedly, and signed, "Hello," and then he showed her the personal sign for his name.

She smiled back pleasantly, and signed to him, "Let me know if you ever need anything," to which Tab thanked her in sign language.

Both teens paid, and then sat at the end of a long table inside the cafeteria to eat. As soon as he finished his snack, Tab guzzled the remnants of his soft drink. Suddenly, the cafeteria burst into bedlam. Stunned, Tab watched in his soundless existence as people rushed from their seats and acted outrageously. Several family members collided into each other, while deciding where to rush next.

Confused by the sudden chaos, Tab looked at Brian for help. With his head cocked to one side as if listening, Brian suddenly stood and started urging for Tab to follow him.

Karalee raced from behind the establishment's counter signing to Tab, "The fire alarm is ringing. We need to exit the building now!"

Close behind the cashier, the teens followed her from the cafeteria and into the main lobby, where they spotted the student girls rushing out of the gift shop. Together, they each merged within the thronging crowd through the front doors, until they once more huddled outside the Museum beneath the enormous portico.

Brian faced Tab, and spoke loud enough for Leslie, Melinda, and Ruth Ann to hear over the noise of the alarm, "Did you ever think a Museum could be this exciting? Here we go again."

Tab nodded his agreement to Brian, while the students left the area and proceeded back to stand by the railing, waiting to see what transpired next.

***

Brock, while making his daily museum security rounds, favored coming down the back stairs during this time of the day. He frequently found bored teenagers loitering in the stairwell. However, all was clear today as he descended the nearly hidden steps.

The retired navy man moved lightly to his right and quickly peeked into the Australian hall without expecting to see a problem. With the comfort of knowing everything appeared fine, he retreated and passed under a grand archway leading into the Asian gallery area. While meandering through the massive room crowded with magnificent Chinese artifacts, he smiled, having a personal fondness for the culture.

He thought, *"It's amazing these guys were shooting fireworks into the skies over three thousand years ago."*

Without haste, he transitioned from one exhibit hall to the next by moving beneath another sizable doorway leading into the Japanese hall. At the gallery's end, he rounded the final corner of the giant room that led directly into the entrance of the Egyptian hall when he heard an unusual metallic scrape.

Suspicious without seeing the forthcoming menace in the next room, Brock quickly stepped towards the growing sounds of heavy clanking footsteps.

WHISH!

His Navy Seal reflexes suddenly awoke as an intense surge of adrenalin took charge of his normally carefree movements. He lurched backwards with uncertain steps, while gaping stupidly at a complete outfit of medieval battle armor walking towards him, trying to grasp the unexpected sight of the knight. A broadsword rose above its head. Brock watched with panic as the long blade severed the air towards where he stood immobilized. With a sudden perseverance to survive, Brock swiftly dove away from the falling unchallenged blade, which cut deeply and stuck into the imposing wooden archway, barely missing him.

Tangled in the flagpoles that framed the immense archway, he doubted his own senses and wiped his eyes to be sure of the reality in front of him, and instantly wished for the metal man to melt from what must be his mental delusion. The sound of invisible laughter rose nastily from within the helmeted head, when Brock accidentally stumbled into a display and tripped backwards.

"It isn't real," Brock told himself right before he shuddered from the sudden impact to his backside against the floor, and then rolled away to avoid the oncoming man in armor. Too slow to escape, he winced as a shiny metal boot kicked him squarely in his ribs. By tightening his side and stomach muscles, he reinforced his rib cage from the kick's damage, but could not prevent a burst of burning pain from racing up his spine. He grunted inadvertently when the pain exploded sharply inside his head, causing him to squeeze precious air from his lungs.

Unarmed, the knight moved aggressively towards the downed security man. Brock withdrew backwards at a steady rate from his attacker. Stunned at how quickly the assailant shortened the distance between them, and still lying vulnerable on the ground, Brock rolled onto his back and drew in his knees until they pressed tightly into his chest. Two steps later, when the knight leaned over to grasp at Brock, he blasted his legs outward into the mid-section of the armor-encased man.

Not waiting to see the outcome of his potent kick, Brock spun on the slick marble floor, and quickly rose from his knees. He spent costly seconds drawing his handgun from its holster and sprinted away from his bizarre opponent.

Securely holding his pistol, Brock whirled around to fire at his attacker, yet somehow, a metal fist smashed into his left shoulder, just prior to his squeezing the trigger. Dismayed, he thought, *"How does he move so fast in that heavy armor?"*

Turned around by the painful blow, Brock lurched beneath the great archway leading back into the Egyptian hall, when the dangerous knight grasped the hilt of the sword still buried in the wall and ripped it loose. The knight suddenly thrust his hand at Brock, as if he were drawing the blade from a scabbard at his waist. Twisting his wrist, the sword's deadly tip arched straight toward the security guard.

Brock dove to the polished floor to avoid certain death as the blade viciously passed over him. He instantly felt the sharp edge slice through the back of his shirt. The cold wisp of steel brushed across his shoulder blades in a way that made Brock shift to immediately shuffle away crablike from the warrior's boots.

In an attempt to rise and fire his gun at the medieval man, too quickly again, Brock was pinned down by the slicing blade, and dove behind a wooden sarcophagus to escape another arching swing. Unable to pull the blade free from the ancient casket barely gave Brock enough time to stand on his feet, while he bobbed about the metal man's flying fists, until an iron glove connected painfully into his right clavicle. The sudden pain felt like a hard-thrown baseball and had the sting of an angry hornet.

Brock's lips went suddenly colorless from the pain, and a searing numbness relieved Brock of any of his right hand's dexterous movements. Now unable to elevate the gun from the intense pain, Brock faltered alongside a long glass case displaying hammered gold armbands. He shifted the military made firearm to his left hand, and noticed a line of his sweat running down the barrel from the effort. Swiftly he raised the gun, and fired loudly once — twice — nothing happened.

Brock steadily triggered two more rounds into the seemingly unstoppable approaching breast armor. For an instant, he thought the Knight hesitated, but then it became determined in its oncoming steps to grasp him.

Misshapen metal fingers lurched forward hoping to strangle Brock, as sweat ran into the security man's eyes. Once more, he fired as the now leaping Knight collapsed onto him. Crumpled under the unknown Knight's heaviness, Brock stumbled backwards until he lost his balance and crashed against a granite pedestal, which supported a stone Egyptian Eagle. With the sound of a hysterical scream in the background, Brock's head felt a weighty thud. Everything turned upside down, and Brock collapsed into unconsciousness on the floor.

***

Upon hearing the dreadful uproar, the plump security room's female employee hurried into the vicinity barely in time to see Brock plummet backwards after firing his weapon. Unsure of his target, the woman screamed a warning to him, however, too late, the stone eagle dropped upon his cranium.

Shaken with fear, she staggered frantically to push the hidden security alarm button.

Considerable metal doors immediately rolled shut, followed by a high-pitched siren blare. Lights instantly dimmed within the hall as heavy metal cage bars encased with bulletproof glass lowered from the ceiling to quarantine the area. The security employee rushed to where Brock lay unconscious on the floor, the whole time wishing she had hurried back faster after taking her break to know what had happened.

Chapter Seventeen

VANISHED

Brock's first awareness of returning to consciousness was that of his boots dragging along the smooth polished floor. With the next feeling of floating in mid-air, his feet soon lifted from off the ground. Through blurry slits for eyes, he watched as familiar Egyptian artifacts raced past him at an accelerated rate.

The momentum continued throughout a white tunnel. He streaked above and across the marble floor of the Museum's main lobby, wondering how this was possible. Foggy and funny thoughts inside Brock made him smile from speeding towards the upside-down stairs, until realizing he was the one upside down.

With his head lifted upward over his chest instead of hanging backwards to view the racing floor, Al's smile warmed at his seemingly vacant stare. Cheerful, he closed his eyes again. Unable to feel his legs moving, he was succumbing to an intense sleepiness while hearing the pounding of quick steps down the stairs.

"Brock — Brock! Can you hear me?"

Amid the painful aching inside his skull, Brock focused hard on Al's blurry and apprehensive face as though he were seeing him through a dusty window.

"Wheeere…I?" he asked, trying to rise.

"Brock, don't go to sleep! Tell me what happened before the police arrive."

"Policcce," Brock stammered slowly coming to attention.

Al felt Brock's grip had strength when the Navy Seal caught his elbow during another intense wave of pain. He helped the injured man recline on a cot in the security area, allowing him time to collect himself.

Within minutes, Brock recovered some strength and asked Al, "Did I get him? Who was it? Man that guy was fast!"

"What guy? There was no one else in the room!"

Shocked at hearing the startling words, the wounded man stared at Al's face with an open mouth, trying to read his expression.

"That can't be…I shot him five times in the chest…there's no way he could have gotten up."

"What did he look like?" Al fervently asked.

Unsure, Brock answered with a concentrated effort to overcome his nausea, "His helmet hid his face…, but I think the armor has to still be there."

"Armor! You're not making any sense," Al said with mounting concern.

Slowly swinging his legs to the floor, Brock gaped into space telling the big man, "I don't understand. Can we go look? I can show you!"

Al nodded his acknowledgement, and assisted Brock to his feet. They slowly gained momentum ascending the stairs to the main hall lobby.

In response to the activated security alarm, police contained the lobby. At the sight of Al and Brock, senior officer Lieutenant Gomez ran over to them, "I wasn't expecting to see you guys this soon. What happened?"

Al replied, "I'm not sure, Lieutenant. Brock is showing us the problem. Tell your men to cover us."

At the bark of the leader's orders, the officers understood and responded. Brock led both men through the long alabaster tunnel, until they halted near the Egyptian vestibule entrance. With a careful inspection of the area through the bulletproof glass, and seeing nothing suspicious, Al entered his lockdown override code into the blinking security panel.

Impatient to pass by the security gate, Brock squeezed past the other two and led them to the place where he had fought off the knight.

"Right here! I tell ya, he should be right here! I shot him five times in the chest."

"WHAT?" the Lieutenant exclaimed. "You shot who?"

Brock shook his head in confusion as he led his two companions towards the grand archway, which separated the Egyptian and Japanese chambers.

"Here is where I almost got a haircut, when the guy swung that sword at me," Brock said pointing at the large gash in the doorway.

Al and the Lieutenant easily saw the deep damage to the wood archway, as if created from a hatchet or axe.

"What happened next? What did he look like?" The Lieutenant blitzed him with questions.

Brock spun red in the face to stare at both men.

"This will sound crazy, but it was a knight!"

"A what?" cried the Lieutenant.

"I didn't see any part of him because he was wearing a full set of armor, but that didn't stop him from swinging a sword at me," Brock said sheepishly.

With a raised hand to gain control, Al asked the foggy man, "You're telling us you fought with a knight? A guy dressed in real armor?"

"Right, — that's what I'm trying to say."

"OK, slow down, and tell us what happened next," Al coached.

After concluding the story, his companions were equally unsure of what to believe.

Massaging the back of his giant neck, Al stated, "It's strange, but finding you unconscious, I know you didn't have time to make up that story, and the evidence matches your depiction of the struggle.

"As hard as it is to believe, the deep cuts are real in the archway and besides your sliced shirt, which would be hard to do to yourself, there are scratches in the marble floor. So where did the armor come from, and where did it go?"

With a sudden turn towards the front lobby stairs, Brock yelled, "It had to come from upstairs — follow me!"

Above in the Arms and Amour Room, they widened out to search the enormous area.

All appeared ordinary. Pedestals displayed entire sets of unaffected armor. There were no empty visible places, and nothing seemed out of order. In the room's core, while continuing to study the vast area, the Lieutenant announced, "I got nothing here…is there another section of armor?"

"No, this is the only spot," Al replied.

"What about your surveillance tapes, have you watched them yet?"

Exhaling an agonizing sigh, Al winced, "We only received the new cameras this morning, and they're not up yet. They're scheduled for installation tonight."

"Oooh, blind too...we better investigate the rest of the building," the lead officer suggested.

"Where do you want my men to search?" the Lieutenant questioned him.

"Your group's larger, so have them check the top two floors. Brock and my team will search the bottom floor. Meet you back in the auditorium."

Separated from the officer to follow the plan, Brock and big Al were in the motion of jogging quickly towards the front of the building, when they both heard "AL!"

Dr. Swinford was glaring at Al and Brock, while he stomped across the top of the main stairs towards the executive area, and then yelled, "IN MY OFFICE NOW!

Looking like children knowing they are guilty, both men followed slowly behind him into his office.

Slamming his office door shut, Dr. Swinford yelled, "AL, THIS IS NOT ACCEPTABLE! I HAVE NO EARTHLY IDEA WHAT THE BLAZES IS GOING ON AROUND THE MUSUEM LATELY, BUT NOT HAVING OPERATIONAL CAMERAS IS NOT AN EXCUSE!"

Dr. Swinford paused to catch his breath after their explanation of the previous events, and then continued his bellow, "FIND THE CULPRIT AND THEN GET THOSE CAMERAS INSTALLED ASAP! I WANT AN ONGOING REPORT AS SOON AS EACH ONE IS WORKING AND ON-LINE! AM I MAKING MYSELF CLEAR?"

Surprised, Al had never seen the man so furious. Red in the face, Dr. Swinford's veins popped out of his neck and temples.

Al and Brock hastened speechless from his office.

Behind his desk, Dr. Swinford slowly slid into his chair. With his head cupped into his hands and his elbows on his desk, he muttered to himself, "How am I going to explain this to the press? First, a tiger hoax and now we are shooting at the exhibits! Ahhh, I just don't believe this!"

Chapter Eighteen

SHADOW PEOPLE

"No Mother, I'm fine! Really, everything here is very safe.... It was in another..., what? You don't understand. It's good they have guns in the Museum to protect us; ok, if there's one more problem, I promise to call you before you hear something about it on the news again. All right Mom, I love you too. Tell Dad I'm fine...thanks, bye." Melinda clicked off her cell phone and slipped it into her purse, having reassured her mother of her safety.

When the two girls departed from the Museum's student center and walked through the magnificent alabaster passageway, Leslie flipped her highlighted blonde hair and asked Melinda, "Do your folks want you to leave here too?" Her playful snicker eased a response from her friend.

"Yeah, they wanted me to fly home tonight." With a puzzled look developing a few paces later, Melinda continued, "I guess I'm somewhere in the middle. It's a bit scary with all of the creepy stuff happening around here — but it's kind of exciting too," Melinda smiled mischievously, and leaned her head sideways to gauge Leslie's reaction.

"I know! Who would have thought a Museum could be so cool!"

Melinda hesitated for a moment in the Roman chamber to adjust her bangs within the reflection of a polished battle shield. Satisfied with the impromptu style revision, Melinda smiled at Leslie to follow her as they navigated rows of ancient statues and display cases filled with painted pottery, dishware, and aged scrolls.

Both girls slowed their pace to a halt when they noticed Al directing three of his staff high above them on a rolling scaffold.

"What are they doing?" Melinda asked the huge man while watching his underlings perform their balancing act.

"We're installing new video cameras," Al responded while he ogled over his new toys and gadgets, now a part of the completed work. "The other cameras were outdated...but these babies," he proudly grinned with excitement to put the new ones to work, "will pick up everything."

Clueless about electronics, Leslie blinked indifferently at him and asked, "Are they a new digital kind or something?"

"It's true they have exceptional digital clarity, but what I mean is *these cameras* can decipher other things like temperature fluctuations."

"Oh — so they can tell me if I have a fever," the cute blonde-haired teen said, giggling at him.

"That's a funny way to state it — but actually — yes! Here, try to think of it in this way. Pretend you were a thief attempting to steal a priceless artifact in here, and you crawled slowly beneath a blanket that was the same color as the floor. Our older cameras might be tricked into thinking you were part of the flooring, but the new cameras will register your body's temperature from that of the room. This way we can determine if you were outside the pre-set parameters, immediately setting off the alarm. We also added EMF sensors to them too."

"EMF?" Melinda repeated with a confused expression.

"Think of the cameras as capturing electrical signals as well. In addition to filming ghosts or other paranormal energy slinking around the Museum at night," he said jokingly, "more importantly, we know your body's temperature would register on the camera's sensitive sensors, but what about if you had a bomb in your bag. We need a way to detect electrical differences beside heat, and relay the findings to us in the control room. An early lead could help us proactively diffuse the situation before it became a problem," Al finished proudly.

"Do you have more cameras to install?" Leslie queried him, as her eyes searched up at the performed work near the ornate ceiling.

"These are the last two," he said pointing above and towards the corner behind them.

"Well, it sounds stimulating," Leslie said to be polite, yet wanting her and

Melinda to leave, "good luck with them — we're on our way to the gift shop," she announced, to make their getaway.

"See you later," Melinda added cheerily, as she gave a short wave to Al.

Outside of Al's hearing, Leslie told Melinda in a solemn tone, "I don't know how you feel about it, but with all of the weird things around here lately, I hope these new cameras work; otherwise, I think the contest will be closed down this year." Then bumping her elbow against Melinda's, Leslie giggled saying, "Meaning, we'll be out of here faster than you can say 'supernatural activity'."

***

After they purchased personal items in the Museum's gift shop, Leslie sorted their individual things near the gift store doorway. Melinda waited impatiently for Leslie to remove her stuff from the bag, when she spotted the extremely heavy boy, Matt Faraday, leaving the Museum cafeteria across the expansive main entrance hall.

"Let's try to catch up with Matt. He might be headed towards the student area," Melinda said to Leslie.

Approximately forty paces in front of the girls, Matt's generous size was easy to follow in the midst of much smaller Museum visitors as they traveled towards the interior atrium. Nearly at the entrance, the large teen rounded right, walking towards the Egyptian area, where the ghostly disappearing Knight had attacked Brock. Moments later as if remembering the incident, he changed his direction and instead exited through the thick glass doors, which led outside into the Museum's courtyard gardens.

Reaching the doors a few seconds after Matt, they looked outside and saw Matt heading away.

Suddenly rigid with attention, Melinda grabbed Leslie's arm and pointed, "LOOK! THERE! What's that guy doing?" she cried out.

Leslie immediately saw the undersized shirtless man, hiding in the bushes where Melinda pointed. His blue-black hair matched the style of leaves hanging around his waist and covering most of his bare legs. Tribal tattoos circled around his arms like wrapped fabric, and spread across his face and chest. Nevertheless, what actually caught their attention was the menacing blowgun the miniature man raised to his lips, and his focused stare — at Matt.

Melinda, closely followed by Leslie, rushed the glass doors screaming, "MATT! Watch out!"

It took their combined weight pressed solidly against the glass door's metal lever to burst them outside, exactly as the tribal man blew his dart. Startled by the girl's sudden appearance, the clannish man leapt backwards into the shrubbery to hide. Quickly, a second new face resembling the first poked through the leaves to peer anxiously at the girls.

Focused on their friend, Melinda saw Matt turn slowly at hearing their screams, but without recognition of them, he dropped expressionless onto his thick right knee. Inactive in that position, he stared vacantly with glazed eyes at the fast-approaching girls. Melinda watched the color ebb from his skin as they neared him, and he finally fell drearily onto his face.

"Matt, Matt!" both girls shrieked in tandem, running to his aid.

Nearby Museum patrons, hearing the girl's cries, hurried to help. Leslie in despair, sighted a middle-aged man in tan shorts and a red polo shirt, and urged him, "Call 911! Call 911!"

Startled by the demand, the man dropped his phone, but caught it and quickly dialed the emergency number.

Leslie ran back to Melinda, and it took both girls together to roll Matt to his side and off his face, where they waited with him for help to arrive. Matt's labored breathing became erratic, and he turned ashen. Trying urgently, neither of the girls could wake him.

A pale freckle faced man bent over Melinda's shoulder, and asked her, "What's that thing? Is that some kind of a dart?"

The man recoiled at the thought, and then suddenly retreated, afraid of getting too close to the deadly tool. However, a fit woman in her mid-thirties knew exactly what to do. Removing the dart quickly from Matt's bulky neck, she inspected the gray-colored dart, which revealed a homemade tail using a bird's feather.

"See here," the woman, explained to Melinda, "this stained quill tip is like the types used with ink wells in the 1700s for writing with."

Suddenly, a paramedic appeared and authoritatively stated to the gathered crowd as he and his partner approached to help Matt, "Everyone, please move back!"

While the emergency medical technicians worked to stabilize Matt's deteriorating condition, Melinda and Leslie, with a few others, observed the dangerous situation from a distance.

Al and Brock, running from the security office, arrived right after the EMT unit. The big leader quickly conferred with the medical personnel, who informed him of the disappointing news. The concern growing on his face, Al maintained control by keeping the crowd safely back as the paramedics placed an oxygen mask over Matt's face.

A thin blonde paramedic updated his partner, "He's at three liters now! Then the young man asked his medical associate, "What's his pulse?"

"It's falling fast!" his Asian partner exclaimed. "We need to move him to Memorial Hermann Hospital quick!"

Melinda watched the paramedics lower the gurney to the ground once they stabilized Matt enough for transport to the hospital. Together, the two smaller medical workers tried to lift him onto the gurney with great difficulty, using a stretcher board. They strapped him in place, and wheeled the pale teen across the garden area to an exit near the ambulance.

Al searched the slowly dispersing crowd hoping to gain needed details, and blazed away, "Did anyone see what happened? If so, please follow me," as he stepped backwards to stand in front of a large water fountain.

Only Melinda and Leslie trailed in his direction.

"We saw what happened," Melinda volunteered nervously, unsure how to explain the small-sized men they saw hiding in the shrubs.

"Yea, the guy who shot Matt was right behind those bushes," Leslie emphasized while she pointed at the exact spot.

Al asked her, "You mean someone did this to him…right behind us?"

Forcefully nodding yes, both friends again pointed at the same location.

"They were both really short, and neither wore a shirt. The first one stood up in some kind of a grass skirt, and shot a blow gun at Matt," Melinda informed the security leader and gingerly handed him the dart.

"What did you say — a blow gun?" Al asked in amazement, as he cautiously retrieved the deadly dart from Melinda's extended fingers to examine the evidence.

"It was about this long," Leslie showed him, by holding her hands almost three feet apart.

After instantly unsnapping his semi-automatic case, Al placed a huge hand on the gun's grip, and pointed to Brock, to cover the far side of the hedge where the men hid. He quickly responded to cover the jungle men's expected route of escape.

With a quick stride towards the shrubbery, and understanding Matt's serious condition, Al proceeded in a wide semi-circle to utilize the best view of the open space behind the undergrowth. He could not see the tiny jungle men, and assumed both were hiding near Brock's side of the bushes. The giant man crouched down to fit below the top of the vegetation, and then accelerated like a freight train, bulldozing into the greenery.

Instantly, Brock grasped the stock of his own firearm with his hand, and waited to react if the men came out fighting or running. The tall bushes rustled in all directions, and then parted when Al crashed into view.

"Did you see them?" Al hollered at Brock.

"No!" Brock replied, urgently scanning the area.

Both trained security men approached the area where the attackers hid, and searched for signs of the retreating men without success. Without an indication to determine which direction the treacherous men had fled, Al barked, "Let's check the security cameras. You girls follow me, and show me if you see the two men in the video. I need you both to identify the men, so we know which direction they fled."

***

When Melinda and Leslie arrived at the Museum's lower level, Al easily held the heavy glass door open as they entered the security area, and then led the teens down a long corridor towards the control room. Video monitors congruently displayed various Museum exhibit halls.

"Was it only this specific area?" the burly leader asked Melinda, while he pointed at the garden view monitor.

"Yes," she rapidly replied.

Al placed a behemoth hand on the younger operator's shoulder sitting before the command module, and looking at his wristwatch ordered him, "Key a thirty minute reverse into 21."

When the worker turned a large dial, the digital image raced backwards in time. At the appointed location, he pushed 'play', and the video started. Both of the girls stared at the screen, trying to detect the small men in the bushes, when abruptly, the two tiny men materialized.

"Where did they come from?" Al asked, suddenly confused by what he saw.

Both tribal men squatted discreetly within the dense undergrowth of the Museum courtyard. Within seconds, Matt appeared inside the left edge of the camera's view. Unaware of the jungle natives who watched him, Matt strolled calmly towards the student center.

"There!" cried Melinda, as the front man raised the blowgun to his lips and shot the deadly dart.

The video reminded Melinda of how Matt turned ashen and faltered for breath, while she and Leslie ran to his aid on the monitor. A blank space remained behind the bushes when Al scanned the screen from Matt to the small men.

"Where did they go? Did either of you see them leave?" the enormous man demanded.

"No," Melinda said, while Leslie shook her head side-to-side with a concerned expression.

Al ordered the AV man, "Reverse the video again in slow motion!"

When the junior officer pressed play, the screen re-activated, and the images scrolled forward at a snail's pace, frame-by-frame. Just as before, the girls ran to help Matt, however, this time, no one looked where Matt lay helpless on the ground; all eyes paid attention to the strange men. With a flicker like slow motion flash photography, and surrounded by a sputtering electrical mist like melting fireflies, the two small men gradually faded into nothingness.

"This can't be — there must be a malfunction," Al muttered at the mystery. "How could they suddenly show up, and then simply vanish?"

"Rewind it," he commanded his employee crossly, "let's see it again. Only this time, utilize the heat signature view."

The flat panel monitor shifted into an illuminated version of its former image, when the technician pushed a glowing button. The video screen at first was indiscernible, until Matt entered the depiction. Instantly, a radiant patchwork of yellows, reds, and shades of orange appeared. The girls, displaying comparable color patterns, soon followed the heavily built boy; however, the gap where the tribal men crouched in the bushes remained obscure and dark.

"Notice the injured student and the girls' vibrant colors," the younger security man stated purposefully, "the system's working properly."

Al pointed at the monitor and said as he turned sideways "Ok, let's try this."

He pushed a square gray button. Immediately, the screen transformed into a black and white version. Once more as they played the video, Matt walked by again, only this time, he scarcely registered as a dark outline, yet, where the two small men ducked, in slow motion they glowed with a brilliant aura, and shone radiantly. Vivid silvery outlines surrounded both of the visible jungle men, and grew into an unexpected large and bright bubble. The air shimmered and popped in a final intense burst of light, as both attackers dematerialized and vanished.

Perplexed expressions showed on all of their faces, as each person gaped wide-eyed at the others to validate what they witnessed was real. Al swiftly grabbed the phone on the desk in front of them, and called Dr. Swinford's office. Melinda faintly heard the Museum Curator's administrative assistant inform Al in a buzzing voice, "I'm sorry Al, but Dr. Swinford is on a very important call. You should try back again later."

The extraordinary man gritted his teeth, and after biting his lip said, "Alice, you're a great gal, but if you don't get him on the phone straight away, I won't be able to hold back his anger at you when he finds you prevented him from knowing what just happened."

"What happened?" she asked, suddenly apprehensive.

"Not now! Please get him on the phone."

"Ok!"

Fifteen seconds later, they all heard, "AL! What's so blasted important it can't wait?"

"Sir, we had another incident — only this time one of the students was seriously hurt."

"SAY AGAIN!"

"Come down to the control room. We finally caught this one on video."

The group jointly heard the phone drop to the older Curator's desk, but none heard the phone hang up. Shortly, Dr. Swinford rushed into the Museum's security command center, and after viewing the recorded video, he had no idea what to say either.

"What's the status on the boy?" Dr. Swinford asked, scratching his left ear as he paced the overcrowded security space.

"Not sure, we were trying to find these perpetrators before they could harm anyone else."

"Good — ok, keep searching for the little scoundrels, and I'll check on the boy."

"Sir, should we call for local police backup to help find them?"

Astounded by the unexpected comment, Dr. Swinford spit out, "Not yet! I do *not* want the journalists in on this one until we know more. Something is seriously wrong around this place to cause all of these abnormal phenomenons, and right now, we don't know what is going on, or who to ask for help. For now, stay in touch with me on your progress, and I'll inform you on Matt's condition as soon as I can," he said with a glum expression as he spun and then left the control room.

Too late to attend the students' evening meal because of the sad incident, Melinda and Leslie both ate sandwiches in the public cafeteria. Between bites, Melinda updated the rest of their team members on the most recent puzzling events.

Melinda explained, "Leslie, Al, and I searched almost every inch of this Museum this afternoon, but we found zilch. We never saw those little creeps again."

"Will Matt be ok?" Brian asked Leslie.

"I don't know, we haven't heard anything new yet — but that's what the local reporters kept asking us today." Leslie answered earnestly.

Melinda added "Yeah, they kept asking us if we were petrified by the attack — if we knew the men — if covert work was conducted here in the Museum — and if so, what were our roles."

Leslie's forehead furrowed as she explained further, "At first it was fun to feel important and believe we would be on TV, since we were the only witnesses when Matt was hurt, but when those reporters kept asking us all of those stupid questions about secret experiments and stuff, it got annoying real fast."

Leslie continued after wrinkling her nose, "It did seem they loved Melinda. The camera operator filmed her most of the time. I'll bet you're probably famous by now," she joked to Melinda.

Tab flashed his incredible blue eyes between Leslie and Melinda to get their attention, and then he signed to his older brother. Trent translated his question, "Show us where it happened, so we can keep our eyes open too and look for clues."

Staring among the group, and eager to help the situation in any way possible, Melinda replied, "Ok, follow me."

She led her friends outside of the Museum and into the garden area, through the same glass door Matt used before the strange men shot him with the toxic dart.

Leslie pointed first at the spot where Matt lay and said, "Here's where Matt was shot with the blowgun dart — and over there are the bushes..."

Immediately, a side door into the courtyard popped open, and the alluring Dr. Yvonne Kirchappel waved to them, "Come along now! Dr. Swinford wants to speak to us in the lecture auditorium."

"Has he heard anything about Matt?" Brian asked the attractive professor.

"Yes, he plans to provide us with an update. Come along now, they're waiting for us."

Quickly following her inside the lecture theater, they sat in their usual seats.

Directly behind them, Cheryl Broom, one of the friendly competitors from team three, leaned forward and whispered to Leslie, "What's going on? There's a rumor one of the students was injured!"

"More than injured — it was Matt! He was shot in the neck by a little weirdo with a blowgun," Leslie informed her.

"A real blowgun?" she questioned in disbelief.

"That's exactly what we saw," Melinda echoed the look in Cheryl's heartfelt eyes.

Satisfied Dr. Swinford was not ready to begin his report, Melinda continued, "It was terrible. Leslie and I saw the whole thing. Matt is really sick. The paramedics seemed very concerned about his condition when they took him away in the ambulance."

"Oh!" Cheryl exhaled, "I wonder if this will affect the program, especially after the other scary incidents. They'll shut things down for sure. It'd be horrible if anyone else got hurt too!"

"We're about to find out," Brian whispered when Dr. Swinford entered the extra-large space.

The Museum's curator did not waste time with pleasantries, but stood in the front of the room to give an updated explanation.

"Today, Matt Faraday was seriously harmed by two unknown men. I have spoken with his doctors, and they have informed me the poison on the dart is very deadly. Due to Matt's size, the ratio dose of poison was much smaller than it might be for a lighter person, which saved his life. Matt currently remains in critical care; however, his doctors feel he will fully recover.

"The hospital's toxicology department struggled to determine the type of toxin used in this attack; however, after great skill and effort on their part, they traced it to a type exclusively found deep in the jungles of South America. How it came into these men's hands, and why they chose to use it here, is still a mystery.

"Matt's parents are en route to the hospital at this time. Upon consideration of the recent publicity the Museum has received including the tiger scare, the medieval dressed fanatic who damaged priceless artifacts, and today's disappointing situation, I expect I shall be speaking with most of your parents soon. I can't predict the next twenty-four to forty-eight hours; however, I can share with you that many desire this year's program to conclude, and return everyone home immediately due to the current situation."

At hearing the alarmed tone in his normally authoritative voice, several students became distressed with the leader's uncertainty.

"Until we know more, we will continue our course as planned, but under no circumstances will any of you go into the garden grounds, or outside of the building for your own safety. If you must travel anywhere within the building, only pass through open public areas, and with at least one other person. The police, with

- 140 -

our assistance, have been unable to apprehend these men, or for that matter, the other radical who attacked Brock before he mysteriously disappeared. Unfortunately, this is all of the information I have at this time."

The room remained silent, as all eyes watched Dr. Swinford step down from the stage and depart the lecture theater. The indecisiveness and heaviness of the situation was clearly visible on his face.

Chapter Nineteen

MISSING

Worry splashed across Dale Bradan's face as he raced around the corner only to abruptly crash into Brian and Leslie speaking with Melinda and the brothers in the hallway on their way to get breakfast. Out of breath, Dale wheezed "Sorry…real sorry…have…any of you…seen my father?"

Aggravated from retrieving her books and cell phone from off the floor, Leslie brashly said, "No!"

The rest confirmed the same message to the disheveled teen.

Dale glumly voiced, "Thanks," and began to jog again in his original direction.

Disappointed in her reaction to the accident, Leslie called to him, "Dale, I'm sorry I got upset at you. If we see him, do you want us to say you're looking for him?"

Dale stopped in his tracks, and turned back with a somber look, "If you see him, let anyone know! He's been missing for days, and doesn't answer his phone!"

Melinda questioned the younger boy, "When did you see him last?"

"Three days ago," Dale replied on his way back to the group. "I went to bed thinking my dad was working late. When I woke up the next morning, he wasn't at home, but I blew it off thinking he'd left early, because he's been working long hours lately."

"What's he working on?" Trent asked curiously.

"I'm not sure. He only tells me that some big questions will be answered if he's right. I'm really worried; will you guys help me look around the museum for him?"

Sincerely wanting to help Dale, and yet required to attend the re-scheduled Asian lecture later that morning, the friends glanced at each other hoping someone knew what to do.

Tab signed to Trent, who explained, "My brother suggested we split up. Brian and Leslie, why don't you two take notes for our group during the lecture, while the rest of us help Dale look for his dad."

Satisfied with the straightforward solution, all of the program friends agreed with the plan and then parted ways. Melinda, Trent, and Tab arrived with Dale at his father's office within minutes. Dale reached into the front right pocket of his jeans and removed a key dangling on the end of a rubber band. Inserting it into the lock, he twisted the key, and the door clicked opened. Inside his dad's office, the room was dark and silent.

"DAD!" he yelled, as the sound of his voice echoed in the quiet space "are you here?"

Dale flipped on the overhead lights and walked to the other side of the modest place to open a supply room door that revealed a mostly empty area. Cast in shadows from the position of the open door and the overhead lighting were an assortment of artifacts, papers, boxes, and rolled maps. Lost in thought after slowly closing the door, Dale stared vacantly at the world map on the wall behind Dr. Bradan's desk.

Finally, Dale said, "Ok, I don't really understand what he's trying to prove, but it has something to do with the fluctuations that have been recorded in the Earth's energy. Last week he told me how the Earth is made of different layers. Are any of you familiar with this?"

Melinda and the group stared back at him indecisively.

Dale continued, "Ok, so from what little I understand, somehow the heat and energy deep inside the center of the earth creates a movement in the liquid magma."

Dale noticed that the blank faces remained.

"Look, I'm no expert on this stuff, but I think magma is made up of melted rocks and metal. Don't ask me how, but supposedly, super hot and bubbling pressure pushes the magma around inside the Earth's core, which somehow causes it to rotate the planet as it circles the Sun. When there's too much heat, I think it leaks to the surface like lava, or it becomes lava.

"Ah — shoot, I wish I had paid more attention to how it all works, but somehow different types of magnetic lava spread out across the Earth, depending on the course of the flowing magma. My dad has been tracking these to see if they create any patterns, and if so, maybe see if they map to any big events throughout history."

"What does lava have to do with studying ancient civilizations?" Melinda asked the confused boy.

"What do I know?" Dale sighed. "I feel bad because lately, I have been missing my mom who passed away two years ago this month. We both miss her a lot. During the last few months, I think my dad has been working more than usual to avoid feeling sad too. Plus, when he wanted to talk to me about what he was doing to get our minds off missing my mom, I was too busy playing video games. Now I'm really worried about him," he said regretfully.

Trent consoled him, "It's ok Dale, we've all been there by not listening to our parents as much as we should. I'm really sorry to hear about your mother, I didn't know — but don't worry, we will do our best to help you find him," he said, smiling in a positive manner.

He continued, "Since we're not exactly sure what your dad is working on, we need to figure that part out first if we're going to look for him later. I suggest we spread out in here and search his office."

Pausing to look at the possible search locations, Trent directed, "Dale, since he's your dad, why don't you search his desk drawers. Melinda, you should look through these folders while Tab and I will be in the supply room. If anyone finds something, call it out to the others."

Arranged in their various assignments, Melinda sat cross-legged on the floor next to the cardboard box of folders. Opening the top, she scanned each file. Inside each folder were both typed and hand-written summary notes. The first typed one read:

"It is widely accepted by modern science that the exterior of the Earth's crust surrounds thousands of miles of scorching rock and iron. The contained heat and force intermingle to generate an internal churning that rotates much of the volcanic iron rich fluid around the Earth's nucleus. The irregular speeds form positively and negatively charged magnetic fields throughout the Earth's outer layers. Computer analysis has suggested that the perceived solid iron core may in fact be a giant iron crystal, while other theories advocate the core is a huge nuclear energy source similar to that of a nuclear reactor facility. Today, no one truly understands the Earth's center; however, the result is clear when pressed magma and energy travels upward through the Earth's crust, sometimes resulting in devastation such as volcanoes and earthquakes.

"The impact can be seen in the vast ridges that are produced deep along the ocean's floor to press immeasurably against enormous sections of the Earth's crust. These floating or suspended sections, called continents, can be up to two hundred and fifty miles thick. The largest sections are termed as tectonic plates. Major tectonic plates have drifted away and into each other during hundreds of millions of years, creating new cracks in the earth's surface for the rising magma to pierce through and into the ocean floor. When this occurs, deep freezing waters solidify the magma into fresh Earth, and continue to push older tectonic plate land away to make more room for the new ground."

She read more:

"The Earth's internal movements alter magnetic fields. For example, magnetic north that conventionally navigates a compass to point north, has in fact slipped south over long periods. Magnetic north and magnetic south have swapped positions many times throughout the history of the world, and is commonly known as a geomagnetic reversal. Interchanging reversals do affect huge swings in the Earth's magnetic fields. Predicted reversals can last from a few hundred to possibly several thousand years.

"Science is uncertain on the underlying principle that triggers these incidents. One theory suggests that unusual movements within the liquid magma itself activate the reversals. Still others believe the reversals of the North Pole and South Pole is impulsive, and happens for no clear reason."

The third page of notes read:

"Recent studies do not connect previous polar reversals with any of the major natural extinctions during Earth's past. Excavations today conclude that early man survived several magnetic reversals. Yet, current investigations are inconclusive to forecast how today's modern electrical technology will react during the present reversal progression. The existing polar reversal is already shifting the North Pole down into Siberia. This movement may well cause earth-shattering electrical unsteadiness.

"Some data supports possible reductions in the geomagnetic field during the past two millennia, which should be viewed as serious warnings. Scientific calculations conclude it may completely cave in sometime between now and the next coming centuries."

Tense from what she read, Melinda called, "Hey you guys, what do you make of this?"

Everyone reviewed the file, and after sifting through the contents, the group stared at each other in surprise, and then at Dale.

"Why does your father have these notes?" Melinda asked.

Dale shrugged his shoulders, "I wish I knew!"

"I remember seeing a movie at school about some of this stuff," Trent offered. "Instead of the continents we have today, supposedly the Earth was once a giant single piece of land down until the time of the dinosaurs, before it broke up into smaller continents."

"But I thought a giant asteroid impacted the Earth around the Gulf of Mexico, and it killed the dinosaurs," Melinda said."

"HA! Wait a second; I'm remembering something," Dale sputtered.

"My dad told me that the giant asteroid did crash into the Gulf of Mexico …now what was he saying…oh yeah, something about how it might have caused the continents to break apart sooner than they would have on their own…Oooh, I can't remember the rest! I'm so dumb for not listening. Now I'll never find him," Dale frowned.

"We can't give up. Let's keep thinking about this. What do we know about this stuff?" Trent asked almost rhetorically.

No one responded.

Finally, Trent added, "When Tab and I played with magnets as kids, sometimes they would push away from each other, and other times, snap together..."

Melinda cut him off, "Instead of guessing, let's get back to finding clues."

Dale reached for another desk drawer as he supported her, "She's right."

A few minutes later Dale yelped, "I've got something! Has anyone heard about this place? Here, read this article." Melinda gazed over his arm after he moved the file closer to her, and then she read aloud to the group:

"The Enchanted Rock is the second largest individual rock exposed by ordinary erosion within the United States. At an altitude just below nineteen hundred feet, it resides north of San Antonio, Texas. Its monumental size displaces nearly six hundred and forty five acres of land, and stands roughly half as tall as the Eiffel Tower. Early humans are theorized to have lived around the pink granite, for more than ten thousand years."

"Wow, that's one big rock," Trent whistled.

Dale stated, "Yea, let her keep reading." Melinda looked down at the paper and continued aloud:

"Nearby Native Americans tell of supernatural yellow and blue 'ghost fires', which habitually flicker at night around the area and at the crest of the gigantic rock. Stories flourish of daring warriors who never returned to the tribe after they investigated the strange lights. Myths describe that when angered, the Great Spirit causes un-worldly groans throughout the massive rock. However, recent geologists now believe these sounds come from the sun raising the rock's temperature by day, and cooler nighttime temperatures contracting the granite.

"One of the earliest documented stories about the giant rock is from a Spanish conquistador, who claimed that he had been previously captured by the area's Native American tribe. The Spaniard testified on several occasions how he escaped from his captors by passing through a mysterious veil, or conduit that led into a vast spirit world inside the granite rock's interior. Curiously, countless Indian versions validate his story by reciting that the gigantic formation swallowed a 'ghost man'. They also claim he later became one of their own tribe's people.

"Elder clansmen believe that the conquistador endowed the entire area with magical enchantments, which later led to the naming of the mammoth rock, but the soldier insisted it had nothing to do with him, but that the pink rock was the genuine source of the magic. The conquistador also claimed that numerous spirits eerily haunted the miraculous rock's interior.

"Sought after by unfamiliar personages, his spirit friends inside the rock sheltered him in their paranormal world from capture, and later again from the Indian people who chased him in this world. Unfortunately, no part of his story was ever substantiated or his early comments validated that the spirit world had its own version of the sun and moon, or of the unbelievable creatures he described."

"Sounds like a creepy place to me," Melinda said as she shivered.

Trent asked Dale, "Is your dad superstitious?"

"Not that I know about. In fact, as a scientist, he always talks about what the evidence shows, or he tries to understand all the facts before drawing a conclusion. I don't know why he would have something like this in his desk."

"Well, let's keep looking," Melinda, suggested. "Everyone keep searching in your designated areas."

A few minutes later Trent called to Dale, "Hey, Tab found something!"

"What is it?" Dale questioned in suspense.

"Hold on, we're bringing it out of the supply room."

Together, Trent and Tab carried out a heavy box marked 'Important' in large blue marker letters.

"What's in it?" Dale asked eagerly.

"Not sure — it's not open yet," Trent, replied.

Using scissors, Trent removed the securing tape, and then lifted the lid to reveal additional internal files. Melinda reached down to remove the file lying on top of the others. Inside the green folder, she examined the photos, notes, measurements, and both of the articles.

A typewritten summary was paper-clipped on the outside front of the folder. Trent took the folder from her and read it loudly, "The title is,

Japan

- **Ancient Underwater Temple**
- **13,000+ years old**
- **Long, straight exacting carved stone steps**
- **Steps observed to be carved above water**
- **Controversial; they may be natural**
- **No matching broken rock pieces found below steps to prove the steps were created naturally**
- **Un-natural circular type patterns / pictures carved in side walled areas**
- **Builders - vanished!"**

Dale pulled out another file and unhooked the fastener. Unfolding it to read the contents, Melinda noticed it had the title **Stonehenge**. Reading the typewritten summary sheet to himself first, he cleared his throat and shared the details, "Ok, it says,

- **Ancient England**
- **160 enormous stones form the oversized ring**
- **Carbon dating suggest portions as old as 4200 BC**
- **Two types of stones are used in the construction - sandstone and blue stones**
- **Weight - some as much as thirty tons (60,000 lbs) - how were they moved?**
- **Theories**
  - **Built to predict sun and moon celestial positions**
  - **Orientation suggests knowledge of the universe**
- **Builders - vanished!"**

Finished reading the note, Dale handed the file folder to Trent and walked to the other side of Dr. Bradan's desk. After Trent reviewed the inner file material, he sighed loudly, suggesting he was having a difficult time making sense of the information.

"Guys, wait till you read this!" Trent declared.

Dale excited to learn more flew around the desk, and accidentally knocked two manila folders off his father's desk onto the floor. Closest to the desk, Tab stooped and picked them up from off the ground.

"What do you mean? What is it?" Dale asked.

Trent said as he read, "Alright, it's like this,

Philadelphia Experiment

- **U.S. Warship became invisible at the Philadelphia Naval station**
- **Ship and sailors instantly disappeared while teleported from the Naval Yard**
- **The experimental project happened in 1943**
- **Unsure how to manage the event, or find part of the missing crewmen, the project was terminated**
- **Some Crewmen - vanished!"**

Dale's expression increasingly represented his confusion with each new item they evaluated.

"Do any of these article topics mean much to you, Dale?" Melinda asked him as she placed her hand on his arm.

"I have no idea," he said dejectedly.

Dale exhaled loudly and then turned away to think, when Tab waved his hands hysterically. Dale and Melinda saw the movements first.

"Trent!" Melinda snapped.

He looked up at Tab from reading another file as his brother signed quickly. Trent soon smiled, and quickly stepped next to his brother. When he saw what Tab pointed towards, Trent motioned for Melinda and Dale to join them. On the other side of the desk, Tab again pointed at Dr. Bradan's desk calendar, which showed hand-written details in the date boxes. Suddenly visible from when Dale knocked the files onto the floor, they clearly read:

1. **Gas the car**
2. **Pack camping gear**
3. **Buy food**
4. **Program address into GPS**
5. **Charge cell phone**

Three large circles surrounded the entire Saturday date box, which read:

Enchanted Rock

(830-555-ROCK)

"THAT'S IT!" Dale yelled. "I'm calling the number right now."

He lifted up the desk phone handset and dialed the number. Holding his breath, Dale heard the ring on the other end.

"It's ringing!" he smiled warmly to everyone.

A woman answered and said, "Enchanted Rock State Park, how may I help you?"

Dale blurted, "Is my dad there?"

"I'm sorry sir," the voice sounded confused, "is he staying with us?

"Ah, I think so — is this Enchanted Rock?"

"Yes, this is the on-site store. Who is your father?"

"Dr. Bradan, I mean—Mr. Bradan," Dale stuttered.

At this point, the woman said, "I'm sorry; it's still early, and I don't see the visitor's list around here at the moment. Was your dad staying overnight?"

Dale hesitated, so Melinda took the phone from him and said, "Sorry, he's very excited to see his dad again. We want to come and surprise him; but we're not sure where you're located. Oh, I see...yes, he *is* hard to follow sometimes. Thank you, I would like the address."

Melinda continued, "I'm ready. Right...ok, I believe I have it. Thank you, you have been very helpful...alright, bye."

"Here's the address," Melinda sang happily. "Now that we have it, can we get on the computer and print out the directions?"

"Easy," Dale beamed, "I know my dad's password. He downloaded computer games on it to keep me from being bored when I used to wait for him at night."

Dale got online and before printing the directions, they looked at the screen for the distance between the state park and the Museum.

"Wow, that's four hours one way," Trent, complained, "We're never going to get there from the Museum. I wonder if the bus even goes there, and if it does, where do we catch the right one?"

At hearing Trent's comments, Dale's elation began to fizzle.

He seemed confused about what to do next when Melinda asserted, "Ok, I have a plan, but we need to move fast. Trent, see if you can find anything we might need to help us look for Dr. Bradan at the state park. Tab, you head to the cafeteria and buy enough breakfast food for us to eat on the way to the Enchanted Park. Dale, find a picture of your dad so that we can show it to the park people."

"What are you going to do?" Trent asked.

"I'm going to get us to Enchanted Rock. But, we'll have to split up from each other so no one notices us sneaking outside, because of Dr. Swinford's new curfew rule. Meet me in the parking lot on the far side corner in twenty minutes."

With the new assignments given, they separated to execute the plan.

Chapter Twenty

ESCAPE

Television described much of the mixed-up world to the black dog when she watched it with the Nelxon family. She was comfortable in their home, and during the past several months, had begun to feel a harmony swell inside the household. Yet, masked deep within her mind, strange memories hauntingly disturbed her sleep, which often caused her to wake, feeling she was forgetting something important. With each greater effort to remember, a silencing fog arose within her thoughts.

Unable to recall anything before living with this family, she remained befuddled with her feelings. Easily learning to understand English from watching TV, still watching and listening to the Nelxon family's behavior often surprised her. Much of it seemed wrong to her instincts. It was effortless to communicate with Butch on a higher extrasensory level, as all dogs use similar body language and sounds, yet fully grown, he lacked the aptitude to serve and protect. The big dog expected the desire to be fundamental or instinctual within him; however, he amazed her with his deficiency of awareness.

Butch never realized the approach of strangers at the front door, until after the doorbell rang. His behavior became even worse after a family member opened the door. Instead of observing the master for a reaction, Butch immediately overstepped his place, and wagged a welcome for the unfamiliar person to enter.

In opposition, she knew precisely when and how many people approached the door, long before they arrived at the front porch. Not sure why, she followed a simple three step strategy. First, conceal her position beside the door. Second, take direction from the master, and third, if required, attack and provide a defense against possible intruders.

Rarely did Butch survey the perimeter of the house and yard, and when he did, he failed miserably in his watchdog duties by seldom noticing *any* new changes. With her keen senses, she evaluated the safety of up-to-the-minute objects left in the front yard. She was able to decipher residual pheromones from the last person to handle them. If the item contained the lingering smell of alarm or irritation, she immediately disposed of the article inside one of the trashcans; however, if smelling contentment or joy from kids playing with the item, she left it alone.

Play fighting with Butch was unsatisfactory to her too. He projected his attack moves on her far too early to be successful. Upon her early arrival in the family, eager for a new dog pal to play with, Butch's gusto was short lived. Within moments, he yelped like a frightened banshee. Close enough to nip her neck during the play fight, she had speedily twisted away from his teeth, and simultaneously using her long nose, pushed the back of his neck towards the ground.

The bigger dog's sudden actions became blurred movements to Butch. By the time he registered the neck pressure from her pointed nose, closely followed by a separate bump to his front legs from one of hers to flip him, his slow working brain never connected the two feelings together. Prior to the Earth shifting beneath his paws, he felt an unforeseen weightlessness as he tumbled forward through the air, to land squarely on his side with a dull thud.

She easily tracked beside him during his complete airborne revolution as if he seemingly moved through the air in slow motion. As his shoulder contacted the ground, she darted in and placed her teeth around his throat proving she had won, long before his rear legs came to a rest in the grass. Horrified by the unbelievable experience, Butch exhaled blood-curdling yelps. Astonished at his odd visible reaction, the black dog tagged close behind him with concern through the house and into the family room. With a rush to identify the reason for such a ruckus, Jennifer's parents noticed her pursuit during Butch's terrified yelps and believed she had hurt him.

After that episode, she drastically checked her speed and strength when they played together.

While forced to watch an assortment of TV from Mr. Nelxon's perpetual clicking between the cable stations, Jennifer's mom prepared buttered popcorn for her family to enjoy. After removing the steaming popcorn from the microwave, she placed it in a huge bowl. Mrs. Nelxon crisscrossed melted butter across the top. To distribute the butter evenly, she stirred the popcorn around inside the bowl with a large frosting spatula, and then scooped the warm mixture into smaller cereal bowls.

Jennifer's mom placed a tablespoon within each bowl, and passed one to Jennifer, her brother, and their dad. All ate their popcorn using the spoons to prevent butter from transferring onto their hands and everything else too.

As the family's remote control ranger, Jennifer's dad clicked through several channels between mouthfuls, and hesitated on a station to watch a 'Late Breaking News Announcement' with interest. He listened as a local reporter updated the studio anchor concerning a sequence of adverse events at a prestigious Houston Museum.

"...dispatching trained zoo personnel to locate and capture a loose tiger inside the historic building, it was later determined to be a practical joke. Days later, an un-apprehended intruder, outfitted in an entire medieval suit of armor, damaged priceless artifacts using a broadsword.

"Earlier today, two petite and deranged men hospitalized an archeological program student using a blowgun and dart dipped in toxin from a South American Blue Poison Dart Frog. No arrests have been made in connection with the incidents, however, police recently issued a statement these were separate and isolated events. Fortunately, the injured student is expected to fully recover."

The shot changed to a view of the Museum from an earlier filmed clip of two female students, who explained the recent events during an interview. A blonde girl stood next to her attractive brunette friend, and as both knew the injured boy, described the occurrence.

Jennifer's dad reached for the remote to flip the channel again after chewing another spoonful of popcorn, when the big dog suddenly sprung forward, and peered directly into the big screen at the two student girls. Frozen in place before the TV, the black dog did not blink, bark, or move. Jennifer's brother and dad cracked up at her latest craziness, and then zipped through even more shows after the newsbreak.

Quietly, the big dog lay on her pillow, and never watched the TV again that night.

***

"Jennifer!" her mom called the next morning.

"Yeah," Jennifer huffed at the top of the stairs.

"I'm picking up a few things at the store. Is there anything you need?"

"No!"

"Alright I'm leaving. Make sure you feed the dogs, and let them out before you leave...did you hear me?"

"I heard you," Jennifer moaned.

Her mom's voice faded down the first floor hall when Jennifer yelled, "Bring me some ice cream please! I think we're out."

"Alright, see you later," her mom yelled distantly.

Early for a Saturday morning, Jennifer struggled from her bed. She descended downstairs in an oversized t-shirt and after stretching in the doorway, placed both dog bowls on the kitchen counter.

She then scooped dry dog food into each bowl, and pulled open the refrigerator door. Choosing a day-old tuna casserole, she mixed part of it in with the dry food. She then warmed both bowls of food in the microwave.

"Butch, come eat your breakfast!"

Not knowing what type of food the bowl contained, he scrambled around the counter to inhale the mixture without chewing. Missed for the first time since arriving in their home, the black dog did not wait behind Jennifer for her food as expected.

"How strange," Jennifer muttered to herself, and called, "Come here girl!"

With no response from the big dog, Jennifer opened the back door believing she might be waiting in the backyard to re-enter the house, when her mom unexpectedly returned into the kitchen from the garage, and asked, "Jennifer, did you go out through the garage this morning?"

"No, why?"

"The garage door was up."

"Maybe Dad left it open?"

"He's still asleep, so I know it wasn't him," her mother countered.

Noting that Butch had completely finished his breakfast, Mrs. Nelxon spoke in toddler talk to him, "Guud morning Butchie, was that a guud breakfast? Yeah, he's a guud boy!"

"Where's Sheba?" her mom asked, seeing the uneaten food in the big dog's bowl.

"I don't know; I just called her before you came back," Jennifer mentioned.

"That's odd," her mom whispered to herself.

With the corner of her mouth turned down to form a wrinkle, Jennifer entered the family room and called, "Sheba!"

Neither found her when they separated and searched throughout the house. Mrs. Nelxon called into the backyard again in vain, and then returned into the kitchen.

Worried at the non-response, Jennifer checked in the family room where Sheba slept at night and hollered, "*MOM!* You better see this!"

As soon as her mother arrived, Jennifer pointed to the floor. During the night, Sheba had neatly stacked her chews and stuffed animal toys to form the amazing shape of a 12-inch tall pyramid in the middle of her pillow bed.

Unsure of its meaning, her mom's expression changed suddenly, "The garage door. She must have gotten out through the garage!"

***

Riding her bike throughout the day while her parents drove around their neighborhood, each put up 'Lost Dog' signs. Later they received a few calls by those who had seen a giant black dog early that Saturday morning. When each call came, the people described seeing Sheba further away from their home.

Finally, the calls stopped.

Chapter Twenty-One

ENCHANTED ROCK

Hiding between a maroon Honda and a white XJ Jaguar in the Museum's parking lot, Trent noticed movement near the front bumper of a silver Ford pickup truck. Unsure who it was, Trent jerked backward out of sight. He spied around the white car's tire once more, and the sudden flash confirmed his thoughts, *"There it is again!"*

The third time it moved, he realized the person peeking from behind the bumper was Tab. Uncertain if any Museum staff were nearby in the parking lot; Trent located a small pebble and threw it to where Tab waited. The pebble hit the truck's front panel and bounced unnoticed to the ground. Tab remained motionless, not hearing the noise.

Next, he spotted a dime in front of the Honda, and tossed it like a Frisbee. It skipped in front of the truck and instantly, Tab's vivid blue eyes stared at him beside the truck's grill.

"Tab," he whispered so his brother could see his lips, "I'm coming to you."

Quickly skirting around the white sedan, watching carefully behind him to make sure he was unseen, he accidentally collided into a mother pushing her stroller. The young woman's face suddenly wrinkled in anger as she realized her daughter was scared.

Trent hastily told the woman, "I'm awful sorry — I'm playing a hiding game with my brother, and I didn't see you guys. I didn't mean to scare you," which smoothed the mother's ruffled feathers.

"Have you seen a thin boy about my age nearby?" he asked her to dispel the

- 157 -

situation further.

She glanced around the Museum's parking lot saying, "No, I don't see anyone — except a security guard who seems to be looking for someone — hey, are you hiding from him?" she asked suspiciously.

"No, really, I'm playing a game with my brother."

She raised her hand above her head in alarm to alert the guard, when Tab silently arrived and knelt beside his older brother.

Trent pointed in Tab's direction, and scolded the woman as if sharing the rules from a real hiding game as his only defense, "Shoot! You let him reach me first!" Trent pressed it harder hoping she would leave, "I would have gotten him, if you hadn't given away my position. Thanks a lot, lady."

Suddenly embarrassed by the twist of the situation, she huffed and pushed her daughter rapidly away from the brothers.

Trent asked Tab, "Have you seen Melinda yet?"

Moving his head side-to-side, Tab smiled, and then patted the stuffed bag of food under his arm.

Trent smelled the aroma from the bag appreciatively, and winked at Tab saying, "It smells great. Good job."

Slowly, Trent realized what the young mother pushing the stroller had said, and quickly put a finger to his own lips for Tab to see.

Trent rose slowly, and through the Jaguar's windows, noticed the security guard was Brock, intently looking for someone. Wondering if it was for them, Trent squatted down to avoid the security man from seeing him, because of the new rule requiring students not to leave the Museum building.

As he pondered their next step, a long stretch limousine passed by their location and pulled over into the corner of the parking lot. It waited with its engine running.

With a quick look once more in Brock's direction, Trent rapidly drew in his breath. Brock had moved closer to their hiding place. Unsure of what to do, he debated pulling Tab around the car when he glanced up again to check on Brock.

His blood chilled. Brock was now only two cars over and walking toward them.

"Trent! Trent!" a voice whispered.

Surprised to hear his name called in the area; he spun and saw no one nearby. *"Must be Brock,"* he thought, and raised his head once more. To his sudden relief, he noticed that Brock had moved one row back and almost five cars away. *"It couldn't be Brock,"* Trent reflected as he searched the immediate vicinity desperately again with his eyes.

"If only that limousine would move," he contemplated. It was right where they needed to meet Melinda. Suddenly Tab squeezed his arm. He faced his brother, fearing that Brock had again reversed his direction, when he noticed Tab's smiling eyes and his impish grin. Trent's eyes followed Tab's pointing finger, and noticed the limousine's lowered rear window. Cracked open only a few inches, the window was low enough for him to recognize Melinda's happy face. She waved for them to hurry.

Tab was already in motion when Trent glanced back towards Brock one last time. Seeing that he was closer than before, Trent quickly shuffled on his hands and feet to the long black car. In a flash, both brothers were safely inside the automobile.

Trent couldn't see clearly in the car's darker interior after leaving the bright sunlight outside, yet he quickly heard words that brought him a great sense of relief.

Melinda said, "Carl, we're only missing one more boy. He's wearing a light green shirt."

A deep Scottish voice replied, "I might see him up ahead. I'll pull closer te him te avoid that security guard."

Without a sound, the stretched car crawled forward towards Dale. Carl had pulled forward three rows and stopped exactly where Dale headed. Trent's eyes, now attuned to the interior's ambiance, easily saw Dale jogging their way.

Trent pressed the button to lower the window and waved at Dale to speed up. Delighted to see Trent in the elongated vehicle, Dale hurried towards the car when he caught sight of Brock moving fast in his direction.

Dale stooped to avoid Brock seeing him, but it was too late.

"Go! Brock's coming!" Dale yelled at Carl after he opened the door and jumped inside.

All eyes turned towards the security guard chasing the car; however, Carl got it moving too quickly for Brock to reach them in time. Although close enough to peer inside, the presidential looking dark tinted windows proved too much for the security man to make out anything within.

"Wow, when you say you have a plan, you have a plan!" Dale exclaimed, turning in his seat and smiling at the plush interior.

"Actually, we have Carl to thank for our ride," Melinda replied. "Do you remember him? He was with me when I arrived that first day of the program."

Trent brightened, "Yea, I remember him. How do you guys know each other?"

"He works for my dad's company. He drove me from the airport to the Museum."

Carl said smoothly, "Pleasure te sees ye lads again."

"Likewise, and thanks for helping us," Trent replied.

Dale asked Melinda, "Does Carl know where we're going?"

Before she responded, Carl answered, "Don't worry, Enchanted Rock is programmed into the GPS navigation, so we'll not be seeing problems findin' the park today."

Melinda immediately sniffed the air and asked, "Tab, what's in the bag for us to eat? I didn't know I was so hungry."

Tab handed everyone his or her foodstuff.

Each enjoyed the soft leather seats, and soon began to feel the effects of a full stomach after finishing their breakfast while they watched the highway miles zoom past.

Trent spoke first, "Dale, are those the rest of your dad's files?"

"Yeah, they're inside his briefcase. I only brought the ones we didn't read in his office. Wait a second and I'll pass them out."

A hush continued in the car while each student read more of the printed summaries. The more they read, the more confused they became from the puzzling information.

Trent's face scrunched with down turned lips as he read his aloud first, "All right, listen here:

- **Caused by extinct volcanoes**
- **Hundreds of giant stone heads reside on the island**
- **Some statues rise up 40 feet high**
- **Carved with unusually long ears and noses**
- **No idea why the monolithic heads were produced**
- **Islanders have no records of the builders**
- **Builders - vanished!"**

"I remember seeing some of those huge heads on TV a few months ago. It's strange that no one knows why they were carved. They face the ocean like they're guarding the island from something," Melinda said.

"They're spooky," Dale, agreed browsing through the stack of folders.

"Here's another one," he exclaimed and read:

"Ten Tribes of Israel

- **10 tribes lost out of 12 tribes of Israel**
- **Only two have known whereabouts in recent history**
- **Destination of remaining ten tribes unknown**
- **Unaccounted for after Assyrians conquered Israel**
- **Much debate on their current location**
- **Scattered to form the earliest seeds of other nations?**
- **Ten Tribes - vanished!"**

Melinda read hers next, "This one is about Egypt:

- **Pyramids built between 2650 BC to about 1100 BC**
- **Early archaeologists thought the Sphinx was built at the same time**
- **New theories explain it was constructed much earlier, perhaps 8,000+ years prior to pyramids**
- **No records of its builders, or of its purpose**
- **Sphinx builders - vanished!"**

"Did you know the Sphinx was built that long before the pyramids?" Melinda asked aloud as she flipped through the file.

"Of course, don't you remember in Dr. Koffin's lecture, when he told us it was older than the pyramids and had a secret tunnel and chamber, but no one knows why it was built," Trent reminded her.

"Yea, that's right, I remember now."

Trent chuckled and said, "Here, listen to this:

Mexico

- **Bull Mountain Mexico – thousands of clay relics found beneath burial grounds in the 1950's.**
  - o **Radiocarbon dating their age up to 3,500 years old**
  - o **Statues of cows, camels, elephants, & horses not native to the geographic area**
  - o **Included precise examples of dinosaurs that have been extinct for fifty million years**
    - **Showed T-Rex & Stegosaurus living in harmony with humans**
- **Problem – Dinosaurs were excavated, revealed, and assembled by scientist only in the last 200+ years, not 3,500 years ago**
- **All valid attempts are unable to clarify why living humans in that time period are connected to dinosaurs**
- **Mexican Government determined the statues must be fakes**
  - o **Decided it was impossible for people and dinosaurs to be seen together, regardless of significant data the statues are authentic**
- **Was man alive at the time of the dinosaurs?**
- **Did giant reptiles live until the time of man?**
- **Makers - vanished!"**

"Dale, I'm not trying to be rude or anything like that, but your dad is starting to freak me out a little. Why does he have all of these files? Everyone seems to disappear," Melinda said quietly.

"Hey, this whole thing is bizarre to me too. I had no idea he was working on most of this stuff — at least I don't remember him telling me," Dale said weakly.

"Don't worry guys, we only have a few more files to go, let's see what else we can find." Trent coached.

"Ok," Dale whispered, feeling worse than he had before asking for their help.

A few minutes later, Trent bursted out, "Oooh, listen to this one:

- **Mysterious Carved Stones**
- **Older than figures in Mexico**
- **Carved rocks display people riding dinosaurs**
- **Carved pictures of planes, medical organ transplants, and viewing a shooting star through a telescope**
- **World-wide drawing of the modern science of Tectonic Plates (Note: Tectonic science is only from the 20th century)**
- **Represents highly developed ancient society in South America**
- **Makers - vanished!"**

"Where is all of this going?" Melinda queried Trent.

"Good question — I'm not sure I see any connection between these folders, other than everyone vanishes. And these pictures of the carved rocks are weird ..."

"Excuse me," Carl informed them over the limousine's intercom, "we've arrived at Enchanted Rock State Park."

"Really! What does it look like?" Dale chirped, excited to see it out the windows.

Melinda peeked out of both sides to see the famous rock.

Trent chuckled, "Wow, it is big, but overall it looks pretty normal to me. At least for a giant rock that moans, and has ghosts running around inside it at night," he said, hoping to evoke a laugh.

No one laughed or spoke until Carl pulled the long sedan to the side of the parking area.

Melinda stepped out of the car and asked while she stretched, "Does anyone see a bathroom? That was a long ride."

Tab pointed towards the front of the parking area at a small building.

"Nice work Tab," Melinda said with approval as she walked towards the washrooms.

Everyone else soaked in the incredible view.

"What's our plan now?" Trent asked the group after Melinda returned from the restrooms.

Melinda suggested, "Let's start looking for Dale's dad."

When Dale turned back towards the limousine, the youth blasted out,

"THAT'S MY DAD'S CAR!" and ran over to a dark green Range Rover sitting across the parking lot.

Dust obviously covered the SUV's exterior.

Using his hand, Dale wiped off the driver's window and shouted, "Yep, this is it! It's our car!"

With a quick pull of the door handle, the vehicle remained locked, but with a giant smile on his face, Dale said sincerely, "We're on the right track. Thanks everyone, I would never have made it this far without your help."

Trent replied, "Now that we found his car, we better find your dad too."

At the limousine, Trent opened one of the rear doors to remove a small canvas duffle bag. With its contents emptied on the ground, he displayed a silver flashlight, a long rope, two flares, and a pocketknife.

"Where did you find that stuff?" Dale asked in amazement.

"You don't want to know!"

"Seriously, where did you get it?" Melinda supported Dale.

"Ok, right after we all arrived at the Museum, I was exploring the place when I noticed Brock looking around to make sure no one saw him. I knew he couldn't see me standing behind a big display. When he climbed up the side of a Greek stone arch, he felt around with his hand, and when he seemed happy to feel something, he stepped down and quickly left the area.

"I was curious, so I went to the same spot, and when I reached up there too, my hand touched this small canvas bag. Inside were matches, bullets, and these things."

"Bullets? Why did he hide bullets in the Greek gallery?" Dale asked with a crumpled face.

"You got me. I left them and took the bag with this stuff."

Carl approached them saying, "Maybe 'tis will help," and popped open the limo's trunk. He bent down, and extracted a long flashlight, a tire iron, and three more flares.

"These are compliments of Global Star-Aviation! All company cars are equipped with these items in the trunk. Maybe they'll help," Carl said, and handed the items to the kids.

"While ye search for Dale's father up the trail, I'll show the photo of Dr. Bradan te find a park employee knowin' about him."

"Excellent — this is good stuff," Trent voiced his opinion.

Trent quickly offered the tire iron to Dale, and the three flares to Tab before he handed the flashlight to Melinda.

Carl added, "If yer not back in three hours I want ye to call my cell phone. If I don't hear from ye, I'll make a rescue call, and then come find ye. Are we clear aboot calling me or coming back te check in?" he asked in a concerned tone.

Everyone agreed and entered his number into their phones.

The four friends followed the parking lot towards Enchanted Rock while waving good-bye to Carl.

Chapter Twenty-Two

ALTERNATE STATES

Inside the park entrance, a sign read:

Loop Trail - Four Miles

Below it was another that read:

Summit Trail Climbs 420 feet

"How high is 420 feet? Is that a little or a lot?" Melinda asked.

"Well, a football field is 100 yards long, and a yard is about three feet, so it's almost a football field and a half high. It may be more to climb than we thought," Trent stated.

Across the Sandy Creek Bridge, an arrow pointed at the campsites directly ahead. They stopped to read a wooden information kiosk, which displayed the camp rules. Below the rules was a complete layout map of the campsites, from one through forty-six. Melinda read the rules:

1. **Numbered sites are for overnight camping only**
2. **Campfires are permitted only in provided fire rings**
3. **Prohibited - gathering and burning park wood**

"Forty-six campsites, it's going to take a ton of time to find your dad's site," Trent frowned at Dale.

"What about if we get questioned by a ranger when they see us snooping around?" Melinda asked in a worried tone.

Tab signed to Trent. He turned to face Dale and Melinda and explained,

"Apparently, Tab is the only one using his head. He noticed a campsite number hanging in your dad's SUV," and then Trent pointed towards the bottom of the sign where it read:

Valid Campsite Permit is required inside each car's windshield

"All we have to do is go back and look at the number in my dad's car to know what campsite is his!" Dale yelled, starting to run back towards the parking lot.

"Wait!" Trent called to Dale, "Come back!"

"I've got to get the number," Dale fired back.

"Tab remembered the number laying on the dash of your dad's car — it's twenty nine."

"All right," Dale exclaimed, "Let's go!"

Close to the campsites, the students speedily found number twenty-nine, the last campground in its row. When they arrived at the site, Melinda noticed a blue and white ice chest pushed underneath a small aluminum table, and that both were next to a drab green and burgundy tent. The aluminum camping table had two matching folding chairs.

Dale confirmed, "Yep, this is our stuff."

"Dad — Dad?" he hastily shouted.

No one responded. A light layer of dust covered the tent's exterior, but otherwise, all else looked normal.

"Guys, should this much dust be on the tent?" Melinda asked as she pulled the zipper open to peer inside the tent.

A dust film covered the sleeping bag, which suggested it had been unused recently. Next to a battery-operated lantern was a paperback book, and in the middle of the floor was a pair of tennis shoes.

When they stepped outside, Dale zipped up the tent.

"I don't think he's been in camp for a couple of days. Where do we look now?" Dale whined with worry.

Trent asked Dale after he translated the hand signs from Tab, "Does your dad wear hiking boots?"

"Sometimes — why do you ask?" Dale questioned him back.

"Tab noticed your dad's tennis shoes were still inside the tent, which he thinks means your dad must be wearing his hiking boots. Tab is wondering if he maybe went hiking!"

"If he did, which way do you think he went?" Melinda asked.

"Not sure," Trent pondered, "but if he came here to see the Enchanted Rock, we should head in that direction first."

"Ok, let's go," Dale said promptly.

***

At the main lane, they merged onto the Loop Trail. After a short distance, another sign read:

Pond and Summit Trail

Five minutes later, a larger sign read:

Required – One Quart of Water per Person

"Wish they told us sooner about the water, I'm already thirsty," Melinda said dryly.

The domed top of the enormous rock appeared smoother in contrast with the lower half, which remained covered with scattered bushes and small boulders.

"It reminds me of a giant pink turtle," Dale chuckled.

"Or a large pink bird egg in a nest!" Melinda added.

At a crossroad in the trail, a blue metal sign read:

Summit Trail Left - Turkey Peak Right

"I'm guessing it's the Summit Trail. What do you guys think?" Trent asked.

They were all silent until Melinda said, "If he was interested in Turkey Peak, he would have written it on his desk calendar, but he wrote Enchanted Rock. I bet he went up the Summit Trail."

"Does everyone agree?" Trent validated.

No one spoke; they simply hiked up the trail behind the older boy. Soon steeper and harder to climb, the trail wound towards the top, but instead of going higher as planned, Trent abandoned his original intention by veering onto a small animal path.

No one questioned Trent for leading them off the main trail; they simply followed until Dale asked a quarter of a mile later, "Trent, why are we going this way? I don't see anything around here. Don't you think we should climb up the Enchanted Rock and look around first to get our bearings?"

As he stopped to rest, Trent replied, "I thought so at first, but I kept asking myself, if I were trying to explore something never before seen, would I go where everyone hikes? Or would I search somewhere different? From the dust in the camp, we know it hasn't rained here lately, but I thought I saw some waffle footprints head down this trail. On a hunch, I followed them and we're here now," while he opened his arms wide to include the ample area.

"I'm thirsty," Melinda complained. "Let's stand in the shade under that big stone outcropping for a few minutes. I could use the rest," she added while scanning the wild and rugged landscape.

"That's a good idea — let's rest over there," Trent agreed.

The initial outcrop turned out to be a long flat rock lodged between the granite and above a large boulder. Behind the great stone, a small crevice folded inward into the pink surface.

Out of the direct sun, Dale praised Melinda, "You can't really see this place from the trail until you get right here. This is a good find."

Unable to see into the crevice from where he sat, Trent pulled out the silver flashlight from his back pocket, and shined it inside the gap. Sitting too far away to see much, he stood and pressed his arm through the opening. With squinted eyes, he flashed the light around inside.

Freezing in place, he shouted, "LOOK!"

Everyone jumped up to look with him. Ten feet inside of the crevice, waffle footprints disappeared around a bend from their sight.

"This is it," Dale cheered, "Let's hurry!"

"Wait," Trent restrained him. "We need a plan. Melinda and I have the only two flashlights, so we need to stay together."

Melinda pleaded, "I don't want to lead us in there — or be the last person.

Here's my flashlight Dale."

Trent spoke up quickly, "Ok, I'll go in first, and then Melinda, Tab, and Dale you cover the rear."

"Don't you want Tab closer to you?" Melinda asked genuinely.

"Tab can't hear if there are any noises ahead in the dark, but you can. He's better back a few paces."

Nodding her head at his logic, Melinda stood in single file behind Trent. When Tab and Dale stood behind her, Trent entered the crevice first.

The narrow opening required some squeezing through the first turn, however, thirty-five feet inside, it widened with room for the four students to stand side-by-side. Shortly, their formation turned into a huddle, as the friends cautiously inched forward through the blackness.

With his flashlight shining at the ceiling above, Dale nervously asked, "Do you think there are bats in here?"

"Don't worry about it, they're not interested in us," Melinda said confidently.

The path changed into a spacious chamber, and Trent was soon unsure of which direction to follow. When he used his flashlight to view the ground, it was evident that waffle prints circled in all directions.

"Which is the right way?" he asked, spinning in a circle.

Hesitant to move and disturb the tracks, Melinda added, "Let's spread out to explore the room, but be careful not to step on the footprints."

As Dale shifted his flashlight beam to shine it on the walls, thousands of tiny alluring twinkles filled their sight.

"Whoa, look at that," Trent exclaimed.

"What is it?" Dale asked.

Examination of the miniature flickers revealed the walls were full of tiny bits of quartz and metal.

"I wonder if this stuff is worth anything," Melinda said merrily. "I could make some great jewelry with it."

"Over here!" Trent urgently called.

Along the far side of the cave, the crevice rounded a wall and continued.

"Do you think we should tie our rope to something solid and pull it behind us?" Dale said fearfully as his voice echoed in the dark.

"That's a good idea. Going in will be easy, but coming back might not be. Here, give me the rope," Trent requested to Dale.

With one end, Trent tied it to a large rock on the ground that had fallen from the ceiling, and then he handed the bulk of the rope back to Dale.

"Let's go onward" Trent's voice reverberated in the cave.

In a single file again, Dale slowly lowered the rope to the ground behind them, like a woven breadcrumb trail.

"Quiet everyone…do you hear that?" Trent quizzed.

Melinda whispered, "I don't hear anything unless you mean that humming noise?"

"Exactly, it gets louder the deeper in we go."

"Do rocks conduct vibrations? Perhaps it's coming from a nearby train," Dale volunteered.

"Maybe, but it sounds different to me," Trent whispered back.

Melinda suddenly felt strange. She was listening to Trent and Dale talk to each other as if from a great distance, as an odd sensation washed over her being like the misty spray from a waterfall, giving her the feeling she had been here before. No, not here, but somewhere like it. Instinctive caution prompted her to touch her necklace, only to release it instantly. *"Was it hot?"* she thought.

Instead of the accustomed feel of her jewelry, the pendant felt strangely hot against her skin. Worried she was feeling the effects of dehydration; Melinda feared her rising temperature had over-heated the necklace. Lost in the moment, her mind shifted into autopilot. Hardly listening to Trent, Tab, and Dale, she noticed the sound of the vibration grew with powerful intensity until she felt the tangible ripple in the air mixed with a chilly sensation until dazzling flashes of yellow and blue light suddenly blinded her.

Instantly the blinking lights and vibration evaporated into nothingness as Melinda felt herself swaying back and forth before passing through something, which seemed to physically envelope her completely like entering a hot bathtub of water. Another frightened step forward gave her the feeling of walking on air. Panic flung her eyes open to see dizzying spots before her eyes that quickly melted together into a sudden brighter intensity. She quickly blocked stinging sunshine from her eyes using only her hands until they slowly adjusted to the brightness. In addition to seeing the yellow sunlight above her, a slight breeze caressed her neck, drawing from her a surprising chill. Able to see through her now-squinting eyes, she had forgotten to answer her own thoughts, distracted by the breathtaking pasture in which she now stood.

Emerald, knee-high grass produced light and dark shadow movements from swaying peacefully in the gentle breeze, and covered low rolling hills that rose gradually towards large stately trees. A nearby buzzing shifted her attention from a birdcall to a flying bumblebee inspecting wild flowers of various descriptions and colors.

"WHAT HAPPENED TO US?" Dale blasted noisily.

Shaken from her trance by the sound, Melinda again scanned the unfamiliar rolling hills around her, under the deep azure blue sky.

Concern and tension flooded into her mind when she thought, "*I shouldn't be seeing these things. How can I see this in the middle of a cave? Why isn't it dark? Did I bump my head? Am I dreaming?*"

The smart of the bright sunlight softened as her formerly watering eyes cleared to view the expansive sky and surrounding area.

"LOOK!" she cried, pointing at a large oak tree behind them.

The last remaining few inches of the rope's red-taped end floated stiffly outward from the center of the thick tree bark, suspended four feet above the grass.

Shocked at the realization of what she saw, Melinda thought, "*How did the bark grow so tightly around the rope? There isn't any gap between the outside edge of the rope or the inside edge of the bark.*"

Frozen with astonishment, she stared at the mysterious sight.

Dizzy from comprehension of what she observed, Melinda asked, "How is this possible?"

Tab was the first to move. Cautiously he approached the rope, while at the same time he studied it carefully before pacing behind the tree.

He waved urgently and signed at them when he jumped back into sight.

Tentatively Dale followed him while looking squarely at Tab, and then with a shrug of his thin shoulders stated, "What? I don't see anything."

"He's asking us what happened to the other end of the rope. We see one end poking out through the front of tree, but there's nothing behind the tree — including the cave." Trent translated.

Melinda stepped backwards to view the whole tree at once, and plainly saw the red-taped end of the yellow rope stuck out of the tree's bark on one side, but the remaining length was missing inside the tree.

"Does anyone know where we are? Is this a dream, or did something strange happen to us?" Melinda asked with questioning eyes.

Everyone remained quiet; no one knew what to say. She followed Tab as he circled back around the tree to return to the visible piece of rope, where he touched it gingerly. With a smile at Trent to indicate it felt normal, he then froze when he soaked in their dismayed expressions. Dale's face displayed a look of terror. Melinda's face froze in an incredulous stare, and Trent's face drained of color, while he reached towards his brother.

Afraid to glance at his hand, Tab forced himself. "NO!" he yelled in an off-key voice, realizing his entire hand and wrist had vanished with the end of the rope.

Both were no longer visible.

With a rush of unreasoned panic, Tab jerked back his hand. To his great relief, his hand reappeared. Uncertain of his physical condition, he felt his right hand with his left, and smiled when he knew it had feeling.

"I am all right!" he thought.

Breathlessly, Melinda, Trent, and Dale inspected Tab's hand too, and the spot where it had recently disappeared.

"This is weird — this is REALLY WEIRD!" Dale shouted. "I don't know about you guys, but I'm scared!" He turned, and snickered, "This is not arid San Antonio either; this place is green! I'm not even sure if this is Texas anymore!"

No one disagreed with his comments. The bleak landscape from when they entered the cave, and where they stood now, were noticeably different.

"How do we get back?" Melinda asked with a nervous stammer.

Trent deciphered Tab's signing, "Tab says when his hand was missing, he didn't feel any pain. But he also thinks he felt something else inside too."

Reaching towards the visible five-inch portion of the rope, Trent slowly dabbed at its end with his fingers, and when he felt nothing wrong, he pushed his hand forward. His fingers mysteriously disappeared, and then his entire hand.

"I don't feel anything except the rope," Trent said glancing back to his friends.

Confident, Trent pushed his arm in deeper to his elbow, and again, without feeling any discomfort, he pushed his other arm into the tree too. Soon, he looked like an armless boy trying to hug a tree.

"I can't reach in any further. The opening seems to be about the size of a Frisbee."

Trent stepped easily back, and pulled out his arms until both appeared from the inside of the bizarre tree. He shook them as if slinging imaginary water drops from his hands, and then stared at his exercising fingers.

Convinced he was in good health; Trent smiled and said, "I could definitely feel a hard boundary that felt like solid rock. Whatever we came through is still there, but it's only about this big," he said, holding up his hands with a gap.

"You know, I think we passed through that tree into this field. This may sound crazy but I'm worried that if we can't get back inside the tree, maybe we should call someone for help, or at least find some water. Someone has to live around here, and maybe they'll know what we should do," Dale suggested.

Tab pulled out his text phone and looked quizzically at Trent when he did not have any signal. Instantly, Trent looked at his signal strength and with a wheeze asked, "I don't have any bars on my phone, does anyone else?"

Melinda confirmed, "I don't have a signal either and my battery is low."

Dale shook his head in disappointment.

Without any cell phone signals to call Carl, or squeeze through the small portal to return, their need for water drove them forward. In agreement with Dale to search for help, Melinda was lost in thought about how to re-find their tree from a distance, when she removed a scarf from her purse saying, "Trent, tie this onto that lower branch. Once we're across the pasture, this will help us to know our tree from a distance."

With the scarf in place, and moving slightly in the breeze, Melinda was satisfied the tree would be identifiable, so they began their trek. Halfway across the spacious meadow, Melinda watched the wavy emerald colored grass wrap around her legs with each step.

Secure in the need for food and water, the search was underway.

"I hope we find water soon, because my throat feels like it's swelling up," Dale complained.

"As green as the grass is around here, there has to be a stream or a pond nearby. Just keep your eyes sharp," Trent instructed.

Along the way, Melinda saw no signs of water or people and she asked, "Where do we go now? Do you think we should split up to cover more ground, or should we stay together?"

"I vote we stay together," Dale panted immediately.

"Dale's right — we don't know where we're at, and if we get separated now, this could go from bad to worse. My guess is we should circle the field first as a group, and see if we can get a hint of which direction to go next," Trent suggested while using his hand to block the sun from his eyes.

Melinda was able to see their tree from across the sea of green grass, and noticed the overall landscape appeared similar in each direction; however, looking directly back across the grassland at the scarf, she felt the left half of the field seemed a shorter return to the tree.

"Let's try this way first," Melinda said while she marched to the left. Without hesitation, her friends followed.

A few minutes later, Tab clapped his hands together excitedly. When his fellow students stared at him, the deaf boy held up one finger, and then he tilted his head as if listening.

"What's he doing? He can't hear anything, can he?" Dale asked.

Trent shrugged his shoulders in a question-type manner at Tab who signed to him.

"Tab feels vibrations coming from deep inside that grove of trees."

"I don't feel anything," Melinda stated while moving her head from side-to-side.

"We hear with our ears, but some hearing-impaired people feel vibrations better than we do, so I know Tab might be on to something," Trent countered.

Nodding his head in a knowing manner, Tab again pointed into the trees.

"Maybe he feels vibrations coming from a factory, or a road construction crew. Let's follow him!" Dale said excitedly.

Trent warned them first, "If we go into those trees, we might get turned around or lost from finding our way back. Are you sure you want to leave the field?"

After a pause, he assumed the answer and added, "We shouldn't split up, so I guess we have no choice."

"I don't see any other way," Melinda, said to confirm his reasoning.
With a solid push, Trent pressed the tire iron into the ground, and turned it so it pointed in the direction of the tree's position. Then they followed Tab.

Chapter Twenty-Three

STRANGE WORLD

Thirty minutes later, Melinda wondered if her eyes were playing tricks on her, or if the environment was actually altering around them. The area appeared darker, as if a giant cloud overhead had blocked the sun's rays, yet when she glanced upward, she saw only a wide-open, blue sky.

Before she heard the noise, she felt the tremors.

Melinda moved her head to the side, hoping to hear better, when she said, "It kind of sounds like a celebration over that next ridge...I think I hear people cheering...does that sound like fireworks to you guys?"

Without waiting to receive an answer, she continued in the same direction, and as before, they followed.

"I wonder if it's an air show?" she whispered to herself.

"Why do you think it's an air show?" Dale asked.

Embarrassed to be overheard; she explained, "I went to an air show with my parents last year, and some of the jets flew fast enough to make sonic booms. Each time we heard the boom, the crowd cheered similar to what we're hearing right now. I don't really know, it just sounded the same to me."

Melinda was certain the air was changing, as she now noticed a mass of billowing gray vapor moving towards them that veiled the treetops, and was in the process of blotting out the sunlight. The roar of people, mixed with the sharp popping sounds of firecrackers, grew deafening.

Dale coughed and Melinda realized her throat felt rough too. In fact, it was hard to breathe due to an acidic smell that clung to the air. Piercing whistles, high above their heads, led to thunderous explosions. As soon as they climbed up the short ridge, they froze as if hypnotized.

Military men faced each other from both sides of an open field. Soldiers wearing dark navy uniforms knelt upon one knee in long rows to their right, and each fired their rifles to the rhythmic rumble of war drums playing across the field. Upon discharging his weapon, each kneeling man stood, and allowed the soldier waiting behind him to kneel in his place and then shoot. Melinda realized this was the source of the firecracker sounds.

Immediately the signal of a bugle cut through the sounds of yelling and shooting. Profound booms erupted from large firing cannons, shaking the ground beneath their feet. Great smoke plumes hid each cannon when it rocked backward from the powerful recoil of each thunderous explosion. Cannon balls and artillery shells whistled across the haze-filled sky, far above the noise of the battle below.

Across the field between drifts of smoke, Melinda watched as men in dreary gray uniforms returned an equal barrage of firepower. The battle raged before them amidst furious shouts and the sounds of metal clashing as countless soldiers fought by shooting guns and stabbing at each other with rifle-mounted bayonets. Without warning, a second bugle recalled both sides, to retreat and flee for protection within the trees near each camp. Within seconds, both groups of soldiers had melted from her sight, except for the bodies left behind on the field.

Incredibly, scores of men lay everywhere, while a few called vainly for aid.

"I know this looks like a war, but that can't be real! It has to be some film crew making a movie or a re-enactment," Trent uttered in disbelief.

Soon, all remained quiet. Smoke faded with the vibrations in the ground, and except for dead and dying men on the field, nothing more resembled the chaos they had just witnessed.

"If it's a re-enactment, I'll bet it must be a celebration…which means they have FOOD AND DRINKS! Come on, let's hurry before I pass out from thirst," Dale's voice trailed while he ran towards the gray side.

"Wait!" Melinda shouted fearfully from assessing the situation, but he kept running further away.

Every so often, he slowed and motioned for them to follow.

"We can't split up, so let's go," Trent groaned.

Without a glance at Tab or Melinda, he jogged after Dale.

Melinda squeezed Tab's elbow, and together they trotted behind Trent. She could hear Tab as he ran behind her, but felt too uneasy crossing the corner of the field to glance back.

Injured men stirred in the field and called to her for water, but most lay still. Melinda picked up her pace to close the gap between her and Trent. As they neared the far edge of the trees, she became aware of several soldiers in gray, pointing guns in their direction. When Dale shortened the remaining distance to the trees, three of the soldiers in gray ran towards him, with long rifles in their hands — of which two had bayonets.

Excited to see the oncoming men, Dale ran faster. His breathing came out in heavy gasps as he called, "Hey…sure glad…to see you guys…we're starting to…"

SMACK! The front soldier cracked Dale over the head with his rifle barrel.

"STOP HURTING HIM!" Melinda heard her voice scream.

Unsure of what to do, she halted when the remaining two tackled Trent. While Trent lay on the ground from the attack, two new soldiers emerged from the trees and raced to intercept Melinda's route. Worn rifles soon rose in her direction as if to fire at both Melinda and Tab. Together, both teens stood in place. With their hands held above their heads, they watched the two latest soldiers run toward them.

The lead soldier reached Melinda first and grabbed her tightly around the knees with his bloodstained hands. Hoisting her waist over his shoulder in one fluid motion, the man ran towards his camp carrying Melinda. Unable to see Tab in her upside-down position, she choked down the desire to vomit when her nose filled with a revolting smell.

Saturated with dirt, blood, tobacco, and sweat, the man's scratchy uniform gave off a strong stench. In addition, his sweat-smeared face suggested he had not bathed in weeks. Nauseous from his reeking odor, Melinda gagged as she watched the ground bob up and down from bouncing over his shoulder.

Approaching the cover of trees revealed more soldiers dressed in gray. The man carrying Melinda threw her to the ground, and she tumbled into Trent. Circled by a half-dozen raggedy unshaven men, their visibly thin and tired bodies blazed with passions of fear and hatred.

"Whoos side are yer on?" the lead man yelled into their faces, his hazel eyes burning in anger.

Not understanding the question, Melinda stared blankly into his face.

Another man gave Trent a hard kick in the leg and yelled, "Whoos side yer be on?"

More confused by their reactions, Melinda searched for help from the rest of the nearby soldiers, but the red glow in their eyes made her suspicious; they were asking a trick question. Without hearing any response from the kids, the lead soldier raised his gun above his head with both hands, as if to bash Trent with its end.

Melinda screamed to save him, "WE'RE ON YOUR SIDE! Didn't you see us run over here?"

The soldier continued, "Wer do yer live? Wat state?"

Finally in control of her emotions, she replied, "Arizona," while she met his gaze squarely.

"Him?" He asked her when he pointed at Dale, who remained unconscious with blood trickling down the side of his head.

"Texas," she said coolly.

The man seemed satisfied at hearing the answer, and a young blue-eyed man in his early twenties reached down to assist her to her feet.

"Sorry ma'am — can't be too careful. I'm S'gent Halversen, Theodore Halversen. Bin ketchen spies round here latly during these perilous times. Sorry 'bout yer friend. He'll be fine! Ya'll come along now."

With a tin cup filled with water from a nearby barrel, a bad-mannered soldier drenched Dale's face until he sputtered and opened his eyes wide, bolting upright in shock, which caused the man to laugh.

"Where...what...oh my head," he whined as he held his bleeding scalp.

Trent pinched Dale's arm, while simultaneously speaking loudly, "These are our friends, Dale, who are fighting for us. Good news, we made it to them!"

Dale caught the look on Trent's face, and glanced around at the men staring angrily at him. He answered slowly by saying, "Good — I'm glad...," which further set the fighters at ease.

After following Sergeant Halversen through a sea of canvas tents, Melinda soon felt lost in the maze. Many tents were quite large, but the majority resembled dirty pup tents. Everywhere she looked, pain and fear reflected from the soldiers' expressions. Desperate wounded men, unable to imagine surviving another day without their side decisively winning the next battle, littered the area around them. Many seemed to know their lives were uncertain, after suffering grievous losses already.

Some were without arms and legs, while most received bandages from others scarcely able to move under their own effort. A middle-aged man rocked a young teenager in his arms as he spoke softly, "Hang in thar son, the doc will be here soon."

The youth's blank stare made Melinda think he was already dead. Soldiers sat wearily on the ground and pulled out bits of food to eat from small canvas bags tied around their waists. A few played cards, while most of the injured men lay collapsed on the ground from exhaustion, trying to rebuild their little remaining strength.

Finally, they arrived at a very large tent in the center of the camp, as two men argued in front. One pointed to a map that lay between them on a small wooden table.

Both senior officers were older and slightly cleaner than most of the surrounding men.

"Sir, I don't recommend breaking through there..."

"Captain, I don't believe we have a choice," the older man rebutted. "They only have a few ten pound Parrott cannons positioned there. It is our best chance! Now get the men informed. I want to press our advantage in that area, and attack before nightfall!"

The tall dusty captain stood at attention, and saluted the elder man, "Yes sir, right away!" Melinda had to step from his path as he briskly walked past her with an expression of stern determination.

The older man in charge hesitated in thought as he contemplated the kids standing beside the young sergeant. Deep grooved stress lines framed his weathered face and neck. His tan face sported a short gray and white beard with a handlebar moustache. The officer insignia covered hat he wore remained turned up on the right side only, and boasted a thick strip of perspiration beneath the gold braded hatband. While the strong-minded man said nothing more, Melinda realized he was evaluating them like an eagle, with his pewter-gray eyes. She felt herself suddenly become nervous under his powerful and penetrating gaze.

Sergeant Halversen addressed the man, "Sir, the boyz an' me found these young-uns maken ther way te us."

Silent, the commander scrutinized them while he calculated his next move. Melinda knew deep down he was not one to be fooled.

"Captain David feels Cemetery Hill would be a better spot to rush these damn Union Yankees! What do you think?" the leader asked the sergeant, while watching the student's reactions.

Melinda blinked thinking, "*Yankees! These worn-out gray uniforms would mean these people are Confederate soldiers in the Civil War.*"

The man in charge hardly heard the sergeant's response; instead, he paid closer attention to their reactions from the Union insult he cast at them. Dale's face became contorted. Melinda could not decide if he was in pain, or going to throw up.

Mentally dissecting their clothing, the older man walked closer to the students. Melinda immediately smelled tobacco smoke mingled with sweat exuding from the leader.

He abruptly introduced himself without warning, "I'm Major McGregor!" and then he demanded, "Whom might I have the curiosity to meet?"

Melinda shot a fleeting glance at Trent, who was already staring back at her.

Both knew they seemed very out of place in this camp.

Major McGregor's voice, rough from years of yelling at troops over gunfire rumbled, "What would you care to tell me?"

A hush filled the area until Dale blurted, "Was that a real battle? Did those people really die?"

The man's eyes squinted into a hard gaze suddenly filled with fury, "Son — this here stinking war's been going on for some two years, and is becoming harder still. Do you think their flowing blood is not real?"

With an angry glare at Dale, the Major squinted further, causing Dale to ask a question better left unasked.

"What year is this?"

"Ya mean what munth?" the young sergeant offered.

"No, I mean what year?" Dale corrected.

The major stopped the sergeant from answering the question by holding up his hand.

"What year do you believe it is?" the major threw back coldly at Dale.

Dale's face reminded Melinda of how a deer might actually look in an oncoming car's headlights. Without answering, sweat beaded on his brow, while Dale stared at the leader with an involuntary shudder, unsure how to respond.

Slowly, the major scratched out, "Sergeant — I believe these troublemakers deserve further investigation."

Tab signed at Trent, which caused the major's teeth to clench together and his face to harden like steel.

"Whoa boy, what trickery is this?" the leader demanded.

Trent jumped in, "Sir, my brother is deaf. We learned to communicate with our hands when we were kids."

"What did he say?" the major commanded, and displayed his irritated disbelief by gritting his brown teeth.

"He wants to answer your question that it's the 1860's, sir," Trent replied, sounding a bit brittle and hollow to Melinda.

With a darker countenance after taking in Trent with his cold calculating eyes, the major questioned him further, "1860 what?"

Visibly uncomfortable under the man's harsh glare, Melinda stood silent in the tenseness of the unspoken moment. Major McGregor turned slightly to his side, and easily retrieved a pistol from off the small table.

"Sergeant, we don't have time now to take this further. Put them under guard immediately!" he barked, and pointed the barrel of his pistol squarely at the kids.

Shaken by the major's unpredictable reaction, the sergeant saluted his superior quickly, and then pointed his long rifle at the kids.

He said to the students while nodding to another soldier, "Fallow him!"

Without change of expression, Major McGregor ordered, "Bind their hands tight!"

***

Guarded in a large supply tent, Melinda couldn't feel her hands any longer. After losing the feeling in her fingers first, she was now sure her arms were numb too. Junior soldiers had shoved them around and tied the team up as prisoners of war. Fortunately, a kinder teenage soldier gave them water to drink and corn meal to eat.

It had been several hours since using the bathroom at the state park. The longer Melinda sat as a bound prisoner, the more aware she was of her filling bladder, and almost wished she'd refused to accept the kind soldier's earlier offer to quench her mounting thirst.

Sweat gathered on his face, Dale stared blankly ahead, slowly rambling a repeating phrase from fright, "We're gone...we're gone...we're gone," leaving only Trent to talk with her in hushed voices.

"How do we get out of here?" Melinda whispered.

"Do you mean this tent, or this whole place?"

She frowned and mumbled, "Both!"

"I don't know. Even if we can escape from the tent, I don't know where to go, or what to do next. There are soldiers surrounding us. This is looking bad for us now that they've taken our stuff away. Do you have any idea...?"

Suddenly, cannon fire at the edge of the trees in the Union camp instantly transitioned into the oncoming missile sounds of cannonballs in flight. Within seconds, the rain of shells and bullets rumbled the ground about them. The impacts felt close by, and Melinda thought dirt crumbled onto the tent. The air quickly filled with an eruption of yelling men and cursing rebel officers running in all directions.

Another cannon blast followed by crashing sounds caused Melinda to imagine that a giant bowling ball raced through the camp causing damage. Large chunks of dirt pummeled the tent's exterior, and strained the ropes holding the canvas in place.

Melinda screamed above the roar of urgent voices, gunfire, and cannons, "WE HAVE TO GET OUT OF HERE! CAN YOU MOVE?"

Trent did not respond, instead, he was straining against the cords fastened around his wrists. Dale continued to mutter, oblivious to the flying dangers.

From the corner of her eye, Melinda thought she saw Tab playing a trick on her. One second Tab was holding up his bound hands, and the next, they seemed to slip easily from the leather cords. She blinked to make sure she was not dreaming as she saw him unfasten Trent's bindings next.

Together, the brothers quickly untied their feet. Moments later, they untied Dale and Melinda. She attempted to stand, and the complete numbness created thousands of needle stabs that shot throughout her feet and hands.

A large saddled buckskin colored horse, frightened by the subsequently close cannon blast, stamped in fear outside of their tent. Rearing up on its hind legs, it pulled its reins loose from the makeshift post and rushed headfirst through their tent, almost trampling them.

Adrenalin shot through the nearly 1,200-pound animal, which made the horse oblivious that the tent's canvas had caught on its saddle horn. While it pulled the tent spikes from out of the ground, it next dragged the tent and main pole between rows of the camp, until the drum of its swirling hooves faded into the smoke and sounds of rifle fire. Without the tent's meager cover for protection, the four friends ran. Unsure of the right direction, they swerved and changed their course several times.

At the camp's rear edge, Trent and Tab dashed towards the nearest clump of trees, when Melinda looked back and noticed Dale abruptly reverse his course, to head directly back into the chaos. Unsure of whom to follow, she stopped and watched as Dale ran straight into harm's way. While the brothers unknowingly left them both behind, Melinda lowered her head and sprinted as fast as possible after Dale.

Lost from her sight when he ran behind a covered wagon, she thought she heard the faint sound of Dale's voice. A glance into a sizable tent she ran past proved valuable, when she spotted Dale in the process of untying a man from its center wooden pole. As Dale raced to free the first man, she hurried inside to help untie a second.

In a torn and dusty navy uniform, with elaborate gold braids sewn horizontally across his chest and stomach, Melinda guessed the second prisoner was about twenty-five years old. The elaborate uniform made her believe him to be an important prisoner to the rebel troops, so she helped the wobbly man to regain his feet. As he used the tent's interior pole for support, another close explosion rocked the ground under their feet, which caused the first stranger to swing around and face her. In astonishment, Melinda realized whom she was saving.

"Dr. Bradan! You're alive!" she rang out above the raging conflict noise.

The professor yelled, "WE NEED TO GET OUT FAST BEFORE THEY FIND US!"

Dale squeezed his father tight with happiness, while Melinda watched the tender scene.

Not able to say anything during the moment, both smiled at each other until Dr. Bradan yelled again, "LET'S GO!"

Cautiously they proceeded to step through the tent's opening, when an unknown instinct warned Dr. Bradan to shrink back suddenly as a Confederate soldier ran past the tent flaps, firing two pistols in rapid succession. After the man rushed past, Melinda led them from the tent and towards the rear trees where she had seen the brothers escape. Focused on searching for a quick glimpse of Trent and Tab, Melinda was unaware of two soldiers dressed in gray, running towards them from a right angle.

Using a buckboard for cover, Melinda dashed behind it and collided into the chest of the first running soldier. The unexpected and sudden hard impact exhaled her breath in a single whoosh.

Strong hands caught Melinda from behind, when Dr. Bradan helped her to regain her feet.

"RUN!" he screamed at her and Dale.

Together, the three dashed towards the trees where Trent and Tab had disappeared. Scared, she glanced backwards, and to her horror, she observed the two soldiers angrily pursuing them.

"FASTER!" she screamed over the racket. "They're chasing us!"

Inside the initial border of trees, Melinda fearfully realized both men were closing on them fast. Dr. Bradan had difficulty keeping up the continuous pace, from being bound for days as a prisoner of war. No sooner had they entered the thicket of trees, than it became more difficult to see in the overcast area, now filled with cannon and rifle smoke.

With no easy escape in sight, Melinda watched helplessly as the two Confederate soldiers sprinted at them with raised rifles. Without forewarning, a full-sized tree branch dropped from above and plowed directly onto the top of the soldier's heads, driving both of them to the ground. She stared upward in disbelief, to see the brothers grinning wildly at her from the success of their plan.

Dropping down onto the ground from their higher position, they excitedly shook Dr. Bradan's hand.

WHAP!

Tree splinters sprayed at the students from a bullet impact, closely followed by the sound of a cannonball exploding about 25 yards directly behind where the two soldiers remained on the ground and echoed its force within Melinda's belly. War sounds blasted around them, adding to the confusion of their next plan of action.

The cannonball, filled with solid metal marbles, scattered the iron spheres about them unpredictably from the explosion's impact. Large chunks of tree bark fractured in all directions simultaneously, including into the students' exposed skin. Filled with fear and pain, they all ran until they could go no more. When they fell to the ground gasping for breath, it seemed to Melinda they had been running for the past hour.

With his composure slowly regained, Dr. Bradan scolded his son, "I can't believe you put yourself or these students in danger coming here," and then pausing with relief added, "However, I'm extremely glad to see everyone! I thought I'd never see you again after the Confederacy caught me."

"Was that real, Dad?" he asked pointing back towards the battle, "How'd we become part of a battle fought so long ago?"

"I would tell you, but it's going to be hard for you to believe — however, you're here, so maybe you know most of what's happening."

"Sir, we have no idea what's going on around here. We only followed some clues that got us — to wherever we are?" Trent said with his arms open wide.

"That is amazing — well; this may take some time to explain…"

"Wait! I thought I saw something," Melinda whispered intently.

Her gaze focused in the direction they had recently traveled, when she saw another slight flicker.

"I'm not sure, but it kind of looked like those same guys chasing us."

Suddenly, both Confederate soldiers burst from their tree cover, and sprinted furiously towards them.

"HURRY!" Trent screamed at the top of his lungs.

Everyone hustled to their feet and ran out of the small clearing, but it seemed to Melinda as if they were running in slow motion to reach the other side. Trent, who remained in the lead, angled their escape towards a natural opening in the brush. Past the opening, he next veered onto a small trail, which descended along a steeper slope. At the bottom of the ravine, they all slowed to decide where to run next. In less than a moment, a bullet ricocheted off a large rock in front of Dale. Frightened, they ran faster.

While the soldiers halted and reloaded their rifles, the group raced ahead of the two historic pursuers.

Dr. Bradan grunted, "Get off the trail! Make it harder to follow...."

Immediately, Trent broke from the trail, and led them up another sharp ravine.

Chapter Twenty-Four

CHASING THE FUTURE

Climbing over the last ridge, it seemed to Melinda that the trees had thinned; however, in direct proportion, thicker green brush flourished with varied life. She was incapable of seeing very far behind them, because of the immediate tangle of lush vines that housed a menagerie of sounds.

"It sounds as if we're in the jungle," Dr. Bradan stated to his son.

"And it looks like one too," Dale agreed.

Once the group had progressed deeper into the newer jungle environment, the sunlight soon faded, blocked by the substantial overhead canopy. When they passed around a bend in the trail, they saw a large ground hole filled with bubbling mud.

"It reminds me of chocolate pudding coming to a boil," Melinda laughed.

Everyone was hungry, so at the thought, no one commented further walking beyond the dark bubbling ooze. After a few minutes, Trent followed the sound of running water without seeing the source, until they reached the edge of a small stream. Parched from their long ordeal, he fell to his knees, and scooped up water in his cupped hands to drink. Before the anticipated feel of cool wetness touched his lips, Tab slapped the water from his hands. Hurt and confused by the unpredicted action, Trent soon relaxed when he saw Tab point downstream at a mystery.

The small brook abruptly ended into an ethereal pool of water about fifteen feet across at the widest point. Akin to a whirlpool, the water swirled in circles, and rapidly disappeared deep into the ground. The outer edge resembled yellow broken crystals, which had a distinct separation from the inner electric blue water draining from their sight into some kind of hidden outlet. Trent lacked an understanding of the pond's significance, and quickly wiped the stream's moisture from his hands onto his pant legs. Fearful of the possible consequences within the mystic world, Melinda leapt across the running water, to avoid touching it further.

Whizzz!

The air split with the sound of the soldier's racing bullet. Behind them, the Confederate soldier rapidly re-loaded his single fire weapon, as his buddy chased them, hoping for clear area to fire at the fleeing students. Melinda and her friends dashed ahead along the open animal trail behind Trent, until he abruptly veered right and abandoned the worn corridor within the brush. Slowed from the effort of running through heavy foliage, the group zigzagged through the few open spaces in the vegetation when possible, and following no marked course, hoped they would lose their pursuers.

Hundreds of bamboo leaves sliced paper-thin cuts into their exposed skin, but that was not the worst of the present escape. Most alarming were the substantial spider webs. Melinda realized that in some places, the thick webbing resembled stretched white cotton candy. She was afraid to slow down in fear of discovering an incredibly large and poisonous stowaway; she picked up the pace and fled faster.

Trent, who remained in the lead, halted within a small clearing when they could run no more. Melinda checked her heavy breathing to listen for what she feared, but could only hear the thunderous pumping of her own heartbeat and breathing. Deep in the jungle, she had lost all sense of direction from the race to escape from their historic hunters. Melinda felt her senses relax slightly when Trent veered onto a narrow pathway that wound among the leaves, and she heard only the normal background drum of jungle noises.

The narrow path overflowed with wild growth from the recent lack of traffic. Occasional dirt patches peeked up at her through the greenery. The narrow trail forced the team into a single file, and Melinda was thankful to discover that walking between the lush leaves was much easier than shoving her way through the previous dense plants. Soon, the trail widened into an overgrown clearing. A hut, constructed out of heavy bamboo, confirmed to her that people had lived in this camp for some time.

Woven rope hammocks, now badly shredded and discolored, were visible to her through sizable gaps between the poles forming the front walls. Outside and to the right of the shelter, a sun-faded green canvas hung partially tied between several of the surrounding trees. Melinda believed it had once provided cover from the sun; however, thick moss and black mold overran the still-hanging portion. She was unsure if the remnants of a small, roughly crafted fence meant the camp's occupants tried to keep animals in, or out of the encampment.

The center of the campsite contained a small rock fire ring, but without a caretaker and time, it remained entirely overgrown with underbrush and weeds. Together, the small party approached the hut out of curiosity. Inside the debris-filled hut's doorway, a set of antique binoculars with busted lenses lay on the shoddy flooring. Trent reached down to grasp them and suddenly jumped backwards, when a strange green and black striped lizard poked its head out of the hollow left lens. It turned its tiny head to view them with rotating oversized eyes, and then scurried through a hole in the hut floorboards.

"I wonder who lived here — and why?" Dr. Bradan asked rhetorically.

"I'm more concerned with what happened to them," Dale said anxiously.

"Whatever happened, it was a long time ago by the looks of this place." Melinda offered, more to lift her spirits than to help Dale feel secure.

After sizing up the run-down site, Dr. Bradan faced everyone, "I suppose this is as good a place as any to figure out our next move," he said, hoping to bolster their collective morale.

"Let's take an inventory of what we have to…."

"Quiet — I heard a noise," Trent whispered softly.

The shock of the words caused Melinda to hear only her own heart beating loudly inside her ears once more. Not expecting to hear more with her recent experiences, she was surprised to hear a faint click of metal on metal. As quietly and fast as possible, the student group disappeared into the thick overgrown jungle, which surrounded the open campground. After hiding under the substantial plant life, Melinda peered through the leaves, and was amazed how her friends had disappeared like ghosts into the vegetation, when she heard voices drawing closer.

"Thay wint this way I tel yer. See, the grass bin stepped down here."

Inside the encampment, both of the soldiers tracking the group scoured the area as they had recently done themselves. Efficiently rummaging for anything of use, but seeing nothing of value, the two war men exited through the other side of the encampment.

Once they were both outside of the students' sight, with the exception of Tab, everyone returned into the open area from his or her recent hiding place. Trent, out of habit, quickly peeked around the side of the hut, and waved for Tab to join them. Anxious to join his older brother and without seeing a small metal box hidden under the deep growth, Tab kicked it unexpectedly and hurt his foot. Unable to hear the clanging rattle of metal inside the concealed storage container, Tab was unsure of the reason for Trent's startled expression.

As feared, the relentless soldiers' howls alerted the teens that both of their pursuers were returning to investigate the unexpected sudden noise. Quickly as before, Melinda dove with the team into the flora. Tab's lack of hearing did not alert him of the soldiers' return, as he leaned forward to rub his foot, and observe what he had kicked. Trent thought Tab had quickly ducked down out of view once more.

Inside the metal box, the deaf boy first noticed a pair of rusty pliers and two small wrenches. When he turned the container over to look within it, a worn palm-sized leather book and an aged pair of aviator goggles slid into the open. With his left hand, Tab picked up the goggles and shook the dust off them, and then he grasped the book with his right. Once Tab stood upright, he found himself starring into the killing ends of two militia rifles, pointing at his face.

With the soldier's beards and cheeks resting on their rifle stocks, Tab could not read their lips, while they screamed at him to walk towards them. In his silent world, he helplessly looked into the faces of escalating danger, as he watched the two men become visibly agitated.

Their tone froze the blood in Trent's veins, sensing the two men were unpredictable. Too much for Trent as a protective brother, he called out to the soldiers in a loud clear voice, "I'm coming out of hiding. My hands are raised high above my head."

"Guys, my brother is deaf. He cannot hear. He does not know what you are saying. He can sometimes read lips, but he has to see the…"

They wanted none of his explanation and the lead soldier yelled, "QUIET!" dealing with Trent's arrival. With the man's rifle pointed at the middle of Trent's stomach, the second soldier moved closer to Tab. On impulse, the deaf brother held out the goggles and the small book in his hands to the man. Uncertain of their purpose, and saying nothing to the teen, the closest soldier slapped them from his hands to land in the tall grass. The angry expression on the man's face pre-manifested his following forceful movements to shove Tab around to face in the opposite direction.

With a long piece of rawhide, the smaller Confederate soldier tied Tab's hands together, and when bound tight, the shorter man did the same to Trent, and questioned the older brother, "Where be the rest hidin'?"

Trent remained silent in his response, causing the second man to pull a large knife from its sheath at his waist, and rubbed the cold flat side against Trent's neck, below his ear.

At seeing his reaction to the feel of the dangerous cold steel, the filthy man mocked him, "Ain't yoo a purty young boy. Be a shame to cutz ya. Tell me or lose an ear!"

Melinda had the inspiration that this was a critical juncture. Both of the brother's lives hung in the balance of the moment, and without regret, she yelled, "Here! I'm right here," stepping from behind the giant leaves to save them after realizing the treacherous man was genuinely capable of hurting the boys.

Dr. Bradan and Dale comprehended the same reality, and appeared from their hiding places knowing the men would continue with the interrogation, and injure Melinda too. After the soldiers had tied everyone up as their prisoners, with each person's hands tied to the back of the person in front of them, the two herded Melinda and her friends' single-file. The two soldiers returned the team from the direction they all had approached the vacant camp.

The older and larger soldier led the student string by pulling them aggressively to keep his pace, while his younger partner followed at the rear of the procession.

"Here's the weird water," Dale quacked like a duck when they crossed over the small stream, still disappearing down into the odd blue and yellow drain.

At the sound of the comment, the rear soldier jerked Dale's rope and grunted, "Shut yer face boy!"

None of the students spoke again, while the string of prisoners retraced their steps towards the upcoming bubbling mud. Nearly at the mire, a terrifying scream rose above the jungle floor when a full-grown panther savagely pounced upon and bit the rear soldier on the neck. Traumatized by the force of the cat's attack, the injured soldier lifted his rifle. However, the heavy burden of the powerful feline forced him to shoot prematurely and harmlessly into the trees. The jungle shrieked in objection to the thunderous report.

The other lead soldier spun and shoved past Dr. Bradan to gun down his friend's killer. Scattered from fear of attack by the looming panther, the connected students unwittingly became a human vine across the soldier's path.

The lead soldier thrashed to break through the chain of students, and instead knocked Dr. Bradan off balance, who unexpectedly grabbed hold of the struggling captor to avoid tipping over onto his side. Together the remaining soldier and Dr. Bradan fell together in the middle of the trail, causing a chain reaction that pulled both Tab and Trent on top of Dr. Bradan's back.

Dale and Melinda remained standing at each tangled end, fully exposed to the hungry danger. Frozen in fear, Melinda realized the powerful animal was crouching to spring directly at her.

In a burst of motion, Melinda watched the panther's muscles tighten and release. Extended claws pointed at her from the two massive front paws, its hazardous mouth opened to exhibit lethal teeth. Before she clasped her eyes tightly together, she saw the cat's fur ripple as it leapt towards her. She ducked at the final moment, hoping the cat would fly over her. However, the heavy weight of its rear legs drove her to the ground.

Expecting to feel the warm sensation of her blood running down her back, Melinda tightened her muscles, waiting for the moment. 5 seconds…10 seconds…15 seconds…went by, and then she neither heard, nor felt the cat.

Fearfully she glanced up, expecting the pounce to come at any moment, until she spied the dead cat lying on its side. Powerless to move and gripped with fear, the makeshift rope still connected to her wrists, jerked her back into the present moment, as she watched Tab, Trent, and Dr. Bradan wrestle with the bigger soldier to regain control of the situation.

Unsure of what transpired, Melinda stood dazed until the soldier was their prisoner. It was impossible for Melinda to hold back a jittery laugh while Dr. Bradan tightly bound the man's feet and hands. Dale, relieved to be safe, nervously twitched as adrenaline continued pumping through his veins.

"Wow, did you see that?" he speedily asked her.

Dale, who had a taste for the dramatic, simply pointed one finger at the man lying on the ground and said, "He barely had time to cock his rifle, let alone raise it to his shoulder. I can't believe it; he just pointed his rifle and fired. I don't know who was more surprised that he shot the thing — him or me. We just stood there staring at the panther until Trent and my dad wrestled him down."

After cutting the ropes from their wrists with the soldier's hunting knife, Dr. Bradan grew quiet in his thoughts.

"What do we do now?" Dale asked his father with an inquisitive tone.

Anxious to know his fate, the dirty soldier listened intently to the professor.

"Well, we don't have time to bury the dead man, so we're going to leave that job to his buddy. I think it's best we find our way out of here as soon as possible," he said with resolve.

"What do we do with this guy?" Trent asked as he picked up both of the soldiers rifles from off of the ground.

Dr. Bradan reinforced his position, "We need to leave him here to take care of his friend, but he needs to remain tied up to give us a real chance to escape."

"YOU KENT LEEVE ME!" the new prisoner hollered from the ground. "Nut tyed up. Wut if one of 'em cats comes along, wut am I ta do?"

"I'm very sorry, but there's not much we can do except to leave your rifle behind. After you untie yourself, it will be here for you to protect yourself while you care for your friend."

To Trent, Dr. Bradan instructed, "Place the man's rifle against that tree behind you so he has it." He then turned and threw the man's knife deep into the thick brush.

Coughing slightly, the professor added, "I hate to do this to him, but I don't want him free to chase us until we're far from this spot. I don't know about you guys, but I'm ready to go home," the educator said as he scratched his tousled hair, and smiled warmly at the group once again.

Home, Melinda thought; it seemed like months since she sat in the kitchen eating Louisa's brownies. So much had happened. Yet, she had no trouble agreeing to return to the tree portal. With the man tied up in the jungle, they retraced their way back to the original grass field. Along the way, the friends shared their individual details of the story with Dr. Bradan. Shortly, they reached the few inches of rope, still suspended out of the tree, just as it was when they left to find water.

"See, watch my hands," Trent informed the professor.

With his hands held above the end of the rope, Trent grabbed it, and his hands quickly disappeared.

"Even though you can't see my hands, the portal's not working. Something is still wrong, because I can't get through it. Watch what I mean," Trent said as he pushed against the outer edges, but he was still unable to extend the hole.

"Dale, you try next," Dr. Bradan said, urging his son towards the tree.

Scared, Dale hesitated, but with quivering movements, grabbed the rope as his father requested. As expected, his hands disappeared, but he bravely pushed them further inside the small circle.

"I'm trying to pry it open, but it feels…locked."

"Let me try," Dr. Bradan said when he approached the rope.

Even with his adult strength, the portal remained unchanged. Puzzled, his expression changed when he removed his hands. Minutes later, he pointed at Tab to take his turn, which provided the same results.

Leaning with his back to the tree, Dr. Bradan stared vacantly at the lush green field.

"I'm very surprised you kids came through the portal without knowing what you were doing. This means something *is* different. Think hard this time — tell me again how you came through to this place?"

After rehearsing the story once more, he was still unable to see the key to the mystery.

"Something about one of you opened that gate…" was all the muttering

Melinda heard, when the professor paced around the tree, and circled towards her from the opposite side. "...rope keeps it open because our hands disappear, but it remains in a suspended state. Not opening, not closing...," he said, as he rounded the tree again.

"We need more power!" he exclaimed when he returned to stand by the group.

"Power, what do you mean we need more power?" Dale asked in doubt.

"When I came through the Enchanted Rock portal, I used a series of crystals with different harmonic resonances or energy, which pulled me into this dimension. As I think about it, I believe the metal and crystal flecks inside the cavern amplified my crystals. When the Confederate army captured me, they confiscated everything from my pack. Because we fled so fast to escape from them, there was no time to retrieve them. So, since none of you used any crystals to come through, there must be another answer."

While the professor drifted again in his thoughts, they stood quietly waiting for him to speak.

Dr. Bradan suddenly asked, "One more time, which of you put their arms into the tree?"

"Me," Trent said.

Tab raised his hand too.

"What about you Melinda, have you tried?"

"Not yet."

"Ok it's your turn."

Melinda cautiously walked up to the tree, and reached out her hands to place them on the rope. Similar to the guys, her hands speedily disappeared. She turned to say, "What now?" when her shoulder vanished too.

"DON'T MOVE!" Dr. Bradan yelled. "Hold still! Your shoulder just went in. Slowly, try to walk into the tree."

Melinda carefully stepped forward, which caused more of her to disappear.

"It works! Everyone line up. Melinda, stay where you are, and slide over a little to keep the doorway open, until we squeeze past you. Once we get past, you come through into the cave, OK?" he coached.

"Trent, you and Tab go first."

"Alright, here we go," Trent, said as he moved next to Melinda, and grasping Tab's elbow, he stepped past Melinda.

Slowly, Trent inched inside the tree, and then Tab moved past Melinda too.

"It tickles. I feel funny when you go through." Melinda gasped, and then blushed.

Nevertheless, neither heard her comments because they had departed from the strange world.

"Now it's your turn, Dale," his father instructed.

"Gladly, I'm ready to leave this place!"

Similar to the brothers, Dale slipped past her and disappeared through the tree.

"Melinda, since I'm bigger than the boys, I'm not sure if you should go through the tree first, or me. If I go first, there may not be enough room for us both at the same time. However, if you go first, the portal may close, and leave me on this side."

Worried, Melinda challenged him, "If you can't get through, we can't leave you here alone. You try next. I'll step backwards as much as I can to make more room for you to pass by me."

In accord to her statement, Melinda pushed against the invisible wall, sucking in her stomach to hold her breath, she whispered, "Now!"

Dr. Bradan stuck one arm through the portal in front of her face, and next poked his leg through. While his torso was moving though the opening, he came to a stop. Not moving further, he panicked, and sucking in his stomach he exclaimed, "I'm stuck! I can't move!"

Fear escalated in his mind at the thought of never leaving the place, when Dr. Bradan felt a sharp pain in his arm on the other side of the portal.

"Ouch," he winced, which caused Melinda to blink at him with desperation, and then he disappeared.

Suddenly alone in the odd world, and unsure how long to wait before she followed the team, Melinda was startled when only Dr. Bradan's head poked back through the portal to stare at her.

"It worked! Now let's get you out of here," he said, grabbing her hand in his.

"On the count of three," Dr Bradan instructed.

"One — two —," Melinda took a lasting look at the beautiful green field, until she heard, "THREE!"

Instantly, everything went dark. As her eyes adjusted to the dark interior of the cave, Melinda's eyes slowly focused on the twinkling along the walls. Able to see slightly, she worked her way through the gloomy passage to the cave's entrance.

Once she arrived, her excitement bloomed at seeing the growing intensity of the light until she heard, "Humph."

Suddenly, the appearance of a rough-looking man threw her into a panic. He grabbed Melinda's arm in a threatening manner, and pulling her into the blinding sunlight, quickly flattened her face against the rock wall in front of her.

Melinda screamed, but no one came to her rescue.

Chapter Twenty-Five

CAPTURED

Shoved around the corner of the cave entrance, Melinda stumbled and fell from having her arms tied tightly behind her back. Rising to one knee, she was distracted from standing by the sight of a second gruff character guarding her friends at gunpoint. The way the other man waved the pistol about him in the air, she could not decide if he was some kind of an experienced spectacle shooter, or an idiot. Focused on the man's gruff exterior, Melinda's gaze dropped to observe a bound person lying on the ground.

Instantly she recognized him, and raising her voice with concern, asked, "Carl, what happened?"

Hogtied with his legs bent backwards at his knees, and his ankles bound tightly to his wrists behind his back, Carl lay awkwardly on his side. With a defeated countenance, the chauffer replied, "While waiting fer yer return, my good man here knocked me over the head, and when I revived, I discovered I wez tied up as ye see me now. Sorry fer letting ye down," he said in a disappointed tone.

Before Melinda could respond, a slow deep laugh with an evil edge rose mockingly into the air directly behind her. Melinda stood and twisted at the waist to look over her shoulder to identify the source. She immediately noticed contemptuous teardrop-shaped eyes burning into hers. Unlike the other two thugs, something about his expression and the manner of his folded arms drove her to stare at him defiantly.

Maybe in his early 50's, his South American looking weathered features and deep grooved wrinkles suggested his five foot seven inch frame was older; yet, in contrast to his appearance, physically, he carried the years lightly in his movements with the exception of a limp as he approached her.

The eyes! Something about them captivated Melinda from the moment her gaze connected with his. They were eager — no, they peered hungrily at her with a hint of bitterness and cruelty, while dwelling on the details of her face. She oddly knew these were dangerous eyes.

His face was new to Melinda, yet his broad face and wide shallow nose had a bizarre familiarity she could not place. His mischievous smile had a crooked bend to it, which made Melinda feel he was laughing at her without her understanding why.

"You are the striking image of your mother! Did you know that?" he said and then laughed triumphantly while watching the change in her expression.

Melinda noticed the man's deep, rasping voice, with a peculiar accent like an uncharacteristic mix of various tribal dialects and Portuguese, but abnormally thick. It almost sounded ancient, yet she oddly felt his hypnotic words echo within her mind beyond just hearing them, and amazingly, she understood him as clearly as she might with anybody else.

As he stepped closer to Melinda, he held up his hand to point out the difference in height by saying, "You are not yet as tall as she, but you have a remarkable image of her face."

"My mother! How do you know my mother? Do you work for my father?" Melinda angrily spat at the way he spoke about her mother.

"All in good time," he said, as his wicked eyes twinkled with enchantment until he continued, "I have been searching many years for you, so now it is your turn to be patient."

Unexpectedly, the stranger spun around and pointed at the student team when he ordered his two companions, "Tie the rest up quickly. This must finish before we're discovered."

"Finish with what?" Dr. Bradan quizzed the uncommon looking man in a concerned tone, "What are you after here?"

The strange man began to speak, but then changed his mind by saying indifferently, "Nothing from you…nothing from you."

After the dark man was satisfied that everyone's hands were securely joined, he slowly limped back to face Melinda, this time stepping much closer.

"Now *you* on the other hand, *you* have much that I want," he said with a low husky chuckle.

"*Me*, what could I possibly have that you want? I don't even know you, how could you want something from me?" Melinda challenged with a curious tone.

"Don't you remember me?" the older man asked as his voice raised a few degrees.

Melinda glared at him, and while shaking her head, she authoritatively alleged "No..."

"Of course you don't, I should have realized it's been too long since our last encounter, and you were much too small...yet, try to think again!"

Melinda took another long hard look at him, and again she felt there was something memorable about him, but nothing specific entered her mind.

Once again, she shook her head no, and added, "I still don't remember you. Who are you?"

The unusual man stepped nearer to stare into Melinda's questioning eyes, as if he were trying to prompt her memories or hypnotize her into recollection, when Trent broke the tension between her and the captor, "Is this a kidnapping? Are you trying to get money from her parents?"

"SILENCE!" he roared as he spun to scowl at Trent.

For a smaller man, his voice amazingly filled the open area with surprising amplitude.

Without moving in Trent's direction, the captor spit to the ground in the older brother's direction, before he raved angrily, "You have no value to me! Remain quiet, or you will be discarded without delay."

"What do you want from me? Have I done something to you? *Is* this a kidnapping?" Melinda rattled the questions at him like machine gun fire while he continued to face Trent.

"You have something of great value to me, but it is no mere money. With what I want, I shall have the power to obtain riches beyond all of the great kings," he smiled an evil smirk, and then turned his gaze back to stare at Melinda.

"How did you pass through the time rift back into this world when no one else could?" the older man immediately hissed while pointing in the direction of the cave.

"How should I know," Melinda annoyed him with her attitude, "it just happened."

"Nonsense, there is a reason!" he snapped back hastily, and clenched his teeth, illustrating to her he was serious.

Uncertain of how to follow the dialog of the rash natured man and feeling as if she were floundering, Melinda simply asked him, "Why?"

The eccentric man's pacing slowed until he replied cryptically, "I have waited many centuries for this moment, so a few minutes more to explain my purpose will not matter."

Melinda expected to hear his reason, yet after pausing as still as a statue, he surprised her with a sudden burst of enthusiasm that broke through his icy veneer, "Let us see what you can remember," he declared fiercely.

After limping with his back to her, Melinda noticed the uneven wear of the heels of his shoes when the man stopped and sat on a large rock. Without a prelude, he said, "Thousands of years ago, the great God of the dawn, *Itzamna*, changed my people's feudal and warring ways of decimating each other's villages. He welded together the earliest Olmec tribes, and transformed our turmoil by refining it through instructing my people to grow cacao, becoming skilled as merchants, and afterwards training them in the secret power of calendars. These were potent secrets to learn, and they fueled our growth until we spread across the land.

"His judgments brought harmony to my people by separating the ruling government from the widespread high priest's duty to preserve the greatest of our secrets from misuse. These highest priests, you would call Governors in your language, were keepers of the most significant secrets. They counseled our elected leaders who guided my people to enormous success, until they eliminated all famine, war, iniquity, and poverty.

"In time the Olmec became as numerous as the sands of the seas, and built great cities across what you call Central America to display my people's impressive achievements, long before the Mayans arrived. Vast wealth and prolonged peace should have been enough; however, the privileged leaders gained more than the rest of the people and were soon lifted up the most in their pride and narcissism. Self-interest and indulgence shifted the loyalties of these nobles from fulfilling their elected positions of protecting all of the peoples' welfare to sustaining their personal greed. In time, two distinct classes of Olmec emerged; those who sought domination of the land, and those fighting to defend the peoples' rights.

"Unable to persuade our influential Governors to align and support their greedy plans of Olmec dominance, the elected nobles devised secret and sinister alliances with criminals, to swindle the Governors' mystical powers from them and keep it for themselves. Convinced the richest were the rightful rulers over time and space, their mounting lust for authority ensnared their misguided minds. Overzealous to rule the kingdom, when their frauds failed, they raised armies to overtake the land, and then city marched against city.

"Their mad lust for power drove them to annihilate cities, and their victory rapidly perverted into sacrificing their opposing city brothers, to illustrate their dominant control of the people. Sadly, the misconception of this evil influenced later Mayans and Incans long after my people vanished," he said.

"What secret power are you talking about? Nothing has been established to indicate what you describe as a mythical secret or other source of power in Mesoamerica," Dr. Bradan stated with knowledgeable authority.

"Wait a minute, who were the Olmec people?" Trent asked the malicious man.

Annoyed by Trent again, the older man regained his feet and refused to answer the question.

Dr. Bradan responded, "Remember Trent, that many leading archeological experts describe the Olmec to be the great forefathers of the pre-Mayan civilization, while others believe they were the earliest Mayans. Either way, they are fully recognized as Mesoamerica's foundational influence to all later empires, including the later Mayans, Toltec's, Aztecs, and ..."

"Silence!" the spiteful man cut off the professor in mid-sentence.

Glaring and exasperated at Dr. Bradan, their captor continued his discourse by asking the educator, "Long before my people, the Earth has shifted from the endless movements of...what do you call the giant pieces of land?"

Dr. Bradan replied cautiously, "Do you mean the continents?"

"No and yes," the older man said irritated, "much bigger."

"Ah, you're referring to the Tectonics Plates?" Dr. Bradan offered.

"Yes, yes, as they move, the Earth's energy also moves from the top of the world to the bottom of the world, which causes the opening of doorways..."

"What do you mean when you say move down?" Dr. Bradan interrupted the man.

"How do you say in your language...when the compass points north, over a great period of time it then points south?"

"Do you mean when magnetic north does a polar reversal?

The aged man paused to digest the meaning of the words and stated, "Yes!"

"Dad, we read the notes in your office. Isn't the North Pole falling, and is really somewhere in Canada right now, and moving south on its way to flip with the polar South Pole?"

"That's right Dale!" Dr. Bradan agreed, pleased his son grasped the details of his work. "Evidence proves that the world's polarity is currently shifting south — just as it has done many times before."

No longer facing his son, Dr. Bradan returned his attention back to their captor, and stated, "Explain how your secret power is connected with polarity, or for that matter, Tectonic Plates?"

"I have read this in your world's books. First tell me what happens in the ocean bottom when the tectonic land moves!" he demanded to re-address the topic.

"If you're referring to events like the Mid-Atlantic ridge, it is created when the Earth's magnetized magma escapes up through cracks in the ocean floor, and then forms new earth after it hardens from contact with the ocean's freezing water currents."

"Yes, yes, but tell me what metal it is!"

Dr. Bradan hesitated, "I'm not sure I'm following you, are you asking me if magma is made of mostly nickel and iron?"

"Yes!" the crooked man said gleefully. "Keep going!"

Dr. Bradan relented to the man, and added, "As far as I understand how the overall process works, when the blistering hot magma meets with the freezing ocean currents, the two react and the magma or lava solidifies to become new land within the ocean's floor. With limited space, the process of creating newly formed earth pushes against the old earth, and spreads the sea floor wider, which causes a domino effect by pushing the giant tectonic plates against and away from each other very slowly over millions and millions of year...."

Dale cut him off, "Oh yeah, that makes sense, because when you look at a map of the world, the continents look like giant jigsaw puzzle pieces that could fit together."

"Again that's right," Dr. Bradan, said pleased with Dale's appraisal, "North America, South America, Africa, Europe, and Asia are all being pushed and tugged in multiple directions at the same time, from the magma filling cracks in the ocean's flooring. Remember, magma is mostly liquid metal and rock, so it can be magnetized just like a magnet. Sometimes it's magnetized with a positive charge; and sometimes it can be negatively charged..."

Dr. Bradan's face lit up and exclaimed, "That's it! I understand now!"

"WHAT?" yelled Dale caught up in the excitement.

Eagerly, Dr. Bradan cascaded his formed conclusion to their un-welcomed host, "So as the tectonic plates are shifted in their movements, for lack of better clarification, the positive and negative sections of the polarized magma are laid out in alternating strips across the Earth. This would be analogous to the wooden beams of a gigantic railroad track, or like an enormous barcode-type pattern. During a polar reversal, when the Earth's magnetic field reverses across the charged sections, the union of the two amplifies the positive or negative charges."

Still animated, the professor paused to digest and organize his new theory thoughts, until he asked, "But what precisely happens at these special times?"

Their captor's grin quickly evolved into a cackle at the euphoric sight of the professor, and validated him, "You may yet understand."

"Through the eras of time, when the position of the ancient tectonic plates moved across the Earth, they generated openings leading into other dimensions, capable of causing an overlap in space within different times. *Itzamna*, our great living God, revealed and taught my ancestors how to use positively charged crystals and ironstones to open these travel portals as you call them. Years later, he trained our Governors to map them to past and future calendar dates and star movements. Negatively charged crystals and ironstone artifacts could open and control time within the multiple overlapping dimensions."

"So you used ancient calendars to calculate where a dimension portal opening would or did exist? I still don't understand what value this brought the Olmec?" Dr. Bradan questioned the strange man.

He replied, "At first our Governors avoided earlier famines by traveling back in time to pre-warn the Olmec people to store great reservoirs of food. Later as the Governor's understanding of the power grew, they re-routed streams and waterfalls through time in order to prevent the loss of large agriculture crops. Where dry earth remained in this world, freshwater lakes and streams covered its exact location in the overlapping dimension. If you traveled far enough forward or backwards in time, because of the constant movements of the tectonic plates you would discover the existence of suitable irrigation water. This gave the Governors of my people a great advantage over their environment. They used the portal's power to irrigate inland arid crops, using this knowledge of past or future water sources."

Fascinated and almost pleased with himself at his comprehension, Dr. Bradan validated the theory, "So in summary, what you're telling us is there are multiple dimensions which overlap in both time and space on Earth, and the overlap can be accessed from our world and controlled. As the polar reversals combine with the tectonic plate movements, mutually, they affect the varying strengths in the electromagnetic fields. The changeable strengths open different types of windows, worm holes, portals, or whatever you want to call them, which can be mapped to star movements and tracked as calendar events."

Without speaking to the professor, the dangerous man's only reply was with a distasteful shrug of his shoulders.

"How can anyone harness those types of forces?" Dr. Bradan asked him in awe.

Annoyed by the questioning tone of the educator, he said, "Come now Doctor, how did you pass through the portal within this small cave, and reach your destination within another time?"

Dr. Bradan answered defensively, "I understand the importance of needing to use a positive or negatively charged energy frequency to pass beyond the veil of this world into another; what I can't discern is the right amounts of either which are needed at the right time. Alternatively, how to open a porthole great enough to move millions of gallons of irrigation water to save lives, as you just described. I don't have any idea which of my crystals pulled me through the curtain of time."

"That is the marvelous secret guarded by the Governors!" he answered as his facial features darkened with anger and self-righteousness. With a quick snap of his wrists, the man held up his two index fingers shoulder-width apart, and explained to Dr. Bradan, "The fusion of certain types of negative crystals together with positively charged metal pieces can fashion both energies simultaneously together as one."

With a pause to emphasize the importance, the man slowly drew his index fingers together and added, "Which will open both space and time portals on command, without the need to wait for specific calendar dates in the right location. However, that tightly guarded secret was only passed from within each generation of the divine Governors from father to son, securing their reign of influence over the administering elected officials."

At this point, Dr. Bradan was intensely interested in the details, and forgetting he was still the man's prisoner, asked, "If what you say can be supported with evidence, it would provide answers to many of Earth's mysteries. But how do you know this information?"

He replied in a snobbish tone, "Your world has great academic knowledge, far more than my people, but very little understanding. The evidence has forever been in front of your experts, and yet they remain blind."

"Evidence — what evidence?" Dr. Bradan challenged the man.

"What you call Egypt's Great Sphinx, was their main portal entrance into the dimensions. The country known today as England created Stonehenge for their gateway through time. Do you not clearly see the similarities between the pyramids of my lands and those of Egypt?" the arrogant man questioned. "How do I know this information? Where did I learn these details? You are not listening to me; these great ancient nations used the dimensions to gain power through trade. The portals connection to man has existed throughout the ages."

With a sense of pride, and feeling overconfident, Dr. Bradan attacked the premise, and shot out, "If the power you speak of is so great, why did your people disappear?"

Frustrated, the self-indulgent man reminded him, "As I have already said, my people the Olmec were once a peaceful people, who were enslaved by their own prominence and greed. Unsatisfied and desiring more, our rulers became suspicious and paranoid causing them to create secret pacts, which eventually overthrew many of the Governors in our cities."

Perceiving the visible uncertainty in the educator's eyes, the angered captor sarcastically joked, "Your people and time astonish even me. Unless you watch something on television, it becomes too complex for you to grasp. So be it with that weakness…watch and learn!"

As the dark lines in the man's face deepened, he raised his arms above his head and suddenly waved them in a serpentine rhythm. Melinda started to think their keeper had lost his marbles when he suddenly yelled in an ancient and foreign language, "LIEPATON SIDOM DARAUMNN!"

When he stopped his arm writhing and lowered his hands together in front of his chest, a small shimmer of light grew between his palms and slowly filled the space directly in front of him as he spread his hands apart.

Astonished at the incredible sight, Melinda unconsciously leaned away from the mysterious glow, as if it were deadly radiation. Intensely, she watched the orb of light rapidly grow in volume. Pulsating colors formed multiple shapes within a glowing cloud. As the man spoke normally to them, each word amazingly materialized as ghostly three-dimensional holographic images in front of her eyes. Flabbergasted by the hovering images, Melinda peered at them without fear.

"In Egypt, many tried to also overthrow the rulers, yet their priests were wiser than my people, and prohibited the devastation of their culture. In fear of the portal's misuse, the priests buried the powerful Sphinx. Once the main portal was sealed, all remaining charged metals and crystals were gathered and sealed inside the crypts of their rulers, which they considered impregnable.

"Yet, similar to my people, influential Egyptians who feared the loss of this power used backhanded ways to retain the knowledge for themselves. In their deception, those in high power created mummification as a religious disguise to shield their activities from the people, by burying slaves in their place to lie within their sarcophagus, inside the fortified tombs.

"Once they were assumed dead and buried, they traveled back in time along with their valuable possessions through the portals, to bestow their vast knowledge and wealth to younger versions of themselves. Each recycled lifetime began with greater treasures and understanding than the previously lived life.

"Able to live over and over without unveiling their rituals, and capitalizing on future facts presented to them by their older selves, they grew in wealth and splendor until they became the great High Priests and Pharaohs. Eventually, under their rule, mummification cascaded as the applied and accepted religion where the truth became lost as legend. However, because they hid a great quantity of charged power sources in burial chambers, the lower Egyptian lords and priests caused an energy tear in reality, which created domino style time fractures within the other dimension."

Melinda jumped in her shoes when the depraved man abruptly snapped his fingers loudly and cried out, "HEPOPUMTA!" instantly causing the mesmerizing vision to pop like a soapy bubble in the sunlight.

Caught off-guard by what each had witnessed, Melinda and her friends gawked with looks of pure astonishment at each other. It took several seconds for reality to replace the bewilderment in their combined expressions. Still looking at the mysterious captor, Dr. Bradan quizzed the man with puzzled hesitation, "Wait, wait. If Governors could travel back through time to change history or prevent wars, why did they allow the demise of your people?"

As his eyes squinted at the professor, he nodded his agreement to the question and appeared to want to share something urgent, but instead added, "Time resembles rings similar to those found inside a tree. Each year fits precisely between other numbered rings. The correct negative charge can open a predictable year inside of a time dimension. Yet after the time disruption tear, moments in time had become unbalanced. It was as if a time quake split the tree in half from top to bottom, and left all years open to merge inside the dimension. The Governors used various energy entrances to enter a dimension inside the split-open tree, but once inside, they could not progress as before, and now circled inside fixed time loops.

"Unlike the ancient Egyptians who sealed their secret knowledge of time dimensions and control from their public, foolish Romans soldiers later burned much of the details kept inside the great library of Alexandria. In my time, similar upheavals forced many Olmec to flee into alternate states to escape their own destruction, and were unable to return, as they lacked many of the powerful time traveling tools. In later years, without the previous infrastructure to support our cities, our way of life dwindled into nothing."

"Even if only part of the story is true, it explains a great deal," said Dr. Bradan. Carried away in his thoughts, Dr. Bradan asked, "But what does it have to do with us? This is just a group of students. If you know so much, why do you need us?"

Amused by the professor's growing insight, the mystic man replied, "Many powerful Egyptian, and Mesoamerican artifacts were stolen by grave robbers, or were later discovered by archeologists, and now reside in museum displays around the world. These fantastic powers have collected through the years, and while housed together, have multiplied their massed frequency, thus thinning the shroud between this world and other time dimensions. Soon the increasing energy disruptions will flood this world like a gigantic broken dam of water."

"What do you mean? I've never heard of anything happening like that," Melinda contradicted him.

"You have not, say you! You have not wondered at the paranormal events?" he replied.

"What paranormal events?" she asked mockingly.

"How do you describe ghost sightings?" he queried in a smug manner to Melinda.

Melinda looked at him in disbelief after hearing the question, but said nothing, believing he was a serious mental case.

He then continued, "Partial thinning of the veil reveals other times and dimensions. What your time describes as a haunted site is merely a thinning of the veil, revealing the so-called ghost, which lives during its normal time and location. A full breach between worlds can only occur with the correct magnetic source."

"Wow…so now we know that ghosts are only people living in another time, and not weird dead people trying to scare us all the time," Dale blissfully whispered to his father.

Upon hearing Dale's comments, Dr. Bradan asked their captor, "I'm not sure I'm following you exactly; are there other types of examples?"

"What of the well-known Bermuda Triangle or of Japan's Dragon Triangle?" the spiritualist replied. "Is there not almost a direct strip of travel between each place on either side of the world? These two places on Earth similarly disrupt compass readings. Is this only a coincidence? Or, could giant amounts of highly charged metals, perhaps remnant pieces from the asteroid that destroyed the dinosaurs, remain in those waters? Is it possible the direction of the impact created the straight line between both mysterious triangles, which is perhaps capable of opening larger pockets of time and space, or is it something else causing hundreds of ships and airplanes to disappear?"

Dr. Bradan agreed thoughtfully, "I see your point; you are correct — there seems to be a strange connection between those two locations, and as you said, both have similar longitude placement, and align on almost a direct 35-degree latitude line of travel along the Tropic of Cancer. Although there are far more disappearances in the Dragon's Triangle than in the Bermuda Triangle, no one really knows why radio reports before the disappearance from either location claim to see strange lights and portal-type openings in the cloudy skies. There seems to be unknown forces at work in the triangles."

With a smirk, the increasingly sinister man continued, "UFOs are simply future technology viewed through time from the harness of their great energy. Do you not wonder why all of the recorded evidence of them is blurry?"

Dr. Bradan nodded his head in agreement, but also shrugged his shoulders at the mystery when the shorter man touched his index finger to his eye, and said, "Eyes see the UFO and the ghost sightings, but the camera captures their images only through the shimmering veil."

Dr. Bradan startled the man, "AHH, which explains…"

"ENOUGH OF THIS!" the older man shouted domineeringly. "I've wasted too much time! Why unlock your unknowing minds! You will never live to use this information."

"Wait, one more question," Dr. Bradan asked on purpose. "If it doesn't matter, at least tell me how this all began? I have spent my professional career researching for this truth, and you provided so many answers in only a little time," the professor said, hoping to feed the man's ego and buy more time to loosen his ropes without notice. "Only you know of such things. Surely you wish to speak of them again, even with someone who knows as little as I know."

"NO MORE!" the vile man shouted, causing the rocks around the area to vibrate. When the echo of his voice quieted, he concluded, "I tire from your prying questions!"

Filled with resentment, the loathsome captor pointed a short dull finger at Melinda as his quivering voice and face became more menacing, "I have wasted more than two thousand years traveling into this dreadful future, chasing you!"

Chapter Twenty-Six

BAD TO WORSE

With the exception of Melinda and the older man, everyone else was jolted speechless as if feeling an electric shock at hearing these words.

"How ridiculous," Melinda scolded him, "that's a lie and you know it! I've never seen you before in my life, so how could *you* be chasing me? My parents adopted me when I was little. Why are you trying to trick us?"

The apathetic leader remained unfazed by her comments. In fact, he smiled a devious smile. The ends of his puffy lips curled, which suggested he was ready to attack for the pleasure.

"Adopted you say...not sure of your true origins? Well now, that presents something of a hole in your story. Let us see what you can remember. As I recall...you would have been about three — no, perhaps four years old when I last saw you together with your mother. Old enough I believe to remember certain details," he said coyly. "One final tale for you today...think carefully about what I say because if you are right, then I have made a mistake, however..."

With another wave of his arms high over his head, he muttered strange words again. The earlier shimmer returned and hovered in place between his hands, and as he spoke, his words became visions they observed.

"A young Olmec, quite wise for his age, gained the voice of the people, and rapidly rose up through the political ranks of city Elders, to become the great city's Magistrate. Second only to the Chief Magistrate in the administration of the government, where our municipal laws demanded the Magistrate replace the Chief Magistrate when he died, or he could no longer manage the people's affairs. As to be expected, the young man had political opponents. One in particular, a rival, persuaded the region's Sovereign Governor to change the rightful law of ascension through an influential vote, to have him elevated above the young ambitious Magistrate to sit on the Chief Magistrate's throne.

"Unable to legally reclaim that which was rightfully his, the young Magistrate plotted his deadly revenge. Hate, greed, and selfish aspiration drove him relentlessly. He dedicated the rest of his life to becoming a terrible Shaman with the power to cast wicked spells. By learning dark and mystical magic from a powerful jungle wizard, he was capable of shape shifting into various creatures. Motivated by vengeance, the Shaman planned to become the Chief Magistrate by kidnapping the Sovereign Governor's wife. He would then return her to the Sovereign Governor after he repealed the law that prevented the Shaman from obtaining the Chief Magistrate's throne. In addition, the Shaman intended to kill the Sovereign Governor's young daughter as revenge for her father's meddling in his political affairs. One chosen night, the Shaman, with four of his supporters, carried forth their preparations while the Sovereign Governor traveled away from the city."

As the image continued to hover, the picture froze in place as he paced back and forth with quivering excitement until he continued, "Bribing the Governor's fortress guards, they crept inside during the black of night. Somehow, the Shaman's plan was exposed too early, and the Governess and her daughter were already escaping. Without their capture, the sorcerer's plans would fail. Most importantly, he would not obtain the two time pendants they wore to traverse between times, and therefore wouldn't be able to change the past voting results if the Governor failed to alter the new law.

"The Governess and her daughter were protected by extremely powerful Guardians. After having barely overcome a male Guardian at the great fortress, the Shaman and his final colossal follower pursued the royal pair deep into a tunnel only to discover a female Guardian..."

"I hope the other Guardian gave them plenty of trouble!" Dale interrupted the edgy leader, recovering some of his confidence.

Exasperated by the disruption that caused the images to disappear, the loathsome man displayed a savage grimace and backhanded Dale across the face, throwing him onto the ground. He snarled like a hissing cat at the now-frightened boy and cried out, "As if ferocious four-inch fangs and deep penetrating talons weren't enough," he stopped in mid-sentence, and wavered in his speech, as if personally remembering the grim episode.

Blood oozed from Dale's split lip as he cowered on his back. Dr. Bradan viewed the event and vividly displayed his disgust at the calloused man.

After a short pause, a smirk of intense satisfaction grew on the wicked man's face as he completely ignored Dale. With a drop in the level of his voice, he launched into the end of his story to Melinda, "Losing the battle to the Guardian, all hope was lost until the unexpected emergence of a time portal. The Shaman, Governor's wife, and her daughter fell through time during the battle."

Melinda expected there to be more, however, as the contemptible man studied her features, he also noticed the team's concentration to absorb his words. After pausing further to create additional tension, and revel in his long awaited success, he rose his shaking hands skyward and screamed, "*I* AM THE SHAMAN!" with his nostrils flaring in an angry and threatening manner, "AND *YOU* ARE THAT DAUGHTER!"

The silence felt tangible! Skeptical of the man's abrupt and unexpected announcement, but quickly losing her conviction, Melinda's mind raced with the thoughts, *"Could this be true? How is it possible?"*

Mostly in denial, Melinda clenched her eyes together tightly to block her view of the Shaman, and desperately tried to remember some hint or clue within the mixture of various mental pictures from her young past. Deep in the recesses of her recollection, she remembered having feared monsters creeping around in the dark hallways while at the orphanage, until the fear changed into horrid nightmares. Unable to speak or understand English at that time, the friendly staff could not easily console her fears without knowing the problem. Adopted by her parents, she later rewrote over her young memories.

Melinda was surprised that in the past few weeks her childhood nightmares of long forgotten shadows and fighting had returned twice, late at night since attending the Museum's program. Thoughts ricocheted around in her brain as she dug deeper to ask herself, *"What was the blue light? Did I fall to this time — did my mother fall through the portal?"* In her nightmare, a woman's outstretched arms reached towards her as she wondered, *"Was that my real mother?"*

When an incredulous look formed on Melinda's face, her eyes snapped open to stare directly into his eyes. They reminded her of the former monsters from her childhood past. Once again, she closed her eyes and visualized the haunting eyes she remembered within her mind, only this time, the outlines of a face appeared around them.

Slowly Melinda opened her eyes, yet the dream remained. Before her was the same nightmare from her childhood. The hair, styled differently and graying, and the face older with age, yet the numbing actuality of his shocking claim assailed her.

"It's true," she marveled, as she felt her hair standing on end. Wilting like a hanging leaf on a dehydrated tree, she whispered again, "It's true! I thought you were just a dream, but…you're real!"

The Shaman was elated, and roared like an untamed man.

"WE'RE THE LAST OF OUR TIME!" he shouted at her. Smiling again, his tone softened when he confided, "I'm the only living person in the entire world who knows your true name."

Melinda's blurry eyes looked at him with genuine interest at his latest comment.

"Your name is Maynaya! Moreover, *you* are the daughter of the Sovereign Governor, the Chief Time Keeper of our most powerful pendants. Yes, I knew your family!"

Melinda hesitated to believe him, and then urgently asked the Shaman, "What was my mother like?"

He let the question hang almost visibly in the air between them, wanting her to taste the emotional words to allure her to his wrongful cause.

"Maynaya, if you would like, together we can find her! She is alive in the other dimension! Join me, and we'll find her. Give me the pendant you carried as a small child, and with it, we can find her swiftly."

Unsure what to do, Melinda stared hard into his evil eyes. She knew this strange man could not be trusted, yet she desperately wished to learn more from him, and possibly find her birth mother. Torn with indecision, the longer she tried to decide on the right thing to do; new questions raced though her mind, which only he could answer. Her internal debate seemed to linger like hours to her, but only seconds had actually passed from his request.

With her glances passing between her new student friends, and back to him, she asked the Shaman, "How can you know my mother is alive, or even if she is still in the dimension?"

For a small second, the Shaman smiled with a strange pride as he shook his head at her in approval, before he allowed himself to answer, "One must enter into the other dimension from night or from darkness on this side. For this reason, ancient Egyptians only buried their dead late at night, and in very dark tombs while performing the crossover ceremonies to pass their nobility into the alternate dimensions. When coming into this world from the other side, one must step from daylight and into daylight, unless you possess the most powerful type of pendants to traverse freely anywhere or anytime, which you do.

"You and I passed into a daylight portal, while your mother fell into a night time portal. I can't guarantee she still lives but I will promise to help you search for her. You do want to meet her don't you?"

About to answer, and wondering if she would be a fool for doing so, chaos erupted to shatter the moment.

Chapter Twenty-Seven

HAZARDOUS HIEROGLYPHICS

The Shaman's thug, still guarding Carl and the team with his revolver, suddenly levitated off his feet. Flying backwards through the air he landed unconscious onto the ground amidst a cloud of dust. Startled, and then astounded by what she witnessed, Melinda gaped wide-eyed with new hope.

Security Chief Al, with nearly the strength of a full-grown bull, loomed gigantically where the mugger had recently stood. Unbeknownst to those present, he had used the outcrop of the cave to sneak up and flatten the guard with a single punch.

Dressed in faded blue jeans and a tight fitting long sleeve shirt, Al swiftly spun, and leapt almost eight feet from his standing position to grapple with the second thug. Al easily hoisted the startled ruffian high into the air above his own head and launched the startled man as easily as a javelin. The hired assailant hit the hard earth and rolled to a stop. Al knocked both henchmen insensible in a matter of seconds.

"YEAH!" rang from the student group.

Overlapping questions blitzed at Al from the team, "When did you get here? How did you find us? Who's with you?'

When the sound of the questions retreated, Al pointed first at Carl, and then at the Shaman during his answer, "It's because of them I'm here! After running through a role call at the Museum several days after the blowgun incident, we discovered that Dr. Bradan, Trent, Tab, and you were missing from the Museum," he nodded to each as he spoke their names, Melinda being last.

"No one knew where to find you guys until Leslie came clean with me about your helping Dale to find his dad. When I was unable to locate Dale either, Brock informed us he had seen Dale enter a limousine. We ran the license plates, and discovered the car belonged to Global Star Aviation — assigned to Carl.

"I called and left a message for Carl on his car phone, which was closely followed by someone demanding to see Melinda and claiming to be her uncle, so the front desk paged me, and I arrived to handle the situation. It turns out that this joker," Al pointed at the Shaman, "told me he had seen Melinda's interview on the news about the blowgun incident with Matt, and how he was deeply concerned for her safety. During our conversation, Carl returned my earlier call, and the switchboard patched him directly to me at the front desk. We agreed during our phone call, that I would drive up here to Enchanted Rock to help him find and return you kids back to the Museum.

"With Mr. Joker standing in close proximity, he overheard the entire conversation. I asked him to wait a few minutes for me until I could update Brock to cover for me. When I returned to the main hall, our new friend here was gone. After gathering my gear, by the time I reached the security van, I discovered that both front tires had been cut with a knife."

Al glared at the Shaman and added, "No doubt you were the culprit!"

Dr. Bradan asked, "But how did you know *exactly* where to look for us? Enchanted Rock is so vast, and this place is off the normal path...we could have been anywhere."

"Carl planned ahead and taped a note inside the limousine's windshield that explained the way. When I first reached the turnoff, I missed it and searched up around the summit. On my way down, I took a moment to view the area, and I almost passed it again, but then I noticed the fresh footprints leading this way. After following the trail for awhile, it was clear it was the right way."

As if from some internal inferno boiling deep inside the Shaman, he began to pace back and forth, his momentum increasing, until he cleared his throat to gain their attention to say, "Sorry to disturb this happy reunion, but Melinda was about to join me in finding her mother...am I right Melinda?"

Before she answered, Trent yelled a caution, "MELINDA! Don't go along with him — he's lying!"

Instantly, the Shaman's dilated eyes burned red with hate and he screamed, "BOY, I WARNED YOU NOT TO INTERFERE. NOW YOU WILL DIE AN AGONIZING DEATH!"

Shocked and then infuriated by the Shaman's unexpected and seemingly irrational comments, Al marched directly towards the much smaller man to intercept his path towards Trent, pulling out his handcuffs.

With flickering eyes darting between Trent and Al's hulking figure closing fast upon him, the Shaman muttered something under his breath, and then yelled, "WAIT MELINDA — you must know more!"

Al hesitated with momentary indecision while he cast a quick glance at Melinda's expression. The Shaman pounced on the awkward moment between them, and produced a small glass vial from his pocket.

He held it up into the air for all to see, as a sinister expression crossed his face when he said, "This *too* is part of your story Melinda." He stepped back a few paces, putting his back against the rock wall and then grunted loudly, "Watch!"

Comparable to a bottle of metallic gray fingernail polish, he unscrewed the black lid, which displayed a small applicator brush. On the rock behind him, the Shaman outlined a six-inch stick figure with the silvery liquid and chanted an unfamiliar incantation. The shiny lines immediately pulsed into a brilliant neon orange, and then transitioned into a shimmering green; all the while emitting smoldering scarlet sparks. Blue-black smoke billowed from within the drawing and expanded in an upward spiral, where it partially hid the vicious expression on the Shaman's face.

He bellowed a sinister laugh from behind the supernatural smoke, and then mocked them with cruel mirth, "I promised this was part of your story...now meet the *end* of your story!"

Melinda noticed that miniature life motions quivered within the drawing, as the initial distinct outlines faded. The drawn figure resembled a primordial monster that grew taller and more appalling with each breath of its new life. In a matter of seconds, the disturbed hieroglyph had reached a height of three feet. The two-dimensional illustration then pushed out one of its eerie arms to grasp the top of its head. Next, it peeled itself from the rock's face, brought to life by a perverted and long-forgotten dark magic.

Before Melinda's eyes, the unsightly gray-green figure leaped from the rock face onto the ground, and raised its ugly head skyward, growing rapidly all the while. Soon, at nearly six feet tall, five-inch spikes grew to crown its scalp between oversized bat-like ears that rose above its nasty gargoyle-shaped face. Throughout the adaptation, three slanted purplish-blue colored eyes glared wickedly at the group. Two horizontal eyes stared up and down, while a third vertical eye, located above the other two, panned from right to left.

Two enormous pairs of black vampire-type fangs pointed down from double upper rows of greenish gums when the creature flicked its tongue, tasting the air for their scent. However, nothing prepared them for the sight of its arms. Both sinuous arms produced a pair of forearms, jutting out from both of the misshapen elbows. All four hands dangled long ice pick-shaped fingers. Chunky bloated skin reflected a rubber type shine across the entire body. Lean powerful legs bent at a sickening angle. Small snakes and venomous vipers replaced normal toenails, hissing and darting furiously.

Melinda was amazed at the repugnant sight and Al, standing closest to the expanding beast, watched it grow taller with each passing moment. An assortment of shrunken human and animal heads formed a deadly necklace, each snapping hungrily towards Al with sharp teeth.

Gruesome at full height, it stood inches taller than Al, yet remained significantly thinner compared to the huge bodybuilder. With an icy feeling flowing through his veins, Al realized he was staring into the face of peril, and he was the only person currently not a prisoner of the Shaman. The thought produced a cold sweat on the back of his broad neck, knowing he alone must defeat the incredible monster and save the others.

Swiftly, Al snapped out his 45 semi-automatic and fired four rapid bullets into the sneering creature's ashen chest. Reeling from the forceful impacts of the gunshots, the beast glared at the new bullet holes, now oozing deep indigo-black streams of blood, and then back at Al. It clenched its evil teeth and screeched inhumanly, while it contracted steely muscles within its chest and ribs, slowly squeezing the lead slugs outward from its rubbery skin.

Wordlessly, Melinda watched the wounds miraculously close. In awe at the mysterious experience, Al starred down at the four mushroom-shaped bullets when the creature sprang at him. The appalling monstrosity forcefully slammed Al in his chest, using its four malformed open hands in chorus, which knocked the breath from the big man in one sudden explosion. Launched backwards nearly twenty feet, Al's muscular 320 pounds crashed heavily onto the rocky ground. He shook his head to stop the piercing ringing. Meanwhile, grasshopper style, the breathing nightmare sprung on its hinged legs, landing next to him.

From behind, Dr. Bradan yelled, "Al, Watch out!"

Too late for Al to move away, Melinda watched in horror as the fiend stretched its sinewy arms to grasp him. The top right upper hand of dagger-like fingers reached under and gripped Al by his belt, while the lower hand of the same arm grasped him by one of his legs. Without effort, the monstrosity lifted Al far above the ground with incredible power. As the goblin-faced beast dangled the Security Chief upside down, it pounded Al's torso with alternating left fists, brutally shaking his brawny body.

After flinging Al headlong to the ground like a useless bag-of-trash, the walking death stalked towards Melinda, who shook visibly at the coming hideous sight. When it stomped near her, the ancient threat grasped both of Melinda's arms in its right hands directly below the shoulder. She cowered away with repulsion from the icy wet sensation gripping her skin, which caused her flesh to crawl like writhing worms.

Melinda screamed in fear, "NO — LET ME GO!" Quickly, the lower left hand darted to strangle her throat.

Choked, Melinda instantly stopped breathing within the tight python-style clench. While she sagged in the harsh grip compressing her neck, the top left hand tapped a pointed finger against the skin on her forehead. Both Trent and Dr. Bradan strained hardily against their ropes to aid her, but were both unable. Tab miraculously freed his hands, only a moment before the horrendous beast was about to drive the single revolting dagger-like finger through Melinda's skull.

Tab rushed to the side of the beast with a fistful of dirt, crying loudly with his off-tone voice, "Ahhhhhh!"

The murdering atrocity spied Tab's rapid movements when its ghastly center eye rolled left. At the same time, the deaf teen pitched his handful of gritty sand into the beast's hideous face. The third eye snapped shut, to avoid the clever injury, while the remaining two open eyes independently glared wide open at Melinda. Once the creature's open eyes filled with the stinging grit, it seemed temporarily blinded. With blinking eyes, it exhaled a vile hiss and released Melinda's neck from its rigid grip.

The hellish beast reopened the third unaffected eye, which quickly targeted Tab. With both of its creepy right hands, the evil-conjured menace promptly brushed sand from its blinded eyes, while the lower left hand darted out and snatched Tab. The younger brother struggled to regain his freedom as the creature curled its upper second left hand into a dreadful fist, and then unfolded a rigid index finger like a switchblade.

Tab pulled and jerked his arm fiercely from the beast, but could not free himself from the monster's iron grip. When the brute pulled back a long deadly finger, the teen realized it intended to kill him. Attuned to using his tactile senses and due to his compensated visual perception from being deaf, Tab fastened his eyes closed to avoid the coming shock before the stiletto finger point would blast through his face. He waited for the belated imminent thrust, and unable to hear the reason of the delay, Tab cracked open his eyes to peek at his death.

Upon recovering from the grisly beating, Al stood dazed and shaken to catch the left elbow of the monster with one of his immense hands. In tandem, he stooped to grasp the back of the fiend's knee and lifted it overhead like an Olympic power lifter. Still in the creature's tightening grasp, Tab closed his eyes again from the nausea rising from within his stomach.

Stunned from Al's sudden comeback, the creature's face cringed from the disadvantage of kicking its feet at only empty air. Its clenched fingers released Tab to focus its retaliation at Al.

Like a giant pro-wrestler dropping down onto one knee, Al forcefully slammed the evil creature's backbone onto the top of his other bent knee. A nerve-shattering crack emanated from deep within the foul body. Before Al moved, a terrifying screech issued from the monster.

After rolling the rubbery body from his knee and onto the ground, Al stood; fully expecting it to remain immobile from a fractured backbone. However, the furious fiend startled him by lifting itself up from the ground with an ugly twist of its frame. Hurt and angry, it rushed at him, bent over crab-like.

The vampire looking creature overcame its disadvantage by placing both of its left hands onto the ground in front of its feet, and supported its weakened condition with the stability of seemingly four legs. Twisted into the perverted position, the lowest of the withered heads on its awful necklace scraped along the ground, snapping their teeth at any rocks or branches within their reach.

Al positioned one enormous hand on the back of the brute's neck, and applying all of his weight and strength, drove it face-first into the dirt. As the curved deformity pushed up from off of the ground, both of its free right hands snatched at Al, hoping to clutch his calves. The Security Chief expected such a reaction, and leaped over them to move quickly behind its bent form to wrap his gargantuan arms around the beast's chest, pinning both sets of deformed elbows against the monster's gray-green sides.

With a new planned attack, the evil imp tried to impale the Herculean man once more by throwing his crown of deadly spikes backwards. In time, Al ducked underneath the beast's abysmal-looking shoulders to avoid the stabbing prongs. With a terrible shriek of fury, it hung its feet hoping to envenom Al's legs with the long serpentine toes. Al countered the lethal feet by leaning slightly backward at his waist, causing the freakish legs to push away from his.

The pinning force Al applied to the creature's arms and shoulders prevented the creature's cannibalistic heads from swinging around as dangerous chewing weapons. Without the benefit of a fully functioning backbone or grounded feet, the creature's only recourse was to expand its bizarre arms outward in an effort to rupture the locking arm clamp by Al.

Stronger than hardened steel, the semi-human arms pressed outward. Nevertheless, in savage opposition, Al crushed inward with all of his controlling might. Usual smooth rolling titanic muscles flexed rigid and stretched his shirt's threads to their bursting points when the upper portion of his sleeves shredded, as he conflicted with his opponent's astonishing force. For nearly a solid minute, huge amounts of Al's blood pumped through his thick veins, flushing the security man's skin bright crimson with vitality. As if he were in great pain, Al cried out heartily and squeezing inward with his immeasurable strength, crushed the monster's chest. The brute's collapsing chest punctured its internal vital organs with the serrated shards of its broken rib cage. Al heaved the beast to the ground. The beaten monster's defeated eyes now burned hatefully at him, with the realization that it was finished in this life.

Al exhaled a gusty sigh of relief to be alive and wiped large drops of perspiration away from his brow, while carefully watching the nearly motionless figure gasp for breath.

Relieved by the outcome, Melinda reminded herself to breathe while she observed it snarl at her to reveal the horrid gnashing fangs, as it wheezed a final breath and stared with lifeless eyes.

Successively, the creature's body emitted a sound like a lit book of matches igniting as it became engulfed inside reddish-purple flames. Summoned into this world through an unnatural smoke, it dissipated the same way.

Al glared back purposely at the beast's invoker while he regained some of his vigor after the intense ordeal. While the Shaman glared hatefully at the bigger man, Al viewed a sickening expression of madness, envelop the Shaman's face. Al rushed forward to subdue the wrongdoer from drawing another hazardous picture on the rocks. The despicable Shaman instantly inscribed a bizarre symbol in the air between them while intoning under his breath and suddenly, Al froze in mid-stride.

Immoveable by jungle magic forces, Al remained in suspended animation. His facial features held to the exact moment the Shaman had snapped his fingers together. With a nonchalant wave of the wizard's wrist, the giant man toppled sideways onto the ground and remained in the same catatonic state. Tension filled everyone's emotions like ice water. Fear gripped Melinda when she had the same collective thought as her friends, *"If he can control Al so easily, what can he do to us?"*

While the older Shaman gloated at Melinda, he said with an intimidating tone, "You see, I have numerous powers to help you find your mother. For the final time, will you give me the mystic pendant?"

Rising anger suddenly replaced Melinda's fear of the man as she verbally lashed out at him, "It's because of you my mother was lost, and I never knew my father! No, I will never help you!"

Caught off-guard by her unexpected declaration, he internalized her spontaneous reaction while his mind whirled with a new resentment. Again, he muttered another spell, and faced his left palm at her. The palm turned into a fist, as he curled his fingers closed in the air between them. Immediately Melinda felt her body compress inward by an unseen force, as if in the grip of a great invisible vice. Tighter and tighter, the pressure mounted as it squeezed the life from her.

The jungle sage lifted his fist upward in the air, and likewise, Melinda's feet rose from off the ground, and she levitated with his movements. Using his other index finger and thumb, the Shaman reached forward in the air and made nimble movements. Melinda's top blouse button popped off. He lowered his thumb and forefinger together, then quickly drew them back.

Melinda felt the awful burning spread throughout her oxygen depleted lungs, and noticed her necklace, the final item she retained from her true childhood, tug suddenly from her neck and hover before her eyes. Slowly, it moved away from her face and floated into the Shaman's other open palm as she felt a hollow ache fill her heart at the loss. Melinda's lips turned blue, and her sight faded into black dots as she noiselessly began to faint. Straight away, when he relaxed his closed palm, the grinding pressure released her, and she crumpled to the ground.

The scandalous Olmec held the pendant into the air, and he crowed, "At last! The power of the ages belongs to me!"

Instantly, a gold aura shrouded the hand that grasped her necklace. He laughed passionately while limping towards Melinda, now gasping for air and struggling to her knees.

"I will find your mother, and this will lead me to her! Each pendant has the power to find the other," he smiled insanely before he continued, "and I shall find her, and have her necklace too. Together with the knowledge from this age, I shall return to conquer my world in my time."

Boastful, the Shaman held the shining pendant high overhead, and as he stared at the students he added, "Here are the secrets long forgotten. The ancients understood how to use their full power. I shall use them as they did before, to cause all kings, wizards, governors, and presidents to serve me! With this time pendant combined with the other, I will destroy those that opposed me. My enemies will fall under my wrathful footsteps. I will become powerful and merciless. Who would stand before me? I shall ensnare and change my past world, to lay ruin to this one, as if it had never existed!"

Slowly Melinda stood on her wobbly feet, and challenged his ranting, "What will you do to my mother when you find her?"

"That is for me alone to decide because you rejected my offer," he smiled fiercely with unconcealed relish at taunting her.

"Your mother's value will be nothing to me after I posses her necklace," he told her, and then added, "However, as I have been trapped for years in this absurd time, I *do* owe her something extra for my extensive troubles."

The Shaman looked piercingly at Melinda, and held the pendant in front of him for her to see as he exclaimed in an eerily quivered voice, "This shall be her last memory just before I kill her too," and licking his lips animal-like, delivered his fearful statement to her, "the long trail I followed ends here now, with your death."

The vile Shaman hobbled towards Melinda, filled with evil merriment. His dark eyes sparkled as he enjoyed various thoughts of how he would destroy her, when his cerebral hold on Al temporarily relaxed. Two steps closer to Melinda, in view of everyone, the sage shuddered suddenly as if he were under considerable stress. Briefly forgotten, Al strained against the invisible barrier. His face had become taut from the excruciating effort to move his magically frozen fingers.

Melinda spotted Al's minute fingertip movements, and stared at him motionlessly as his huge physique bunched into a mass of muscles in an effort to get out of his invisible bindings. His brow furrows deepened and revealed the veins bulging outward from his temples. Al pressed his hands slowly outward with clenched fists, until he fully extended his arms.

Gripped in a heart attack-like pain, the jungle wizard clutched his chest before he wheeled and staggered in a direct line towards Al.

"NO!" he shouted at Al as he gasped, "You will not escape!"

With increasing determination, the Shaman's distorted features showed his resolve to crush Al within his mental trap. Equally resolute to smash free, Al's reservoir of physical power had nearly reached its limit against the mental crushing from the wizard, during their war of wills.

Without uttering a noise while sweat beaded on his face, the Shaman made ghastly mystical gestures in the air like that of a tiger unsheathing its great talons. Fleetingly, Al's arms bent backwards by his foe's psychic emanations, until with a massive groan, he exploded outward exerting super energy to break the unseen barrier.

Visibly shaken backwards, Al's incredible physical valor rocked the degenerate Shaman's cerebral opposition. Hunched over, the Shaman's clothing immediately stretched and ripped at the seams. Melinda wondered in horror, "*Is he growing?*"

Short screams escaped the Shaman's constricted lips, as his pain-stricken face rolled sideways to gaze at Melinda. He was hideous. Glazed bloodshot eyes stretched vertically. Large uneven bumps budded everywhere on his forehead and features. However, his evil smile frightened her most.

Unbeaten, he happily wanted this eerie transmutation. Pleased with the results, he threw his head back, exposing his lengthening throat to utter a howl, until a spasm of agony creased his expression. Yellow fur rushed from every pore to swathe his formerly brown skin. Staring at him in repulsion, Melinda felt her blood quicken throughout the change. Dramatically increased in size, his ripped clothing hung in tatters on his massive new frame.

The small man had transformed into an enormous, malformed spotted jaguar man. Immense arms ended in gleaming black talons, which replaced his formerly clenched fists. Part bestial and part man, the most gruesome part was the alteration of his head. The shape-shifted Shaman adopted neither jaguar nor human features, as hard leathery bumps covered the noxious head of a deformed crocodile. Jagged teeth overflowed from his gaping mouth.

He was terrifying! Standing upright as a man would, his huge size and toxic image overpowered Melinda's senses. No longer fearing his human foes in his transformed state, the dreamlike horror completely ignored the incredibly muscular

Al and his feeble efforts to escape. Roaring terribly, the beast slowly shifted its massive weight and walked heavily towards her.

Melinda fully believed the shape-shifting Shaman's preceding murderous words. She cowered with fear and looked frantically to Al for help when she noticed his arms were free. Nevertheless, her hopes dashed when she realized he remained unmoving from the waist down. Carl, Dr. Bradan, and Trent were straining to break their knotted ropes. Tab remained comatose on the ground.

The giant morphed creature stepped closer to Melinda, and in desperation she stepped back. Her unbelief of what she saw, jumbled with panic, radiated from her wide eyes. Melinda wished she could block out the dreadful sight of his evil head, rather than be captivated by his archaic gaze and razor fangs. She easily accepted her demise in his foreign eyes as she stepped backward again and toppled over a rock. Lying merely three paces from his advancing position, she waited as the primal brute brandished curved talons to rend her apart.

Both of the Shaman's hired criminals had regained their earlier awareness after Al's brilliant attack, and together they ducked in fear directly behind Carl, Trent, and Dr. Bradan, during the Shaman's gruesome transformation. Melinda saw their involuntarily quaking, and knew they were too terrified of their shape-shifting leader to provide her with assistance.

He jeered in blood-freezing tones, ripping her glance from the thugs, and rasping while he towered above her, "This is where we ended 2,000-years before!"

While he unhurriedly raised his claws above her head with concentrated spite, she saw a wicked smile curve upon his misshapen lips when she clamped her eyes to shut out the petrifying sight. She could feel his hot, humid breath burning her skin as he leaned down to strike when a frenzied scream broke through her fear and startled her further. Melinda thought it had escaped from her mouth. With a tiny peek through her tightly closed eyelids, she now faced the back of the massive transfigured Shaman. Cursing in a nameless language and filled with rage, he made indiscernible gestures that moved him sideways to reveal a most peculiar sight.

The first of the Shaman's goons that Al had punched remained utterly frozen in place just before a black blur pounced upon him. The vague impression of a fast-moving rocket-bike slamming into his side jerked the clueless hoodlum into reality before he felt a sudden crushing pressure on his elbow. In fearful exasperation, the surprised henchman instinctively recoiled from the sudden clench of sharp teeth, which felt to him like burning hot embers melting into his skin. A giant black dog permitted the injured thug to pull his arm back to a certain point. Then with a full-bodied muscular wrench, the powerful dog pulled the hardened man headfirst onto the ground. The assault ended as the dog carefully bit a key location on the man's neck to pinch a nerve and temporarily immobilize him, ensuring he would not be an ongoing threat.

With a huge leap away from the first defeated ruffian, the huge dog sped next towards the second mobster Al had hurled earlier like a javelin. After watching how easily the approaching dog overcame his partner, the remaining thug sprinted away from the speeding black ferocity. Without falter, he impressively stooped and grasped a broken tree branch from off the ground while still running. He slid to a stop and readied for the black creature's charge by lifting the branch over his shoulder like a baseball bat.

The trajectory offered the thug a perfect swing angle in the dog's direction, when the fast moving blur suddenly darted to his left while rising in a leap. The branch swung murderously at the black shape, but with helpless fury. Batting merely at air, the uncontested force shifted his weight around his hips.

The female dog easily avoided the weapon's pathway. Blazing forward with the momentum of a rumbling boulder, the four-legged defender drove her massive shoulder into the hoodlum's hip. Shrieks quickly followed the dislocating pop of the downed man's hip socket; both remained concealed behind a dust cloud created by the current clash.

The suspended dirt hovered until it severed in half from the pointed nose of the prevailing dog. Bellowing a menacing growl, she whirled and charged towards the Shaman. Traumatized from unexpectedly seeing the amazing hero, the valiant big dog shook him to his morbid foundation. Rapidly regaining his senses from the sudden appearance, the Shaman's toxic mind searched frantically for a cosmic magic to defeat her, while bracing for the paw-pounding onslaught. He clicked his raised right talons in the air, ready to slash down at her, while concurrently he lifted Melinda's amulet in his monstrous left grip.

The Shaman rasped in frustration, "Guardian! How did you find me?"

Past the shock of their meeting again after 2,000 years earlier in a dark tunnel, the transformed Shaman extended his jaws to mouth a horrible primitive curse. With the ground rapidly shrinking between them, the nefarious jaguar man marveled at the Guardian's quickening pace. He admired her as both a perfect weapon and powerful force. Yet he loathed her completely with jealous hate.

Focused on the incredible animal's pursuit of the Shaman, Melinda felt strangely drawn to it.

A voice saying, "I will protect you," gently filled her mind. Strangely, Melinda was instantly soothed. She felt it, but it made no sense to her, as only seconds before she was terrified for her life.

Unsure of the message's origination, vivid mental pictures materialized within her mind of a tiny child cuddled asleep against a soft and caring dog-like animal. She knew she had communicated telepathically with the same being now in front of her before she was capable of speaking words, and that it had cared and watched over her as a toddler.

Spellbound inside her own thoughts, raging events gripped Melinda back to her dangerous reality, realizing Al had recently risen to his feet. Now close enough to the Shaman; Melinda noticed the transformed man's gape had focused entirely on the Guardian. Al winked at Melinda and moved undetected behind the beast-man.

Afraid to glance at Al, fearing the shocking Shaman would notice her tiny eye movements and give away his position, Melinda stared blindly ahead in the final seconds. Her young mind whirled to solve the problem confronting each of them, as all three were rapidly merging into an unpredictable finale. The presence of a jungle wizard was almost understandable from what she had learned today, but his towering foulness was nearly beyond her rationale. Without looking in the direction of the female Guardian, Melinda heard her thundering steps almost upon them, while she also realized Al now remained only a step behind the transmuted beast. The terrible Shaman's paranormal spell hissed in the air through his jagged teeth when Melinda darted her hand!

Only a stab of movement in front of the beast's path, the crocodile eyes fleetingly looked in her direction, and then flashed back to the leaping Guardian. Al, again using strength that seemed impossible for a mortal man, landed a solid two-handed sledgehammer blow to the base of the Shaman's leathery covered skull, which crumpled the hideous form into a state of unconsciousness.

With only Al's smiling face hovering above hers after lifting her to her feet, a cold nose happily greeted Melinda's hand, as the female Guardian's rippling shoulder rubbed against her side. Instant sensations of warm, burning love filled Melinda entirely. Hardly leaning to stare into the magnificent animal's caring eyes, she recognized and hugged the enormous protector.

The mental feelings of distress that radiated from the Guardian at losing Melinda as a child, suddenly changed into elation at finding her again. Memories from the Guardian flowed from a telepathic electrical energy into Melinda's mind's eye, as if she watched images from an internal DVD player. Minutes later, Melinda stood speechless as she realized she had just relived her young life through the eyes of this wonderful life form, which had cared and protected her family since before her birth.

Forgotten memories of her formative years were now unsealed by the Guardian and crackled like burning sparklers in her mind, allowing Melinda to re-imprint the beautiful voice of her birth mother into her soul. For the first time since she was a toddler, Melinda basked in the comforting voice of her former father, cradling her after awaking during the night.

Bombarded with countless feelings and emotions, Melinda understood the female Guardian truly loved her parents. As a trusted equal in their innermost circle, the incredible protector had watched over and shared Melinda's forgotten childhood with her frame-by-frame.

Using a direct brain-to-brain type connection, the transfer speed was unbelievable. Nevertheless, unlike watching a silent home movie, these vicarious visions provided Melinda with the ability to experience the actual emotions, smells, sounds, and sensations felt during the Guardian's cerebral recording of their experiences.

Thousands of years later, the female Guardian reintroduced Melinda to the texture of her favorite blanket, the sweet smell of her mother, and the caring affection from her father — always at her family's side.

The fresh visions of her birth mother and father swirled inside Melinda's thoughts, mixing with the childhood provided by her adopted parents. Filled with fantastic joy, Melinda's mind lingered with the desire to absorb additional new memories of her lost mother, until her thoughts changed.

Suddenly worried, questions if her birth mother survived after the fall through the ancient time portal crept into Melinda's mind. Instantly they were replaced with warm peaceful sensations from the Guardian using its telepathy, the devoted beast assured her, "We will find your mother, do not fear — I will always be here for you," which strengthened Melinda's confidence.

Together, they joined her student friends.

***

Later, as Al placed the bound henchmen together on the exit path leading back to the cars, both noisily complained of their injuries. Unconscious, the Shaman's magic had faded, and he had returned into his human form where he lay in his ripped clothing, bound in front of the cave's entrance. Carl, Dr. Bradan, Dale, Trent, and Tab excitedly relived the recent incredible adventure to each other.

Melinda searched the ground to find her necklace, and walked by the comatose Shaman, now incapable of being their tormentor. Unable to locate the pendant near him, she retraced her steps back to where he had approached her in his morphed state. Still unable to see the necklace anywhere on the ground, Melinda returned to where her family's traitor remained on the dirt, and reached into his tattered shirt pocket hoping to find it.

Immediately, the Shaman's eyes flung open. He stared into hers. Melinda lurched back in surprise and witnessed the ropes that bound his hands radiate a bright yellow, and then melt quickly from his wrists. The outrageous Shaman scrambled to his feet and caught her tightly around the neck in a chokehold.

From this vantage point, Melinda noticed her pendant's chain peeking out from the bottom of his other hand. The jungle man strangled her by tightening his arm around her soft neck, when an excruciating pain emanated from his side.

Able to see the Shaman's abysmal eyes open from Melinda's thoughts, the female Guardian calculated the situation, and leapt to Melinda's rescue. Before the

Shaman applied deadly pressure to Melinda's neck, the highly skilled Guardian bit a sensitive pressure point under the incessant man's arm, crippling it.

Dreadful pain forced the Shaman to release his grip, while Melinda, following her Guardian's mental instructions, shoved the edge of her shoe along his shin the exact moment he felt the biting pain in his side. The contemptible man howled with rage from the intense pain, while he staggered backwards into the cave's opening. Clasping the slack in Melinda's blouse, he jerked her into the Guardian's path. The thoughtless selfish movement prevented the Guardian from reading his mind and gave the Shaman time to hasten deeper into the cave.

When Melinda regained her balance, a quick step to the side allowed the female Guardian room to shoot past her into the cave's darkness. Urgently following both, Melinda slowed her speed slightly in the gloomy cave's interior as her eyes adjusted, having come from the recent sunlight. Unable to see clearly, she heard deep growls mixed with yells and cursing.

She doubled her effort to reach the cave's rear wall. When she arrived, the area was empty, except for the entire rope lying on the cave floor, no longer jammed inside the portal doorway.

Trent sped behind her and puffed, "Looks like they crashed through the portal, and knocked the rope out to close the opening."

With the dimension doorway closed, devastating stillness filled the cave.

Chapter Twenty-Eight

RUNNING SCARED

As the seething pain from the bite spread throughout his torso, the Shaman fled into the cave, hoping to evade the pursuing female Guardian. In addition to his limp, the agonizing bite slowed his progress. As the pursuing footsteps echoed louder along the narrow cavern walls, he knew she was quickly overtaking him. He was close to the portal's exit; however, the female Guardian gained on him with each step. He imagined her hot snarling breath on his back when her penetrating mental attacks sent overruling wavelengths into his skull.

Despite his intellectual effort to wrestle his mind away from her deadly thoughts, they forcefully drilled deeper into his cognitive core. The Shaman reeled from the invisible suggestions within his brain, and felt her gaining imminent control of his body. Dread of her drove him onward.

Distraught, he shouted at her, "LEAVE MY MIND!"

However, powerful telepathic energy from the Guardian engulfed his panicked thoughts while she communicated her control of his movements, "...*Legs slow down — I will stop you — you will pay for your crimes!*"

Her dominant mental submission commands to trip and fall abruptly seized the jungle man's brain, filling his frightened mind! Instantly, his feet tangled within imaginary vines. Before he could re-direct his own thoughts in opposition, the female Guardian tightened her psychological trap. Unable to defend against her commands still burrowing into his wits, her controlling thoughts literally tripped him forward. Fiercely grasping at the thin ray of light directly in front of his hands, he braced for the painful impact of the cave's rear wall, but it never came. The air thickened about him for long seconds, as darkness replaced his vision. Suddenly, intense overhead sunlight blinded him the instant his weary body crashed onto the ground. Rolling onto his back, he remained slightly dazed at the edge of the open green field, and stared up at the azure blue sky, gasping for enough air to enunciate peculiar words.

Fleecy clouds hovered high above, as his thoughts rapidly filled with a glaring mental transmission, *"I will protect her from you."*

He jerked his head off the ground to face the black dealer of pain. Fear snaked up his bowels and retched past his throat, to ignite his mind with alarm. He stared deeply at her for the first time in two thousand years without a battle raging about them. She was a faultless weapon of intellect and power. Her Egyptian hieroglyphic Jackal-shaped ears stood erect and attentive on her glossy wedge-shaped head, reminding him of her fabled breeding and link to the Great Sphinx.

Afternoon sunlight sifted through the overhead tree branches, creating a mixture of shadows that highlighted her perfect lion-sized physique. He absorbed her muscular agile ability while she stood over him in authority. The Shaman froze when she bore razor-sharp fangs below her long nose. Her retractable claws grew eagerly from thick paw casings.

She lowered her head into an attack position and psychically declared, *"As your verdict, I condemn you to pay for your crimes against the Sovereign Governor's family."*

The guilty Shaman knew firsthand this astounding high-ranking protector was loyal to the governing Olmec Timekeeper's family, and had commanded a pack of similar animals located strategically throughout the Olmec civilization. He feared her abilities as she stood with shoulders bristling, poised to discharge her lawfully appointed judgment after having pursued him for so long.

However, the supernatural transition into this dimension had broken the female Guardian's controlling linkage before she could mentally stop his spell casting. Quickly she re-sent psychic messages to derail his thoughts from mumbling an ancient spell. Too late, the completed spell created a force field around him.

Safely contained within the nearly invisible sphere, the female Guardian's thoughts only partially penetrated his safety bubble. Temporarily protected from her inside the sparkling ball, he began his former horrible transformation once more. The female Guardian knew his deadly intention, and patiently waited for the change. Shape shifting into the previous half man, half beast appearance, his monstrous looking eyes stared painfully at her until the conversion was complete.

The female Guardian looked within the ugly recesses of his deformed skull cavity and observed him rise to his full height, when the force field suddenly dissolved.

Quickly the female Guardian darted abruptly left, then paused to allow the beast to track her with its eyesight, only to flash back to the right in a hard to follow blur.

She darted towards the opening between his raptor-shaped legs, passing through them easily. Slowed by her pressing mental command, the slicing actions of his downward talons struck viciously at the empty space between his knees.

The terrible creature roared and twisted at the waist to grasp at her, only to miss once more when she sprung up and latched onto his back. Her unsheathed sharp claws dug deep into the brute's immense shoulder muscles, while her hind claws buried into the yellow and black fur near his hips. He screeched from the excruciating pain. She leveraged the movement to crunch below the leather portion of his crocodile head with her fangs; bits of his golden fur flew everywhere, as she shook her head.

Unable to reach her clinging onto his mammoth back, he tried to jab his own treacherous talons into her paws, still latched securely onto his broad muscles. Upon reading his mental intentions, the sleek Guardian retracted her claws at the last instant before he thrust his longer talons deep into his own flesh.

With the new additional self-inflicted sting beyond his previous injuries, the beast roared with fury. Frustrated, he jerked out his talons dripping in his own blood to swipe ferociously where he expected her to be. However, dropping low to the ground, her razor fangs instead wedged into his calf muscle. The evil being lifted his transformed leg high off the ground, trying to shake her off with unimaginable power. Gladly, she waited for the mistake, and swung her heavy body sideways without releasing her potent bite.

The Shaman lost his balance, and dropped to his knees from the excruciating pain of tearing tendons. Panicked at losing the battle, he reacted with thoughtless fright by springing upward on powerful legs in one continuous motion to land high above her position on a thick tree branch.

Trapped above with blood draining freely from his recent injuries, he hated the female Guardian with all of his alien ability, as he wheezed with great gasps.

Telepathically, she spoke to him, "*You have lost! Come down, and I shall be merciful, otherwise I will recall every evil deed locked in the darkest reaches of your mind, and punish each with deserved restitution.*"

"Never," the beast hissed with ragged breath, "you did not avert me in our time from destroying the Sovereign family. Hang your head in shame *Guardian!*"

Firing back at him, "*Maynaya is safe from you. After your elimination, I will instruct her how to use the pendant to find the Governess if she still lives and reunite them with their Governor in our time.*"

"Fool," he shot back callously, "When attacking the inner sanctuary that night, my additional brothers pursued the High Governor during his travels and killed him. Even if you go back in time, *we* will be there, and I will succeed to retain what is rightfully mine!"

"*Prepare to breathe your last breath,*" she advised, and leapt upwards to attach onto the exterior tree shaft.

The trapped monster, observing her resolve, cursed in a tainted language and uttered a new magic enchantment to grow wings. The Guardian absorbed his thoughts of flying to escape her and doubled her labor to ascend the tree. Even as the Shaman watched her steady ascent, he too leapt to an elevated altitude to gain precious moments for his freshly grown wings to dry.

Pouncing from branch-to-branch, she raced to reach him in time. With an ultimate burst, she launched upward to fasten her front talons into his foot and lower leg. Her extra weight combined with his sturdy mass snapped the tree limb.

Interlocked they fell. He flapped his newly produced sinister wings, still damp, and as one, they slowly hovered in flight. He kicked at the Guardian's paws with his other misshapen foot. She shifted her grip into another portion of his leg to avoid the kicking blows. They both lost altitude during the airborne scuffle. To avert her from climbing further up his leg, he drew it upward to rake her with his arm talons. The added movement twisted his foot and caused her razor-like fangs to slice deeper down his leg. Finally, the soft tissue tore from supporting her heavy weight, and she dropped to the ground.

"You may have bettered me; yet, I'm still free! Next time I will be ready!" he squawked coldly while climbing higher in the wind.

Then he cackled, "Soon I will find and destroy the mother — and then the daughter too! They will all be gone! You will be alone Guardian!"

With an evil laugh, the newly shaped creature circled upward like a hawk, until reaching the height needed to soar into the distance. Below him, the Guardian trailed beneath the trees.

"The daughter!" drifted down to the Guardian's ears as the Shaman sailed overhead with his sickening laughter.

***

Gripped by what they had witnessed in the cave, Melinda hung her head in despair. Her thoughts and emotions sunk as never before. Struggling to comprehend that another world overlapped ours in space and time, she relived the new details about her birth parents and their mysterious past. It was too much for her to grapple with in one day. Melinda had a vast amount of questions, but few answers. Instead of leaning on her telepathic companion for support; now the female Guardian, was lost again to her.

Melinda vacantly trailed Trent outside of the cave's entrance, struggling with her internal quandary of feelings. Her friends' curious eyes scanned her expression for the details. Aware something tragic had occurred within the cave, none dared to solicit facts from her now. Trent waved at the group to join him away from Melinda, for an update.

"The Guardian and the Shaman went through the portal with her necklace. When they passed into the other side, they somehow knocked out the rope that kept the doorway open. Without her pendant, there's no way for us to follow," Trent whispered as he watched Melinda pace in her forlorn state.

Al said with a feeble smile, feeling terrible for Melinda, "Why don't you guys collect the rest of our stuff, while the professor and I turn this pair of losers over to the authorities at the ranger station."

Unsure how Melinda might receive the delivery of his words, Al tacked on, "When you're ready," staring in her direction, "follow us."

Everyone remained silent, knowing Melinda's mother was vulnerable to the Shaman inside the dimension; however, Trent nodded in agreement with Al's comments and said, "Don't worry about us — we may take a little time, but we'll be along."

Al walked towards the two injured thugs and gave a slight push to the man with the injured arm to begin the trek back to the park's entrance. The other thug, still immobilized from his newly dislocated hip, remained on the ground. Without animosity, Al effortlessly lifted the injured man from the ground. Placing the ruffian over his broad shoulder in a firefighter carry, he tagged closely behind Dr. Bradan and the first hooligan until they departed out of the students' view.

Ten minutes later, Melinda looked longingly at the cave's entry with a resigned sigh.

Still in despair, Melinda stated obediently, "There's nothing we can do here now — I guess we should hike back to the park entrance. We're safe now, and we should be grateful for that at least."

Without looking at the rest of the small band of friends, Trent urged them, "OK everyone, it's a bit of a walk from here — let's get going."

Shortly into their return trip, Tab unexpectedly stopped and turned to wait for Trent to catch up to him on the trail. When they were near enough, Tab signed.

"Tab said we forgot the rope inside the cave. He's going back to get it, and wants us to wait until he catches up."

Reading Trent's lips, Tab knew they understood and jogged back the way they came. When Tab reached the cave entrance, he switched on a flashlight that Carl had handed him. Once inside, he proceeded through the meandering path, until he spied the rope lying in the dirt. He squatted to position the flashlight on the ground in order to coil the rope around his hand and elbow. The uncoiled rope's red tapered end, which had previously held the time portal open, whipped back and forth in the dust flipping the flashlight to the right when they touched. Pushed aside, the pale beam of light pointed in a new direction on the ground.

Unconcerned, Tab placed the twisted rope over his left shoulder, and bent low to retrieve the flashlight with his right hand. The leaning movement positioned his eyes to see a sudden fleeting glimpse of a bright twinkle further inside the cave. Stopped in mid-motion, Tab raised his head and watched as the flicker disappeared. Ducking down, it reappeared. Without disturbing the flashlight, he stepped forward cautiously, and caught his breath within his silent world.

***

Winded from the rapid retreat from the cave to return to the other students, Tab sped up when his friends came into view. Melinda glanced over her shoulder and saw Tab in the distance, saying, "Hey, Tab's coming."

They waited patiently for Tab to catch up.

Together again, Tab signed wildly to Trent.

"NO WAY!" Trent exclaimed, "That's incredible!"

"What?" What did he say?" Dale asked, excited.

"You're not going to believe this, but when Tab found the rope inside the cave, he saw something shiny." Trent turned towards Melinda and said, "Get ready for this — when he walked over to look at it — he found your necklace."

Stunned by the potential meaning of the words, Melinda was unsure what to feel. She wondered if Trent was teasing her about the pendant, hoping to make her smile, or if Tab discovered something similar, and made a mistake without having seen her necklace up close. Without hesitation, Tab sensed her apprehension and hastily reached into his jeans pocket. He beamed brightly as he retrieved the necklace.

"How..." Melinda exhaled the word at seeing her amulet.

The silence was intense, as her friends tried to grasp what made this moment possible.

"Ha, ha!" Dale said laughing. "The Shaman must have dropped it before he fell through the portal. Serves him right..."

Enthusiastic about the find, Trent accidentally cut Dale off by saying, "Wow, we're lucky Tab remembered the rope, otherwise, we might never know what happened."

Melinda snapped around to stare at Trent. Something about what he said dredged up her concern.

"You're right, we'd never have known — but now we can," she whispered enthusiastically to herself.

"Come again?" Dale asked.

"We know the Shaman went through the portal, right? And, we're familiar with his plans to harm my mother and steal her pendant. If we don't hurry back inside the dimension to stop him, what happens if he does find her? You heard him talk about traveling back into the past and making changes to eliminate our world as if it never existed. If we don't stop him now, while we know where he is, we might all be in trouble later," Melinda said with an alarmed countenance.

"But the Guardian went through with him, maybe she killed him," Dale suggested hopefully.

"Yeah, but...you saw the guy when he turned into that monster! What if *he* killed the Guardian? Unless we return, how will we ever know for sure?" Trent alleged by accepting Melinda's implication.

"And even if you're right, Dale, and the Guardian is alive, with my necklace we can bring her back to this side. It's not right to abandon her on the other side, especially if she saved us again by stopping the Shaman in the other world," Melinda said with growing fervor.

"Should we go back now, or wait for Al and my dad to come with us?" Dale questioned nervously.

"The Shaman was pretty scary after he turned into that creature. I don't think we could take him on alone. We better have Al and your dad there to help us," Trent hummed.

Dale expressed his anxiousness by walking away and saying, "You guys better wait here until I bring them back."

"Wait," Carl called, "I should be the one te return and inform Al and Dr. Bradan. My best value is te provide a secure base of communication should we need help."

"That's not a bad idea," Trent decided.

"Ok then, ye kids return back te the cave, and STAY PUT. I'll tell Al and

Dr. Bradan about the plan. No one do anything until both join ye in the cavern! Are we clear?"

They all nodded their agreement.

After watching Carl fade into the distance, the students returned to the cave and waited.

Chapter Twenty-Nine

REWIND

Regrouped inside the cave, Dr. Bradan and Al shared sandwiches and drinks with the parched team. Al additionally bought enough water canteens, hiking backpacks, and an assortment of snacks for everyone from the state park's on-site store to revive them.

Finished with his sandwich, and standing to put on his backpack, Dr. Bradan said, "We need to hurry before it gets too late, otherwise, we might be hiking back to the cars in the dark."

"Alright, is everyone ready?" Al asked, looking each student in the eye. "Let's get moving in a single file."

Quickly they passed through the cave's interior, and reached the portal wall.

"Ok — it might be best for Melinda and Al to pass through first! This way if Al can squeeze through beside her, we already know the rest of us can. Line up behind me," Dr. Bradan planned.

Positioned as instructed, Melinda explained to Al, "Last time when we returned, I entered first and held the doorway open for the others to slip past me. I'm not sure if it will work because you're so big, so maybe this time, I'll only hold out my hand in front of me to open the doorway, which should give you more room to pass by me."

"Is there anything special I need to do to pass through the portal?" Al asked.

"Not that I know of — we just walked through," Melinda coached him.

"Ok, here goes…," the giant man stated, somewhat apprehensive.

Holding out her necklace, Melinda pressed it into the wall. Instantly, her hand vanished.

"That's freaky," Al confessed, watching Melinda's arm partly fade into nothing, "I'm glad you told me about this earlier, otherwise, I'm not sure I would be doing this right now," he said, trying to sound confident.

Pushing her arm in further, it soon disappeared. Within the edge of the portal, Al stepped forward until he departed from their view. In turn, each person slipped past her through the portal's opening. As the last person to cross over, Melinda turned inward to follow, and once more, daylight instantly blinded her.

"...GUYS, LOOK AT THIS!" she heard Dale's energetic voice.

After allowing her eyes to adjust to the brightness of the sun, Melinda stared around them in surprise. Instead of finding the tranquil green field as before, they stood in the middle of churned grass, as if wild hogs had rooted up the pasture looking for food. Blood and fur remained in countless places within the area.

Concerned from seeing the dried reddish-purple spots, Melinda asked, "What happened here? Why is there blood everywhere?"

"It appears that after the Guardian and the Shaman passed into this dimension, they fought each other," Dr. Bradan surmised.

Fearful to find her Guardian badly hurt, Melinda quickly scanned the vicinity looking for her protector's injured body. Relieved at finding nothing, the pre-Mayan girl was still mystified with the puzzling discovery. Without any obvious signs or clear directions to follow, the team spread out hoping to find more clues to clarify the situation.

Suddenly, Tab signed and then Trent said, "Guys, come here!"

When Melinda neared the two brothers, Tab pointed at the grass. Oversized distinct footprints matching the Shaman's horrendous morphed feet mingled with comparatively smaller paw prints.

"Clearly the two fought here because of all of the ripped-out yellow fur. Plus, we seem to be finding little, if any, of the Guardian's black fur. I wonder what actually happened," Dr. Bradan asked, scrutinizing the area. "Wait — look here!" he cried.

Melinda saw what the professor pointed at instantly. Broken branches hung in the tree above them, and twigs littered the ground. Deep penetrating claw marks trailed up into the higher parts of the tree branches. Nearing the base of the tree portal, everyone searched the ground, hoping to discover more answers.

"Hey — here are more prints," Dale exclaimed.

Pressed into the smashed grass near Dale's feet, the Guardian's paw prints perceptibly raced into the forest of oak trees.

"That's strange," Al, said, "where are the Shaman's prints? I only see the Guardian's prints leaving in that direction. Can anyone find his prints leaving the area? He's obviously not here!"

"It's hard to decipher by the markings alone," Dr. Bradan said, "at this point in our analysis, we don't appear to have enough information. The only choice seems to be for us to follow the prints and see where they lead. The good news is that at least we know the Guardian is safe."

"How can you tell?" Melinda asked in an optimistic tone.

"Judging by the amount of space in between her tracks, she was loping away at a rapid pace, which means to me she was in good shape, plus, without seeing a blood trail near her prints, I believe she's not injured badly, if at all," the professor explained.

"So, most of the blood stains belong to the Shaman?" Trent questioned.

"I hope you're right," she said, partially relieved.

Staring at the marred dirt and torn up grass, Melinda's feelings calmed as they entered the trees.

"Come on everyone, let's follow these tracks. They might be close by," Al ordered.

Melinda felt hope rush within her veins. However, after passing each tree or rock, Melinda paused to search the area with her eyes, hoping to find the Guardian. Yet, as they continued scrounging for clues, she became anxious with each crack of a stick or flutters of birds, and hoped the next noise they heard would be the Guardian.

Later, the paw tracks became faded and less perceptible as the immediate countryside altered from a shelter of trees into stony foothills. At the forefront, Melinda followed the prints as they lead down into and around a bend in a gorge, until forced to stop. Stunned by what she witnessed, lower inside the ravine, the Guardian's path led over the edge of a cliff.

When Melinda stood at the rim, she overlooked a 30-foot drop to where sand nestled perfectly against the bottom of the sheer rock wall. Scanning hundreds of square miles of sand in front of them, she noticed the Guardian's prints going into the desert. Enough time had lapsed that her paw prints were already blowing away from the hot breeze.

"We need to hurry, because the tracks are fading in this wind! The Guardian could be hurt and need our help!" she said, fearing the trail would soon be lost.

"I agree with Melinda, it's better to follow the prints while we can. Come on people, let's hurry it up — stand behind me now," Al advised.

Once Al formed a secure loop at one end of the rope brought from the cave, he announced, "After I lower each of you using this rope, I'll climb down it myself. Nobody run ahead," he said looking at Melinda. "We all go together."

The Security Chief cinched one end around his washboard stomach, and easily lowered each team member to the waiting sand below. As the last person to follow, he removed the rope from around his waist and circled it loosely around a large nearby rock. Suddenly halfway down the sheer wall, his considerable weight caused the rope to slip on the rock from the strain.

Shocked by the sudden drop in his altitude, Al held still until he jerked on the rope a few times, and felt comfortable it would hold. Finished with climbing down, he stood in the sand to catch his breath. Whipping the rope free from the above rock with an undulating movement, he nodded at Melinda to proceed. She eagerly followed the vanishing prints to find her precious, four-legged hero.

***

An hour of hiking beneath the scorching sun, and the Guardian's large paw prints faded completely in the desert wind. Without an observable path to guide them forward across the scorching sand, Melinda and her friends were undecided of which direction to advance.

Dr. Bradan said aloud what they were all thinking, "It appears we can't follow this trail any longer. The good news is, she still seems to be going strong, but if we don't backtrack soon, we may lose our own tracks too."

Melinda glared up at the sun, fully aware that perspiration dampened her face and neck. Suddenly she felt an unexpected chill run up her spine. Amazed by the fact, she noticed that the wind was quickly building around them.

Together, she and Al glanced back in the direction they had recently traveled. Although she had never seen one, it was unmistakable. In unison, they yelled, "SAND STORM!"

Staring at the imminent hazard, the advancing sand forced her eyes to water, and with a dry cough, she swallowed dust while grasping her hair in a fist on the side of her head to stop it from blowing into her eyes. Directly in their return path, the sky turned the color of burnt caramel as a tsunami-sized wave of sand rushed at them. Stunned by the immense sight, indecisiveness gripped Melinda. The sand sped towards them too fast to flee from its path, and glancing around their vicinity, only small sand dunes offered any visible protection. Hesitating about which way to run, and dreading the coming wall of sand, too quickly, it knocked Melinda down and barreled over her.

Al saw her go down in front of him, and scooped her up around the waist. He wheeled around and sprinted behind a short dune to their right. Dropping to the ground with his back absorbing the majority of the sandblasting windstorm, he positioned Melinda on the protected side of his body, away from the oncoming danger. Al quickly covered her head with one of his massive arms, and clenched his jaw from the painful stinging as the flash flood of rolling sand washed completely over them.

Shielded by the enormous man, and gasping for breath amid the flying dust, howling winds pelted Melinda with thousands of tiny pricks, as each sand granule cut against her skin.

***

Melinda awoke to the angry voice of Dale, "…you believe it. Now we're stuck here in the middle of nowhere!"

Startled when she moved, Al sat up, completely blanketed by sand. Except for a small space made from his huge arms across her face, the sand saturated Melinda too. Al was confused until Melinda spoke to him, "Are you ok?"

"Fine, I guess. How long did the storm last?" Al asked her.

"I'm not sure; I remember choking, and either I dozed off or I passed out."

After a few moments, Melinda rubbed her head when she grumbled to Al, "My head hurts, does yours?"

"I'm fine," Al replied while rising to his knees.

Under the weight of the quilt of sand, Melinda slowly rose into a kneeling position. The movement caused buckets of sand to stream down from her head, neck, and clothes. She blew air through her lips to remove the gritty feeling from her teeth. Al scrubbed the top of his head using his thick fingers to rid it of most of the clinging sand. Melinda stood and followed his actions by running in place and shaking her hair back and forth like a rock star on stage to release trapped sand from inside her clothes. Melinda then groaned with sudden nausea from fatigue and dehydration after the effort, and sat down.

When Melinda felt better, she decided to join Dr. Bradan and Dale on top of a large dune, but slid back with each step from the smooth sheets of loose sand. When she finally reached the crest, she froze, amazed by what she saw.

The landscape had changed radically. The previous smaller easy-to-navigate sand dunes that once provided views of nearly a mile, had morphed into massive 30 to 50 foot tall mounds of sand, blocking their visibility in every direction. Confused by the drastic change, Melinda stood with a blank expression on her face, and wondered which direction would be the right one to travel. Under the intense temperature of the late afternoon sun, Melinda instead searched for an exposed tree or rock for shade to prevent her skin from drying out in the still sweltering environment.

"Dad, where are we?" Dale broke the strange tranquility of the desert scene.

Dr. Bradan hesitated before replying. He first scooped up a handful of sand. With the help of the sunlight, he examined the sand particles trickling between his fingers while Dale looked at him as if he were crazy.

"I'm not sure son, but if I guessed…based on what we see around us…this may be the Sahara Desert."

"How can you be sure, Dr. Bradan?" Melinda asked.

"As funny as it sounds, in spite of the vast amounts of sand in the Sahara Desert, local people haul in large loads of sand from other places to use for construction."

"What? You mean with all of this sand, they don't have enough to build stuff?" she teased.

"No silly, because the native sand particles of the Sahara have rolled across the desert for thousands of years, they are nearly round. This prevents them from gripping properly to make solid plaster walls. From what I can tell, the sand grains in this area are rounded," Dr. Bradan said with a slight chuckle.

"What year do you think it is?" Trent asked the professor.

Dr. Bradan answered, "Who can say with any amount of certainty? For all I know, this could be our time, just as easily as it could be ten million years earlier."

Al stood in one spot and slowly turned around to observe their entire surroundings, before he asked the professor, "Which direction do you think we should walk?"

"Without any identifiable land marks, and getting turned around during the sand storm, it will be difficult to determine the correct way. Right now, one direction may be just as good as another may. We may need to use some criteria," the professor projected.

"Huh? What do you mean by 'criteria'?" Dale sighed loudly. Bored with his father's gigantic version of a simple explanation, he readied himself further.

"For example, would you prefer to walk with the sun directly in your face, or shine on your back? Me personally, I would prefer to have the sun facing my back rather than my face," Dr. Bradan illustrated. "So depending on what we decide is best, we may also consider which direction might offer us the longest survival support. We have no idea how long we could be in this terrible desert, meaning it would be helpful to determine the most comfortable route to help conserve our strength. Those are some of the criteria I imagine we need to figure out, before hiking in any direction."

Surprised that his father did not take longer, Dale said proudly, "So if I understand correctly, you're suggesting we walk with the setting sun at our backs. Because if the sun sets in the west, and we walk towards the east, that might mean the sun could set slightly sooner on us."

"Good idea. Maybe by the time the sun sets, we'll know what our next step should be," Trent said hopefully.

"However, it also means we'll be engulfed in a faster temperature variance. The hottest deserts in the world can get extremely cold at night," Dr. Bradan warned.

Melinda said, "My vote is to get cooler faster, and I think we should start moving now — the sooner the better!"

Tab signed quickly to Trent who translated, "Tab suggested we take off our shirts and tie them around our heads, to make a type of turban like the desert people do. This way, we'll remain cooler during the day, without baking our brains. Also, he thinks our back packs will act as insulation from the sun's direct rays."

Dr. Bradan agreed, "Tab's right, our uncovered heads will overheat first; it's a very good point. Let's do as he says."

Immediately, the guys removed their outer shirts, keeping their white tees on. Bumbling away with their male chatter, they finally assembled their Ali Baba look-a-like coverings. Melinda quietly stood off to the side, hoping someone would not see. She was already sunburned, so her embarrassment went unnoticed. She needed a turban too, but she could not use her shirt. Somehow, she did not think a lacy bra would pass for a bikini top! She was mortified and thought, *"It's so easy being a guy. They probably just expect me to 'wrap my hair over my head' or something."*

Dr. Bradan noticed Melinda's face, and quickly realized her concern. Walking next to Al, he motioned for the bigger man to follow him.

About ten yards away, Dr. Bradan informed him, "Al, I believe Melinda needs part of your shirt more than you need it right now. Would you mind giving her one of your ripped shirt sleeves to cover her head, instead of her having to use her only shirt?"

Eager to help, Al quickly said, "No problem! She can have both sleeves if it helps her from getting heatstroke."

Without having a second shirt under her blouse, Melinda was unsure of what to do for a solution, until she received Al's sleeve. She slid the oversized sleeve on her head like a snow-skiing stocking cap, and then tied the remaining shredded lengths in a bow below her chin, tucking in the loose ends.

Melinda told Al 'thank you' more with her eyes, than her words, and off they went. Trent and Tab dangled behind a few feet and then caught up, obviously quarreling. Trent's eyes grew wide with annoyance. Tab smirked, and Trent gave him a shove. They simmered down for a short while, until out of nowhere, Tab made big eyes at Trent with his tongue hanging out, and made kissing gestures to Trent, all the while laughing uncontrollably. Trent smacked him on the shoulder, his lips forming a scowl, and huffed off ahead of Tab by several paces. Everyone ignored them — mostly because they could see Trent was embarrassed, and they had never seen Tab be the aggressor before. None of the team wanted to add to whatever it was about, especially with Tab still chortling with amusement in the background.

To change the disposition of the group, Dr. Bradan told everyone, "Remain in a single file because sand is more difficult to walk on than pavement. When the leader gets tired, we will switch places to give each person their turn packing the sand down for the others who are following. This will help the group better conserve our energy overall."

"Dad, why'd we have to climb down the rock wall so far to end up at the lower sand level, instead of both places being at the same height as the green field?" Dale asked curiously.

"I have been wondering that myself. Regarding the green field versus here, I'm not sure I know the answer, unless it depended on what year it is. The green field was about 150 years back from our time, so there would be very little change in the elevation. However, if we went back hundreds of thousands, or even millions of years into the past to this location, perhaps the sand did not have enough time to build up, or as the tectonic plates constantly move, perhaps we landed in a valley, which could also cause a difference in the altitude."

Dr. Bradan stopped and faced the students saying, "We must stop speaking while we hike in this tremendous heat. You may not realize it, but with each spoken word, you exhale some of your body's moisture, which is the absolute wrong thing to do out here. Do not speak unless it's absolutely necessary."

With the added understanding, each took a final look around the area to ensure none of their gear remained in the sand before continuing.

***

Further, into their trek across the sizzling sand dunes, Melinda realized she was exhausted. Pursued by Civil War soldiers, captured by a beastly Shaman, discovering her past, finding and losing her Guardian, and hiking in difficult sand, had ground her down mentally and physically.

Feeling her energy had drained, Melinda called out, "Hey, I'm beat. Can we take a short break? My legs really hurt."

Weary grunts of approval met her query. Worn out, everyone rested on the burning sand after removing his or her meager gear. Melinda watched as the heat waves danced in the distance. Unconsciously, she pushed her hands under her legs to keep as much of her out of the boiling sun as possible, and quickly noticed the deeper sand felt much cooler on her fingers below the surface.

"Everyone, stick your hands underneath the sand. It's not as hot as the sand on top. Maybe we should dig into the cooler layer and cover ourselves. We could stay out of the high temperature during the rest of the day, and at night, even though it might be colder, the walking will keep us from getting too chilly. I assume it will be easier than hiking under this scorching sun. At least at night, we won't dehydrate as fast as we would in the sun."

"That's a great idea; I'm up for it. What about you, Doc?" Al asked.

"I agree. Everyone, cover yourselves with sand, and situate your backpack to shade your head from the remaining direct sunlight," Dr. Bradan directed.

Melinda struggled with weariness in the melting heat to dig a trench large enough to fit inside, and then arranged her pack to block the lowering sun from off of her head. Finished, she sat down, and by means of her hands, covered her feet and legs first. The sand produced a weighty sensation after she was sheltered.

The edges of her exposed skin tickled while tiny sand granules trickled over her stomach, feeling like water drops running down her skin. Next, she wiggled her shoulders beneath a shallow layer of sand. With only her neck exposed under her chin, she pulled her hands beneath the sand too, and enjoyed the sudden coolness.

***

Awakened with a start, Melinda noticed sparkling stars, like diamonds filling the black sky. Unsure how long she had slept; she almost closed her eyes from fatigue, when the annoying images of trudging through the roasting sun the next day forced her to rise. Shaking sand away another time from her body and clothes, she approached Trent as the closest person in the sand to her. Once Trent was alert, together they awoke the rest of the team, and prepared to trek onward yet again.

Before proceeding with the single file hiking, Dr. Bradan advised the group, "Without the sun behind our backs to guide our direction, we need an indicator or star to direct ourselves in the dark; otherwise, as large sand dunes tend to travel in curved formations, it would be easy to lose our direction and backtrack. I suggest we utilize that small cluster of stars up there on the right side of the brighter one, to be our guide."

"What's the plan if someone gets lost?" Trent asked.

"I don't believe that will occur, however, it's better to make preparations just in case. If you find yourself separated from the group, yell loudly for help. Your voice can travel reasonably far in the desert. If you fail to perceive a response, remain consistent in following the path of those stars. After daylight, if you see footprints in front of your position, then pursue them. If you don't, cover yourself in the sand once more, and stay in place until the rest of us trail your footprints to you," Dr. Bradan coached.

Three hours later, Melinda felt chilled from the night wind blowing around her clammy skin.

Unexpectedly Dale shouted, "Hey, what's that sparkle?"

Near him, Melinda peered where he pointed, far away into the desert.

"I don't see anything," she said. "What was it?"

"I'm not sure, but for a second, it sort of flickered like when somebody uses a mirror to reflect the sunlight," he replied.

Ten minutes further, and the flash remained a mystery.

Dale felt foolish, and alleged with insecurity, "It might have just been a star, and I only thought I saw something."

"Hold on; let's wait longer before we get going again. Everyone please look up," Dr. Bradan pointed skyward. "It's a clear night, yet you can still detect a few high clouds. Perhaps one temporally shielded the moonlight from reflecting on the source of the shimmer."

They waited as first fifteen minutes passed, and then thirty. As the troop gathered their belongings, ready to depart, Trent gripped Dale's arm, and yelled, "IT'S STILL THERE! I see it too!"

As Dr. Bradan predicted, when the fleeting clouds drifted into the distance, radiant moonbeams blanketed the area they spied, producing the intermittent flashes.

"At this moment, we know someone, or something, is situated over there. Let's hike towards it before the sun rises, or worse, before whomever it might be leaves prior to our arrival," Dr. Bradan instructed.

"Should we pick a new star to follow for going in this direction?" Al questioned.

"Exactly, let's use...how about those?" Dr. Bradan said, pointing at two minor stars lower in the sky. "Can everybody distinguish them above the blinking?"

With agreement on the new sky markers, the crew marched into the darkness. Several hours later, they had not arrived at the hoped-for goal.

"I recognize we're weary, but we must increase our pace, because over there, you'll notice the sun is beginning to rise. We have very little time to find the sparkle, and if we lose sight of it, we will have no choice but to dig ourselves a new sand ditch," Dr. Bradan urged the squad.

Filled with negative motivation to discover the source of the flashing, Melinda and her friends pushed themselves harder towards the two low hanging stars. At the summit of another steep rise, Dr. Bradan said, "We're still not there. I believe we better dig our trenches..." when Dale froze in his spot on the sand dune.

When Dr. Bradan noticed his son's rigidity, he looked across the sand with skepticism. To his surprise, beyond a cluster of shallow sand dunes, palm trees unmistakably bordered an oasis of water. Afraid to believe it was real, no one moved thinking the hallucination would quickly disappear back into the desert. However, undaunted, and with a loud hoot, Dale sprinted towards the water.

Chapter Thirty

TRANSITIONS

Absolute exhaustion overcame Melinda knowing their desperate trip through the Sahara Desert may have finally brought them to a water-filled oasis. Melinda scurried faster to keep pace with Dale, who both ran and stumbled across the sand. She knew the decisive moment was seconds away, as Dale tripped forward into the edge of the seeming mirage. He gladly plunged in headfirst, until his head and shoulders sank beneath the shiny surface. Stunned with relief that it was real, Melinda rushed forward too.

When the rest of the friends splashed into the water's edge, each had their fill of the desert water. Invigorated from the smell of moisture lingering in the dry air combined with the feel of water upon her sunburned face and neck, Melinda crawled backwards to relax upon the sand. After she rolled over onto her back, Melinda used her fingers to screen her eyes from the rising sun. As she glanced to her right, Dale and Trent had jovial faces. On her left, Dr. Bradan smiled wide at Dale.

To no one in particular, Trent exploded with a huge groan of release, "I'm so thankful we found water. I'm not sure how much further I could have marched."

Melinda agreed blissfully, "Me too! I was prepared to quit two sand dunes back. Dale, I'm so glad you spotted this place last night."

Thrilled to listen to the flattering remark, Dale felt some of his self-assurance return, and hoisted himself unhurriedly to his feet. When he turned about to overlook the lifesaving water he had discovered, a surprise ripple at the other end of the oasis captured his attention. He thought an animal made the swell in the water, and he watched the area intently. Unable to discern the type of creature, his curiosity grew until he walked the length of the water in suspense.

To Dale's surprise, rather than spotting a fish or animal causing the large ripples, he peered deep into a threatening and spinning whirlpool that led to the bottom of the lagoon. Advancing cautiously for a closer look, it reminded him of a water twister after he removed a drain stopper from a full bathtub.

"DAD — COME QUICK!" Dale shouted. "LOOK AT THIS!"

Dr. Bradan looked tiredly across the water and yelled, "WHAT IS IT?"

Dale waved his arms while jumping up and down energetically, eager to show it to the group. Al effortlessly lifted Melinda, Trent, and Tab to their feet and Melinda smiled up at the pleasant man. Al politely signaled for the students to pass before him.

Their sluggish walking became unacceptable to Dale, and he walked further into the ripples and leaned forward to point his index finger at the rotating surface. Next, he made revolving motions with his arms in the air, when he felt his foot slip below the water. Dale felt his shoe suctioned into the swirling water, and hastily jerked it aloft, hoping to free it from the current. The single exertion pulled his foot up explosively; however, the sudden wobbly liberation shifted his balance.

Melinda and Dr. Bradan, still in the lead, did not comprehend that Dale was in danger while wildly flapping his hands and arms. Both believed he was still trying to hurry them with his excited movements. Melinda instead paid attention to her damp clothing, amazed to see it drying before her eyes in the growing intense heat.

Surprised to hear a sudden splash, Melinda shot a glance in Dale's direction. Unconcerned with his disappearance, she laughed at the unanticipated, frenzied actions when he surfaced. Strangely, she noticed as Dale paddled frantically towards the dry beach, in opposition, he traveled backwards, away from the sand.

Curious, Melinda grabbed the professor's arm and pointed at Dale saying, "Look, I think he's in trouble."

Prior to hearing her entire warning, she felt the professor's arm suddenly grow stiff with concern. Instantly, he sprinted across the loose sand, and rounded the corner of the oasis towards his son.

To Melinda's distress, Dale yelled, "HELP! HELP!" when his course quickly changed.

Instead of moving backwards in a straight line as before, Dale now swirled upright in a circular motion. Melinda stared in an effort to comprehend the severity of the crisis, until the gigantic splash to her side grabbed her attention. Quickly, Al shortened the distance to Dale, swimming with long powerful strokes.

Abruptly, Trent yelled next to her, "Something's got him!"

Concerned for Dale, Trent, Tab, and Melinda dashed across the sweltering sand. True to Trent's words, Dale swirled about as if gripped in the mouth of a great predator. Melinda wondered, *"What's down there?"*

Suddenly, Dale vanished beneath the surface. Together Al and Dr. Bradan converged upon Dale's last seen location, and rather than lunge forward to help him, his father shrank back while peering into the water, hoping to see signs of Dale. When Melinda approached the spot where Dale disappeared, she, alongside with the rest of the team, watched an amazing spectacle. The dark rushing water made it impossible to see Dale below.

Formerly unnoticed at the far side of the oasis, the large vortex drained hundreds of gallons of oasis water per second. Shaken, Melinda cried out, "Dale, can you hear me?"

Unseen, they could hear Dale calling to them, yet his voice seemed far away. Melinda was undecided where the bottomless pool drained beneath their location. For a long moment, Dr. Bradan panicked at losing Dale, fearing the worst.

Without warning, they heard Dale's voice, "Get me out of here!"

Dr. Bradan yelled happily, "Dale — Dale can you hear me?"

Again, Dale's voice rang out, muffled by the noise of the speeding water, "I hear you! Stop talking and help me!"

Al called, "Dale, where are you? We can't see you."

Astonished without any physical indication of Dale, they heard him clearly shout, "I'm okay. I'm just in the water."

"How far down did you go? What happened?" Trent hollered.

Except for the churning sound of the twisting torrent, it remained eerily quiet for several long moments before Dale replied, "Maybe about 15 or 20 feet down. I landed in the middle of the ocean."

Dr. Bradan yelled, "Dale, try to remain calm, and tell us what happened!"

"Dad, I'm okay. Once I fell into the water, it swirled around me, and the next thing I knew, I fell out of the bottom of the whirlpool. Now I'm floating in the sea. There's no way I can climb up to the whirlpool."

Al yelled, "Can you see us?"

"I see bubbly water floating above my head, but I can't see you guys."

Dale shouted again, "Hurry up; I'm drifting away, and can't stay underneath the whirlpool much longer."

The two men stared hard at each other, thinking the same thing. The longer they waited, the faster Dale could float away from their position, and perhaps become lost forever.

Al said with certainty, "We can't split up! We need to join him!"

Dr. Bradan's eyes went wide with an impulsive idea as he blared, "Throw down the rope so we can pull him up!"

Al quickly snapped at Trent, "Run back and bring us the rope from your backpack!"

Once Trent returned, Al unrolled the nylon rope, and holding one end, threw the rest of it into the whirlpool while Dr. Bradan called above the rushing water, "Dale, we're dropping the rope! See if you can grab it."

Dale shouted happily, "I see it!"

Once Dale doggedly gripped the end of the rope, he wrapped it about his elbow to avoid floating away and then shouted, "I got it! Pull me out!"

Dr. Bradan pulled the rope with all of his strength. Nevertheless, to his great surprise, it seemed as if an obstruction stopped the rope from inching up.

With a firmer grip on the line, Dr. Bradan jerked back harder than he did before, yet the rope would not budge in his direction. Briefly, he wondered if he was the only person pulling the cable, and quickly spun to look at Al. Suddenly distressed by what he witnessed, the extraordinary man, full of immense power, strained with all of his might to drag the rope backwards. The awareness made the professor quiver in fear.

His mind worried, *"If Al, with all of his strength, can't pull Dale up from the ocean, it must mean the whirlpool is linked with the portals."*

It was a feeble attempt, yet refusing to give up, the professor grabbed the rope again, and the young students pulled as well. With their united exertion, the rope would not budge; instead, they lost several additional inches of it into the vortex when they relaxed. Dr. Bradan yelled, "Dale, Dale, is there anything below to snag the rope?

"No! But I'm not moving up at all. Are you people pulling or not?" Dale responded testily.

"Dale, hold on a moment! Don't let go for any reason," Dr. Bradan ordered.

When the professor turned to face Al, now coated in perspiration, he realized the bigger man had not stopped trying to pull his son up.

Dr. Bradan uttered, "Stop," raising his hands to Al. "It's not working. This is a one-way portal…easy to go forward, but impossible to come back without triggering a switch or understanding how Melinda's pendant works. We must think of another way."

Al relaxed his two-handed grip, yet even in his relaxed state, he kept the rope stretched tight in one massive hand. Defeated, there were zero clues to tell them how they could fix the problem.

Concern filled Trent's voice when he validated Al's earlier comments, "We might not be able to lift Dale, but we can't split up; and if we don't know where Dale is going, we may never find each other again."

Dr. Bradan nodded his head in agreement, when he responded, "I agree. However, the real problem is if we follow him down, how will we survive the open seas with him? How can we keep swimming once we tire?"

Melinda, along with her team, pondered the consequences of the problem. Abandon Dale and die of starvation in the current wasteland, or possibly drown below in a vast sea. The conflict raged internally within each of them. Melinda could see no easy answer.

Abruptly, Tab signed eagerly to Trent.

"Wait a second, Tab wants us to drop a few of those dead palm trees laying over there through the whirlpool before we join Dale, and then lash them together with the rope to make a small raft on the other side."

Al smiled luminously and said, "Hang onto this rope for me Trent."

Quickly he sprinted out of the oasis water, and ran to where Trent had pointed. Dr. Bradan trailed close behind the bigger man. Making several trips dragging the largest palm trees, the two Museum leaders stacked them at the edge of the water.

"Dale, move out of the way! We're going to drop a palm tree through the whirlpool. When it splashes into the ocean, it may land onto the rope. Make sure the rope is not wrapped around any part of you," Al directed.

With a grunt, Al and the professor pushed the first tree base down into the whirlpool.

"Dale; on the count of three, the tree's coming your way."

"Okay, you can drop it now."

Al yelled loudly "One…two…three," when they released the palm tree.

From his vantage point below, Dale suddenly saw a rupture in the draining water that filled with flashing lights. Within seconds, the large end of the palm tree became visible as the portal opened.

The tree plummeted into the ocean to explode seawater high in the air, as it disappeared beneath the surface with a huge splash. Immediately Dale swam towards it after it surfaced.

"I've got the tree," Dale hollered.

Dr. Bradan, to his relief, responded, "Dale, same as before, be careful, here comes another one."

Shortly, the lights flashed above, and a second tree appeared inside of the vortex high above Dale's head.

Dale pulled it beside the other after it fell, and the rest soon followed.

In the desert above his son, Dr. Bradan instructed the students, "We must take turns passing through the portal so I will go first. Please listen to me when I'm on the other side, because if I notice anything dangerous, or I see a serious problem, I'll call to make sure everybody is aware of it before you join us."

Everyone agreed. With his backpack hanging over his shoulder, Dr. Bradan stepped into the oasis water, and peered down into the winding distortion. Melinda noticed Dr. Bradan's face grimace, until he slipped beyond their sight, and the vortex again filled with rushing water.

Like Dale, Dr. Bradan was not visible, but heard through the draining water.

The lecturer yelled, "It's okay, I don't see any trouble. I'm with Dale, and we *are* in an ocean. Hurry down."

Al asked Melinda and the two brothers, "Who wants to go next?"

Tab loyally raised his hand, and grinned at Trent to relieve his older brother's nerves. After he too secured his canteen and valuables, Tab entered into the center of the swirling portal. Moments passed while Tab suddenly blew a former teasing kiss at Trent, and then he too departed within the flash of the vortex. Immediately, Trent's face turned pink.

Seconds later Dr. Bradan called, "Tab is fine!"

Melinda noticed the confidence drain away from Trent's expression when his eyes averted hers and he mumbled, "Melinda, I better go next, and make sure Tab's not worried about me."

Melinda skeptically smiled and thought, *"He's acting as if he likes me."* When Trent's eyes met hers, she replied, "Good idea. That would be best."

Trent awkwardly made sure that he had his gear. Certain he was prepared, Trent walked into the swirl to disappear too. Within seconds, he cheerily called back to Melinda and Al, "C'mon down you guys."

Al told Melinda, "You should be okay here, but if there was any problem, I would prefer to be on this side of the portal to help, while Dr. Bradan is helping on that side. Why don't you go next, and I'll follow right behind you."

Melinda trusted him without hesitation, and she impulsively hugged him. She squeezed as hard as she physically could against his strong torso, barely making an impression in Al's powerful muscles. However, inside, her kindness squeezed the air from him, as he felt sincerely moved. With a giant smile at Al, Melinda stepped backwards into the current.

Surprised at the warmth of the swirling outlet, Melinda realized she was able to breathe comfortably after the air thickened until it molded tightly to her body. When she tried to focus on a particular area, illuminations flashed about her until the water disappeared underneath her, as the portal door opened beneath her feet. Suddenly, Melinda plunged into the ocean below and felt the chilly seawater against her skin. She rose to the surface and gasped for air. While sputtering out salt water, Melinda wiped her eyes to see clearly. Pleased at the trouble-free descent, she spotted her team hanging onto the palm trees behind her. Melinda shivered and paddled towards her friends announcing, "This water feels cold on my sunburn!" She dunked back under the seawater, and rinsed out the sand that remained in her hair.

Melinda surfaced near the drenched group when Dale apologized, "Sorry about forcing you guys to come down here, but I'm glad to see everyone."

Dr. Bradan supported him by saying, "Although not part of the original plan, I'm very glad no one was hurt, and we're all together."

Melinda, hearing the sound of draining water, noticed the swirling vortex above them in the air. From this perspective, the swirling cyclone generated a steady twirling cascade of water into the ocean that reminded her of a small waterspout tornado. Immediately she thought, *"How does so much water drain from a small oasis? It must drain other parts of the desert too. Maybe that's why it's a desert in the first place!"*

Suddenly Al's feet, legs, and torso slithered through the opening, and splashed a short distance away to interrupt her thoughts. Seconds later, his smiling face appeared above the surface next to the floating tree trunks.

He laughed, "Quite a difference between that desert and swimming here. Clearly, we're somewhere else. What's next?"

Instantly, everyone searched the horizon, hoping to spot land, a boat, or some other identifiable object to target as their swimming route. Nothing but shimmering swells surged in all directions. The seriousness of the new circumstances settled harshly on Melinda, when she acknowledged the immense distance between their location and any opportunity for safety.

"Which way should we swim?" Melinda asked, suddenly grasping for her pendant, hoping it had not fallen off. Relieved from her immediate panic, she felt the hard familiar shape still hanging around her neck.

Dr. Bradan instructed, "Before we swim in any direction, I suggest we lash these palm trees together with the rope in the meantime. We'll need a raft to sit on, so we can take turns drying off and warming up from the sun. We have to avoid becoming chilled as this could be dangerous."

Dale, having been in the ocean the longest, asked with chattering teeth, "I'm really cold...can I be the first?"

"Can you feel your arms and legs?" Dr. Bradan asked while observing his son.

"Yeah...," he sputtered with blue lips.

Melinda noticed pronounced goose bumps on everyone's skin.

Al next wrapped the nylon rope around the base of the trees, and then strung it along the length, to fasten the far ends collectively to form a makeshift raft.

Afterwards, Dr. Bradan said, "Dale, get on top of the raft, you need to be out of the water before your body's core temperature lowers too quickly. Every 30 minutes or so, we'll take turns drying and hopefully prevent anyone from developing hypothermia."

Chapter Thirty-One

LOST AT SEA

Early the next morning Melinda opened her eyes and lifted her head off the floating palm tree raft. During the hours of darkness, growing sea winds had caused rising swells to form underneath them. Not quite awake, and yet not quite asleep, she and her friends had endured a difficult time paddling throughout the night to slow the development of hypothermia. They took turns perched on the makeshift raft, to lessen the shivering of their bodies. The effort to propel the raft against the previous larger waves drastically decreased their already waning energy.

Dale reminded everyone of his or her miserable condition when he whined, "I can't believe I am so hungry. Can't we eat something soon?"

Similar pangs of starvation made Al suggest, "Because we don't know how long we'll be stranded in this ocean, we need to ration our little bit of food and water, but still, maintain our strength. I want each person to agree right now, we will consume the same quantity of food until we're rescued!"

Melinda's voice quivered, "Agreed."

The brothers signaled their conformity.

Dr. Bradan and Dale confirmed too.

Al persisted, "This way, we'll know how much food each pack has at any given time. Now everyone remove one of the energy bars we brought with us."

Dr. Bradan supported Al by adding, "He's right, this may become fatal if we lose our heads and use up our fresh water or food too quickly. If truth be told, we need mental discipline right now to stay sharp for our survival."

After everyone did as directed, Al explained, "Before we chomp into our bars, since we're famished, the first bite will taste fantastic, and your hunger will be even more noticeable. Now, this is extremely important. Before anyone eats a second bite, it's vital we refold the wrapper on the food bars, and replace them into your packs. If you believe you're ravenous now, the moment the food touches your lips; it will increase your hunger pains a lot."

Irritable, Melinda complained, "I'm not sure if I want to take a bite, and then feel worse. I'm so hungry that I keep hoping a fish will swim close enough for us to catch it, but I haven't seen anything yet."

Trent placed a hand on Melinda's shoulder and genuinely offered, "Al's right, if we eat too much now, it will only make things worse for us later. If that's not enough of a snack, you can have a corner of mine too."

Melinda smiled vibrantly at the thought, but shook her head against the idea, "Trent you're a good friend, and I know you would share your energy bar with me, but I wouldn't be a good friend to eat your food. Thanks for thinking of me though," she smiled bravely.

Somewhat calmed by her comments, Trent replied, "What are friends for, which you just proved by not accepting my offer, so thanks for thinking of me too."

Melinda bit into the chocolate flavored energy bar. For an instant, the satisfying taste took her mind off their desperate situation, as the sugar seemed to instantly course through her veins to invigorate her body. She felt immediately better. Melinda leaned back in the water to rest her head again on the end of the palm trees, and then nearly spat out the lingering food bits yelling, "THERE! WHAT'S THAT?"

Five sets of glazed-over and sunburned eyes followed Melinda's pointed finger. Far into the distance, Melinda spied tiny white triangles. Al pressed his hands down on the raft and effortlessly lifted himself higher out of the water.

The muscle man hesitated with his enhanced view when he said, "I might be hallucinating, but those almost look like the sails you see on old seafaring ships, but I can't be certain from this distance," he said warily.

"Hey, over here, help us!" Dale yelled at the remote movement.

Surprised at Dale's abrupt yell towards the white triangles, Melinda joined him by screaming and waving an arm as high as possible in the air.

Not wanting to get her hopes up, she wondered if the triangles had grown somewhat larger when she asked, "Is it just me, or do they look bigger, and if so, does that mean they're getting closer?"

Dr. Bradan smiled at her across the palm trees, "They do appear larger than from before, which means you're right about them coming in our direction. This may be the break we've been waiting for out here."

"Yes!" Dale stated with delight, "We're saved! Wahoo! We're saved!"

Ten minutes transpired, which lapsed into fifteen. The obviously larger triangles billowed in the wind as Al predicted. When the ship sailed within easy viewing proximity, Melinda thought it was either an old type of schooner, or one of the newer Windjammer type vessels. Joyful at the sight, Melinda and her friends increasingly waved their hands as much as possible after enduring a hard night and lack of food. The white sails expanded in the continuous ocean breeze, as the craft cut through the swells and sped in their direction.

While the minutes unhurriedly ticked by, fear suddenly dashed Melinda's hopes when the vessel dramatically angled away from their location. Noticing the unforeseen course alteration, she shrieked, "NO! COME BACK THIS WAY!"

As if on command, the ship responded to Melinda's tone, and corrected its path towards their raft. Melinda's eyes filled with small tears of happiness when the swift sailing vessel glided their way. When the mesmerizing ship drew near, people hung over the bow railing, to point in their direction, while shouts caused smaller groups of people to scramble with preparation for their arrival on board.

Melinda watched with excitement as the ship closed the gap to their rickety craft, and looked at Dale across the trees saying, "You see it too right? The ship is really there?"

Dale smiled brighter when he said, "Melinda, it's for real. We're saved!"

Animated, Melinda's attention turned to how perfectly the water parted on either side of the ship's front edge keel. Trent and Tab busily signed to express their good fortune.

Before long, the yacht sized vessel drew near enough to clearly hear a man's voice call to them, "Ahoy!"

The former miniature white triangles on the horizon now soared in the sky above them, as the colossal masts and sails towered over their heads. Practically 90 feet in length, and more than 25 feet wide, the striking ship lowered its large sails to avoid overshooting the castaways. Soon an aged rowboat carrying two middle-aged men rowed towards them.

When the rowboat reached the crude raft, two scruffy sailors greeted them happily, with large smiles and many handshakes.

Melinda and the rescued friends filled with adrenaline, and nearly spoke over each other to express thanks to the men for the rescue.

Melinda's cheerfulness calmed down when she had trouble comprehending one of the sailors, when the man announced, "No entiendo."

Her friends instantly recognized that he spoke in Spanish to them. Wanting to communicate with the rescuers, Trent signed to the men while vocalizing aloud, "Can you understand sign language?

The sight of his rapid hand signals compelled each sailor to study the other, wondering at the meaning. With a courteous gesture, the front man shook his head without comprehending.

Melinda stared wide-eyed in astonishment at the magnitude of the remarkable and historic ship when the seasoned rowboat returned to tie up with the larger vessel. New faces peered over the railing at Melinda and her friends with matched readiness to assist them, as well as the original two sailors. A rope ladder with wooden steps quickly rolled down the side of the ship. Melinda felt weak and cold from the ordeal, but climbed up the steps using a small burst of vigor that gave her added strength to flee their conditions.

Eager to be away from the ocean below, Melinda hastily dragged herself over the ship's rail, aided by several worn and capable hands. Onboard the wooden deck, she stood on wobbly legs with aid from the helpful Spaniards. When friends arrived over the railing to join her, Melinda gave them a huge embrace. The happy band stood dripping in their soggy clothing.

Safely on board the ship, warning bells started to ring in their minds.

Melinda soon viewed the hardened men, most dressed in ragged linen shirts and tatty pants belted with weapons. Melinda worried as one of the men pressed closer to her. She watched the leader point at their garments before speaking excitedly to the others surrounding them in a semi-circle. Unkempt sailors tightened the ring of their unwashed bodies about the group to inspect and touch the group's garments.

Touching Melinda's hair and blouse, a man received a sharp slap on the hand from her as she promptly pulled away from him. Al sensed the immediate change of the men's mood, and stretched out his immense arms to safeguard Melinda and the rest behind him. Al's protective movement caused an alarm to pass among the grubby Spaniards as if from a non-spoken signal. Discerning his motions to shield the students emphasized Al's huge size and muscles, which forced many of the lean seafarers to grip their weapons and suddenly step backwards, unsure of his intentions.

Uncertain of what to anticipate during the subsequent minutes, Al noticed a freshly whittled wooden oar remained on the deck where someone dropped it during their rescue. Heroically, he snatched up the solid wood apparatus and positioned it above one of his immense shoulders, like a power-hitting baseball player. Inadvertently, each side raised the stakes of the heated moments by reacting to the other's actions. Melinda wondered, *"Did these people rescue us, or have we been captured?"*

Melinda was about to step backwards from the predictable angry outburst between Al and the front man when the air filled with the sound of a commanding voice, "DEJEN DE LUCHAR!"

Awestruck by the new person's sharp tone, the entire deck of people turned to stare captivated towards a dark haired and well-built middle-aged man. The commanding Spaniard took Melinda aback. Instantly drawn to the great silver buckles gleaming over his high-heeled black footwear, he stood proudly in dark woolen stockings and garters beneath tan-colored velvet knee-length breeches.

Melinda thought, *"My grandmother would wear those heels and tights."*

Silver braids lined the lapel of his thick velvet jacket. Beneath the coat, the man wore a white fringed silk scarf tied around his neck, which draped over most of the front of his linen shirt. Melinda's eyes rested on his silver sword, supported in a thick leather band by his side.

Long white feathers shot into the air from the brown band of his matching hat, and his tapered face was refined with a tiny goatee. While he paused in his assessment of the waterlogged students, Melinda noticed he had eyes similar to those of the observant Civil War major.

Without introductions, it was obvious this was the ship's true leader, from the receding steps of the men taunting Al. The Spanish captain boldly rested his hands upon his hips to glare equally at both sides, and then proceeded to within a few feet of Al. The striking overseer pointed to the oar held in the Security Chief hands, and affirmed in a governing voice, "Éste es mi nave, por lo tanto que es la mía!"

Melinda was incapable to distinguish the individual words, but his meaning was plain. Without wavering, Al lowered the oar onto the deck floorboards. In respect of the man's position on the ship, Al too backed up a few feet, herding the students that still hovered behind him. He was hopeful the captain would favorably understand his good intentions.

The captain ignored the oar, and inspected the foreigners now aboard his ship. He concluded that the rest of the group presented a feeble risk to his crew and their craft, with the exception of Al. Suddenly, the captain's face brightened with awareness when he noticed Trent and Tab sign to each other.

The man's demeanor changed abruptly, and this time he observed Melinda, along with her drenched friends, to understand they had been floating at sea. Compassion for their weary circumstances became the captain's top concern, and he motioned for Melinda and Al to tag along. Warily, Al remained in front of his companions to protect them from any sailors that got out of hand.

Crossing the main deck, they entered through a large set of red painted doors near the railing. Al relaxed his former notion when they realized the Spanish captain led the group into the ship's galley. Though the dishware appeared to have been scarcely wiped clean from the previous mealtime, Melinda was too famished to care, and ate voraciously to regain her strength.

The delectable flavor of the pot roast overflowed within her mouth causing Melinda to eat as rapidly as she could chew. Seeing this, one of the Spanish cooks placed his weathered hand on hers, to slow down her eating actions saying, "No coma demasiado rápidamente o usted hará enfermo." Melinda showed him that she understood his meaning, and began chewing more slowly to keep the food down.

After the feast, the team followed an elderly man into another large space, where a long table appeared nailed to the floorboards, as well as the encircling wooden chairs. The aging Spaniard instructed, "Por favor. Mi capitán quisiera hablar con ustedes," and then lowered both of his palms in a downward motion two times, to impress upon them to stay.

Able to understand the man's meaning, Melinda and the team sat around the table, and enjoyed the wonderful feeling of sitting upright in a chair in contrast to the constant hiking and swimming over the past few days.

After the man departed from the room, Dale asked, "Dad, what kind of ship is this? It seems a little old to be sailing in the middle of the ocean."

"I'm not sure Dale, but right now I'm more disturbed with the meaning of being aboard this ship," Dr. Bradan replied.

"The meaning?" Melinda asked, unable to follow the professor.

"I'm not precisely sure, but one of my early university classes studied a variety of ship structures. We learned how to classify a range of earlier ship building techniques. European vessels were not my area of proficiency, but the Spanish language combined with the authentic style of this ship, and including the crew's attire, I presume we're on a seafaring ship during the mid to late 1600's."

"How can that be?" Al asked what everyone was thinking.

"Well, we never identified what time period we were in throughout the Sahara Desert. Even while we were adrift on our raft, I wondered how we exited land on one side of the portal doorway and entered water on the other side. Based on what the Shaman explained to us, it is reasonable we passed through significant time changes during both occasions."

Trent asked pensively, "How far back did we go in the desert?"

"My speculation is we may have traveled back *millions* of years at the sand dunes, however, it's hard for me to summarize exactly how far, considering the area may have had its waters draining for eons into the sea," Dr. Bradan conveyed.

Al asked, "So do you have any idea which ocean…"

Instantly, the door to the room opened, and the ship's captain floated into the area like a blue peacock when he twirled to sit at the table. Despite their previous meeting only an hour before, the leader had changed his clothing, and now wore a large blue hat that matched his jacket and knickers.

Glancing and nodding at each of the museum friends around the table, the Spaniard straightforwardly offered a broad smile while he introduced himself to the group, "Hola. Soy Ferdinand mayor Sanchez, el dueño de la estrella del mar."

"Hola, Señor Ferdinand Sanchez," Dr. Bradan replied.

Smiling at the professor, the Spanish captain asked him, "Hay alguien aquí que habla español?"

Shaking his head no, Dr. Bradan said, "No, sorry."

Realizing Dr. Bradan understood his meaning in spite of what he said, he asked, "Es usted Inglés?"

Shaking his head no again, Dr. Bradan raised his hand saying, "American," and then tapped his chest with his hand.

Puzzled, Captain Sanchez squinted and replied, "Usted no es Inglés?"

Dr. Bradan confirmed, "American."

Tab signed to the captain, when the former smile returned at the action, and Sanchez held up one finger for Tab to wait. Turning in his seat, the leader bellowed to the guard outside the door, "Traigame el cocinero que utiliza señales de la mano inmediatamente. Necesito su servicio."

At once, one of the pre-assigned sentries announced, "Sí señor."

While the man hurried off to fulfill the Spanish captain's orders, their host smiled again. The guard returned quickly with an older, shorter crewmember clothed nearly in rags.

Tentative to enter into the presence of the captain, the lookout sentry gave the older man a gentle push in their direction while the captain appraised the destitute Cook's appearance and said, "Entre. Necesito ayuda,"

The captain ordered him, "Usted hable con sus manos con ellos. No son Inglesa?"

Displaying a nervous demeanor, the petite man used brief, awkward sign language movements.

Smiling, Trent said, "He's using a hesitating manner, so I'll do my best to fill in the gaps as I translate. Right now, he's asking, "Who are you people? Where do you come from?""

Trent replied using similar hand signals to the cook, while saying the words he signed aloud for the benefit of the team, "We are from America."

The man repeated the words quickly in Spanish to his captain.

Sullen, the ship's leader grunted at the short man, who signed the captain's remarks to Trent. Translating, Trent said, "My lord has not been to this place. Is this a part of England?"

Trent signed saying, "Once, a long time ago, but our people fought the English for their independence, and broke away to form our own land."

After the translation into Spanish, Captain Sanchez slapped his knee, smiling, and rapidly rattled off a string of words to the cook. Trent translated the cook's conversion with the captain, "My lord is pleased we both have the English as enemies. He requests to know more from you later, perhaps tonight. He wishes you to feel liberated to travel about the ship. Come, I show where you may sleep."

Rising, the Spanish captain grinned in a pleasant way, while Melinda and her friends reveled in the news this was truly a rescue, and that they could move freely aboard the sailing schooner. Happy, Melinda smiled politely at the captain as the man bowed to her and then left the room. Once the captain had departed, the nervous cook signed at the group to follow him. As they exited the room, Melinda enjoyed feeling the warm sunshine and studied her surroundings. She was enthralled with the romantic nature of the sailing ship. Watching the sailors work, she noticed most were barefoot.

Surprised by this revelation, she asked, "Why don't the men wear shoes?"

Trent passed on the question, and repeated the answer aloud from the weathered cook, "Too dangerous! Shoes are slippery on wet decks."

Soon, they walked past the quartermaster's cabin, and then descended a narrow set of wooden stairs into the hold.

Below the main deck, the ship produced unusual smells. Sweat lingered in the musty air, combined with various whiffs of strong spices, which eventually overpowered the initial previous odors. Next, their guide escorted them past stalls crammed with barrels and crates, until they reached an open area of rope hammocks.

Their new host pointed towards the hammocks, and signed to Trent who translated, "Sleep here. These extras are distant from the crew's quarters in front. I return when my lord wishes to speak with you later tonight."

He started to leave when Trent stopped him by signing, "Wait, can I ask you a few questions to know where we are?"

The man smiled a nearly toothless grin, and sat heavily on a box crate.

Trent verbalized what he was signing, "What is your name?"

The man spelled, "Felipe."

Trent continued, "We drifted in the ocean. What land are we close to?"

The seasoned man grinned, signing, "Passing Tortugas. We are not Corsair, but come onward across the West Ocean from Spain with supplies to the colonies."

"Where are we headed?"

Animated, Felipe replied, "We sail for the Isthmus of Panama!"

"Where is that place?" Trent signed.

Shocked at the question, the older man looked suspiciously at Trent, who spotted the sudden tenseness in the man's posture, so he quickly added, "I meant where the bathrooms are?"

"Ship's head is near the bow before reaching the figurehead."

"What about food and drink? When can we eat again?"

"Tortillas, beans, and biscuits will be fit to be eaten soon. I make more tonight. No one drinks until mealtime."

Trent hesitated, but felt compelled to ask, "Can you tell me what year it is?"

Undaunted by the question, the veteran cook signed, "1669."

Before Trent could ask another question, the cook stood and waved his arms saying, "I'm late in cooking, and will explain more later."

Once the older man had departed, Melinda and the team, with the exception of Tab, were eager to know more by asking Trent, "What else did he say?"

Trent updated them with minor additional details, when Dr. Bradan said, "I wondered if we were in the late 1600's when I saw this ship. Wow, what historians would give to watch actual sea-faring activities." After a short pause the professor added, "Well, since we can't eat now, we better rest while we have the chance."

Melinda felt hypnotized with the mention of sleep. Among her friends, she chose a hammock, and soon fell fast asleep to the gentle rising and falling motion of the ship.

Chapter Thirty-Two

EERIE DREAMS

Just below the surface of consciousness, the female Guardian's almond-shaped eyelids twitched rapidly as she telepathically received thoughts of foul conspiracy from the menacing mind of a younger version of the Shaman. He led other secretive figures that were lurking within the depths of the jungle's imposing stone and jade stronghold.

Awakened from absorbing their sinister intentions, the female Guardian reacted swiftly. Alerted to the Shaman's presence within the sanctuary, the female Guardian instinctively broadcasted a psychic warning to the Sovereign Governess asleep in her chamber, *"Awake! A menace threatens you and the child!"* In addition, she projected her thoughts to the larger and hulking muscular male Guardian busily patrolling the perimeter, *"Five death stalkers approach us inside the outer chamber —, and one is truly evil!"*

Together with the male Guardian, both had evolved from the bloodlines of mammoth sized telepathic ancestors.

Superbly built for strength and speed, she ran purposefully into the hallway. Powerful strides stretched out her long retractable claws to sharpen them on the stone floor, while on her way to protect the good nobles that she served.

By her urging the Olmec Governess to gather up her small daughter Maynaya, together the fearful mother and her tiny child readied hastily, and then anxiously met the female Guardian at the entry of an underground hidden passageway.

Near the escape access, the trio stood in front of massive carved stone blocks lining the inner chamber's rear wall; however, it was an illusion. Perfectly overlapping each other, the walls concealed stone steps leading downward and through a heavy wooden door. The incredible animal searched the gloom behind them to ensure their safety, before leading her dear companions deep into the getaway tunnel.

***

Cloaked within the muted and wavering torchlight of the barely-lit palace, in restless silence, his black ink-colored iridescent eyes and smooth close-lying fur permitted the enormous and tailless male Guardian to evaporate like a mist into the shadows. He inspected his vicinity after receiving the telepathic forewarning from the female Guardian. Vigilantly, he emerged from the darkness, with the nagging awareness that the Shaman and his grim followers spied him beneath the dimness of the lofty stone ceiling.

Savagely, four barbarous figures with the Shaman rushed the devoted protector; one was not truly human. The male Guardian bore his frightening fangs, and with the swiftness of an arrow in flight, stepped effortlessly from the path of the foremost warrior. The insistent assassin rushed unpredictably past the skilled four-legged silhouette, and slashed viciously at the huge animal with a sudden gleam in the moonlight.

The male Guardian ducked the razor-sharp blade, and fastened his powerful jaws around the fighter's ankle. Using colossal strength, the male Guardian drove his massive head and neck up. Vaulted skyward, the now-desperate combatant lost his grip of a deadly scimitar shaped weapon before slamming unconscious onto the jade inlaid floor.

Telepathically forcing the next opponent to discard his machete, the black mass of fury pounced upon him to clamp his front claws over the intruder's shoulders, and then wrapped his vice-like teeth securely around his enemy's neck. The scared man could not free himself from the brute even with forceful side-wrenching throes. Still clinging with unyielding talons onto his opponent's shoulders throughout a powerful launch backward, the male Guardian twisted in the air and thrust out his heavily built legs like a Judo champion, to fling the criminal into the sweeping gloom.

The male Guardian quickly rose and leapt over the *whoosh* of the Shaman's streaking sword, and slammed forcefully into the broad chest of the next rushing foe. As if stricken by lightning, the attacker flew backwards. His unprotected head crashed heavily against a sandstone column, and then he wilted to the ground. Blood promptly trickled on the floor beneath his slumped head.

The magnificent beast drew in the smell of the fresh blood, when again, peril telepathically flashed throughout his brain. After dropping into a tigerish crouch, the male Guardian's sharp eyes observed the flowing actions of a powerfully built giant. With incredible might, the grisly giant easily hurled a 400-pound limestone jaguar statue at him. Despite his own massive size, the male Guardian sprung catlike to change his direction to avoid the oncoming sculpture.

The speeding limestone projectile would have crushed the skull of his broad head, without forewarning from reading the Giant's mind; nevertheless, even with fantastic footwork, the male Guardian's huge legs slipped when aged floor tiles broke free from weakened mortar beneath his mighty claws.

Unable to recoil away from the racing statue in time, the heavy wallop of the glancing blow knocked the male Guardian unconscious. Plummeting lifelessly to the ground, he slid across the floor and lay motionless. The vile goliath and Shaman left him for dead, as they dashed away before the current clash attracted unwanted attention from the palace sentry.

***

The female Guardian guided the Governess, who was now carrying her frightened three-year-old daughter, through the insect-infested dark tunnel. The impressive animal knew her cherished companions were directly behind her, by collecting what they indistinctly saw in the gloom as pictures within her own mind.

Unexpectedly, the female Guardian's fur hackles bristled intensely, when she sensed a pulsation. Mentally probing the murky area ahead, she raced forward through the rough corridor to confront the reason. Around a tunnel bend, an irregular eerie glow of living fire blazed and swirled from the side of the stone hallway.

With gleaming black opal eyes, the female Guardian's fierce gaze appraised the shining yellow and blue lights with burning interest. Diffused illuminations revealed strange, alien images, through the translucent shimmer, until those she sheltered arrived by her side. Collectively, the inseparable royal companions and their loyal protector viewed the portal's streaming imagery of outlandish people, buildings, and landscapes, swirling into a point of blended confusion. Mysterious shapes filled with expressionless humans crossed and faded into the distance.

Riveted by the hovering mystery of what they witnessed, none of the three companions heard the stealthy footsteps of their relentless pursuers, trailing them like phantoms through the gloominess. Aware of a sudden mounting sensation, the previous deadly thoughts flashed within the mind of the gifted female Guardian.

She whirled to meet the oncoming stalkers before actually seeing the two threatening figures closing steadily on her precious pair. Within sight of each other, the Shaman stepped aside when the goliath extracted a heavy blade from the scabbard slung over his shoulder. He pointed the razor-sharp tip at the child. Intent on killing the tiny girl, the bald gargantuan did not see the female Guardian partially hidden by the Governess's long flowing robes. The Guardian faithfully lunged into a shielding stance between the giant and the girl. She remained unmoved waiting to strike at the huge man after understanding his murderous thoughts.

Alarmed by the unexpected appearance of the second protective Guardian, the assailant's eyes shot wide-open with surprise. Telepathically warning the mother and daughter to run, they turned to observe the strobe-like movements of the battle that broke through the darkness, randomly lit by the quick flashes from the mysterious portal's spinning radiance.

The hulking figure wielded his great sword, while yearning for their defender's blood. Without alarm, the female Guardian stopped his charge by rushing him. With agile swiftness, she boldly avoided the mighty blows of his bare steel. Brilliant blue-white sparks glittered on the whirling blade each time it raked the walls and ceiling from the giant's tremendous force.

During a huge sword thrust at the female Guardian, pain shot up his arm. The giant felt an agonizing sting emanate from his wrist, now held tightly within the female Guardian's powerfully clenched fangs. She quickly dislocated his elbow using her full strength with a mighty snap and a tug.

His wrist remained locked firmly within her fangs during the brief engagement. Before he could recover, she twisted sideways in a semi-circle, and authoritatively led him, doubled over, by his sagging forearm. Mentally forcing his footsteps to go faster, she used a telepathic attack to immobilize the goliath, by causing him to pitch headfirst into a four-ton stone block.

At the precise moment of his collapse onto the stone floor, the female Guardian relaxed her bite, and used the momentum from his immense swinging arm to fly airborne until she slammed into the weight-bearing knee of the Shaman.

The cold-blooded killer's leg twisted into an unnatural angle, and stopped him from viciously plunging a dagger into the now-horrified and screaming toddler. Inflicted with great physical pain by the force of the female Guardian, his countenance quickly filled with dread, after witnessing her effortless elimination of the war-skilled titan.

Now alone to face the royal protector, the Shaman's desperation grew when he realized the tables had turned, and he was now fighting for his own life. Helpless to escape from his injury, his uncontrollable fear throbbed heavily within his temples from having no place or ability to run. With hate-filled eyes, he slashed furiously at the female Guardian with a grimacing pain surging within his leg. Losing his balance, the pain caused a sound of agony to escape his lips, stopping his muttered spell as he staggered uncontrollably at the terrified youngster.

The girl's mother fearfully dragged her only child from the path of the stumbling Shaman. Entirely focused on the evil man's approach, she turned sharply to pull away from his outstretched hands. Unintentionally stepping on the inside of her extensive robes, she tripped backwards. Losing her clammy grip on the child, the unexpected sudden movements reeled her and the youngster directly into the spinning vortex.

The Governess vanished completely into a dark night setting, while the small girl tumbled through the air until she passed through the portal into a shimmering sunrise. At the same time, the female Guardian launched herself upwards to pounce upon the Shaman, still stumbling in direction of the fading majestic duo.

Shadows began to shrink back into the darkness of his newly conscious mind, when the wavering torchlight gradually intensified within his recovered vision. The flickering illumination slowly outlined shapes about him, within the humid shelter. Abruptly, the male Guardian scrambled to regain his footing. Racked with an intense pain that tore at the inside of his head like jagged knives, the great beast shook his head back and forth to clear the aching fog.

Three figures lay motionless about him in the large hall, amongst the smashed pieces of the jaguar sculpture from the recent commotion. Silence prevailed in the area. Filled with impatient dedication, the male Guardian charged across the stunning jade floor tiles, making his way towards the tunnel's hidden stairs.

New images packed his mind's eye an instant before his hearing confirmed the struggle further ahead. After traversing the tunnel's concluding bend, he saw the Governess and her daughter falling backwards only to instantly disappear within moments of each other into the swirling blue and yellow gateway. The enormous male Guardian soared over the still fallen giant in the direction of the stumbling Shaman. Racing towards the wicked man, he watched him evaporate entirely through the gateway, shortly followed by the female Guardian.

A final oversized leap carried the powerful male Guardian into the diminishing sparks of the withdrawing light; and with a thunderous thud, the fearsome animal crashed painfully into the wall, tearing a gash into his shoulder. Unaware of the bleeding now matting his dark fur, he peered deeply into the departing remnants of the flashing lights, until only a minuscule dot of blue flickered on the wall.

Then all went black.

Suddenly Melinda bolted upright out of her deep sleep in a panic. Shaken by a smaller hand, she distantly heard, "Señora. Coma por favor."

Wearily, her eyes fluttered, uncertain if she was coming to consciousness, or still dreaming of the terrible events that happened 2,000 years before in the far-away tunnel. She wondered at the newly added details of her dream, now refreshed within her unconscious mind by the female Guardian's previous mind transmission, when the tiny voice spoke again, "Señora. Coma por favor el alimento!"

Awakened, Melinda realized the ship's cabin boy shook her arm. The distressed boy stepped back from her dismayed reaction, fearful he had wrongly touched her arm. Realizing she was not angry with him, he then pressed his skinny fingers to his mouth, mimicking the actions of eating food. When Melinda realized the boy was explaining it was mealtime, she ran her fingers through her hair, and pushed her bangs out of her eyes as she swung her feet to the floorboards. The boy next awoke Dr. Bradan and Tab.

Melinda watched her friends wobble from the residue of their sleep until the boy signaled for all to tag along. Similar to their route down to the hammocks below deck, he soon brought them back to the same narrow set of wooden stairs to go above deck. As a mildly refreshed and wide-eyed group, they gawked in all directions while they crossed the open deck, and ascended three more steps between the ship's railing and the side of the poop deck. The elementary school age lad soon halted in front of the red painted doors. Hesitating to ensure all arrived; he pulled open the door to the galley.

Inside, Melinda counted twenty-seven haggard faces showing the strain of voyaging for months in all types of sea conditions. A few greeted them with a small speck of curiosity. The boy pointed at a vacant side table to sit. Uneasily, Melinda peered at the toughened men while they conversed with each other in Spanish. She scanned the sailors, but could not locate the captain or any of his officers among the unruly looking group.

At the table, Melinda made a decision to sit down on the wooded bench with her back to the ship's wall, so she could study the other tables.

Trent leaned over to speak in low tones saying, "I didn't see the Captain. Tab thinks he eats with his officers inside his cabin."

Dr. Bradan whispered across the table, "I was wondering the same thing. This is a rough-looking bunch. I hope the captain is firmly in charge, because as you know, many times crews would mutiny under the pressure of ocean crossings."

Dale winced, "Do you think we'll have to walk the plank?"

Dr. Bradan chuckled and consoled his son, "No, Dale, not with this group, however, we need to bear in mind how fortunate we are to be found by this ship instead of pirates during this time. The 1600's to the early 1700's were part of the

Golden Age of Piracy. We would most certainly endure much bigger troubles from them."

Unhurriedly, the stubby cook entered the dining area, carrying an iron pot, and a wooden ladle. After placing the steaming pot onto their table, he then returned with a woven container filled with biscuits and a stack of bowls. Once each team member had acquired a bowl, the older man filled it with one ladle of the concoction.

The cook left them, but soon returned with a large bowl of beans and a mound of tortillas. Quiet the entire time, he again departed when the cabin boy brought out various pewter mugs. When the youth returned with an aged wooden bucket, he poured a shadowy liquid into each mug.

At first, Melinda thought it was juice, but the pungent odor soon convinced her it was something more. Subtly, Melinda gazed back at the group of sailors, where a few men occasionally stared awkwardly at them. She waited for the lad to return with spoons, but when he didn't, she looked at the sailors to see how they ate. It was soon clear they used the tortillas to scoop up the beans, the biscuits to dip into the soup, or they drank directly from the bowl.

Melinda whispered to those at her table, "Watch what I do. This is how they're eating behind you guys."

After completing the meal, Melinda felt very tired from the combination of her stress prior to being onboard the ship, and the effects from the warm food. She assumed by seeing the same sagging eyelids on the faces of her friends that they also would trail her back to their hammocks for additional rest.

Smiling at Trent, Melinda stood up saying, "I'm ready for more sleep," when the ship violently shuddered and careened.

Chapter Thirty-Three

PIRATES

Instantly, the sailors' voices filled the dining galley with breathless yells as they rushed out to the main deck. Unsure what to do next because of the sudden excitement, foreboding filled Melinda's thoughts as she and her friends nervously remained at their table, until the squat cook raced from the kitchen and made hand signals to Trent.

Trent translated, "Hide! Ship is under attack. Go below deck!"

His warning made clear, the man pointed at the galley door. The team scrambled over one another to follow his urgent directions. Melinda hurried towards the doorway, when powerful explosions rocked the ship again. Awkward from leaning to one side during the sudden impacts, Melinda and Dale tried to regain their sense of balance, as they trailed Al and the professor beyond the door.

Blinded by the shimmering water from the setting sun, Melinda distinctly heard Captain Sanchez bark orders to the Spanish sailors. Instantly, the large sailing craft made another sharp turn. Melinda braced herself during the tilt throughout the turn, while enemy cannon balls blasted chunks from the ship's starboard side. Melinda shielded her eyes with her hands to avoid injury from flying debris, and peeking through her fingers, noticed the dark outline of a larger ship sailing towards them.

The Spanish Captain commanded, "FUEGO!"

Three onboard cannons fired at the fast forthcoming ship and vibrated the air with blasting sounds and newly billowing smoke. With the approaching ship sailing directly to ram them, it provided a narrow target for the firepower of the

Spanish guns. Melinda saw the first ball rip through the large main sail of the enemy ship, while the other two shots splashed harmlessly into the ocean.

Accurately aimed cannon balls shot back from the invading ship, causing their vessel to shake forcefully upon each concussion. Each shudder from the enemy's cannon fire caused the Spanish captain to yell new orders to his crew. Sailors nearly trampled Melinda when she failed to move during their rush.

The sailors worked in unison to unfurl the ship's top sail. As it stretched out and captured the wind, the lighter Spanish ship sped away from the fast-approaching foe, still firing upon them. Melinda believed they were about to escape when they began pulling away from the trailing pirates.

However, to everyone's alarm, a forward cannon on the pirates' ship blasted two cannon balls welded together in the middle with a chunky iron bar. The well-aimed shot punched through the Spanish mainmast with a loud snap, cracking it in half. With a giant moan, the mainmast lurched forward, snapping the higher half of the tall beam, and crashed down heavily onto the lower sail. Roped together, the topsails of the mast pulled free and tumbled below to cause more damage.

Though a few minutes earlier all felt they would escape, the damage to their ship from the pirate's cannons stopped them dead in the water. The tangle of broken timbers, ropes, and wooden debris upon the main deck rendered the sailors powerless to execute many of Captain Sanchez's commands.

Melinda appraised the situation, and then climbed over broken timbers to ascend stairs leading up to the top deck. With the improved view, she saw that the aggressive ship had shortened the distance between them. Alarmed, she started searching through the deck's wreckage for her friends. Melinda spotted Al removing huge pieces of cracked lumber near the warping capstan where she had seen Tab and Trent duck for cover. She then observed Dr. Bradan, closely followed by Dale, hurrying towards her yelling, "It's coming…the pirate ship is coming!"

A large Spaniard rushed past them and pried open the stockroom cabinet door behind Melinda, with a thick metal bar. Once he backed out of the shallow room, the large sailor held a ship's short handled axe. Other Spaniards rushed around him to remove muskets, swords, knives, and powder horns.

The armed sailors then rushed near the railing and dropped to their knees to load their weapons. With newly loaded muskets, they readied for the approaching ship. As the pirate craft neared, the Spanish sailors stood and fired their muskets.

Melinda noticed that with each shot, a pirate dropped to the deck on the other ship. When the larger vessel drew closer still, pirates threw large metal hooks tied to ropes over the side of the smaller ship's railing. Within minutes, that side of the ship's main deck looked like a spidery web of ropes.

Spaniards carrying swords and axes quickly cut the ropes secured to each hook, hoping to prevent the pirates from lashing both ships together. Yet each time a Spaniard sliced a rope, new pirates appeared to toss more of the metal hooks as replacements. After the front sections of the ships came together, the invaders fought back by firing at the Spanish sailors with pistols and muzzleloaders.

Suddenly, the rear sections of both vessels collided with a gut-wrenching shudder, knocking Melinda and Dr. Bradan onto the deck floorboards. Al and the brothers moved quickly to help them to their feet. The two ships now secured side-by-side, Melinda glanced up in time to see pirate sea-rats swinging onto the Spanish ship's main deck. With a rush to hold back the boarders, the brave Spaniards met the pirates in swordplay.

In less than a minute, the pirates remaining on their ship shot at the fighting Spaniards, cutting them down. Swiftly outnumbered by the boarding enemy, the valiant Spaniards were defeated.

Above the noise and confusion of the battle, Captain Sanchez bellowed orders to the rest of his men to fire muskets and pistols at the robbers on their deck. Successfully killing some of the men, the horde of foul pirates turned their attention to the remaining Spanish leader and his surrounding officers. One by one, they shot down his gathered lieutenants, leaving Captain Sanchez to stand alone.

Melinda, knowing the Spaniards were beaten, shouted to Al, "We need to run to the back of the ship and hide!"

Without waiting for Al's response, Melinda ran towards the stern of the ship and glanced over her shoulder in time to see Captain Sanchez charge towards the oncoming pirates. Extremely outnumbered, the passionate man held guns in both hands. He fired each quickly, then dropped the empty ones, and rapidly removed more from the bandolier draped across his chest.

A fierce-looking Chinese pirate dodged Captain Sanchez's next shot, and thrust his sword at the Spanish leader's stomach. With a quick leap backwards, the Spanish captain dodged the stabbing tip. Bent slightly at the waist to avoid the attack put the lone leader in an awkward position to defend against the pirate's next assault. The Chinese man faked a deeper slash, forcing Sanchez to lean further forward, but instead of sticking him with the blade, the Chinese man instead spun around quickly in a roundhouse style movement to strike the Spanish captain on the side of his head with the handle of his sword. The battle ended when Captain Sanchez lost awareness.

When Melinda returned to the ship's galley, the quickest place to hide was behind a half-wall inside the large dining space. Her friends trailed her, believing the attack was over. Melinda peeked around the side of their protective barrier, and saw the ship's injured and dead laying on the deck through the open doorway.

Melinda watched the invaders hoist a gangplank in place to link the two ships. She spotted a bulky man crossing the makeshift bridge, while the other pirates outside the galley silently waited for new orders. Melinda decided this must be the pirate captain, not only because of his commanding presence, but also because of the respect shown to him by the others.

Without matching her expectation of a ruthless pirate's appearance, this man seemed a complete surprise to her. Although he stood with a stiff military posture, his pose did not match his long wavy hair neatly parted in the middle. He had large eyes and a straight nose that ran down to his trimmed handlebar mustache. It widened, as the ends were thicker than the middle section under his nose. On his chin, the man sported the tiny triangle of a miniature goatee. The new leader's embroidered clothing far surpassed the extravagant outfits of Captain Sanchez, as the tailoring was unique for his form. As the setting sun shined on the gold braid fringes of his jacket, a sudden breeze lifted the rich exterior to show a burgundy silk lining.

The man didn't speak angrily to his men, but coolly signaled them into action with a wave of his hand. Many hurried to gather and toss lifeless Spaniards over the ship's railing. Melinda noticed the movements of a few injured men, who now had a slim chance to survive once thrown into the ocean.

Melinda was startled when the pirate captain abruptly roared, "Ahoy! Stand by t' search th' ship. Shake a leg, and brin' e'erythin' — Now turn 't!"

Under his watchful eyes, the pirates scattered in many directions to obey his orders. Some men lifted the fallen sails to search underneath for goods, while more followed the giant Chinese raider into the lower depths of the ship. Within a short time, those below deck returned with chests filled with Spanish gold pieces-of-eight, and stacked them next to wooden drums filled with salt, beef, corn, rum, candles, and gunpowder.

As Melinda and her friends squatted nervously behind the bulkhead wall, Dale, stunned by what he witnessed, stood in the open to watch the overwhelming amount of plunder spread out across the center of the ship's main deck.

Suddenly the galley doorway went dark, and a disfigured olive-skinned pirate with a horrible slash across his face pointed a crooked and dirty finger at Dale. He commanded with a tremendous roar, "AHOY, YOU THAR — AVAST!"

The echo resonated back to the main deck, where several pirates scanned the area, until they too spotted Dale hovering in fear through the large dining area window. Two muscular pirates shouted frightening curses, and rushed towards the galley, striking terror into Dale's heart. Seeing that Dale was riveted with fear into place, Al jumped up from his hiding place and grabbed Dale securely about the waist, while he bellowed over his shoulder to the rest, "FOLLOW ME!"

Energetically running at the man in front of him, the former football player barreled his shoulder fully into the surprised man's chest, propelling him off his feet and through the single glass-paned window. The flying pirate's momentum carried him beyond the broken frame and into the oncoming sea-rats, knocking both of the surprised pirates to the deck floorboards. With the pathway cleared, Melinda raced after Al through the open doorway.

Outside the galley, another pirate lifted his deadly sword to chop at Al. Instinctively the bigger man lifted up his leg and kicked the attacking pirate in the stomach, tumbling him backwards. Quickly turning the corner, Al led the friends through a hatchway entrance and down a set of steps into a lower cargo section. From somewhere behind them, a pistol fired, lodging a deadly lead ball into the deck beam next to Melinda's head. She screamed from the unexpected blast, and fled down the steps behind Al, still carrying Dale.

Even with Dale's additional 120-pounds of weight, Al effortlessly skipped two and sometimes three wooden steps as a time. The small band passed through a double set of locking doors and entered into a large hold filled with barrels and crates. Strangely, instead of hearing the pounding footsteps of the chasing pirates, silence followed them. Everyone's hearts beat furiously in fear.

Several pensive minutes later, the area remained quiet, until leisurely, slow heavy steps sounded down the stairs and stopped. Melinda peeked from around a large wooden barrel, and watched the gigantic Chinese pirate point two pistols in their direction, one in each hand.

"Ahoy there," his voice immediately broke the hush. "Hidin' behind gunpowder be a filthy decision on yer part!"

Melinda and Al swiftly looked at each other to confirm the meaning of what the pirate said. Within the dimly lit room, branded imprints on each crate and barrel were suddenly visible. Their vulnerability by ducking behind the gunpowder crashed down on their thoughts.

Al, Dr. Bradan, and Melinda stared amongst themselves, trying to come up with a possible next move. Unexpectedly, the Chinese pirate split open the top of a small barrel marked *Gunpowder* in front of him with a hatchet. Everyone froze in fear of his next action. He then pushed the barrel onto its side with his foot, and rolled it towards the large barrel in front of them, leaving a trail of gunpowder.

Abruptly, Melinda moved back from the barrel when she heard the sound of tearing fabric, closely followed by the sound of a lit match.

The room illuminated, as the pirate said, "I know yer here. Come out or be blasted t' th' bottom o'de sea."

Melinda glanced at Dr. Bradan and Trent, frightened at the man's icy tone. Dr. Bradan realized the hopelessness of their situation, and called out, "Wait — we're coming out! Everyone, we're coming out."

Slowly rising from behind the explosives with one hand held high above his head, Dr. Bradan pulled on Dale's shoulder, urging him to stand too. Melinda, Al, and the brothers followed. Instantly two more of the vicious pirates came down the stairs and strode past the Chinese brute.

A Corsair pirate painfully jerked Dale's arm, and pulled him away from Dr. Bradan, wrapping his arm forcefully under Dale's chin. The other renegade drew his cutlass and urged the brothers to follow behind Dr. Bradan up the stairway, and out of the ammunition room. Prodded from behind, Melinda remained sandwiched behind Trent and in front of Al, until they all reached the top deck.

When Al passed through the small doorway and stepped onto the open quarterdeck, the massive Chinese pirate took serious interest in him at once. Melinda watched, as the pirate appeared genuinely happy by Al's appearance and grinned at him. The smaller pirate who forcefully held Dale by the neck stepped to where the waiting captain stood. Scared for Dale's well-being, Dr. Bradan stepped cautiously towards his son, when the second pirate used his cutlass handle to knock the professor over the head. Slowly, the educator slumped to the deck.

Al quickly grasped the wrist of the man who had hit the professor with one hand, and using his other powerful hand, squeezed the man's neck in his remarkable grip, choking off his air. The pain in the man's wrist forced him to drop the sword onto the ship's deck. Al's sudden movements startled the pirates standing by the captain, but they quickly recovered and moved aggressively towards the big man. Al responded to their violent advance by easily lifting the weaker pirate higher into the air, using only one hand about the man's neck, illustrating the plan to snap his neck, if they came closer. For several moments, the standoff was clear and silent, until the terrible captain bellowed a sinister laugh, and raised his own pistol to fire at Al.

Reactively, Al stepped backwards when the captain fired the weapon. Instantly, the man's upper body tightened within Al's grip, and then wilted. Stunned by the leader's unconcerned expression, Al lowered the wounded pirate to the deck, and realized the captain had purposely shot his own man, to prove his wicked ability.

Aware of the captain's unpredictable nature, even with his own men, Al surrendered, to avoid causing further hostility toward the students.

The captain glared at Al and demanded, "Who be ye? Ye be not Spanish!"

"We were lost at sea for several days before being discovered. This crew saved us, and showed us kindness. They did not deserve what you have done to them." Al scolded the man.

As soon as Al spoke, the captain cocked his head as if trying to distinguish his accent. Not quite knowing what he heard, he asked, "Whose people be ye?"

With a moan, Dr. Bradan tried to warn Al while he rubbed his injured head.

Ignoring the dazed professor, the captain queried, "Ye speak English, but not as I e'er heard before."

Al told him, "Once, we were part of England," then unwittingly added, "years later, we fought England and its government, to become a new country…"

Immediately the leader's face scrunched hard into a dark expression, and he blasted, "Aye, and traitors! Traitors against th' Crown. It be well that I find ye with th' Spaniards!" Glancing around the ship angrily, he yelled, "TAKE TH' GIRL T' ME CABIN, AND PUT TH' LADS T' WORK!"

Melinda watched the captain spin and storm back toward his ship, which she noticed was called the *Oxford*, when the gigantic Chinese pirate caught up to the captain, and whispered in his ear while smiling.

Laughing boldly, the buccaneer chief turned to his men and added, "These two traitors, I care not if ye maroon on th' next patch o' desolate hell we see, or strap 'em t' th' masthead and kill 'em."

The pirate chief turned and quickly disappeared from Melinda's eyesight. Escorted by two new pirates, they pressed her to walk forward towards the much larger ship. Separated from her friends, Melinda was amazed to see the huge amounts of chests, food, clothing, and barrels of gunpowder piled together, that had recently belonged to the Spaniards. All of it ready for hauling across the main plank bridging the two ships.

Hurried over the suspension bridge, and onto the *Oxford*, Melinda watched as freebooters energetically moved the stolen items to a pre-determined hold below deck. Lost in her thoughts from watching the nearby activity, one of the pirates jerked Melinda's arm, leading her towards the rear of the bigger ship. She knew they were taking her to the pirate leader's quarters, and glanced backwards at Trent, Tab, and Dale, now led in an opposite direction.

She also noticed that Al and Dr. Bradan were escorted in a third direction at sword point. Scared and uncertain, she cried out involuntarily when one of the leering pirates pushed her through the cabin door into the captain's quarters. Hearing Melinda scream, Al reacted to her plea, but the Chinese brute grabbed a gun from his waistband and slammed it down on Al's head. He collapsed unconscious to the deck.

Chapter Thirty-Four

COW ISLAND

Al slowly opened his unfocused eyes, and immediately raised a hand to caress a large bump on the back of his head. He withdrew his fingers from the pain shooting across his scalp, and noticed remnants of dried blood on his fingertips. Drowsy, the oversized man rolled onto his back with a groan, from the pain of his throbbing head. As Al's eyes focused, he noticed Dr. Bradan grinning down at him from a cot like a Cheshire cat.

"Did you have a nice nap?" the professor happily asked the dazed man.

Al squinted against the sharp pain stabbing behind his eyes to ask, "What happened? Melinda yelled something, and now I have this splitting headache."

Dr. Bradan replied, "Your scalp took quite a blow, but fortunately, this time it paid off to have such a thick, hard, head. You sound as if you'll be fine," the professor said with amusement.

Giving the unsteady man a chance to become more alert, Dr. Bradan said, "It seems your large Chinese friend has an unusual interest in you."

"I'm not sure why Doc, but I noticed that too. He must mistake me for somebody else, or because of my size, he's wondering who would win in a fight."

"I hope it doesn't come to that, because I'm not sure this group would give you the opportunity to have a fair fight," Dr. Bradan said dolefully.

"What's going on here? Do you have any idea who these people are, because if we did, we might guess their real intent for not killing us?" Al asked.

"I'm not positive big guy, but I have a strong suspicion. From the uneasy reaction we saw in this new captain when you explained how we fought against

England leads me to believe the man is not just a pirate, but also a privateer. In fact, my hypothesis based on his behavior, language, and description, is that he may be the legendary Sir Henry Morgan."

"Sorry professor, I should know my history better, but first of all, what's the difference between a pirate and a privateer? And I do remember something about the name Henry Morgan, but I can't recollect exactly who he was, or what he did," Al confessed.

"Again, it's not my area of expertise, but from what I can recall, privateers may go back as far as Sir Francis Drake. Morgan must have been within the first few to sail the known world fully authorized for his line of work. Due to his earlier achievements, the English colony based in Jamaica granted him a commission...I believe it was called a *Letter of Marque*...to attack Spanish vessels. Moreover, as payment for those deeds, he and his crew kept most, if not all, of the plunder to fulfill the agreement.

"Fierce raids were committed by the privateers, because they could act just like the known pirates from the Caribbean, but still travel freely inside much of the civilized world too."

Al replied, "So what you're saying Doc, is these guys had authority from England to be legal pirates against England's enemies. They freely attacked other nation's ships just to keep the captured cargo?"

"That's exactly what happened. It was an inexpensive form of indirect war upon Spain by England. From the perspective of England's leaders, these men were legalized servants of the Crown; however, from Spain's perspective, Morgan was one of the cleverest pirates to attack their ships and colonies. Those he felt kept information from him about hidden money knew him for his cruelty. He was brutal in order to achieve his goals.

"If I remember correctly, he had a sailing base on the island of Tortuga, which we passed if you remember what the old Spaniard cook told us. Morgan was very brazen and ruthless in his planning and is best remembered in our time for his sinister raid at Portobello and sacking Panama."

Al thoughtfully mentioned, "Sounds to me as if during this time period, a privateer was really what we called bounty hunters during the Wild West, except in this case, some of their victims were honest merchants."

Dr. Bradan agreed, "You're correct, and if successful, which Morgan was, as a reward for his rough treatment upon the Spanish, he later became the Lieutenant Governor of Jamaica. I am not sure if this *is* Morgan, but I'm almost positive he is, and if so, I hope we're better off with him than with a conventional pirate.

"I did not want to share this with the students, but this strange dimension is confusing to me. Passing from one time into another, I'm not convinced we will find our way back home. After our wandering in the desert and drifting in the ocean, we need to consider the possibility that we could remain trapped here. Therefore, for the moment at least, it may be to our advantage to help Morgan understand we're not traitors to England, and we are *not* against the English."

The dim room remained silent while Al thought about the professor's concerns until he asked, "So, where's Dale, Melinda, and the brothers?"

Professor Bradan hesitated before he replied, "I'm not sure exactly. I'm not as concerned about Dale or the brothers so much, because Morgan commanded the boys remain on board to do whatever the crew members want them to do as work, so I assume they will be fine.

"However, I don't know about Melinda. Morgan separated her, and had her escorted to his cabin. If Morgan were an authentic pirate, I would be gravely concerned for her well-being, however if this is Morgan, he may have separated her from the crew for her safety."

"I hope you're right Doc. I would feel awful if anything bad happened to Melinda."

Lying in the faintly lit room, Al realized he could do nothing but wait, and slowly rolled onto his side to kill time. Looking around the room, he noticed it was larger than he had expected. In addition to the iron cage for their prison, he counted 16 oversized wooden barrels marked as gunpowder lining the far wall.

Several hours later, a new rough-looking character entered their room carrying a small pail. The filthy man approached the iron cage, and smiled at their helpless condition, all the while showing several gaps from his missing teeth. The few remaining teeth were stained yellow and brown.

The buccaneer placed his grimy hand into the container, and with a curling grin that spread along his lips, removed a hard tack biscuit. He stood barely outside of their reach through the bars and ate the baked food, enjoying the expressions of hunger on Al and Dr. Bradan's faces. Recognizing that the pirate enjoyed the moment too much, both men turned their backs to him, acting indifferent to his presence and the food.

Sensing the loss of his fun, the angered man tossed the remaining biscuits out of the pail at the cage bars and then left. Although stale and difficult to eat, both men felt thankful for the nourishment. Neither of them allowed thoughts of the man's grubby hands to ruin the meal. Filled with the poor sustenance, Al and the professor soon drifted to sleep.

***

Startled from his sleep, Dr. Bradan awoke from feeling something brush against his leg, and quickly peered around in the murkiness. Unsure of the cause of his awareness, the professor heard the sound of a faint scratching behind him, followed by a tiny squeak. He immediately zoned in on the rats, startled by their size.

Two large brown rats acted unafraid of his movements, and remained focused on the biscuit crumbs sprinkled on the floor inside the cage. Slightly concerned with the appearance of the small thieves, Dr. Bradan watched closely to ensure the rats were not interested in them. He watched them scurry around and decided they were only interested in the food, so he quietly went back to sleep.

***

Later a sixth sense awoke Dr. Bradan abruptly in the early light of a new day. First, he heard Al snore comfortably on his back, and then realized they were not alone. Across the room, the mammoth Chinese man sat quietly atop one of the huge drums of gunpowder. The pirate calmly stared motionless at them in their iron cage, even as Dr. Bradan peered directly back at him. The man made no sign he was interested in Dr. Bradan; however, he seemed intensely aware of Al sleeping.

Unsure of the man's potential actions, Dr. Bradan reached out and shook Al until he quit snoring. Al slowly raised his head and threw a heavy-eyed glance in the doctor's direction. Dr. Bradan simply nodded his head towards the mysterious visitor. Drowsily, Al turned his head slightly, and focused upon the giant pirate, who stared contently back at him, unconcerned that he was now in their spotlight. Shortly the strong pirate stood, and leisurely left the room.

"What was that about?" Dr. Bradan asked as he thought about the reason. Then he smiled and teased Al, "Do you have a new secret admirer?"

Laying his head back onto the floor, Al ignored the overtone, and replied halfheartedly, "I hope he's only wondering who's the strongest between us."

Several quiet minutes passed before Al continued, "Do you remember when I told you that I noticed his interest in me right away? Well, I've seen this type of behavior, from would be 'tough guys' during my college football days. Most guys, usually dropped ideas of fighting me when they saw my true size up close, but others wanted to know how hard-hitting they were, and tried to push me into a fight. I'm guessing that this man has never been beaten before, and he wants to fight me."

Dr. Bradan joked, "Fortunately, that's not a problem I've had a lot of experience with. Do you think you would win?"

"Let's hope I'm not forced to find out, but if it did come to that Doc, I would do my best…again, considering it was a fair fight."

Dr. Bradan suggested, "Well then, we better not lose sight of him while we're on board this ship, or allow him to sneak up behind you. He seems to me to be the type of person who would try to stack the odds in his favor."

Al agreed, "I was thinking the same thing…"

Suddenly two sets of loud footsteps echoed down the stairs in the adjoining room, before a pair of never-before-seen privateers entered the cell room. The taller of the two men resembled a grim no nonsense English undertaker, having a bent posture as if he had dug too many graves during his lifetime. Even with his bad stance, he glared crossly at them, while holding a firearm in one hand and a short, wicked blade in his other.

The second Maltese pirate displayed pockmarks across his round face. He lifted up his striped shirt to remove a ring of iron keys that he carried on his belt. Sifting through the keys, he found one to unlock the iron cage door.

As the tall bowed pirate, still handling the pistol and blade, came closer to the prisoners, he said, "Morgan wants t' speak wi' ye. Come wi' us," and staring into

Al's eyes warned harshly, "ye be a big one, but dasn't try me hand. Ye'll jus' make a bigger target fer me barkers to shoot ya, ye horn-slogging bilge rat."

Al chuckled at the man's solemn face as he replied with a lighthearted sarcasm, "Why would I, and if I did, where would I go?

"Just dasn't forget ye be standin' between th' two o' us," the smaller pirate stated seriously while turning the key in the lock. The door squealed open from the weight of the heavy door on the rusty hinges.

Without another word, the man withdrew the ring of keys from the lock and led the way from the room. The taller sailor followed directly behind Al and Dr. Bradan, with his loaded pistol aimed at the small of their backs. Above on the main deck, both museum employees were astonished at the flurry of activity.

Neither Al nor the professor could distinguish much difference between the activity on this larger ship and the Spaniards' craft they had sailed on. Hardened men polished cannons, or refilled stockpiles of cannon balls used during the recent battle. Others sawed and shaved wood to repair damaged parts of the vessel. Still others secured loose ropes, essentially preparing their war ship for the next assault.

While Dr. Bradan paused to admire the stitching ability of a pirate repairing a torn sail, Al spotted the huge Chinese privateer.

"Get t' work, or I'll cut yer gullet, an' feed it t' th' buzzards," the immense man ordered his men, and then smiled maliciously at Al for several moments. After releasing his stare, he barked more threats to his subordinates, "I'll be keelhaulin' th' next one of ye fer not finishin' on time!"

Led by their two guides towards the leader's quarters, the taller pirate knocked on the door. Melinda opened it at once and felt relieved to see Al and Dr. Bradan were both unharmed. She gave each a cheerful expression when the taller man directed, "Ye two, wait fer th' captain in thar."

"Are you guys okay?" Melinda asked.

Dr. Bradan replied, "We're below deck in a jail cell, however, we ate a few biscuits, and spent the night with some of our rat friends — it could be much worse."

"How about you?" Al questioned her with a raised eyebrow.

"Believe it or not, but Captain Morgan insisted I remain in his cabin, and showed me how to dead bolt the door from the inside..."

Suddenly, the cabin door burst open, and Henry Morgan entered the room. Although Melinda had previously seen a personable side of the man when they were alone, his dark eyes and hard stare frightened her. Morgan strolled across the room, and plopped heavily onto a chair beside his desk.

Silent until now, Morgan waved at the other two pirates to act as his sentries by commanding, "Boots — Cricket, wait fer me outside!"

Reluctantly, they departed from the cabin room, and closed the door.

Dr. Bradan stepped beside Melinda, and then turned to express gratitude to Morgan by saying, "Thank you sir. We appreciate your generous hospitality and kindness towards Melinda. She's very dear to us." Morgan considered the words, but did not acknowledge the flattering remarks.

He replied, "Melinda enlightened me ye be advocates t' England, an' yer intentions be sincere. As such, I have a proposition for th' two o' ye. On th' one hand, ye can be me prisoners, an' on th' other, ye can join me crew. If ye choose against me, I'll feed ye t' th' fishes, or sell ye in Port Royal."

Dr. Bradan smiled, as Al tried to guess the captain's true intentions.

Morgan noticed the movement yet acted uninterested by continuing, "Port Royal be excitin', but it be a place that has its dangers. There be myriad o' good times t' be had, but not a place t' wander th' streets alone. I be known in those parts, so I could probably fetch a good price — especially on ye," he said pointing to Al. "And she would make an excellent work slave, or a buxom beauty," he added nodding his head towards Melinda's direction, "dependen' on yer decision."

Al and Dr. Bradan looked at each other. Based on the previous experience with Morgan, they didn't want their situation to worsen by giving a wrong answer.

Morgan sensed their indecision, and raised a goblet off the desk to offer, "Search th' ship, an' work with th' crew. Decide yer fates when I ask ye again."

Without uttering a word, Morgan stood and marched towards the cabin's door. Instantly, Boots opened the door, and motioned for Al and Dr. Bradan to follow.

Melinda came forward too, but the taller pirate known as Cricket, still holding his pistol, waved her back, "Ye be staying here! Morgan's orders! He'll not be wantin' th' men distracted by a woman."

Saying quick good-byes to Melinda, Dr. Bradan, and Al followed the two guards out onto the main deck. With a sea breeze rustling his hair, Dr. Bradan felt relaxed and searched the surrounding deck to find Dale.

Without seeing his son nearby, the professor turned and asked Al, "Can you see Dale anywhere..." when they both heard Dale's voice.

Around the corner behind them, a French looking deck swab illustrated to Dale, Trent, and Tab how to scrub the deck with a bucket of water and brushes.

Thankful that the boys were in good health; Dr. Bradan went to the training area, and while hugging Dale, whispered to him, "Keep working hard until we get everything figured out. I suppose we're ok for now."

Excited to see his father again, Dale responded with a bright smile, "I understand," as Tab and Trent cheerfully grinned at the professor.

"Get t' work scaly wags! Thar be no time fer rest. If ye be wantin' t' eat, finish yer work," another privateer yelled at the boys as he walked by.

While Al and Dr. Bradan inspected the soapy area, an older buccaneer called to them with a gruff voice, "Ye, come here!"

The darkly tanned man had a slight build for the work of a pirate. Deep ruts for wrinkles sunk heavily into his forehead, and broad age lines framed his mouth. He instructed Al and Dr. Bradan, "Get t' work ya landlubbers! Help me replace th' cannon balls we used durin' th' swashbuckle wi' th' Spaniards. Go below, and find th' shot stack. Fetch 'em up here and stack 'em as ye be seein' me do."

Al and Dr. Bradan nodded their understanding, and went below deck to find the main powder room and shot locker. Only a thin wall separated the numerous barrels of gunpowder from the extra gunpowder drums taken from the Spanish ship, and placed inside the storage hold next to their detention room with the iron cage.

Al and Dr. Bradan returned up to the seasoned privateer, and unloaded four of the round cannon balls between them, when the older man said, "Stack 'em here in these wooded frames. Fill th' broadside edges first, and then fill th' middle."

When they observed him point at a stacked pyramid of the round steel, he added, "One stack o' cannon balls, fer ever' three cannons," and as he stood upright, he dictated, "Hasten, ya scurvy curs!"

**

Alone in Morgan's cabin, Melinda looked outside of the windows to catch occasional glimpses of the boys, or hear them talking. Bored from watching them soap and scrub the deck; she scanned around the room once more. Walking across the floor, Melinda sat down in the chair next to Morgan's wooden desk to decide how to pass the time. A glance at the disheveled desk revealed a number of maps, ocean charts, letters, and pictures of old style sailing ships.

At first, each of the ships looked identical to her, but upon closer inspection, she saw that each ship was uniquely different. Melinda read more and learned about *Schooners, Frigates, Barques, and Sloops.* From the diagram, she decided they were now sailing aboard a Frigate warship.

In the margin space below each craft sketch, she evaluated numbers written in cursive ink, which Melinda believed showed the length and width of each ship type. Beneath that, different numbers showed the traditional crew size, along with the expected cannon firepower.

Underneath the ship drawings, she discovered two different portraits of a woman. Melinda's thoughts turned romantic considering the era, *"I wonder if this is his wife, and where they live when he returns from sea."* Searching through the maps and other pictures, she enjoyed herself throughout the afternoon.

***

Upon his return to check on the new crewmates, the older privateer was pleased with their completed effort of hauling cannon balls up from the deck below, and introduced himself, "Most around th' ship' call me John. What be ye called?"

The professor introduced them by saying, "I'm Doc Bradan, and this is Al."

Al asked John, "Can you tell us how the crew is structured on this ship?"

John answered, "Like most, th' ship has articles or rules t' be followed. Unless appointed as Morgan had been, many leaders are elected by th' crew, and be replaced dependin' on if th' crew felt th' captain did not give what he promised. If th' captain is unable t' secure enough booty t' satisfy th' crew, he might walk th' plank, or be marooned on a small island."

Al wondered aloud, "So what drives everyone to follow Morgan?"

The man replied, "It's th' Law o' th' Sea gave Morgan license t' attack merchant and pirate ships. Doin' so, put him and ship in th' service o' England. Tis' only way a commoner like me have th' attention o' royalty."

Al asked, "What would our roles be if we joined the crew, or what other duties could we perform onboard the ship?"

The privateer scratched his ear before saying, "First thar be th' captain, and he gets two full shares o' treasure. Below th' captain be th' first mate or Master. Him gets one share and a half. Th' master's role be t' enforce th' captain's orders, divide up th' booty, and give punishment t' those that break th' rules. After him be th' gunners and boatswain. Both gets one share, and a quarter. Th' boatswain has men keep th' ship in top runnin' order, and keeps th' decks clean. They works width' ship's carpenter t' repair most broken tings."

Dr. Bradan asked the man, "What is your trade?"

John responded proudly with a smile and a pat to his own chest, "While th' ship remains afloat, I'm a gunner. Gunners like me make th' captain's job easy or difficult t' attack an enemy ship. Master gunners aim and fire many guns at once. Me be like a treasure among men, and be hard t' find. It takes year's t' learn what me knows. "Th' best be tradin' their services from captain t' captain, depends on who pays th' most."

"Who takes care of the injured?" Dr. Bradan asked.

"Thar's th' surgeon who takes care o' th' bullet holes, cutlass cuts, or t' amputate any arm or leg as he deems fit. Th' surgeon's share o' treasure be one share and a quarter, which is th' same as me."

"Are there other jobs on board the ship?" Al questioned the man.

"There be powder monkeys," he said with a reluctant grimace, "which be a lowly job for lads. They clean and load th' guns, or they be cabin boys. Takes orders from almost any o' th' crew fer any duty needs doin'.."

Dr. Bradan asked, "What happens when a crew member is hurt, or loses an arm as an example. How will he thrive or fail with the crew?"

"You be talkin' 'bout compensation. If a ship citizen be injured in battle and maybe loses an eye, arm, finger or e'en a leg, thar be a fee he receives with each. When a man loses a leg, he receives 350 pieces o' eight for th' wound. If he lost a finger or an eye, that man receives 85 pieces o' eight. If he lost a fightin' arm, it would be a sum of 550 pieces o' eight, but only 450 for th' non-fightin' arm, so thar would be no fear fer th' men in battle.

"What types of punishment can the master choose?" Dr. Bradan asked the thin man with curiosity.

"Let's be seein' — thar be the dance o' th' hempen which be t' hang a man, and thar's floggin' sometimes called th' cat-o-nine-tails. Ye can be fed t' th' fishes, or marooned width' one bullet, one powder horn, and one tub o' water, or be tied t' th' main brace fer days. Ye can be tied o'er a cannon when 'tis bein' fired in battle. Thar be more, but ye get th' fact none be wanted."

Changing the gruesome subject, Al inquired, "Who's the Chinese fellow?"

"That be Foon. He's th' boatswain. He keeps th' ship afloat," the man said. "Ne'er lost a fight, not from boardin' ships, or fightin' in taverns. A brute he is. Knows not th' limit t' his own strength. Good width' guns, blades, or hands."

"That's why he's interested in me," Al whispered to Dr. Bradan. "He sounds lethal with everything. That, combined with his strength, has made him unbeatable."

After a lengthy pause, Al broke the silence to ask the gunner, "Why is he interested in me? I've done nothing to him."

The man laughed loudly, "Ahhh, ye haven't done anythin' t' him yet, but he knows ye will. There be none else on th' ship t' challenge him except ye. He will soon pick a time t' have a quarrel. You just wait!" he warned gleefully, and then continued onward with his work.

Lost in thought from what he learned from the gunner, Al continued his work during the afternoon. When he rolled one of the heavy cannons back into place, a yell came from high above them in the crow's nest at the top of the mainmast, "LAAAND HOOOHH!"

All work ground to a halt while the crew peered over the ship's railing. Far into the distance, a shadowy outline of land was noticeable. At the sound of the long call, Melinda pushed aside the heavy curtains, to admire the far-off foothills. Soon she saw that the island appeared overgrown with tropical foliage, and began listening to a conversation between two privateers, Trent, and Dale.

A squat buccaneer with long dark sideburns stood next to Trent and rattled in excitement while he said, "Can't wait t' get t' Port Royal t' find a few maidens."

His cynical Corsair mate teased him, "Ye be spendin' all yer doubloons on them an' be spliced t' th' main brace, 'fore too long."

"Tell us about this place. I've never been here before," Trent asked them.

The second older privateer proudly said, "This be one o' th' busiest harbors in these seas. Look out at th' ships' round us."

Melinda, too, gazed where the man pointed. She spotted crafts of all kinds, both large and small.

The first privateer added, "Ye can tell by th' many ship's flags this be a port o' many people from about th' world."

"What is this place, some kind of a distribution port?" Dale asked the man.

The second man replied, "Ye be findin' anythin' ye desire 'ere, as many o' th' innkeepers offer a blind eye t' th' sea goin' vessels an' smugglers, which be a thrivin' part o' th' city's way o' life."

Melinda's thoughts drifted across the harbor towards the enchanting looking waterfront district. Excited by the enlarging vision, she opened the rear windows, and drew in a deep breath of sea air, which intensified her overall experience.

When the *Oxford* neared the docks, Melinda peered out the side windows at the broad array of houses overlooking the town. She was surprised to see several fine homes.

Cube-shaped cutouts contained massive cannons along the heavily built front of the harbor fort. A few of the fort's corners boasted flat roofed turrets. Two mixed-period bridges connected the fortification to the city.

Vines grew from cracks in the mortar around part of the stone foundation. Melinda noticed large rock steps circling around one of the towers to reach a huge wooden door. Their ship soon reached the wharfs and piers, where she watched an international array of dockworkers performing various jobs.

Thick braided ropes served as railings along the entire length of the pier, and rope netting stretched between the poles to prevent mercantile goods from falling into the harbor. Ready to dock alongside the wooden pier, local shore men caught heavy ropes tossed to them by the privateers to secure the ship. Excited for the arrival, Melinda opened the cabin door and walked over to the ship's railing.

Melinda saw winding cobblestone streets, and easily recognized a tavern chimney by the thick black soot layered from decades of burning fires. A second-story arched window remained sheltered by pots filled with multihued flowers, showing where the owners resided.

Melinda watched throughout the afternoon, as crates of various shapes and sizes were unloaded and loaded onto the *Oxford*. Several cargo crates had pointed metal spikes for legs, while others had metal veneer etchings on them. She thought one intricate design was distinctly Mediterranean, while two other ornate versions seemed Asian. When the men took a break from their work, her attention shifted to a few of the square town buildings. Made of a type of stucco, most roofs had layered handcrafted shingles, providing a watertight seal.

A heightened sense of excitement was rising among the sailors as they finished the work, and prepared to debark and enjoy the town, when a call rang out near the bow of the ship, "Ahoy, is Captain Morgan among you?"

Melinda followed the sound, and spotted a small band of dignified men on the pier below, two clad in black capes, approached the warship.

The verbal message immediately passed from one man to another on the ship. When the message traveled below deck, it found Sir Henry Morgan. Melinda spied him after he appeared on deck, and looked down at the group from over the side of his ship. Morgan recognized the waiting men, and shouted an incoherent statement to them. With a broad smile on his face, the Captain quickly turned to bark final orders to his crew, before he quickly disappeared down the gangway.

***

After the *Oxford* was fully loaded with new sailing supplies, Dr. Bradan rested on a wooden barrel, weary from the heavy work and wished for food to recharge his energy, while Al spoke to John.

Al asked the veteran sailor, "How long have you been with Morgan?"

"Six voyages now," the old hand replied.

"What has your experience been on the ship? Would you still join up with Morgan or someone else if you had a choice to do it again?"

Staring directly into Al's face, their experienced friend alleged, "Because I be a top-notch gunner, I shoulda' joined one o' th' Swashbucklers long ago. Had I done so, I be havin' made more treasure, but seein' how them like Morgan hunt down and destroy them very same sea dog ships, I live t' spend me legal-made gold."

"So, basically you're pleased with how Morgan treats you and the crew?" Al validated, as he folded his great arms across his chest.

"He treats a swabbie well, as long as th' swabbie does their work," the veteran replied, and then inquired, "Why be ye askin' me these things?"

Al quickly rehearsed the proposal from Captain Morgan.

John replied in a serious tone of voice, "It dasn't seem much o' a choice t' me t' be part o' a successful crew or fed t' th' fishes. I know Morgan might give ye th' benefit o' th' doubt," and lowering his voice continued, "but he be pitiless, and if ye cross him, ye lads be indeed fed t' th' fishes..."

Dr. Bradan interrupted, "Should we tell Morgan straight out that we want to be part of the crew, or is it best to tell him we still need to think about it?"

John laughed, but his tone quickly became solemn when he whispered, "If Morgan spake ye be havin' wee hours t' make yer decision, ye had best be havin' made yer decision — fishes always be hungry. Now when he asks ye, clearly tell him ye want t' be part o' th' crew. Don't hold back, be straight fore as ye say."

Thirsty from their labors, Dr. Bradan changed the topic, "John, where can I find drinking water? I'm thirsty after all of the hard work today."

"Head t' th' galley, and inside be a water cask. Use th' tin cup on th' nail."

Dr. Bradan stood up to go when Al informed him, "I better get a drink too."

Nodding at the older man, they left together for the galley and soon felt refreshed after drinking water. Returning to where they left John, Cricket and Boots intercepted them. Cricket pointed his pistols again at Al and the professor.

Dr. Bradan asked incredulously, "Why are you holding us at gunpoint? Morgan offered us the chance to work on the ship. We want to be part of the crew."

"Ye may have decided t' join th' crew, but dat doesn't mean Morgan accepted th' decision. Th' captain intends t' question ye further, but has business now. Wait in yer cell, because thar be no jumpin' overboard once th' men be in Port Royal an' ye be tryin' t' escape," the hardened pirate stated with authority, never taking his eyes off them.

"We have a good thing here, which is why we don't want to escape," Al countered the man.

"Enough o' ye talk, 'tis time t' march," Boots, the other pirate, sneered.

Dismayed by the treatment, Al and Dr. Bradan watched as other seaman led Dale, Trent, and Tab, to join them in the iron cage. Together, they all squeezed into the iron cell.

The next day the team groggily awoke after a crowded night in the cramped space, to the clang of metal on metal. Dr. Bradan cracked open his eyes to see Boots, but this time, he was without his partner Cricket. Boots raked the heavy keys along the bars to make a deafening noise while yelling, "Up, ye sorry bunch o' scallywags, 'tis time fer work. We be off t' sea, so only a fool be lily livered enough t' jump overboard. Up th' stairs an' get t' work!"

Hungry and tired from the physical work done the day before, all struggled up the ship's stairs to resume their tasks.

***

During the previous days since the *Oxford* had sailed the Caribbean Sea after leaving Port Royal, Melinda learned from a crewman that England had given the warship to Morgan to help protect Jamaica, and that they were on their way to meet up with the rest of his armada. Otherwise, she spent the majority of her time locked inside Morgan's cabin with the exception of mealtimes. Early that morning, their ship reached Cow Island and anchored in deeper water away from the end of a small pier.

Melinda noticed ships anchored around them when she left Morgan's cabin for her noontime walk with the thin cabin boy named Sheamus.

She decided to ask Sheamus a few questions. Each time Melinda had spoken to the boy, he responded to her questions in a physical way, but never spoke. Melinda had seen him speak with several of the crewmembers, but he had yet to respond verbally to her, so she kept trying.

She asked the bony boy, "Why do they call it Cow Island?"

He shrugged his thin shoulders, but said nothing more.

"Do all of these vessels belong to Morgan's fleet?" she asked, looking around the sparkling bay, framed by white sandy beaches.

Again, the small boy refused to respond, but nodded his head yes to her question. She then asked him, "Do you know why we're here?"

She hoped that by not looking at the youth, he would speak, and she would finally hear the sound of his voice. After an awkward pause, Melinda gave in, and turned around to see his answer. To her surprise, he had vanished.

***

At the same time, below deck, Dr. Bradan demanded, "Wait!" of the parting men. Cricket, with double pistols supported in a bandolier, stepped near the cage when the professor continued, "During the time we left Port Royal, we have worked, eaten, and slept in the crew's quarters. We have done nothing wrong, so why are we back to this cage now?"

Before Cricket answered, Al demanded, "And what's the meaning for Morgan's fleet to be at Cow Island?"

"'Tis none o' yer concern bein' first timers aboard ship, but Morgan be rewardin' all o' th' officers in his armada wi' a dinner party on board th' *Oxford* this night. This means most o' th' crew will be havin' time off from their duties t' drink an' gamble in th' crew quarters so as nay t' disturb th' party. Morgan wishes naught for any problems — especially from ye, so ye be stayin' in here 'til mornin'.'"

Dr. Bradan queried the sea-rat further, "What about the girl with us? Will she be at tonight's dinner?"

The man replied with a wink, "She'll be accompanin' Morgan t' supper as his guest," and while viciously laughing, Cricket unexpectedly twirled like a girl, and pinching the sides of his pants at his mid-thigh, pulled them outward as if he curtsied, while batting his eyelashes at the professor. He then leaned backwards, and bellowed another cruel laugh, before turning to leave the room.

Once they heard Cricket and Boots' footsteps ascend the stairs and fade, Al said, "I did *not* like the way he sneered at your question Doc. I think something's up. We'd better come up with an escape plan fast, because if we don't, who knows what will happen when we leave this harbor. Besides, I get the gut feeling that Morgan is planning to split us apart among the different ships in his fleet."

Dr. Bradan said in support, "Assuming there will be a dinner party tonight, and that jerk is not just pulling our chain, Morgan and his officers will attend the affair. Now, I'm guessing that only a few junior crewmembers will remain on duty to serve up meals at the event. If we're lucky, maybe this is the perfect time to break out of this prison."

"What can we do? I mean, we're stuck in this pen. How do you plan for us to get out?" Trent asked the professor.

"I haven't figured that part out yet," Dr. Bradan answered truthfully. "I know this will be our biggest problem. We must figure a way out of this cage tonight during the dinner party, when the ship will have the fewest crewmen at large, and before they sober up and notice we're missing."

"No need to worry about breaking out from the cage. I can easily enough solve that problem," Al said.

He clarified, "These bars are rusty...I'm positive I can bend them enough for us to escape," he said plainly.

"Excellent," Dr. Bradan cheered quietly. "Now we need to determine how to find Melinda, and free her from Morgan before we jump off the ship. All without being caught!"

"Okay Doc, I'm up for getting us out of this cell *and* saving Melinda, however, I don't believe this is a big island. Once we're off the ship, what do you propose we do then?" Al asked with raised eyebrows.

Dr. Bradan explained, "If we can bring some food and water with us, once overboard, I believe we can conceal ourselves until things settle down. Later, after Morgan and his fleet leave, we can secure passage on another ship departing out of the harbor...perhaps towards the Bahamas. After that, I'm not sure."

"So Dad, when should we make our break? And don't we need a diversion, like they always have in the movies?"

Dr. Bradan agreed, "No doubt you're right. If we can create an opportunity to isolate Melinda, it would be much easier for us to reach her and then escape together."

"What kind of distraction are you planning, Doc?" Al asked.

Before the professor could respond, Tab signed rapidly to Trent who interpreted, "Remember when we hid on the Spanish ship behind those kegs of gunpowder?"

Everyone nodded yes, "Tab and I found another room of ammunition like that near the front of the ship. If we light one of those barrels, when it explodes, the crew and everybody at the party should rush towards it to investigate the blast. All we have to do is wait in the rear of the ship and free Melinda."

"Hmm... there's merit in your plan, however, what will happen if you run into some of the crew on your way back to the galley?" Dr. Bradan quizzed Trent.

"Easy; if we ignite a long enough fuse, we just keep outrunning them to the rear of the ship and then up the back steps into the galley from the food storeroom below. By the time anyone catches up to us, the explosion will have occurred. With Morgan and his captains rushing from the galley room on the main deck, we can grab Melinda during the confusion and then slip overboard."

"It's a good plan for short notice. If the boys make it back with someone tagging along, I can take care of them too," Al said excitedly, and winked at Tab. "If we wait until their dinner is in full swing, it just might work. We've each seen enough of this ship to find our way below deck."

Dale asked, "Who should light the fuse, and when?"

Immediately Trent volunteered, "Al, if you, Dr. Bradan, and Tab hide in the food storeroom until you're ready to free Melinda, Dale and I can sneak into the ammunition room and light the fuse."

Dale suddenly went white around the lips at the suggestion. Expecting this reaction, Trent added before Dale refused, "While Dale acts as a lookout, I'll light the fuse. Plus," Trent said jokingly, "I've seen Dale run, so the two of us can quickly meet you guys in the rear of the ship as fast as anyone can."

Dr. Bradan hesitated while trying to decide about Dale's capability, and then he agreed, "I guess it would be best to wait until the guests are onboard and eating before we light the fuse. Hopefully, we will know the right time."

***

At sunset, Morgan's guests boarded the *Oxford*. Echoes from visitors dressed in stiff-soled shoes traveled throughout the ship. Occasional bursts of laughter carried down to their iron cage. The noise and mirth diminished a half-hour later.

"It sounds like the social portion of the evening is winding down. Let's start our plan while the guests are eating their meal. If we wait too long, the banquet may end before we're ready, and everyone will spread about the ship, increasing our risk," Al advised.

Dr. Bradan nodded his agreement to Al to initiate the rescue plan. Al shifted his position and moved toward the iron bars furthest from the room's doorway. He placed his feet shoulder width apart and grasped the bars with his massive hands. Instantly, his shirt tightened as his titanic muscles swelled. The metal easily relented to form a gap large enough for them to exit the cage.

Freed from their jail, Dr. Bradan hurried to the doorway to see if anyone heard the groan of the bars during their breakout. Satisfied the escape had gone unnoticed; Dr. Bradan asked Trent, "How will you light the gunpowder?"

The older brother replied, "I thought we'd use one of the hanging lanterns on our way to the Ammunition room."

"Good idea!" Dr. Bradan said before he turned and gave his son a bear hug. "You two should leave now, before we're all discovered."

Trent smiled at Dale, and motioned for him to follow. Together, they scurried through the adjoining powder room and up the stairs, on their way to light one of the small kegs of gunpowder near the bow. Dale and Trent took turns as the lead person, while they stealthily crept throughout the hull.

Halfway to the room, Dale leaned through a doorway in order to listen for sounds of nearby activity, when suddenly a Mediterranean pirate leisurely climbed up the stairs next to them, hauling a sack of flour from the lower deck. Surprised by the soundless steps of the barefoot man, Dale froze in his place like a figurine, clearly visible to the sailor. Fortunately lost in his thoughts, the man spoke to himself, and passed Dale's position without spotting him.

Trent realized after the freebooter disappeared from their view, that Dale's eyes remained wide with panic. Aware of Dale's capacity to burst out in speech during the worst times, Trent placed a finger over his own lips, to remind the nervous teenager not to speak. Trying to calm him, Trent immediately replaced him as the lead lookout, and motioned for him to remain close by.

Their pace progressed slower than before, as Trent carefully inched them forward to the arsenal housing the smaller gunpowder kegs. Near the targeted room, Trent stooped and quickly passed underneath the radiant glow made by a hanging lantern. Assured no one else was nearby in the dimly lit area, Trent gradually reached an arm from out of the shadows and gently removed the light.

Holding the lamp in front of them, their slow moving shadows stretched and shrunk through the spooky cargo spaces in the lantern's flickering light.

On a hunch, Trent stopped to listen for potential danger. Not hearing anything suspicious, he whispered to Dale, "Let's keep going."

Their patience seemed rewarded when they entered the small armaments room. Dale sighed with relief at the end of the reconnaissance, and quickly pointed at the small kegs of gunpowder stacked along the far wall.

Trent nudged Dale with his elbow and whispered, "Stand by the door, and listen for sounds of anyone coming this direction. If you hear anything at all, snap your fingers behind your back, so I know to stop what I'm doing."

"Ok," Dale whined nervously. "Just hurry," he urged.

Trent stalked past labeled box crates, until he reached the closest keg of gunpowder, and searched the container for an opening to access the black granules inside. Not finding one, he stepped to the next keg, and was disappointed again when he did not find a stopper. After exploring a third keg, Trent decided the small barrels did not have an opening. Trent knew the small kegs would create a perfect bomb, but only if he could create an opening and insert a fuse, so he searched for a device to open the little barrel.

On tiptoes, Trent repositioned the keg next to the doorway and informed Dale, "None of these barrels have a way to remove the gunpowder. I need something to open the barrel, but I can't find anything in this room. Without something sharp, we're not going to make the diversion happen."

"Hey — I remember a room we passed by tonight that had lots of tools. I'm not exactly sure what kind they are, but if you wait here, I'll bring one back," Dale volunteered softly.

"How far away is the room?" Trent asked in a hushed tone.

"Maybe one deck down and…I'm guessing three or four cargo spaces back from the stairs," Dale explained.

"Whoa — that's too risky to go all that way, and then come back here again. It's better if we carry the gunpowder with us, and light it there," Trent said with some doubt.

Dale's eyes twinkled and he said, "Plus, from there, it would be a shorter run to the back of the ship to meet Dad and Al."

"Ok, let's go," Trent, urged.

He handed the candle lantern to Dale, who immediately led their return into the previous hallway. Guardedly, Trent followed his friend and nestled the small keg like a football near his stomach so it would not accidentally bump against a doorway and alert anyone of their presence. Silent like mice, Dale and Trent carefully listened at various intervals. Without hearing or seeing any privateers, they retraced their route towards the center of the ship.

A lone privateer sulking quietly in the dark noticed the bobbing lantern flame that Dale carried on the other side of the hull, past the waist of the ship. Suspicious, the man made his way quietly in their direction.

Unaware the sailor followed them; Trent and Dale reached and entered the room next to the ship's pumps, where Dale had seen the tools. Together, they looked for a chisel and hammer to use, but instead, found a metal spike lying near a wooden club.

After placing the barrel on the floorboards, Trent instructed, "Hold the barrel while I give the spike a solid strike to pierce the top. It should make a perfect hole between these two wood sections," he said as he pointed at the spot.

Dale knelt and squeezed the small drum between his hands and knees to hold it firmly in place. Trent positioned the sharp tip on a knot in the wood, and raised the wood club as a hammer. Trent thought, "*I hope one strike is enough to get the powder out of this stupid drum.*"

Suddenly, Dale blew out the candle in the lantern, throwing the room into darkness.

Immediately, Trent and Dale heard the floorboards outside the room creak, and both wordlessly ducked behind the worktable next to the powder keg. Seconds passed that seemed like minutes, when Trent peeked through the table legs to see a pair of bare feet standing in the doorway. His heart instantly raced within his chest, while he fought the yearning to gasp for breath. Afraid to move during the predicament, Trent paced his breathing and froze, hoping Dale would not accidentally reveal their location. Fortunately, the person in the shadows stepped back, and left the room.

Listening inside the blackness, they heard the man's footsteps grow fainter, until the only sound was the ebb and flow of the tide that splashed against the ship's exterior hull. Dale whispered to Trent, "WOW — that was close. I thought for sure he found us in here. I can't believe he didn't see us!"

"Well, he'll be back when he doesn't find anything further down the hallway. We have to hurry, but how will we light the powder without the flame?" Trent questioned Dale.

"Easy, we just find another flame. I'll relight the wick with another lantern, while you punch the hole in the drum and pour out the powder," Dale excitedly said.

Without waiting for Trent's response, Dale slipped into the shadows of the hallway to find a lantern. Trent sat silently in the darkness, and waited for his friend to return.

***

Al, Dr. Bradan, and Tab snuck towards the ship's stern until they arrived at the provisions pantry, situated underneath the galley. Huddled together in the food storeroom, they found it filled with containers of corn, beef, sugar, salt, and pork. As they had so desperately hoped, they heard loud conversation and laughter above, confirming the social occasion was in full session. *"This is perfect, but can we do it?"* Al wondered.

Dr. Bradan patted Tab once on the arm, and applied his right index finger to his own lips after the deaf teenager faced him. Then the professor whispered, "The dinner party is directly above us now. We must be ready to dash up these back stairs," he said pointing to the nearby steps, "and free Melinda when everyone runs to the front of the ship. I will signal you as soon as we hear the diversion."

Tab acknowledged with a positive nod of his head, that he understood. Then without warning, Dr. Bradan suddenly gripped the front of Tab's shirt and jerked him behind a storage bin. Behind Al, heavy footsteps descended the rear stairs, growing louder by the moment. He looked around but could not find a hiding spot large enough to conceal his massive frame.

With no other choice, he quickly stepped through the doorway into the adjoining room, and crouched flat against the wall several feet from the door. He thought, *"Hopefully this guy's hurrying, and doesn't see me."*

The sound of the footsteps grew closer, until the doorway filled with the outline of the huge Chinese privateer. Surprised to see the Asian man below the festivities, Al instinctively knew the man was on his way to their former jail. The man rapidly passed through the room where Al was hiding. Fearful the buccaneer would find the empty cage too soon and sound an alarm; Al stood quietly and whispered to Dr. Bradan, "You two stay here to free Melinda after the distraction, while I follow our big friend, before he ruins our single chance to escape."

Smiling good luck to the professor, Al stealthily followed the full-size adventurer. As he trailed the malicious man, Al realized his suspicions were correct when his rival proceeded towards the staircase leading down into their captivity area. Al, deliberated with himself, *"Should I tackle him now, or wait until he goes below,"* when the choice was made by someone else.

Without warning, the man suddenly stopped. Shocked to see each other during such an unexpected moment, the Chinese privateer and Dale stared awkwardly at each other.

Frightened, Dale swung the newly re-lit lantern into the freebooter's face to escape. In tandem, the ferocious man reached for Dale, but missed the teen in order to swipe the brass lamp from out of his face. Giving Dale a chance to run, Al circled his arms about his opponent from behind. With a jerk, he lifted the pirate's feet off the floorboards.

Skilled in battle, the Asian warrior quickly twisted sideways and shifted his excessive weight forward to break away from Al, before the security man could lock his grip. Astonished by the swift and powerful movement, Al could only influence the man's heavy momentum. With an incredible heave, the Security Chief pushed his opponent down the stairs towards the stored gunpowder and their jail room.

Mindful not to follow Dale to assist him in his assignment, Al watched the teen disappear around a corner, and then rushed downward to deal with the infuriated privateer. Nearly halfway down the stairs, the Chinese adversary plunged his cutlass at Al's knees through the spindles. Fortunately, most of Al's tall length remained above the upper deck floor, when his peripheral vision caught the flicker of the stabbing blade. His instincts placed his hands on the stair rails, and he hoisted up his legs, allowing the sword to pass harmlessly beneath his feet.

Before the Asian man withdrew the weapon from the missed attempt, Al stomped on it to prevent its withdrawal. Incensed at the missed opportunity to injure Al, the powerful pirate yanked his cutlass with full force from beneath Al. Expecting this, Al swiftly raised his feet, causing the pirate to fall back clumsily. Al laughed hardily at the bumbling man, hoping to fuel his foe's anger. Adrenalin surged through the furious privateer's muscles and he regained his feet swiftly. Lowering his head like a battering ram, he plowed headfirst into Al near the bottom step.

The man's weight slammed the ex-football star backwards until he landed heavily onto the floorboards. Al saw his opponent quickly bend and easily lift one of the enormous wooden drums of gunpowder above his head, intending to smash it down on him. Al remained stationary until the last moment, and then blasted his legs into the barrel's widest part. With a thudding rupture, the total area filled with sparkling black granules as the drum exploded at its seams, knocking the surprised freebooter backwards and onto the hard floor.

Scurrying onto his feet before the pirate, Al was still defenseless. Using his extraordinary strength, he grasped and ripped one of the bulky spindles from the staircase railing, then dashed through the open doorway into the room containing his familiar iron cage. Following Al, the Chinese pirate seethed in anger and screamed an Asian curse. Shaking his drawn sword above his head with a clenched fist, he charged at Al, overflowing with hate.

Al faced the advantaged opponent with only his meager piece of wood. In a series of thrusts and slashes, the determined privateer hacked enough wood away from Al's spindle so that it was soon ineffective as a weapon. After the loss of his club, Al threw the chunk, striking the pirate in the arm. The buccaneer charged him again, and with a boxer's bob-and-weave combo, Al tried to dodge the vigorous blade swipes, until the trained warrior swung his sword downward.

Powered by the vision of the arching steel, Al caught his combatant's wrist above their heads in his left hand, instantly stopping the deadly cutting edge. With his right hand, Al punched the man squarely in his jaw, shaking the fighting man to his core. Bolted off his feet, the rebel shook the stupor away, and warily circled Al to decide his next attack.

The antagonist rushed at Al again, forcing him to wrench the cutlass from the pirate's hand, but the clever enemy staged the move, and pulled his arm backward, bringing Al with it. He then reached around and circled his free arm around Al's neck from behind. Al quickly realized his intent and drew in a deep breath of air. Then he grasped the Asian's wrist in one of his hands and the handle of the sword in his other.

Neither gained advantage to control the blade. Al determined there was no benefit to his effort, and rapidly released the man's wrist around his throat. Using his newly free hand to grasp the back of the cutlass tip's non-cutting edge, Al pushed his knee upward just as he shoved the flat side of the rapier down. The middle of the weapon broke against his knee, and was no longer useful to the pirate.

The warrior swiftly squeezed his elbow around Al's esophagus, trying to finish him with a chokehold. Al blocked the tactic by bending the man's fingers downward to create a gap and spun around, facing his foe. With no other weapons besides their bodies, they locked arms in an attempt to control one another.

While Al tried to get a superior hand position on the man's neck, the pirate spun and bent at his waist intending to flip Al over his shoulder. Instead of being tossed over onto the floor, Al wrapped his leg over the other man's thigh to halt the martial art tactic. Stopped from his original intention, the enemy rushed backwards, expecting to slam Al's back against the iron cage. Al twisted around at the last moment, which caused both to crash heavily into the confine forcing a breach between two of the bars.

Slightly dazed, Al knew he had to end this struggle now if he was to free Melinda. This thought supplied him with a burst of energy and he broke free from the other man's grasp. Sweeping behind the man, Al pinned the man's arms behind him. Using his excessive strength, Al pressed the pirate's head through the new space in the bars. Raising his knee to prevent the man from backing out, Al squeezed the wrenched bars together around his opponent's neck.

The buccaneer violently shook the cage. Furious, he kicked at Al, and then pulled at the metal bars to escape. Al knew the man would shortly free himself, and hurried from the room, exhausted from the powerful struggle. His muscles feeling like putty, Al climbed the stairs and staggered towards the ship's stern to help Dr. Bradan.

***

The huge Chinese rival broke free from his temporary prison, raging mad. He charged from the room in pursuit of Al. Retrieving the lit lantern previously discarded by Dale, he scanned the dimly lit corridors to determine which way Al had gone. Peering into each murky direction, he couldn't decide, and in a fit of anger, threw the lamp to the ground. The powerful impact sprung open the metal latch of the lantern releasing the candle. It ricocheted against the wall and flew down the stairs. The Chinese privateer watched in horror as the flaming candle bounced off the bottom stair and landed onto the shiny gunpowder spilt across the floor of the room below.

***

Al ran as fast as he could inside the ship until abruptly, he heard a loud "BOOM!" Within moments, the entire ship rocked savagely from a second, massive explosion, tossing Al across the cargo-filled hold. Dazed, Al scrambled to his feet when he heard shrieks of panic from the privateer leaders and their guests above on the top deck. Gradually he staggered into the food pantry where both of the Bradan's and the two brothers waited. Noticing Al's cuts and bruises, they assisted the larger man up the rear steps as they went in search of Melinda.

Melinda had remained in the dining room as her friends expected, nevertheless, two of Morgan's naval officers kept watch over her. When the waiting officers heard the noisy footsteps rushing up the back stairs from the provisions store, one of the officers withdrew his sword and lunged at them. Supported in front of the group, Al jumped out of the way of the sharp blade with a quick burst of

- 317 -

adrenaline and quickly caught the man's smaller wrist with one hand. Jerking him forward, he then punched the commander's jaw, instantly knocking him out cold.

Dr. Bradan, Trent, Tab, and Dale encircled the second privateer leader, who swung his sword about him, eager to slash any person that rushed at him. Dr. Bradan waited until the man's spinning back was nearer to him, then grasped the man's hair and pulled his head backward while bringing his elbow down onto the man's nose. The officer released his sword and dropped to the floor, his eyes watering.

Delighted to see her rescuers, Melinda gave them a group embrace right as the ship twisted violently. A massive crack resonated throughout the huge ship followed by sounds of snapping cables. Moments later, sections of the galley floor broke apart and dropped towards the sloping midpoint of the ship.

"FOLLOW ME!" Al yelled, as he grabbed a dinner bench sliding towards him across the splitting floorboards. Lifting it, he ran up the slanting flooring towards the dining room's rear window, and heaved the long bench up and through the stained glass. Instantly, the floor tilted steeper as shattered glass tumbled past him. As everyone rushed upward to escape through the smashed window, Dale lost his traction, and slipped back towards the disintegrating floorboards, as the galley rapidly filled with salt water.

Al reached out his long arm to catch Dale's belt as the frightened teen slid near him, and with a mighty one-armed hurl, he flung Dale up and through the broken window. Climbing up the now nearly vertical floor, Al jumped and grasped the open window frame. Bit-by-bit, he pulled his hulking torso up and through the window just as the room bubbled completely with water. The large ship then careened violently and tossed Melinda and the others into the dark harbor water.

From her new vantage point treading water in the cove, Melinda saw by the illuminating blue and yellow glare, that the ship had broken in half near the middle, and both ends now bobbed in the waves. Flames continued burning on several of the floating timbers. The stern of the vessel rose skyward from a pocket of escaping air, before it surrendered, sinking beneath the waves.

Melinda and her friends swam away from the downed ship and towards the shore.

"Are you alright? Are you hurt?" Dr. Bradan asked Dale in gasping breaths.

"I'm fine. But what just happened?" Dale responded.

Hearing cries of surprise in the sea behind them and along the short wharf, Al urged, "Use the debris as cover to swim towards the pier, so no one sees us!"

Melinda pushed a small crate before her as she remained close to the giant hero, as they quietly paddled through the surf and wreckage to hide beneath the end of the dock.

"Are we all here? I see Trent, Tab, Melinda, Dale, and Al. Excellent, we didn't lose anyone. Ok everyone, head towards the beach, and avoid making any splashing noises. Dale, you lead, but stay underneath the pier," Dr. Bradan directed.

From their location below the jetty, Melinda heard footsteps and quizzical calls from the people above them running towards the calamity. While numerous sailors and dockworkers peered in the darkness for survivors, Melinda slipped out of the waves with her friends, and they carefully worked their way along the beach. Melinda easily followed Al around and behind stacked freight.

Melinda hid with him behind a grounded overturned rowboat, waiting for their friends to gather again. Once the small group re-assembled, Dale asked Al, "Where do we go now?"

"Right now, we need to avoid everyone. Look for a good place to leave the beach," Al coached.

"What about that old building over there? I saw it earlier today," Melinda offered, and then added, "I think it's close enough to the jungle that we should run to it and then hide in the trees."

"I can't see it from here…what type of building is it?" Dr. Bradan asked.

"It was too far away to tell for sure, but if I guessed, I would say maybe an old school," Melinda explained.

Suddenly they heard a woman scream hysterically, "William — William!" Melinda turned to see two men restraining a woman at the far end of the pier. One man yelled to her, "Beth, yer husband's gone, I'm sorry."

The scene intensified the calamity and Al whispered, "A school's good enough for me. Let's go!"

Afraid to meet any surprise visitors on their way to the dark building, Melinda and her group carefully crouched along the sand and higher grass like military trainees in a boot camp. On the near side of the rundown structure, Melinda spotted a cross hanging on the outside. Narrow spires stretched above the roofline at each of its four corners, and huge metal hinges supported a heavyset timber door. The small windows were made of simple stained glass, and more of the tall golden grass overran the church grounds. Using the waist-high weeds, she and her friends sneaked quietly, until they reached the far side of the building.

Together, they scanned the surrounding beach area, and finding that no one had noticed them, sprinted into the tropical jungle directly behind the church. Melinda turned and looked back at the harbor. In the distance, she watched as men holding lanterns in rowboats from the neighboring ships, rescued survivors still swimming in the deeper water.

Dr. Bradan called to her, "Melinda, come along now."

Turning, she made her way to him in the shadows. Hidden within the immense foliage, without a flashlight, the darkness made it difficult for them to see each other.

To avoid an accidental separation, Al explained, "It's too dark in here and we don't want to lose anybody. We are going to walk in a single file, with me in the front and Dr. Bradan bringing up the rear. Ok, let's go."

Exhausted, wet, and emotionally drained from the past week's events, Melinda was grateful when they discovered a small clearing to lie down and rest. She knew no one would search for them, believing others had rescued them, or that they had died in the explosion. With that sense of security, Melinda covered herself with banana tree leaves, and slept deeply.

Chapter Thirty-Five

REDISCOVERED

Melinda eventually felt her limbs and joints loosen from the ongoing hike through the tropical rain forest. By mid-morning, she was suffering from the inescapable humidity underneath the thick foliage.

The trail led to an immense fallen tree, lying diagonally across their pathway. Al sensed the students needed a rest, as they were falling behind in their march, so he sat restfully on the tree to wait until everyone had caught up with him. After several silent minutes of respite, Tab anxiously signed to Trent, who translated, "Tab wants to know why there were two explosions, instead of only the diversion blast?"

Dale faced Tab with a quizzical look, and shrugged his shoulders in response. Shortly he suggested, "I don't know why there were two blasts, let alone one! By the time Trent and I reached the room with the gunpowder, it turned out we needed a tool just to open the keg. All I know is we had to carry a small drum of it to another room near the middle of the ship, where we opened it, but we had no way to light the powder."

"That's true," Trent supported. "We never did light the gunpowder, so I have no idea why there was any blast either. The reason we couldn't light the gunpowder was that Dale had to blow out the lantern for us to hide from one of the sailors. After the coast was clear, Dale went to relight the candle, while I used a metal pick to open a small hole in the barrel."

Dale agreed, "After I left Trent in the tool supply room, I found another lit lantern almost right away, but on my way back, I ran into that big Chinese pirate. I dropped the light and ran — but for some reason — he never chased me," Dale said with recollection. "I found Trent again and told him we needed to run, so we hoofed it out of there," Dale concluded.

Al grinned and said, "I can explain why he didn't chase you. I had followed that guy right before you bumped into him at the top of the stairs. I was right behind him, and almost laughed when you threw your lamp at his face. When he stepped back to avoid it, I tackled him from behind."

"So are those cuts and bruises from the explosion, or from that guy?" Dale asked in awe.

"I wish they were only from the ship, however, that chap really gave me a run for my money. If we had fought much longer, I'm sure he would have won. I got a lucky break and trapped him in the cage bars. On my way back to warn everyone we needed a plan B, everything went KABOOM," Al emphasized with his wide-open arms and eyes.

Dr. Bradan finally spoke after listening during the ongoing conversation, "With the overflow cannon powder next door to our jail room, did you say that you and Trent opened a powder keg near the center of the ship — not far from where you collided with the big privateer?"

"Yea, I'm pretty sure," Dale, confirmed.

"Then the first explosion must have been close to those huge wooden drums of gunpowder by us. That would explain why there were two separate explosions. The first blast triggered the second storage area or the main supply that then devastated the *Oxford*. It would appear we're very lucky to have been at the rear of the ship when it happened, otherwise, we would *not* be alive right now."

Al digested the professor's comments and wondered aloud, "So if the boys didn't cause the first explosion, then who did?"

"Wait," Melinda said, "I'm not sure if this has anything to do with what happened — but remember when Morgan attacked the Spaniard's ship, and we hid in the ammunition room? I remember thinking after they caught us, that there were way too many explosives on board, even for a merchant ship. When Morgan's men sacked everything from off the Spanish ship, they must have added the additional gunpowder to what they already kept on board, which might explain how the second blast was large enough to sink the ship."

Tab signed once more while Trent verbalized the message, "Tab believes Melinda is right, because he helped move some of the unused powder into another cargo area, right behind the storage room next to our jail cage. So apparently, there were even more gunpowder crates on board than we thought."

"You must be right Dad; but what triggered the second explosion?"

Trent translated Tab's signs, "This is kind of weird. Tab recalls reading in a history book, about how Morgan really did host a celebration banquet on the night the *Oxford* exploded in real life and sunk."

Amazed at the coincidence, Melinda asked, "What happened to Morgan?"

Tab easily read her lips, and signed his reply to his brother, "Although Morgan survived the blast with most of the crew, to this day — I mean in our time — no one ever learned why the ship exploded. It's still a big mystery."

Al immediately broke out with a stunned face, "You're kidding!" Then with an almost contented look, he said, "That really happened in the past?"

Tab nodded it did.

"So the real question is, was that fate we just experienced, or a coincidental similar explosion, or do you think there really is some kind of a time loop which continues to explode the ship no matter what?" Al asked the group.

Uncertain of the answers, each silently pondered the events.

Dr. Bradan looked up and noticed the rising position of the sun above the jungle canopy, and stood to say, "We're not going to figure this mystery out here. I vote we put more distance behind us and the harbor just to be safe, in case we *were* seen by someone."

***

The sun had slowly dragged itself into a blinding arch high above them in the sky, when Melinda complained, "Can we spread out from each other to search for some food and water? I don't know about you guys, but I'm really thirsty."

Dale agreed, "Yeah, I'm starving too. We should find some coconuts."

"OK, let's fan out in a straight line to continue in our original direction, but still give us an opportunity to spot something to eat or drink outside of the path we're on," Dr. Bradan suggested.

Soon Melinda became concerned they wouldn't find any food, because the trees began to shorten and thin out. She thought, *"I haven't seen any coconuts for a while; in fact, I haven't seen palm trees lately."*

Twenty minutes later, Trent suddenly raised his hand above his head and said, "Quiet everyone! I think I hear something."

Melinda remained quiet too, listening for a sound beyond the normal jungle noise. Distinctly in the distance, she heard what she thought sounded like water dripping onto a hard surface.

Unsure of the exact direction, Melinda suggested, "Hey, let's search over there."

After minutes of searching, Trent pointed to his left and shouted, "GUYS, IT'S GETTING LOUDER OVER HERE!"

Huddled together where Trent waited for them, Melinda distinctly heard the dripping sound. For some reason, it seemed familiar.

The group progressed closer to the noise, and Trent exclaimed with a shocked expression, "No way! This can't be true!"

Amazed by his unusual comment, Melinda asked, "Trent what d…"

Trent never heard the question as he dashed out of their view, deeper into the brush. Stunned by his unexpected actions, the team hastily followed. After trudging through a thick clump of trees, everyone halted in bewilderment and stared at the bubbling pool of mud before them.

Baffled, Melinda's thoughts whirled. Her mind raced for the unexplainable answer. She wondered, *"How did we cross the Sahara Desert, float in the ocean, and sail from Port Royal to Cow Island, only to arrive…?"*

Melinda scanned their surroundings in disbelief as she double-checked to make sure it was the same location. Able to recognize certain landmarks, it hit her so hard she had to catch her breath to accept the unexplainable truth, *"We returned to the same exact spot as before, from a completely different direction!"*

Not alone in her bewilderment, Dr. Bradan voiced his thoughts, "This is truly implausible…however, maybe not if we consider what the Shaman told us."

"What are you talking about Dad? I don't remember what he said!"

The professor paused for a moment, and then added, "The Shaman said that time, inside the dimension, had in some way splintered during ancient Egypt...no, he used a phrase. It was something like...oh yes, the tree split in half cracking from the top to the bottom! Instead of moving through time in a progressive year-to-year ring method, somehow, the entire time dimension became altered or fractured, opening all of the individual time rings at once to create...oh — what did he call it again...."

"Do you mean a Time Loop?" Trent offered.

"Right," Dr. Bradan confirmed, "so apparently, we only traveled within the times and locations associated with the Enchanted Rock's cave portal — located in that section of the split tree."

Melinda's face wrinkled in thought when she added, "In a bizarre way that kind of makes sense. There must be a link or loop from when we originally entered into this dimension, because we can see our footprints from the last time we were here...."

The truth of Melinda's statement caught her by sudden surprise. Apprehension quickly replaced amazement, as she wondered if the remaining Civil War soldier might still be nearby.

"What's wrong?" Dale asked her in panic, when he noticed her expression change.

Melinda glanced quickly around them, and then whispered, "What if the Confederate soldier is still here? By now he's free, and has his rifle!"

Instantly, dread filled the darting eyes of her friends, who glanced back and forth to check the shadows surrounding them in the jungle.

"We better check to see if he escaped," Dr. Bradan said worriedly.

They crept further down the pathway at a snail's pace, trying to remain quiet. Melinda spied the recently dug gravesite first. The outer surface of the dirt was dry, showing that it had aged. She guessed the soldier had dug the grave about a week earlier. Melinda felt a sense of relief and hoped the survivor had returned to those he knew during the Civil War.

Next, a rancid smell rose to her nostrils, and assaulted her stomach's composure. Melinda scanned the area for the remains of the panther that had attacked and killed the soldier. Flies buzzed about the area, and she saw the remainder of the carcass picked-clean by wild animals or vultures. Everyone took small breaths to avoid the sickening smell as they hurried past the area.

Certain of both their exact location and their good fortune, Trent suggested, "You know — that hut we found is close to here. Maybe they built it near water. Before we hike all the way back to the portal thirsty, I wonder if we can at least find the water first."

"Yeah, plus we can show Al the hut where the Confederate guys caught us. That would be fun," Dale suggested.

Al expressed his agreement, "Before you found the bubbling mud, we had no idea where we were, or where to hike next. If ya'll know we're not too far from the portal, I say let's try it. I'm on the thirsty side too."

When they retraced their way to the previous clearing, to Melinda, it looked precisely the same as it did only a week before.

Trent pointed at the bamboo hut saying, "Al, this is the first thing we found. There is nothing valuable inside, but it seems the people lived here for a while. The Confederate soldiers, who tracked us here, left the camp over there — until they heard Tab accidentally kick that metal box lying over there. When they raced back, we heard them and hid in those bushes again, but Tab had no idea they returned, and that's how they found him."

Tab was reading Trent's lips, and at the part about kicking the metal box, his face flushed crimson. He reluctantly remembered the incident, and then he remembered the flying goggles. While Trent explained to Al what happened after the students came out of hiding, Tab re-discovered the leather flying spectacles, and he correctly positioned them on his head.

Melinda noticed Tab first, and burst out laughing, "Look at him; he looks like a dog fighter pilot from World War I."

Trent turned to see Tab pretending he was zipping through the sky. He enjoyed the lighthearted release, and then his stomach growled, causing him to get serious and say, "Let's split up into teams of two and find some water."

Still smiling from his role-playing, with a quick step towards the team, Tab felt something solid slip beneath his shoe. Lifting up his foot, he spotted the small leather book that he had seen earlier inside the metal box. Realizing he had never inspected it, he quickly scooped it up. Planning to show it to his brother, he was surprised with the sudden departure of his friends, until he saw Trent stepping back into view at the edge of the campsite to look for him.

Trent signed to Tab, "Let's go this way to find some water. Spread out about thirty feet from me to cover more ground."

Tab slipped the book in his back pocket and then signed to Trent, "Don't get too far away; it's hard for me to see you in these thick trees."

Trent smiled caringly, and they searched the area together.

***

An hour of crisscrossing through the tropical forest, neither Melinda nor anyone else had located the hoped-for food and water. Unhappy, Dr. Bradan suggested, "Although our intentions were good, this is not working. Since we know where the portal is from here, I recommend we return through it, and then eat and drink at the Enchanted Rock on-site store. I vote we head back now."

"I agree," Al reinforced, and then chuckled at the thought when he added, "Dr. Swinford probably had kittens by now wondering what happened to us. The Museum's almost certainly shut down from losing half of the program students without a clue about where we went."

"That's a good point. I wonder how Carl is too. We should return through the portal as fast as we can," Dr. Bradan urged.

On the trail back to the tree portal, Melinda worried about Carl thinking, "*What if my dad fired him for driving us to Enchanted Rock?*"

Lost deep in thought, Melinda quietly followed her friends, scarcely listening to their conversation along the way. Strolling across the emerald green field once more, Melinda easily recognized the important tree, because of broken branches from the clash between the female Guardian and the Shaman.

Melinda was incredibly disheartened that they had not located the Guardian before returning through the portal into their world. She stood to one side and wondered what had happened to the Guardian, before realizing her friends were waiting on her.

Without a word from anybody, Melinda, still wearing her pendant, stepped

- 327 -

into the portal's opening, and allowed each of her friends to pass by her as before in the cave.

***

As they neared the park entrance, Dale shouted, "Hey, isn't that the limo?"

Melinda felt her mood immediately soar at the news saying, "Where...no wait, I see it too!"

A hand-written note was visible, taped inside the windshield. It simply read:

I am at site 29

Melinda quickly turned to Dr. Bradan, and said, "Wow, can you believe Carl stayed at the park to watch your stuff? What a great guy!"

With a rush, the team quickly located Carl for a heartfelt reunion. After the initial excitement died down, Carl updated them, "It's been a three-ring circus around here after I alerted the authorities ye kids were missing. The park rangers searched the cave and every inch of the park fer three days.

"However, without any indication of foul play, the search ended without authorities saying where ye were. The Museum continued te post an Amber Alert; however, I stayed in Dr. Bradan's tent te search fer ye each day." Relieved to see Carl and hear the news, Melinda soon worried about returning to the Museum.

***

Melinda fell into deep reflection during the return ride to the Museum. With the state park, on-site store closed when they returned, and the security van towed back to the Museum by Dr. Swinford earlier in the week, Al and Dr. Bradan followed behind in the professor's Range Rover, while all of the students rode comfortably in the limo.

To refrain from thinking about food, Trent occupied their attention by saying, "I still can't believe we were in the middle of the Civil War, or that we saw that crazy Shaman dude turn into a monster!"

Dale paused with a pleased expression, and added, "I can't wait to tell everyone at the Museum about sailing with pirates on the high seas. I know Scott and *his girlfriend* Mea will turn green with envy when they hear about our stories."

Something about Dale's comments caught Melinda's attention.

"Wait a minute," she said, with a concerned tone. "If we tell them exactly what happened, will anyone believe us? I mean, what proof do we have that any of those things happened?"

A hush hovered in the passenger area of the limousine, as they thought about her words.

Within a few moments, Trent supported Melinda by saying, "Yeah, she's right, Dr. Swinford will use any reason to expel us from the program to help Scott's team win the competition. Everybody will assume we invented a make-believe story, just to stay out of trouble."

"No way," Dale scoffed, "Al will tell them what really happened, so stop worrying!"

"Maybe...even so, Al never went through the portal with us the first time. How could he validate that portion of the story? Dr. Swinford might believe he's part of the scheme because he never came back to the Museum either." Trent added.

"Ok, I understand your point, but my dad was in the portal longer than we were...he'll vouch we're on the level."

"I'm not sure if that will count. Do you really think Dr. Swinford will believe your dad *isn't* covering for you, especially after you seemingly dragged students from the Museum against his rules, and then we all disappear for a week? In fact, your father might get into a lot of trouble too. Everyone knows we were supposed to remain inside the Museum. The courtyard and anywhere outside of the building were off-limits with the penalty that the entire team would be expelled from the program," Trent reminded.

Dale's confident expression seemed to melt when he screeched, "Oh no, my dad's going to get fired, and I'm to blame. You guys will be disqualified, all because I asked for your help."

"Hold on a minute — I have an idea," Trent said.

"We were all held against our will by the Shaman and his two goons, including your dad! Al turned them over to the state police, so everyone knows that part of the story is fact because of the police report. In addition, the Museum employees working at the front desk when the Shaman asked for Melinda can verify the conversation between him and Al. Maybe we can focus on how he made us prisoners against our will, which is certainly true!"

"Yeah...that would cover my dad too! You've got the right idea," Dale said, elated with anxious eyes.

"Well, it still doesn't explain why we deliberately broke the rules by sneaking out of the Museum, and for traveling to the Enchanted Rock state park without permission. Remember, we never told anybody where we were going. You heard Carl explain how Dr. Swinford falsely accused him of fabricating the story about the portals, to avoid being fired by my dad's airline," Melinda injected, not wanting to burst their bubble.

Dale felt miserable, and lowered his eyes.

Melinda once again drifted into her own painful thoughts. While leaving the Museum was the worst problem for the rest of her friends, for her, it was only the tip of a huge iceberg. This excursion had now mushroomed into a huge scandal. With the dreadful press coverage the Museum had endured from the media before they had vanished, Melinda worried how far the media disapproval had escalated now that almost an entire student team had been 'misplaced.' She could hardly envision what Dr. Swinford must have tolerated after their parents had learned about the team's disappearance.

Melinda wondered how her parents would react when the energy account CFO in Houston confronted them about her expulsion from his darling program, or worse, if Dr. Swinford had cancelled the competition. What would her father think about her causing one of his customers so much trouble? This was serious; this could even hurt her dad's career to become the CEO of the airline. In addition, she would still need to explain everything about her birth parents.

Melinda visualized the scene with her parents as she rehearsed the details in her mind. She saw them flipping out after telling both, "By the way, Mom and Dad; instead of going to Hawaii, I would like to search for my two thousand year-old biological mom, somewhere inside a broken time dimension."

The more she thought about it, the worse it sounded. She watched mile after mile of the long road disappear, staring blankly out the window.

Trent broke the drone of the car's vibrations.

"What's that?" he asked when Tab looked up from the book he was reading.

Melinda turned her head to see what Tab was holding.

To Melinda, it looked like a small tan leather notebook, riddled with age cracks.

Tab opened it further, allowing all to see the handwriting. Delicate pages had yellowed with years. Mold spots mottled several pages. The large cursive writing reminded her of black and white movies.

Sitting closer to Tab than Trent was, she reached over and took hold of the book from him. Opening the book, it fell to a page almost in the middle:

I estimate it has been three months since the crash. Swimming to shore, we pushed our way northeast on the island. Fred is fighting a fever from a deep cut. I am of the opinion we are not on Howland Island. Our travel has been too extensive, and we have passed through various landscapes and climates for one small island..

Flipping the page Melinda read:

I am more confused than ever. Fred followed the LOP course directly. However, I am unsure if we were on target for the Howland area, or the Phoenix Islands. Because of the difficulty we had with flawed maps, Fred's navigation was not perfect. This was complicated due to the overcast skies and rainstorms. It is possible our course veered nearer to the Gilbert or the Tarawa Islands, but we have seen no evidence of the British. We traversed north and south trying to determine an actual fix; however, it seems to be a desolate island, which may indicate the Gardner Islands.

Skimming more pages, Melinda continued reading:

We are still unable to determine the cause of the distortion storm that caused our crash right before running out of fuel. Even dropping to an altitude below nine hundred feet, we remained in the direct path of unusual yellow and blue blinding lights. Fred and I believe the disturbance affected our radio communication with the Itasca. After passing through the lights, neither 3105 nor 6210 were operable at the time even with sudden clear skies, as there seemed to be some unexpected magnetic activity in the atmosphere. We were in vocal contact with the Itasca, and seemed close enough we should have seen signs of smoke residue rising into the air from her pipes before the Electra sputtered, and became difficult to control.

Amelia Mary Earhart

Turning another page, Melinda continued to read:

We have sustained ourselves with minimal food and water, as both are in short supply. Today I am severely missing my thermos of hot chocolate. If I had the chance to redo any of my actions, I would have brought additional thermos bottles with me from New Guinea. If any person shall ask in the future about my decision to attempt this epic flight plan, I continue to believe the goal has been worth the risks we are facing. I must not worry. Worry retards reactions, making clear-cut decisions virtually impossible to achieve.

I must admit, this is not how I expected to spend the commencement of my 40th year. I truly miss George. I am sure by now he has read my last letter in the event something should happen to me during this flight. No matter what befalls us, we have not failed yet. George, you knew I was aware this could happen, but you supported me to do what I wanted. If we do fail, for anyone who finds my diary, know it was because of our preparation. We are seeing a sour outlook as of late, yet I continue to look for a delightful break around the next corner.

Flipping more pages, Melinda noticed that the ink color of her handwriting was progressively fading.

I believe we have been wandering several months, but I am without certainty. We were never able to determine our longitude and latitude position, or calculate the many miles that we have sojourned in this land. It is becoming increasingly difficult to continue. I am beginning to doubt myself. Nearly depleted, we erected a small hut for protection. Fred continues to insist I am taking this hardship as well as a man, but I believe he is just trying to keep up my spirit.

Fred is gone. They took him early this morning. I could not save him in time. God help me to survive. I will try to lead them away from our camp, and come back later to gather what I need to continue homeward. If I fail, and my diary is found, please George, know I love you for loving me.

Amelia

Melinda, looked up in awe mumbling, "This is impossible."

Trent jolted her from her thoughts by asking, "Well — what is it?"

She peered closely at Tab's face when she asked him, "Where did you get this?"

Tab signed to Trent.

"He found it by that old hut, when he accidentally kicked the metal box. This was inside with that pair of flying goggles. After the soldiers pointed their rifles at him, he forgot about it until we went back to show Al the camp. He picked it up and just remembered that he had it in his back pocket."

Waiting until he finished, Melinda stated, "This is the diary of that lost woman pilot Amelia Earhart."

Dale gasped in disbelief, and then he screeched, "*THE* AMELIA EARHART!!!?"

"I only skimmed it, but her name is signed several times. Also, there's several flight references about how they got lost. Amelia and her navigator Fred built the hut. Something happened to the navigator, and she had to get away. That's where it ends."

"No way, I watched a documentary about her. It's a huge mystery as to what happened to her," Dale told them, leaning back in his seat.

Melinda said, "It seems they saw flashing yellow and blue lights in a storm, and the next thing they knew, they were somewhere else with clear skies. I bet they passed through a dimension portal, but apparently they didn't leave."

The remainder of the ride was hushed. Each person remained lost in their own thoughts, trying to digest the recent events. Noticing that they were slowing down, Melinda glanced out the window, as the limousine headed up the long drive to the Museum. Circling under the magnificent portico, Carl stopped the car.

It was dusk. Exiting, Melinda was amazed at how fast the return four hours had gone by. Everyone stretched, and Carl stepped next to Melinda and smiled.

Returning his smile, Melinda gave him a giant hug.

He said, "I hope none of ye get into serious trouble."

"I hope you're right Carl, but we did break the rules. I'm positive that I'm in *big* trouble. At the very least, I know we're going home tomorrow. Was my father hard on you?"

"I didn't want te say anything earlier, but the reason why I'd so much time te stay at the park and search fer ye, is because once he discovered I drove ye te Enchanted Rock, I wez fired immediately. I am even being sued by the airline fer not bringing back the car straight away, but in case I found ye, I needed a way te rush ye back here or te a hospital."

"Oh no Carl! I'm so sorry I dragged you into this mess."

"No worries. Let's focus on tomorrow. If yer parents make ye return, it would be my pleasure te drive ye and yer friends te the airport."

Looking up, Melinda said, "Thanks Carl; you're a wonderful friend."

Al, in his usual good spirits, bellowed for all to hear him, "Sure feels good to be back!"

Dale ran to where his dad stood, and told him, "We found Amelia Earhart's diary in the portal," he said excitedly.

"What do you mean?" Dr. Bradan asked in astonishment.

Melinda handed the diary to Dr. Bradan, and filled in the absent details.

"Tab found it in that camp. We think it's the real deal."

"This...would be amazing if it's authentic," Dr. Bradan said, smiling.

He was about to hand it back, when the relief and exhilaration of the moment was shattered.

"WHAT IN BLAZES DID YOU IMAGINE YOU WERE DOING?" Dr. Swinford yelled frantically, storming in their direction.

"You were given explicit instructions never to leave this facility; yet each of you defied my orders. Not only did you disappear from the Museum, you never notified anyone of your location for almost a week. If you thought we had negative publicity before you left, times that by 100 after you immature students ran away!"

"Sir, if you will let me explain..." Al started.

"You're still deep in the woods too! Most of our trouble is a direct result from not having operational cameras on line to catch the perpetrators who ruined the reputation of this Museum. Then, you high tail it to a state park hours away without a single phone call until tonight. What's the purpose for having a two-way radio with our security office if you don't use it?"

Pointing at the teens, he added, "I have been drowned in calls from their parents, police detectives, and every news reporter from across the country. Your fault in all of this will be discussed, you can be assured," he growled crossly at Al.

With squinted eyes, Dr. Swinford squawked at Trent, Melinda, and Tab, "I told you — one more step out of line, and your time here would end. This is VERY out of line! Pack your things tonight; I spoke with your parents after Al called me, and all of you are leaving for home first thing in the morning."

The three disheartened students hesitated, unsure what to say.

Dr. Swinford yelled for them to scurry out of his sight, "INSIDE NOW!"

He looked back over his shoulder at Al and the professor, and then he demanded while striding away, "You two, in my office! Two minutes!"

With the raggedy friends heading into the Museum front doors, Al and Dr. Bradan thanked Carl by nearly shaking off his arm.

After following the students into the main entrance, Al walked silently beside Dr. Bradan as the professor hung his head and stared at his shuffling feet. The pressure he felt weighed upon him more tangible than Al's massive hand on his shoulder.

Chapter Thirty-Six

BROKEN HEROES

Physically, and emotionally exhausted, Melinda, Dale, and the brothers slowly trudged through the museum hallways towards the student dining area, totally famished. Barely able to climb the rear steps from feeling fatigue and hopelessness, they perked up a little as they caught the lingering smells of dinner.

Trent focused on his hunger pains, when he tiredly said, "We may be kicked out of the competition and on our way home tomorrow, but what can Dr. Swinford do to us if we wait until after we eat to pack our stuff?"

Melinda said, "Right now, I only care about eating and then falling asleep."

Past the final corner, they came face-to-face with Scott, Mea, and Dino.

"Look what the cat dragged in," laughed Scott.

"Smells like something the cat left behind," Mea sniffed and cackled.

"I told you we would win the competition, and with you guys kicked out, it's going to be easier than ever. You'll be reading about *us* this summer," Scott, gloated.

Too tired and hungry to be bothered, Melinda, Trent, and Tab ignored the antagonistic comments, and sidestepping past the irritating trio, proceeded into the student dining room.

***

Following dinner, Melinda was slowly placing her newly folded clothing into her luggage, when a surprise rap sounded at the door. Too weary to answer it, she looked pleadingly at Leslie, who was excited for her return, and quickly bounced off her bed to answer the door.

On the other side were the tired, yet beaming faces of Al and Dr. Bradan.

"May we come in?" Al requested.

Melinda gave them her best smile, but it was apparent her eyelids were drooping.

"Yeah, sure, but I'm afraid I'm not going to be very good company right now."

Dr. Bradan said, "Trust me, I know how you feel. But we thought you'd like to know what we discovered speaking with Dr. Swinford before you depart in the morning."

"At this point, I'm ready to hear anything, no matter how unpleasant it is," Melinda yawned.

"There is some potential good news too, if you're interested," Al baited her.

"Oh," Melinda tried to sound pleased.

"Frankly, good and bad," Dr. Bradan teased.

"What is it?" Leslie clamored with interest. "Tell us!"

"Do you want the good or bad news first?" Al questioned Melinda in good spirits.

"Start with the bad," Melinda sighed while sitting on the edge of her bed.

"Ok, you tell them Doc," Al whispered folding his great arms in an attempt to look pitiful.

"The bad news is that Al is being forced to take a compulsory leave of absence from his job. This means Brock will now be in charge of the Museum's security."

"Ahh Al, I'm sooo sorry, really I am," Melinda said tenderly.

"And, since our team took an unauthorized field excursion into Enchanted Rock, there will be no further project trips for our team. The rules are exact about one project site visit per team."

With a frown forming on her face, Leslie remembered the rules and began to worry.

"Oh no, so if even one person gets into trouble, the whole team will be sent home! I'm going home too!" she raised her voice in a pout.

Melinda sprung from the bed with concern, "Leslie, I'm so sorry, I forgot this would happen. You don't deserve to be part of this mess!"

Suddenly full of fire and energy, Melinda faced Dr. Bradan exclaiming, "This is not fair! Leslie and Brian did nothing wrong. We have to talk to Dr. Swinford right now; he has to listen to us!"

"Wait, wait, before you jump to the wrong conclusions, there's more…" Al interjected.

"I can hardly wait to hear *more* good news," Melinda interrupted him sarcastically.

"It may not be what you think, Melinda," Dr. Bradan continued. "Both of you sit and listen to me," he said, pulling over and sitting in one of the desk chairs.

Staring into the faces of each girl, he blurted, "You're not going home. No one is being kicked out of the competition!"

"That's right," Al reinforced, "no one is going home tomorrow!"

Leslie's face beamed, "Really, we can stay?"

"Yes! It took us quite awhile, but we finally helped Dr. Swinford simmer down enough to listen to us. Once he realized what we placed onto his desk in front of him, he started to understand we were telling him the truth about the past week."

"Understand what? Put what in front of him?" Leslie fired off.

Ignoring the two questions, Dr. Bradan smiled at the blonde girl, and went on.

"Flipping through Amelia Earhart's diary, which explained what happened to her final flight was nearly too much for him to handle. He didn't believe it was real. Before we explained exactly how we acquired it, we asked him to validate its authenticity.

"How can he do that?" Melinda asked in surprise.

"The Museum has two early letters written by Amelia Earhart, long before her disappearance. He took the journal to their display location, and compared the handwriting and signature."

"What did he find?" Melinda asked, suddenly energized at knowing about the letters.

Dr. Bradan said, "Exactly what he anticipated to find — the handwriting appears to be very similar, and matches the era. The quotes were representative of her personality, and the signatures were more or less a perfect match to our eyes," he said.

Taking over the explanation, Al added, "Plus, knowing what's closest to his heart, we emphasized that the Museum's board will be delighted with him for reducing the overall curriculum expenses, by not funding our entire squad to travel around the world to someplace exotic, and compile research for a different project. Our trip into Enchanted Rock fits the profile description perfectly with assigned instructor supervision," he said, smiling.

"No way, you're teasing us right?" Melinda questioned.

After a short pause, Dr. Bradan continued, "The best part is that our team is so far ahead of the other teams in project selection, quality, and now evidence, that we may be able to potentially provide answers based on what we learned from the Shaman, to solve the other student team projects too. So, Dr. Swinford will announce tomorrow that we're the winning team because we have outdistanced the other teams by a long shot, with real and potentially undeniable evidence!"

Ready to burst at the seams, Al held up one of his massive hands, and said, "However, before it's announced publicly, we still need to account for and document the results."

Melinda validated what she heard by saying, "So you're telling us that we won the team competition? And we only need to document how and where the diary was found, prior to broadcasting our project to the world as part of the contest program?"

"Are you serious? We won?!" Leslie sang out in astonishment.

Dr. Bradan finished, "If we confirm its legitimacy, this would be one of the greatest finds of our time, and the student program would become the envy of the Museum community."

"That got Dr. Swinford over the edge, but just to make sure, we added that if you students were expelled from the program for leaving the Museum, then technically the diary was found on your personal time, and so theoretically it's yours. It would be an enormous loss to J-MA if you were forced to align with a competitive Museum for being expelled," Al said, grinning.

Melinda and Leslie were glowing inside. Jumping up, Leslie cried out, "Really?"

"Really," Al and Dr. Bradan validated in unison.

"What do we do next?" Melinda wondered.

"That's the best part yet," Al said excitedly. "Dr. Bradan is your project mentor, so he will remain with the team, however, at Dr. Swinford's energetic insistence; I'm to become your new bodyguard when the team goes back to explore Enchanted Rock. We need to learn how the portals work in order to make the diary public."

"Why is that important?" Melinda asked.

"We must have definable proof to support where and how the diary was discovered."

"This is really serious! You're not teasing us?" Melinda reinforced, almost bursting inside with happiness.

"Unless you don't want to go back inside the portal," Al joked with her. "You know we're going to look for your mother — right?" Al added in a serious tone.

"Mother! Whose mother? What do you mean looking for?" Leslie spit out.

"I'll tell you later," Melinda said hurriedly.

"So when do we start?" Melinda asked, searching their faces for additional answers.

"It's kind of up to you and your parents. Dr. Swinford told us how upset they were when they heard you were missing from the program. We'll need to do a lot of explaining to them later, so for now, I suggest we all get some rest, and tomorrow, we'll inform our entire team about the good news," Dr. Bradan said.

Leslie complained, "Yeah you guys, someone needs to tell me what's going on around here. I feel left out."

"Better unpack your things, and plan what you want to bring when we return into the portal...*if* you get to stick around for a few more days," Al advised. "I will do some research and buy us some professional expedition gear, so we're better prepared the next time."

Melinda stood up.

"This is way too much to believe," she said. "Instead of being disqualified from the competition, we're now going to find my mother as part of the team's project — sanctioned by Dr. Swinford?" For a moment, she appeared lost in her good fortune, when a depressing thought crossed her mind.

Al perceived the gloominess behind her eyes and overflowing with concern asked, "What's wrong?"

"What about the Shaman? Is he still out there somewhere looking for my mom's necklace so he can use it to find mine?" Melinda asked. "We still don't know if the Guardian stopped him or not."

"What is it with you guys — has everyone gone bonkers? What is a Guardian? Who is a Shaman? What does this have to do with your necklace, and what do you mean by a portal — into what?" Leslie fired off desperately as her mind would not rest from what she had heard.

Except for Leslie, the rest broke out in genuine laughter. It felt good to Melinda after their recent trials.

"I promise; you'll find out everything," Melinda said, trying to appease her roommate's feelings.

She then added, "We need to search for proof to link with the diary for sure, but my mother is still in serious danger...if she's still alive."

Dr. Bradan said, "I'm not sure if we will ever find her, but I know Al and I won't rest until we know what happened to her, once we go back through the portal."

Staring into his eyes, Melinda smiled her appreciation.

Standing expectantly, Dr. Bradan said to Melinda, "I have a growing feeling that tonight's briefing will not hold until we meet with the rest of the team and may take some time," as he looked in Leslie's direction. "She's not going to wait until tomorrow," he said with a wide grin.

Suddenly appearing as serious as he could, Dr. Bradan directed Leslie, "Every word she's about to tell you is one thousand percent true — no matter how crazy or unbelievable it may sound to you."

Smiling at Melinda, he said to her, "This is going to take some time to explain, so I imagine you two will be up late discussing the whole thing after we leave tonight. I will notify the rest of the team to sleep in tomorrow. Let's not plan to meet again until after lunch."

Together the two men moved closer to the door, and then left upon saying goodbye.

Melinda said, "Leslie, we better find a way to stay awake, because for what I'm about to tell you, it's going to take most of the night."

***

Much later into the early morning hours, Melinda rested in her comfortable Museum bed.

As unbelievable as the past weeks had been, she wondered what their future, or past, held for them starting tomorrow. Closing her eyes, she drifted to sleep, smiling.

THE END

CPSIA information can be obtained at www.ICGtesting.com
Printed in the USA
BVOW001558210613

323986BV00006B/43/P

1 MONTH OF FREE READING

at

www.ForgottenBooks.com

By purchasing this book you are eligible for one month membership to ForgottenBooks.com, giving you unlimited access to our entire collection of over 700,000 titles via our web site and mobile apps.

To claim your free month visit:

www.forgottenbooks.com/free99786

VOLUME XIII

Autobiography in the Middle of the Nineteenth Century

(1820—1870)

INCLUDING THE SELF-NARRATIVES OF

CARDINAL NEWMAN, the famed English convert to Catholicism; VICTOR HUGO, the greatest of French romantic writers; MARIE ASMAR, a modern princess of Babylon; HANS CHRISTIAN ANDERSEN, most beloved of Danish writers; EUGENIE DE GUERIN, a gentle French Catholic devotee; JOHN STUART MILL, sternest of utilitarian philosophers; and LONGFELLOW, foremost of American poets.

WITH INTRODUCTORY ESSAYS BY

REV. ALPHONSUS J. DONLON
President of Georgetown University

REV. CHARLES FRANKLIN THWING
President of Western Reserve University

CONTENTS OF VOLUME XIII

ILLUSTRATIONS IN VOLUME XIII

INTRODUCTION TO VOLUME XIII

AUTOBIOGRAPHY IN THE MIDDLE OF THE NINETEENTH CENTURY

1820—1870

THE period of the present volume includes one of the very great autobiographies of all time, that of Cardinal Newman. For a parallel to his deep heart-searching study of himself and of the spiritual meaning of life, we must look back to Saint Augustine, that earliest, mightiest of the "Christian Fathers." Equally earnest with Augustine, perhaps equally able-minded, and certainly as profoundly convinced of his finally accepted doctrines, Newman offers a striking resemblance to his predecessor.

He was an Englishman who grew to manhood during that strange period of reaction which we have described as paralyzing the democratic forces of Europe after 1815. The period of complete reaction ended with the second French revolution, that of 1830. A milder, wiser, and hence stronger, Democracy then took control of France. Its example and encouragement gradually spread to Germany and Italy and even to that ancient center of all reactionary principles, Austria. Hence in 1848 there ensued uprisings of the people all over Europe; and though these revolts were by no means everywhere successful, yet from 1848 onward the people had everywhere some voice in their own government. Probably future ages looking back on the long battle of Democracy against Autocracy which began in America in 1775 and has reached even into our time, will mark as the central focus, the decisive moment of Democracy's control, this year 1848. Up to then Democracy had been a new force in civilization, one little understood and much distrusted. From then on it was an accepted principle, slowly but surely establishing itself everywhere, while all the ancient forces of "privilege" and the "divine right" of the powerful fought against it in an ever receding battle.

In France, the leader of this mighty movement, we can perhaps see its meaning best in the life of Victor Hugo. Many voices have acclaimed him the greatest man of the age. Certainly he was the leader of the protesting or ''Romantic'' party in his country. There the battle was to be waged chiefly by the pen. Education had become the dominant factor in life. And to the war of argument, Hugo brought a splendid fiery genius which made him invincible. More than once his plays or poems were suppressed by the reactionary government; but suppression has proven in our day but a feeble method of warring against intellect. If a man have any real thing to say to Democracy, then Democracy will hear it somehow, even though the voice be that of a Turgenef or a Tolstoi crying out in darkest Russia.

So Hugo made himself heard not only by France but by all the world. We have no autobiography from him; but his intimate personal letters show us well the ardent, clear-eyed youth just entering on his life-long struggle, looking back, as it were, to take stock of himself and his resources before he undertakes the fight.

Along with this great struggle of the period for material and political freedom, there arose also in this momentous epoch a struggle for intellectual freedom. Men refused to accept doctrines merely because of having been taught them in childhood. They insisted on examining for themselves the sources of their teaching and the evidence on which it all was based. Newman's famous autobiography illustrates this tendency as it affected the religious mind. Almost equally remarkable, though not equally famed, is the autobiography of John Stuart Mill. He displays the same persistency to reach the depths of understanding as Newman, but on other lines.

John Mill was a materialist, or ''utilitarian,'' to use the word which he himself made popular. He sought to measure all things by their results, accept only what could be proven, attempt only where he could see logically that the achievement was good, would be ''worth while.'' Some very noble-minded men have thus refused to be led along by undemonstrable visions, dreams of what may come; but in Mill's day such an attitude was held to be essentially unreligious, and his life was not an easy one.

In fullest, gentlest antagonism to the stern spirit of Mill, and perhaps almost equally to that of Newman, let us turn to a third remarkable autobiography of the period, the Journal of Eugenie de Guerin. Mlle. de Guerin was the most loving, the most devoted of French Catholic maidens. She had a younger brother Maurice whom she guided almost as a mother; and Maurice was, like Hugo, a poet and a thinker. He left the ancient church, he married an outsider opposed to all his family's manners and ideas, and then he died, leaving his sister Eugenie broken-hearted. She had written chiefly for him, and she continued until her death soon after, a journal of her pure thoughts day by day. Often she turns back to tell some incident of his or her childhood, the days they had shared together in full harmony. There is perhaps no more beautiful, and no more unreasoning, book within the century. Her words are just pure faith from end to end. One likes to know in this toiling, shifting, devious world, to carry close at heart amid the effort of life, the knowledge that such a simple, steadfast soul as that of Eugenie de Guerin existed, and can still exist.

Of somewhat similar type is the beautiful autobiography of Hans Christian Andersen, the Danish teller of fairy tales, the lover of children. With Andersen we feel as with that earlier Dane, Baron Holberg, that we are swinging a bit outside the circle of established European life. Andersen is in it, but not of it. He is a traveler; he visits Germany and France and England, and tells us what he saw there. But he looks upon it all as a stranger, as one who smiles upon a struggle meaningless to him, empty words wherein he has no part. He knows as little of spiritual doubt or of scientific rules of evidence as does Mlle. de Guerin. He looks only for the sweetness and tenderness and nobility of life. In one edition of his autobiography he truly named it *The Fairy Story of My Life*. By this title he meant to indicate how wonderfully everybody had helped him and how he had risen from obscurity; but would not life always be a fairy story to one who forever sought, like Andersen, and forever saw, the beautiful?

In one way the Danish story teller was as over-sensitive as Rousseau or Haydon or any of the mass of self-conscious, over-imaginative artists. He never reaches the saintliness and self-sacrifice of Eugenie de Guerin. So with him we meet yet another kind of mind to convince us of the infinite variety and complexity of humanity.

From the abnormal we may turn with somewhat of relief to the more easily appreciated normal. If we look for the best known American of this immediate period we may perhaps find him in the poet Longfellow. No name is better known to every American household; and Longfellow is known just because he was what all good men sought to be and could appreciate. It has often been pointed out by critics that Longfellow wrote no really wonderful poetry; and the answer is that he did a better thing, he put into poetry, such poetry as people could remember and recite, all the good little ordinary things, all the commonplaces of righteousness. If his are not the supreme words which may inspire some great soul in a great crisis, they are the much more useful axioms which we all need day by day and every day, whereby to mold our common lives. Hence the fragments of autobiography here culled from Longfellow's letters, though they are but scanty, have a value for us all.

One other narrative makes up our volume. It is an oddity indeed, the story of a Princess of Babylon. The ancient Babylon, dead for two thousand years, has been so much discussed, that it is hard for us quite to realize that there is a Babylonia to-day, and that people live there. They are Arabs, and in the 1840's they were sorely abused by Turkish overlords. They had petty Arab princes of their own; and the daughter of one of these, feeling herself particularly abused, fled to England and there wrote her story. In later years, resolute European travelers risked their lives to journey through these distant regions and bring home some scant account of how their people lived. But here we have, from an earlier date than any of the travels, an account by one of the Arabs themselves, a princess' own account of how an Eastern princess lived in the nineteenth century. It is very interesting, and, if we pause to contrast its primitive poverty with the splendor of the *Arabian Nights,* it is whimsically entertaining. To the West this had become an age of easy living and hence an age of thought; to the ancient East it was still an age of material considerations.

NEWMAN'S "APOLOGIA"

By Alphonsus J. Donlon, S.J.

In his *Apologia* Newman has left to posterity an imperishable heritage. The book will withstand the disintegrating influences of time, because of its irresistible appeal to the heart of humanity, because of its stern and uncompromising opposition to man-made religions and shallow philosophies, and because of the high position its literary power has secured for it among the classics of the language.

We have in the *Apologia* the phenomenon, probably unique in history, of a man writing his autobiography against his will and in self-defense. In *Macmillan's Magazine* for January, 1864, Charles Kingsley, a popular writer of the day, charged Newman with saying that truth for its own sake need not, and on the whole ought not to be, a virtue with the Roman clergy. Newman indignantly protested against the accusation and challenged Kingsley to prove it. Kingsley did not attempt to prove it; and the only reparation he offered was to say that he was sorry at having mistaken the meaning of Newman's words; and this he did without indicating any words of Newman's which could even apparently justify the accusation. Newman replied in a humorous and satirical pamphlet which completely turned the tables on Kingsley. Kingsley then published a rejoinder entitled, "What, then, does Dr. Newman mean?" This pamphlet of Kingsley's was the occasion of the writing of the *Apologia*.

Newman's was one of those great and noble souls which make their appearance but once or twice in a century. Mankind takes but a superficial interest in men who are absorbed in themselves, who hunger for notoriety, and are consumed with self-pity when it is denied them. But the world knows that such is not the character of the man whose soul is revealed in the *Apologia*. There is no striving after notoriety here.

Newman passed his whole life doing good to others. When the interests of religion or the needs of his fellow-man called for a sacrifice on his part, he made it freely and ungrudgingly. Even when publicly put upon his defense by the reckless and unjust attack of Kingsley, his chief thought was not for himself, but for the Church of his adoption and the good name of his fellow-priests.

The man of right principle and tender heart cannot but be touched by the evident struggle and pain with which Newman sets himself to bare his soul to the world. "It is not at all pleasant," he says, "for me to be egotistical; or to be criticized for being so. It is not pleasant to reveal to high and low, young and old, what has gone on within me from my early years." "Who can afford to be leisurely and deliberate, while he practises on himself a cruel operation, the ripping up of old griefs, and the venturing again upon the 'infandum dolorem' of years, in which the stars of this lower heaven were one by one going out? I could not in cool blood, nor except upon the imperious call of duty, attempt what I have set myself to do. It is both to head and heart an extreme trial."

The generous souls of the world will always admire and love Newman for his transparent honesty and his simple and disinterested devotion to truth, a devotion which led him to sacrifice all that he held dear on earth rather than be unfaithful to it. He gave up "much that he loved and prized and could have retained, but that he loved honesty better than name, and Truth better than dear friends."

He has a word of rebuke for those superficial observers who ascribed to cunning and double-faced practice his conduct of the Oxford Movement and his conversion to the Catholic Church. "As if forsooth a Religion which has flourished through so many ages, among so many nations, amid such varieties of social life, in such contrary classes and conditions of men, and after so many revolutions, political and civil, could not subdue the reason and overcome the heart, without the aid of fraud in the process and the sophistries of the schools."

A striking feature of the *Apologia* is the unequivocal testimony it bears in behalf of dogmatic religion, and that, the religion of traditional Christianity. The giant intellect of

Newman, conceded by those who had little sympathy with his convictions to be possessed of almost unrivaled logical powers, pronounces in favor of dogma, and thus emphatically gives the lie to the arrogant and sneering assertion of the agnostic that Christianity is the badge of the illiterate and the weak-minded.

Eleven years before his death Newman said that for fifty years he had resisted with all his power the spirit of liberalism in religion. But we need not go beyond the *Apologia* for a proof of his opposition to this spirit. It is his fight against the anti-dogmatic principle which illuminates and gives a meaning to the pages of the *Apologia*. To Newman more than any one else the Protestant of the English-speaking world owes it that some remnant of dogmatic Christianity is preserved to him. When the hosts of liberalism and skepticism, who had had such a singular success in continental Europe, were threatening to overrun England, they were met by Newman and his little party of the Oxford Movement, and Christianity was saved for Protestant England for many years to come.

Unlike the proud and self-satisfied theorist of the present day, Newman did not painfully elaborate a religious system out of his own head. When he was searching for the true religion of Christ, he did not start by laying down an arbitrary hypothesis which made a farce of Revelation and contradicted the facts of history during two thousand years. He made it his rule to be guided by evidence alone; and it was his nufaltering adherence to this rule which finally brought him into the Catholic Church.

Not that he was ignorant or unmindful of the arguments of the skeptic. On the contrary, no one has mastered the skeptic's position more thoroughly than Newman, or could give it more powerful and persuasive expression. But the reasonings of the skeptic left him untouched; for he saw their fundamental weakness and the fallacies upon which they rely for their plausibility. He saw the inconsistency between the skeptic's theory and his practice, and the complicated system of balances and props by which he endeavors to maintain himself in an unnatural position. He saw how the skeptic applies to the evidences of Christianity a method of reasoning which he would be ashamed to employ in the ordinary affairs of life. Newman gives some hint of his answer to the skeptic in the first chapter of the *Apologia;* but the full development of this answer must be looked for in his *Grammar of Assent.*

The singular grace and unaffected simplicity with which Newman recounts the story of his life captivated the English reading public from the start, and everywhere the *Apologia* was accepted as a classic. On its first publication the *Saturday Review* pronounced it "one of the most interesting works of the present literary age. Dr. Newman is one of the finest masters of language, his logical powers are almost unequalled, and, in one way or other, he has influenced the course of English thought more perhaps than any of his contemporaries." "I have just been going through Newman's *Apologia* for the twentieth time," writes "T. B." in *The Upton Letters,* "and as usual have fallen completely under the magical spell of that incomparable style; its perfect lucidity, showing the very shape of the thought within, its simplicity, . . . its appositeness, its dignity, its music. I oscillate between supreme contentment as a reader and envious despair as a writer; it fills one's mind up slowly and richly, as honey fills a vase from some gently tilted bowl." "In England," wrote Matthew Arnold, "there needs a miracle of genius like Shakespeare's to produce balance of mind, and a miracle of intellectual delicacy like Dr. Newman's to produce urbanity of style." Gladstone said of Newman's style: "It is a transporting style. I find myself constantly disposed to cry aloud and vent myself in that way as I read. It is like the very highest music, and seems sometimes in beauty to go beyond the human."

THE AUTOBIOGRAPHY OF JOHN STUART MILL: AN APPRECIATION

By Charles F. Thwing, LL.D., Litt.D.

THERE hangs before me as I write a photograph of Watt's portrait of John Stuart Mill. Regarding the portrait an American philosopher who knew Mill once said that "The painter of that face knew more about his subject than any man had the right to know about another." The portrait does seem to be an expression of Mill himself. It gives evidence of those qualities, fundamental and structural, which Mill possessed, or which rather possessed and constituted him.

The most eminent of these qualities is the love of truth and the consequent determination to find truth. As to Bishop Butler, so also to John Stuart Mill the search of truth was the business of his life and the object of his unconquerable passion. No desire for a certain conclusion influenced his judgment. No hope for a specified verdict colored the evidence presented. No friendliness and no enmity was suffered for an instant to turn by a hair's breadth the rigor of logical procedure. No warmth of passion or of emotion was allowed to alter the coldness of the plain fact. The personal equation was eliminated. His mind was just in analyzing and in synthesis, in seeing the fact and in inferring truth from the fact.

The fields which Mill cultivated in this sublime quest were among the greatest. Government, economics, logic and philosophy were among them. To each he made contributions which for a generation profoundly and vitally moved the thoughtful world of English speech,—contributions too which are still influencing forces. His work on political economy is the foundation of much of the economic thinking of our time. His views on government and the whole social and socialistic movement have proved to be in many respects a true and inspiring prophecy. His logic still stands not only as a monument but also as a formative and instructive force in thinking. In other fields as well, such as education, art, music, his thoughts especially as embodied in the St. Andrew's Address touch the high water mark of interpretation.

The search for truth was impregnated with a passion for righteousness. To Mill revelation spelled dedication, and truth duty. The intellectual quest was supported by the ethical motive. The intellectual vision was clear in part at least because the heart was pure. In a narrow way the beatitude, "Blessed are the pure in heart, for they shall see God," may be applied to Mill, to Mill who thought of himself as an agnostic. The passion for righteousness seemed to be quite as deep as the passion for truth. It is reported of him that once he said, "If to Hell I must go for doing right, to Hell I will go."

Neither truth nor righteousness as incarnated in Mill was remote from human concerns. Both were colored and charged with the social feeling. His interpretation of truth, his desire to be and to do the right, was not a personal matter only. It had relations to men, to all men. The race-passion was his, and especially strong was the passion for that portion of the human family whose environment is hard, narrow, oppressed. His chapter on the future of the working classes illustrates one of the best endeavors of the mid-Victorian age to alleviate and to serve the people. No soul was more responsive, no hand more generous, than Mill's in helping forward the great cause of human betterment.

For the formation of such a character and for the creation and nurturing of such a force, many and mighty conditions contributed. His education by his father, also a man of unique part and place, still remains one of the unique endeavors for the training of the individual boy. He began to learn Greek when he was three years old, although Latin was deferred to the eighth year! Before he had entered his teens he had received an education of far greater value than most boys receive at the close of this period. The experience which would have killed most boys, even if possible for them, seems to have been inspiring and really educative to young Mill. The reason lies quite as much in the character of the teacher as in the character of the student.

It is also to be said that Mill's interest in individual men was quite as intense as his interest in truth and in righteousness. He was fortunate in his friendships. In a group which included Carlyle, Ruskin, George Grote, Maurice, Bentham and John Sterling his place was central. His letters recently published show that his heart was as warm and big as his intellect was inspiring. Apparently it would be hard to find two men of personalities more opposite than Carlyle and Mill, yet immediately after his death Carlyle said to Charles Eliot Norton:

"I never knew a finer, tenderer, more sensitive or modest soul among the sons of men."

The only one of his special group still remaining, Lord Morley, wrote immediately after his death in terms of deep feeling and regard. His memory claims "the affectionate veneration of sons, and he is himself an example of unselfish and magnanimous living." And Morley writes of his friends describing "Their pain at the thought that they will see him no more." His letters to John Sterling,—that unique, beautiful, moving, tragic personality,—are among the most touching letters ever written by a man to a man.

In Mill were united the greatest qualities of human nature,—the desire for truth, the desire for righteousness, the desire for service. Each of these qualities found in him a high degree of power and of development; and the union of them in his character and work was as unique as it was beautiful and inspiring.

In a generation which embraced names so distinguished and so diverse in government as Gladstone, Peel, Palmerston, Disraeli, in science as Darwin, Huxley, Spencer, in literature as Tennyson, Browning, Wordsworth, Coleridge,—John Stuart Mill has a great and lasting place.

JOHN, CARDINAL NEWMAN

THE MOST FAMED OF ENGLISH CONVERTS TO CATHOLICISM

1801-1890

(INTRODUCTORY NOTE)

In the year 1845, convinced that the Roman Catholic faith was the only true one, the Very Reverend John Henry Newman, one of the foremost men in the Anglican Church, sent for a humble Italian monk, Father Dominic, Passionist, and, falling at his feet, pled for reception into the fold of St. Peter. Home, friends, preferment, leadership—all were forgotten in his desire to embrace what he considered to be the original, authentic Christian religion. And his determination had not been arrived at idly. Long had been his mental and spiritual battle, and this "Apologia" is mainly the record of it. What a dramatic soul-dissection he gives us!

We see him affiliating himself with the "Oxford Movement," in 1833, which strove toward high-church principles, in the Church of England, against the marked tendency toward radicalism and liberalism. He wrote many of the celebrated "Tracts of the Times" which so stirred up the Protestants in Great Britain, both lay and clergy. For several years he devoted himself to proving the possibility of a middle ground between the Roman Catholic Church and Protestantism, only to discover his *via media* impracticable and an object of derision.

In 1843 he resigned his living in the Anglican Church, and two years afterwards became a Roman Catholic, accepting comparative poverty in the change. In 1849 he founded an English branch of St. Philip Neri, the "Oratory." He wrote voluminously, and all his work is distinguished for scholarship, analytical penetration, and beauty of language. The "Apologia pro Vita Sua," or "Explanation of His Life," his masterpiece, appeared in 1864. It came out in parts, and each part was looked forward to with eagerness by the public. Wide-sweeping was its effect, and Father Newman had the unique privilege of determining the judgment of his age concerning himself, fairly compelling his contemporaries, by his persuasive powers and sincere conviction, to accept his interpretation of himself to himself. Personally, he seemed to exercise a mesmeric influence over friends and associates, and in his writings there is some-

A. V. 13—1

thing of the same uncanny quality. Needless to add, the whole Catholic Church, Anglican as well as Roman, owes a vast debt to the powerful defense that he made of all the great fundamentals of the Catholic faith. In a latitudinarian era he battled in behalf of the great verities contained in Holy Scripture and the creeds.

Newman was created a Catholic cardinal in 1879. As an orator he was not ideal, for his manner was rather awkward and his voice thin, but his discourse was ever admirable and concise. Physically, he was almost emaciated, with a sharp, eagle look about his face. There was also a monkish austerity in his make-up oddly mingled with a quality of great sweetness.

The ''Apologia'' as a sincere revelation of a human soul ranks beside the ''Confessions'' of St. Augustine.

APOLOGIA PRO VITA SUA

CHAPTER I

HISTORY OF MY RELIGIOUS OPINIONS TO THE YEAR 1833

IT may easily be conceived how great a trial it is to me to write the following history of myself; but I must not shrink from the task. The words, ''Secretum meum mihi,'' keep ringing in my ears; but as men draw towards their end, they care less for disclosures. Nor is it the least part of my trial, to anticipate that, upon first reading what I have written, my friends may consider much in it irrelevant to my purpose; yet I cannot help thinking that, viewed as a whole, it will effect what I propose to myself in giving it to the public.

I was brought up from a child to take great delight in reading the Bible; but I had no formed religious convictions till I was fifteen. Of course I had a perfect knowledge of my Catechism.

After I was grown up, I put on paper my recollections of the thoughts and feelings on religious subjects, which I had at the time that I was a child and a boy,—such as had remained on my mind with sufficient prominence to make me then consider them worth recording. Out of these, written in the Long Vacation of 1820, and transcribed with additions in 1823, I select two, which are at once the most definite among them, and also have a bearing on my later convictions.

1. ''I used to wish the Arabian Tales were true: my imagi-

nation ran on unknown influences, on magical powers, and talismans. . . . I thought life might be a dream, or I an Angel, and all this world a deception, my fellow-angels by a playful device concealing themselves from me, and deceiving me with the semblance of a material world."

Again: "Reading in the Spring of 1816 a sentence from [Dr. Watts's] *Remnants of Time,* entitled 'the Saints unknown to the world,' to the effect, that 'there is nothing in their figure or countenance to distinguish them,' &c., &c., I supposed he spoke of Angels who lived in the world, as it were disguised."

2. The other remark is this: "I was very superstitious, and for some time previous to my conversion" [when I was fifteen] "used constantly to cross myself on going into the dark."

Of course I must have got this practice from some external source or other; but I can make no sort of conjecture whence; and certainly no one had ever spoken to me on the subject of the Catholic religion, which I only knew by name. The French master was an *émigré* Priest, but he was simply made a butt, as French masters too commonly were in that day, and spoke English very imperfectly. There was a Catholic family in the village, old maiden ladies we used to think; but I knew nothing about them. I have of late years heard that there were one or two Catholic boys in the school; but either we were carefully kept from knowing this, or the knowledge of it made simply no impression on our minds. My brother will bear witness how free the school was from Catholic ideas.

I had once been into Warwick Street Chapel, with my father, who, I believe, wanted to hear some piece of music; all that I bore away from it was the recollection of a pulpit and a preacher, and a boy swinging a censer.

When I was at Littlemore, I was looking over old copybooks of my school days, and I found among them my first Latin verse-book; and in the first page of it there was a device which almost took my breath away with surprise. I have the book before me now, and have just been showing it to others. I have written in the first page, in my school-boy hand, "John H. Newman, February 11th, 1811, Verse Book;"

then follow my first Verses. Between "Verse" and "Book" I have drawn the figure of a solid cross upright, and next to it is, what may indeed be meant for a necklace, but what I cannot make out to be anything else than a set of beads suspended, with a little cross attached. At this time I was not quite ten years old. I suppose I got these ideas from some romance, Mrs. Radcliffe's or Miss Porter's; or from some religious picture; but the strange thing is, how, among the thousand objects which meet a boy's eyes, these in particular should so have fixed themselves in my mind, that I made them thus practically my own. I am certain there was nothing in the churches I attended, or the prayer books I read, to suggest them. It must be recollected that Anglican churches and prayer books were not decorated in those days as I believe they are now.

When I was fourteen, I read Paine's *Tracts against the Old Testament,* and found pleasure in thinking of the objections which were contained in them. Also, I read some of Hume's *Essays;* and perhaps that on *Miracles.* So at least I gave my Father to understand; but perhaps it was a brag. Also, I recollect copying out some French verses, perhaps Voltaire's, in denial of the immortality of the soul, and saying to myself something like "How dreadful, but how plausible!"

When I was fifteen, (in the autumn of 1816,) a great change of thought took place in me. I fell under the influences of a definite Creed, and received into my intellect impressions of dogma, which, through God's mercy, have never been effaced or obscured. Above and beyond the conversations and sermons of the excellent man, long dead, the Rev. Walter Mayers, of Pembroke College, Oxford, who was the human means of this beginning of divine faith in me, was the effect of the books which he put into my hands, all of the school of Calvin. One of the first books I read was a work of Romaine's; I neither recollect the title nor the contents, except one doctrine, which of course I do not include among those which I believe to have come from a divine source, viz. the doctrine of final perseverance. I received it at once, and believed that the inward conversion of which I was conscious, (and of which I still am more certain than that I have hands and feet,) would last into the next life, and that I was elected

to eternal glory. I have no consciousness that this belief had
any tendency whatever to lead me to be careless about pleasing God. I retained it till the age of twenty-one, when it
gradually faded away; but I believe that it had some influence
on my opinions, in the direction of those childish imagina-
tions which I have already mentioned, viz. in isolating me
from the objects which surrounded me; in confirming me in
my mistrust of the reality of material phenomena, and making
me rest in the thought of two and two only absolute and
luminously self-evident beings, myself and my Creator;—
for while I considered myself predestined to salvation, my
mind did not dwell upon others, as fancying them simply
passed over, not predestined to eternal death. I only thought
of the mercy to myself.

The detestable doctrine last mentioned is simply denied and
abjured, unless my memory strangely deceives me, by the
writer who made a deeper impression on my mind than any
other, and to whom (humanly speaking) I almost owe my
soul,—Thomas Scott of Aston Sandford. I so admired and
delighted in his writings, that, when I was an Under-graduate, I thought of making a visit to his Parsonage, in order to
see a man whom I so deeply revered. I hardly think I could
have given up the idea of this expedition, even after I had
taken my degree; for the news of his death in 1821 came upon
me as a disappointment as well as a sorrow. I hung upon the
lips of Daniel Wilson, afterwards Bishop of Calcutta, as in
two sermons at St. John's Chapel he gave the history of
Scott's life and death. I had been possessed of his *Force of
Truth* and *Essays* from a boy; his *Commentary* I bought
when I was an Under-graduate.

What, I suppose, will strike any reader of Scott's history
and writings, is his bold unworldliness and vigorous independence of mind. He followed truth wherever it led him,
beginning with Unitarianism, and ending in a zealous faith
in the Holy Trinity. It was he who first planted deep in my
mind that fundamental truth of religion. With the assistance
of Scott's *Essays*, and the admirable work of Jones of Nay-
land, I made a collection of Scripture texts in proof of the
doctrine, with remarks (I think) of my own upon them, before
I was sixteen; and a few months later I drew up a series of

texts in support of each verse of the Athanasian Creed. These papers I have still.

Besides his unworldliness, what I also admired in Scott was his resolute opposition to Antinomianism, and the minutely practical character of his writings. They show him to be a true Englishman, and I deeply felt his influence; and for years I used almost as proverbs what I considered to be the scope and issue of his doctrine, *Holiness rather than peace,* and *Growth the only evidence of life.*

Calvinists make a sharp separation between the elect and the world; there is much in this that is cognate or parallel to the Catholic doctrine; but they go on to say, as I understand them, very differently from Catholicism,—that the converted and the unconverted can be discriminated by man, that the justified are conscious of their state of justification, and that the regenerate cannot fall away. Catholics on the other hand shade and soften the awful antagonism between good and evil, which is one of their dogmas, by holding that there are different degrees of justification, that there is a great difference in point of gravity between sin and sin, that there is the possibility and the danger of falling away, and that there is no certain knowledge given to any one that he is simply in a state of grace, and much less that he is to persevere to the end:—of the Calvinistic tenets the only one which took root in my mind was the fact of heaven and hell, divine favor and divine wrath, of the justified and the unjustified. The notion that the regenerate and the justified were one and the same, and that the regenerate, as such, had the gift of perseverance, remained with me not many years, as I have said already.

This main Catholic doctrine of the warfare between the city of God and the powers of darkness was also deeply impressed upon my mind by a work of a character very opposite to Calvinism, Law's *Serious Call.*

From this time I have held with a full inward assent and belief the doctrine of eternal punishment, as delivered by our Lord Himself, in as true a sense as I hold that of eternal happiness; though I have tried in various ways to make that truth less terrible to the imagination.

Now I come to two other works, which produced a deep

impression on me in the same Autumn of 1816, when I was fifteen years old, each contrary to each, and planting in me the seeds of an intellectual inconsistency which disabled me for a long course of years. I read Joseph Milner's *Church History,* and was nothing short of enamored of the long extracts from St. Augustine, St. Ambrose, and the other Fathers which I found there. I read them as being the religion of the primitive Christians: but simultaneously with Milner I read Newton *On the Prophecies,* and in consequence became most firmly convinced that the Pope was the Antichrist predicted by Daniel, St. Paul, and St. John. My imagination was stained by the effects of this doctrine up to the year 1843; it had been obliterated from my reason and judgment at an earlier date; but the thought remained upon me as a sort of false conscience. Hence came that conflict of mind, which so many have felt besides myself;—leading some men to make a compromise between two ideas, so inconsistent with each other, —driving others to beat out the one idea or the other from their minds,—and ending in my own case, after many years of intellectual unrest, in the gradual decay and extinction of one of them,—I do not say in its violent death, for why should I not have murdered it sooner, if I murdered it at all?

I am obliged to mention, though I do it with great reluctance, another deep imagination, which at this time, the autumn of 1816, took possession of me,—there can be no mistake about the fact; viz. that it would be the will of God that I should lead a single life. This anticipation, which has held its ground almost continuously ever since,—with the break of a month now and a month then, up to 1829, and, after that date, without any break at all,—was more or less connected in my mind with the notion, that my calling in life would require such a sacrifice as celibacy involved; as, for instance, missionary work among the heathen, to which I had a great drawing for some years. It also strengthened my feeling of separation from the visible world, of which I have spoken above.

In 1822 I came under very different influences from those to which I had hitherto been subjected. At that time, Mr. Whately, as he was then, afterwards Archbishop of Dublin, for the few months he remained in Oxford, which he was leaving for good, showed great kindness to me. He renewed it in 1825, when he became Principal of Alban Hall, making me his Vice-Principal and Tutor. Of Dr. Whately I will speak presently: for from 1822 to 1825 I saw most of the present Provost of Oriel, Dr. Hawkins, at that time Vicar of St. Mary's; and, when I took orders in 1824 and had a curacy in Oxford, then, during the Long Vacations, I was especially thrown into his company. I can say with a full heart that I love him, and have never ceased to love him; and I thus preface what otherwise might sound rude, that in the course of the many years in which we were together afterwards, he provoked me very much from time to time, though I am perfectly certain that I have provoked him a great deal more. Moreover, in me such provocation was unbecoming, both because he was the Head of my College, and because, in the first years that I knew him, he had been in many ways of great service to my mind.

He was the first who taught me to weigh my words, and to be cautious in my statements. He led me to that mode of limiting and clearing my sense in discussion and in controversy, and of distinguishing between cognate ideas, and of obviating mistakes by anticipation, which to my surprise has been since considered, even in quarters friendly to me, to savor of the polemics of Rome. He was a man of most exact mind himself, and he used to snub me severely, on reading, as he was kind enough to do, the first Sermons that I wrote, and other compositions which I was engaged upon.

Then as to doctrine, he was the means of great additions to my belief. As I have noticed elsewhere, he gave me the *Treatise on Apostolical Preaching*, by Sumner, afterwards Archbishop of Canterbury, from which I was led to give up my remaining Calvinism, and to receive the doctrine of Baptismal Regeneration. In many other ways too he was of use to me, on subjects semi-religious and semi-scholastic.

It was Dr. Hawkins too who taught me to anticipate that, before many years were over, there would be an attack made upon the books and the canon of Scripture. I was brought to the same belief by the conversation of Mr. Blanco White, who also led me to have freer views on the subject of inspiration than were usual in the Church of England at the time.

There is one other principle, which I gained from Dr. Hawkins, more directly bearing upon Catholicism, than any that I have mentioned; and that is the doctrine of Tradition. When I was an Under-graduate, I heard him preach in the University Pulpit his celebrated sermon on the subject, and recollect how long it appeared to me, though he was at that time a very striking preacher; but, when I read it and studied it as his gift, it made a most serious impression upon me. He does not go one step, I think, beyond the high Anglican doctrine, nay he does not reach it; but he does his work thoroughly, and his view was in him original, and his subject was a novel one at the time. He lays down a proposition, self-evident as soon as stated, to those who have at all examined the structure of Scripture, viz. that the sacred text was never intended to teach doctrine, but only to prove it, and that, if we would learn doctrine, we must have recourse to the formularies of the Church; for instance to the Catechism, and to the Creeds. He considers, that, after learning from them the doctrines of Christianity, the inquirer must verify them by Scripture. This view, most true in its outline, most fruitful in its consequences, opened upon me a large field of thought. Dr. Whately held it too. One of its effects was to strike at the root of the principle on which the Bible Society was set up. I belonged to its Oxford Association; it became a matter of time when I should withdraw my name from its subscription-list, though I did not do so at once.

It is with pleasure that I pay here a tribute to the memory of the Rev. William James, then Fellow of Oriel; who, about the year 1823, taught me the doctrine of Apostolical Succession, in the course of a walk, I think, round Christ Church meadow; I recollect being somewhat impatient of the subject at the time.

It was at about this date, I suppose, that I read Bishop Butler's *Analogy;* the study of which had been to so many, as it was to me, an era in their religious opinions. Its inculcation of a visible Church, the oracle of truth and a pattern of sanctity, of the duties of external religion, and of the historical character of Revelation, are characteristics of this great work which strike the reader at once; for myself, if I may attempt to determine what I most gained from it, it lay

in two points, which I shall have an opportunity of dwelling
on in the sequel; they are the underlying principles of a great
portion of my teaching. First, the very idea of an analogy
between the separate works of God leads to the conclusion
that the system which is of less importance is economically or
sacramentally connected with the more momentous system,[1]
and of this conclusion the theory, to which I was inclined as
a boy, viz. the unreality of material phenomena, is an ultimate
resolution. At this time I did not make the distinction between matter itself and its phenomena, which is so necessary
and so obvious in discussing the subject. Secondly, Butler's doctrine that Probability is the guide of life, led
me, at least under the teaching to which a few years later I
was introduced, to the question of the logical cogency of
Faith, on which I have written so much. Thus to Butler I trace those two principles of my teaching, which have
led to a charge against me both of fancifulness and of skepticism.

And now as to Dr. Whately. I owe him a great deal. He
was a man of generous and warm heart. He was particularly
loyal to his friends, and to use the common phrase, ''all his
geese were swans.'' While I was still awkward and timid
in 1822, he took me by the hand, and acted towards me the
part of a gentle and encouraging instructor. He, emphatically, opened my mind, and taught me to think and to use my
reason. After being first noticed by him in 1822, I became
very intimate with him in 1825, when I was his Vice-Principal
at Alban Hall. I gave up that office in 1826, when I became
Tutor of my College, and his hold upon me gradually relaxed.
He had done his work towards me or nearly so, when he had
taught me to see with my own eyes and to walk with my own
feet. Not that I had not a good deal to learn from others
still, but I influenced them as well as they me, and coöperated
rather than merely concurred with them. As to Dr. Whately,
his mind was too different from mine for us to remain long
on one line. I recollect how dissatisfied he was with an Article
of mine in the London Review, which Blanco White, good-
humoredly, only called Platonic. When I was diverging from

[1] It is significant that Butler begins his work with a quotation from
Origen.

him in opinion (which he did not like), I thought of dedicating my first book to him, in words to the effect that he had not only taught me to think, but to think for myself. He left Oxford in 1831; after that, as far as I can recollect, I never saw him but twice,—when he visited the University; once in the street in 1834, once in a room in 1838. From the time that he left, I have always felt a real affection for what I must call his memory; for, at least from the year 1834, he made himself dead to me. He had practically indeed given me up from the time that he became Archbishop in 1831; but in 1834 a correspondence took place between us, which, though conducted especially on his side in a friendly spirit, was the expression of differences of opinion which acted as a final close to our intercourse. My reason told me that it was impossible we could have got on together longer, had he stayed in Oxford; yet I loved him too much to bid him farewell without pain. After a few years had passed, I began to believe that his influence on me in a higher respect than intellectual advance, (I will not say through his fault,) had not been satisfactory. I believe that he has inserted sharp things in his later works about me. They have never come in my way, and I have not thought it necessary to seek out what would pain me so much in the reading.

What he did for me in point of religious opinion, was, first, to teach me the existence of the Church, as a substantive body or corporation; next to fix in me those anti-Erastian views of Church polity, which were one of the most prominent features of the Tractarian movement. On this point, and, as far as I know, on this point alone, he and Hurrell Froude intimately sympathized, though Fronde's development of opinion here was of a later date. In the year 1826, in the course of a walk, he said much to me about a work then just published, called *Letters on the Church by an Episcopalian*. He said that it would make my blood boil. It was certainly a most powerful composition. One of our common friends told me, that, after reading it, he could not keep still, but went on walking up and down his room. It was ascribed at once to Whately; I gave eager expression to the contrary opinion; but I found the belief of Oxford in the affirmative to be too strong for me; rightly or wrongly I yielded to the general voice; and I have never heard, then or since, of any disclaimer of authorship on the part of Dr. Whately.

The main positions of this able essay are these; first that Church and State should be independent of each other:—he speaks of the duty of protesting "against the profanation of Christ's kingdom, by that *double usurpation,* the interference of the Church in temporals, of the State in spirituals," p. 191; and, secondly, that the Church may justly and by right retain its property, though separated from the State.

I am not aware of any other religious opinion which I owe to Dr. Whately. In his special theological tenets I had no sympathy. In the next year, 1827, he told me he considered that I was Arianizing. The case was this: though at that time I had not read Bishop Bull's *Defensio* nor the Fathers, I was just then very strong for that ante-Nicene view of the Trinitarian doctrine, which some writers, both Catholic and non-Catholic, have accused of wearing a sort of Arian exterior. This is the meaning of a passage in Froude's *Remains,* in which he seems to accuse me of speaking against the Athanasian Creed. I had contrasted the two aspects of the Trinitarian doctrine, which are respectively presented by the Athanasian Creed and the Nicene. My criticisms were to the effect that some of the verses of the former Creed were unnecessarily scientific. This is a specimen of a certain disdain for Antiquity which had been growing on me now for several years. It showed itself in some flippant language against the Fathers in the Encyclopædia Metropolitana, about whom I knew little at the time, except what I had learnt as a boy from Joseph Milner. In writing on the Scripture Miracles in 1825-6, I had read Middleton *On the Miracles of the early Church,* and had imbibed a portion of his spirit.

The truth is, I was beginning to prefer intellectual excellence to moral; I was drifting in the direction of the Liberalism of the day. I was rudely awakened from my dream at the end of 1827 by two great blows—illness and bereavement. In the beginning of 1829, came the formal break between Dr. Whately and me; the affair of Mr. Peel's reëlection was the occasion of it. I think in 1828 or 1827 I had voted in the minority, when the Petition to Parliament against the Catholic Claims was brought into Convocation. I did so mainly on the views suggested to me in the Letters of an Episcopalian. Also I shrank from the bigoted "two-bottle-orthodox," as they were invidiously called. When then I took part against Mr. Peel, it was on an academical, not at all an ecclesiastical or a political ground; and this I professed at the time. I considered that Mr. Peel had taken the University by surprise; that his friends had no right to call upon us to turn round on a sudden, and to expose ourselves to the imputation of time-serving; and that a great University ought not to be bullied even by a great Duke of Wellington. Also by this time I was under the influence of Keble and Froude; who, in addition to the reasons I have given, disliked the Duke's change of policy as dictated by Liberalism.

Whately was considerably annoyed at me, and he took a humorous revenge, of which he had given me due notice beforehand. As head of a house he had duties of hospitality to men of all parties; he asked a set of the least intellectual men in Oxford to dinner, and men most fond of port; he made me one of this party; placed me between Provost This and Principal That, and then asked me if I was proud of my friends. However, he had a serious meaning in his act; he saw, more clearly than I could do, that I was separating from his own friends for good and all.

Dr. Whately attributed my leaving his *clientela* to a wish on my part to be the head of a party myself. I do not think that this charge was deserved. My habitual feeling then and since has been, that it was not I who sought friends, but friends who sought me. Never man had kinder or more indulgent friends than I have had; but I expressed my own feeling as to the mode in which I gained them, in this very year 1829, in the course of a copy of verses. Speaking of my blessings, I said "Blessings, of friends, which to my door *unasked, unhoped,* have come." They have come, they have gone; they came to my great joy, they went to my great grief. He who gave took away. Dr. Whately's impression about me, however, admits of this explanation:—

During the first years of my residence at Oriel, though proud of my College, I was not quite at home there. I was very much alone, and I used often to take my daily walk by myself. I recollect once meeting Dr. Copleston, then

Provost, with one of the Fellows. He turned round, and with the kind courteousness which sat so well on him, made me a bow and said, "Nunquam minus solus, quàm cùm solus.". At that time indeed (from 1823) I had the intimacy of my dear and true friend Dr. Pusey, and could not fail to admire and revere a soul so devoted to the cause of religion, so full of good works, so faithful in his affections; but he left residence when I was getting to know him well. As to Dr. Whately himself, he was too much my superior to allow of my being at my ease with him; and to no one in Oxford at this time did I open my heart fully and familiarly. But things changed in 1826. At that time I became one of the Tutors of my College, and this gave me position; besides, I had written one or two Essays which had been well received. I began to be known. I preached my first University Sermon. Next year I was one of the Public Examiners for the B.A. degree. In 1828 I became Vicar of St. Mary's. It was to me like the feeling of spring weather after winter; and, if I may so speak, I came out of my shell; I remained out of it till 1841.

The two persons who knew me best at that time are still alive, beneficed clergymen, no longer my friends. They could tell better than any one else what I was in those years. From this time my tongue was, as it were, loosened, and I spoke spontaneously and without effort. One of the two, Mr. Rickards, said of me, I have been told, "Here is a fellow who, when he is silent, will never begin to speak; and when he once begins to speak, will never stop." It was at this time that I began to have influence, which steadily increased for a course of years. I gained upon my pupils, and was in particular intimate and affectionate with two of our probationer Fellows, Robert Isaac Wilberforce (afterwards Archdeacon) and Richard Hurrell Froude. Whately then, an acute man, perhaps saw around me the signs of an incipient party, of which I was not conscious myself. And thus we discern the first elements of that movement afterwards called Tractarian.

The true and primary author of it, however, as is usual with great motive-powers, was out of sight. Having carried off as a mere boy the highest honors of the University, he had turned from the admiration which haunted his steps, and sought for a better and holier satisfaction in pastoral work in

the country. Need I say that I am speaking of John Keble?
The first time that I was in a room with him was on occasion
of my election to a fellowship at Oriel, when I was sent for
into the Tower, to shake hands with the Provost and Fellows.
How is that hour fixed in my memory after the changes of
forty-two years, forty-two this very day on which I write!
I have lately had a letter in my hands, which I sent at the
time to my great friend, John William Bowden, with whom I
passed almost exclusively my Under-graduate years. "I had
to hasten to the Tower," I said to him, "to receive the congratulations of all the Fellows. I bore it till Keble took my
hand, and then felt so abashed and unworthy of the honor
done me, that I seemed desirous of quite sinking into the
ground." His had been the first name which I had heard
spoken of, with reverence rather than admiration, when I
came up to Oxford. When one day I was walking in High
Street with my dear earliest friend just mentioned, with what
eagerness did he cry out, "There's Keble!" and with what
awe did I look at him! Then at another time I heard a
Master of Arts of my College give an account how he had just
then had occasion to introduce himself on some business to
Keble, and how gentle, courteous, and unaffected Keble had
been, so as almost to put him out of countenance. Then too
it was reported, truly or falsely, how a rising man of brilliant
reputation, the present Dean of St. Paul's, Dr. Milman,
admired and loved him, adding, that somehow he was strangely
unlike any one else. However, at the time when I was elected
Fellow of Oriel he was not in residence, and he was shy of
me for years in consequence of the marks which I bore upon
me of the evangelical and liberal schools. At least so I have
ever thought. Hurrell Froude brought us together about
1828: it is one of the sayings preserved in his *Remains*,—"Do
you know the story of the murderer who had done one good
thing in his life? Well; if I was ever asked what good deed
I had ever done, I should say that I had brought Keble and
Newman to understand each other."

The *Christian Year* made its appearance in 1827. It is
not necessary, and scarcely becoming, to praise a book which
has already become one of the classics of the language. When
the general tone of religious literature was so nerveless and

impotent, as it was at that time, Keble struck an original note and woke up in the hearts of thousands a new music, the music of a school, long unknown in England. Nor can I pretend to analyze, in my own instance, the effect of religious teaching so deep, so pure, so beautiful. I have never till now tried to do so; yet I think I am not wrong in saying, that the two main intellectual truths which it brought home to me, were the same two, which I had learned from Butler, though recast in the creative mind of my new master. The first of these was what may be called, in a large sense of the word, the Sacramental system; that is, the doctrine that material phenomena are both the types and the instruments of real things unseen,—a doctrine, which embraces in its fullness, not only what Anglicans, as well as Catholics, believe about Sacraments properly so called; but also the article of "the Communion of Saints;" and likewise the Mysteries of the faith. The connection of this philosophy of religion with what is sometimes called "Berkeleyism" has been mentioned above; I knew little of Berkeley at this time except by name; nor have I ever studied him.

On the second intellectual principle which I gained from Mr. Keble, I could say a great deal; if this were the place for it. It runs through very much that I have written, and has gained for me many hard names. Butler teaches us that probability is the guide of life. The danger of this doctrine, in the case of many minds, is, its tendency to destroy in them absolute certainty, leading them to consider every conclusion as doubtful, and resolving truth into an opinion, which it is safe indeed to obey or to profess, but not possible to embrace with full internal assent. If this were to be allowed, then the celebrated saying, "O God, if there be a God, save my soul, if I have a soul!" would be the highest measure of devotion: —but who can really pray to a Being, about whose existence he is seriously in doubt?

I considered that Mr. Keble met this difficulty by ascribing the firmness of assent which we give to religious doctrine, not to the probabilities which introduced it, but to the living power of faith and love which accepted it. In matters of religion, he seemed to say, it is not merely probability which makes us intellectually certain, but probability as it is put to account by faith and love. It is faith and love which give to probability a force which it has not in itself. Faith and love are directed towards an Object; in the vision of that Object they live; it is that Object, received in faith and love, which renders it reasonable to take probability as sufficient for internal conviction. Thus the argument from Probability, in the matter of religion, became an argument from Personality, which in fact is one form of the argument from Authority.

In illustration, Mr. Keble used to quote the words of the Psalm: "I will guide thee with mine *eye*. Be ye not like to horse and mule, which have no understanding; whose mouths must be held with bit and bridle, lest they fall upon thee." This is the very difference, he used to say, between slaves, and friends or children. Friends do not ask for literal commands; but, from their knowledge of the speaker, they understand his half-words, and from love of him they anticipate his wishes. Hence it is, that in his Poem for St. Bartholomew's Day, he speaks of the "Eye of God's word;" and in the note quotes Mr. Miller, of Worcester College, who remarks in his Bampton Lectures, on the special power of Scripture, as having "this Eye, like that of a portrait, uniformly fixed upon us, turn where we will." The view thus suggested by Mr. Keble, is brought forward in one of the earliest of the *Tracts for the Times*. In No. 8 I say, "The Gospel is a Law of Liberty. We are treated as sons, not as servants; not subjected to a code of formal commandments, but addressed as those who love God, and wish to please Him."

I did not at all dispute this view of the matter, for I made use of it myself; but I was dissatisfied, because it did not go to the root of the difficulty. It was beautiful and religious, but it did not even profess to be logical; and accordingly I tried to complete it by considerations of my own, which are to be found in my University Sermons, Essay on Ecclesiastical Miracles, and Essay on Development of Doctrine. My argument is in outline as follows: that that absolute certitude which we were able to possess, whether as to the truths of natural theology, or as to the fact of a revelation, was the result of an *assemblage* of concurring and converging probabilities, and that, both according to the constitution of the human mind and the will of its Maker; that certitude was a habit of mind, that certainty was a quality of propositions; that probabilities which did not reach to logical certainty, might suffice for a mental certitude; that the certitude thus brought about might equal in measure and strength the certitude which was created by the strictest scientific demonstration; and that to possess such certitude might in given cases and to given individuals be a plain duty, though not to others in other circumstances:—

Moreover, that as there were probabilities which sufficed for certitude, so there were other probabilities which were legitimately adapted to create opinion; that it might be quite as much a matter of duty in given cases and to given persons to have about a fact an opinion of a definite strength and consistency, as in the case of greater or of more numerous probabilities it was a duty to have a certitude; that accordingly we were bound to be more or less sure, on a sort of (as it were) graduated scale of assent, viz. according as the probabilities attaching to a professed fact were brought home to us, and as the case might be, to entertain about it a pious belief, or a pious opinion, or a religious conjecture, or at least, a tolerance of such belief, or opinion or conjecture in others; that on the other hand, as it was a duty to have a belief, of more or less strong texture, in given cases, so in other cases it was a duty not to believe, not to opine, not to conjecture, not even to tolerate the notion that a professed fact was true, inasmuch as it would be credulity or superstition, or some other moral fault, to do so. This was the region of Private Judgment in religion; that is, of a Private Judgment, not formed arbitrarily and according to one's fancy or liking, but conscientiously, and under a sense of duty.   .

Considerations such as these throw a new light on the subject of Miracles, and they seem to have led me to reconsider the view which I had taken of them in my Essay in 1825-6. I do not know what was the date of this change in me, nor of the train of ideas on which it was founded. That there had been already great miracles, as those of Scripture, as the Resurrection, was a fact establishing the principle that the laws of nature had sometimes been suspended by their Divine Author, and since what had happened once might happen again, a certain probability, at least no kind of improbability, was attached to the idea taken in itself, of miraculous intervention in later times, and miraculous accounts were to be regarded in connection with the verisimilitude, scope, instrument, character, testimony, and circumstances, with which they presented themselves to us; and, according to the final result of those various considerations, it was our duty to be sure, or to believe, or to opine, or to surmise, or to tolerate, or to reject, or to denounce. The main difference between my Essay on Miracles in 1826 and my Essay in 1842 is this: that in 1826 I considered that miracles were sharply divided into two classes, those which were to be received, and those which were to be rejected; whereas in 1842 I saw that they were to be regarded according to their greater or less probability, which was in some cases sufficient to create certitude about them, in other cases only belief or opinion.

Moreover, the argument from Analogy, on which this view of the question was founded, suggested to me something besides, in recommendation of the Ecclesiastical Miracles. It fastened itself upon the theory of Church History which I had learned as a boy from Joseph Milner. It is Milner's doctrine, that upon the visible Church come down from above, at certain intervals, large and temporary *Effusions* of divine grace. This is the leading idea of his work. He begins by speaking of the Day of Pentecost, as marking "the first of those *Effusions* of the Spirit of God, which from age to age have visited the earth since the coming of Christ." Vol. i. p. 3. In a note he adds that "in the term 'Effusion' there is *not* here included the idea of the miraculous or extraordinary operations of the Spirit of God;" but still it was natural for me, admitting Milner's general theory, and applying to it the principle of analogy, not to stop short at his abrupt *ipse dixit*, but boldly to pass forward to the conclusion, on other grounds plausible, that as miracles accompanied the first effusion of grace, so they might accompany the later. It is surely a natural and on the whole, a true anticipation (though of course there are exceptions in particular cases), that gifts and graces go together; now, according to the ancient Catholic doctrine, the gift of miracles was viewed as the attendant and shadow of transcendent sanctity: and moreover, since such sanctity was not of every day's occurrence, nay further, since one period of Church history differed widely from another, and, as Joseph Milner would say, there have been generations or centuries of degeneracy or disorder, and times of revival, and since one region might be in the mid-day of religious fervor, and another in twilight or gloom, there was no force in the popular argument, that, because we did not see miracles with our own eyes, miracles had not happened in former times, or were not now at this very time taking place in distant places:—but I must not dwell longer on a subject, to which in a few words it is impossible to do justice.

Hurrell Froude was a pupil of Keble's, formed by him, and in turn reacting upon him. I knew him first in 1826, and was in the closest and most affectionate friendship with him from about 1829 till his death in 1836. He was a man of the highest gifts,—so truly many-sided, that it would be presumptuous in me to attempt to describe him, except under those aspects in which he came before me. Nor have I here to speak of the gentleness and tenderness of nature, the playfulness, the free elastic force and graceful versatility of mind, and the patient winning considerateness in discussion, which endeared him to those to whom he opened his heart; for I am all along engaged upon matters of belief and opinion, and am introducing others into my narrative, not for their own sake, or because I love and have loved them, so much as because, and so far as, they have influenced my theological views. In this respect then, I speak of Hurrell Froude,—in his intellectual aspect,—as a man of high genius, brimful and overflowing with ideas and views, in him original, which were too many and strong even for his bodily strength, and which crowded and jostled against each other in their effort after distinct shape and expression. And he had an intellect as critical and logical as it was speculative and bold. Dying prematurely, as he did, and in the conflict and transition-state of opinion, his religious views never reached their ultimate conclusion, by the very reason of their multitude and their depth. His opinions arrested and influenced me, even when they did not gain my assent. He professed openly his admiration of the Church of Rome, and his hatred of the Reformers. He delighted in the notion of an hierarchical system, of sacerdotal power, and of full ecclesiastical liberty.

He felt scorn of the maxim, "The Bible and the Bible only is the religion of Protestants;" and he gloried in accepting Tradition as a main instrument of religious teaching. He had a high severe idea of the intrinsic excellence of Virginity; and he considered the Blessed Virgin its great Pattern. He delighted in thinking of the Saints; he had a vivid appreciation of the idea of sanctity, its possibility and its heights; and he was more than inclined to believe a large amount of miraculous interference as occurring in the early and middle ages. He embraced the principle of penance and mortification. He had a deep devotion to the Real Presence, in which he had a firm faith. He was powerfully drawn to the Medieval Church, but not to the Primitive.

He had a keen insight into abstract truth; but he was an Englishman to the backbone in his severe adherence to the real and the concrete. He had a most classical taste, and a genius for philosophy and art; and he was fond of historical inquiry, and the politics of religion. He had no turn for theology as such. He set no sufficient value on the writings of the Fathers, on the detail or development of doctrine, on the definite traditions of the Church viewed in their matter, on the teaching of the Ecumenical Councils, or on the controversies out of which they arose. He took an eager courageous view of things on the whole. I should say that his power of entering into the minds of others did not equal his other gifts; he could not believe, for instance, that I really held the Roman Church to be Antichristian. On many points he would not believe but that I agreed with him, when I did not. He seemed not to understand my difficulties. His were of a different kind, the contrariety between theory and fact. He was a high Tory of the Cavalier stamp, and was disgusted with the Toryism of the opponents of the Reform Bill. He was smitten with the love of the Theocratic Church; he went abroad and was shocked by the degeneracy which he thought he saw in the Catholics of Italy.

It is difficult to enumerate the precise additions to my theological creed which I derived from a friend to whom I owe so much. He taught me to look with admiration towards the Church of Rome, and in the same degree to dislike the Reformation. He fixed deep in me the idea of devotion to the

Blessed Virgin, and he led me gradually to believe in the Real Presence.

There is one remaining source of my opinions to be mentioned, and that far from the least important. In proportion as I moved out of the shadow of that Liberalism which had hung over my course, my early devotion towards the Fathers returned; and in the Long Vacation of 1828 I set about to read them chronologically, beginning with St. Ignatius and St. Justin. About 1830 a proposal was made to me by Mr. Hugh Rose, who with Mr. Lyall (afterwards Dean of Canterbury) was providing writers for a Theological Library, to furnish them with a History of the Principal Councils. I accepted it, and at once set to work on the Council of Nicæa. It was to launch myself on an ocean with currents innumerable; and I was drifted back first to the ante-Nicene history, and then to the Church of Alexandria. The work at last appeared under the title of *The Arians of the Fourth Century;* and of its 422 pages, the first 117 consisted of introductory matter, and the Council of Nicæa did not appear till the 254th, and then occupied at most twenty pages.

I do not know when I first learned to consider that Antiquity was the true exponent of the doctrines of Christianity and the basis of the Church of England; but I take it for granted that the works of Bishop Bull, which at this time I read, were my chief introduction to this principle. The course of reading, which I pursued in the composition of my volume, was directly adapted to develop it in my mind. What principally attracted me in the ante-Nicene period was the great Church of Alexandria, the historical center of teaching in those times. Of Rome for some centuries comparatively little is known. The battle of Arianism was first fought in Alexandria; Athanasius, the champion of the truth, was Bishop of Alexandria; and in his writings he refers to the great religious names of an earlier date, to Origen, Dionysius, and others, who were the glory of its see, or of its school. The broad philosophy of Clement and Origen carried me away; the philosophy, not the theological doctrine; and I have drawn out some features of it in my volume, with the zeal and freshness, but with the partiality, of a neophyte. Some portions of their teaching, magnificent in themselves, came like music to my inward ear, as if the response to ideas, which, with little external to encourage them, I had cherished so long. These were based on the mystical or sacramental principle, and spoke of the various Economies or Dispensations of the Eternal. I understood these passages to mean that the exterior world, physical and historical, was but the manifestation to our senses of realities greater than itself. Nature was a parable: Scripture was an allegory: pagan literature, philosophy, and mythology, properly understood, were but a preparation for the Gospel. The Greek poets and sages were in a certain sense prophets; for "thoughts beyond their thought to those high bards were given." There had been a directly divine dispensation granted to the Jews; but there had been in some sense a dispensation carried on in favor of the Gentiles. He who had taken the seed of Jacob for His elect people had not therefore cast the rest of mankind out of His sight. In the fullness of time both Judaism and Paganism had come to nought; the outward framework, which concealed yet suggested the Living Truth, had never been intended to last, and it was dissolving under the beams of the Sun of Justice which shone behind it and through it. The process of change had been slow; it had been done not rashly, but by rule and measure, "at sundry times and in divers manners," first one disclosure and then another, till the whole evangelical doctrine was brought into full manifestation. And thus room was made for the anticipation of further and deeper disclosures, of truths still under the veil of the letter, and in their season to be revealed. The visible world still remains without its divine interpretation; Holy Church in her Sacraments and her hierarchical appointments, will remain, even to the end of the world, after all but a symbol of those heavenly facts which fill eternity. Her mysteries are but the expressions in human language of truths to which the human mind is unequal. It is evident how much there was in all this in correspondence with the thoughts which had attracted me when I was young, and with the doctrine which I have already associated with the *Analogy* and the *Christian Year*.

It was, I suppose, to the Alexandrian school and to the early Church, that I owe in particular what I definitely held about the Angels. I viewed them, not only as the ministers employed by the Creator in the Jewish and Christian dispensations, as we find on the face of Scripture, but as carrying on, as Scripture also implies, the Economy of the Visible World. I considered them as the real causes of motion, light, and life, and of those elementary principles of the physical universe, which, when offered in their developments to our senses, suggest to us the notion of cause and effect, and of what are called the laws of nature. This doctrine I have drawn out in my Sermon for Michaelmas day, written in 1831. I say of the Angels, "Every breath of air and ray of light and heat, every beautiful prospect, is, as it were, the skirts of their garments, the waving of the robes of those whose faces see God."

Also, besides the hosts of evil spirits, I considered there was a middle race, δαιμόνια, neither in heaven, nor in hell; partially fallen, capricious, wayward; noble or crafty, benevolent or malicious, as the case might be. These beings gave a sort of inspiration or intelligence to races, nations, and classes of men. Hence the action of bodies politic and associations, which is often so different from that of the individuals who compose them. Hence the character and the instinct of states and governments, of religious communities and communions. I thought these assemblages had their life in certain unseen Powers. My preference of the Personal to the Abstract would naturally lead me to this view. I thought it countenanced by the mention of "the Prince of Persia" in the Prophet Daniel; and I think I considered that it was of such intermediate beings that the Apocalypse spoke, in its notice of "the Angels of the Seven Churches."

While I was engaged in writing my work upon the Arians, great events were happening at home and abroad, which brought out into form and passionate expression the various beliefs which had so gradually been winning their way into my mind. Shortly before, there had been a Revolution in France; the Bourbons had been dismissed: and I held that it was unchristian for nations to cast off their governors, and, much more, sovereigns who had the divine right of inheritance. Again, the great Reform Agitation was going on around me as I wrote. The Whigs had come into power; Lord Grey had told the Bishops to set their house in order, and some of the

Prelates had been insulted and threatened in the streets of London. The vital question was, how were we to keep the Church from being liberalized? there was such apathy on the subject in some quarters, such imbecile alarm in others; the true principles of Churchmanship seemed so radically decayed, and there was such distraction in the councils of the Clergy. Blomfield, the Bishop of London of the day, an active and open-hearted man, had been for years engaged in diluting the high orthodoxy of the Church by the introduction of members of the Evangelical body into places of influence and trust. He had deeply offended men who agreed in opinion with myself, by an off-hand saying (as it was reported) to the effect that belief in the Apostolical succession had gone out with the Non-jurors. "We can count you," he said to some of the gravest and most venerated persons of the old school. And the Evangelical party itself, with their late successes, seemed to have lost that simplicity and unworldliness which I admired so much in Milner and Scott. It was not that I did not venerate such men as Ryder, the then Bishop of Lichfield, and others of similar sentiments, who were not yet promoted out of the ranks of the Clergy, but I thought little of the Evangelicals as a class. I thought they played into the hands of the Liberals. With the Establishment thus divided and threatened, thus ignorant of its true strength, I compared that fresh vigorous Power of which I was reading in the first centuries. In her triumphant zeal on behalf of that Primeval Mystery, to which I had had so great a devotion from my youth, I recognized the movement of my Spiritual Mother. "Incessu patuit Dea." The self-conquest of her Ascetics, the patience of her Martyrs, the irresistible determination of her Bishops, the joyous swing of her advance, both exalted and abashed me. I said to myself, "Look on this picture and on that;" I felt affection for my own Church, but not tenderness; I felt dismay at her prospects, anger and scorn at her do-nothing perplexity. I thought that if Liberalism once got a footing within her, it was sure of the victory in the event. I saw that Reformation principles were powerless to rescue her. As to leaving her, the thought never crossed my imagination; still I ever kept before me that there was something greater than the Established Church, and that that was the Church Catholic and Apostolic, set up from the beginning, of which she was but the local presence and the organ. She was nothing, unless she was this. She must be dealt with strongly, or she would be lost. There was need of a second reformation.

At this time I was disengaged from College duties, and my health had suffered from the labor involved in the composition of my Volume. It was ready for the Press in July, 1832, though not published till the end of 1833. I was easily persuaded to join Hurrell Froude and his Father, who were going to the south of Europe for the health of the former.

We set out in December, 1832. It was during this expedition that my Verses which are in the Lyra Apostolica were written;—a few indeed before it, but not more than one or two of them after it. Exchanging, as I was, definite Tutorial work, and the literary quiet and pleasant friendships of the last six years, for foreign countries and an unknown future, I naturally was led to think that some inward changes, as well as some larger course of action, were coming upon me. At Whitchurch, while waiting for the down mail to Falmouth, I wrote the verses about my Guardian Angel, which begin with these words: "Are these the tracks of some unearthly Friend?" and which go on to speak of "the vision" which haunted me:—that vision is more or less brought out in the whole series of these compositions.

I went to various coasts of the Mediterranean; parted with my friends at Rome; went down for the second time to Sicily without companion, at the end of April; and got back to England by Palermo in the early part of July. The strangeness of foreign life threw me back into myself; I found pleasure in historical sites and beautiful scenes, not in men and manners. We kept clear of Catholics throughout our tour. I had a conversation with the Dean of Malta, a most pleasant man, lately dead; but it was about the Fathers, and the Library of the great church. I knew the Abbate Santini, at Rome, who did no more than copy for me the Gregorian tones. Froude and I made two calls upon Monsignore (now Cardinal) Wiseman at the Collegio Inglese, shortly before we left Rome. Once we heard him preach at a church in the Corso.

I do not recollect being in a room with any other ecclesiastics except a Priest at Castro-Giovanni in Sicily, who called on me when I was ill, and with whom I wished to hold a controversy. As to Church Services, we attended the Tenebræ, at the Sistine, for the sake of the Miserere; and that was all. My general feeling was, "All, save the spirit of man, is divine." I saw nothing but what was external; of the hidden life of Catholics I knew nothing. I was still more driven back into myself, and felt my isolation. England was in my thoughts solely, and the news from England came rarely and imperfectly. The Bill for the Suppression of the Irish Sees was in progress, and filled my mind. I had fierce thoughts against the Liberals.

It was the success of the Liberal cause which fretted me inwardly. I became fierce against its instruments and its manifestations. A French vessel was at Algiers; I would not even look at the tricolor. On my return, though forced to stop twenty-four hours at Paris, I kept indoors the whole time, and all that I saw of that beautiful city was what I saw from the Diligence. The Bishop of London had already sounded me as to my filling one of the Whitehall preacherships, which he had just then put on a new footing; but I was indignant at the line which he was taking, and from my Steamer I had sent home a letter declining the appointment by anticipation, should it be offered to me. At this time I was specially annoyed with Dr. Arnold, though it did not last into later years. Some one, I think, asked, in conversation at Rome, whether a certain interpretation of Scripture was Christian? it was answered that Dr. Arnold took it; I interposed, "But is *he* a Christian?" The subject went out of my head at once; when afterwards I was taxed with it, I could say no more in explanation, than (what I believe was the fact) that I must have had in mind some free views of Dr. Arnold about the Old Testament:—I thought I must have meant, "Arnold answers for the interpretation, but who is to answer for Arnold?" It was at Rome, too, that we began the *Lyra Apostolica* which appeared monthly in the *British Magazine.* The motto shows the feeling of both Froude and myself at the time: we borrowed from M. Bunsen a Homer, and Froude chose the words in which Achilles, on returning to the battle, says, "You shall know the difference, now that I am back again."

Especially when I was left by myself, the thought came upon me that deliverance is wrought, not by the many but by the few, not by bodies but by persons. Now it was, I think, that I repeated to myself the words, which had ever been dear to me from my school days, "Exoriare aliquis!"—now too, that Southey's beautiful poem of Thalaba, for which I had an immense liking, came forcibly to my mind. I began to think that I had a mission. There are sentences of my letters to my friends to this effect, if they are not destroyed. When we took leave of Monsignore Wiseman, he had courteously expressed a wish that we might make a second visit to Rome; I said with great gravity, "We have a work to do in England." I went down at once to Sicily, and the presentiment grew stronger. I struck into the middle of the island, and fell ill of a fever at Leonforte. My servant thought that I was dying, and begged for my last directions. I gave them, as he wished; but I said, "I shall not die." I repeated, "I shall not die, for I have not sinned against light, I have not sinned against light." I never have been able quite to make out what I meant.

I got to Castro-Giovanni, and was laid up there for nearly three weeks. Towards the end of May I left for Palermo, taking three days for the journey. Before starting from my inn in the morning of May 26th or 27th, I sat down on my bed, and began to sob violently. My servant, who had acted as my nurse, asked what ailed me. I could only answer him, "I have a work to do in England."

I was aching to get home; yet for want of a vessel I was kept at Palermo for three weeks. I began to visit the Churches, and they calmed my impatience, though I did not attend any services. I knew nothing of the Presence of the Blessed Sacrament there. At last I got off in an orange boat, bound for Marseilles. Then it was that I wrote the lines, "Lead, kindly light," which have since become well known. We were becalmed a whole week in the Straits of Bonifacio. I was writing verses the whole time of my passage. At length I got to Marseilles, and set off for England. The fatigue of traveling was too much for me, and I was laid up for several days at Lyons. At last I got off again, and did not stop night or day, (except a compulsory delay at Paris,) till I reached England, and my mother's house. My brother had arrived from Persia only a few hours before. This was on the Tuesday. The following Sunday, July 14th, Mr. Keble preached the Assize Sermon in the University Pulpit. It was published under the title of "National Apostasy." I have ever considered and kept the day, as the start of the religious movement of 1833.

CHAPTER II

HISTORY OF MY RELIGIOUS OPINIONS FROM 1833 TO 1839

IN spite of the foregoing pages, I have no romantic story to tell; but I have written them, because it is my duty to tell things as they took place. I have not exaggerated the feelings with which I returned to England, and I have no desire to dress up the events which followed, so as to make them in keeping with the narrative which has gone before. I soon relapsed into the every-day life which I had hitherto led; in all things the same, except that a new object was given me. I had employed myself in my own rooms in reading and writing, and in the care of a Church, before I left England, and I returned to the same occupations when I was back again. And yet perhaps those first vehement feelings which carried me on, were necessary for the beginning of the Movement; and afterwards, when it was once begun, the special need of me was over.

When I got home from abroad, I found that already a movement had commenced, in opposition to the specific danger which at that time was threatening the religion of the nation and its Church. Several zealous and able men had united their counsels, and were in correspondence with each other. The principal of these were Mr. Keble, Hurrell Froude, who had reached home long before me, Mr. William Palmer of Dublin and Worcester College (not Mr. William Palmer of Magdalen, who is now a Catholic), Mr. Arthur Perceval, and Mr. Hugh Rose.

. To mention Mr. Hugh Rose's name is to kindle in the minds of those who knew him a host of pleasant and affectionate remembrances. He was the man above all others fitted by his cast of mind and literary powers to make a stand, if a stand could be made, against the calamity of the times. He was gifted with a high and large mind, and a true sensibility of what was great and beautiful; he wrote with warmth and energy; and he had a cool head and cautious judgment. He spent his strength and shortened his life, Pro Ecclesia Dei, as he understood that sovereign idea. Some years earlier he had been the first to give warning, I think from the University Pulpit at Cambridge, of the perils to England which lay in the biblical and theological speculations of Germany. The Reform agitation followed, and the Whig Government came into power; and he anticipated in their distribution of Church patronage the authoritative introduction of liberal opinions into the country. He feared that by the Whig party a door would be opened in England to the most grievous of heresies, which never could be closed again. In order under such grave circumstances to unite Churchmen together, and to make a front against the coming danger, he had in 1832 commenced the British Magazine, and in the same year he came to Oxford in the summer term, in order to beat up for writers for his publication; on that occasion I became known to him through Mr. Palmer. His reputation and position came in aid of his obvious fitness, in point of character and intellect, to become the center of an ecclesiastical movement, if such a movement were to depend on the action of a party. His delicate health, his premature death, would have frustrated the expectation, even though the new school of opinion had been more exactly thrown into the shape of a party, than in fact was the case. But he zealously backed up the first efforts of those who were principals in it; and, when he went abroad to die, in 1838, he allowed me the solace of expressing my feelings of attachment and gratitude to him by addressing him, in the dedication of a volume of my Sermons, as the man "who, when hearts were failing, bade us stir up the gift that was in us, and betake ourselves to our true Mother."

But there were other reasons, besides Mr. Rose's state of health, which hindered those who so much admired him from availing themselves of his close coöperation in the coming fight. United as both he and they were in the general scope of the Movement, they were in discordance with each other from the first in their estimate of the means to be adopted for attaining it.

I, on the other hand, had out of my own head begun the Tracts; and these, as representing the antagonist principle of personality, were looked upon by Mr. Palmer's friends with considerable alarm. The great point at the time with these good men in London,—some of them men of the highest principle, and far from influenced by what we used to call Erastianism,—was to put down the Tracts. I, as their editor, and mainly their author, was of course willing to give way. Keble and Froude advocated their continuance strongly, and were angry with me for consenting to stop them. Mr. Palmer shared the anxiety of his own friends; and, kind as were his thoughts of us, he still not unnaturally felt, for reasons of his own, some fidget and nervousness at the course which his Oriel friends were taking. Froude, for whom he had a real liking, took a high tone in his project of measures for dealing with bishops and clergy, which must have shocked and scandalized him considerably. As for me, there was matter enough in the early Tracts to give him equal disgust; and doubtless I much tasked his generosity, when he had to defend me, whether against the London dignitaries or the country clergy. Oriel, from the time of Dr. Copleston to Dr. Hampden, had had a name far and wide for liberality of thought; it had received a formal recognition from the *Edinburgh Review*, if my memory serves me truly, as the school of speculative philosophy in England; and on one occasion, in 1833, when I presented myself, with some of the first papers of the Movement, to a country clergyman in Northamptonshire, he paused a while, and then, eyeing me with significance, asked, "Whether Whately was at the bottom of them?"

Mr. Perceval wrote to me in support of the judgment of Mr. Palmer and the dignitaries. I replied in a letter, which he afterwards published. "As to the Tracts," I said to him (I quote my own words from his Pamphlet), "every one has his own taste. You object to some things, another to others. If we altered to please every one, the effect would be spoiled. They were not intended as symbols *ê cathedrâ*, but as the expression of individual minds; and individuals, feeling strongly, while on the one hand, they are incidentally faulty in mode or language, are still peculiarly effective. No great work was done by a system; whereas systems rise out of individual exertions. Luther was an individual. The very faults of an individual excite attention; he loses, but his cause (if good and he powerful-minded) gains. This is the way of things; we promote truth by a self-sacrifice.''

The visit which I made to the Northamptonshire Rector was only one of a series of similar expedients, which I adopted during the year 1833. I called upon clergy in various parts of the country, whether I was acquainted with them or not, and I attended at the houses of friends where several of them were from time to time assembled. I do not think that much came of such attempts, nor were they quite in my way. Also I wrote various letters to clergymen, which fared not much better, except that they advertised the fact, that a rally in favor of the Church was commencing. I did not care whether my visits were made to high Church or low Church; I wished to make a strong pull in union with all who were opposed to the principles of liberalism, whoever they might be. Giving my name to the Editor, I commenced a series of letters in the *Record* newspaper: they ran to a considerable length; and were borne by him with great courtesy and patience. The heading given to them was, ''Church Reform.''

Acts of the officious character, which I have been describing, were uncongenial to my natural temper, to the genius of the Movement, and to the historical mode of its success:—they were the fruit of that exuberant and joyous energy with which I had returned from abroad, and which I never had before or since. I had the exultation of health restored, and home regained. While I was at Palermo and thought of the breadth of the Mediterranean, and the wearisome journey across France, I could not imagine how I was ever to get to England; but now I was amid familiar scenes and faces once more. And my health and strength came back to me with such a rebound, that some friends at Oxford, on seeing me, did not well know that it was I, and hesitated before they spoke to me. And I had the consciousness that I was employed in that work which I had been dreaming about, and which I felt to be so momentous and inspiring. I had a supreme confidence in our cause; we were upholding that primitive Christianity which was delivered for all time by the early teachers of the Church, and which was registered and attested in the Anglican formularies and by the Anglican divines. That ancient religion had well-nigh faded away out of the land, through the political changes of the last 150 years, and it must be restored. It would be in fact a second Reformation:—a better reformation, for it would be a return not to the sixteenth century, but to the seventeenth. No time was to be lost, for the Whigs had come to do their worst, and the rescue might come too late. Bishoprics were already in course of suppression; Church property was in course of confiscation; Sees would soon be receiving unsuitable occupants. We knew enough to begin preaching upon, and there was no one else to preach. I felt as on board a vessel, which first gets under weigh, and then the deck is cleared out, and luggage and live stock stowed away into their proper receptacles.

Nor was it only that I had confidence in our cause, both in itself, and in its polemical force, but also, on the other hand, I despised every rival system of doctrine and its arguments too. As to the high Church and the low Church, I thought that the one had not much more of a logical basis than the other; while I had a thorough contempt for the controversial position of the latter. I had a real respect for the character of many of the advocates of each party, but that did not give cogency to their arguments; and I thought, on the contrary, that the Apostolical form of doctrine was essential and imperative, and its grounds of evidence impregnable. Owing to this supreme confidence, it came to pass at that time, that there was a double aspect in my bearing towards others, which it is necessary for me to enlarge upon. My behavior had a mixture in it both of fierceness and of sport; and on this account, I dare say, it gave offense to many; nor am I here defending it.

I wished men to agree with me, and I walked with them step by step, as far as they would go; this I did sincerely; but if they would stop, I did not much care about it, but walked on, with some satisfaction that I had brought them so far. I liked to make them preach the truth without knowing it, and encouraged them to do so. It was a satisfaction to me that the *Record* had allowed me to say so much in its columns, without remonstrance. I was amused to hear of one of the Bishops, who, on reading an early Tract on the Apostolical Succession, could not make up his mind whether he held the doctrine or not. I was not distressed at the wonder or anger of dull and self-conceited men, at propositions which they did not understand. When a correspondent, in good faith, wrote to a newspaper, to say that the "Sacrifice of the Holy Eucharist," spoken of in the Tract, was a false print for "Sacrament," I thought the mistake too pleasant to be corrected before I was asked about it. I was not unwilling to draw an opponent on step by step, by virtue of his own opinions, to the brink of some intellectual absurdity, and to leave him to get back as he could. I was not unwilling to play with a man, who asked me impertinent questions. I think I had in my mouth the words of the Wise man, "Answer a fool according to his folly," especially if he was prying or spiteful. I was reckless of the gossip which was circulated about me; and, when I might easily have set it right, did not deign to do so. Also I used irony in conversation, when matter-of-fact men would not see what I meant.

This absolute confidence in my cause, which led me to the negligence or wantonness which I have been instancing, also laid me open, not unfairly, to the opposite charge of fierceness in certain steps which I took, or words which I published. In the *Lyra Apostolica*, I have said that before learning to love, we must "learn to hate;" though I had explained my words by adding "hatred of sin." In one of my first Sermons I said, "I do not shrink from uttering my firm conviction that it would be a gain to the country were it vastly more superstitious, more bigoted, more gloomy, more fierce in its religion than at present it shows itself to be." I added, of course, that it would be an absurdity to suppose such tempers of mind desirable in themselves. The corrector of the press bore these strong epithets till he got to "more fierce," and then he put in the margin a *query*. In the very first page of the first Tract, I said of the Bishops, that, "black event though it would be for the country, yet we could not wish them a more blessed termination of their course, than the spoiling of their goods and martyrdom.'' In consequence of a passage in my work upon the Arian History, a Northern dignitary wrote to accuse me of wishing to reëstablish the blood and torture of the Inquisition. Contrasting heretics and heresiarchs, I had said, ''The latter should meet with no mercy: he assumes the office of the Tempter; and, so far forth as his error goes, must be dealt with by the competent authority, as if he were embodied evil. To spare him is a false and dangerous pity. It is to endanger the souls of thousands, and it is uncharitable towards himself.'' I cannot deny that this is a very fierce passage; but Arius was banished, not burned; and it is only fair to myself to say that neither at this, nor any other time of my life, not even when I was fiercest, could I have even cut off a Puritan's ears, and I think the sight of a Spanish *auto-da-fè* would have been the death of me. Again, when one of my friends, of liberal and evangelical opinions, wrote to expostulate with me on the course I was taking, I said that we would ride over him and his, as Othniel prevailed over Chushanrishathaim, king of Mesopotamia. Again, I would have no dealings with my brother, and I put my conduct upon a syllogism. I said, ''St. Paul bids us avoid those who cause divisions; you cause divisions: therefore I must avoid you.'' I dissuaded a lady from attending the marriage of a sister who had seceded from the Anglican Church. No wonder that Blanco White, who had known me under such different circumstances, now hearing the general course that I was taking, was amazed at the change which he recognized in me. He speaks bitterly and unfairly of me in his letters contemporaneously with the first years of the Movement; but in 1839, on looking back, he uses terms of me, which it would be hardly modest in me to quote, were it not that what he says of me in praise occurs in the midst of blame. He says: ''In this party [the anti-Peel, in 1829] I found, to my great surprise, my dear friend, Mr. Newman of Oriel. As he had been one of the annual Petitioners to Parliament for Catholic Emancipation, his sudden union with the most violent bigots was inexplicable to me. That change was the first manifestation of the mental revolution, which has suddenly made him one of the leading persecutors of Dr. Hampden, and the most active and influential member of that association called the

Puseyite party, from which we have those very strange productions, entitled, *Tracts for the Times.* While stating these public facts, my heart feels a pang at the recollection of the affectionate and mutual friendship between that excellent man and myself; a friendship, which his principles of orthodoxy could not allow him to continue in regard to one, whom he now regards as inevitably doomed to eternal perdition. Such is the venomous character of orthodoxy. What mischief must it create in a bad heart and narrow mind, when it can work so effectually for evil, in one of the most benevolent of bosoms, and one of the ablest of minds, in the amiable, the intellectual, the refined John Henry Newman!'' (Vol. iii. p. 131.) He adds that I would have nothing to do with him, a circumstance which I do not recollect, and very much doubt.

I have spoken of my firm confidence in my position; and now let me state more definitely what the position was which I took up, and the propositions about which I was so confident. These were three:—

1. First was the principle of dogma: my battle was with liberalism; by liberalism I mean the anti-dogmatic principle and its developments. This was the first point on which I was certain. Here I make a remark: persistence in a given belief is no sufficient test of its truth: but departure from it is at least a slur upon the man who has felt so certain about it. In proportion, then, as I had in 1832 a strong persuasion of the truth of opinions which I have since given up, so far a sort of guilt attaches to me, not only for that vain confidence, but for all the various proceedings which were the consequence of it. But under this first head I have the satisfaction of feeling that I have nothing to retract, and nothing to repent of. The main principle of the movement is as dear to me now, as it ever was. I have changed in many things: in this I have not. From the age of fifteen, dogma has been the fundamental principle of my religion: I know no other religion; I cannot enter into the idea of any other sort of religion; religion, as a mere sentiment, is to me a dream and a mockery. As well can there be filial love without the fact of a father, as devotion without the fact of a Supreme Being. What I held in 1816, I held in 1833, and I hold in 1864. Please God, I shall hold it to the end. Even when I was

under Dr. Whately's influence, I had no temptation to be less zealous for the great dogmas of the faith, and at various times I used to resist such trains of thought on his part as seemed to me (rightly or wrongly) to obscure them. Such was the fundamental principle .of the Movement of 1833.

2. Secondly, I was confident in the truth of a certain definite religious teaching, based upon this foundation of dogma; viz. that there was a visible Church, with sacraments and rites which are the channels of invisible grace.· I thought that this was the doctrine of Scripture, of the early Church, and of the Anglican Church. Here again, I have not changed in opinion; I am as certain now on this point as I was in 1833, and have never ceased to be certain. In 1834 and the following years I put this ecclesiastical doctrine on a broader basis, after reading Laud, Bramhall, and Stillingfleet and other Anglican divines on the one hand, and after prosecuting the study of the Fathers on the other; but the doctrine of 1833 was strengthened in me, not changed. When I began the *Tracts for the Times* I rested the main doctrine, of which I am speaking, upon Scripture, on the Anglican Prayer Book, and on St. Ignatius's Epistles. (1) As to the existence of˙ a visible Church, I especially argued out the point from Scripture, in Tract 11, viz. from the Acts of the Apostles and the Epistles. (2) As to the Sacraments and Sacramental rites, I stood on the Prayer Book. I appealed to the Ordination Service, in which the Bishop says, "Receive the Holy Ghost"; to the Visitation Service, which teaches confession and absolution; to the Baptismal Service, in which the Priest speaks of the child after baptism as regenerate; to the Catechism, in which Sacramental Communion is receiving "verily and indeed the Body and Blood of Christ"; to the Commination Service, in which we are told to do "works of penance"; to the Collects, Epistles, and Gospels, to the calendar and rubrics, portions of the Prayer Book, wherein we find the festivals of the Apostles, notice of certain other Saints, and days of fasting and abstinence.

(3) And further, as to the Episcopal system, I founded it upon the Epistles of St. Ignatius, which inculcated it in

various ways. One passage especially impressed itself upon me: speaking of cases of disobedience to ecclesiastical authority he says, "A man does not deceive that Bishop whom he sees, but he practices rather with the Bishop Invisible, and so the question is not with flesh, ·but with God, who knows the secret heart." I wished to act on this principle to the letter, and I may say with confidence that I never consciously transgressed it. I loved to act as feeling myself in my Bishop's sight, as if it were the sight of God. It was one of my special supports and safeguards against myself; I could not go very wrong while I had reason to believe that I was in no respect displeasing him. It was not a mere formal obedience to rule that I put before me, but I desired to please him personally, as I considered him set over me by the Divine Hand. I was strict in observing my clerical engagements, not only because they *were* engagements, but because I considered myself simply as the servant and instrument of my Bishop. I did not care much for the Bench of Bishops, except as they might be the voice of my Church: nor should I have cared much for a Provincial Council; nor for a Diocesan Synod presided over by my Bishop; all these matters seemed to me to be *jure ecclesiastico,* but what to me was *jure divino* was the voice of my Bishop in his own person. My own Bishop was my Pope; I knew no other; the successor of the Apostles, the Vicar of Christ. This was but a practical exhibition of the Anglican theory of Church Government, as I had already drawn it out myself, after various Anglican Divines. This continued all through my course; when at length, in 1845, I wrote to Bishop Wiseman, in whose Vicariate I found myself, to announce my conversion, I could find nothing better to say to him than that I would obey the Pope as I had obeyed my own Bishop in the Anglican Church. My duty to him was my point of honor; his disapprobation was the one thing which I could not bear. I believe it to have been a generous and honest feeling; and in consequence I was rewarded by having all my time for ecclesiastical superior a man, whom, had I had a choice, I should have preferred, out and out, to any other Bishop on the Bench, and for whose memory I have a special affection, Dr. Bagot—a man of noble mind, and as kind-hearted and as considerate as he was noble. He ever sympathized with me in my trials which followed; it was my own fault, that I was not brought into more familiar personal relations with him, than it was my happiness to be. May his name be ever blessed!

And now in concluding my remarks on the second point on which my confidence rested, I repeat that here again I have no retractation to announce as to its main outline. While I am now as clear in my acceptance of the principle of dogma, as I was in 1833 and 1816, so again I am now as firm in my belief of a visible Church, of the authority of Bishops, of the grace of the sacraments, of the religious worth of works of penance, as I was in 1833. I have added Articles to my Creed; but the old ones, which I then held with a divine faith, remain.

3. But now, as to the third point on which I stood in 1833, and which I have utterly renounced and trampled upon since,—my then view of the Church of Rome;—I will speak about it as exactly as I can. When I was young, as I have said already, and after I was grown up, I thought the Pope to be.Antichrist. At Christmas 1824-5 I preached a sermon to that effect. But in 1827 I accepted eagerly the stanza in the *Christian Year*, which many people thought too charitable, "Speak *gently* of thy sister's fall." From the time that I knew Froude I got less and less bitter on the subject. I spoke (successively, but I cannot tell in what order or at what dates) of the Roman Church as being bound up with "the *cause* of Antichrist," as being *one* of the "*many* antichrists" foretold by St. John, as being influenced by "the *spirit* of Antichrist," and as having something "very Antichristian" or "unchristian" about her. From my boyhood and in 1824 I considered, after Protestant authorities, that St. Gregory I. about A.D. 600 was the first Pope that was Antichrist, though, in spite of this, he was also a great and holy man; but in 1832-3 I thought the Church of Rome was bound up with the cause of Antichrist by the Council of Trent. When it was that in my deliberate judgment I gave up the notion altogether in any shape, that some special reproach was attached to her name, I cannot tell; but I had a shrinking from renouncing it, even when my reason so

ordered me, from a sort of conscience or prejudice, I think
up to 1843. Moreover, at least during the Tract Movement,
I thought the essence of her offense to consist in the honors
which she paid to the Blessed Virgin and the Saints; and
the more I grew in devotion, both to the Saints and to our
Lady, the more impatient was I at the Roman practices, as if
those glorified creations of God must be gravely shocked, if
pain could be theirs, at the undue veneration of which they
were the objects.

On the other hand, Hurrell Froude in his familiar conversations was always tending to rub the idea out of my mind.
In a passage of one of his letters from abroad, alluding, I
suppose, to what I used to say in opposition to him, he
observes: "I think people are injudicious who talk against
the Roman Catholics for worshiping Saints, and honoring
the Virgin and images, &c. These things may perhaps be
idolatrous; I cannot make up my mind about it; but to my
mind it is the Carnival that is real practical idolatry, as it
is written, 'the people sat down to eat and drink, and rose
up to play.'" The Carnival, I observe in passing, is, in
fact, one of those very excesses, to which, for at least three
centuries, religious Catholics have ever opposed themselves,
as we see in the life of St. Philip, to say nothing of the
present day; but this we did not then know. Moreover, from
Froude I learned to admire the great medieval Pontiffs;
and, of course, when I had come to consider the Council of
Trent to be the turning-point of the history of Christian
Rome, I found myself as free, as I was rejoiced, to speak in
their praise. Then, when I was abroad, the sight of so many
great places, venerable shrines, and noble churches, much impressed my imagination. And my heart was touched also.
Making an expedition on foot across some wild country in
Sicily, at six in the morning, I came upon a small church;
I heard voices, and I looked in. It was crowded, and the
congregation was singing. Of course it was the mass,
though I did not know it at the time. And, in my weary
days at Palermo, I was not ungrateful for the comfort which
I had received in frequenting the churches; nor did I ever
forget it. Then, again, her zealous maintenance of the
doctrine and the rule of celibacy, which I recognized as

Apostolic, and her faithful agreement with Antiquity in so many other points which were dear to me, was an argument as well as a plea in favor of the great Church of Rome. Thus I learned to have tender feelings towards her; but still my reason was not affected at all. My judgment was against her, when viewed as an institution, as truly as it ever had been.

As a matter, then, of simple conscience, though it went against my feelings, I felt it to be a duty to protest against the Church of Rome. But besides this, it was a duty, because the prescription of such a protest was a living principle of my own Church, as expressed not simply in a *catena*, but by a *consensus* of her divines, and by the voice of her people. Moreover, such a protest was necessary as an integral portion of her controversial basis; for I adopted the argument of Bernard Gilpin, that Protestants "were *not able* to give any *firm and solid* reason of the separation besides this, to wit, that the Pope is Antichrist." But while I thus thought such a protest to be based upon truth, and to be a religious duty, and a rule of Anglicanism, and a necessity of the case, I did not at all like the work. Hurrell Froude attacked me for doing it; and, besides, I felt that my language had a vulgar and rhetorical look about it. I believed, and really measured, my words, when I used them; but I knew that I had a temptation, on the other hand, to say against Rome as much as ever I could, in order to protect myself against the charge of Popery.

And now I come to the very point, for which I have introduced the subject of my feelings about Rome. I felt such confidence in the substantial justice of the charges which I advanced against her, that I considered them to be a safeguard and an assurance that no harm could ever arise from the freest exposition of what I used to call Anglican principles. All the world was astounded at what Froude and I were saying: men said that it was sheer Popery. I answered, "True, we seem to be making straight for it; but go on awhile, and you will come to a deep chasm across the path, which makes real approximation impossible." And I urged in addition, that many Anglican divines had been accused of Popery, yet had died in their Anglicanism;—now, the ecclesiastical principles which I professed, they had professed also; and the judgment against Rome which they had formed, I had formed also. Whatever deficiencies then had to be supplied in the existing Anglican system, and however boldly I might point them out, anyhow that system would not in the process be brought nearer to the special creed of Rome, and might be mended in spite of her. In that very agreement of the two forms of faith, close as it might seem, would really be found, on examination, the elements and principles of an essential discordance.

It was with this absolute persuasion on my mind that I fancied that there could be no rashness in giving to the world in fullest measure the teaching and the writings of the Fathers. I thought that the Church of England was substantially founded upon them. I did not know all that the Fathers had said, but I felt that, even when their tenets happened to differ from the Anglican, no harm could come of reporting them. I said out what I was clear they had said; I spoke vaguely and imperfectly, of what I thought they said, or what some of them had said. Anyhow, no harm could come of bending the crooked stick the other way, in the process of straightening it; it was impossible to break it. If there was anything in the Fathers of a startling character, this would be only for a time; it would admit of explanation, or it might suggest something profitable to Anglicans; it could not lead to Rome. I express this view of the matter in a passage of the Preface to the first volume, which I edited, of the *Library of the Fathers.* Speaking of the strangeness at first sight, in the judgment of the present day, of some of their principles and opinions, I bid the reader go forward hopefully, and not indulge his criticism till he knows more about them, than he will learn at the outset. "Since the evil," I say, "is in the nature of the case itself, we can do no more than have patience, and recommend patience to others, and with the racer in the Tragedy, look forward steadily and hopefully to the *event*, τῷ τέλει πίστιν φέρων, when, as we trust, all that is inharmonious and anomalous in the details, will at length be practically smoothed."

Such was the position, such the defenses, such the tactics,

by which I thought that it was both incumbent on us, and possible for us, to meet that onset of Liberal principles, of which we were all in immediate anticipation, whether in the Church or in the University. And during the first year of the Tracts, the attack upon the University began.

Such was the commencement of the assault of Liberalism upon the old orthodoxy of Oxford and England; and it could not have been broken, as it was, for so long a time, had not a great change taken place in the circumstances of that counter-movement which had already started with the view of resisting it. For myself, I was not the person to take the lead of a party; I never was, from first to last, more than a leading author of a school; nor did I ever wish to be anything else. This is my own account of the matter; and I say it, neither as intending to disown the responsibility of what was done, or as if ungrateful to those who at that time made more of me than I deserved, and did more for my sake and at my bidding than I realized myself. I am giving my history from my own point of sight, and it is as follows:—I had lived for ten years among my personal friends; the greater part of the time, I had been influenced, not influencing; and at no time have I acted on others, without their acting upon me. As is the custom of a University, I had lived with my private, nay, with some of my public, pupils, and with the junior fellows of my College, without form or distance, on a footing of equality. Thus it was through friends, younger, for the most part, than myself, that my principles were spreading. They heard what I said in conversation, and told it to others. Under-graduates in due time took their degree, and became private tutors themselves. In their new *status,* they in turn preached the opinions, with which they had already become acquainted. Others went down to the country, and became curates of parishes. Then they had down from London parcels of the Tracts, and other publications. They placed them in the shops of local booksellers, got them into newspapers, introduced them to clerical meetings, and converted more or less their Rectors and their brother curates. Thus the Movement, viewed with relation to myself, was but a floating opinion; it was not a power. It never would have been a power, if it had remained in my hands. Years after, a friend, writing to me in remonstrance at the excesses, as he thought them, of my disciples, applied to me my own verse about St. Gregory Nazianzen, ''Thou couldst a people raise, but couldst not rule.'' At the time that he wrote to me, I had special impediments in the way of such an exercise of power; but at no time could I exercise over others that authority, which under the circumstances was imperatively required. My great principle ever was, Live and let live. I never had the staidness or dignity necessary for a leader. To the last I never recognized the hold I had over young men. Of late years I have read and heard that they even imitated me in various ways. I was quite unconscious of it, and I think my immediate friends knew too well how disgusted I should be at such proceedings, to have the heart to tell me. I felt great impatience at our being called a party, and would not allow that we were such. I had a lounging, free-and-easy way of carrying things on. I exercised no sufficient censorship under the Tracts. I did not confine them to the writings of such persons as agreed in all things with myself; and, as to my own Tracts, I printed on them a notice to the effect, that any one who pleased, might make what use he would of them, and reprint them with alterations if he chose, under the conviction that their main scope could not be damaged by such a process. It was the same with me afterwards, as regards other publications. For two years I furnished a certain number of sheets for the British Critic from myself and my friends, while a gentleman was editor, a man of splendid talent, who, however, was scarcely an acquaintance of mine, and had no sympathy with the Tracts. When I was Editor myself, from 1838 to 1841, in my very first number I suffered to appear a critic unfavorable to my work on Justification, which had been published a few months before, from a feeling of propriety, because I had put the book into the hands of the writer who so handled it. Afterwards I suffered an article against the Jesuits to appear in it, of which I did not like the tone. When I had to provide a curate for my new church at Littlemore, I engaged a friend, by no fault of his, who, before he had entered into his charge, preached a sermon, either in depreciation of baptismal regeneration, or of Dr. Pusey's view of it. I showed a similar easiness as to the Editors who helped me in the separate volumes of Fleury's *Church History;* they were able, learned, and excellent men, but their after-history has shown how little my choice of them was influenced by any notion I could have had of any intimate agreement of opinion between them and myself. I shall have to make the same remark in its place concerning the *Lives of the English Saints,* which subsequently appeared. All this may seem inconsistent with what I have said of my fierceness. I am not bound to account for it; but there have been men before me, fierce in act, yet tolerant and moderate in their reasonings; at least, so I read history. However, such was the case, and such its effect upon the Tracts. These at first starting were short, hasty, and some of them ineffective; and at the end of the year, when collected into a volume, they had a slovenly appearance.

It was under these circumstances, that Dr. Pusey joined us. I had known him well since 1827-8, and had felt for him an enthusiastic admiration. I used to call him ὁ μέγας. His great learning, his immense diligence, his scholarlike mind, his simple devotion to the cause of religion, overcame me; and great of course was my joy, when in the last days of 1833 he showed a disposition to make common cause with us. His Tract *On Fasting* appeared as one of the series with the date of December 21. He was not, however, I think, fully associated in the Movement till 1835 and 1836, when he published his Tract *On Baptism,* and started the *Library of the Fathers.* He at once gave to us a position and a name. Without him we should have had little chance, especially at the early date of 1834, of making any serious resistance to the Liberal aggression.

Dr. Pusey's influence was felt at once. He saw that there ought to be more sobriety, more gravity, more careful pains, more sense of responsibility in the Tracts and in the whole Movement. It was through him that the character of the Tracts was changed. When he gave to us his Tract *On Fasting,* he put his initials to it. In 1835 he published his elaborate *Treatise on Baptism,* which was followed by other Tracts from different authors, if not of equal learning yet of equal power and appositeness. The Catenas of Anglican divines, projected by me, which occur in the Series were executed with a like aim at greater accuracy and method. In 1836 he advertised his great project for a Translation of the Fathers:—but I must return to myself. I am not writing the history either of Dr. Pusey or of the Movement; but it is a pleasure to me to have been able to introduce here reminiscences of the place which he held in it, which have so direct a bearing on myself, that they are no digression from my narrative.

I suspect it was Dr. Pusey's influence and example which set me, and made me set others, on the larger and more careful works in defense of the principles of the Movement which followed in a course of years,—some of them demanding and receiving from their authors, such elaborate treatment that they did not make their appearance till both its temper and its fortunes had changed. I set about a work at once; one in which was brought out with precision the relation in which we stood to the Church of Rome. We could not move a step in comfort, till this was done. It was of absolute necessity and a plain duty from the first, to provide as soon as possible a large statement, which would encourage and reassure our friends and repel the attacks of our opponents. A cry was heard on all sides of us, that the Tracts and the writings of the Fathers would lead us to become Catholics, before we were aware of it. This was loudly expressed by members of the Evangelical party, who in 1836 had joined us in making a protest in Convocation against a memorable appointment of the Prime Minister. These clergymen even then avowed their desire, that the next time they were brought up to Oxford to give a vote, it might be in order to put down the Popery of the Movement. There was another reason still, and quite as important. Monsignore Wiseman, with the acuteness and zeal which might be expected from that great Prelate, had anticipated what was coming, had returned to England by 1836, had delivered Lectures in London on the doctrines of Catholicism, and created an impression through the country, shared in by ourselves, that we had for our opponents in controversy, not only our brethren, but our hereditary foes. These were the circumstances, which led to my publication of *"The Prophetical Office of the Church viewed relatively to Romanism and Popular Protestantism."*

This work employed me for three years, from the beginning of 1834 to the end of 1836, and was published in 1837. It was composed, after a careful consideration and comparison of the principal Anglican divines· of the 17th century. It was first written in the shape of controversial correspondence with a learned French Priest; then it was recast, and delivered in Lectures at St. Mary's; lastly, with considerable retrenchments and additions, it was re-written for publication.

It attempts to trace out the rudimental lines on which Christian faith and teaching proceed, and to use them as means of determining the relation of the Roman and Anglican systems to each other. In this way it shows that to confuse the two together is impossible, and that the Anglican can be as little said to tend to the Roman, as the Roman to the Anglican.

But this Volume had a larger scope than that of opposing the Roman system. It was an attempt at commencing a system of theology on the Anglican idea, and based upon Anglican authorities. I wished to build up an Anglican theology out of the stores which already lay cut and hewn upon the ground, the past toil of great divines. To do this could not.be the work of one man; much less, could it be at once received into Anglican theology, however well it was done. This I fully recognized; and, while I trusted that my statements of doctrine would turn out to be true and important, still I wrote, to use the common phrase, ''under correction.''

There was another motive for my publishing, of a personal nature, which I think I should mention. I felt then, and all along felt, that there was an intellectual cowardice in not finding a basis in reason for my belief, and a moral cowardice in not avowing that basis. I should have felt myself less than a man, if I did not bring it out, whatever it was. This is one principal reason why I wrote and published the *Prophetical Office*. It was from the same feeling, that in the spring of 1836, at a meeting of residents on the subject of the struggle then proceeding against a Whig appointment, when some one wanted us all merely to act on college and conservative grounds (as I understood him), with as few published statements as possible, I answered, that the person whom we were resisting had committed himself in writing, and that we ought to commit ourselves too. This again was a main reason for the publication of Tract 90. Alas! it was my portion for whole years to remain without any satisfactory basis for my religious profession, in a state of moral sickness, neither able to acquiesce in Anglicanism, nor able to go to Rome. But I bore it, till in course of time my way was made clear to me. If here it be objected to me, that as time went on, I often in my writings hinted at things which I did not fully bring out, I submit for consideration whether this occurred except when I was in great difficulties, how to speak, or how to be silent, with due regard for the position of mind or the feelings of others. However, I may have an opportunity to say more on this subject. But to return to the *Prophetical Office*.

The subject of the Volume is the doctrine of the *Via Media*, a name which had already been applied to the Anglican system by writers of repute. It is an expressive title, but not altogether satisfactory, because it is at first sight negative. This had been the reason of my dislike to the word "Protestant"; viz. it did not denote the profession of any particular religion at all, and was compatible with infidelity. A *Via Media* was but a receding from extremes,—therefore it needed to be drawn out into a definite shape and character: before it could have claims on our respect, it must first be shown to be one, intelligible, and consistent. This was the first condition of any reasonable treatise on the *Via Media*. The second condition, and necessary too, was not in my power. I could only hope that it would one day be fulfilled. Even if the *Via Media* were ever so positive a religious system, it was not as yet objective and real; it had no original anywhere of which it was the representative. It was at present a paper religion.

I had brought out in the *Prophetical Office* in what the Roman and the Anglican systems differed from each other, but less distinctly in what they agreed. I had indeed enumerated the Fundamentals, common to both, in the following passage:—"In both systems the same Creeds are acknowledged. Besides other points in common, we both hold, that certain doctrines are necessary to be believed for salvation; we both believe in the doctrines of the Trinity, Incarnation, and Atonement; in original sin; in the necessity of regeneration; in the supernatural grace of the Sacraments; in the Apostolical succession; in the obligation of faith and obedience, and in the eternity of future punishment." So much I had said, but I had not said enough. This enumeration implied a great many more points of agreement than were found in those very Articles which were fundamental. If the two Churches were thus the same in fundamentals, they were also one and the same in such plain consequences as were contained in those fundamentals and in such natural observances as outwardly represented them. It was an Anglican principle that "the abuse of a thing doth not take away the lawful use of it"; and an Anglican Canon in 1603 had declared that the English Church had no purpose to forsake all that was held in the Churches of Italy, France, and Spain, and reverenced those ceremonies and particular points which were Apostolic. Excepting then such exceptional matters, as are implied in this avowal, whether they were many or few, all these Churches were evidently to be considered as one with the Anglican. The Catholic Church in all lands had been one from the first for many centuries; then, various portions had followed their own way to the injury, but not to the destruction, whether of truth or of charity. These portions or branches were mainly three:—the Greek, Latin, and Anglican. Each of these inherited the early undivided Church *in solido* as its own possession. Each branch was identical with that early undivided Church, and in the unity of that Church it had unity with the other branches. The three branches agreed together in *all but* their later accidental errors. Some branches had retained in detail portions of Apostolical truth and usage, which the others had not; and these portions might be and should be appropriated again by the others which had let them slip. Thus, the middle age belonged to the Anglican Church, and much more did the middle age of England.

A. V. 13—4

The Church of the 12th century was the Church of the 19th. Dr. Howley sat in the seat of St. Thomas the Martyr; Oxford was a medieval University. Saving our engagements to Prayer Book and Articles, we might breathe and live and act and speak, as in the atmosphere and climate of Henry III.'s day, or the Confessor's, or of Alfred's. And we ought to be indulgent to all that Rome taught now, as to what Rome taught then, saving our protest. We might boldly welcome, even what we did not ourselves think right to adopt. And, when we were obliged on the contrary boldly to denounce, we should do so with pain, not with exultation. By very reason of our protest, which we had made, and made *ex animo,* we could agree to differ. What the members of the Bible Society did on the basis of Scripture, we could do on the basis of the Church; Trinitarian and Unitarian were further apart than Roman and Anglican. Thus we had a real wish to coöperate with Rome in all lawful things, if she would let us, and if the rules of own Church let us; and we thought there was no better way towards the restoration of doctrinal purity and unity. And we thought that Rome was not committed by her formal decrees to all that she actually taught: and again, if her disputants had been unfair to us, or her rulers tyrannical, we bore in mind that on our side too there had been rancor and slander in our controversial attacks upon her, and violence in our political measures. As to ourselves being direct instruments in improving her belief or practice, I used to say, "Look at home; let us first (or at least let us the while) supply our own shortcomings, before we attempt to be physicians to any one else."

And now I have said enough on what I consider to have been the general objects of the various works, which I wrote, edited, or prompted in the years which I am reviewing. I wanted to bring out in a substantive form a living Church of England, in a position proper to herself, and founded on distinct principles; as far as paper could do it, as far as earnestly preaching it and influencing others towards it, could tend to make it a fact;—a living Church, made of flesh and blood, with voice, complexion, and motion and action, and a will of its own. I believe I had no private motive, and no personal aim. Nor did I ask for more than "a fair stage and no favor," nor expect the work would be accomplished in my days; but I thought that enough would be secured to continue it in the future, under, perhaps, more hopeful circumstances and prospects than the present.

I will mention in illustration some of the principal works, doctrinal and historical, which originated in the objects which I have stated.

I wrote my *Essay on Justification* in 1837; it was aimed at the Lutheran dictum that justification by faith only was the cardinal doctrine of Christianity. I considered that this doctrine was either a paradox or a truism,—a paradox in Luther's mouth, a truism in Melanchthon's. I thought that the Anglican Church followed Melanchthon, and that in consequence between Rome and Anglicanism, between high Church and low Church, there was no real intellectual difference on the point. I wished to fill up a ditch, the work of man. In this Volume again, I express my desire to build up a system of theology out of the Anglican divines, and imply that my dissertation was a tentative Inquiry. I speak in the Preface of "offering suggestions towards a work, which must be uppermost in the mind of every true son of the English Church at this day,—the consolidation of a theological system, which, built upon those formularies, to which all clergymen are bound, may tend to inform, persuade, and absorb into itself religious minds, which hitherto have fancied, that, on the peculiar Protestant questions, they were seriously opposed to each other."

In my *University Sermons* there is a series of discussions upon the subject of Faith and Reason; these again were the tentative commencement of a grave and necessary work, viz. an inquiry into the ultimate basis of religious faith, prior to the distinction into Creeds.

In like manner in a Pamphlet, which I published in the summer of 1838, is an attempt at placing the doctrine of the Real Presence on an intellectual basis. The fundamental idea is consonant to that to which I had been so long attached: it is the denial of the existence of space except as a subjective idea of our minds.

The *Church of the Fathers* is one of the earliest productions of the Movement, and appeared in numbers in the *British Magazine*, being written with the aim of introducing the religious sentiments, views, and customs of the first ages into the modern Church of England.

The Translation of Fleury's *Church History* was commenced under these circumstances:—I was fond of Fleury for a reason which I express in the Advertisement; because it presented a sort of photograph of ecclesiastical history without any comment upon it. In the event, that simple representation of the early centuries had a good deal to do with unsettling me in my Anglicanism; but how little I could anticipate this, will be seen in the fact that the publication of Fleury was a favorite scheme with Mr. Rose. He proposed it to me twice, between the years 1834 and 1837; and I mention it as one out of many particulars curiously illustrating how truly my change of opinion arose, not from foreign influences, but from the working of my own mind, and the accidents around me. The date, from which the portion actually translated began, was determined by the Publisher on reasons with which we were not concerned.

Another historical work, but drawn from original sources, was given to the world by my old friend Mr. Bowden, being a *Life of Pope Gregory VII.* I need scarcely recall to those who have read it, the power and the liveliness of the narrative. This composition was the author's relaxation, on evenings and in his summer vacations, from his ordinary engagements in London. It had been suggested to him originally by me, at the instance of Hurrell Froude.

The Series of the *Lives of the English Saints* was projected at a later period, under circumstances which I shall have in the sequel to describe. Those beautiful compositions have nothing in them, as far as I recollect, simply inconsistent with the general objects which I have been assigning to my labors in these years, though the immediate occasion which led to them, and the tone in which they were written, had little that was congenial with Anglicanism.

At a comparatively early date I drew up the Tract *On the Roman Breviary.* It frightened my own friends on its first appearance; and several years afterwards, when younger men began to translate for publication the four volumes *in extenso,* they were dissuaded from doing so by advice to which from a sense of duty they listened. It was an apparent accident, which introduced me to the knowledge of that most wonderful and most attractive monument of the devotion of saints. On Hurrell Fronde's death, in 1836, I was asked to select one of his books as a keepsake. I selected Butler's *Analogy;* finding that it had been already chosen, I looked with some perplexity along the shelves as they stood before me, when an intimate friend at my elbow said, "Take that." It was the Breviary which Hurrell had had with him at Barbados. Accordingly I took it, studied it, wrote my Tract from it, and have it on my table in constant use till this day.

That dear and familiar companion, who thus put the Breviary into my hands, is still in the Anglican Church. So, too, is that early venerated long-loved friend, together with whom I edited a work which, more perhaps than any other, caused disturbance and annoyance in the Anglican world,— Fronde's *Remains;* yet, however judgments might run as to the prudence of publishing it, I never heard any one impute to Mr. Keble the very shadow of dishonesty or treachery towards his Church in so acting.

The annotated Translation of the *Treatises of St. Athanasius* was of course in no sense of a tentative character; it belongs to another order of thought. This historico-dogmatic work employed me for years. I had made preparations for following it up with a doctrinal history of the heresies which succeeded to the Arian.

I should make mention also of the *British Critic.* I was Editor of it for three years, from July, 1838, to July, 1841. My writers belonged to various schools, some to none at all. The subjects are various,—classical, academical, political, critical, and artistic, as well as theological, and upon the Movement none are to be found which do not keep quite clear of advocating the cause of Rome.

So I went on for years up to 1841. It was, in a human point of view, the happiest time of my life. I was truly at home. I had in one of my volumes appropriated to myself the words of Bramhall, "Bees, by the instinct of nature, do love their hives, and birds their nests." I did not suppose that such sunshine would last, though I knew not what would be its termination. It was the time of plenty and, during its seven years, I tried to lay up as much as I could for the dearth which was to follow it. We prospered and spread.

The first threatenings of what was coming were heard in 1838. At that time, my Bishop in a Charge made some light animadversions, but they *were* animadversions, on the *Tracts for the Times.* At once I offered to stop them. What took place on the occasion I prefer to state in the words in which I related it in a Pamphlet addressed to him in a later year, when the blow actually came down upon me.

"In your Lordship's *Charge* for 1838," I said, "an allusion was made to the *Tracts for the Times.* Some opponents of the Tracts said that you treated them with undue indulgence. . . . I wrote to the Archdeacon on the subject, submitting the Tracts entirely to your Lordship's disposal. What I thought about your Charge will appear from the words I then used to him. I said, 'A Bishop's lightest word *ex cathedrâ* is heavy. His judgment on a book cannot be light. It is a rare occurrence.' And I offered to withdraw any of the Tracts over which I had control, if I were informed which were those to which your Lordship had objections. I afterwards wrote to your Lordship to this effect, that 'I trusted I might say sincerely, that I should feel a more lively pleasure in knowing that I was submitting myself to your Lordship's expressed judgment in a matter of that kind, than I could have even in the widest circulation of the volumes in question.' Your Lordship did not think it necessary to proceed to such a measure, but I felt, and always have felt, that, if ever you determined on it, I was bound to obey.'"

That day at length came, and I conclude this portion of my narrative, with relating the circumstances of it.

From the time that I had entered upon the duties of Public Tutor at my College, when my doctrinal views were very different from what they were in 1841, I had meditated a comment upon the Articles. Then, when the Movement was in its swing, friends had said to me, "What will you make of the Articles?" but I did not share the apprehension which their question implied. Whether, as time went on, I should have been forced, by the necessities of the original theory of the Movement, to put on paper the speculations which I had about them, I am not able to conjecture. The actual cause of my doing so, in the beginning of 1841, was the restlessness, actual and prospective, of those who neither liked the *Via Media,* nor my strong judgment against Rome. I had been enjoined, I think by my Bishop, to keep these men straight, and I wished so to do: but their tangible difficulty was subscription to the Articles; and thus the question of the Articles came before me. It was thrown in our teeth; "How can you manage to sign the Articles? they are directly against Rome." "Against Rome?" I made answer, "What do you mean by 'Rome'?" and then I proceeded to make distinctions, of which I shall now give an account.

By "Roman doctrine" might be meant one of three things: 1, the *Catholic teaching* of the early centuries; or 2, the *formal dogmas of Rome* as contained in the later Councils, especially the Council of Trent, and as condensed in the Creed of Pope Pius IV.; 3, the *actual popular beliefs and usages* sanctioned by Rome in the countries in communion with it, over and above the dogmas; and these I called "dominant errors." Now Protestants commonly thought that in all three senses, "Roman doctrine" was condemned in the Articles: I thought that the *Catholic teaching* was not condemned; that the *dominant errors* were; and as to the *formal dogmas,* that some were, some were not, and that the line had to be drawn between them. Thus, 1. The use of Prayers for the dead was a Catholic doctrine,—not condemned in the Articles; 2. The prison of Purgatory was a Roman dogma,—which was condemned in them; but the infallibility of Ecumenical Councils was a Roman dogma,—not condemned; and 3. The fire of Purgatory was an authorized and popular error, not a dogma,—which was condemned.

Further, I considered that the difficulties, felt by the persons whom I have mentioned, mainly lay in their mistaking, 1, Catholic teaching, which was not condemned in the Articles, for Roman dogma which was condemned; and 2,

Roman dogma, which was not condemned in the Articles, for dominant error which was. If they went further than this, I had nothing more to say to them.

A further motive which I had for my attempt, was the desire to ascertain the ultimate points of contrariety between the Roman and Anglican creeds, and to make them as few as possible. I thought that each creed was obscured and misrepresented by a dominant circumambient "Popery" and "Protestantism."

The main thesis then of my Essay was this:—the Articles do not oppose Catholic teaching; they but partially oppose Roman dogma; they for the most part oppose the dominant errors of Rome. And the problem was, as I have said, to draw the line as to what they allowed and what they condemned.

Such being the object which I had in view, what were my prospects of widening and of defining their meaning? The prospect was encouraging; there was no doubt at all of the elasticity of the Articles: to take a palmary instance, the seventeenth was assumed by one party to be Lutheran, by another Calvinistic, though the two interpretations were contradictory of each other; why then should not other Articles be drawn up with a vagueness of an equally intense character? I wanted to ascertain what was the limit of that elasticity in the direction of Roman dogma. But next, I had a way of inquiry of my own, which I state without defending. I instanced it afterwards in my *Essay on Doctrinal Development*. That work, I believe, I have not read since I published it, and I do not doubt at all I have made many mistakes in it;—partly, from my ignorance of the details of doctrine, as the Church of Rome holds them, but partly from my impatience to clear as large a range for the *principle* of doctrinal Development (waiving the question of historical *fact*) as was consistent with the strict Apostolicity and identity of the Catholic Creed. In like manner, as regards the 39 Articles, my method of inquiry was to leap *in medias res*. I wished to institute an inquiry how far, in critical fairness, the text *could* be opened; I was aiming far more at ascertaining what a man who subscribed it might hold than what he must, so that my conclusions were negative rather than positive. It was but a first essay. And I made it with the full recognition and consciousness, which I had already expressed in my *Prophetical Office,* as regards the *Via Media,* that I was making only "a first approximation to the required solution";—"a series of illustrations supplying hints for the removal" of a difficulty, and with full acknowledgment "that in minor points, whether in question of fact or of judgment, there was room for difference or error of opinion," and that I "should not be ashamed to own a mistake, if it were proved against me, nor reluctant to bear the just blame of it."—*Proph. Off.* p. 31.

I will add, I was embarrassed in consequence of my wish to go as far as was possible in interpreting the Articles in the direction of Roman dogma, without disclosing what I was doing to the parties whose doubts I was meeting; who, if they understood at once the full extent of the license which the Articles admitted, might be thereby encouraged to proceed still further than at present they found in themselves any call to go.

1. But in the way of such an attempt comes the prompt objection that the Articles were actually drawn up against "Popery," and therefore it was transcendently absurd and dishonest to suppose that Popery, in any shape,—patristic belief, Tridentine dogma, or popular corruption authoritatively sanctioned,—would be able to take refuge under their text. This premise I denied. Not any religious doctrine at all, but a political principle, was the primary English idea of "Popery" at the date of the Reformation. And what was that political principle, and how could it best be suppressed in England? What was the great question in the days of Henry and Elizabeth? The *Supremacy;*—now, was I saying one single word in favor of the Supremacy of the Holy See, in favor of the foreign jurisdiction? No, I did not believe in it myself. Did Henry VIII. religiously hold Justification by faith only? did he disbelieve Purgatory? Was Elizabeth zealous for the marriage of the Clergy? or had she a conscience against the Mass? The Supremacy of the Pope was the essence of the "Popery" to which, at the time of the composition of the Articles, the Supreme Head or Governor of the English Church was so hostile.

2. But again I said this:—let ''Popery'' mean what it would in the mouths of the compilers of .the Articles, let it even, for argument's sake, include the doctrines of that Tridentine Council, which was not yet over when the Articles were drawn up, and against which they could not be simply directed, yet, consider, what was the object of the Government in their imposition? merely to get rid of ''Popery''? No; it had the further object of gaining the ''Papists.'' What then was the best way to induce reluctant or wavering minds, and these, I supposed, were the majority, to give in their adhesion to the new symbol? how had the Arians drawn up their Creeds? was it not on the principle of using vague ambiguous language, which to the subscribers would seem to bear a Catholic sense, but which, when worked out on the long run, would prove to be heterodox? Accordingly, there was great antecedent probability, that, fierce as the Articles might look at first sight, their bark would prove worse than their bite. I say antecedent probability, for to what extent that surmise might be true, could only be ascertained by investigation.

3. But a consideration came up at once, which threw light on this surmise:—what if it should turn out that the very men who drew up the Articles, in the very act of doing so, had avowed, or rather in one of those very Articles themselves had imposed on subscribers, a number of those very ''Papistical'' doctrines, which they were now thought to deny, as part and parcel of that very Protestantism, which they were now thought to consider divine? and this was the fact, and I showed it in my Essay.

4. And here was another reason against the notion that the Articles directly attacked the Roman dogmas as declared at Trent and as promulgated by Pius the Fourth:—the Council of Trent was not over, nor its Canons promulgated at the date when the Articles were drawn up,[1] so that those Articles must be aiming at something else? What was that something else? The Homilies tell us: the Homilies are the best comment upon the Articles. Let us turn to the Homilies,   .

[1] The Pope's Confirmation of the Council, by which its Canons became *de fide*, and his Bull *super confirmatione* by which they were promulgated to the world, are dated January 26, 1564. The Articles are dated 1562.

and we shall find from first to last that, not only is not the Catholic teaching of the first centuries, but neither again are the dogmas of Rome, the objects of the protest of the compilers of the Articles, but the dominant errors, the popular corruptions, authorized or suffered by the high name of Rome. The eloquent declamation of the Homilies finds its matter almost exclusively in the dominant errors. As to Catholic teaching, nay as to Roman dogma, of such theology those Homilies, as I have shown, contained no small portion themselves.

5. So much for the writers of the Articles and Homilies; —they were witnesses, not authorities, and I used them as such; but in the next place, who were the actual authorities imposing them? I reasonably considered the authority *imponens* to be the Convocation of 1571; but here again, it would be found that the very Convocation, which received and confirmed the 39 Articles, also enjoined by Canon that "preachers should be *careful,* that they should *never* teach aught in a sermon, to be religiously held and believed by the people, except that which is agreeable to the doctrine of the Old and New Testament, and *which the Catholic Fathers and ancient Bishops have collected* from that very doctrine." Here, let it be observed, an appeal is made by the Convocation *imponens* to the very same ancient authorities, as had been mentioned with such profound veneration by the writers of the Homilies and the Articles, and thus, if the Homilies contained views of doctrine which now would be called Roman, there seemed to me to be an extreme probability that the Convocation of 1571 also countenanced and received, or at least did not reject, those doctrines.

6. And further, when at length I came actually to look into the text of the Articles, I saw in many cases a patent justification of all that I had surmised as to their vagueness and indecisiveness, and that, not only on questions which lay between Lutherans, Calvinists, and Zuinglians, but on Catholic questions also; and I have noticed them in my Tract. In the conclusion of my Tract I observe: The Articles are "evidently framed on the principle of leaving open large questions on which the controversy hinges. They state broadly extreme truths, and are silent about their adjustment. For

instance, they say that all necessary faith must be proved from Scripture; but do not say *who* is to prove it. They say, that the Church has authority in controversies; they do not say *what* authority. They say that it may enforce nothing beyond Scripture, but do not say *where* the remedy lies when it does. They say that works *before* grace *and* justification are worthless and worse, and that works *after* grace *and* justification are acceptable, but they do not speak at all of works *with* God's aid *before* justification. They say that men are lawfully called and sent to minister and preach, who were chosen and called by men who have public authority *given* them in the Congregation; but they do not add *by whom* the authority is to be given. They say that Councils called by *princes* may err; they do not determine whether Councils called in the name of Christ may err.''

Such were the considerations which weighed with me in my inquiry how far the Articles were tolerant of a Catholic, or even a Roman interpretation; and such was the defense which I made in my Tract for having attempted it. From what I have already said, it will appear that I have no need or intention at this day to maintain every particular interpretation which I suggested in the course of my Tract, nor indeed had I then. Whether it was prudent or not, whether it was sensible or not, anyhow I attempted only a first essay of a necessary work, an essay which, as I was quite prepared to find, would require revision and modification by means of the lights which I should gain from the criticism of others. I should have gladly withdrawn any statement, which could be proved to me to be erroneous; I considered my work to be faulty and open to objection in the same sense in which I now consider my Anglican interpretations of Scripture to be erroneous; but in no other sense. I am surprised that men do not apply to the interpreters of Scripture generally the hard names which they apply to the author of Tract 90. He held a large system of theology, and applied it to the Articles: Episcopalians, or Lutherans, or Presbyterians, or Unitarians, hold a large system of theology and apply it to Scripture. Every theology has its difficulties; Protestants hold justification by faith only, though there is no text in St. Paul which enunciates it, and though St. James expressly denies it; do we therefore call Protestants dishonest? they deny that the Church has a divine mission, though St. Paul says that it is "the Pillar and ground of Truth"; they keep the Sabbath, though St. Paul says, "Let no man judge you in meat or drink or in respect of . . . the sabbath days." Every creed has texts in its favor, and again texts which run counter to it: and this is generally confessed. And this is what I felt keenly:—how had I done worse in Tract 90 than Anglicans, Wesleyans, and Calvinists did daily in their Sermons and their publications? how had I done worse, than the Evangelical party in their *ex animo* reception of the Services for Baptism and Visitation of the Sick?[2] Why was I to be dishonest and they immaculate? There was an occasion on which our Lord gave an answer, which seemed to be appropriate to my own case, when the tumult broke out against my Tract:—"He that is without sin among you, let him first cast a stone at him." I could have fancied that a sense of their own difficulties of interpretation would have persuaded the great party I have mentioned to some prudence, or at least moderation, in opposing a teacher of an opposite school. But I suppose their alarm and their anger overcame their sense of justice.

In the sudden storm of indignation with which the Tract was received throughout the country on its appearance, I recognize much of real religious feeling, much of honest

[2] For instance, let candid men consider the form of Absolution contained in that Prayer Book, of which all clergymen, Evangelical and Liberal as well as high Church, and (I think) all persons in University office declare that "it containeth *nothing contrary to the Word of God.*"

I challenge, in the sight of all England, Evangelical clergymen generally, to put on paper an interpretation of this form of words, consistent with their sentiments, which shall be less forced than the most objectionable of the interpretations which Tract 90 puts upon any passage in the Articles.

"Our Lord Jesus Christ, who hath left *power* to His Church to absolve all sinners who truly repent and believe in Him, of His great mercy forgive thee thine offenses; and by *His authority committed to me, I absolve thee from all thy sins,* in the Name of the Father, and of the Son, and of the Holy Ghost. Amen."

I subjoin the Roman form, as used in England and elsewhere: "Dominus noster Jesus Christus te absolvat; et ego auctoritate ipsius te absolvo, ab omni vinculo excommunicationis et interdicti, in quantum possum et tu indiges. Deinde ego te absolvo à peccatis tuis, in nomine Patris et Filii et Spiritûs Sancti. Amen."

and true principle, much of straight-forward ignorant common sense. In Oxford there was genuine feeling too; but there had been a smoldering, stern,. energetic animosity, not at all unnatural, partly rational, against its author. A false step had been made; now was the time for action. I am told that, even before the publication of the Tract, rumors of its contents had got into the hostile camp in an exaggerated form; and not a moment was lost in proceeding to action, when I was actually fallen into the hands of the Philistines. I was quite unprepared for the outbreak, and was startled at its violence. I do not think I had any fear. Nay, I will add, I am not sure that it was not in one point of view a relief to me.

I saw indeed clearly that my place in the Movement was lost; public confidence was at an end; my occupation was gone. It was simply an impossibility that I could say anything henceforth to good effect, when I had been posted up by the marshal on the buttery-hatch of every College of my University, after the manner of discommoned pastry-cooks, and when in every part of the country and every class of society, through every organ and opportunity of opinion, in newspapers, in periodicals, at meetings, in pulpits, at dinner-tables, in coffee-rooms, in railway carriages, I was denounced as a traitor who had laid his train and was detected in the very act of firing it against the time-honored Establishment. There were indeed men, besides my own immediate friends, men of name and position, who gallantly took my part, as Dr. Hook, Mr. Palmer, and Mr. Perceval; it must have been a grievous trial for themselves, yet what after all could they do for me? Confidence in me was lost;—but I had already lost full confidence in myself. Thoughts had passed over me a year and a half before in respect to the Anglican claims, which for the time had profoundly troubled me. They had gone: I had not less confidence in the power and the prospects of the Apostolical movement than before; not less confidence than before in the grievousness of what I called the "dominant errors" of Rome: but how was I any more to have absolute confidence in myself? how was I to have confidence in my present confidence? how was I to be sure that I should always think as I thought now? I felt that by this event a kind Providence had saved me from an impossible position in the future.

First, if I remember right, they wished me to withdraw the Tract. This I refused to do: I would not do so for the sake of those who were unsettled or in danger of unsettlement. I would not do so for my own sake; for how could I acquiesce in a mere Protestant interpretation of the Articles? how could I range myself among the professors of a theology, of which it put my teeth on edge even to hear the sound?

Next they said, "keep silence; do not defend the Tract"; I answered, "Yes, if you will not condemn it,—if you will allow it to continue on sale." They pressed on me whenever I gave way; they fell back when they saw me obstinate. Their line of action was to get out of me as much as they could; but upon the point of their tolerating the Tract I *was* obstinate. So they let me continue it on sale; and they said they would not condemn it. But they said that this was on condition that I did not defend it, that I stopped the series, and that I myself published my own condemnation in a letter to the Bishop of Oxford. I impute nothing whatever to him, he was ever most kind to me. Also, they said they could not answer for what some individual Bishops might perhaps say about the Tract in their own charges. I agreed to their conditions. My one point was to save the Tract.

Not a line in writing was given me, as a pledge of the observance of the main article on their side of the engagement. Parts of letters from them were read to me, without being put into my hands. It was an "understanding." A clever man had warned me against "understandings" some thirteen years before: I have hated them ever since.

In the last words of my letter to the Bishop of Oxford I thus resigned my place in the Movement:—

"I have nothing to be sorry for," I said to him, "except having made your Lordship anxious, and others whom I am bound to revere. I have nothing to be sorry for, but everything to rejoice in and be thankful for. I have never taken pleasure in seeming to be able to move a party, and whatever influence I have had, has been found, not sought after. I have acted because others did not act, and have sacrificed a quiet which I prized. May God be with me in time to come, as He has been hitherto! and He will be if I can but keep my hand clean and my heart pure. I think I can bear, or at least will try to bear, any personal humiliation, so that I am preserved from betraying sacred interests, which the Lord of grace and power has given into my charge.''

CHAPTER III

HISTORY OF MY RELIGIOUS OPINIONS FROM 1839 TO 1841

AND now that I am about to trace, as far as I can, the course of that great revolution of mind, which led me to leave my own home, to which I was bound by so many strong and tender ties, I feel overcome with the difficulty of satisfying myself in my account of it, and have recoiled from the attempt, till the near approach of the day, on which these lines must be given to the world, forces me to set about the task. For who can know himself, and the multitude of subtle influences which act upon him? And who can recollect, at the distance of twenty-five years, all that he once knew about his thoughts and his deeds, and that, during a portion of his life, when, even at the time his observation, whether of himself or of the external world, was less than before or after, by very reason of the perplexity and dismay which weighed upon him,—when, in spite of the light given to him according to his need amid his darkness, yet a darkness it emphatically was? And who can suddenly gird himself to a new and anxious undertaking, which he might be able indeed to perform well, were full and calm leisure allowed him to look through everything that he had written, whether in published works or private letters? yet again, granting that calm contemplation of the past, in itself so desirable, who could afford to be leisurely and deliberate, while he practices on himself a cruel operation, the ripping up of old griefs, and the venturing again upon the ''infandum dolorem'' of years, in which the stars of this lower heaven were one by one going out? I could not in cool blood, nor except upon the imperious call of duty, attempt what I have set myself to do. It is both to head and heart an extreme trial, thus to analyze what has so long gone by, and to bring out the results of that examination. I have done various bold things in my life: this is the boldest: and, were I not sure I should after all succeed in my object, it would be madness to set about it.

In the spring of 1839 my position in the Anglican Church was at its height. I had supreme confidence in my controversial *status,* and I had a great and still growing success, in recommending it to others. I had in the foregoing autumn been somewhat sore at the Bishop's Charge, but I have a letter which shows that all annoyance had passed from my mind. In January, if I recollect aright, in order to meet the popular clamor against myself and others, and to satisfy the Bishop, I had collected into one all the strong things which they, and especially I, had said against the Church of Rome, in order of their insertion among the advertisements appended to our publications. Conscious as I was that my opinions in religion were not gained, as the world said, from Roman sources, but were, on the contrary, the birth of my own mind and of the circumstances in which I had been placed, I had a scorn of the imputations which were heaped upon me. It was true that I held a large bold system of religion, very unlike the Protestantism of the day, but it was the concentration and adjustment of the statements of great Anglican authorities, and I had as much right to hold it, as the Evangelical, and more right than the Liberal party could show, for asserting their own respective doctrines. As I declared on occasion of Tract 90, I claimed, in behalf of who would in the Anglican Church, the right of holding with Bramhall a comprecation with the Saints, and the Mass all but Transubstantiation with Andrewes, or with Hooker that Transubstantiation itself is not a point for Churches to part communion upon, or with Hammond that a General Council, truly such, never did, never shall err in a matter of faith, or with Bull that man had in paradise, and lost on the fall, a supernatural habit of grace, or with Thorndike that penance is a propitiation for post-baptismal sin, or with Pearson that the all-powerful name of Jesus is no otherwise given than in the Catholic Church. "Two can play at that," was often in my mouth, when men of Protestant sentiments appealed to the Articles, Homilies, or Reformers; in the sense that, if they had a right to speak loud, I had the liberty to speak out as well as they, and had the means, by the same or parallel appeals, of giving them tit for tat. I thought that the Anglican Church was tyrannized over by a mere party, and I aimed at bringing into effect the promise contained in the motto to the Lyra, "They shall know the difference now," I only asked to be allowed to show them the difference.

What will best describe my state of mind at the early part of 1839, is an Article in the *British Critic* for that April. I have looked over it now, for the first time since it was published; and have been struck by it for this reason:—it contains the last words which I ever spoke as an Anglican to Anglicans. It may now be read as my parting address and valediction, made to my friends. I little knew it at the time. It reviews the actual state of things, and it ends by looking towards the future. It is not altogether mine; for my memory goes to this,—that I had asked a friend to do the work; that then, the thought came on me, that I would do it myself: and that he was good enough to put into my hands what he had with great appositeness written, and that I embodied it in my Article. Every one, I think, will recognize the greater part of it as mine. It was published two years before the affairs of Tract 90, and was entitled *The State of Religious Parties*.

I concluded the Article by saying, that all who did not wish to be "democratic, or pantheistic, or popish," must "look out for *some* Via Media which will preserve us from what threatens, though it cannot restore the dead. The spirit of Luther is dead; but Hildebrand and Loyola are alive. Is it sensible, sober, judicious, to be so very angry with those writers of the day, who point to the fact, that our divines of the seventeenth century have occupied a ground which is the true and intelligible mean between extremes? Is it wise to quarrel with this ground, because it is not exactly what we should choose, had we the power of choice? Is it true moderation, instead of trying to fortify a middle doctrine, to fling stones at those who do? . . . Would you rather have your sons and daughters members of the Church of England or of the Church of Rome?"

And thus I left the matter. But, while I was thus speaking of the future of the Movement, I was in truth winding up my accounts with it, little dreaming that it was so to be;—while I was still, in some way or other, feeling about for an available *Via Media,* I was soon to receive a shock which was to cast out of my imagination all middle courses and compromises for ever. As I have said, this Article appeared in the April number of the *British Critic;* in the July number, I cannot tell why, there is no Article of mine; before the number for October, the event had happened to which I have alluded.

But before I proceed to describe what happened to me in the summer of 1839, I must detain the reader for a while, in order to describe the *issue* of the controversy between Rome and the Anglican Church, as I viewed it. This will involve some dry discussion; but it is as necessary for my narrative, as plans of buildings and homesteads are at times needed in the proceedings of our law courts.

I have said already that, though the object of the Movement was to withstand the Liberalism of the day, I found and felt this could not be done by mere negatives. It was necessary for us to have a positive Church theory erected on a definite basis. This took me to the great Anglican divines; and then of course I found at once that it was impossible to form any such theory, without cutting across the teaching of the Church of Rome. Thus came in the Roman controversy.

When I first turned myself to it, I had neither doubt on the subject, nor suspicion that doubt would ever come upon me. It was in this state of mind that I began to read up Bellarmine on the one hand, and numberless Anglican writers on the other. But I soon found, as others had found before me, that it was a tangled and manifold controversy, difficult to master, more difficult to put out of hand with neatness and precision. It was easy to make points, not easy to sum up and settle. It was not easy to find a clear issue for the dispute, and still less by a logical process to decide it in favor of Anglicanism. This difficulty, however, had no tendency whatever to harass or perplex me: it was a matter which bore not on convictions, but on proofs.

First I saw, as all see who study the subject, that a broad

distinction had to be drawn between the actual state of belief and of usage in the countries which were in communion with the Roman Church, and her formal dogmas; the latter did not cover the former. Sensible pain, for instance, is not implied in the Tridentine decree upon Purgatory; but it was the tradition of the Latin Church, and I had seen the pictures of souls in flames in the streets of Naples. Bishop Lloyd had brought this distinction out strongly in an Article in the *British Critic* in 1825; indeed, it was one of the most common objections made to the Church of Rome, that she dared not commit herself by formal decree, to what nevertheless she sanctioned and allowed. Accordingly, in my *Prophetical Office*, I view as simply separate ideas, Rome quiescent, and Rome in action. I contrasted her creed on the one hand, with her ordinary teaching, her controversial tone, her political and social bearing, and her popular beliefs and practices, on the other.

While I made this distinction between the decrees and the traditions of Rome, I drew a parallel distinction between Anglicanism quiescent, and Anglicanism in action. In its formal creed Anglicanism was not at a great distance from Rome: far otherwise, when viewed in its insular space, the traditions of its establishment, its historical characteristics, its controversial rancor, and its private judgment. I disavowed and condemned those excesses, and called them "Protestantism" or "Ultra-Protestantism": I wished to find a parallel disclaimer, on the part of Roman controversialists, of that popular system of beliefs and usages in their own Church, which I called "Popery." When that hope was a dream, I saw that the controversy lay between the book-theology of Anglicanism on the one side, and the living system of what I called Roman corruption on the other. I could not get further than this; with this result I was forced to content myself.

These then were the *parties* in the controversy:—the Anglican *Via Media* and the popular religion of Rome. And next, as to the *issue,* to which the controversy between them was to be brought, it was this:—the Anglican disputant took his stand upon Antiquity or Apostolicity, the Roman upon Catholicity. The Anglican said to the Roman: "There

is but One Faith, the Ancient, and you have not kept to it";
the Roman retorted: "There is but One Church, the Catholic,
and you are out of it." The Anglican urged: "Your special
beliefs, practices, modes of action, are nowhere in Antiquity"; the Roman objected: "You do not communicate
with any one Church besides your own and its offshoots, and
you have discarded principles, doctrines, sacraments, and
usages, which are and ever have been received in the East
and the West." The true Church, as defined in the Creeds,
was both Catholic and Apostolic; now, as I viewed the controversy in which I was engaged, England and Rome had
divided these notes or prerogatives between them: the cause
lay thus, Apostolicity *versus* Catholicity.

However, in thus stating the matter, of course I do not
wish it supposed that I allowed the note of Catholicity really
to belong to Rome, to the disparagement of the Anglican
Church; but I considered that the special point or plea of
Rome in the controversy was Catholicity, as the Anglican plea
was Antiquity. Of course I contended that the Roman idea
of Catholicity was not ancient and apostolic. It was in my
judgment at the utmost only natural, becoming, expedient,
that the whole of Christendom should be united in one visible
body; while such a unity might, on the other hand, be nothing
more than a mere heartless and political combination. For
myself, I held with the Anglican divines, that, in the Primitive Church, there was a very real mutual independence between its separate parts, though, from a dictate of charity,
there was in fact a close union between them. I considered
that each See and Diocese might be compared to a crystal,
and that each was similar to the rest, and that the sum
total of them all was only a collection of crystals. The unity
of the Church lay, not in its being a polity, but in its being
a family, a race, coming down by apostolical descent from
its first founders and bishops. And I considered this truth
brought out, beyond the possibility of dispute, in the Epistles
of St. Ignatius, in which the Bishop is represented as the
one supreme authority in the Church, that is, in his own
place, with no one above him, except as, for the sake of
ecclesiastical order and expedience, arrangements had been
made by which one was put over or under another. So much

for our own claim to Catholicity, which was so perversely appropriated by our opponents to themselves:—on the other hand, as to our special strong point, Antiquity, while, of course, by means of it, we were able to condemn most emphatically the novel claim of Rome to domineer over other Churches, which were in truth her equals, further than that, we thereby especially convicted her of the intolerable offense of having added to the Faith. This was the critical head of accusation urged against her by the Anglican disputant; and as he referred to St. Ignatius in proof that he himself was a true Catholic, in spite of being separated from Rome, so he triumphantly referred to the Treatise of Vincentius of Lerins upon the "Quod semper, quod ubique, quod ab omnibus," in proof that the controversialists of Rome, in spite of their possession of the Catholic name, were separated in their creed from the Apostolical and primitive faith.

Of course those controversialists had their own mode of answering him, with which I am not concerned in this place; here I am only concerned with the issue itself, between the one party and the other—Antiquity *versus* Catholicity.

Now I will proceed to illustrate what I have been saying of the *status* of the controversy, as it presented itself to my mind, by extracts from my writings of the dates of 1836, 1840, and 1841. And I introduce them with a remark, which especially applies to the paper, from which I shall quote first, of the date of 1836. That paper appeared in the March and April numbers of the *British Magazine* of that year, and was entitled *Home Thoughts Abroad*. Now it will be found, that, in the discussion which it contains, as in various other writings of mine, when I was in the Anglican Church, the argument in behalf of Rome is stated with considerable perspicuity and force. And at the time my friends and supporters cried out, "How imprudent!" and, both at the time, and especially at a later date, my enemies have cried out, "How insidious!" Friends and foes virtually agreed in their criticism; I had set out the cause which I was combating to the best advantage: this was an offense; it might be from imprudence, it might be with a traitorous design. It was from neither the one nor the other; but for the following reasons. First, I had a great impatience, whatever was the subject, of not bringing out the whole of it, as clearly as I could; next I wished to be as fair to my adversaries as possible; and thirdly I thought that there was a great deal of shallowness among our own friends, and that they undervalued the strength of the argument in behalf of Rome, and that they ought to be roused to a more exact apprehension of the position of the controversy. At a later date, (1841,) when I really felt the force of the Roman side of the question myself, as a difficulty which had to be met, I had a fourth reason for such frankness in argument, and that was, because a number of persons were unsettled far more than I was, as to the Catholicity of the Anglican Church. It was quite plain that, unless I was perfectly candid in stating what could be said against it, there was no chance that any representations, which I felt to be in its favor, or at least to be adverse to Rome, would have had any success with the persons in question. At all times I had a deep conviction, to put the matter on the lowest ground, that "honesty was the best policy."

It is plain, then, that at the end of 1835 or beginning of 1836, I had the whole state of the question before me, on which, to my mind, the decision between the Churches depended. It is observable that the question of the position of the Pope, whether as the center of unity, or as the source of jurisdiction, did not come into my thoughts at all; nor did it, I think I may say, to the end. I doubt whether I ever distinctly held any of his powers to be *de jure divino*, while I was in the Anglican Church;—not that I saw any difficulty in the doctrine; not that in connection with the history of St. Leo, of which I shall speak by and by, the idea of his infallibility did not cross my mind, for it did,—but after all, in my view the controversy did not turn upon it; it turned upon the Faith and the Church. This was my issue of the controversy from the beginning to the end. There was a contrariety of claims between the Roman and Anglican religions, and the history of my conversion is simply the process of working it out to a solution. In 1838 I illustrated it by the contrast presented to us between the Madonna and Child, and a Calvary. The peculiarity of the Anglican theology was this,—that it "supposed the Truth to be en-

tirely objective and detached, not'' (as in the theology of
Rome) ''lying hid in the bosom of the Church as if one with
her, clinging to and (as it were) lost in her embrace, but as
being sole and unapproachable, as on the Cross or at the
Resurrection, with the Church close by, but in the background.''

As I viewed the controversy in 1836 and 1838, so I viewed
it in 1840 and 1841. In the *British Critic* of January 1840,
after gradually investigating how the matter lies between the
Churches by means of a dialogue, I end thus: ''It would
seem, that, in the above discussion, each disputant has a strong
point: our strong point is the argument from Primitiveness,
that of Romanists from Universality. It is a fact, however it is
to be accounted for, that Rome has added to the Creed; and
it is a fact, however we justify ourselves, that we are estranged
from the great body of Christians over the world. And each
of these two facts is at first sight a grave difficulty in the
respective systems to which they belong.'' Again, ''While
Rome, though not deferring to the Fathers, recognizes them,
and England, not deferring to the large body of the Church,
recognizes it, both Rome and England have a point to clear
up.''

And still more strongly, in July 1841:

''If the Note of schism, on the one hand, lies against England, an antagonist disgrace lies upon Rome, the Note of
idolatry. Let us not be mistaken here; we are neither ac-
cusing Rome of idolatry nor ourselves of schism; we think
neither charge tenable; but still the Roman Church practices
what is so like idolatry, and the English Church makes much
of what is so very like schism, that without deciding what is
the duty of a Roman Catholic towards the Church of England
in her present state, we do seriously think that members of
the English Church have a providential direction given them,
how to comport themselves towards the Church of Rome,
while she is what she is.''

The Long Vacation of 1839 began early. There had been a
great many visitors to Oxford from Easter to Commemora-
tion; and Dr. Pusey's party had attracted attention, more, I
think, than in any former year. I had put away from me the
controversy with Rome for more than two years. In my

Parochial Sermons the subject had at no time been introduced: there had been nothing for two years, either in my Tracts or in the *British Critic,* of a polemical character. I was returning, for the Vacation, to the course of reading which I had many years before chosen as especially my own. I have no reason to suppose that the thoughts of Rome came across my mind at all. About the middle of June I began to study and master the history of the Monophysites. I was absorbed in the doctrinal question. This was from about June 13th to August 30th. It was during this course of reading that for the first time a doubt came upon me of the tenableness of Anglicanism. I recollect on the 30th of July mentioning to a friend, whom I had accidentally met, how remarkable the history was; but by the end of August I was seriously alarmed.

I have described in a former work, how the history affected me. My stronghold was Antiquity; now here, in the middle of the fifth century, I found, as it seemed to me, Christendom of the sixteenth and the nineteenth centuries reflected. I saw my face in that mirror, and I was a Monophysite. The Church of the *Via Media* was in the position of the Oriental communion, Rome was where she now is; and the Protestants were the Eutychians. Of all passages of history, since history has been, who would have thought of going to the sayings and doings of old Eutyches, that *delirus senex,* as (I think) Petavius calls him, and to the enormities of the unprincipled Dioscorus, in order to be converted to Rome!

Now let it be simply understood that I am not writing controversially, but with the one object of relating things as they happened to me in the course of my conversion. With this view I will quote a passage from the account, which I gave in 1850, of my reasonings and feelings in 1839:

"It was difficult to make out how the Eutychians or Monophysites were heretics, unless Protestants and Anglicans were heretics also; difficult to find arguments against the Tridentine Fathers, which did not tell against the Fathers of Chalcedon; difficult to condemn the Popes of the sixteenth century, without condemning the Popes of the fifth. The drama of religion, and the combat of truth and error, were ever one and the same. The principles and proceedings of the Church

now, were those of the Church then; the principles and proceedings of heretics then, were those of Protestants now. I
found it so,—almost fearfully; there was an awful similitude,
more awful, because so silent and unimpassioned, between the
dead records of the past and the feverish chronicle of the
present. The shadow of the fifth century was on the sixteenth. It was like a spirit rising from the troubled waters
of the old world, with the shape and lineaments of the new.
The Church then, as now, might be called peremptory and
stern, resolute, overbearing, and relentless; and heretics were
shifting, changeable, reserved, and deceitful, ever courting
civil power, and never agreeing together, except by its aid;
and the civil power was ever aiming at comprehensions, trying
to put the invisible out of view, and substituting expediency .
for faith. What was the use of continuing the controversy,·or
defending my position, if, after all, I was forging arguments
for Arius or Eutyches, and turning devil's advocate against
the much-enduring Athanasius and the majestic Leo? Be my
soul with the Saints! and shall I lift up my hand against
them? Sooner may my right hand forget her cunning, and
wither outright, as his who once stretched it out against a
prophet of God! anathema to a whole tribe of Cranmers,
Ridleys, Latimers, and Jewels! perish the names of Bramhall, Ussher, Taylor, Stillingfleet, and Barrow from the face
of the earth, ere I should do aught but fall at their feet in
love and in worship, whose image was continually before my
eyes, and whose musical words were ever in my ears and on
my tongue!"

Hardly had I brought my course of reading to a close, when
the *Dublin Review* of that same August was put into my
hands, by friends who were more favorable to the cause of
Rome than I was myself. There was an article in it on the
"Anglican Claim" by Dr. Wiseman. This was about the
middle of September. It was on the Donatists, with an application to Anglicanism. I read it, and did not see much
in it. The Donatist controversy was known to me for some
years, as has appeared already. The case was not parallel to
that of the Anglican Church. St. Augustine in Africa wrote
against the Donatists in Africa. They were a furious party
who made a schism within the African Church, and not·be-

yond its limits. It was a case of Altar against Altar, of two occupants of the same See, as that between the Non-jurors in England and the Established Church; not the case of one Church against another, as of Rome against the Oriental Monophysites. But my friend, an anxiously religious man, now, as then, very dear to me, a Protestant still, pointed out the palmary words of St. Augustine, which were contained in one of the extracts made in the *Review,* and which had escaped my observation. "Securus judicat orbis terrarum." He repeated these words again and again, and, when he was gone, they kept ringing in my ears. "Securus judicat orbis terrarum;" they were words which went beyond the occasion of the Donatists: they applied to that of the Monophysites. They gave a cogency to the Article, which had escaped me at first. They decided ecclesiastical questions on a simpler rule than that of Antiquity; nay, St. Augustine was one of the prime oracles of Antiquity; here then Antiquity was deciding against itself. What a light was hereby thrown upon every controversy in the Church! not that, for the moment, the multitude may not falter in their judgment,—not that, in the Arian hurricane, Sees more than can be numbered did not bend before its fury, and fall off from St. Athanasius,—not that the crowd of Oriental Bishops did not need to be sustained during the contest by the voice and the eye of St. Leo; but that the deliberate judgment, in which the whole Church at length rests and acquiesces, is an infallible prescription and a final sentence against such portions of it as protest and secede. Who can account for the impressions which are made on him? For a mere sentence, the words of St. Augustine, struck me with a power which I never had felt from any words before. To take a familiar instance, they were like the "Turn again Whittington" of the chime; or, to take a more serious one, they were like the "Tolle, lege,— Tolle, lege," of the child, which converted St. Augustine himself. "Securus judicat orbis terrarum!" By those great words of the ancient Father, interpreting and summing up the long and varied course of ecclesiastical history, the theory ·of the *Via Media* was absolutely pulverized.

I became excited at the view thus opened upon me. I was just starting on a round of visits; and I mentioned my state of mind to two most intimate friends: I think to no others. After a while, I got calm, and at length the vivid impression upon my imagination faded away. What I thought about it on reflection, I will attempt to describe presently. I had to determine its logical value, and its bearing upon my duty. Meanwhile, so far as this was certain,—I had seen the shadow of a hand upon the wall. It was clear that I had a good deal to learn on the question of the Churches, and that perhaps some new light was coming upon me. He who has seen a ghost, cannot be as if he had never seen it. The heavens had opened and closed again. The thought for the moment had been, "The Church of Rome will be found right after all;" and then it had vanished. My old convictions remained as before.

At this time, I wrote my Sermon on Divine Calls, which I published in my volume of *Plain Sermons*. It ends thus:—

"O that we could take that simple view of things, as to feel that the one thing which lies before us is to please God! What gain is it to please the world, to please the great, nay even to please those whom we love, compared with this? What gain is it to be applauded, admired, courted, followed, —compared with this one aim, of not being disobedient to a heavenly vision? What can this world offer comparable with that insight into spiritual things, that keen faith, that heavenly peace, that high sanctity, that everlasting righteousness, that hope of glory, which they have, who in sincerity love and follow our Lord Jesus Christ? Let us beg and pray Him day by day to reveal Himself to our souls more fully, to quicken our senses, to give us sight and hearing, taste and touch of the world to come; so to work within us, that we may sincerely say, 'Thou shalt guide me with Thy counsel, and after that receive me with glory. Whom have I in heaven but Thee? and there is none upon earth that I desire in comparison of Thee. My flesh and my heart faileth, but God is the strength of my heart, and my portion forever.'"

Now to trace the succession of thoughts, and the conclusions, and the consequent innovations on my previous belief, and the general conduct, to which I was led upon this sudden visitation. And first, I will say, whatever comes of saying it, for I leave inferences to others, that for years I must have had something of an habitual notion, though it was latent, and had never led me to distrust my own convictions, that my mind had not found its ultimate rest, and that in some sense or other I was on journey. During the same passage across the Mediterranean in which I wrote *Lead, kindly light*, I also wrote the verses, which are found in the *Lyra* under the head of *Providences*, beginning, "When I look back." This was in 1833; and, since I have begun this narrative, I have found a memorandum under the date of September 7, 1829, in which I speak of myself, as "now in my rooms in Oriel College, slowly advancing, &c. and led on by God's hand blindly, not knowing whither He is taking me." But, whatever this presentiment be worth, it was no protection against the dismay and disgust which I felt, in consequence of the dreadful misgiving, of which I have been relating the history. The one question was, what was I to do? I had to make up my mind for myself, and others could not help me. I determined to be guided, not by my imagination, but by my reason. And this I said over and over again in the years which followed, both in conversation and in private letters. Had it not been for this severe resolve, I should have been a Catholic sooner than I was. Moreover, I felt on consideration a positive doubt, on the other hand, whether the suggestion did not come from below. Then I said to myself, Time alone can solve that question. It was my business to go on as usual, to obey those convictions to which I had so long surrendered myself, which still had possession of me, and on which my new thoughts had no direct bearing. That new conception of things should only so far influence me, as it had a logical claim to do so. It came from above, it would come again;—so I trusted,—and with more definite outlines and greater cogency and consistency of proof. I thought of Samuel, before "he knew the word of the Lord;" and therefore I went, and lay down to sleep again. This was my broad view of the matter, and my *primâ facie* conclusion.

However, my new historical fact had already to a certain point a logical force. Down had come the *Via Media* as a definite theory or scheme, under the blows of St. Leo. My *Prophetical Office* had come to pieces; not indeed as an argument against "Roman errors," nor as against Protestantism, but as in behalf of England. I had no longer a distinctive plea for Anglicanism, unless I would be a Monophysite. I had, most painfully, to fall back upon my three original points of belief, which I have spoken so much of in a former passage,—the principle of dogma, the sacramental system, and anti-Romanism. Of these three the first two were better secured in Rome than in the Anglican Church. The Apostolical Succession, the two prominent sacraments, and the primitive Creeds, belonged, indeed, to the latter; but there had been and was far less strictness on matters of dogma and ritual in the Anglican system than in the Roman: in cousequence, my main argument for the Anglican claims lay in the positive and special charges, which I could bring against Rome. I had no positive Anglican theory. I was very nearly a pure Protestant. Lutherans had a sort of theology, so had Calvinists; I had none.

However, this pure Protestantism, to which I was gradually left, was really a practical principle. It was a strong, though it was only a negative ground, and it still had great hold on me. As a boy of fifteen, I had so fully imbibed it, that I had actually erased in my *Gradus ad Parnassum,* such titles, under the word "Papa," as "Christi Vicarius," "sacer interpres," and "sceptra gerens," and substituted epithets so vile that I cannot bring myself to write them down here. The effect of this early persuasion remained as, what I have already called it, a "stain upon my imagination." As regards my reason, I began in 1833 to form theories on the subject, which tended to obliterate it; yet by 1838 I had got no further than to consider Antichrist, as not the Church of Rome, but the spirit of the old pagan city, the fourth monster of Daniel, which was still alive, and which had corrupted the Church which was planted there. Soon after this indeed, and before my attention was directed to the Monophysite controversy, I underwent a great change of opinion. I saw that, from the nature of the case, the true Vicar of Christ must ever to the world seem like Antichrist, and be stigmatized as such, because a resemblance must ever exist between an original and a forgery; and thus the fact of such a calumny was almost one of the notes of the Church. But we cannot unmake ourselves or change our habits in a moment. Though my reason was convinced, I did not throw off, for some time after,—I could not have thrown off,—the unreasoning prejudice and suspicion, which I cherished about her at least by fits and starts, in spite of this conviction of my reason. I cannot prove this, but I believe it to have been the case from what I recollect of myself. Nor was there anything in the history of St. Leo and the Monophysites to undo the firm belief I had in the existence of what I called the practical abuses and excesses of Rome.

To her inconsistencies then, to her ambition and intrigue, to her sophistries (as I considered them to be) I now had recourse in my opposition to her, both public and personal. I did so by way of a relief. I had a great and growing dislike, after the summer of 1839, to speak against the Roman Church herself or her formal doctrines. I was very averse to speaking against doctrines, which might possibly turn out to be true, though at the time I had no reason for thinking they were; or against the Church, which had preserved them. I began to have misgivings, that, strong as my own feelings had been against her, yet in some things which I had said, I had taken the statements of Anglican divines for granted without weighing them for myself. I said to a friend in 1840, in a letter, which I shall use presently, "I am troubled by doubts whether as it is, I have not, in what I have published, spoken too strongly against Rome, though I think I did it in a kind of faith, being determined to put myself into the English system, and say all that our divines said, whether I had fully weighed it or not." I was sore about the great Anglican divines, as if they had taken me in, and made me say strong things, which facts did not justify. Yet I *did* still hold in substance all that I had said against the Church of Rome in my *Prophetical Office.* I felt the force of the usual Protestant objections against her; I believed that we had the Apostolical succession in the Anglican Church, and the grace of the sacraments; I was not sure that the difficulty of its isolation might not be overcome, though I was far from sure that it could. I did not see any clear proof that it had committed itself to any heresy, or had taken part against the truth; and I was not sure that it would not revive into full Apostolic purity and strength, and grow into union with Rome herself (Rome explaining her doctrines and guarding against their abuse), that is, if we were but patient and hopeful. I began to wish for union between the Anglican Church and Rome, if, and when, it was possible; and I did what I could to gain weekly prayers for that object. The ground which I felt to be good against her was the moral ground: I felt I could not be wrong in striking at her political and social line of action. The alliance of a dogmatic religion with liberals, high or low, seemed to me a providential direction against moving towards Rome, and a better "Preservative against Popery," than the three volumes in folio, in which, I think, that prophylactic is to be found. However, on occasions which demanded it, I felt it a duty to give out plainly all that I thought, though I did not like to do so. One such instance occurred, when I had to publish a Letter about Tract 90. In that Letter, I said, "Instead of setting before the soul the Holy Trinity, and heaven and hell, the Church of Rome does seem to me, as a popular system, to preach the Blessed Virgin and the Saints, and Purgatory." On this occasion I recollect expressing to a friend the distress it gave me thus to speak; but, I said, "How can I help saying it, if I think it? and I *do* think it; my Bishop calls on me to say out what I think; and that is the long and the short of it." But I recollected Hurrell Froude's words to me, almost his dying words, "I must enter another protest against your cursing and swearing. What good can it do? and I call it uncharitable to an excess. How mistaken we may ourselves be on many points that are only gradually opening on us!"

Instead then of speaking of errors in doctrine, I was driven, by my state of mind, to insist upon the political conduct, the controversial bearing, and the social methods and manifestations of Rome. And here I found a matter ready to my hand, which affected me the more sensibly for the reason that it lay at our very doors. I can hardly describe too strongly my feeling upon it. I had an unspeakable aversion to the policy and acts of Mr. O'Connell, because, as I thought, he associated himself with men of all religions and no religion against the Anglican Church, and advanced Catholicism by violence and intrigue. When then I found him taken up by the English Catholics, and, as I supposed, at Rome, I con-

sidered I had a fulfillment before my eyes how the Court of
Rome played fast and loose, and justified the serious charges
which I had seen put down in books against it. Here we saw
what Rome was in action, whatever she might be when quiescent. Her conduct was simply secular and political.

And here came in another feeling, of a personal nature,
which had little to do with the argument against Rome,
except that, in my prejudice, I viewed what happened to
myself in the light of my own ideas of the traditionary conduct of her advocates and instruments. I was very stern in
the case of any interference in our Oxford matters on the part
of charitable Catholics, and of any attempt to do me good
personally. There was nothing, indeed, at the time more
likely to throw me back. "Why do you meddle? why cannot
you let me alone? You can do me no good; you know nothing
on earth about me; you may actually do me harm; I am in
better hands than yours. I know my own sincerity of purpose; and I am determined upon taking my time." Since I
have been a Catholic, people have sometimes accused me of
backwardness in making converts; and Protestants have
argued from it that I have no great eagerness to do so. It
would be against my nature to act otherwise than I do; but
besides, it would be to forget the lessons which I gained in the
experience of my own history in the past.

This is the account which I have to give of some savage and
ungrateful words in the *British Critic* of 1840 against the
controversialists of Rome: "By their fruits ye shall know
them. . . . We see it attempting to gain converts among us
by unreal representations of its doctrines, plausible statements, bold assertions, appeals to the weaknesses of human
nature, to our fancies, our eccentricities, our fears, our frivoli-
ties, our false philosophies. We see its agents, smiling and
nodding and ducking to attract attention, as gypsies make up
to truant boys, holding out tales for the nursery, and pretty
pictures, and gilt gingerbread, and physic concealed in jam,
and sugar-plums for good children. Who can but feel shame
when the religion of Ximenes, Borromeo, and Pascal, is so
overlaid? Who can but feel sorrow, when its devout and
earnest defenders so mistake its genius and its capabilities?
We Englishmen like manliness, openness, consistency, truth.

Rome will never gain on us, till she learns these virtues, and uses them; and then she *may* gain us, but it will be by ceasing to be what we now mean by Rome, by having a right, not to 'have dominion over our faith,' but to gain and possess our affections in the bonds of the gospel. Till she ceases to be what she practically is, a union is impossible between her and England; but, if she does reform, (and who can presume to say that so large a part of Christendom never can?) then it will be our Church's duty at once to join in communion with the continental Churches, whatever politicians at home may say to it, and whatever steps the civil power may take in consequence. And though we may not live to see that day, at least we are bound to pray for it; we are bound to pray for our brethren that they and we may be led together into the pure light of the gospel, and be one as we once were one. It was most touching news to be told, as we were lately, that Christians on the Continent were praying together for the spiritual well-being of England. May they gain light, while they aim at unity, and grow in faith while they manifest their love! We too have our duties to them; not of reviling, not of slandering, not of hating, though political interests require it; but the duty of loving brethren still more abundantly in spirit, whose faces, for our sins and their sins, we are not allowed to see in the flesh.''

No one ought to indulge in insinuations; it certainly diminishes my right to complain of slanders uttered against myself, when, as in this passage, I had already spoken in disparagement of the controversialists of that religious body, to which I myself now belong.

I have thus put together, as well as I can, what has to be said about my general state of mind from the autumn of 1839 to the summer of 1841; and, having done so, I go on to narrate how my new misgivings affected my conduct, and my relations towards the Anglican Church.

When I got back to Oxford in October 1839, after the visits which I had been paying, it so happened, there had been, in my absence, occurrences of an awkward character, compromising me both with my Bishop and also with the authorities of the University; and this drew my attention at once to the state of the Movement party there, and made me very anxious for the future. In the spring of the year, as has been seen in the Article analyzed above, I had spoken of the excesses which were to be found among persons commonly included in it:— at that time I thought little of such an evil, but the new views, which had come on me during the Long Vacation, on the one hand made me comprehend it, and on the other took away my power of effectually meeting it. A firm and powerful control was necessary to keep men straight; I never had a strong wrist, but at the very time, when it was most needed, the reins had broken in my hands. With an anxious presentiment on my mind of the upshot of the whole inquiry, which it was almost impossible for me to conceal from men who saw me day by day, who heard my familiar conversation, who came perhaps for the express purpose of pumping me, and having a categorical *yes* or *no* to their questions,—how could I expect to say anything about my actual, positive, present belief, which would be sustaining or consoling to such persons as were haunted already by doubts of their own? Nay, how could I, with satisfaction to myself, analyze my own mind, and say what I held and what I did not hold? or how could I say with what limitations, shades of difference, or degrees of belief, I still held that body of Anglican opinions which I had openly professed and taught? how could I deny or assert this point or that, without injustice to the new light, in which the whole evidence for those old opinions presented itself to my mind?

However, I had to do what I could, and what was best, under the circumstances; I found a general talk on the subject of the Article in the *Dublin Review;* and, if it had affected me, it was not wonderful, that it affected others also. As to myself, I felt no kind of certainty that the argument in it was conclusive. Taking it at the worst, granting that the Anglican Church had not the Note of Catholicity; yet there were many Notes of the Church. Some belonged to one age or place, some to another. Bellarmine had reckoned Temporal Prosperity among the Notes of the Church; but the Roman Church had not any great popularity, wealth, glory, power, or prospects, in the nineteenth century. It was not at all certain as yet, even that we had not the Note of Catholicity; but, if not this, we had others. My first business then, was to examine this question carefully, and see, whether a great deal could not be said after all for the Anglican Church, in spite of its acknowledged short-comings. This I did in an Article "on the Catholicity of the English Church," which appeared in the *British Critic* of January 1840. As to my personal distress on the point, I think it had gone by February 21st in that year, for I wrote then to Mr. Bowden about the important Article in the Dublin, thus: "It made a great impression here [Oxford]; and, I say what of course I would only say to such as yourself, it made me for a while very uncomfortable in my own mind. The great speciousness of his argument is one of the things which have made me despond so much," that is, as anticipating its effect upon others.

But, secondly, the great stumbling-block lay in the 39 Articles. It was urged that here was a positive Note *against* Anglicanism:—Anglicanism claimed to hold, that the Church of England was nothing else than a continuation in this country, (as the Church of Rome might be in France or Spain,) of that one Church of which in old times Athanasius and Augustine were members. But, if so, the doctrine must be the same; the doctrine of the Old Church must live and speak in Anglican formularies, in the 39 Articles. Did it? Yes, it did; that is what I maintained; it did in substance, in a true sense. Man had done his worst to disfigure, to mutilate, the old Catholic Truth; but there it was, in spite of them, in the Articles still. It was there,—but this must be shown. It was a matter of life and death to us to show it. And I believed that it could be shown; I considered that those grounds of justification, which I gave above, when I was speaking of Tract 90, were sufficient for the purpose; and therefore I set about showing it at once. This was in March 1840, when I went up to Littlemore. And, as it was a matter of life and death with us, all risks must be run to show it. When the attempt was actually made, I had got reconciled to the prospect of it, and had no apprehensions as to the experiment; but in 1840, while my purpose was honest, and my grounds of reason satisfactory, I did nevertheless recognize that I was engaged in an *experimentum crucis*. I have no doubt that then I acknowledged to myself that it would be a trial of the Anglican Church, which it had never undergone before,—not that the Catholic sense of the Articles had not been held or at least suffered by their framers and promulgators, not that it was not implied in the teaching of Andrewes or Beveridge, but that it had never been publicly recognized, while the interpretation of the day was Protestant and exclusive. I observe also, that, though my Tract was an experiment, it was, as I said at the time, "no *feeler*"; the event showed this; for, when my principle was not granted, I did not draw back. but gave up. I would not hold office in a Church which would not allow my sense of the Articles. My tone was, "This is necessary for us, and have it we must and will, and, if it tends to bring men to look less bitterly on the Church of Rome, so much the better."

This then was the second work to which I set myself; though when I got to Littlemore, other things interfered to prevent my accomplishing it at the moment. I had in mind to remove all such obstacles as lay in the way of holding the Apostolic and Catholic character of the Anglican teaching; to assert the right of all who chose, to say in the face of day, "Our Church teaches the Primitive Ancient faith." I did not conceal this: in Tract 90, it is put forward as the first principle of all, "It is a duty which we owe both to the Catholic Church, and to our own, to take our reformed confessions in the most Catholic sense they will admit: we have no duties towards their framers." And still more pointedly in my Letter, explanatory of the Tract, addressed to Dr. Jelf, I say: "The only peculiarity of the view I advocate, if I must so call it, is this—that whereas it is usual at this day to make the *particular belief of their writers* their true interpretation, I would make the *belief of the Catholic Church such*. That is, as it is often said that infants are regenerated in Baptism, not on the faith of their parents, but of the Church, so in like manner I would say that the Articles are received, not in the sense of their framers, but (as far as the wording will admit or any ambiguity requires it) in the one Catholic sense."

A third measure which I distinctly contemplated, was the resignation of St. Mary's, whatever became of the question of the 39 Articles; and as a first step I meditated a retirement to Littlemore. Littlemore was an integral part of St. Mary's

Parish, and between two and three miles distant from Oxford. I had built a Church there several years before; and I went there to pass the Lent of 1840, and gave myself up to teaching in the Parish School, and practicing the choir. At the same time, I had in view a monastic house there. I bought ten acres of ground and began planting; but this great design was never carried out. I mention it, because it shows how little I had really the idea at that time of ever leaving the Anglican Church. That I contemplated as early as 1839 the further step of giving up St. Mary's, appears from a letter which I wrote in October 1840, to Mr. Keble, the friend whom it was most natural for me to consult on such a point.

Mr. Keble's judgment was in favor of my retaining my living; at least for the present; what weighed with me most was his saying, "You must consider, whether your retiring either from the Pastoral Care only, or from writing and printing and editing in the cause, would not be a sort of scandalous thing, unless it were done very warily. It would be said, 'You see he can go on no longer with the Church of England, except in mere Lay Communion;' or people might say you repented of the cause altogether. Till you see [your way to mitigate, if not remove this evil] I certainly should advise you to stay."

Such was about my state of mind, on the publication of Tract 90 in February 1841. I was indeed in prudence taking steps towards eventually withdrawing from St. Mary's, and I was not confident about my permanent adhesion to the Anglican creed; but I was in no actual perplexity or trouble of mind. Nor did the immense commotion consequent upon the publication of the Tract unsettle me again; for I fancied I had weathered the storm, as far as the Bishops were concerned: the Tract had not been condemned: that was the great point, and I made much of it.

In the summer of 1841, I found myself at Littlemore without any harass or anxiety on my mind. I had determined to put aside all controversy, and I set myself down to my translation of St. Athanasius; but, between July and November, I received three blows which broke me.

1. I had got but little way in my work, when my trouble

returned on me. The ghost had come a second time. In the *Arian History* I found the very same phenomenon, in a far bolder shape, which I had found in the Monophysite. I had not observed it in 1832. Wonderful that this should come upon me! I had not sought it out; I was reading and writing in my own line of study, far from the controversies of the day, on what is called a "metaphysical" subject; but I saw clearly, that in the history of Arianism, the pure Arians were the Protestants, the semi-Arians were the Anglicans, and that Rome now was what it was then. The truth lay, not with the *Via Media*, but with what was called "the extreme party." As I am not writing a work of controversy, I need not enlarge upon the argument; I have said something on the subject in a Volume, from which I have already quoted.

2. I was in the misery of this new unsettlement, when a second blow came upon me. The Bishops one after another began to charge against me. It was a formal, determinate movement. This was the real "understanding;" that, on which I had acted on the first appearance of Tract 90, had come to nought. I think the words, which had then been used to me, were, that "perhaps two or three of them might think it necessary to say something in their charges;" but by this time they had tided over the difficulty of the Tract, and there was no one to enforce the "understanding." They went on in this way, directing charges at me, for three whole years. I recognized it as a condemnation; it was the only one that was in their power. At first I intended to protest; but I gave up the thought in despair.

On October 17th, I wrote thus to a friend: "I suppose it will be necessary in some shape or other to re-assert Tract 90; else, it will seem, after these Bishops' Charges, as if it were silenced, which it has not been, nor do I intend it should be. I wish to keep quiet; but if Bishops speak, I will speak too. If the view were silenced, I could not remain in the Church, nor could many others; and therefore, since it is *not* silenced, I shall take care to show that it isn't."

A day or two after, Oct. 22, a stranger wrote to me to say, that the *Tracts for the Times* had made a young friend of his a Catholic, and to ask, "would I be so good as to convert him back;" I made answer:—

"If conversions to Rome take place in consequence of the *Tracts for the Times*, I do not impute blame to them, but to those who, instead of acknowledging such Anglican principles of theology and ecclesiastical polity as they contain, set themselves to oppose them. Whatever be the influence of the Tracts, great or small, they may become just as powerful for Rome, if our Church refuses them, as they would be for our Church if she accepted them. If our rulers speak either against the Tracts, or not at all, if any number of them, not only do not favor, but even do not suffer the principles contained in them, it is plain that our members may easily be persuaded either to give up those principles, or to give up the Church. If this state of things goes on, I mournfully prophesy, not one or two, but many secessions to the Church of Rome."

Two years afterwards, looking back on what had passed, I said, "There were no converts to Rome, till after the condemnation of No. 90."

3. As if all this were not enough, there came the affair of the Jerusalem Bishopric; and, with a brief mention of it, I shall conclude.

I think I am right in saying that it had been long a desire with the Prussian Court to introduce Episcopacy into the new Evangelical Religion, which was intended in that country to embrace both the Lutheran and Calvinistic bodies. I almost think I heard of the project, when I was at Rome in 1833, at the Hotel of the Prussian Minister, M. Bunsen, who was most hospitable and kind, as to other English visitors, so also to my friends and myself. The idea of Episcopacy, as the Prussian king understood it, was, I suppose, very different from that taught in the Tractarian School: but still, I suppose also, that the chief authors of that school would have gladly seen such a measure carried out in Prussia, had it been done without compromising those principles which were necessary to the being of a Church. About the time of the publication of Tract 90, M. Bunsen and the then Archbishop of Canterbury were taking steps for its execution, by appointing and cousecrating a Bishop for Jerusalem. Jerusalem, it would seem, was considered a safe place for the experiment; it was too far from Prussia to awaken the susceptibilities of any party at home; if the project failed, it failed without harm to any one; and, if it succeeded, it gave Protestantism a *status* in the East, which, in association with the Monophysite or Jacobite and the Nestorian bodies, formed a political instrument for England, parallel to that which Russia had in the Greek Church, and France in the Latin.

Accordingly, in July 1841, full of the Anglican difficulty on the question of Catholicity, I thus spoke of the Jerusalem scheme in an Article in the *British Critic:* "When our thoughts turn to the East, instead of recollecting that there are Christian Churches there, we leave it to the Russians to take care of the Greeks, and the French to take care of the Romans, and we content ourselves with erecting a Protestant Church at Jerusalem, or with helping the Jews to rebuild their Temple there, or with becoming the august protectors of Nestorians, Monophysites, and all the heretics we can hear of, or with forming a league with the Mussulman against Greeks and Romans together."

I do not pretend, so long after the time, to give a full or exact account of this measure in detail. I will but say that in the Act of Parliament, under date of October 5, 1841, (if the copy, from which I quote, contains the measure as it passed the Houses,) provision is made for the consecration of "British subjects, or the subjects or citizens of any foreign state, to be Bishops in any foreign country, whether such foreign subjects or citizens be or be not subjects or citizens of the country in which they are to act, and . . . without requiring such of them as may be subjects or citizens of any foreign kingdom or state to take the oaths of allegiance and supremacy, and the oath of due obedience to the Archbishop for the time being" . . . also "that such Bishop or Bishops, so consecrated, may exercise, within such limits, as may from time to time be assigned for that purpose in such foreign countries by her Majesty, spiritual jurisdiction over the ministers of British congregations of the United Church of England and Ireland, and over *such other Protestant* Congregations, as may be desirous of placing themselves under his or their authority."

Now here, at the very time that the Anglican Bishops were directing their censure upon me for avowing an approach to the Catholic Church not closer than I believed the Anglican formularies would allow, they were on the other hand, fraternizing, by their act or by their sufferance, with Protestant bodies, and allowing them to put themselves under an Anglican Bishop, without any renunciation of their errors or regard to their due reception of baptism and confirmation; while there was great reason to suppose that the said Bishop was intended to make converts from the orthodox Greeks, and the schismatical Oriental bodies, by means of the influence of England. This was the third blow, which finally shattered my faith in the Anglican Church. That Church was not only forbidding any sympathy or concurrence with the Church of Rome, but it actually was courting an intercommunion with Protestant Prussia and the heresy of the Orientals. The Anglican Church might have the Apostolical succession, as had the Monophysites; but such acts as were in progress led me to the gravest suspicion, not that it would soon cease to be a Church, but that, since the 16th century, it had never been a Church all along.

On October 12th, I thus wrote to Mr. Bowden:—"We have not a single Anglican in Jerusalem; so we are sending a Bishop to *make* a communion, not to govern our own people. Next, the excuse is, that there are converted Anglican Jews there who require a Bishop; I am told there are not half-a-dozen. But for *them* the Bishop is sent out, and for them he is a Bishop of the *circumcision*" (I think he was a converted Jew, who boasted of his Jewish descent), "against the Epistle to the Galatians pretty nearly. Thirdly, for the sake of Prussia, he is to take under him all the foreign Protestants who will come; and the political advantages will be so great, from the influence of England, that there is no doubt they *will* come. They are to sign the Confession of Augsburg, and there is nothing to show that they hold the doctrine of Baptismal Regeneration.

"As to myself, I shall do nothing whatever publicly, unless indeed it were to give my signature to a Protest; but I think it would be out of place in *me* to agitate, having been in a way silenced; but the Archbishop is really doing most grave work, of which we cannot see the end."

I did make a solemn Protest, and sent it to the Archbishop

of Canterbury, and also sent it to my own Bishop with the following letter:—

"It seems as if I were never to write to your Lordship, without giving you pain, and I know that my present subject does not specially concern your Lordship; yet, after a great deal of anxious thought, I lay before you the inclosed Protest.

"Your Lordship will observe that I am not asking for any notice of it, unless you think that I ought to receive one. I do this very serious act in obedience to my sense of duty.

"If the English Church is to enter on a new course, and assume a new aspect, it will be more pleasant to me hereafter to think, that I did not suffer so grievous an event to happen, without bearing witness against it.

"May I be allowed to say, that I augur nothing but evil, if we in any respect prejudice our title to be a branch of the Apostolic Church? That Article of the Creed, I need hardly observe to your Lordship, is of such constraining power, that, if *we* will not claim it, and use it for ourselves, *others* will use it in their own behalf against us. Men who learn whether by means of documents or measures, whether from the statements or the acts of persons in authority, that our communion is not a branch of the One Church, I foresee with much grief, will be tempted to look out for that Church elsewhere.

"It is to me a subject of great dismay, that, as far as the Church has lately spoken out, on the subject of the opinions which I and others hold, those opinions are, not merely not *sanctioned* (for that I do not ask), but not even *suffered*.

"I earnestly hope that your Lordship will excuse my freedom in thus speaking to you of some members of your Most Rev. and Right Rev. Body. With every feeling of reverent attachment to your Lordship,

"I am, &c."

PROTEST

"Whereas the Church of England has a claim on the allegiance of Catholic believers only on the ground of her own claim to be considered a branch of the Catholic Church:

"And whereas the recognition of heresy, indirect as well as direct, goes far to destroy such claim in the case of any religious body:

"And whereas to admit maintainers of heresy to communion, without formal renunciation of their errors, goes far towards recognizing the same:

"And whereas Lutheranism and Calvinism are heresies, repugnant to Scripture, springing up three centuries since, and anathematized by East as well as West:

"And whereas it is reported that the Most Reverend Primate and other Right Reverend Rulers of our Church have consecrated a Bishop with a view to exercising spiritual jurisdiction over Protestant, that is, Lutheran and Calvinist congregations in the East (under the provisions of an Act made in the last session of Parliament to amend an Act made in the 26th year of the reign of his Majesty King George the Third, entitled, 'An Act to empower the Archbishop of Canterbury, or the Archbishop of York for the time being, to consecrate to the office of Bishop persons being subjects or citizens of countries out of his Majesty's dominions'), dispensing at the same time, not in particular cases and accidentally, but as if on principle and universally, with any abjuration of error on the part of such congregations, and with any reconciliation to the Church on the part of the presiding Bishop; thereby giving some sort of formal recognition to the doctrines which such congregations maintain:

"And whereas the dioceses in England are connected together by so close an intercommunion, that what is done by authority in one, immediately affects the rest:

"On these grounds, I in my place, being a priest of the English Church and Vicar of St. Mary the Virgin's, Oxford, by way of relieving my conscience, do hereby solemnly protest against the measure aforesaid, and disown it, as removing our Church from her present ground and tending to her disorganization.

"JOHN HENRY NEWMAN.

"November 11, 1841."

Looking back two years afterwards on the above-mentioned and other acts, on the part of Anglican Ecclesiastical authorities, I observed: "Many a man might have held an abstract theory about the Catholic Church, to which it was difficult to adjust the Anglican,—might have admitted a suspicion, or even painful doubts about the latter,—yet never have been impelled onwards, had our Rulers preserved the quiescence of former years; but it is the corroboration of a present, living, and energetic heterodoxy, that realizes and makes such doubts practical; it has been the recent speeches and acts of authorities, who had so long been tolerant of Protestant error, which has given to inquiry and to theory its force and its edge.''

As to the project of a Jerusalem Bishopric, I never heard of any good or harm it has ever done, except what it has done for me; which many think a great misfortune, and I one of the greatest of mercies. It brought me on to the beginning of the end.

CHAPTER IV

HISTORY OF MY RELIGIOUS OPINIONS FROM 1841 TO 1845

FROM the end of 1841, I was on my death-bed, as regards my membership with the Anglican Church, though at the time I became aware of it only by degrees. I introduce what I have to say with this remark, by way of accounting for the character of this remaining portion of my narrative. A death-bed has scarcely a history; it is a tedious decline, with seasons of rallying and seasons of falling back; and since the end is foreseen, or what is called a matter of time, it has little interest for the reader, especially if he has a kind heart. Moreover, it is a season when doors are closed and curtains drawn, and when the sick man neither cares nor is able to record the stages of his malady. I was in these circumstances, except so far as I was not allowed to die in peace,—except so far as friends, who had still a full right to come in upon me, and the public world which had not, have given a sort of history to those last four years. But in consequence, my narrative must be in great measure documentary, as I cannot rely on my memory, except for definite particulars, positive or negative. Letters of mine to friends since dead have come into my hands; others have been kindly lent me for the occasion; and I have some drafts of others, and some notes which I made, though I have no strictly personal or continuous memoranda to consult, and have unluckily mislaid some valuable papers.

And first as to my position in the view of duty; it was this:
—1. I had given up my place in the Movement in my letter
to the Bishop of Oxford in the spring of 1841; but 2. I could
not give up my duties towards the many and various minds
who had more or less been brought into it by me; 3. I expected or intended gradually to fall back into Lay Communion; 4. I never contemplated leaving the Church of England; 5. I could not hold office in its service, if I were not
allowed to hold the Catholic sense of the Article; 6. I could
not go to Rome, while she suffered honors to be paid to the
Blessed Virgin and the Saints which I thought in my conscience to be incompatible with the Supreme, Incommunicable
Glory of the One Infinite and Eternal; 7. I desired a union
with Rome under conditions, Church with Church; 8. I called
Littlemore my Torres Vedras, and thought that some day we
might advance again within the Anglican Church, as we had
been forced to retire; 9. I kept back all persons who were
disposed to go to Rome with all my might.

And I kept them back for three or four reasons; 1. because
what I could not in conscience do myself, I could not suffer
them to do; 2. because I thought that in various cases they
were acting under excitement; 3. because I had duties to my
Bishop and to the Anglican Church; and 4. in some cases,
because I had received from their Anglican parents or superiors direct charge of them.

This was my view of my duty from the end of 1841 to my
resignation of St. Mary's in the autumn of 1843. And now
I shall relate my view, during that time, of the state of the
controversy between the Churches.

As soon as I saw the hitch in the Anglican argument, during my course of reading in the summer of 1839, I began to
look about, as I have said, for some ground which might
supply a controversial basis for my need. The difficulty in
question had affected my view both of Antiquity and Catholicity; for, while the history of St. Leo showed me that the deliberate and eventual consent of the great body of the Church
ratified a doctrinal decision as a part of revealed truth, it
also showed that the rule of Antiquity was not infringed,
though a doctrine had not been publicly recognized as so revealed, till centuries after the time of the Apostles. Thus,

whereas the Creeds tell us that the Church is One, Holy, Catholic, and Apostolic, I could not prove that the Anglican communion was an integral part of the One Church, on the ground of its teaching being Apostolic or Catholic, without reasoning in favor of what are commonly called the Roman corruptions; and I could not defend our separation from Rome and her faith without using arguments prejudicial to those great doctrines concerning our Lord, which are the very foundation of the Christian religion. The *Via Media* was an impossible idea; it was what I had called "standing on one leg"; and it was necessary, if my old issue of the controversy was to be retained, to go further either one way or the other.

Accordingly, I abandoned that old ground and took another. I deliberately quitted the old Anglican ground as untenable; though I did not do so all at once, but as I became more and more convinced of the state of the case. The Jerusalem Bishopric was the ultimate condemnation of the old theory of the *Via Media:*—if its establishment did nothing else, at least it demolished the sacredness of diocesan rights. If England could be in Palestine, Rome might be in England. But its bearing upon the controversy, as I have shown in the foregoing chapter, was much more serious than this technical ground. From that time the Anglican Church was, in my mind, either not a normal portion of that One Church to which the promises were made, or at least in an abnormal state; and from that time I said boldly (as I did in my Protest, and as indeed I had even intimated in my Letter to the Bishop of Oxford), that the Church in which I found myself had no claim on me, except on condition of its being a portion of the One Catholic Communion, and that that condition must ever be borne in mind as a practical matter, and had to be distinctly proved. All this is not inconsistent with my saying above that, at this time, I had no thought of leaving the Church of England; because I felt some of my old objections against Rome as strongly as ever. I had no right, I had no leave, to act against my conscience. That was a higher rule than any argument about the Notes of the Church.

Under these circumstances I turned for protection to the Note of Sanctity, with a view of showing that we had at least one of the necessary Notes, as fully as the Church of Rome;

or, at least, without entering into comparisons, that we had it in such a sufficient sense as to reconcile us to our position, and to supply full evidence, and a clear direction, on the point of practical duty. We had the Note of Life,—not any sort of life, not such only as can come of nature, but a supernatural Christian life, which could only come directly from above.

To bring out this view was the purpose of *Four Sermons preached at St. Mary's* in December of that year. Hitherto I had not introduced the exciting topics of the day into the Pulpit; on this occasion I did. I did so, for the moment was urgent; there was great unsettlement of mind among us, in consequence of those same events which had unsettled me. One special anxiety, very obvious, which was coming on me now, was, that what was "one man's meat was another man's poison." I had said even of Tract 90, "It was addressed to one set of persons, and has been used and commented on by another;" still more was it true now, that whatever I wrote for the service of those whom I knew to be in trouble of mind, would become on the one hand matter of suspicion and slander in the mouths of my opponents, and of distress and surprise to those on the other hand who had no difficulties of faith at all. Accordingly, when I published these *Four Sermons* at the end of 1843, I introduced them with a recommendation that none should read them who did not need them. But in truth the virtual condemnation of Tract 90, after that the whole difficulty seemed to have been weathered, was an enormous disappointment and trial. My protest also against the Jerusalem Bishopric was an unavoidable cause of excitement in the case of many; but it calmed them too, for the very fact of a Protest was a relief to their impatience. And so, in like manner, as regards the Four Sermons, of which I speak, though they acknowledged freely the great scandal which was involved in the recent episcopal doings, yet at the same time they might be said to bestow upon the multiplied disorders and shortcomings of the Anglican Church a sort of place in the Revealed Dispensation, and an intellectual position in the controversy, and the dignity of a great principle, for unsettled minds to take and use,—a principle which might teach them to recognize their own consistency, and to be reconciled to themselves, and which might absorb and dry up a multitude of their grudgings, discontents, misgivings, and questionings, and lead the way to humble, thankful, and tranquil thoughts;—and this was the effect which certainly it produced on myself.

The point of these Sermons is, that, in spite of the rigid character of the Jewish law, the formal and literal force of its precepts, and the manifest schism, and worse than schism, of the Ten Tribes, yet in fact they were still recognized as a people by the Divine Mercy; that the great prophets Elias and Eliseus were sent to them; and not only so, but were sent to preach to them and reclaim them, without any intimation that they must be reconciled to the line of David and the Aaronic priesthood, or go up to Jerusalem to worship. They were not in the Church, yet they had the means of grace and the hope of acceptance with their Maker. The application of all this to the Anglican Church was immediate;—whether, under the circumstances, a man could assume or exercise ministerial functions, or not, might not clearly appear (though it must be remembered that England had the Apostolic Priesthood, whereas Israel had no priesthood at all), but so far was clear, that there was no call at all for an Anglican to leave his Church for Rome, though he did not believe his own to be part of the One Church:—and for this reason, because it was a fact that the kingdom of Israel was cut off from the Temple; and yet its subjects, neither in a mass, nor as individuals, neither the multitudes on Mount Carmel, nor the Shunammite and her household, had any command given them, though miracles were displayed before them, to break off from their own people, and to submit themselves to Judah.

It is plain, that a theory such as this,—whether the marks of a divine presence and life in the Anglican Church were sufficient to prove that she was actually within the covenant, or only sufficient to prove that she was at least enjoying extraordinary and uncovenanted mercies,—not only lowered her level in a religious point of view, but weakened her controversial basis. Its very novelty made it suspicious; and there was no guarantee that the process of subsidence might not ·continue, and that it might not end in a submersion. Indeed, to many minds, to say that England was wrong was even to say that Rome was right; and no ethical or casuistic reasoning whatever could overcome in their case the argument from prescription and authority. To this objection, as made to my new teaching, I could only answer that I did not make my circumstances. I fully acknowledged the force and effectiveness of the genuine Anglican theory, and that it was all but proof against the disputants of Rome; but still like Achilles, it had a vulnerable point, and that St. Leo had found it out for me, and that I could not help it;—that, were it not for matter of fact, the theory would be great indeed; it would be irresistible, if it were only true. When I became a Catholic, the Editor of the *Christian Observer,* Mr. Wilkes, who had in former days accused me, to my indignation, of tending towards Rome, wrote to me to ask, which of the two was now right, he or I? I answered him in a letter, part of which I here insert, as it will serve as a sort of leave-taking of the great theory, which is so specious to look upon, so difficult to prove, and so hopeless to work.

"Nov. 8, 1845. I do not think, at all more than I did that the Anglican principles which I advocated at the date you mention, lead men to the Church of Rome. If I must specify what I mean by 'Anglican principles,' I should say, e.g. taking *Antiquity,* not the *existing Church,* as the oracle of truth; and holding that the *Apostolical Succession* is a sufficient guarantee of Sacramental Grace, *without union with the Christian Church throughout the world.* I think these still the firmest, strongest ground against Rome—that is, *if they can be held"* [as truths or facts]. "They *have* been held by many, and are far more difficult to refute in the Roman controversy, than those of any other religious body.

"For myself, I found *I could not* hold them. I left them. From the time I began to suspect their unsoundness, I ceased to put them forward. When I was fairly sure of their unsoundness, I gave up my Living. When I was fully confident that the Church of Rome was the only true Church, I joined her.

"I have felt all along that Bp. Bull's theology was the only theology on which the English Church could stand. I have felt, that opposition to the Church of Rome was *part* of that theology; and that he who could not protest against the

Church of Rome was no true divine in the English Church. I have never said, nor attempted to say, that any one in office in the English Church, whether Bishop or incumbent, could be otherwise than in hostility to the Church of Rome.''

The *Via Media* then disappeared forever, and a Theory, made expressly for the occasion, took its place. I was pleased with my new view. I wrote to an intimate friend, Samuel F. Wood, Dec. 13, 1841: ''I think you will give me the credit, Carissime, of not undervaluing the strength of the feelings which draw one [to Rome], and yet I am (I trust) quite clear about my duty to remain where I am; indeed, much clearer than I was some time since. If it is not presumptuous to say, I have . . . a much more definite view of the promised inward Presence of Christ with us in the Sacraments now that the outward notes of it are being removed. And I am content to be with Moses in the desert, or with Elijah excommunicated from the Temple. I say this, putting things at the strongest.''

However, my friends of the moderate Apostolical party, who were my friends for the very reason of my having been so moderate and Anglican myself in general tone in times past, who had stood up for Tract 90 partly from faith in me, and certainly from generous and kind feeling, and had thereby shared an obloquy which was none of theirs, were naturally surprised and offended at a line of argument, novel, and, as it appeared to them, wanton, which threw the whole controversy into confusion, stultified my former principles, and substituted, as they would consider, a sort of methodistic self-contemplation, especially abhorrent both to my nature and to my past professions, for the plain and honest tokens, as they were commonly received, of a divine mission in the Anglican Church. They could not tell whither I was going; and were still further annoyed when I persisted in viewing the condemnation of Tract 90 by the public and the Bishops as so grave a matter, and when I threw about what they considered mysterious hints of ''eventualities,'' and would not simply say, ''An Anglican I was born, and an Anglican I will die.''

While my old and true friends were thus in trouble about me, I suppose they felt not only anxiety but pain, to see that

I was gradually surrendering myself to the influence of others, who had not their own claims upon me, younger men, and of a cast of mind in no small degree uncongenial to my own. A new school of thought was rising, as is usual in doctrinal inquiries, and was sweeping the original party of the Movement aside, and was taking its place. The most prominent person in it, was a man of elegant genius, of classical mind, of rare talent in literary composition:—Mr. Oakeley. He was not far from my own age; I had long known him, though of late years he had not been in residence at Oxford; and quite lately, he has been taking several signal occasions of renewing that kindness, which he ever showed towards me when we were both in the Anglican Church. His tone of mind was not unlike that which gave a character to the early Movement; he was almost a typical Oxford man, and, as far as I recollect, both in political and ecclesiastical views, would have been of one spirit with the Oriel party of 1826-1833. But he had entered late into the Movement; he did not know its first years; and, beginning with a new start, he was naturally thrown together with that body of eager, acute, resolute minds who had begun their Catholic life about the same time as he, who knew nothing about the *Via Media,* but had heard much about Rome. This new party rapidly formed and increased, in and out of Oxford and, as it so happened, contemporaneously with that very summer, when I received so serious a blow to my ecclesiastical views from the study of the Monophysite controversy. These men cut into the original Movement at an angle, fell across its line of thought, and then set about turning that line in its own direction. They were most of them keenly religious men, with a true concern for their souls as the first matter of all, with a great zeal for me, but giving little certainty at the time as to which way they would ultimately turn. Some in the event have remained firm to Anglicanism, some have become Catholics, and some have found a refuge in Liberalism. Nothing was clearer concerning them, than that they needed to be kept in order; and on me who had had so much to do with the making of them, that duty was as clearly incumbent; and it is equally clear, from what I have already said, that I was just the person, above all others, who could not undertake it. There are no friends like old friends; but of those old friends, few could help me, few could understand me, many were annoyed with me, some were angry, because I was breaking up a compact party, and some, as a matter of conscience, could not listen to me. When I looked round for those whom I might consult in my difficulties, I found the very hypothesis of those difficulties acting as a bar to their giving me their advice. Then I said, bitterly, "You are throwing me on others, whether I will or no." Yet still I had good and true friends around me of the old sort, in and out of Oxford too, who were a great help to me. But on the other hand, though I neither was so fond (with a few exceptions) of the persons, nor of the methods of thought, which belonged to this new school, as of the old set, though I could not trust in their firmness of purpose, for, like a swarm of flies, they might come and go, and at length be divided and dissipated, yet I had an intense sympathy in their object and in the direction in which their path lay, in spite of my old friends, in spite of my old lifelong prejudices. In spite of my ingrained fears of Rome, and the decision of my reason and conscience against her usages, in spite of my affection for Oxford and Oriel, yet I had a secret longing love of Rome the Mother of English Christianity, and I had a true devotion to the Blessed Virgin, in whose College I lived, whose Altar I served, and whose Immaculate Purity I had in one of my earliest printed Sermons made much of. And it was the consciousness of this bias in myself, if it is so to be called, which made me preach so earnestly against the danger of being swayed in religious inquiry by our sympathy rather than by our reason. And moreover, the members of this new school looked up to me, as I have said, and did me true kindnesses, and really loved me, and stood by me in trouble, when others went away, and for all this I was grateful; nay, many of them were in trouble themselves, and in the same boat with me, and that was a further cause of sympathy between us; and hence it was, when the new school came on in force, and into collision with the old, I had not the heart, any more than the power, to repel them; I was in great perplexity, and hardly knew where I stood; I took their part; and, when I wanted to be in peace and silence, I had to speak out, and I incurred the charge of weakness from some men, and of mysteriousness, shuffling, and underhand dealing from the majority.

Now I will say here frankly, that this sort of charge is a matter which I cannot properly meet, because I cannot duly realize it. I have never had any suspicion of my own honesty; and, when men say that I was dishonest, I cannot grasp the accusation as a distinct conception, such as it is possible to encounter. If a man said to me, "On such a day and before such persons you said a thing was white, when it was black," I understand what is meant well enough, and I can set myself to prove an *alibi* or to explain the mistake; or if a man said to me, "You tried to gain me over to your party, intending to take me with you to Rome, but you did not succeed," I can give him the lie, and lay down an assertion of my own as firm and as exact as his, that not from the time that I was first unsettled, did I ever attempt to gain any one over to myself or to my Romanizing opinions, and that it is only his own coxcombical fancy which has bred such a thought in him: but my imagination is at a loss in presence of those vague charges, which have commonly been brought against me, charges, which are made up of impressions, and understandings, and inferences, and hearsay, and surmises. Accordingly, I shall not make the attempt, for, in doing so, I should be dealing blows in the air; what I shall attempt is to state what I know of myself and what I recollect, and leave to others its application.

While I had confidence in the *Via Media*, and thought that nothing could overset it, I did not mind laying down large principles, which I saw would go further than was commonly perceived. I considered that to make the *Via Media* concrete and substantive, it must be much more than it was in outline; that the Anglican Church must have a ceremonial, a ritual, and a fullness of doctrine and devotion, which it had not at present, if it were to compete with the Roman Church with any prospect of success. Such additions would not remove it from its proper basis, but would merely strengthen and beautify it: such, for instance, would be confraternities, particular devotions, reverence for the Blessed Virgin, prayers for the dead, beautiful churches, munificent offerings to them and in them, monastic houses, and many other observances and institutions, which I used to say belonged to us as much as to Rome, though Rome had appropriated them and boasted of them, by reason of our having let them slip from us. The principle, on which all this turned, is brought out in one of the Letters I published on occasion of Tract 90. "The age is moving," I said, "towards something; and most unhappily the one religious communion among us, which has of late years been practically in possession of this something, is the Church of Rome. She alone, amid all the errors and evils of her practical system, has given free scope to the feelings of awe, mystery, tenderness, reverence, devotedness, and other feelings which may be especially called Catholic. The question then is, whether we shall give them up to the Roman Church or claim them for ourselves. . . . But if we do give them up, we must give up the men who cherish them. We must consent either to give up the men, or to admit their principles." With these feelings I frankly admit, that, while I was working simply for the sake of the Anglican Church, I did not at all mind, though I found myself laying down principles in its defense, which went beyond that particular kind of defense which high-and-dry men thought perfection, and even though I ended in framing a kind of defense, which they might call a revolution, while I thought it a restoration. Thus, for illustration, I might discourse upon the "Communion of Saints" in such a manner (though I do not recollect doing so,) as might lead the way towards devotion to the Blessed Virgin and the Saints on the one hand, and towards prayers for the dead on the other. In a memorandum of the year 1844 or 1845, I thus speak on this subject: "If the Church be not defended on establishment grounds, it must be upon principles, which go far beyond their immediate object. Sometimes I saw these further results, sometimes not. Though I saw them, I sometimes did not say that I saw them: —so long as I thought they were inconsistent, *not* with our Church, but only with the existing opinions, I was not unwilling to insinuate truths into our Church, which I thought had a right to be there."

To so much I confess; but I do not confess, I simply deny that I ever said anything which secretly bore against the Church of England, knowing it myself, in order that others might unwarily accept it. It was indeed one of my great difficulties and causes of reserve, as time went on that I at length recognized in principles which I had honestly preached as if Anglican, conclusions favorable to the cause of Rome. Of course I did not like to confess this; and, when interrogated, was in consequence in perplexity. The prime instance of this was the appeal to Antiquity; St. Leo had overset, in my own judgment, its force as the special argument for Anglicanism; yet I was committed to Antiquity, together with the whole Anglican school; what then was I to say, when acute minds urged this or that application of it against the *Via Media?* it was impossible that, in such circumstances, any answer could be given which was not unsatisfactory, or any behavior adopted which was not mysterious. Again, sometimes in what I wrote I went just as far as I saw, and could as little say more, as I could see what is below the horizon; and therefore, when asked as to the consequences of what I had said, I had no answer to give. Again, sometimes when I was asked, whether certain conclusions did not follow from a certain principle, I might not be able to tell at the moment, especially if the matter were complicated; and for this reason, if for no other, because there is great difference between a conclusion in the abstract and a conclusion in the concrete, and because a conclusion may be modified in fact by a conclusion from some opposite principle. Or it might so happen that my head got simply confused, by the very strength of the logic which was administered to me, and thus I gave my sanction to conclusions which really were not mine; and when the report of those conclusions came round to me through others, I had to unsay them. And then again, perhaps I did not like to see men scared or scandalized by unfeeling logical inferences, which would not have troubled them to the day of their death, had they not been forced to recognize them. And then I felt altogether the force of the maxim of St. Ambrose, "Non in dialecticâ complacuit Deo salvum facere populum suum;"—I had a great dislike of paper logic. For myself, it was not logic that carried me on; as well might one say that the quicksilver in the barometer changes the weather. It is the concrete being that reasons; pass a number of years, and I find my mind in a new place; how? the whole man moves; paper logic is but the record of it. All the logic in the world would not have made me move faster towards Rome than I did; as well might you say that I have arrived at the end of my journey, because I see the village church before me, as venture to assert that the miles, over which my soul had to pass before it got to Rome, could be annihilated, even though I had been in possession of some far clearer view than I then had, that Rome was my ultimate destination. Great acts take time. At least this is what I felt in my own case; and therefore to come to me with methods of logic had in it the nature of a provocation, and, though I do not think I ever showed it, made me somewhat indifferent how I met them, and perhaps led me, as a means of relieving my impatience, to be mysterious or irrelevant, or to give in because I could not meet them to my satisfaction. And a greater trouble still than these logical mazes, was the introduction of logic into every subject whatever, so far, that is, as this was done. Before I was at Oriel, I recollect an acquaintance saying to me that "the Oriel Common Room stank of Logic." One is not at all pleased when poetry, or eloquence, or devotion, is considered as if chiefly intended to feed syllogisms. Now, in saying all this, I am saying nothing against the deep piety and earnestness which were characteristics of this second phase of the Movement, in which I had taken so prominent a part. What I have been observing is, that this phase had a tendency to bewilder and to upset me; and, that, instead of saying so, as I ought to have done, perhaps from a sort of laziness I gave answers at random, which have led to my appearing close or inconsistent.

There was another source of the perplexity with which at this time I was encompassed, and of the reserve and mysteriousness, of which that perplexity gained for me the credit. After Tract 90 the Protestant world would not let me alone; they pursued me in the public journals to Littlemore. Reports of all kinds were circulated about me. "Imprimis, why did I go up to Littlemore at all?. For no good purpose certainly; I dared not tell why." Why, to be sure, it was hard that I should be obliged to say to the Editors of newspapers that I went up there to say my prayers; it was hard to have to tell the world in confidence, that I had a certain doubt about the Anglican system, and could not at that moment resolve it, or say what would come of it; it was hard to have to confess that I had thought of giving up my Living a year or two before, and that this was a first step to it. It was hard to have to plead, that, for what I knew, my doubts would vanish, if the newspapers would be so good as to give me time and let me alone. Who would ever dream of making the world his confidant? yet I was considered insidious, sly, dishonest, if I would not open my heart to the tender mercies of the world. But they persisted: "What was I doing at Littlemore?" Doing there! have I not retreated from you? have I not given up my position and my place? am I alone, of Englishmen, not to have the privilege to go where I will, no questions asked? am I alone to be followed about by jealous prying eyes, which take note whether I go in at a back door or at the front, and who the men are who happen to call on me in the afternoon? Cowards! if I advanced one step, you would run away; it is not you that I fear: "Di me terrent, et Jupiter hostis." It is because the Bishops still go on charging against me, though I have quite given up: it is that secret misgiving of heart which tells me that they do well, for I have neither lot nor part with them: this it is which weighs me down. I cannot walk into or out of my house, but curious eyes are upon me. Why will you not let me die in peace? Wounded brutes creep into some hole to die in, and no one grudges it them. Let me alone, I shall not trouble you long. This was the keen feeling which pierced me, and, I think, these are the very words in which I expressed it to myself. I asked, in the words of a great motto, "Ubi lapsus? quid feci?" One day when I entered my house, I found a flight of Under-graduates inside. Heads of Houses, as mounted patrols, walked their horses round those poor cottages. Doctors of Divinity dived into the hidden recesses of that private tenement uninvited, and drew domestic conclusions from what they saw there. I had thought that an Englishman's house was his castle; but the newspapers thought otherwise, and at last the matter came before my good Bishop. I insert his letter, and a portion of my reply to him:—

"April 12, 1842. So many of the charges against yourself

and your friends which I have seen in the public journals have been, within my own knowledge, false and calumnious, that I am not apt to pay much attention to what is asserted with respect to you in the newspapers.

"In" [a newspaper] "however, of April 9, there appears a paragraph in which it is asserted, as a matter of notoriety, that a 'so-called Anglo-Catholic Monastery is in process of erection at Littlemore, and that the cells of dormitories, the chapel, the refectory, the cloisters all may be seen advancing to perfection, under the eye of a Parish Priest of the Diocese of Oxford.'

"Now, as I have understood that you really are possessed of some tenements at Littlemore,—as it is generally believed that they are destined for the purposes of study and devotion,—and as much suspicion and jealousy are felt about the matter, I am anxious to afford you an opportunity of making me an explanation on the subject.

"I know you too well not to be aware that you are the last man living to attempt in my Diocese a revival of the Monastic orders (in anything approaching to the Romanist sense of the term) without previous communication with me, —or indeed that you should take upon yourself to originate any measure of importance without authority from the heads of the Church,—and therefore I at once exonerate you from the accusation brought against you by the newspaper I have quoted, but I feel it nevertheless a duty to my Diocese and myself, as well as to you, to ask you to put it in my power to contradict what, if uncontradicted, would appear to imply a glaring invasion of all ecclesiastical discipline on *your* part, or of inexcusable neglect and indifference to my duties on *mine*."

I wrote in answer as follows:—

"April 14, 1842. I am very much obliged by your Lordship's kindness in allowing me to write to you on the subject of my house at Littlemore; at the same time I feel it hard both on your Lordship and myself that the restlessness of the public mind should oblige you to require an explanation of me.

"It is now a whole year that I have been the subject of incessant misrepresentation. A year since I submitted entirely to your Lordship's authority; and, with the intention of following out the particular act enjoined upon me, I not only stopped the series of Tracts, on which I was engaged, but withdrew from all public discussion of Church matters of the day, or what may be called ecclesiastical politics. I turned myself at once to the preparation for the Press of the translations of St. Athanasius to which I had long wished to devote myself, and I intended and intend to employ myself in the like theological studies, and in the concerns of my own parish and in practical works.

"With the same view of personal improvement I was led more seriously to a design which had been long on my mind. For many years, at least thirteen, I have wished to give myself to a life of greater religious regularity than I have hitherto led; but it is very unpleasant to confess such a wish even to my Bishop, because it seems arrogant, and because it is committing me to a profession which may come to nothing. For what have I done that I am to be called to account by the world for my private actions, in a way in which no one else is called? Why may I not have that liberty which all others are allowed? I am often accused of being underhand and uncandid in respect to the intentions to which I have been alluding: but no one likes his own good resolutions noised about, both from mere common delicacy and from fear lest he should not be able to fulfill them. I feel it very cruel, though the parties in fault do not know what they are doing, that very sacred matters between me and my conscience are made a matter of public talk. May I take a case parallel though different? suppose a person in prospect of marriage; would he like the subject discussed in newspapers, and parties, circumstances, &c., &c., publicly demanded of him, at the penalty of being accused of craft and duplicity?

"The resolution I speak of has been taken with reference to myself alone, and has been contemplated quite independent of the coöperation of any other human being, and without reference to success or failure other than personal, and without regard to the blame or approbation of man. And being a resolution of years, and one to which I feel God has called me, and in which I am violating no rule of the Church any more than if I married, I should have to answer for it, if I did not pursue it, as a good Providence made openings for it. In pursuing it then I am thinking of myself alone, not aiming at any ecclesiastical or external effeets. At the same time of course it would be a great comfort to me to know that God had put it into the hearts of others to pursue their personal edification in the same way, and unnatural not to wish to have the benefit of their presence and encouragement, or not to think it a great infringement on the rights of conscience if such personal and private resolutions were interfered with. Your Lordship will allow me to add my firm conviction that such religious resolutions are most necessary for keeping a certain class of minds firm in their allegiance to our Church; but still I can as truly say that my own reason for anything I have done has been a personal one, without which I should not have entered upon it, and which I hope to pursue whether with or without the sympathies of others pursuing a similar course. . . .

"As to my intentions, I purpose to live there myself a good deal, as I have a resident curate in Oxford. In doing this, I believe I am consulting for the good of my parish, as my population at Littlemore is at least equal to that of St. Mary's in Oxford, and the *whole* of Littlemore is double of it. It has been very much neglected; and in providing a parsonage-house at Littlemore, as this will be, and will be called, I conceive I am doing a very great benefit to my people. At the 'same time it has appeared to me that a partial or temporary retirement from St. Mary's Church might be expedient under the prevailing excitement.

"As to the quotation from the [newspaper], which I have not seen, your Lordship will perceive from what I have said, that no 'monastery is in process of erection'; there is no 'chapel'; no 'refectory,' hardly a dining-room or parlor. The 'cloisters' are my shed connecting the cottages. I do not understand what 'cells of dormitories' means. Of course I can repeat your Lordship's words that 'I am not attempting a revival of the Monastic Orders, in anything approaching to the Romanist sense of the term,' or 'taking on myself to originate any measure of importance without authority from the Heads of the Church.' I am attempting nothing ecclesiastical, but something personal and private, and which can only be made public, not private, by newspapers and letter-writers, in which sense the most sacred and conscientious resolves and acts may certainly be made the objects of an unmannerly and unfeeling curiosity.''

One calumny there was which the Bishop did not believe, and of which of course he had no idea of speaking. It was that I was actually in the service of the enemy. I had forsooth been already received into the Catholic Church, and was rearing at Littlemore a nest of Papists, who, like me, were to take the Anglican oaths which they disbelieved, by virtue of a dispensation from Rome, and thus in due time were to bring over to that unprincipled Church great numbers of the Anglican Clergy and Laity. Bishops gave their countenance to this imputation against me. The case was simply this:—as I made Littlemore a place of retirement for myself, so did I offer it to others. There were young men in Oxford, whose testimonials for Orders had been refused by their Colleges; there were young clergymen, who had found themselves unable from conscience to go on with their duties, and had thrown up their parochial engagements. Such men were already going straight to Rome, and I interposed; I interposed for the reasons I have given in the beginning of this portion of my narrative. I interposed from fidelity to my clerical engagements, and from duty to my Bishop; and from the interests which I was bound to take in them, and from belief that they were premature or excited. Their friends besought me to quiet them, if I could. Some of them came to live with me at Littlemore. They were laymen, or in the place of laymen. I kept some of them back for several years from being received into the Catholic Church. Even when I had given up my living, I was still bound by my duty to their parents or friends, and I did not forget still to do what I could for them. The immediate occasion of my resigning St. Mary's, was the unexpected conversion of one of them. After that, I felt it was impossible to keep my post there, for I had been unable to keep my word with my Bishop.

Such fidelity, however, was taken *in malam partem* by the high Anglican authorities; they thought it insidious. I happen still to have a correspondence which took place in 1843, in which the chief place is filled by one of the most eminent Bishops of the day, a theologian and reader of the Fathers, a moderate man, who at one time was talked of as likely on a vacancy to succeed to the Primacy.   A young clergyman in his diocese became a Catholic; the papers at once reported on authority from "a very high quarter," that, after his reception, "the Oxford men had been recommending him to retain his living."   I had reasons for thinking that the allusion was made to me, and I authorized the Editor of a Paper, who had inquired of me on the point, to "give it, as far as I was concerned, an unqualified contradiction";— when from a motive of delicacy he hesitated, I added "my direct and indignant contradiction."   "Whoever is the author of it," I continued to the Editor, "no correspondence or intercourse of any kind, direct or indirect, has passed between Mr. S. and myself, since his conforming to the Church of Rome, except my formally and merely acknowledging the receipt of his letter, in which he informed me of the fact, without, as far as I recollect, my expressing any opinion upon it.   You may state this as broadly as I have set it down." My denial was told to the Bishop; what took place upon it is given in a letter from which I copy.   "My father showed the letter to the Bishop, who, as he laid it down, said, 'Ah, those Oxford men are not ingenuous.'   'How do you mean?' asked my father.   'Why,' said the Bishop, 'they advised Mr. B. S. to retain his living after he turned Catholic.   I know that to be a fact, because A. B. told me so.' "   "The Bishop," continues the letter, "who is perhaps the most influential man on the bench, believes it to be the truth."

Upon this Dr. Pusey wrote the Bishop in my behalf; and the Bishop instantly beat a retreat.   "I have the honor," he says in the autograph which I transcribe, "to acknowledge the receipt of your note, and to say in reply that it has not been stated by me, (though such a statement has, I believe, appeared in some of the Public Prints), that Mr. Newman had advised Mr. B. S. to retain his living, after he had forsaken our Church.   But it has been stated to me, that Mr. Newman was in close correspondence with Mr. B. S., and, being fully aware of his state of opinions and feelings, yet ad-

vised him to continue in our communion. Allow me to add,"
he says to Dr. Pusey, "that neither your name, nor that of
Mr. Keble, was mentioned to me in connection with that of
Mr. B. S."

I was not going to let the Bishop off on this evasion, so
I wrote to him myself. After quoting his Letter to Dr. Pusey,
I continued, "I beg to trouble your Lordship with my own
account of the two allegations" [*close correspondence* and
fully aware, &c.] "which are contained in your statement,
and which have led to your speaking of me in terms which
I hope never to deserve. 1. Since Mr. B. S. has been in
your Lordship's diocese, I have seen him in Common rooms
or private parties in Oxford two or three times, when I
never (as far as I can recollect) had any conversation with
him. During the same time I have, to the best of my memory,
written to him three letters. One was lately, in acknowledgment of his informing me of his change of religion. Another
was last summer, when I asked him (to no purpose) to come
and stay with me in this place. The earliest of the three
letters was written just a year since, as far as I recollect, and
it certainly was on the subject of his joining the Church of
Rome. I wrote this letter at the earnest wish of a friend
of his. I cannot be sure that, on his replying, I did not send
him a brief note in explanation of points in my letter which
he had misapprehended. I cannot recollect any other correspondence between us.

"2. As to my knowledge of his opinions and feelings, as
far as I remember, the only point of perplexity which I knew,
the only point which to this hour I know, as pressing upon
him, was that of the Pope's supremacy. He professed to be
searching Antiquity whether the See of Rome had formerly
that relation to the whole Church which Roman Catholics
now assign to it. My letter was directed to the point, that it
was his duty not to perplex himself with arguments on [such]
a question, . . . and to put it altogether aside. . . . It is
hard that I am put upon my memory, without knowing the
details of the statement made against me, considering the
various correspondence in which I am from time to time un-
avoidably engaged. . . . Be assured, my Lord, that there are
very definite limits, beyond which persons like me would

never urge another to retain preferment in the English Church, nor would retain it themselves; and that the censure which has been directed against them by so many of its Rulers has a very grave bearing upon those limits." The Bishop replied in a civil letter, and sent my own letter to his original informant, who wrote to me the letter of a gentleman. It seems that an anxious lady had said something or other which had been misinterpreted, against her real meaning, into the calumny which was circulated, and so the report vanished into thin air. I closed the correspondence with the following Letter to the Bishop:—

"I hope your Lordship will believe me when I say, that statements about me, equally incorrect with that which has come to your Lordship's ears, are from time to time reported to me as credited and repeated by the highest authorities in our Church, though it is very seldom that I have the opportunity of denying them. I am obliged by your Lordship's letter to Dr. Pusey as giving me such an opportunity.". Then I added, with a purpose, "Your Lordship will observe that in my Letter I had no occasion to proceed to the question, whether a person holding Roman Catholic opinions can in honesty remain in our Church. Lest then any misconception should arise from my silence, I here take the liberty of adding, that I see nothing wrong in such a person's continuing in communion with us, provided he holds no preferment or office, abstains from the management of ecclesiastical matters, and is bound by no subscription or oath to our doctrines.'"

This was written on March 8, 1843, and was in anticipation of my own retirement into lay communion. This again leads me to a remark:—for two years I was in lay communion, not indeed being a Catholic in my convictions, but in a state of serious doubt, and with the probable prospect of becoming some day, what as yet I was not. Under these circumstances I thought the best thing I could do was to give up duty and to throw myself into lay communion, remaining an Anglican. I could not go to Rome, while I thought what I did of the devotions she sanctioned to the Blessed Virgin and the Saints. I did not give up my fellowship, for I could not be sure that my doubts would not be reduced or overcome, however unlikely I might consider such an event. But I gave up my living; and, for two years before my conversion, I took no clerical duty. My last Sermon was in September 1843; then I remained at Littlemore in quiet for two years. But it was made a subject of reproach to me at the time, and is at this day, that I did not leave the Anglican Church sooner. To me this seems a wonderful charge; why, even had I been quite sure that Rome was the true Church, the Anglican Bishops would have had no just subject of complaint against me, provided I took no Anglican oath, no clerical duty, no ecclesiastical administration. Do they force all men who go to their Churches to believe in the 39 Articles, or to join in the Athanasian Creed? However, I was to have other measure dealt to me; great authorities ruled it so; and a great controversialist, Mr. Stanley Faber, thought it a shame that I did not leave the Church of England as much as ten years sooner than I did. He said this in print between the years 1847 and 1849. His nephew, an Anglican clergyman, kindly wished to undeceive him on this point. So, in the latter year, after some correspondence, I wrote the following letter, which will be of service to this narrative, from its chronological notes:—

"Dec. 6, 1849. Your uncle says, 'If he (Mr. N.) will declare, *sans phrase*, as the French say, that I have labored under an entire mistake, and that he was not a concealed Romanist during the ten years in question,' (I suppose, the last ten years of my membership with the Anglican Church,) 'or during any part of the time, my controversial antipathy will be at an end, and I will readily express to him that I am truly sorry that I have made such a mistake.'

"So candid an avowal is what I should have expected from a mind like your uncle's. I am extremely glad he has brought it to this issue.

"By a 'concealed Romanist' I understand him to mean one, who, professing to belong to the Church of England, in his heart and will intends to benefit the Church of Rome, at the expense of the Church of England. He cannot mean by the expression merely a person who in fact is benefiting the Church of Rome, while he is intending to benefit the Church of England, for that is no discredit to him morally, and he (your uncle) evidently means to impute blame.

"In the sense in which I have explained the words, I can simply and honestly say that I was not a concealed Romanist during the whole, or any part of, the years in question.

"For the first four years of the ten, (up to Michaelmas, 1839,) I honestly wished to benefit the Church of England, at the expense of the Church of Rome:

"For the second four years I wished to benefit the Church of England without prejudice to the Church of Rome:

"At the beginning of the ninth year (Michaelmas, 1843) I began to despair of the Church of England, and gave up all clerical duty; and then, what I wrote and did was influenced by a mere wish not to injure it, and not by the wish to benefit it:

"At the beginning of the tenth year I distinctly contemplated leaving it, but I also distinctly told my friends that it was in my contemplation.

"Lastly, during the last half of that tenth year I was engaged in writing a book (*Essay on Development*) in favor of the Roman Church, and indirectly against the English; but even then, till it was finished, I had not absolutely intended to publish it, wishing to reserve to myself the chance of changing my mind when the argumentative views which were actuating me had been distinctly brought out before me in writing.

"I wish this statement, which I make from memory, and without consulting any document, severely tested by my writings and doings, as I am confident it will, on the whole, be borne out, whatever real or apparent exceptions (I suspect none) have to be allowed by me in detail.

"Your uncle is at liberty to make what use he pleases of this explanation."

I have now reached an important date in my narrative, the year 1843.

In 1843, I took two very significant steps:—1. In February, I made a formal Retractation of all the hard things which I had said against the Church of Rome. 2. In September, I resigned the Living of St. Mary's, Littlemore included:—I will speak of these two acts separately.

1. The words, in which I made my Retractation, have given rise to much criticism. After quoting a number of passages

from my writings against the Church of Rome, which I withdrew, I ended thus:—"If you ask me how an individual could venture, not simply to hold, but to publish such views of a communion so ancient, so wide-spreading, so fruitful in Saints, I answer that I said to myself, 'I am not speaking my own words, I am but following almost a *consensus* of the divines of my own Church. They have ever used the strongest language against Rome, even the most able and learned of them. I wish to throw myself into their system. While I say what they say, I am safe. Such views, too, are necessary for our position.' Yet I have reason to fear still, that such language is to be ascribed, in no small measure, to an impetuous temper, a hope of approving myself to persons I respect, and a wish to repel the charge of Romanism."

These words have been, and are, again and again cited against me, as if a confession that, when in the Anglican Church, I said things against Rome which I did not really believe.

For myself, I cannot understand how any impartial man can so take them; and I have explained them in print several times. I trust that by this time their plain meaning has been satisfactorily brought out by what I have said in former portions of this Narrative; still I have a word or two to say in addition to my former remarks upon them.

In the passage in question I apologize for *saying out* in controversy charges against the Church of Rome, which withal I affirm that I fully *believed* at the time when I made them. What is wonderful in such an apology? There are surely many things a man may hold, which at the same time he may feel that he has no right to say publicly, and which it may annoy him that he has said publicly. The law recognizes this principle. In our own time, men have been imprisoned and fined for saying true things of a bad king. The maxim has been held, that, "The greater the truth, the greater is the libel." And so as to the judgment of society, a just indignation would be felt against a writer who brought forward wantonly the weaknesses of a great man, though the whole world knew that they existed. No one is at liberty to speak ill of another without a justifiable reason, even though he knows he is speaking truth, and the public knows it too.

Therefore, though I believed what I said against the Roman Church, nevertheless I could not religiously speak it out, unless I was really justified, not only in believing ill, but in speaking ill. I did believe what I said on what I thought to be good reasons; but had I also a just cause for saying out what I believed? I thought I had, and it was this, viz. that to say out what I believed was simply necessary in the controversy for self-defense. It was impossible to let it alone: the Anglican position could not be satisfactorily maintained, without assailing the Roman. In this, as in most cases of conflict, one party was right or the other, not both; and the best defense was to attack. Is not this almost a truism in the Roman controversy? Is it not what every one says, who speaks on the subject at all? does any serious man abuse the Church of Rome, for the sake of abusing her, or because that abuse justifies his own religious position? What is the meaning of the very word "Protestantism," but that there is a call to speak out? This then is what I said; "I know I spoke strongly against the Church of Rome; but it was no mere abuse, for I had a serious reason for doing so."

But, not only did I think such language necessary for my Church's religious position, but I recollected that all the great Anglican divines had thought so before me. They had thought so, and they had acted accordingly. And therefore I observe in the passage in question, with much propriety, that I had not used strong language simply out of my own head, but that in doing so I was following the track, or rather reproducing the teaching, of those who had preceded me.

I was pleading guilty to using violent language, but I was pleading also that there were extenuating circumstances in the case. We all know the story of the convict, who on the scaffold bit off his mother's ear. By doing so he did not deny the fact of his own crime, for which he was to hang; but he said that his mother's indulgence when he was a boy, had a good deal to do with it. In like manner I had made a charge, and I had made it *ex animo;* but I accused others of having, by their own example, led me into believing it and publishing it.

I was in a humor, certainly, to bite off their ears. I will freely confess, indeed I said it some pages back, that I was angry with the Anglican divines. I thought they had taken me in; I had read the Fathers with their eyes; I had sometimes trusted their quotations or their reasonings; and from reliance on them, I had used words or made statements, which by right I ought rigidly to have examined myself. I had thought myself safe, while I had their warrant for what I said. I had exercised more faith than criticism in the matter. This did not imply any broad misstatements on my part, arising from reliance on their authority, but it implied carelessness in matters of detail. And this of course was a fault.

But there was a far deeper reason for my saying what I said in this matter, on which I have not hitherto touched; and it was this:—The most oppressive thought, in the whole process of my change of opinion, was the clear anticipation, verified by the event, that it would issue in the triumph of Liberalism. Against the Anti-dogmatic principle I had thrown my whole mind; yet now I was doing more than any one else could do, to promote it. I was one of those who had kept it at bay in Oxford for so many years; and thus my very retirement was its triumph. The men who had driven me from Oxford were distinctly the Liberals; it was they who had opened the attack upon Tract 90, and it was they who would gain a second benefit, if I went on to abandon the Anglican Church. But this was not all. As I have already said, there are but two alternatives, the way to Rome, and the way to Atheism: Anglicanism is the halfway house on the one side, and Liberalism is the halfway house on the other. How many men were there, as I knew full well, who would not follow me now in my advance from Anglicanism to Rome, but would at once leave Anglicanism and me for the Liberal camp. It is not at all easy (humanly speaking) to wind up an Englishman to a dogmatic level. I had done so in good measure, in the case both of young men and of laymen, the Anglican *Via Media* being the representative of dogma. The dogmatic and the Anglican principle were one, as I had taught them; but I was breaking the *Via Media* to pieces, and would not dogmatic faith altogether be broken up, in the minds of a great number, by the demolition of the *Via Media?* Oh! how unhappy this made me! I heard once from an eye-witness the account of a poor sailor whose legs were shattered by a ball, in .the action off Algiers in 1816, and who was taken below for an operation. The surgeon and the chaplain persuaded him to have a leg off; it was done and. the tourniquet applied to the wound. Then, they broke it to him that he must have the other off too. The poor fellow said, "You should have told me that, gentlemen," and deliberately unscrewed the instrument and bled to death. Would not that be the case with many friends of my own? How could I ever hope to make them believe in a second theology, when I had cheated them in the first? with what face could I publish a new edition of a dogmatic creed, and ask them to receive it as gospel? Would it not be plain to them that no certainty was to be found anywhere? Well, in my defense I could but make a lame apology; however, it was the true one, viz. that I had not read the Fathers cautiously enough; that in such nice points, as those which determine the angle of divergence between the two Churches, I had made considerable miscalculations. But how came this about? why, the fact was, unpleasant as it was to avow, that I had leaned too much upon the assertions of Ussher, Jeremy Taylor, or Barrow, and had been deceived by them. Valeat quantum,—it was all that *could* be said. This then was a chief reason of that wording of the Retractation, which has given so much offense, because the bitterness, with which it was written, was not understood;—and the following letter will illustrate it:—

"April 3, 1844. I wish to remark on William's chief distress, that my changing my opinion seemed to unsettle one's confidence in truth and falsehood as external things, and led one to be suspicious of the new opinion as one became distrustful of the old. Now in what I shall say, I am not going to speak in favor of my second thoughts in comparison of my first, but against such skepticism and unsettlement about truth and falsehood generally, the idea of which is very painful.

"The case with me, then, was this, and not surely an unnatural one:—as a matter of feeling and of duty I threw myself into the system which I found myself in. I saw that the English Church had a theological idea or theory as such, and I took it up. I read Laud on Tradition, and thought it (as I still think it) very masterly. The Anglican Theory was

very distinctive. I admired it and took it on faith. It did
not (I think) occur to me to doubt it; I saw that it was able,
and supported by learning, and I felt it was a duty to maintain it. Further, on looking into Antiquity and reading the
Fathers, I saw such portions of it as I examined, fully confirmed (e.g. the supremacy of Scripture). There was only
one question about which I had a doubt, viz. whether it
would *work,* for it has never been more than a paper system. . . .

"So far from my change of opinion having any fair tendency to unsettle persons as to truth and falsehood viewed as
objective realities, it should be considered whether such
change is not *necessary,* if truth be a real objective thing, and
be made to confront a person who has been brought up in a
system *short of* truth. Surely the *continuance* of a person,
who wishes to go right, in a wrong system, and not his *giving
it up,* would be that which militated against the objectiveness
of Truth, leading, as it would, to the suspicion, that one thing
and another were equally pleasing to our Maker, where men
were sincere.

"Nor surely is it a thing I need be sorry for, that I defended the system in which I found myself, and thus have had
to unsay my words. For is it not one's duty, instead of beginning with criticism, to throw oneself generously into that
form of religion which is providentially put before one?
Is it right, or is it wrong, to begin with private judgment?
May we not, on the other hand, look for a blessing *through*
obedience even to an erroneous system, and a guidance even
by means of it out of it? Were those who were strict and
conscientious in their Judaism, or those who were lukewarm
and skeptical, more likely to be led into Christianity, when
Christ came? Yet in proportion to their previous zeal, would
be their appearance of inconsistency. Certainly, I have always contended that obedience even to an erring conscience
was the way to gain light, and that it mattered not where a
man began, so that he began on what came to hand, and in
faith; and that anything might become a divine method of
Truth; that to the pure all things are pure, and have a self-
correcting virtue and a power of germinating. And though I
have no right at all to assume that this mercy is granted to

me, yet the fact, that a person in my situation *may* have it granted to him, seems to me to remove the perplexity which my change of opinion may occasion.

"It may be said,—I have said it to myself,—'Why, however, did you *publish?* had you waited quietly, you would have changed your opinion without any of the misery, which now is involved in the change, of disappointing and distressing people.' I answer, that things are so bound up together, as to form a whole, and one cannot tell what is or is not a condition of what. I do not see how possibly I could have published the Tracts, or other works professing to defend our Church, without accompanying them with a strong protest or argument against Rome. The one obvious objection against the whole Anglican line is, that it is Roman; so that I really think there was no alternative between silence altogether, and forming a theory and attacking the Roman system."

2. And now, in the next place, as to my Resignation of St. Mary's, which was the second of the steps which I took in 1843. The ostensible, direct, and sufficient reason for my doing so was the persevering attack of the Bishops on Tract 90. I alluded to it in the letter which I have inserted above, addressed to one of the most influential among them. A series of their *ex cathedra* judgments, lasting through three years, and including a notice of no little severity in a Charge of my own Bishop, came as near to a condemnation of my Tract, and, so far, to a repudiation of the ancient Catholic doctrine, which was the scope of the Tract, as was possible in the Church of England. It was in order to shield the Tract from such a condemnation, that I had at the time of its publication in 1841 so simply put myself at the disposal of the higher powers in London. At that time, all that was distinctly contemplated in the way of censure, was contained in the message which my Bishop sent me, that the Tract was "objectionable." That I thought was the end of the matter. I had refused to suppress it, and they had yielded that point. Since I published the former portions of this Narrative, I have found what I wrote to Dr. Pusey on March 24, while the matter was in progress. "The more I think of it," I said, "the more reluctant I am to suppress Tract 90, though *of*

course I will do it if the Bishop wishes it; I cannot, however, deny that I shall feel it a severe act.'' According to the notes which I took of the letters or messages which I sent to him on that and the following days, I wrote successively, ''My first feeling was to obey without a word; I will obey still; but my judgment has steadily risen against it ever since.'' Then in the Postscript, ''If I have done any good to the Church, I do ask the Bishop this favor, as my reward for it, that he would not insist on a measure, from which I think good will not come. However, I will submit to him.'' Afterwards, I got stronger still and wrote: ''I have almost come to the resolution, if the Bishop publicly intimates that I must suppress the Tract, or speaks strongly in his charge against it, to suppress it indeed, but to resign my living also. I could not in conscience act otherwise. You may show this in any quarter you please.''

All my then hopes, all my satisfaction at the apparent fulfillment of those hopes was at an end in 1843. It is not wonderful then, that in May of that year, when two out of the three years were gone, I wrote on the subject of my retiring from St. Mary's to the same friend, whom I had consulted upon it in 1840. But I did more now; I told him my great unsettlement of mind on the question of the Churches. I will insert portions of two of my letters:—

''May 4, 1843. . . . At present I fear, as far as I can analyze my own convictions, I consider the Roman Catholic Communion to be the Church of the Apostles, and that what grace is among us (which, through God's mercy, is not little) is extraordinary, and from the overflowings of His dispensation. I am very far more sure that England is in schism, than that the Roman additions to the Primitive Creed may not be developments, arising out of a keen and vivid realizing of the Divine Depositum of Faith.

''You will now understand what gives edge to the Bishops' Charges, without any undue sensitiveness on my part. They distress me in two ways:—first, as being in some sense protests and witnesses to my conscience against my own unfaithfulness to the English Church, and next, as being samples of her teaching, and tokens how very far she is from even aspiring to Catholicity.

"Of course my being unfaithful to a trust is my great subject of dread,—as it has long been, as you know."

When he wrote to make natural objections to my purpose, such as the apprehension that the removal of clerical obligations might have the indirect effect of propelling me towards Rome, I answered:—

"May 18, 1843. . . . My office or charge at St. Mary's is not a mere *state*, but a continual *energy*. People assume and assert certain things of me in consequence. With what sort of sincerity can I obey the Bishop? how am I to act in the frequent cases, in which one way or another the Church of Rome comes into consideration? I have to the utmost of my power tried to keep persons from Rome, and with some success; but even a year and a half since, my arguments, though more efficacious with the persons I aimed at than any others could be, were of a nature to infuse great suspicion of me into the minds of lookers-on.

"By retaining St. Mary's, I am an offense and a stumbling-block. Persons are keen-sighted enough to make out what I think on certain points, and then they infer that such opinions are compatible with holding situations of trust in our Church. A number of younger men take the validity of their interpretation of the Articles, &c. from me on *faith*. Is not my present position a cruelty, as well as a treachery towards the Church?

"I do not see how I can either preach or publish again, while I hold St. Mary's;—but consider again the following difficulty in such a resolution, which I must state at some length.

"Last Long Vacation the idea suggested itself to me of publishing the Lives of the English Saints; and I had a conversation with [a publisher] upon it. I thought it would be useful, as employing the minds of men who were in danger of running wild, bringing them from doctrine to history, and from speculation to fact;—again, as giving them an interest in the English soil, and the English Church, and keeping them from seeking sympathy in Rome, as she is; and further, as tending to promote the spread of right views.

"But, within the last month, it has come upon me, that, if the scheme goes on, it will be a practical carrying out of No.

90, from the character of the usages and opinions of ante-reformation times.

"It is easy to say, 'Why *will* you do *any*thing? why won't you keep quiet? what business had you to think of any such plan at all?' But I cannot leave a number of poor fellows in the lurch. I am bound to do my best for a great number of people both in Oxford and elsewhere. If *I* did not act, others would find means to do so.

"Well, the plan has been taken up with great eagerness and interest. Many men are setting to work. I set down the names of men, most of them engaged, the rest half engaged and probable, some actually writing." About thirty names follow, some of them at that time of the school of Dr. Arnold, others of Dr. Pusey's, some my personal friends and of my own standing, others whom I hardly knew, while of course the majority were of the party of the new Movement. I continue:—

"The plan has gone so far, that it would create surprise and talk, were it now suddenly given over. Yet how is it compatible with my holding St. Mary's, being what I am?"

Such was the object and the origin of the projected Series of the English Saints; and, since the publication was connected, as has been seen, with my resignation of St. Mary's, I may be allowed to conclude what I have to say on the subject here, though it may read like a digression. As soon then as the first of the Series got into print, the whole project broke down. I had already anticipated that some portions of the Series would be written in a style inconsistent with the professions of a beneficed clergyman, and therefore I had given up my Living; but men of great weight went further in their misgivings than I, when they saw the *Life of St. Stephen Harding,* and decided that it was of a character inconsistent even with its proceeding from an Anglican publisher: and so the scheme was given up at once. After the two first numbers, I retired from the Editorship, and those Lives only were published in addition, which were then already finished, or in advanced preparation.

I resigned my living on September the 18th. I had not the means of doing it legally at Oxford. The late Mr. Goldsmid was kind enough to aid me in resigning it in London.

I found no fault with the Liberals; they had beaten me in a fair field. As to the act of the Bishops, I thought, to borrow a Scriptural image from Walter Scott, that they had "seethed the kid in his mother's milk."

I said to a friend:—

"Victrix causa diis placuit, sed victa Catoni."

And now I may be almost said to have brought to an end, as far as is necessary for a sketch such as this is, the history both of my changes of religious opinion and of the public acts which they involved.

I had one final advance of mind to accomplish, and one final step to take. That further advance of mind was to be able honestly to say that I was *certain* of the conclusions at which I had already arrived. That further step, imperative when such certitude was attained, was my *submission* to the Catholic Church.

This submission did not take place till two full years after the resignation of my living in September 1843; nor could I have made it at an earlier day, without doubt and apprehension, that is, with any true conviction of mind or certitude.

In the interval, of which it remains to speak, viz. between the autumns of 1843 and 1845, I was in lay communion with the Church of England, attending its services as usual, and abstaining altogether from intercourse with Catholics, from their places of worship, and from those religious rites and usages, such as the Invocation of Saints, which are characteristics of their creed. I did all this on principle; for I never could understand how a man could be of two religions at once.

What I have to say about myself between these two autumns I shall almost confine to this one point,—the difficulty I was in, as to the best mode of revealing the state of my mind to my friends and others, and how I managed to reveal it.

Up to January 1842, I had not disclosed my state of unsettlement to more than three persons, as has been mentioned above, and as is repeated in the course of the letters which I am now about to give to the reader. To two of them, intimate and familiar companions, in the Autumn of 1839: to the third, an old friend too, whom I have also named above,

I suppose, when I was in great distress of mind upon the affair of the Jerusalem Bishopric. In May 1843, I made it known, as has been seen, to the friend, by whose advice I wished, as far as possible, to be guided. To mention it on set purpose to any one, unless indeed I was asking advice, I should have felt to be a crime. If there is anything that was abhorrent to me, it was the scattering doubts, and unsettling consciences without necessity. A strong presentiment that my existing opinions would ultimately give way, and that the grounds of them were unsound, was not a sufficient warrant for disclosing the state of my mind. I had no guarantee yet, that that presentiment would be realized. Supposing I were crossing ice, which came right in my way, which I had good reasons for considering sound, and which I saw numbers before me crossing in safety, and supposing a stranger from the bank, in a voice of authority, and in an earnest tone, warned me that it was dangerous, and then was silent, I think I should be startled, and should look about me anxiously, but I think too that I should go on, till I had better grounds for doubt; and such was my state, I believe, till the end of 1842. Then again, when my dissatisfaction became greater, it was hard at first to determine the point of time, when it was too strong to suppress with propriety. Certitude of course is a point, but doubt is a progress; I was not near certitude yet. Certitude is a reflex action; it is to know that one knows. Of that I believe I was not possessed, till close upon my reception into the Catholic Church. Again, a practical, effective doubt is a point too, but who can easily ascertain it for himself? Who can determine when it is, that the scales in the balance of opinion begin to turn, and what was a greater probability in behalf of a belief becomes a positive doubt against it?

In considering this question in its bearing upon my conduct in 1843, my own simple answer to my great difficulty had been, *Do* what your present state of opinion requires in the light of duty, and let that *doing* tell: speak by *acts*. This I had done; my first *act* of the year had been in February. After three months' deliberation I had published my retractation of the violent charges which I had made against Rome: I could not be wrong in doing so much as this; but I did no more at the time: I did not retract my Anglican teaching. My second *act* had been in September in the same year; after much sorrowful lingering and hesitation, I had resigned my Living. I tried indeed, before I did so, to keep Littlemore for myself, even though it was still to remain an integral part of St. Mary's. I had given to it a Church and a sort of Parsonage; I had made it a Parish, and I loved it; I thought in 1843 that perhaps I need not forfeit my existing relations towards it. I could indeed submit to become the curate at will of another, but I hoped an arrangement was possible, by which, while I had the curacy, I might have been my own master in serving it. I had hoped an exception might have been made in my favor, under the circumstances; but I did not gain my request. Perhaps I was asking what was impracticable, and it is well for me that it was so.

These had been my two acts of the year, and I said, "I cannot be wrong in making them; let that follow which must follow in the thoughts of the world about me, when they see what I do." And, as time went on, they fully answered my purpose. What I felt it a simple duty to do, did create a general suspicion about me, without such responsibility as would be involved in my initiating any direct act for the sake of creating it. Then, when friends wrote me on the subject, I either did not deny or I confessed my state of mind, according to the character and need of their letters. Sometimes in the case of intimate friends, whom I should otherwise have been leaving in ignorance of what others knew on every side of them, I invited the question.

And here comes in another point for explanation. While I was fighting in Oxford for the Anglican Church, then indeed I was very glad to make converts, and, though I never broke away from that rule of my mind, (as I may call it,) of which I have already spoken, of finding disciples rather than seeking them, yet, that I made advances to others in a special way, I have no doubt; this came to an end, however, as soon as I fell into misgivings as to the true ground to be taken in the controversy. For then, when I gave up my place in the Movement, I ceased from any such proceedings: and my utmost endeavor was to tranquilize such persons, especially those who belonged to the new school, as were unsettled in

their religious views, and, as I judged, hasty in their conclusions. This went on till 1843; but, at that date, as soon as
I turned my face Romeward, I gave up, as far as ever was
possible, the thought of in any respect and in any shape
acting upon others. Then I myself was simply my own concern. How could I in any sense direct others, who had to be
guided in so momentous a matter myself? How could I be
considered in a position, even to say a word to them one way
or the other? How could I presume to unsettle them, as I
was unsettled, when I had no means of bringing them out of
such unsettlement? And, if they were unsettled already, how
could I point to them a place of refuge, when I was not sure
that I should choose it for myself? My only line, my only
duty, was to keep simply to my own case. I recollected
Pascal's words, "Je mourrai seul." I deliberately put out of
my thoughts all other works and claims, and said nothing to
any one, unless I was obliged.

But this brought upon me a great trouble. In the newspapers there were continual reports about my intentions; I
did not answer them; presently strangers or friends wrote,
begging to be allowed to answer them; and, if I still kept to
my resolution and said nothing, then I was thought to be
mysterious, and a prejudice was excited against me. But,
what was far worse, there were a number of tender, eager
hearts, of whom I knew nothing at all, who were watching
me, wishing to think as I thought, and to do as I did, if they
could but find it out; who in consequence were distressed,
that, in so solemn a matter, they could not see what was coming, and who heard reports about me this way or that, on a
first day and on a second; and felt the weariness of waiting,
and the sickness of delayed hope, and did not understand
that I was as perplexed as they were, and, being of more
sensitive complexion of mind than myself, were made ill by
the suspense. And they too of course for the time thought
me mysterious and inexplicable. I ask their pardon as far as
I was really unkind to them. There was a gifted and deeply
earnest lady, who in a parabolical account of that time, has
described both my conduct as she felt it, and her own feelings
upon it. In a singularly graphic, amusing vision of pilgrims,
who were making their way across a bleak common in great

discomfort, and who were ever warned against, yet continually nearing, "the king's highway," on the right, she says, "All my fears and disquiets were speedily renewed by seeing the most daring of our leaders, (the same who had first forced his way through the palisade, and in whose courage and sagacity we all put implicit trust,) suddenly stop short, and declare that he would go on no further. He did not, however, take the leap at once, but quietly sat down on the top of the fence with his feet hanging towards the road, as if he meant to take his time about it, and let himself down easily." I do not wonder at all that I thus seemed so unkind to a lady, who at that time had never seen me. We were both in trial in our different ways. I am far from denying that I was acting selfishly both in her case and in that of others; but it was a religious selfishness. Certainly to myself my own duty seemed clear. They that are whole can heal others; but in my case it was, "Physician, heal thyself." My own soul was my first concern, and it seemed an absurdity to my reason to be converted in partnership. I wished to go to my Lord by myself, and in my own way, or rather His way. I had neither wish, nor, I may say, thought of taking a number with me. Moreover, it is but the truth to say, that it had ever been an annoyance to me to seem to be the head of a party; and that even from fastidiousness of mind, I could not bear to find a thing done elsewhere, simply or mainly because I did it myself, and that, from distrust of myself, I shrank from the thought, whenever it was brought home to me, that I was influencing others. But nothing of this could be known to the world.

I could not continue in this state, either in the light of duty or of reason. My difficulty was this: I had been deceived greatly once; how could I be sure that I was not deceived a second time? I thought myself right then; how was I to be certain that I was right now? How many years had I thought myself sure of what I now rejected? how could I ever again have confidence in myself? As in 1840 I listened to the rising doubt in favor of Rome, now I listened to the waning doubt in favor of the Anglican Church. To be certain is to know that one knows; what inward test had I, that I should not change again, after that I had become a Catholic? I had still apprehension of this, though I thought a time would come, when it would depart. However, some limit ought to be put to these vague misgivings; I must do my best and then leave it to a higher Power to prosper it. So, at the end of 1844, I came to the resolution of writing an Essay on Doctrinal Development; and then, if, at the end of it, my convictions in favor of the Roman Church were not weaker, of taking the necessary steps for admission into her fold.

I am now close upon the date of my reception into the Catholic Church; at the beginning of the year a letter had been addressed to me by a very dear friend, now no more, Charles Marriott. I quote some sentences from it, for the love which I bear him and the value that I set on his good word.

"January 15, 1845. You know me well enough to be aware, that I never see through anything at first. Your letter to Badeley casts a gloom over the future, which you can understand, if you have understood me, as I believe you have. But I may speak out at once, of what I see and feel at once, and doubt not that I shall ever feel: that your whole conduct towards the Church of England and towards us, who have striven and are still striving to seek after God for ourselves, and to revive true religion among others, under her authority and guidance, has been generous and considerate, and, were that word appropriate, dutiful, to a degree that I could scarcely have conceived possible, more unsparing of self than I should have thought nature could sustain. I have felt with pain every link that you have severed, and I have asked no questions, because I felt that you ought to measure the disclosure of your thoughts according to the occasion, and the capacity of those to whom you spoke. I write in haste, in the midst of engagements engrossing in themselves, but partly made tasteless, partly embittered by what I have heard; but I am willing to trust even you, whom I love best on earth, in God's hand, in the earnest prayer that you may be so employed as is best for the Holy Catholic Church."

In July, a Bishop thought it worth while to give out to the world that "the adherents of Mr. Newman are few in num-. ber. A short time will now probably suffice to prove this fact. It is well known that he is preparing for secession; and, when that event takes place, it will be seen how few will go with him.''

I had begun my *Essay on the Development of Doctrine* in the beginning of 1845, and I was hard at it all through the year till October. As I advanced, my difficulties so cleared away that I ceased to speak of ''the Roman Catholics,'' and boldly called them Catholics. Before I got to the end, I resolved to be received, and the book remains in the state in which it was then, unfinished.

One of my friends at Littlemore had been received into the Church on Michaelmas Day, at the Passionist House at Aston, near Stone, by Father Dominic, the Superior. At the beginning of October the latter was passing through London to Belgium; and, as I was in some perplexity what steps to take for being received myself, I assented to the proposition made to me that the good priest should take Littlemore in his way, with a view to his doing for me the same charitable service as he had done to my friend.

On October the 8th I wrote to a number of friends the following letter:—

''Littlemore, October 8th, 1845. I am this night expecting Father Dominic, the Passionist, who, from his youth, has been led to have distinct and direct thoughts, first of the countries of the North, then of England. After thirty years' (almost) waiting, he was without his own act sent here. But he has had little to do with conversions. I saw him here for a few minutes on St. John Baptist's day last year.

''He is a simple, holy man; and withal gifted with remarkable powers. He does not know of my intentions; but I mean to ask of him admission into the One Fold of Christ. . . .

''I have so many letters to write, that this must do for all who choose to ask about me. With my best love to dear Charles Marriott, who is over your head, &c., &c.

''P.S. This will not go till all is over. Of course it requires no answer.''

For a while after my reception, I proposed to betake myself to some secular calling. I wrote thus in answer to a very gracious letter of congratulation sent me by Cardinal Acton:—

''Nov. 25, 1845. I hope you will have anticipated, before I express it, the great gratification which I received from

your Eminence's letter. That gratification, however, was
· tempered by the apprehension, that kind and anxious well-
wishers at a distance attach more importance to my step than
really belongs to it. To me indeed personally it is of course
an inestimable gain; but persons and things look great at a
distance, which are not so when seen close; and, did your
Eminence know me, you would see that I was one, about
whom there has been far more talk for good and bad than he
deserves, and about whose movements far more expectation
has been raised than the event will justify.

"As I never, I do trust, aimed at anything else than obedience to my own sense of right, and have been magnified into
the leader of a party without my wishing it or acting as such,
so now, much as I may wish to the contrary, and earnestly as
I may labor (as is my duty) to minister in a humble way to
the Catholic Church, yet my powers will, I fear, disappoint
the expectations of both my own friends, and of those who
pray for the peace of Jerusalem.

"If I might ask of your Eminence a favor, it is that you
would kindly moderate those anticipations. Would it were in
my power to do, what I do not aspire to do! At present certainly I cannot look forward to the future, and, though it
would be a good work if I could persuade others to do as I
have done, yet it seems as if I had quite enough to do in
thinking of myself."

Soon, Dr. Wiseman, in whose Vicariate Oxford lay, called
me to Oscott; and I went there with others; afterwards he sent
me to Rome, and finally placed me in Birmingham.

I wrote to a friend :—

"January 20, 1846. You may think how lonely I am.
'Obliviscere populum tuum et domum patris tui,' has been
in my ears for the last twelve hours. I realize more that we
are leaving Littlemore, and it is like going on the open sea."

I left Oxford for good on Monday, February 23, 1846.
On the Saturday and Sunday before, I was in my house at
Littlemore simply by myself, as I had been for the first day
or two when I had originally taken possession of it. I slept
on Sunday night at my dear friend's, Mr. Johnson's, at the
Observatory. Various friends came to see the last of me;
Mr. Copeland, Mr. Church, Mr. Buckle, Mr. Pattison, and

Mr. Lewis. Dr. Pusey too came up to take leave of me; and I called on Dr. Ogle, one of my very oldest friends, for he was my private Tutor, when I was an Undergraduate. In him I took leave of my first College, Trinity, which was so dear to me, and which held on its foundation so many who had been kind to me both when I was a boy, and all through my Oxford life. Trinity had never been unkind to me. There used to be much snap-dragon growing on the walls opposite my freshman's rooms there, and I had for years taken it as the emblem of my own perpetual residence even unto death in my University.

On the morning of the 23rd I left the Observatory. I have never seen Oxford since, excepting its spires, as they are seen from the railway.[1]

CHAPTER V

POSITION OF MY MIND SINCE 1845

FROM the time that I became a Catholic, of course I have no further history of my religious opinions to narrate. In saying this, I do not mean to say that my mind has been idle, or that I have given up thinking on theological subjects; but that I have had no variations to record, and have had no anxiety of heart whatever. I have been in perfect peace and contentment; I never have had one doubt. I was not conscious to myself, on my conversion, of any change, intellectual or moral, wrought in my mind. I was not conscious of firmer faith in the fundamental truths of Revelation, or of more self-command; I had not more fervor; but it was like coming into port after a rough sea; and my happiness on that score remains to this day without interruption.

Nor had I any trouble about receiving those additional articles, which are not found in the Anglican Creed. Some of them I believed already, but not any one of them was a trial to me. I made a profession of them upon my reception with the greatest ease, and I have the same ease in believing them now. I am far of course from denying that every article of the Christian Creed, whether as held by Catholics or by

[1] At length I revisited Oxford on February 26th, 1878, after an absence of just 32 years.

Protestants, is beset with intellectual difficulties; and it is simple fact, that, for myself, I cannot answer those difficulties. Many persons are very sensitive of the difficulties of Religion; I am as sensitive of them as any one; but I have never been able to see a connection between apprehending those difficulties, however keenly, and multiplying them to any extent, and on the other hand doubting the doctrines to which they are attached. Ten thousand difficulties do not make one doubt, as I understand the subject; difficulty and doubt are incommensurate. There of course may be difficulties in the evidence; but I am speaking of difficulties intrinsic to the doctrines themselves, or to their relations with each other. A man may be annoyed that he cannot work out a mathematical problem, of which the answer is or is not given to him, without doubting that it admits of an answer, or that a certain particular answer is the true one. Of all points of faith, the being of a God is, to my own apprehension, encompassed with most difficulty, and yet borne in upon our minds with most power.

People say that the doctrine of Transubstantiation is difficult to believe; I did not believe the doctrine till I was a Catholic. I had no difficulty in believing it, as soon as I believed that the Catholic Roman Church was the oracle of God, and that she had declared this doctrine to be part of the original revelation. It is difficult, impossible, to imagine, I grant;—but how is it difficult to believe? Yet Macaulay thought it so difficult to believe, that he had need of a believer in it of talents as eminent as Sir Thomas More, before he could bring himself to conceive that the Catholics of an enlightened age could resist "the overwhelming force of the argument against it." "Sir Thomas More," he says, "is one of the choice specimens of wisdom and virtue; and the doctrine of transubstantiation is a kind of proof charge. A faith which stands that test, will stand any test." But for myself, I cannot indeed prove it, I cannot tell *how* it is; but I say, "Why should it not be? What's to hinder it? What do I know of substance or matter? just as much as the greatest philosophers, and that is nothing at all;"—so much is this the case, that there is a rising school of philosophy now, which considers phenomena to constitute the whole of our knowledge in physics. The Catholic doctrine leaves phenomena alone. It does not say that the phenomena go; on the contrary, it says that they remain; nor does it say that the same phenomena are in several places at once. It deals with what no one on earth knows anything about, the material substances themselves. And, in like manner, of that majestic Article of the Anglican as well as of the Catholic Creed,—the doctrine of the Trinity in Unity. What do I know of the Essence of the Divine Being? I know that my abstract idea of three is simply incompatible with my idea of one; but when I come to the question of concrete fact, I have no means of proving that there is not a sense in which one and three can equally be predicated of the Incommunicable God.

But I am going to take upon myself the responsibility of more than the mere Creed of the Church; as the parties accensing me are determined I shall do. They say, that now, in that I am a Catholic, though I may not have offenses of my own against honesty to answer for, yet, at least, I am answerable for the offenses of others, of my co-religionists, of my brother priests, of the Church itself. I am quite willing to accept the responsibility; and, as I have been able, as I trust, by means of a few words, to dissipate, in the minds of all those who do not begin with disbelieving me, the suspicion with which so many Protestants start, in forming their judgment of Catholics, viz. that our Creed is actually set up in inevitable superstition and hypocrisy, as the original sin of Catholicism; so now I will proceed, as before, identifying myself with the Church and vindicating it,—not of course denying the enormous mass of sin and error which exists of necessity in that world-wide multiform Communion,—but going to the proof of this one point, that its system is in no sense dishonest, and that therefore the upholders and teachers of that system, as such, have a claim to be acquitted in their own persons of that odious imputation.

Starting then with the being of a God, (which, as I have said, is as certain to me as the certainty of my own existence, though when I try to put the grounds of that certainty into logical shape I find a difficulty in doing so in mood and figure to my satisfaction,) I look out of myself into the world of men, and there I see a sight which fills me with unspeakable distress. The world seems simply to give the lie to that great truth, of which my whole being is so full; and the effect upon me is, in consequence, as a matter of necessity, as confusing as if it denied that I am in existence myself. If I looked into a mirror, and did not see my face, I should have the sort of feeling which actually comes upon me, when I look into this living busy world, and see no reflection of its Creator. This is, to me, one of those great difficulties of this absolute primary truth, to which I referred just now. Were it not for this voice, speaking so clearly in my conscience and my heart, I should be an atheist, or a pantheist, or a polytheist when I looked into the world. I am speaking for myself only; and I am far from denying the real force of the arguments in proof of a God, drawn from the general facts of human society and the course of history, but these do not warm me or enlighten me; they do not take away the winter of my desolation, or make the buds unfold and the leaves grow within me, and my moral being rejoice. The sight of the world is nothing else than the prophet's scroll, full of "lamentations, and mourning, and woe."

To consider the world in its length and breadth, its various history, the many races of man, their starts, their fortunes, their mutual alienation, their conflicts; and then their ways, habits, governments, forms of worship; their enterprises, their aimless courses, their random achievements and acquirements, the impotent conclusion of long-standing facts, the tokens so faint and broken of a superintending design, the blind evolution of what turn out to be great powers or truths, the progress of things, as if from unreasoning elements, not towards final causes, the greatness and littleness of man, his far-reaching aims, his short duration, the curtain hung over his futurity, the disappointments of life, the defeat of good, the success of evil, physical pain, mental anguish, the prevalence and intensity of sin, the pervading idolatries, the corruptions, the dreary hopeless irreligion, that condition of the whole race, so fearfully yet exactly described in the Apostle's words, "having no hope and without God in the world,"— all this is a vision to dizzy and appal; and inflicts upon the mind the sense of a profound mystery, which is absolutely beyond human solution.

What shall be said to this heart-piercing, reason-bewildering fact? I can only answer, that either there is no Creator, or this living society of men is in a true sense discarded from His presence. Did I see a boy of good make and mind, with the tokens on him of a refined nature, cast upon the world without provision, unable to say whence he came, his birthplace or his family connections, I should conclude that there was some mystery connected with his history, and that he was one, of whom, from one cause or other, his parents were ashamed. Thus only should I be able to account for the contrast between the promise and the condition of his being. And so I argue about the world;—*if* there be a God, *since* there is a God, the human race is implicated in some terrible aboriginal calamity. It is out of joint with the purposes of its Creator. This is a fact, a fact as true as the fact of its existence; and thus the doctrine of what is theologically called original sin becomes to me almost as certain as that the world exists, and as the existence of God.

And now, supposing it were the blessed and loving will of the Creator to interfere in this anarchical condition of things, what are we to suppose would be the methods which might be necessarily or naturally involved in His purpose of mercy? Since the world is in so abnormal a state, surely it would be no surprise to me, if the interposition were of necessity equally extraordinary—or what is called miraculous. But that subject does not directly come into the scope of my present remarks. Miracles as evidence, involve a process of reason, or an argument; and of course I am thinking of some mode of interference which does not immediately run into argument. I am rather asking what must be the face-to-face antagonist, by which to withstand and baffle the fierce energy of passion and the all-corroding, all-dissolving skepticism of the intellect in religious inquiries? I have no intention at all of denying, that truth is the real object of our reason, and that, if it does not attain to truth, either the premise or the process is in fault; but I am not speaking here of right reason, but of reason as it acts in fact and concretely in fallen man. I know that even the unaided reason, when correctly exercised, leads to a belief in God, in the immortality of the soul, and in a future retribution; but I am considering the faculty of reason actually and historically; and in this point of view, I do not think I am wrong in saying that its tendency is towards a simple unbelief in matters of religion. No truth, however sacred, can stand against it, in the long run; and hence it is that in the pagan world, when our Lord came, the last traces of the religious knowledge of former times were all but disappearing from those portions of the world in which the intellect had been active and had had a career.

And in these latter days, in like manner, outside the Catholic Church things are tending,—with far greater rapidity than in that old time from the circumstance of the age,—to atheism in one shape or other. What a scene, what a prospect, does the whole of Europe present at this day! and not only Europe, but every government and every civilization through the world, which is under the influence of the European mind! Especially, for it most concerns us, how sorrowful, in the view of religion, even taken in its most elementary, most attenuated form, is the spectacle presented to us by the educated intellect of England, France, and Germany! Lovers of their country and of their race, religious men, external to the Catholic Church, have attempted various expedients to arrest fierce willful human nature in its onward course, and to bring it into subjection. The necessity of some form of religion for the interests of humanity, has been generally acknowledged: but where was the concrete representative of things invisible, which would have the force and the toughness necessary to be a breakwater against the deluge? Three centuries ago the establishment of religion, material, legal and social, was generally adopted as the best expedient for the purpose, in those countries which separated from the Catholic Church; and for a long time it was successful; but now the crevices of those establishments are admitting the enemy. Thirty years ago, education was relied upon: ten years ago there was a hope that wars would cease forever, under the influence of commercial enterprise and the reign of the useful and fine arts; but will any one venture to say that there is anything anywhere on this earth, which will afford a fulcrum for us, whereby to keep the earth from moving onwards?

The judgment, which experience passes whether on establishments or on education, as a means of maintaining religious truth in this anarchical world, must be extended even to Scripture, though Scripture be divine. Experience proves surely that the Bible does not answer a purpose for which it was never intended. It may be accidentally the means of the conversion of individuals; but a book, after all, cannot make a stand against the wild living intellect of man, and in this day it begins to testify, as regards its own structure and contents, to the power of that universal solvent, which is so successfully acting upon religious establishments.

Supposing then it to be the Will of the Creator to interfere in human affairs, and to make provisions for retaining in the world a knowledge of Himself, so definite and distinct as to be proof against the energy of human skepticism, in such a case,—I am far from saying that there was no other way,—but there is nothing to surprise the mind, if He should think fit to introduce a power into the world, invested with the prerogative of infallibility in religious matters. Such a provision would be a direct, immediate, active, and prompt means of withstanding the difficulty; it would be an instrument suited to the need; and, when I find that this is the very claim of the Catholic Church, not only do I feel no difficulty in admitting the idea, but there is a fitness in it, which recommends it to my mind. And thus I am brought to speak of the Church's infallibility, as a provision, adapted by the mercy of the Creator, to preserve religion in the world, and to restrain that freedom of thought, which of course in itself is one of the greatest of our natural gifts, and to rescue it from its own suicidal excesses. And let it be observed that, neither here nor in what follows, shall I have occasion to speak directly of Revelation in its subject-matter, but in reference to the sanction which it gives to truths which may be known independently of it,—as it bears upon the defense of natural religion. I say, that a power, possessed of infallibility in religious teaching, is happily adapted to be a working instrument, in the course of human affairs, for smiting hard and throwing back the immense energy of the aggressive, capricious, untrustworthy intellect:—and in saying this, as in the other things that I have to say, it must still be recollected that I am all along bearing in mind my main purpose, which is a defense of myself.

I am defending myself here from a plausible charge brought against Catholics, as will be seen better as I proceed. The charge is this:—that I, as a Catholic, not only make profession to hold doctrines which I cannot possibly believe in my heart, but that I also believe in the existence of a power on earth, which at its own will imposes upon men any new set of *credenda*, when it pleases, by a claim to infallibility; in consequence, that my own thoughts are not my own property; that I cannot tell that to-morrow I may not have to give up what I hold to-day, and that the necessary effect of such a condition of mind must be a degrading bondage, or a bitter inward rebellion relieving itself in secret infidelity, or the necessity of ignoring the whole subject of religion in a sort of disgust, and of mechanically saying everything that the Church says, and leaving to others the defense of it. As then I have above spoken of the relation of my mind towards the Catholic Creed, so now I shall speak of the attitude which it takes up in the view of the Church's infallibility.

And first, the initial doctrine of the infallible teacher must be an emphatic protest against the existing state of mankind. Man had rebelled against his Maker. It was this that caused the divine interposition: and to proclaim it must be the first act of the divinely-accredited messenger. The Church must denounce rebellion as of all possible evils the greatest. She must have no terms with it; if she would be true to her Master, she must ban and anathematize it. This is the meaning of a statement of mine, which has furnished matter for one of those special accusations to which I am at present replying: I have, however, no fault at all to confess in regard to it; I have nothing to withdraw, and in consequence I here deliberately repeat it. I said, "The Catholic Church holds it better for the sun and moon to drop from heaven, for the earth to fail, and for all the many millions on it to die of starvation in extremest agony, as far as temporal affliction goes, than that one soul, I will not say, should be lost, but should commit one single venial sin, should tell one willful untruth, or should steal one poor farthing without excuse." I think the principle here enunciated to be the mere preamble in the formal credentials of the Catholic Church, as an Act of

Parliament might begin with a *"Whereas."* It is because of the intensity of the evil which has possession of mankind, that a suitable antagonist has been provided against it; and the initial act of that divinely-commissioned power is of course to deliver her challenge and to defy the enemy. Such a preamble then gives a meaning to her position in the world, and an interpretation to her whole course of teaching and action.

In like manner she has ever put forth, with most energetic distinctness, those other great elementary truths, which either are an explanation of her mission or give a character to her work. She does not teach that human nature is irreclaimable, else wherefore should she be sent? not, that it is to be shattered and reversed, but to be extricated, purified, and restored; not, that it is a mere mass of hopeless evil, but that it has the promise upon it of great things, and even now, in its present state of disorder and excess, has a virtue and a praise proper to itself. But in the next place she knows and she preaches that such a restoration, as she aims at effecting in it, must be brought about, not simply through certain outward provisions of preaching and teaching, even though they be her own, but from an inward spiritual power or grace imparted directly from above, and of which she is the channel. She has it in charge to rescue human nature from its misery, but not simply by restoring it on its own level, but by lifting it up to a higher level than its own. She recognizes in it real moral excellence though degraded, but she cannot set it free from earth except by exalting it towards heaven. It was for this end that a renovating grace was put into her hands; and therefore from the nature of the gift, as well as from the reasonableness of the case, she goes on, as a further point, to insist, that all true conversion must begin with the first springs of thought, and to teach that each individual man must be in his own person one whole and perfect temple of God, while he is also one of the living stones which build up a visible religious community. And thus the distinctions between nature and grace, and between outward and inward religion, become two further articles in what I have called the preamble of her divine commission.

Such truths as these she vigorously reiterates, and perti-

naciously inflicts upon mankind; as to such she observes no
half-measures, no economical reserve, no delicacy or prudence. "Ye must be born again," is the simple, direct form
of words which she uses after her Divine Master: "your
whole nature must be reborn; your passions, and your affections, and your aims, and your conscience, and your will,
must all be bathed in a new element, and reconsecrated to your
Maker,—and, the last not the least, your intellect." It was
for repeating these points of her teaching in my own way,
that certain passages of one of my Volumes have been
brought into the general accusation which has been made
against my religious opinions. The writer has said that I
was demented if I believed, and unprincipled if I did not believe, in my own statement, that a lazy, ragged, filthy, story-
telling beggar-woman, if chaste, sober, cheerful, and religious,
had a prospect of heaven, such as was absolutely closed to an
accomplished statesman, or lawyer, or noble, be he ever so
just, upright, generous, honorable, and conscientious, unless
he had also some portion of the divine Christian graces;—
yet I should have thought myself defended from criticism
by the words which our Lord used to the chief priests, "The
publicans and harlots go into the kingdom of God before
you." And I was subjected again to the same alternative of
imputations, for having ventured to say that consent to an
unchaste wish was indefinitely more heinous than any lie
viewed apart from its causes, its motives, and its consequences: though a lie, viewed under the limitation of these
conditions, is a random utterance, an almost outward act,
not directly from the heart, however disgraceful and despicable it may be, however prejudicial to the social contract, however deserving of public reprobation; whereas, we have the
express words of our Lord to the doctrine that "whoso looketh
on a woman to lust after her, hath committed adultery with
her already in his heart." On the strength of these texts, I
have surely as much right to believe in these doctrines which
have caused so much surprise, as to believe in original sin,
or that there is a supernatural revelation, or that a Divine
Person suffered, or that punishment is eternal.

Passing now from what I have called the preamble of that
grant of power, which is made to the Church, to that power

itself, Infallibility, I premise two brief remarks:—1. on the one hand, I am not here determining anything about the essential seat of that power, because that is a question doctrinal, not historical and practical; 2. nor, on the other hand, am I extending the direct subject-matter, over which that power of Infallibility has jurisdiction, beyond religious opinion:—and now as to the power itself.

This power, viewed in its fullness, is as tremendous as the giant evil which has called for it. It claims, when brought into exercise but in the legitimate manner, for otherwise of course it is but quiescent, to know for certain the very meaning of every portion of that Divine Message in detail, which was committed by our Lord to His Apostles. It claims to know its own limits, and to decide what it can determine absolutely and what it cannot. It claims, moreover, to have a hold upon statements not directly religious, so far as this,—to determine whether they indirectly relate to religion, and, according to its own definite judgment, to pronounce whether or not, in a particular case, they are simply consistent with revealed truth. It claims to decide magisterially, whether as within its own province or not, that such and such statements are or are not prejudicial to the *Depositum* of faith, in their spirit or in their consequences, and to allow them, or condemn and forbid them, accordingly. It claims to impose silence at will on any matters, or controversies, of doctrine, which on its own *ipse dixit*, it pronounces to be dangerous, or inexpedient, or inopportune. It claims that, whatever may be the judgment of Catholics upon such acts, these acts should be received by them with those outward marks of reverence, submission, and loyalty, which Englishmen, for instance, pay to the presence of their sovereign, without expressing any criticism on them on the ground that in their matter they are inexpedient, or in their manner violent or harsh. And lastly, it claims to have the right of inflicting spiritual punishment, of cutting off from the ordinary channels of the divine life, and of simply excommunicating, those who refuse to submit themselves to its formal declarations. Such is the infallibility lodged in the Catholic Church, viewed in the concrete, as clothed and surrounded by the appendages of its high sovereignty: it is, to repeat what I said above, a supereminent prodigious power sent upon earth to encounter and master a giant evil.

And now, having thus described it, I profess my own absolute submission to its claim. I believe the whole revealed dogma as taught by the Apostles, as committed by the Apostles to the Church, and as declared by the Church to me. I receive it, as it is infallibly interpreted by the authority to whom it is thus committed, and (implicitly) as it shall be, in like manner, further interpreted by that same authority till the end of time. I submit, moreover, to the universally received traditions of the Church, in which lies the matter of those new dogmatic definitions which are from time to time made, and which in all times are the clothing and the illustration of the Catholic dogma as already defined. And I submit myself to those other decisions of the Holy See, theological or not, through the organs which it has itself appointed, which, waiving the question of their infallibility, on the lowest ground come to me with a claim to be accepted and obeyed. Also, I consider that, gradually and in the course of ages, Catholic inquiry has taken certain definite shapes, and has thrown itself into the form of a science, with a method and a phraseology of its own, under the intellectual handling of great minds, such as St. Athanasius, St. Augustine, and St. Thomas; and I feel no temptation at all to break in pieces the great legacy of thought thus committed to us for these latter days.

All this being considered as the profession which I make *ex animo,* as for myself, so also on the part of the Catholic body, as far as I know it, it will at first sight be said that the restless intellect of our common humanity is utterly weighed down, to the repression of all independent effort and action whatever, so that, if this is to be the mode of bringing it into order, it is brought into order only to be destroyed. But this is far from the result, far from what I conceive to be the intention of that high Providence who has provided a great remedy for a great evil,—far from borne out by the history of the conflict between Infallibility and Reason in the past, and the prospect of it in the future. The energy of the human intellect "does from opposition grow;" it thrives and is joyous, with a tough elastic strength, under the terrible blows of the divinely-fashioned weapon, and is never so much itself as when it has lately been overthrown. It is the custom with Protestant writers to consider that, whereas there are two great principles in action in the history of religion, Authority and Private Judgment, they have all the Private Judgment to themselves, and we have the full inheritance and the super-incumbent oppression of Authority. But this is not so; it is the vast Catholic body itself, and it only, which affords an arena for both combatants in that awful, never-dying duel. It is necessary for the very life of religion, viewed in its large operations and its history, that the warfare should be incessantly carried on. Every exercise of Infallibility is brought out into act by an intense and varied operation of the Reason, both as its ally and as its opponent, and provokes again, when it has done its work, a reaction of Reason against it; and, as in a civil polity the State exists and endures by means of the rivalry and collision, the encroachments and defeats of its constituent parts, so in like manner Catholic Christendom is no simple exhibition of religious absolutism, but presents a continuous picture of Authority and Private Judgment alternately advancing and retreating as the ebb and flow of the tide;—it is a vast assemblage of human beings with willful intellects and wild passions, brought together into one by the beauty and the Majesty of a Superhuman Power,—into what may be called a large reformatory or training-school, not as if into a hospital or into a prison, not in order to be sent to bed, not to be buried alive, but (if I may change my metaphor) brought together as if into some moral factory, for the melting, refining, and molding, by an incessant, noisy process, of the raw material of human nature, so excellent, so dangerous, so capable of divine purposes.

St. Paul says in one place that his Apostolical power is given him to edification, and not to destruction. There can be no better account of the Infallibility of the Church. It is a supply for a need, and it does not go beyond that need. Its object is, and its effect also, not to enfeeble the freedom or vigor of human thought in religious speculation, but to resist and control its extravagance. What have been its great works? All of them in the distinct province of theology:—

to put down Arianism, Eutychianism, Pelagianism, Manichæism, Lutheranism, Jansenism. Such is the broad result of its action in the past;—and now as to the securities which are given us that so it ever will act in time to come.

First. Infallibility cannot act outside of a definite circle of thought, and it must in all its decisions, or *definitions,* as they are called, profess to be keeping within it. The great truths of the moral law, of natural religion, and of Apostolical faith, are both its boundary and its foundation. It must not go beyond them, and it must ever appeal to them. Both its subject-matter, and its articles in that subject-matter, are fixed. And it must ever profess to be guided by Scripture and by tradition. It must refer to the particular Apostolic truth which it is enforcing, or (what is called) *defining.* Nothing, then, can be presented to me, in time to come, as part of the faith, but what I ought already to have received, and hitherto have been kept from receiving, (if so,) merely because it has not been brought home to me. Nothing can be imposed upon me different in kind from what I hold already, —much less contrary to it. The new truth which is promulgated, if it is to be called new, must be at least homogeneous, cognate, implicit, viewed relatively to the old truth. It must be what I may even have guessed, or wished, to be included in the Apostolic revelation; and at least it will be of such a character, that my thoughts readily concur in it or coalesce with it, as soon as I hear it. Perhaps I and others actually have always believed it, and the only question which is now decided in my behalf, is, that I have henceforth the satisfaction of having to believe, that I have only been holding all along what the Apostles held before me.

Let me take the doctrine which Protestants consider our greatest difficulty, that of the Immaculate Conception. Here I entreat the reader to recollect my main drift, which is this. I have no difficulty in receiving the doctrine; and that, because it so intimately harmonizes with that circle of recognized dogmatic truths, into which it has been recently received;—but if *I* have no difficulty, why may not another have no difficulty also? why may not a hundred? a thousand? Now I am sure that Catholics in general have not any intellectual difficulty at all on the subject of the Immaculate Conception; and that there is no reason why they should. Priests have no difficulty. You tell me that they *ought* to have a difficulty;—but they have not. Be large-minded enough to believe, that men may reason and feel very differently from yourselves; how is it that men, when left to themselves, fall into such various forms of religion, except that there are various types of mind among them, very distinct from each other? From my testimony then about myself, if you believe it, judge of others also who are Catholics: we do not find the difficulties which you do in the doctrines which we hold; we have no intellectual difficulty in that doctrine in particular, which you call a novelty of this day. We priests need not be hypocrites, though we be called upon to believe in the Immaculate Conception. To that large class of minds, who believe in Christianity after our manner,—in the particular temper, spirit, and light (whatever word is used,) in which Catholics believe it,—there is no burden at all in holding that the Blessed Virgin was conceived without original sin; indeed, it is a simple fact to say, that Catholics have not come to believe it because it is defined, but that it was defined because they believed it.

So far from the definition in 1854 being a tyrannical infliction on the Catholic world, it was received everywhere on its promulgation with the greatest enthusiasm.

It was in consequence of the unanimous petition, presented from all parts of the Church to the Holy See, in behalf of an *ex cathedrâ* declaration that the doctrine was Apostolic, that it was declared so to be. I never heard of one Catholic having difficulties in receiving the doctrine, whose faith on other grounds was not already suspicious. Of course there were grave and good men, who were made anxious by the doubt whether it could be formally proved to be Apostolical either by Scripture or tradition, and who accordingly, though believing it themselves, did not see how it could be defined by authority and imposed upon all Catholics as a matter of faith; but this is another matter. The point in question is, whether the doctrine is a burden. I believe it to be none. So far from it being so, I sincerely think that St. Bernard and St. Thomas, who scrupled at it in their day, had they lived into this, would have rejoiced to accept it for its own sake. Their difficulty, as I view it, consisted in matters of words, ideas, and arguments. They thought the doctrine inconsistent with other doctrines; and those who defended it in that age had not that precision in their view of it, which has been attained by means of the long disputes of the centuries which followed. And in this want of precision lay the difference of opinion, and the controversy.

Now the instance which I have been taking suggests another remark; the number of those (so called) new doctrines will not oppress us, if it takes eight centuries to promulgate even one of them. Such is about the length of time through which the preparation has been carried on for the definition of the Immaculate Conception. This of course is an extraordinary case: but it is difficult to say what is ordinary, considering how few are the formal occasions on which the voice of Infallibility has been solemnly lifted up. It is to the Pope in Ecumenical Council that we look, as to the normal seat of Infallibility: now there have been only eighteen such Councils since Christianity was,—an average of one to a century,—and of these Councils some passed no doctrinal decree at all, others were employed on only one, and many of them were concerned with only elementary points of the Creed. The Council of Trent embraced a large field of doctrine certainly; but I should apply to its Canons a remark contained in that University Sermon of mine, which has been so ignorantly criticized in the Pamphlet which has been the occasion of this Volume;—I there have said that the various verses of the Athanasian Creed are only repetitions in various shapes of one and the same idea; and in like manner, the Tridentine Decrees are not isolated from each other, but are occupied in bringing out in detail, by a number of separate declarations, as if into bodily form, a few necessary truths. I should make the same remark on the various theological censures, promulgated by Popes, which the Church has received, and on their dogmatic decisions generally. I own that at first sight those decisions seem from their number to be a greater burden on the faith of individuals than are the Canons of Councils; still I do not believe that in matter of fact they are so at all, and I give this reason for it:—it is not that a Catholic, layman or priest, is indifferent to the subject, or, from a sort of recklessness, will accept any thing that is placed before him, or is willing, like a lawyer, to speak according to his brief, but that in such condemnations the Holy See is engaged, for the most part, in repudiating one or two great lines of error, such as Lutheranism or Jansenism, principally ethical not doctrinal, which are divergent from the Catholic mind, and that it is but expressing what any good Catholic, of fair abilities, though unlearned, would say himself, from common and sound sense, if the matter could be put before him.

I have closed this history of myself with St. Philip's name upon St. Philip's feast-day; and, having done so, to whom can I more suitably offer it, as a memorial of affection and gratitude, than to St. Philip's sons, my dearest brothers of this House, the Priests of the Birmingham Oratory, AMBROSE ST. JOHN, HENRY AUSTIN MILLS, HENRY BITTLESTON, EDWARD CASWALL, WILLIAM PAINE NEVILLE, and HENRY IGNATIUS DUDLEY RYDER? who have been so faithful to me; who have been so sensitive of my needs; who have been so indulgent to my failings; who have carried me through so many trials; who have grudged no sacrifice, if I asked for it; who have been so cheerful under discouragements of my causing; who have done so many good works, and let me have the credit of them;—with whom I have lived so long, with whom I hope to die.

And to you especially, dear AMBROSE ST. JOHN; whom God gave me, when He took every one else away; who are the link between my old life and my new; who have now for twenty-one years been so devoted to me, so patient, so zealous, so tender; who have let me lean so hard upon you; who have watched me so narrowly; who have never thought of yourself, if I was in question.

And in you I gather up and bear in memory those familiar affectionate companions and counselors, who in Oxford were given to me, one after another, to be my daily solace and relief; and all those others, of great name and high example, who were my thorough friends, and showed me true attachment in times long past; and also those many younger men, whether I knew them or not, who have never been disloyal to me by word or deed; and of all these, thus various in their relations to me, those more especially who have since joined the Catholic Church.

And I earnestly pray for this whole company, with a hope against hope, that all of us, who once were so united, and so happy in our union, may even now be brought at length, by the Power of the Divine Will, into One Fold and under One Shepherd.

THE END OF THE AUTOBIOGRAPHY

VICTOR HUGO

1802-1885

(INTRODUCTORY NOTE)

There are few men whose personal lives have so held the interest and the study of mankind as has the life of Hugo. He was one of the most passionately emotional of men. If his writings are surcharged with intense feeling, so also was his life. He was a child of the Napoleonic era. His mother was an aristocrat and a devoted royalist, his father was a champion of the people; and Hugo shared the enthusiasms of both. At an age when most young men are still college students, he became a celebrated writer. He was wedded at twenty, was a father at twenty-one, was honored by the government as a leading poet at twenty-three, and at twenty-five was the recognized leader of the French ''Romanticists,'' a powerful party in politics as well as in literature.

Personally Hugo was one of the most naïvely self-confident of men, fully assured of his own greatness. Hence his letters are so frank, so outspoken they have almost the character of personal conversation. He never wrote an autobiography; but his letters almost supply the place of one in their fullness of self-revelation. For our present autobiographical purpose we include several of the most representative among these letters. First comes a youthful—if we may so discriminate, when it is part of the greatness of Hugo that he was eternally youthful—or at least an early letter to his friend and fellow-poet, De Vigny. Then comes a characteristically fervid letter announcing his approaching marriage, and another rhapsody to his father immediately following the event. Next come the first of a series written to his wife on the occasion of his being summoned away from her to be made a knight of the Legion of Honor at the coronation of King Charles X. To these are added two other letters more public and autobiographical, letters which explain themselves.

151

To COUNT ALFRED DE VIGNY, *5th Regiment of the Royal Guards, Rouen.*

[1821.]

Your letter, Alfred, was written on the 18th, and I am answering it on the 21st! We are separated by three days only, and these three days are like three years; distance is nothing,—it is the separation that matters. Thirty leagues, which prevent us from seeing each other, separate us as much as a thousand. One must be with one's friends to enjoy them. Once parted from them, the amount of the distance is of no account. Therefore, my dear friend, the only consolation I derive from your place of exile being near me is that you will come back from it all the quicker. However, our separation is enough to make me melancholy, and I assure you that I should pity those who survived you if the sun that rose on your grave was no brighter than the friend you have left behind you.

Your letter found me here, overdone, wearied, worried, and, what is worse than all, dull; you can imagine what an impression it made on me, and what a happiness it was to me. I read it over again, word by word, as a beggar counts the coins one by one in the purse which he has picked up. I saw with delight that you have not forgotten me, as you write to me, and that you are doing something better than thinking of me, as you are composing poetry. But that, again, is terribly tantalizing;—what! we are only thirty leagues apart, and I shall not have a chance of hearing these lines. Why don't we have roots instead of feet, since we are fixed like wretched plants to a spot which we cannot leave? Why are our aspirations, our desires, our affections removed so far from us, if we are doomed never to follow them? My dear friend, solve the question, and I will put you some more, for the cup of bitterness is inexhaustible.

I think you must have monopolized all the inspiration this month, for I have not had any for a single moment. I have written nothing. The Government asked me for more lines on the baptism [of the Duc de Bordeaux], which I shall not write unless I get an inspiration. You are a lucky man, Alfred; you never strike the rock in vain, and when you have turned out some hundreds of splendid verses you call them lines, to console those of your friends who cannot even produce any lines which they would call verses.

I had, however, begun a story which amused me but for the trouble of writing it; then came this request about the baptism of the Duc de Bordeaux, and then bothers about the fusion of the *Conservateur littéraire* and the *Annales*. I have let the whole thing slide.

Lefèvre is still undecided, Soumet is writing some superb poetry, Pichot is looking for his manuscript, Emile [Deschamps] goes on promising us *Le fou du roi*, Gaspard [de Pons] is making merry at Versailles, Rochet is weeping at Grenoble, by the bedside of his father, who is dangerously ill, Saint-Valry is spending Easter at Montford; all of them love you and embrace you, but none more tenderly than I do.

It is very disagreeable, Alfred, to be able to communicate by letter only. Here I am compelled to stop for want of paper. Is it really worth while to travel about in order to exchange ideas without getting an answer, to intrude upon one's friend's gay thoughts with melancholy remarks, like two instruments which answer each other from afar off with different airs, because the distance prevents those who are playing on them from striking up the same one? Farewell; I embrace you, ashamed of having told you so little, and tired of having put so many words on paper.

Abel's [Hugo] meetings at the *Bonnes lettres* are a great success. I have not read or had anything read since *Quiberon*. I had a charming letter from M. de Chateaubriand, in which he told me this ode *moved him to tears;* I repeat this praise to you, my friend, because it will convince you as well, you who possess the official record of the interment of this work. What is it by the side of your adorable *Symétha!* I regret that I cannot return your charming mark of friendship by signing myself *Alfred;* but, at all events, as you sign yourself *Victor,* I am sure that that name will be always illustrious.

Your affectionate friend　　　　　　　Victor.

To THE ABBÉ DE LAMENNAIS, *la Chesnaie.*

1st *October,* 1822.

I must write to you, my illustrious friend; I am about to be happy. Something would be wanting to my happiness if you were not the first to hear of it. I am going to be married. I wish more than ever that you were in Paris to make the acquaintance of the angel who is about to convert all my dreams of virtue and bliss into reality. I have not ventured to speak to you before now of what absorbs my existence. My whole future was still unsettled, and I could not divulge a secret which did not belong exclusively to myself. Besides, I was afraid of shocking your lofty austerity by the avowal of an uncontrollable passion, although a pure and innocent one. But now that everything conspires to bestow on me a happiness after my own heart, I do not doubt that all your tender feelings will be interested in an attachment as old as myself, born in early childhood and fostered by the first affliction of youth.   VICTOR M. HUGO.

PARIS, 19*th October*, 1822.

MY DEAR PAPA,—The happiest and the most grateful of sons is writing to you. From the 12th of this month I have enjoyed the most delightful and the most perfect happiness, and I see no end to it in the future; it is to you, dear, kind papa, that I owe these pure and lawful joys, it is you who have given me my happiness; accept then, for the third time, the assurance of my deepest and tenderest gratitude.

I did not write to you during the first days of my bliss, because my heart was too full for words; even now you will make allowance for me, my good father, for I hardly know what I am writing. I am absorbed in a deep feeling of love, and so long as this letter is full of it I have no doubt but that your kind heart will be satisfied. Your angelic Adèle unites with me; if she dared, she would write to you, but now that we two are one, her heart feels as mine for you.

Allow me, in concluding this too short letter, my dear, good father, to commend my brothers' interests to you; I have no doubt you have already decided in their favor, and it is only to hasten the execution of your decision that I mention the subject again.

Farewell then, dear papa, I leave you with regret. Still, it is a pleasure to me to assure you once more of the dutiful love and unchanging gratitude of your happy children.

VICTOR.

To ADÈLE HUGO, *care of* GENERAL COUNT HUGO, *Blois.*

ORLÉANS, 19*th May*, 4 P. M., [1825].

Here I am at Orléans, my Adèle, and before dining, before taking a rest, even before sitting down (for I am standing up), I must write to you. You will receive this unexpected letter to-morrow, and it is a great joy to me, in the midst of all my depression, to think of the pleasure this sheet will give you. Besides, I am really so sad, that it will do me good to open my heart to you, my Adèle. You cannot think how long the time and how great the distance have seemed to me since I left you, my beloved. I feel quite depressed at the thought of the forty miles which already separate you from me, and of the eight hours which have passed without seeing you. How will it be to-morrow, and the day after to-morrow, and the next day, and the next? You must really pray to God, my Adèle, my dearly beloved Adèle, to give me courage, for indeed I need it, and this fortnight is an eternity to me.

But I see that instead of strengthening you it is I who am weak, and that I am saddening instead of consoling you. Forgive me, my Adèle, it is a terrible thing to be alone, isolated, with cold, curious, or indifferent faces around one, with no friend but one's purse, as I am now, when one has got into the sweet habit of finding your tender smile and your consoling glance everywhere.

I shall be in Paris to-morrow, and I will write to you at once. Be brave, my adored one; take great care of your little Didine, who is not a greater angel than you are; see that she has cut two or three teeth by my return; kiss her a thousand times. My love to my good father and his excellent wife; I will give the same messages in your name at the same time in Paris.

We had a very good journey here. The roads are first-rate, the weather fine, though cold. I shall not be hot to-night, but I shall think of you, and that will keep me warm.

Write to me to Paris from to-morrow; I will send you my Reims address from Paris. How trying all these honors are! Many people envy me this journey; and they little know how unhappy I am over the good fortune which excites their jealousy.

Farewell, dear angel; farewell, my Adèle; take care of yourself. I embrace you very tenderly from very far off. Do not cry and spoil your pretty cheeks. I want to find them fresh and rosy on my return.

Tell my good father that I was asked on the journey *if I was going to join my regiment,* etc. This was on account of my ribbon.

Once more, farewell, and once more a thousand kisses and caresses.

Your own   VICTOR.

Open my letters, should any come for me, and give me a brief summary of their contents. Farewell, farewell once more.

To ADÈLE HUGO.

PARIS, *Friday, 20th May,* 7.30 A. M., [1825].

You will not have read my first letter, my beloved Adèle, by the time that I am beginning a second one to you. Here I am in Paris; I breakfasted with your dear parents, whom I found just the same as ever, taking as much care of me here, as mine do of you down there. I still have the sound of the diligence in my ears; I am bruised and stunned by its jolting, still I have no difficulty in collecting my thoughts to write to you; they are all merged in one, and that is you, and always you, and only you! You were the companion of my sleepless night; you amused me during the monotonous and insipid talk on the journey; you gave me the strength of mind to part from you, and you will keep up my courage during this never-ending absence. Do not read all I write to you to any one but our dear parents; others might think our grief ridiculous, and it is no use making them laugh at what gives us pain.

Our journey went off well, though all the arrangements for my places had been so badly made, that I always found myself where I ought not to have been, thanks to the stupidity of the innkeeper's wife at Blois. I had no ill effects from the cold, and hardly any from the fatigue, but my depression and ennui have not left me, and are increasing. If I do get inspiration at the Coronation, it will not be from my Muse.

I find a lot of letters, parcels, papers, books, etc., here. I inclose you Soumet's letter; it will please both you and my good father. Take great care of it. I found most kind congratulations from Villemain *dated April 27th;* he invites me to dine with him on the 1st of *last May,* and begs me not to fail him. So you see, he has had to wait some time for me. I will write to him and explain the reason of my absence and my silence, and I will call on him.

Now I must leave you, my adored angel, for I have a thousand and one things to attend to. I must begin my visits. I gave your letter to your kind mother, who sends you and your Didine many loving kisses, but not as many as I do. Your good father joins us in this; he is still cheerful, cordial, and amusing, like mine, though in a different manner. Give my love to my noble and charming father, and to her who is one flesh and one heart with him. I commend you to their loving care. You must be on even better terms with them than with me. They are so kind that this will be no difficulty to them.

I am writing to you from our bedroom, where everything makes me feel my widowhood more acutely. Everything seems strange to me here without you. Coming into Paris, I admired it like a provincial. It seemed as if it were not my own country. You are my true home. Write to me every day.

Your own   VICTOR.

To ADÈLE HUGO.

PARIS, 21st May, [1825].

This is my only happy time throughout the day, my Adèle. I am going to talk to you and forget for a moment all my troubles, fatigues, worries, and difficulties. You are with me in my mind, and nothing can distract my thoughts from you. You will see this sheet, you will touch it, it will be with you twelve or thirteen days in advance of me, it will be like a messenger of whom you will ask a thousand questions. I envy it!

Well, I have been here since yesterday morning, and I will tell you how I have spent my time. When I arrived I found your father and mother still in bed. Paul threw his arms round me, and then all the questions began. We had

breakfast; your father made me some lobster sauce, the coffee
and milk were excellent. After breakfast I wrote you the letter which you will get to-day. As I returned from posting it
myself, Mlle. Julie was going upstairs to see me. I dressed
and went down to her studio, where the questions began again.
How is Adèle? and Didine? and the General? and his wife?
The good woman is as fond of us as if we belonged to her.
She showed me Didine's portrait, which is nearly finished and
is delightful; and Juju's, which she has begun on a large canvas. I think she will do a small one to match the other, at
least so your mother tells me. Juju's is a very good likeness
and very pretty. Her round face has grown longer, and she
looks quite the little woman. Coming away from Mlle.
Duvidal (with whom we dine on Sunday), I went on foot
to see Beauchêne. Destains and Jules Maréchal congratulated
me. Beauchêne showed me my coat, which fits well; it is very
ugly, but very fashionable. I have still to get my knee-
breeches made, to hire or buy a sword. There were so many
people at M. de la Rochefoucauld's that I did not go in there.
Abel was at Beauchêne's shop. I gave my good old brother
everybody's love. He is always driving about in pursuit of
the six millions, which he hopes to get. Then I went to see
Soumet, who is, as you know, always good and kind; he offered to lend me his knee-breeches. He came back with me
by the Tuileries as far as the beginning of the Rue du Bac.
I went to get my pension at the Home Office, where I was
congratulated on my decoration. After that I went to see
Adolphe and Mme. Duménil, neither of whom was at home.
I have ordered a pair of boots, a pair of shoes, and a pair of
pumps, which I shall have by Sunday evening. Coming
home, I looked in on our porter, who told me that the Abbé
Lamennais had called, among others. I must not forget to
tell you that I have also seen Rabbe, who gave me heaps of
kind and affectionate messages for you and our dear parents
at Blois. Abel and Beauchêne dined with us. After dinner
I refused to go to the theater with your people. It would
have been too sad without you. I have been to see Charles
Nodier. Our poor friend has just lost his mother-in-law. All
the house was draped in black. Still I tried to cheer the
ladies, although I am not very merry myself. Our good

Nodier, who knew I was coming, had been expecting me all day, first at lunch and then at dinner. He is short of money like me. It appears we shall not receive any before the journey. We start Tuesday morning with the artist Alaux. The carriage there and back will cost four hundred francs. If we can get Taylor's room we shall have it for nothing. If not we must take what we can get, and we shall have to pay what we are asked. I hear we shall be in a very good position for seeing the ceremony. Our places, they say, are perhaps the best of all. The journey will only take two days, and we shall arrive early on Wednesday. I am to go and see Nodier again on Monday morning and take him my things.

I got home last night at eleven o'clock, after having been to the play to fetch your mother. I slept last night from sheer fatigue, and I saw you in all my dreams. It was a sad night to me, for it is the first I have passed away from you in a strange bed. This morning I have just seen our good friend the Abbé Lamennais, who is still taken up with his wretched troubles. He asked most affectionately after you, talked to me a great deal of Didine, and was as delightful as he always is. I shall see M. de la Rochefoucauld to-day. I shall order my knee-breeches. And to do all this, I am obliged to finish this letter. Your poor aunt is very ill. M. and Mme. Deschamps, M. and Mme. François, send you and our dear parents all sorts of kind messages. If the Viscount does not give me any money, your father will lend me some, and can repay himself when it is sent to me.

Farewell, dear Adèle, farewell, beloved; what a pang it gives me to close my letter so soon! When shall I receive one from you? Your kind parents are particularly attentive to me. They send their love to you, to your Didine, and to my parents. Tell my good father not to overtire himself with head work, and to go out walking. My love to your Blois father and mother. You know how I love you. Farewell.

To M. DE LA BOURDONNAYE, *Minister of the Interior.*

PARIS, 14*th August,* 1829.

MY LORD,—I am much touched by the King's kindness. My devotion to the King is in truth deep and sincere. My family, ennobled in the year 1531, has long served the State. My father and my two uncles served it for forty years with their swords. I myself have perhaps been fortunate enough to render some humble service to the King and to the cause of royalty. I have sold five editions of a book in which the name of Bourbon occurs on every page.

My Lord, this devotion is purely disinterested. Six years ago the late King deigned to grant me, by royal decree, and simultaneously with my noble friend M. de Lamartine, a pension of two thousand francs on the literary fund of the Minister of the Interior. I received this pension all the more gratefully because I had never asked for it.

My Lord, this pension, modest as it is, is enough for me. It is true that nearly all my father's fortune has been sequestrated by the King of Spain, in contravention of the Treaty of 1814. It is true that I have a wife and three children. It is true that I am supporting widows and relations who bear my name. But I have been fortunate enough to make an honorable and independent living by my pen. This is why the pension of two thousand francs, which I value chiefly as a token of royal favor, is enough for me.

It is, however, also true that, as I live by my pen, I had been obliged to reckon on the legitimate profits of my drama, *Marion de Lorme*. But as the performance of this play—a conscientious, honest work of art—appears to be dangerous, I bow to the decision, hoping that the Sovereign's august will may change in this respect. I had asked to have my play acted; I do not ask for anything else.

Be so good, therefore, my Lord, as to tell the King that I entreat him to allow me to remain in the position in which I was when his fresh favors reached me. Whatever happens—I need not repeat the assurance to you—nothing hostile can ever come from me. The King need expect nothing but proofs of fidelity, loyalty, and devotion from Victor Hugo.

I should be glad, my Lord, if your Excellency will be kind enough to submit this letter to the King, with the expression of my warm gratitude and deep respect.

I have the honor to be, my Lord, your Excellency's most obedient, humble servant,   VICTOR HUGO.

To ALPHONSE DE LAMARTINE, *at his Country-seat of Saint-Point near Mâcon.*

PARIS, *7th September,* 1830.

Between your letter and my reply, my dear friend, has come a Revolution. On the 28th of July, just as I was going to write to you, the cannonade made me drop my pen. Since then, in this vortex which surrounds us and makes us giddy, it has been impossible to devote a thought to poetry or friendship. The fever attacks every one, and you cannot defend yourself against outside impressions; the contagion is in the air. It infects you in spite of yourself; art, poetry, the stage, disappear at such a moment. The chambers, the country, the nation, absorb everything. Politics becomes one's life.

However, when once this earthquake has gone by, I am convinced we shall find our poetical edifice standing, and all the stronger for the shocks which it will have withstood. Our cause is also one of liberty; it is a revolution, too: it will advance unharmed side by side with its political sister. Revolutions, like wolves, do not prey on each other.

Your letter delighted me. It is good, nice, cordial prose, but now I expect the poetry. Do not forget that you promised to send it to me.

Farewell. Where are you? What are you doing? When are you coming back? I had my own domestic anxieties in the middle of the social revolution. My wife's confinement took place while the bullets were shattering the slates on our roof. She was safely delivered, and I am now the father of four children.

They are all flourishing. One day they will all love and admire you as I do. VICTOR HUGO.

THE END

PRINCESS MARIE ASMAR

A MODERN PRINCESS OF BABYLONIA

1804-1854

(INTRODUCTORY NOTE)

In these days when woman is evolving for herself a new place in the world, the life story and ideals of Marie Therese, Babylonian princess, hold a poignant appeal. Born among the ruins of lordly Nineveh, bred in gorgeous Bagdad, daughter of a Babylonian Emir, an ardent Christian, she overrode tradition and was the first woman of her race to forswear marriage and devote herself to religion, to travel in far countries and support herself.

Strong-hearted, valiant in her faith, she tells of strange wanderings, hazardous adventures, and frequent persecutions; yet does she endear herself to the hearts of her readers more by her sweet naturalness and humility and her animated accounts of childish escapades. After her father's death, which left her in poverty, she undertook to establish a college for women in her native Bagdad. This arduous task accomplished, her truth and liberality made her the idol of her pupils. Imagine then her despair when an English missionary, attempting to control the college, so embittered the Mohammedan government that the college was closed and the princess forced to flee. Her wanderings carried her among the Beduin sheikhs, to the Holy Land, and later to Europe and England. Her account of the scenes she witnessed is full of that oriental richness which by its very strangeness intrigues the Western mind. Her tales of the people she lived among are always kind. She recognized all their good qualities, which she joyously extolled; and while realizing their faults she softened them with the brush of sympathy.

Courageous little Babylonian princess, she faced hardships before unheard of, her life was often bitterly disagreeable, yet she had the strength and faith of greatness. Her memoirs are of a consistent, earnest truthfulness, full of brave striving for the right, of keen appreciation of life and joy. She has shown us the true heart of a woman, than which there is nothing finer; and in so doing she has given a deep and lasting value to her unpretentious book.

MEMOIRS OF A BABYLONIAN PRINCESS

I

I AM descended from a family in the East, who derive their origin from the Brahmins, and have long professed the Christian religion in the church of Travancore; a church which, according to history, was originally planted by Saint Thomas, the apostle of our Lord in the Indies. My ancestors, some centuries ago, according to the tradition of our family, left Travancore for Persia, and finally migrated to Bagdad. My grandfather, the Emir Abdallah, was a man of great wealth, consisting of lands and other property; including houses, silkworks, sheep, and camels; of which latter alone he possessed five thousand.

Upon the death of my grandfather this great property descended to my father and his four brothers. It was my father's delight to employ all his influence, and a large portion of his riches, in plans for the propagation of the Christian faith. He himself professed the Chaldaic rite in communion with the church of Rome. His house was nevertheless at all times an asylum for the unfortunate of every denomination, whether Christian, Jew, or Mussulman. He built a house especially for the reception of strangers. He would go himself in quest of them, and, when he had found them, he would bring them in and wash their feet, and serve them at table with his own hands.

One individual, in particular, who sought an asylum in his house, when I was quite a child, I well remember. He was a missionary named Gabriel Dombo, who, for his zeal in the cause of religion, had been condemned to the cruel sentence of having his tongue cut out. This worthy man remained with us two years, and my father afterwards supplied him with sufficient funds to enable him to found a college for the instruction of missionaries.

The plague having broken out at Bagdad in the year 1804 with great malignity, my father found it necessary to retire with his family to a country residence which he possessed amidst the ruins of Nineveh. It was called Kasr el Aza, which signifies the Palace of Delight. This was the period of my birth; which took place in a tent in the desert, a short distance from my father's house, whither my mother had retired to bewail the loss of several members of her family who had been carried off by the plague, as well as that of a beloved brother, who had come to his death by the bite of a serpent received while he was hunting, having first undergone the torture inflicted by a method of cure which has prevailed from the highest antiquity in Mesopotamia. Under this system the patient is prevented from sleeping, for five days, by the beating of drums, and by being pricked with needles, should he show any symptoms of drowsiness. During the whole of this time he is fed entirely on milk, with which he is constantly supplied until it causes him to vomit, when both milk and venom are supposed to be ejected simultaneously from the stomach.

To this torture was my unfortunate uncle subjected during five days, but to no purpose, for the poison had entered too deeply into his system to be removed by any human means.

At length the plague ceased its ravages, but not until, in its destroying course, it had swept away entire families, and filled every house with mourning. My parents then returned to Bagdad, and there I remained until I was four years old. We resided at a spacious country mansion, distant about an hour's ride from the city on the banks of the Tigris, surrounded by gardens of vast extent, abundantly stocked with date trees, sweet lemons, and oranges, and fertilized by numerous streamlets supplied from the neighboring river. In this delightful spot I passed the days of my infancy. Many and many were the games of hide and seek, which I played with my brothers, amongst their numerous labyrinths; and the recollection of them is, I think, at this moment, as fresh on my memory as it was at any period of my existence.

Our next door neighbor was an Osmanli Aga, a truly devout Moslem, noted for his scrupulous observance of all the duties prescribed by the Koran, and his horror of unbelievers, of whatever sect or nation. He detested a Shiàh with as much cordiality as he did a downright Kafir. He never suffered a day to pass without repeating the due number of prayers, and going through the mattaniaths prescribed by the law.

I remember, when I was about eight years old, I was one day playing at hide and seek with my brother—at that age I was as nimble as a kitten; and, after an hour's play in the garden, the fancy took me to climb a large date tree, which was hard by the wall that separated our garden from that of this Mussulman. Here I secreted myself, enchanted with the idea of sending my brother on a fruitless chase after me all over the garden.

My trick succeeded to my utmost wish. Between the leaves of the trees I could see the little fellow running, first here and then there, and stopping at intervals to consider whether he had left any nook or corner unexplored; but never for a moment did he suspect the place of my concealment. After enjoying his embarrassment for a considerable length of time, I bethought me how I should make known to him the place of my concealment. At length, prompted, I suppose, by the genius of mischief, imitating as nearly as I could, the tone of the Mollah, who regularly summoned from the nearest minaret all the true believers to prayer, I cried with a loud voice—"La illahoun ila Allah w' Mahommed rasul Allah."—"There is no God but God, and Mahomet is his prophet." "El salat akhsan min eltaam."—"Prayer is better than food." As it was just about the time of mid-day prayer, my brother supposed it to be the voice of the Mollah himself, until a loud laugh, which I could not repress, at the success of my trick, discovered me perched in my hiding-place. He was as much diverted with it as myself; but when we returned to the house, he was thoughtless enough to relate the story of what had passed to my father.

Now my parent was as pious a Christian as ever existed, and of so peaceable a disposition, that, upon all occasions, he cautiously avoided giving any offense, or offering the slightest insult to his Mahomedan fellow-subjects. Instead, therefore, of being amused at what I had done, he condemned me to a confinement for three days to my own room, and gave directions that dates and water should be my only sustenance, at the same time impressing upon my youthful mind this caution—"Knowest thou not that the very walls have ears?"

Over the garden wall of our Moslem neighbor grew clusters of sweet lemons, of an enormous size. Days and days had I watched them, as they hung ripening in the sun, with a longing eye and a watering mouth, and many were the schemes which I revolved in my mind, to get possession of one of them. At length, like our first mother, whose sin is believed by many to have been committed at no great distance from this very spot, unable any longer to resist the promptings of the evil one, I became a perfect Bedouin. Several times I was foiled in my attempt by the unexpected appearance of my brothers or cousins. One day, however, when there appeared to be no danger of interruption, I directed a servant to place a ladder against the wall, and up I mounted. The forbidden fruit was now within my reach. With a heart beating high with hope and joy, but not unmixed with apprehension, I seized the largest lemon I could lay my hands upon, and descended the ladder with it. Whether the fruit derived its exquisite flavor from the manner in which I had obtained it, or whether it was in reality of superior excellence, I will not venture to decide; but I well remember that I relished it more than any sweet lemon I had ever before eaten, and that I have never since tasted one of equal flavor.

Here, however, my enjoyment ended. Like other transgressors, I paid a heavy penalty for the sin I had committed, in the remorse and stingings of conscience which speedily followed it. My father never omitted to read to his family and household, once, at least, in the day, the ten commandments, and a portion of the Holy Scriptures. Every day, therefore, when he came to the commandment which says, ''Thou shalt not steal,'' my uneasy conscience smarted afresh. But not content with merely reading the commandment, he would frequently enlarge upon it, and pursue it to its most remote application. ''He who is faithful in small things,'' he would say, ''is faithful also in great: he who begins by pilfering trifles, will become in time, by habit, a confirmed thief; the only atonement is immediate restitution of what has been stolen.''

Unable, any longer, to support the load of remorse with which my mind became burdened by this constant appeal to my conscience, I set seriously about thinking in what way I could make reparation for the injury I had done our neighbor; and as it was out of my power to return the Moslem a lemon of so large a size as the one I had purloined, I hit upon the notable expedient of replacing it, by flinging over his wall three or four of smaller dimensions.

With this expiatory act I concluded the affair would have ended. Unfortunately, however, a complaint was shortly afterwards made to my father, that some member of his family had been amusing himself by throwing fruit into his garden, which had alighted on the heads of some of the children who were playing in it. Upon this my father immediately summoned all of us into his presence, and subjected us to a rigid examination. Of course, every one denied having any knowledge of the circumstance, until it came to my turn to be questioned. The maxims he had instilled into me, which forbade the telling an untruth, even though the object of telling it should be the salvation of the world, rushed into my mind, and I at once made a full confession of what I had done. I described the agony I every day endured while at prayers, from remorse of conscience, and I submitted myself to his will, expecting nothing less than a long and severe penance. I was, however, most agreeably mistaken; for so high a value did my parent set upon frankness and openness of character, that he not only freely forgave me for what I had done, but even went so far as to chide my urchins of brothers, who had already bestowed upon me the nickname of "the lemon-stealer."

From that day to this I have never, knowingly, said anything which was not true. It was my first trial; and the mastery which I then obtained over the dread of consequences, has remained with me, through good fortune and through bad; though, I am sorry to say, that my inopportune ingenuousness has frequently made me commit, what the French call, *bêtises,* and been the source of much trouble. Whenever, in traveling in my native country, I have had the misfortune to fall in with a Bedouin, I never could help telling him, not only that I had money about me, but the actual amount of it. Had, however, the Wahabis, the Yezidis, and the other predatory bands of Arabia, been the only beings to take advantage of my failing, the consequence would have been comparatively trifling; but, alas, for civilization! I am grieved to say, that this weakness of mine, if weakness it must be called, has been turned to far greater account in the most enlightened part of educated Europe, where the rays of knowledge are supposed to have dispelled the mists of our Asiatic darkness.

When a child I always preferred the society of my elders to that of those of my own age. I was never so happy as when in the company of my grandmother; an excellent woman, who lived to the age of one hundred and four years. Well do I remember the delight with which I heard the stories she related to me of her long and eventful life.

Of all our family I was my grandmother's chief favorite; so that when she died she bequeathed me her khelkhal, or anklets of silver gilt; her kirdan, or necklace, which was very splendid, having pendant strings of pearls and gold chains all round; her kharanfel, or nose-jewels; and her kamar, or girdle of jeweled gold; all which proofs of her affection for me I kept with religious care, until I was robbed of them in a public conveyance, together with many other valuables, the gifts of my parents, to a considerable amount.

My mother had no fewer than eighteen children, of whom nine only survived, five boys and four girls. I was the youngest daughter but one, who died at the age of ten years. My other two sisters both married. The younger of the two was a girl of rare beauty. Her skin was delicate and fair; her eyes were full and dark; and her hair black, and as soft as the finest silk. Her form was cast in the most perfect mold, and her whole presence was full of dignity and grace. Neither were her mental endowments inferior to those of her person, though they had not had the advantage of European cultivation. Such is the true portrait of my second sister, whose name was Ferida, that is, "the incomparable." At the age of twelve she was married to a wealthy sheikh of sixteen, and at thirteen she had given birth to a son.

This nephew of mine was the most precocious little urchin I ever met with. Before he was three years old he could repeat his paternoster, and go through those compliments which, in eastern countries, make the earliest part of education. Before he was four he could read perfectly well.

My sister lived till she was thirty-five, and had several children. But then, together with her whole family, she was carried off by the plague. In the space of a very few days there was not one living soul remaining in that once happy family. The seal of the Pasha, affixed to the door, to prevent unholy pillage, announced the desolation which reigned within.

II

ACCORDING to the custom of the East, where betrothals take place at a very early age, I had been engaged at my birth to a very young sheikh, a distant relation of the family, he being at that period only three years and a half old. When I was twelve, and he, of course, only fifteen and a half, my father made preparations for the marriage. But I had a strong desire to remain single. From the age of six I had been in the habit of reading the lives of the Fathers, and I had formed a determination to follow their example. There had been many weddings in our family, and the festivities on the occasion generally lasted several days; yet I never participated in them. On the contrary, I betook myself to my favorite books, the histories of saints, hermits, and martyrs; and the more I read, the more intense was my desire to share in their sufferings and their glory. My father, indeed, had rather encouraged me in the course I was pursuing; and upon one occasion, when he accidentally found me reading the Arabian Nights' Entertainments, he reproved me severely, and confined me to my room for three days; during which I was only allowed bread and water. From my love of solitude, and retired habits, I was called by my parents ''Bechmel Biri,'' the Daughter of the Desert; a name given to the turtle-dove, which, according to Oriental tradition, when it has lost its young, flies to the desert, and sings itself to death.

With a presentiment of the career of suffering to which I was destined, I made every effort in my power to induce my father to break off my intended espousal with the young sheikh, but in vain. I thereupon addressed myself to the youth, who, like myself, was under the influence of strong religious impressions; and on expressing my determination to become a nun, he resolved to take the vows of a Trappist; to which Order he attached himself, and now lives in a hermitage on Mount Lebanon, at the foot of the cedar mountain, on a ledge so precipitous, that a bird would hardly dare to make her nest on it. We parted with mutual regrets, and oft-repeated hopes, that, though our religious duties compelled us to separate on earth, we should, when our earthly tribulations were over, be united in heaven.

I was particularly fond of riding, and often accompanied my father and brother in their excursions. We frequently wandered through fields of corn, which grew to so great a height as entirely to conceal us. One day we were riding out, and had taken with us a beautiful young girl, whom I loved with the affection of a sister. We were about a three-hours' ride from Mosul, near a little village called Karagossa, when about fifty armed Arabs surrounded us. My father and brother carried arms; but it would have been madness to attempt anything against a force which could easily have destroyed us, or carried us off prisoners. The chief of the Arabs did not, however, offer us any violence; but, struck with the singular loveliness of Mariam, for that was the name of my friend, he insisted on carrying her away with him. We earnestly expostulated, but our entreaties were unavailing; and, with the deepest anguish, I beheld the loved companion of my youth torn from me by a band of lawless robbers, who, quick as lightning, made off with their prize. My brother lost no time in collecting a force sufficiently strong to have recaptured her; but the Arabs were well mounted, and the swiftness of their steeds rendered it impossible to overtake them.

Mariam had been passing some time with us, and it was intended that she should remain still longer. Her parents, therefore, were entirely ignorant of the peril into which their beloved daughter had fallen; and, as we trusted by active exertions to recover her, we wished to spare them the anguish which the knowledge of her misfortune would have occasioned.

My father caused inquiry to be made in every direction, and succeeded at length in discovering the retreat of the Arabs; who engaged, upon the payment of a heavy ransom, to restore their prize to the arms of her distressed friends. The sum they demanded was fifty purses, or close upon six hundred pounds in English money. This my father most gladly engaged to pay; and, immediately afterwards, I had the happiness to see my beloved friend once more under our roof. She related to us that she had been treated by the Arabs with the utmost consideration, which had greatly diminished the horrors of her captivity. The chief, though ardent in pressing his suit, had offered her no violence; neither had he resorted to any threats, for the purpose of terrifying her into compliance. She declared that she could not avoid being touched by the generosity of his conduct throughout.

Both of us were enthusiastic for the cause of religion. I scarcely know on which side the greater zeal lay. Her personal charms were of a high order, and of that description which, at first sight, strikes the beholder of the other sex with admiration. But she heeded not their attentions, and had no desire to make conquests; her whole soul being absorbed in religious meditation, and nearly her whole time passed in pious observances. At midnight, we frequently rose and passed hours together in acts of devotion. During Lent our food consisted of vegetables, boiled with rice; of which we partook sparingly once a day. On Sundays we frequently walked into the fields, and, collecting around us a number of our own sex, we instructed them in the principles of our faith. Hundreds were sometimes attracted to the spot, where, seated on the grass, they would attentively listen to our discourses. Like myself, Mariam had come to the determination to lead a life of celibacy, and to dedicate herself to the advancement of the true faith. This determination on our part caused us to be regarded with wonder, by all who knew us and were acquainted with our vows; for I was the first woman who, since the Mussulman dominion, had devoted herself solemnly to a life of celibacy in my neighborhood, and my friend was the second.

At this period the Christian Church at Mosul enjoyed singular immunity from persecution, under the mild and tolerant rule of the Pasha at that time in power.

With the good Pasha's death things assumed a different aspect, for his successor was a stern and headlong fanatic; the sworn enemy of Christianity, he panted for an opportunity to wreak his vengeance on the head of its followers.

The reigning Pasha having gained intelligence of my proceeding, and being determined to strike a decisive blow to check the spread of what he regarded as pestilential doctrines, and, if so it might be, to uproot them utterly from the land of Islam, appointed a day, on which all Christians were commanded to repair to a certain spot, there to renounce their faith, and publicly embrace that of Mahomet.

Many rejoiced in the prospect of suffering for Christ's sake, and looked forward to martyrdom as a short and glorious passage to the mansion of glory promised by the great Father of our faith to those who should hold fast to the Rock of Salvation even unto their life's end. My uncle, who was Archbishop of Diarbekir, my father, Mariam, and myself, were amongst this number. In company with those, whom neither chains, torture, nor death could tempt to deny their God, we went in procession, chanting hymns of praise and triumph, and almost believing that we saw the heavens opened, and beheld the crown of martyrdom extended.

We were taken before the Pasha, who had threatened to take our lives, and, I doubt not, would have kept his word, had not the charms of my companion turned aside his fury.

On being arraigned by the Pasha, we boldly entered upon the controversy, maintaining the truth of our faith, and endeavoring to convince him of his errors; but he was not a man of words, nor did he care to assert, still less to prove, the truth of his own faith. He threw us into prison. As for my friend and myself, we were shut up in a room of the Pasha's palace, but our unhappy companions were straightway dragged to a dungeon, and received daily two hundred blows of the bastinado.

I was sometimes allowed to visit them in their dark and loathsome cell, and could not restrain my tears on seeing my beloved parent and relations loaded with heavy chains. They, however, were not cast down, but kissing their chains, exhorted me not to weep, but rather to rejoice, that they were accounted worthy to suffer for Christ's sake, even as his disciples.

They were daily brought out into a court to receive the bastinado, and I was forced to hear the cries of my father, my brothers, and my uncles (one of whom was branded on the forehead with hot irons), without being able to alleviate their sufferings, or even to speak a word of comfort to them under their trials. One of my uncles died under the torture. My father and the rest of his relations were at length released, upon paying enormous sums to the rapacious and cruel tyrant who was the cause of their misfortunes.

The Pasha having enriched himself, and in some measure sated his religious enthusiasm, by this flagrant outrage on my family, and wholesale plunder of their property,—we were permitted to enjoy an interval of repose, and to return to our former way of life, without interference or molestation.

We resided at this time in the town of Alkoush, about twelve hours distant from Mosul, near which was situated a convent of considerable size. To this retreat I obtained my father's permission to retire, and a small room was prepared for me, the furniture of which consisted of a bed, made of the leaves of the palm tree, a small carpet, a skull, and a crucifix, with a number of books, comprising a copy of the Holy Scriptures, and the lives of those holy men who had devoted themselves to prayer and contemplation, among which was the life of St. Anthony of Egypt.

In this sacred asylum my days passed in quiet, if not in happiness. I rose at six, and remained on my knees for two hours engaged in prayer and meditation; then, taking my Bible, I read a certain number of chapters, after which I read for some time portions from the lives of the saints, and concluded by reciting fifty of the Psalms and other canticles, which occupied me till noon, at which hour I left my cell and wandered in the convent gardens, sometimes penetrating beyond them, and climbing the steep mountains which surrounded our dwelling.

As I ascended, magnificent views opened around me on every side, the Tigris was at my feet, and wild romantic scenery surrounded me in every direction. For hours would I remain rambling over these lofty hills, my thoughts employed in the contemplation of nature, thence ascending to the divine Author of all things, till songs of praise would break from my lips.

At four o'clock I usually returned to take a light and simple meal, which consisted of bread and fruit. Every Sunday my parents supplied me with these necessaries. A servant was charged to bring me weekly a large loaf, and enough dried fruits to last till the following Sunday.

III

Six months had passed over my head since I first entered the convent, at the expiration of which my father, brother, and two of my uncles set out for Bagdad, while my mother, with the rest of her family, went to reside a mile or two from Mosul, amid the ruins of Nineveh, in a small village the greater part of which belonged to my father. My mother would not hear of leaving me behind. I therefore accompanied her, and, finding at a short distance from our habitation the remains of a deserted convent, I took up my abode there, passing my time, as before, in prayer, meditation, and fasting. Some portion of every day I devoted to literary pursuits, and composed several books on religious subjects. After some months' residence in this secluded habitation, I formed the determination of founding an establishment of learned women, and prevailed upon two friends, one from Mesopotamia and the other from Persia, to join me in my retreat.

The inequality of the sexes had long been to me a subject of indignation. I saw Christian women treated almost like slaves, their understanding uncultivated and left in the grossest ignorance, while men enjoyed every advantage of education. I, therefore, determined to do all in my power to educate those of my own sex. One of my cousins undertook to give lessons in Kurdish, Chaldee, and Turkish; and I had a friend, a lady of great intelligence, who taught the Persian language. Numbers were attracted to our institution, in which no branch of education was neglected, and we were joined by many ladies of rank.

During this period I did not neglect the poorer classes, but constantly preached to them in the open air, giving them lessons of prudence and piety; thus laboring, as I hoped, not only for their good, but for that of generations to come. A shepherd of my father's, a Bedouin by birth, together with his whole family, was persuaded to embrace the Christian faith.

Whilst I was an inmate of the convent, I was visited by many ladies of consideration from the neighborhood, and, amongst others, by the sister of the Pasha, a woman of some learning, but, nevertheless, a great fanatic.

On one occasion, during a conversation which lasted three hours, I made a strenuous effort to lead her from darkness to the true faith. I expatiated largely and fearlessly on the glorious truths of the Christian religion; I used every argument which my reading could supply; I omitted no means of proof, nor failed to avail myself of any analogy which my fancy could suggest, for the purpose of convincing her of the superiority of the Christian faith over all other creeds, the offspring, as I labored to convince her, of human error and invention.

I did not fail to point out to her how these impositions had been fastened upon the minds of their credulous and ignorant brethren,—who, from the absence of all education and moral enlightenment, were absolutely the prey of any delusion, however absurd, to which they were incapable, alike from ignorance and indifference, of offering any resistance,— by ambitious adventurers, solicitous only for their own advancement, and either instigated by hatred towards their fellow-men, or animated by the lust of conquest and the thirst for fame.

God, the only true God, the everlasting Father, the Creator of the universe, the Giver of life, was, I told her, the Author of the Christian religion, and, in proof of my assertion, I referred her to the Bible, which I knew she was much in the habit of studying, and for which she entertained great respect. I also proved to her that Mahomet himself had borrowed his Koran mostly from the sacred volume—a tribute to, if not a proof of, its truth.

These, and other arguments of a similar kind, which, I hoped, might tend to her conversion, did I unweariedly urge during our long interview. The princess was astounded. Such language had cost many a Christian his head. Had not her brother, in the course of that very year, put to death multitudes of Christians, who had dared to avow their faith, and set at nought the established religion?

What, she asked me, could make me so far regardless of my safety as recklessly to indulge in language which, if carried elsewhere, might cost me my life?

I replied that I had long earnestly desired to suffer martyrdom in the cause of the Christian religion, if such should be the will of God. "God," I exclaimed, "who does all for our good, and disposes events according to his supreme will, will not permit me to suffer, unless it seem good to his Almighty wisdom."

At this display of resignation to the will of Providence, so perfectly Mahomedan in its character, the princess seemed surprised, and began to show me greater respect than before, struck by the exhibition, in a Christian, of a virtue, occupying so high a place in the faith which she herself professed.

After a mutual interchange of the customary compliments, the princess returned to the Zenana, in the same private manner as she had come.

Our conversation seemed to have made no inconsiderable impression on my illustrious visitor; for, at the termination of Ramazan, she sent me an invitation to dine with her. She had already given me repeated invitations, but my friends, apprehensive for my safety during the continuance of the fast, would not permit me to accept them. I was myself far from desirous of paying this visit, for many reasons; one of which was the necessity of putting off my usual dress (that of a recluse) and appearing in a garb more suited to the guest of so distinguished a personage.

Whilst these considerations passed in my mind, my conscience told me that my visit might, perhaps, be the means of reclaiming sinners, and diffusing the saving light of truth, where all before had been dark and without hope: and this admonition quickly putting to flight all personal considerations, and overcoming all personal apprehensions, at once determined me to go, if, peradventure, I might bring into the fold some of the lost sheep of Israel. I should have liked to have taken with me a young friend whom I greatly loved; but the invitation being strictly confined to myself, I did not dare to take any step which might put the Amira to inconvenience.

In a strictly private manner, attended only by two slaves, I set out for the Zenana, with a heart full of joy, elate with the hope of making converts to the true faith.

During the half hour in which we were enjoying our "nerghilahs" we conversed but little. Ten jairiahs stood before us, in an attitude of respect, with their arms reverentially folded before them. Our pipes being finished, the Pasha's sister offered to show me her brother's harem; a proposal to which my curiosity gave a ready assent.

We proceeded first to visit the bed-rooms; which were very numerous. They were covered, for the most part, with magnificent carpets. The beds, the manufacture of Bagdad, were made of the branches of the palm-tree, and were so light, that the whole frame might, without difficulty, be lifted with one hand. On the bed of the Pasha's chief wife were five mattresses, each covered with silk of a different color from the others, filled with the feathers of the peacock.

After spending an hour in this place, the princess conducted me to a salon opening upon the garden, where I was introduced to the wives of her brother, the Pasha, in number twenty-five. In addition to Georgians and Circassians, there were some from Kurdistan. One of them, with whom I conversed, was a beautiful Georgian, with large black eyes, shaded by eyelashes, long, dark, and drooping like a cedar branch, and not more than eighteen years old. She told me she was born of Christian parents, and that at the age of twelve she had been carried off to Constantinople, where she had been compelled, on pain of death, to abjure her faith and embrace that of Islam. She had a brother, a Mamaluke, in the service of the Pasha, who had also been forced to abjure the faith of his fathers. I asked her if she was happy in her present condition? she replied, that, far from rejoicing at her lot, she never ceased to bewail her hard fate, and to mourn the loss of parents and kindred.

Our colloquy was here cut short by the entrance of the Pasha himself. All instantly rose to salute him. He was a man apparently about forty years of age, and of lofty and commanding stature: his eyes were large, dark, and brilliant; his beard, which was black and copious, descended to his girdle, where his "hanjar," or dagger hung, its handle rough and sparkling with jewels. His dress was sumptuous and befitting his rank, and his courteous manner inspired confidence and respect.

The princess presented me to him as the relative of his "kerkhea," or lieutenant, which was the fact; whereupon he received me with distinguished politeness, and made many inquiries respecting my family and kindred, particularly after my father, who was at that time at Bassorah, on his way to Bagdad. Our conversation had lasted a quarter of an hour, when the mollah, from the minaret, began to call all true believers to the "salat al zohor," or mid-day prayer, whereupon the Pasha immediately took his leave, for the purpose of repairing to the adjoining mosque, leaving his "harem'" to say their prayers in the salon.

This summons is repeated five times during the day: at daybreak the mollah calls all true Mussulmans to their devotions, with the words, "prayer is better than sleep;" the summons to the salat al zohor, or mid-day prayer, is, "prayer is better than food;" the third call, at three o'clock, and is named "el assr;" the fourth, called "el muggerib," takes place at sunset; and the fifth at midnight.

Forthwith the ladies gave themselves up to their devotions; first going upon their knees, and then prostrating themselves on the ground, and kissing it, crying aloud, "There is no God but Allah! there is no God but the God of heaven, and Mahomet is his prophet; there is no hope, no refuge, save in the most high and mighty God." During all this time they had before them what they called a relic of the great Prophet himself, which was no less than a fragment of the very "sherwals," or trousers, said to have graced the limbs of Mahomet's sister, enveloped in paper, and encased in a rich gold cover, inlaid with diamonds. This precious relic they repeatedly kissed, and placed on their heads during their prayers.

These pious observances lasted about a quarter of an hour, during the whole of which period I remained seated on the "diwan," regarding the extraordinary scene with mingled curiosity. As soon as it was over, a slave entered and announced dinner. The invitation was promptly attended to, and we all proceeded to the dining-room, which, on account of the great heat of the weather (it being then the month of June) was one of the apartments opening, the whole width of one of its sides, into the court.

As it was late when I quitted the Pasha's palace, I did not return to my home, the convent, that evening, but took up my night's abode at the house of a married sister of mine, who resided at no great distance from the palace, near the mosque Nour el din.

IV

WE had now, for some years, led a life of uninterrupted felicity; when my father resolved to give an entertainment to his relatives and friends, in the open air, at a charming spot, not far from Mosul, on the banks of the Tigris. This was one of the ways in which he greatly loved to show his hospitality; and upon this occasion, as on many similar ones, he had invited, besides his numerous friends from Mosul and the neighborhood, several of the chiefs of the Kurd and Bedouin tribes, with whom he always maintained an intimacy.

The day was extremely splendid. Nature was decked in her holiday garments, for it was the month of May. All around was smiling. Adversity seemed to have taken leave of us for ever. My father had, once more, become wealthy. Everything seemed to promise him a dignified and protracted old age, until the hour when it should please Almighty God to gather him, full of years, to his fathers.

This was the happiest day of my life; my heart was overflowing with gratitude and thanksgiving. I had no wish or thought beyond that which it had pleased Providence to bless *me* with at that moment. All past cares and sorrows were forgotten, as things that had not been.

Seeing my father alone, at a short distance from us, I quitted my companions and flew to his side. He had never remained for so long a time together, in the bosom of his family, as during the last brief interval of tranquillity and peace. I was never so happy as when I could enjoy his society alone. Upon this occasion we wandered for some hours on the banks of the Tigris; our hearts swelling with gratitude to the Almighty Disposer of events for all his mercies.

I besought my father that we might again resort to this lovely spot together alone, and again indulge in pious musings. He cheerfully consented; but this was not to be. While my fond parent was promising to himself and to me many a happy hour of converse in this delightful place, at that very moment a gulf was yawning at our feet, which, ere long, was to close over all our worldly joys for ever.

Information had been carried to the ears of the Pasha, ever ready to entertain any charge against his Christian subjects, that treasure of immense value had been discovered by my father under the ruins of ancient Nineveh, and that he had appropriated it to his own use. In addition to this, he was accused of fomenting projects for the subversion of the Ottoman government and Islam.

A sincere, regular, legal investigation into the truth or false-hood of the charge was entirely out of the question. The bare suspicion was quite enough to justify extreme measures, more especially when the individual suspected happened to be a zealous Christian. With increasing means, my father was naturally enabled to give increased support to the Christian churches around him; and this just zeal in behalf of his own faith was easily perverted by designing men into a desire to undermine that of his rulers. But, whatever might be the impression on the minds of his persecutors, as to the truth of their accusation, there can be no doubt as to the advantages they would derive from the conviction of my father, namely, a second confiscation of his entire property.

Accordingly he was again cast into prison, together with his brothers, his former companions in suffering. Tortures, cruel and unceasing, were resorted to, in order to force from him an acknowledgment of his pretended crime, and a dis-closure as to the spot in which this pretended treasure was hidden. But all was in vain. My poor father had nothing to disclose. The only result of all their barbarity was to prove to his revilers with what calm resignation a Christian, firm in his faith, can endure the direst of sufferings.

But rapacity again prevailed. My beloved parent was set at liberty; the sentence of death having been commuted to that of confiscation of his entire possessions. Broken down both in body and spirit, covered with bruises and wounds, his feet a shapeless mass of black, festering flesh, the effects of the merciless blows of the bastinado, he was at length turned out of his dungeon, and conveyed to his home. Oh, God! what a frightful change! A short month since, and we were planning projects of future happiness and harmless enjoyments, during our happy walk on the banks of the Tigris.

Everything that unremitting attention, aided by the care of the most skillful surgeons, could effect, was resorted to in vain. My dear parent sank gradually. Nature was exhausted. His sufferings had passed the limits of human endurance. From the first his case was pronounced hopeless. Three weeks after his release found him at his last gasp.

From the moment of his liberation, I never quitted his

chamber. The awful moment now drew near. His soul, hovering over the brink of eternity, he called me to his bedside. "Poor child," he said, in faltering accents, "what will become of thee? Who will protect thee from the enemies of thy race, who have slain thy parent, and driven thy kindred to herd with the wild beasts of the desert? Preserve in thy heart, my dear daughter, the lively faith already implanted there, and the fear of the Almighty, and thou wilt have no need to fear the assaults of thy enemies. End thy days as thou hast begun them, a good Christian. God give thee patience in tribulation, and consolation in sorrow, until we again meet in that happy country where the humble followers of Christ need no longer dread the cruelty and oppression of unbelieving rulers."

This last persecution ended in the utter destruction of my family. One of my uncles expired, from the treatment he had· received, shortly after my father. Another, who was Archbishop of Diarbekir, was bound on the back of a wild horse, which was then driven into the desert. Many days he was without food. At last, he succeeded in disengaging himself from his bonds, and, for fifteen days, subsisted on wild herbs, until at length he succeeded in reaching some place of safety. He was so fortunate as to reach a town from whence he traveled much, with varying fortunes, over Persia, and other countries, and finally returned to Diarbekir, where he now resides.

My mother died of grief; surviving my father but a very short time.

The hand of Providence was heavy upon us. Nevertheless, my cup of bitterness was not yet full. Yet a little time, and a pestilence spread throughout the land, carrying off, in its ravages, ninety-five thousand souls in Mosul and its neighborhood. Every one with whom I was connected by blood, in this, to me, ill-omened city, perished by that plague—leaving me an orphan in the wide world. I longed for death, but the destroying angel passed me by. I wandered about the fields, scarcely knowing where I was, or what I did. I passed on, heedless of surrounding objects; save when the sight of some well-known spot lacerated my heart anew, by awakening it to a sense of its bitter loss and mournful desolation.

V

MY father left me all that he had been able to save from the wreck of his fortune, his ring, his hanjar, and his watches; which, together with some pearls and jewels of value and some Persian shawls, were intrusted for security to the hands of a bishop of his acquaintance who, seeing my forlorn and destitute condition, kindly proposed to take me with him to Bagdad. To this I assented, and we left the ill-omened city, the scene of all my woes, a few months after the frightful tragedy which had torn from me all that rendered life desirable.

On arriving at Bagdad, I went to the house of a friend, and there took up my abode.

During the time that I remained at my friend's house, a project entered my head, to which I forthwith directed all my energies; namely, to set on foot an institution for the education of women. This was a project which I had cherished from early life. I was not absolutely destitute of means. With the little property that still remained to me, together with the assistance of my friend, who was wealthy, and whose coöperation I did not despair of obtaining, I confidently hoped to be able to carry my wishes into effect.

On first opening the subject to my protector, he would not listen to it, but treated it as a visionary scheme, which could have been only generated in an over-sanguine and even a disordered imagination, and one which could not possibly lead to any beneficial results. I was not, however, to be easily discouraged. I endeavored to raise his enthusiasm by setting before him, in as glowing colors as I possibly could, the glory that would result from rescuing the weaker sex amongst us from the inferiority, both moral and physical, in which they had hitherto continued, and the happiness that would attend those who should assist in raising them to that condition of usefulness for which they were designed by a beneficent Creator.

By what means, I asked, have they been reduced to this state? By ignorance. Who is it that has suffered them to remain in that ignorance? Who is it that has erected the dam which shuts out the streams of intelligence from their minds? Man. Man alone is the culprit. He first denies to woman the means of attaining knowledge, and then avails himself of her ignorance, the consequence of his own neglect, as a justification for contemning his victim. Let it no longer be said that we imitate the fabled example of our infidel neighbors, in the treatment of our helpmates. Our religion teaches us better things. Let us not be Christians in name only. Where, I asked him, is it taught us by our church, that woman should be the slave of man? Was she not formed to be his companion, his solace, through all the changing scenes of his earthly existence? On what pretense then, does man assert his privilege to tyrannize over our sex? Has not our sex more patient endurance, more tender attention than yours? Like you, have we not an immortal soul? Are not the sensibilities of woman as keen as, nay, keener than, those of her lord and master? Has she not a heart equally alive to gratitude; and a sense of wrong as deep? Notwithstanding all this, she is often treated as if she had neither a head nor a heart.

At last, I succeeded in convincing him of the correctness of my views, and in inducing him to lend his powerful aid towards the accomplishment of my project, which, in the course of a few months after my arrival at Bagdad, gave fair promise of a successful result.

Accordingly we took a spacious house, and here we established our college, to which, in a short time, flocked great numbers of every class in society; for we made no distinction of rank. Young girls, rich as well as poor, and even grown-up women of condition, desirous of obtaining instruction, poured in incessantly. We taught reading, writing, needle-work, and embroidery; and no pains were spared to inculcate the principles of the Catholic religion.

Thus tranquilly and successfully we proceeded, day after day adding to the number of our pupils; actuated by no other ambition than that of making ourselves useful to our fellow-creatures, and if possible, to redeem the female sex from the humiliating position in which they stood in our country. We sought not for celebrity neither did we desire or expect interference; when, suddenly, our labors were interrupted, our plans frustrated, and our institution itself was ultimately destroyed, by the officious intermeddling of a European missionary, who happened, at that time, to be residing in Bagdad.

. This individual, who had obtained his appointment in the East by the influence of an illustrious personage, was of humble origin. His chief object was to amass wealth, of which he made a very foolish parade; rivaling the Pasha himself in the breed of his horses, and in the richness and splendor of their trappings.

It is scarcely possible to conceive the injury, the deadly mischief, that has been done to the true faith in the East, by missionaries, appointed without any adequate investigation into the qualifications they possess for the high and sacred office which they are called upon to fill. Too much caution cannot be exercised in selecting men whose duties are to inculcate the doctrines of meekness, long-suffering, charity, and brotherly love, amongst a people but too well accustomed, alas! to behold and feel the effects of opposite qualities in their infidel rulers and fellow-countrymen.

In so saying, I do but give the results of my own experience, of not a few years, in the East, the land of my birth; during which it has been my lot to meet with numerous persons sent to convert unbelievers, and confirm their Christian brethren in the determination to hold fast the true faith amidst stripes and bondage. None but those who have lived amongst the persecuted Christians of the East can have any conception of the inestimable benefits which would result to the cause of our holy religion, by the appointment of men fitted by vocation, education, and genuine piety, for the high post of missionary; neither can they form a just estimate of the deadly blow inflicted on the righteous cause, by the selection of men distinguished for qualities of an opposite description.

The individual to whom I have alluded, introduced himself into our humble, unpresuming establishment, with the avowed purpose of inculcating the principles of the Christian religion. He was received by us with open arms. He was welcomed as the special messenger of Christ; for such we of the East are ever disposed to view the European missionary—the hem of whose garments we were almost ready to kiss. To Europe we look for final deliverance from the yoke of the oppressor; and every Christian from Europe is therefore regarded and treated by us as a deliverer, and as such honored far beyond his Asiatic brethren.

To this man, alas! I owed the frustration of my darling project. I might, perhaps, have stolen a march on the senseless and heedless Moslem, quaffing the fumes of fatalism on the musnud of security; but the conduct of the European completely baffled me, and once more made me an outcast on the world.

Having no power to resist, I at length yielded; and weary of life, and thoroughly deceived in the estimate I had formed of mankind, I became desperate, and resolved to quit the crowded cities, where men seemed only to congregate for the purpose of vilifying and injuring one another, and betake myself to the desert. I determined to go wherever my fancy or caprice led me; heedless of the consequences, so that I did but escape from the nest of hornets into which my unlucky stars had cast me. "Amongst the wandering hordes of the desert," I said, "I shall at least meet with open friends and open enemies. I shall then meet no wolf in sheep's clothing, to fasten on his unsuspecting prey, who fed and protected him from the wintry blast. At least, I shall not fall by the dagger of him with whom I have broken my bread and eaten my salt."

Fully bent on carrying my purpose into execution, my heart filled with a loathing which had well-nigh driven Christian charity from my breast, I addressed a letter to the chief of the Dryaah tribe, occupying the desert, in the neighborhood of Babylon and Bagdad, with whom my father had been well acquainted, and who had many and many a time been our guest, during our sojourn at Bagdad, in happier days. Not in the least doubting that my letter would meet with a favorable reception, I made preparations for my immediate departure, and forthwith packed up all the valuables I possessed, ready for my journey. I was not disappointed. Shortly after I had dispatched my letter, the chief Dryaah Ebn Shalan, sent his son and daughter for me, with camels to carry my baggage, and his own favorite mare for my especial use.

I was almost moved to tears by this kind attention to one who had nothing but thanks and good wishes to offer in return; and that from a man whom my late persecutors would have despised, to the full extent that their fears would permit them, as a lawless barbarian. Coming after so many injuries, and so much sorrow, it seemed like a ray from heaven, to cheer me on my weary pilgrimage. I set off with the son and daughter of this kind-hearted Bedouin chief, as though I had been going to my own parents; such was my firm reliance on their hospitality, their inflexible honor, and their adherence to their engagements; and it was not long before we reached the encampment of the tribe, who had pitched their tents upon a spot near the Euphrates, hard by the ruins of ancient Babylon; which they had chosen on account of its general fertility, and the abundance and excellent quality of the pasture.

Nothing could exceed the cordiality of my reception at the encampment. I had no sooner arrived at the tent of the chief Dryaah Abn Shalan, than I was introduced to his wife and relatives, and treated with the highest distinction. The spectacle which presented itself to my sight, on approaching the encampment, was most imposing. On the right, and on the left, as far as the eye could reach, the vast plain was covered with tents: while countless flocks of sheep, camels, and horses innumerable, were grazing on the pastures around. No mountain range, no tree intervened to break the level surface of the plain which surrounded us on every side.

The customary compliments being over, we proceeded to make arrangements for my accommodation in the department allotted to the women. By means of putting up a curtain, I managed to secure for myself a sort of private apartment, which was particularly desirable, in order that I might not shock or offend my hostess, by the performance of certain religious duties, for which she might entertain an aversion.

Here I forthwith installed myself, together with my effects. I must, however, confess, that I could not contemplate, without a shudder, the idea of lying down to sleep at night upon the bare ground, with nothing but a carpet to protect me from the attacks of noxious reptiles, of which I always entertained the greatest dread. From infancy upwards I had ever been accustomed to sleep on beds made of palm-leaves, resting on a frame constructed of palm-wood, and therefore I did not at first at all relish the idea of changing this for a simple carpet. Fortunately, there were no scorpions to be dreaded

here, otherwise I do not think, after what I had already suffered from their bite, that any persuasion could have induced me to trust myself on the ground. In Bagdad it was,
I remember, by no means an uncommon thing, on rising in
the morning, to find among the palm-leaves one of these poisonous reptiles, which had been impaled on one of the sharp
spines, in its endeavor to reach the body of the individual
sleeping above. Here, however, there were no fears on this
score.

When we had completed our arrangements, my kind enter-
tainers immediately set about preparing some refreshment.
We all sat down to a repast, consisting of dates fried in butter,
eggs, and camel's milk; to which primeval fare my keen appe-
tite, the result of a long ride, enabled me to do ample justice.

We were not long in dispatching our meal, and passed our
time between that and dinner in taking a walk upon the
banks of the Euphrates, or "Nahr al Fraat," as it is called
by the inhabitants of the country through which it flows. I
never enjoyed a stroll more; the sky was beautifully serene,
the air mild without being oppressive, and all nature clad in
her holiday suit. We came at every step upon vast numbers
of gazelles, which are found here in an abundance almost
incredible; never did I see such immense flocks of them; during our short walk I am sure I beheld thousands. Their
flesh is exceedingly good, and is held in high esteem among
the Bedouins, who constantly make parties to hunt them; the
flavor of their flesh is not unlike that of a goose.

The sun had nearly reached the horizon, which here presented precisely the same appearance as at sea, when we returned to the tent of the sheikh, where we found dinner prepared. The hour for that meal was sunset. It was, therefore,
not long before we were all seated at the chief's hospitable
board. Our repast, it is true, was not distinguished by any of
the refinements of culinary science. There was, however, no
lack of good, substantial dishes; and fastidious indeed must
the individual have been who could not have made a hearty
meal out of the dishes before him. Of roasted meats we had
three different sorts; sheep, lamb, and gazelles, of which I
am particularly fond. Besides these, there was a dish to

which, during my abode with the Bedouins, I could never reconcile myself; and that was the leg of a camel roasted; though I daily saw them partake of it, apparently with infinite relish. To say the truth, these Arabs came to their dinner with appetites so sharpened by severe exercise, that I believe they would not have made wry faces even though it had been served up in an undressed state.

When the solid part of the meal had been disposed of, we were regaled with the fruits of various descriptions. I myself had taken the precaution to bring with me a large supply of lemons, dates, figs, and almonds; besides cakes, dried fruits, and fruits preserved with sugar. So that I was enabled to contribute something to the feast.

The Bedouins eat with hands alone; making use of neither knife, fork, nor spoon. "Allah," they say, "gave man a mouth and a pair of hands to be mutually serviceable to each other. Why, then, should we mock the Eternal Spirit by fashioning to ourselves strange implements of wood or metal? Shall the tooth despise the finger, or shall the finger forget the way to the tooth? What fork is equal to nature's fork—the hand of man? Our ancestors," say they, "used no cunningly fashioned instruments. But did they, therefore, perish with hunger? Were their years not as the sands of the desert? In their bodies was the blood of health, and in their minds the salt of wisdom. Shall we then laugh at the beards of our fathers?"

Thus, with the means at hand of eating with forks of gold, they persist in eating with their fingers. I, who was less accustomed to such primitive usages, had brought with me a spoon; but, on learning the horror in which such contrivances were regarded by my hosts, I determined not to wound their feelings, and consequently conveyed the food into my mouth like themselves, though the consequence of my politeness was not unfrequently a scalded finger.

After dinner, coffee was introduced; for, unlike the Wahabis, whose rigid asceticism forbids them the use of this harmless stimulant, the Dryaahs do not forbid the enjoyment of it. This rejoiced me exceedingly; for I should have regretted the absence of the cup of coffee, to which I had been so long accustomed. There was, nevertheless, still a difficulty to be got over. The Dryaah tribe abhor "the accursed weed," as they call tobacco, and prohibit the use of it.

I had so long been used to enjoy a nargileh after taking my coffee, that the prospect of losing the accustomed indulgence produced by no means a pleasing anticipation in my mind. I had brought all my apparatus with me, but was afraid to produce it, from the dread of shocking the scruples of my host and his friends. His considerate kindness relieved me, however, from my distress. When upon a visit to my father, he observed that, in common with most others, I invariably took a nargileh after dinner. He, therefore, now insisted on my observing the custom, and kindly forbade the sacrifice which I was prepared to make to his own prejudices. The highest bred cavalier of civilized Europe could not have shown more genuine politeness.

After a few days' stay with the Dryaah tribe, I became acquainted with the principal members of all the neighboring tribes, by whom I was, on every occasion on which I visited them, treated with the greatest kindness, hospitality, and distinction; and at this distance of time, gratitude compels me to declare my conviction, that more real friends are to be made in one day amongst these lawless tribes, than could be formed in a century in civilized Europe, where it is possible to live for half a century without knowing your neighbor.

Whatever may be the defects in the Bedouin character, assuredly lukewarm friendship is not one. An attachment once formed, continues through life. In every change of fortune, they cheerfully share their last crust with those to whom they have sworn eternal friendship. Even their bitterest enemy, if overwhelmed with misfortune, is not excluded from their widespread hospitality. Violations of it are punished with death. An instance of this, which occurred in the Dryaah tribe, was related to me. A stranger, who had been a guest of this tribe, after quitting their encampment, placed himself under the protection of a neighboring tribe; by some members of which he was himself maltreated, and his slave killed. The Dryaah tribe, on becoming acquainted with this outrage, this gross violation of the Bedouin laws, immediately made war on their neighbors, and avenged the injury done to their guest. The person of their greatest enemy is ever held sacred, should he seek their tents and claim their protection.

It is impossible to live for any length of time amongst this people, without becoming sensible of the height to which the rare virtues of friendship and hospitality, not the mere parade of them, having for its object rather the gratification of the pride of the giver than the solace of the receiver, are carried.

While I resided with the Dryaah tribe, I was told of an instance of hospitality, which appears to me scarcely inferior to that recorded in holy writ, where the prophet was relieved by the kind charity of the pious widow. The principal actor in this case was also a widow, whose children had all been cut off in a fray with a neighboring tribe; so that she was left, in her old age, without stay or prop, and with barely a sufficiency for her subsistence.

It chanced one day, that two travelers, worn with fatigue, and fainting from thirst and hunger, passed the door of her tent. They were Indians, and on their way to Damascus. The widow, who was sitting before her tent, seeing the pitiable condition of the famished travelers, invited them to repose within, and refresh themselves with what fare she had to offer, saying "See, I have yet a sheep left, which we will straightway kill, that your hunger may be stayed: bread I have none, but there are those around who will give it me; tarry here, therefore, while I hasten to fetch it."

The travelers, seeing that the widow was poor, and had but this one sheep, would have gone away, preferring to suffer yet awhile the pangs of hunger, rather than diminish her scanty store. But the widow heeded them not. She killed her sheep; she sought bread amongst her neighbors; and setting the provisions before them, she said: "Wherefore would ye have grieved me by going away empty? for if ye meet not with hospitality in the tents of the living, it had been as well if ye had sought succor in the graves of the dead. Shall not the Almighty render me that which I give an hundred fold? Allah kerim!"—"God is merciful!"

Seeing daily so many admirable virtues manifested in the conduct of my Bedouin hosts, I was much tempted to make some efforts towards their conversion to the true faith, and to induce them to study Catholic books. I even went so far as to baptize a few children in secret; but I was unsuccessful. Their settled dislike to all established forms of worship, and their aversion to books in general, completely baffled all my efforts. I went to as great lengths as I dared. I spoke to them of a future state; of the rewards which would attend the virtuous hereafter; and of the punishments which would await the wicked. Often had I the commandment "Thou shalt not steal," at the tip of my tongue, but fear prevented my giving it utterance. Many of the other divine commandments I found they knew, and what was still better, constantly practiced.

VI

I HAD long cherished an anxious desire to visit the scenes of the events recorded in holy writ. From a very early age, ever since I was ten years old, I had burned to climb those awful mountains, whence the Creator made known his will to man; and to behold the desert spot, where the Redeemer of the world fed thousands with five loaves and two small fishes; the scene of the passion and the crucifixion for the redemption of man. Often did I dream that I was wandering in those very places, which my soul had so long yearned to visit, until at last I became thoroughly absorbed in this one idea, to the exclusion of nearly every other.

Full of this determination, I no sooner gained the encampment than I went straight to the tent of the good-hearted chief, to announce my intention. The sheikh expressed his regret that I should have resolved on leaving them so soon; adding, however, that if my destiny required me to go, opposition was of course out of the question. I had even more difficulty in reconciling myself to part with my Bedouin female friends, whose simple and unaffected behavior towards me had entirely won my affection, and made a separation from them little less severe than a parting from beloved friends and kindred.

Upon my arrival at Bagdad, I learned that a caravan, consisting of an immense number of travelers, of every nation and calling, had been collecting for the last seven or eight months, the roads being, during the whole of that time, so infested by robbers, that it was impossible to proceed with safety, and would start in the following month of March, for Damascus. By this caravan, therefore, I determined to proeeed to Palestine.

On the third day after our departure from Hid, as we were going, as usual, listlessly on, I saw upon a sudden a great commotion towards the front of our cavalcade. I was, of course, anxious to ascertain the reason of so unusual an occurrence, and inquired of a man, whom I saw hurrying past me, with alarm in his countenance, what had happened. ''The samiri! the samiri!'' he cried, ''is approaching!'' ''The samiri!'' I said to myself, ''how can that be? Not a cloud is to be seen; the sky is clear and bright; not a breath of air is stirring. How can this be? by what means have they come at the knowledge that this scourge of the desert is about to pour its fury on our heads?''

I was not suffered to remain long in doubt. The camels in the front rank had, I was told, refused to proceed, which was an infallible sign that the dreaded wind was not far off. Two hours before its approach they seem to scent its coming; for nothing can induce them to continue their onward course. Though upon all other occasions they are the most docile and obedient of living creatures, they become, under these circumstances, more perverse and obstinate than the ass or the mule. They bury their heads in the sand, and remain crouched down, until the scourge has passed over them. This wonderful instinct bestowed on them by the great Creator of all things for their own preservation, is also instrumental in saving the lives of innumerable travelers, who, ignorant of the approach of the wind, would be overwhelmed and suffocated by it, before they could make any efforts for their own preservation.

No sooner was it known that the samiri was near at hand, than a halt was immediately called, and all became bustle and confusion. The tent camels were quickly unloaded, and the tents pitched, with a rapidity increased by fear and dread. The horses were secured, their heads covered and their ears filled with cotton. As for the camels, the faithful harbingers of danger, they were left to their own sagacity.

The travelers had now betaken themselves to their tents, where they cast themselves on the ground, and covered their heads with the "mashallah." A profound stillness reigned throughout the vast multitude, as if every one expected to escape the fury of the blast, by keeping his very existence a secret.

Still the samiri came not. An hour had passed away, and the sky was yet serene, and the air tranquil. When the intelligence which had thrown us into this state of consternation was first brought to us, a Turkish lady, who was traveling with us, happened to be near me. This lady seemed disposed to laugh at the fears expressed by more experienced travelers. After giving orders for the pitching of her tent, she invited me to join her in a cup of coffee and a chibouk, saying that she was certain the samiri would not reach us for some time to come; perhaps not for an hour or more. From the continued fineness of the weather, and the stillness of the atmosphere, I was much disposed to be of her way of thinking, and accepted her invitation with pleasure, as an agreeable mode of passing the time until the approach of the wind should warn me to fly to my tent.

As I lifted the curtain of it, I thought I perceived a slight motion in the air, but I took no heed of it, and was soon comfortably seated with my Turkish acquaintance, talking over indifferent matters, sipping some excellent coffee, which her slaves had prepared at a very short notice, and enjoying my chibouk. It was, however, not long before I saw the sides of the tent agitated, slightly at first, but gradually increasing in violence. I rose hastily from my cushion, and putting aside the curtain, looked out upon the desert.

Casting my eyes to windward, I beheld a vast column, which seemed to reach from earth to heaven, gradually approaching our encampment. Round and round the huge lurid mass whirled, as it slowly but steadily kept its onward progress, casting a deep shadow across the naked desert. Above my head all was serenity and peace; but, as the column approached, the gusts which had just now produced the slight rustling in the curtains of the Mahomedan lady's tent, became more sudden and violent; now chilling the blood, and now scorching, like the blast of a furnace.

I felt a sensation of terror creeping over me; my strength seemed to have abandoned my limbs; I felt as though I was

suffocated, and gasped for breath. All hopes of gaining my
own tent were vain, for the samiri was now at hand. I closed
the curtain in haste, and, stretching myself on the ground,
covered my head and face with my "mashallah." My companion did the same, and we awaited the passage of the
scourge in silent dread.

The sides of our tent were now shaken with fearful violence.
I expected every moment to see it lifted high in the air, and
ourselves exposed to the destructive fury of the blast, which
makes a speedy tomb for all who oppose its onward progress.
The tent was become like a hot bath, and we breathed with
the greatest difficulty. I remember well the horror with
which, in that moment of terror, I contemplated the idea of
dying in the company of an unbeliever. I have lived to entertain more charitable sentiments.

The storm lasted seven or eight hours, at the end of which
we rose from the ground, and, after returning thanks to
Almighty God for our preservation, each after her own fashion, I went forth from the tent to see what had been the fate
of my own friends. As I passed along the encampment I met
crowds looking like men arisen from the dead, issuing from
their tents, and exchanging congratulations upon their recent
escape; and turning leeward I beheld the deadly dreaded column holding on its desolating course towards the horizon.

The tents being now struck, and the camels loaded, we proceeded on our way. In our progress we beheld, with horror,
the dead bodies of several Arabs, who had been overtaken by
the samiri, scorched to a cinder on the dreary waste.

For several days after this awful visitation we marched
on without meeting with any incident of sufficient moment to
break the monotony of the journey. We had been eight days
without seeing water, and during the whole of that time our
poor camels had not tasted a single drop. Upon the ninth
day they were observed to prick up their ears and snuff the
air, with other demonstrations of restlessness and excitement.
On a sudden they began to utter the most extraordinary cries,
stamping and fidgeting in a way which made it almost impossible to manage them and retain one's seat. At length,
with one accord, they all made a rush forward, and started
off at the pace of which no one who has not seen a thirsty

camel, which scents the water, can have any idea. At first I could not understand this movement; for, look where I would, no water was perceptible by the eye.

As I had taken care to select one of the tallest camels I could meet with, in order to have a better view of the country through which our path lay, I was now, the first in this involuntary camel race, and expected, every moment, to be dashed to the earth. And, sure enough, we at last came to the bank of a stream, into which my camel, altogether forgetful of its accustomed politeness, forthwith plunged up to its middle, and began to drink eagerly.

If I found it difficult to maintain my seat when only the animal and myself had the water to ourselves, I now found it next to impossible to do so, when every minute another and another camel dashed in, and what with their plunging and jostling, I consider it little short of a miracle that I escaped drowning. In this desperate extremity I cried aloud to the driver, whom I saw, looking on with the utmost indifference, at the edge of the bank, to come to my assistance. "Come and save me," I said; "if you do not, I and your camel must both sink together."

"Fear nothing," he replied, "the camel is wise; Allah has given him knowledge that he may not perish in the water." "That may be very true," I rejoined, "but how is it possible that he can know the depth of this stream, in which, most probably, he never was before?" "By the beard of my father, by the light of my eyes," continued he, "you are safe: on my head be it. Which of the dangers of the desert has Providence hidden from the holy animal?"

This calm resignation to the will of destiny, when the danger is another's, I could readily understand; but, notwithstanding his assurances, I felt no little alarm at my perilous position, from which I saw no means of extricating myself. However, as the driver refused to lend me any assistance, and seemed resolved to leave the result to Providence, I could only resign my fate into his hands.

When the camels had drunk their fill they walked out in the calmest manner imaginable, with their bellies swelled to the size of mountains. We then proceeded to unload our beasts and pitch our tents; for we had determined to pass the night at this refreshing spot; where I enjoyed a delightful walk along the banks of the stream before supper.

VII

As we drew near to the Holy City, my impatience increased to such a pitch, that the fatigue of the journey, the roughness of the road, and the danger of attack, were all forgotten. It is impossible for me to describe the feelings which filled my breast, when one of our guides pointed out to me at length the Jebel el Zeitun, the Mount of Olives; my eyes were filled with tears. We entered by the Bab el Ghasali, the Gate of the Beloved, and went straightway to the house of a Hawajah, or noble of Aleppo, who was a Christian, and who had promised us an asylum during our stay in Jerusalem.

The next day I rose early, and went to see the Holy Sepulcher. On entering the church I was greatly surprised on meeting a priest, whom I had known at Alkoush. He related to me some rather curious circumstances connected with his life. He had always been remarkable for his piety; which increased to such a degree, that at length he was filled with a fervent desire to obey the Scripture to the very letter. To this end he determined to eschew all worldly pleasure and gain, and to sever at once all attachments which were incompatible with the practice of the evangelical counsels.

Having visited, in a cursory manner, the principal points of interest contained in the church of the Holy Sepulcher, I returned home, with the full determination to revisit the sanctuary on the morrow.

To my great mortification I learned, on my return, that the plague had broken out in the city; which distressing event would, for a time, utterly prevent the execution of my project. Immediately we were all in a state of bustle, and actively engaged in preparing for our departure, that we might be placed beyond the reach of the pestilence.

On the following day I set out with my companions for Jaffa; where we soon succeeded in finding a vessel that was bound for Alexandria, in which we straightway embarked, about the end of 1825. From Alexandria I proceeded to Grand Cairo; from which place I made an excursion to Mount Sinai.

After a stay of some weeks at Grand Cairo I returned to Alexandria; whence I embarked in a vessel bound for Smyrna; and from Smyrna I proceeded to Constantinople. These excursions occupied me nearly twelve months; but as nothing happened to me of sufficient importance to call for particular notice, and inasmuch as it forms no part of my design to give minute and accurate descriptions of cities, already so faithfully and so ably described by travelers who have visited them note-book in hand, I feel it will far better become me, (my object being merely to give to the British public a plain and unpretending narrative of my misfortunes,) to pass over this period of my history thus briefly, than either to make a feeble attempt to enter into details and disquisitions foreign to my habits of thought, without note or memorandum to refer to, or to weary the reader with a dry catalogue of everyday occurrences, important only to myself.

I returned to Jerusalem just before Holy Week in 1826. The day before Palm Sunday I went to the Holy Sepulcher, and joined with enthusiasm in the pious labor of cleansing the sanctuary for the great and joyous festival which was to take place on the following day. It fell to my lot to sweep away the dust from the Calvary and the Holy Sepulcher itself. Oh, joyous labor! inestimable privilege! With what intense emotion was my breast filled while I performed my sanctified task! With what floods of grateful tears did I water the spot where man's redemption was finally accomplished!

The events of my life, during the twelve years I have been in Europe, would alone fill volumes; but the length to which these memoirs have already extended, warns me that I have already trespassed too long on the patience of the reader; who, I cannot doubt, must, before this, be heartily tired of a recital of occurrences and misfortunes, interesting only to the humble individual who now relates them. Besides these considerations, a series of severe attacks of tic douloureux in my eyes and head almost unnerve me from making the attempt at the present moment. I do not, however, despair of giving to the world a detailed account of the adventures and persecutions which have befallen me during my exile of twelve years in Italy, France, and England; in which period.

circumstances have brought me in contact with persons of considerable note in the different states of Europe, and which have been marked by events of considerable interest.

My expectations of deriving an income by teaching my native language, and translating Oriental works and manuscripts, have by no means been realized. It might possibly have been otherwise had it pleased Providence to spare the kind-hearted nobleman who took so warm an interest in my welfare. I have, moreover, suffered sadly in health since my stay in England, where my formidable enemy, the "tic douloureux," has renewed his attacks with redoubled vigor, occasionally visiting me with paroxysms so violent as well-nigh to deprive me of reason.

What pang is sharper to the warm and sensitive mind than to meet with cold indifference where the heart yearns for affection and sympathy? Calmness and fortitude, when displayed in the endurance of pain and calamity, are heroic virtues; but, when exhibited in the case of injuries sustained by false friends, are no better than a cold, unfeeling egotism, which deadens the feelings, and soon leads to an indifference for all that is virtuous and good. The humble apartment in which I have taken up my abode happens to abut close upon a Roman Catholic chapel; and it has often been a sweet consolation to me, when lying on my bed exhausted with pain and anguish, and unable to hear mass, to catch the pious strains as they arose from the assembled congregation in accents of prayer and thanksgiving. I knew that many of those with whom I was acquainted attended mass and vesper at this chapel, and often I said to myself, "Will they not put in practice the lessons they have just heard, and visit the poor and the sick?" But I waited in vain!

The exertions made by my friends to recover some of my lost property, and to procure me a pension, have also, up to the present time, proved unsuccessful; and God only knows what would have been my lot, had it not been for the repeated kindness and generosity of an illustrious personage, who has only descended from the highest place in the kingdom to rise still higher by the display of unostentatious virtues, the possession of which lifts their owner far above all worldly honors and dignities; and for the generous aid afforded me by a kind and noble-hearted friend, Mr. Hudson Gurney.

It is sweet to relate services received in the time of affliction. During my stay in London I have been much indebted to the kindness of the noble and high-minded Chevalier Bunsen, whose talents and exertions are ever at the service of those whom they can benefit, and to the considerate attentions received from his amiable lady. It has also been my good fortune to become acquainted, through the kind introduction of Sir Robert Inglis, with the widow of the late Mr. Rich, who formerly held the post of British Consul at Bagdad, where he distinguished himself by a frank and dignified fulfillment of his duties, and by his vigorous and learned researches. She has been my comforter in sickness, and my consolation in adversity.

Why should I despair? Has not Providence thrown me at length on a shore whose inhabitants are renowned to the uttermost corners of the earth for their noble institutions, for the relief of every ill to which our nature is subject, where the hungry are fed, the naked clad, and where the destitute and houseless never fail to find shelter?

I will, therefore, take courage, and abide with patience and resignation the progress of events, and, with a fervent prayer that it may be the lot of no one that reads these pages, to encounter one-half of the calamities which have befallen their unfortunate authoress, I now, for the present, respectfully bid the British public farewell.

THE END

HANS CHRISTIAN ANDERSEN

THE MOST WIDELY KNOWN OF DANISH WRITERS; FAMED AS A
LOVER OF CHILDREN AND OF ALL MANKIND

1805-1875

(INTRODUCTORY NOTE)

Hans Christian Andersen, writer of fairy tales and wonder stories,
finds a place in our hearts while we are yet little children, and with the
years our affection for him grows. To read his account of his life is to
understand his universal attraction. His human sympathy and love are
a constant inspiration. He has named his memoirs "The Fairy Story of
My Life," and it is a fairy story. But it is made so, not by his rise
from obscurity to fame, but by his sweetness and humility, his faith and
grateful loyalty.

Andersen was born in the Danish island of Funen in 1805. His father
was a poor shoemaker, but possessed of a powerful and independent
mind which constantly craved education. This desire he communicated
to his son, Hans, who patiently and sunnily endured hardship and priva-
tion in pursuit of learning, and began his formal schooling at the age
of twenty, entering a class with small boys of eight and ten.

His genius, in lyric poetry as well as prose, soon became apparent.
His confrères seem always to have resented his success and were continually disparaging him and his works. Andersen bore this envy, it
seems to have been mere snobbery, with a kindly spirit, and though his
sensitive heart bled at the critics' jibes, he met these with a humorous,
even tender, raillery.

Abroad however he was everywhere acclaimed, and was received with
honor by the European rulers of his day. Naturally then he delighted
to travel, and his memoirs are a colorful account of his wanderings,
stored with tender incidents, exquisite pictures of scenic beauty, and
glowing accounts of famous fêtes. In his pages Dickens, Jenny Lind,
Victor Hugo, Mrs. Browning, all the celebrities of his century, live again
as his honored friends. Andersen's warm-hearted admiration and praise
of their characters as well as their genius, seem to invite us, too, to
know them intimately, to share in the joyous wonder of their charm
and worth. Truly, it is a "fairy story" he offers us, in which the

spirits of Goodness and Truth, Innocence and Eternal Youth wander over a happy world.

THE FAIRY STORY OF MY LIFE

I

My life is a lovely story, happy and full of incident. If, when I was a boy, and went forth into the world poor and friendless, a good fairy had met me and said, "Choose now thy own course through life, and the object for which thou wilt strive, and then, according to the development of thy mind, and as reason requires, I will guide and defend thee to its attainment," my fate could not, even then, have been directed more happily, more prudently, or better. The history of my life will say to the world what it says to me,—There is a loving God who directs all things for the best.

In the year 1805 there lived at Odense, in a small mean room, a young married couple, who were extremely attached to each other; he was a shoemaker, scarcely twenty-two years old, a man of a richly gifted and truly poetical mind. His wife, a few years older than himself, was ignorant of life and of the world, but possessed a heart full of love. The young man had himself made his shoemaking bench, and the bedstead with which he began housekeeping; this bedstead he had made out of the wooden frame which had borne only a short time before the coffin of the deceased Count Trampe, as he lay in state, and the remnants of the black cloth on the wood-work kept the fact still in remembrance.

Instead of a noble corpse, surrounded by crape and wax-lights, here lay, on the second of April, 1805, a living and weeping child,—that was myself, Hans Christian Andersen. During the first day of my existence my father is said to have sat by the bed and read aloud in Holberg, but I cried all the time. "Wilt thou go to sleep, or listen quietly?" it is reported that my father asked in joke; but I still cried on; and even in the church, when I was taken to be baptized, I cried so loudly that the preacher, who was a passionate man, said, "The young one screams like a cat!" which words my mother never forgot. A poor emigrant, Gomar, who stood as god-father, consoled her in the meantime by saying that the louder I cried as a child, all the more beautifully should I sing when I grew older.

Our little room, which was almost filled with the shoemaker's bench, the bed, and my crib, was the abode of my childhood; the walls, however, were covered with pictures, and over the work-bench was a cupboard containing books and songs; the little kitchen was full of shining plates and metal pans, and by means of a ladder it was possible to go out on the roof, where, in the gutters between it and the neighbor's house, there stood a great chest filled with soil, my mother's sole garden, and where she grew her vegetables. In my story of the "Snow Queen" that garden still blooms.

I was the only child, and was extremely spoiled, but I continually heard from my mother how very much happier I was than she had been, and that I was brought up like a nobleman's child. She, as a child, had been driven out by her parents to beg, and once when she was not able to do it, she had sat for a whole day under a bridge and wept. I have drawn her character in two different aspects,—in old *Dominica*, in the "Improvisatore," and in the mother of Christian, in "Only a Fiddler."

My father gratified me in all my wishes. I possessed his whole heart; he lived for me. On Sundays he made me perspective glasses, theaters, and pictures which could be changed; he read to me from Holberg's plays and the "Arabian Tales;" it was only in such moments as these that I can remember to have seen him really cheerful, for he never felt himself happy in his life and as a handicraftsman. His parents had been country people in good circumstances, but upon whom many misfortunes had fallen: the cattle had died; the farm house had been burned down; and lastly, the husband had lost his reason. On this the wife had removed with him to Odense, and there put her son, whose mind was full of intelligence, apprentice to a shoemaker; it could not be otherwise, although it was his ardent wish to attend the grammar school, where he might learn Latin. A few well-to-do citizens had at one time spoken of this, of clubbing together to raise a sufficient sum to pay for his board and education, and thus giving him a start in life; but it never went beyond words. My poor father saw his dearest wish unfulfilled; and he never lost the remembrance of it. I recollect that once, as a child, I saw tears in his eyes, and it was when a youth from the grammar school came to our house to be measured for a new pair of boots, and showed us his books and told us what he learned.

"That was the path upon which I ought to have gone!" said my father, kissed me passionately, and was silent the whole evening.

He very seldom associated with his equals. He went out into the woods on Sundays, when he took me with him; he did not talk much when he was out, but would sit silently, sunk in deep thought, whilst I ran about and strung strawberries on a bent, or bound garlands. Only twice in the year, and that in the month of May, when the woods were arrayed in their earliest green, did my mother go with us, and then she wore a cotton gown, which she put on only on these occasions and when she partook of the Lord's Supper, and which, as long as I can remember, was her holiday gown. She always took home with her from the wood a great many fresh beech boughs, which were then planted behind the polished stone. Later in the year sprigs of St. John's wort were stuck into the chinks of the beams, and we considered their growth as omens whether our lives would be long or short. Green branches and pictures ornamented our little room, which my mother always kept neat and clean; she took great pride in always having the bed linen and the curtains very white.

One of my first recollections, although very slight in itself, had for me a good deal of importance, from the power by which the fancy of a child impressed it upon my soul; it was a family festival, and can you guess where? In that very place in Odense, in that house which I had always looked on with fear and trembling, just as boys in Paris may have looked at the Bastile—in the Odense house of correction.

My parents were acquainted with the jailer, who invited them to a family dinner, and I was to go with them. I was at that time still so small that I was carried when we returned home.

The House of Correction was for me a great storehouse of stories about robbers and thieves; often I had stood, but always at a safe distance, and listened to the singing of the men within and of the women spinning at their wheels.

I went with my parents to the jailer's; the heavy iron-bolted gate was opened and again locked with the key from the rattling bunch; we mounted a steep staircase—we ate and drank, and two of the prisoners waited at the table; they could not induce me to taste of anything, the sweetest things I pushed away; my mother told them I was sick, and I was laid on a bed, where I heard the spinning-wheels humming near by and merry singing, whether in my own fancy or in reality, I cannot tell; but I know that I was afraid, and was kept on the stretch all the time; and yet I was in a pleasant humor, making up stories of how I had entered a castle full of robbers. Late in the night my parents went home, carrying me, the rain, for it was rough weather, dashing against my face.

Odense was in my childhood quite another town from what it is now, when it has shot ahead of Copenhagen, with its water carried through the town and I know not what else! Then it was a hundred years behind the times; many customs and manners prevailed which long since disappeared from the capital. When the guilds removed their signs, they went in procession with flying banners and with lemons dressed in ribbons stuck on their swords. A harlequin with bells and a wooden sword ran at the head; one of them, an old fellow, Hans Struh, made a great hit by his merry chatter and his face, which was painted black, except the nose, that kept its genuine red color. My mother was so pleased with him that she tried to find out if he was in any way related to us, but I remember very well that I, with all the pride of an aristocrat, protested against any relationship with the "fool."

The first Monday in Lent the butchers used to lead through the streets a fat ox, adorned with wreaths of flowers and ridden by a boy in a white shirt and wearing wings.

The sailors also passed through the streets with music and flags and streamers flying; two of the boldest ended by wrestling on a plank placed between two boats, and the one that did not tumble into the water was the hero.

But what especially was fixed in my memory, and is very often revived by being spoken about, was the stay of the

Spaniards in Funen in 1808. Denmark was in alliance with Napoleon, who had declared war against Sweden, and before anybody was aware of it, a French army and Spanish auxiliary troops, under command of Marshal Bernadotte, Prince of Pontecorvo, entered Funen in order to pass over into Sweden. I was at that time not more than three years old, but I remember very well those dark-brown men bustling in the streets, and the cannon that were fired in the market-place and before the bishop's residence; I saw the foreign soldiers stretching themselves on the sidewalks and on bundles of straw in the half-burned St. John's Church. The castle of Kolding was burnt; and Pontecorvo came to Odense, where his wife and his son Oscar were staying. The school-houses all about were changed into guard-rooms, and the mass was celebrated under the large trees in the fields and on the road. The French soldiers were said to be haughty and arrogant, the Spanish good-natured and friendly; a fierce hatred existed between them; the poor Spaniards excited most interest.

A Spanish soldier one day took me up in his arms and pressed against my lips a silvery image, which he carried on his breast. I remember that my mother became angry because, as she said, it was something Catholic, but I was pleased with the image, and the foreign soldier danced with me, kissed me, and shed tears; he had, perhaps, children himself at home. I saw one of his comrades carried to execution for having killed a Frenchman. Many years afterward, in rememberance of that, I wrote my little poem, "The Soldier," which, translated into German by Chamisso, has become popular, and is found in German "Soldier Songs" as an original German song.

Quite as lively as the impression of the Spaniards was a later event, in my sixth year, namely, the great comet of 1811; my mother told me that it would destroy the earth, or that other horrible things threatened us, to be found in the book of "the prophecies of Sibylla." I listened to all these superstitious stories and fully believed them. With my mother and some of the neighboring women I stood in St. Canut's church-yard and looked at the frightful and mighty fire-ball with its large, shining tail.

All talked about the signs of evil and the day of doom.
My father joined us, but he was not of the others' opinion at
all, and gave them a correct and sound explanation; then my
mother sighed, the women shook their heads, my father
laughed and went away. I caught the idea that my father
was not of our faith, and that threw me into a great fright!
In the evening my mother and my old grandmother talked
together, and I do not know how she explained it; but I sat
in her lap, looked into her mild eyes, and expected every moment that the comet would rush down, and the day of judgment come.

The mother of my father came daily to our house, were it
only for a moment, in order to see her little grandson. I was
her joy and her delight. She was a quiet and most amiable
old woman, with mild blue eyes and a fine figure, which life
had severely tried. From having been the wife of a countryman in easy circumstances she had now fallen into great
poverty, and dwelt with her feeble-minded husband in a little
house, which was the last, poor remains of their property. I
never saw her shed a tear; but it made all the deeper impression upon me when she quietly sighed, and told me about
her own mother's mother,—how she had been a rich, noble
lady, in the city of Cassel, and that she had married a "com-
edy-player,"—that was as she expressed it,—and run away
from parents and home, for all of which her posterity had now
to do penance. I never can recollect that I heard her mention the family name of her grandmother; but her own maiden
name was Nommesen. She was employed to take care of the
garden belonging to a lunatic asylum, and every Sunday
evening she brought us some flowers, which they gave her
permission to take home with her. These flowers adorned
my mother's cupboard; but still they were mine, and to
me it was allowed to put them in the glass of water.
How great was this pleasure! She brought them all to me;
she loved me with her whole soul. I knew it, and I understood it.

She burned, twice in the year, the green rubbish of the
garden; on such occasions she took me with her to the asylum,
and I lay upon the great heaps of green leaves and pea-straw.
I had many flowers to play with, and—which was a circum-

stance upon which I set great importance—I had here better food to eat than I could expect at home.

All such patients as were harmless were permitted to go freely about the court; they often came to us in the garden, and with curiosity and terror I listened to them and followed them about; nay, I even ventured so far as to go with the attendants to those who were raving mad. A long passage led to their cells. On one occasion, when the attendants were out of the way, I lay down upon the floor, and peeped through the crack of the door into one of these cells. I saw within a lady almost naked, lying on her straw bed; her hair hung down over her shoulders, and she sang with a very beautiful voice. All at once she sprang up, and threw herself against the door where I lay; the little valve through which she received her food burst open; she stared down upon me, and stretched out her long arm toward me. I screamed for terror —I felt the tips of her fingers touching my clothes—I was half dead when the attendant came; and even in later years that sight and that feeling remained within my soul.

Close beside the place where the leaves were burned the poor old women had their spinning-room. I often went in there, and was very soon a favorite. When with these people, I found myself possessed of an eloquence which filled them with astonishment. I had accidentally heard about the internal mechanism of the human frame, of course without understanding anything about it, but all these mysteries were very captivating to me; and with chalk, therefore, I drew a quantity of flourishes on the door, which were to represent the intestines; and my description of the heart and the lungs made the deepest impression. I passed for a remarkably wise child, that would not live long; and they rewarded my eloquence by telling me tales in return; and thus a world as rich as that of the Thousand and One Nights, was revealed to me. The stories told by these old ladies, and the insane figures which I saw around me in the asylum, operated in the mean time so powerfully upon me, that when it grew dark I scarcely dared to go out of the house. I was therefore permitted, generally at sunset, to lie down in my parents' bed with its long, flowered curtains, because the press-bed in which I slept could not conveniently be put down so early in the evening on account of the room it occupied in our small dwelling; and here, in the paternal bed, lay I in a waking dream, as if the actual world did not concern me.

I was very much afraid of my weak-minded grandfather. Only once had he ever spoken to me, and then he had made use of the formal pronoun, "you." He employed himself in cutting out of wood strange figures,—men with beasts' heads and beasts with wings; these he packed in a basket and carried them out into the country, where he was everywhere well received by the peasant women, because he gave to them and their children these strange toys. One day, when he was returning to Odense, I heard the boys in the street shouting after him; I hid myself behind a flight of steps in terror, for I knew that I was of his flesh and blood.

I very seldom played with other boys; even at school I took little interest in their games, but remained sitting within doors. At home I had playthings enough, which my father made for me. My greatest delight was in making clothes for my dolls, or in stretching out one of my mother's aprons between the wall and two sticks before a currant-bush which I had planted in the yard, and thus to gaze in between the sun-illumined leaves. I was a singularly dreamy child, and so constantly went about with my eyes shut, as at last to give the impression of having weak sight, although the sense of sight was especially cultivated by me.

An old woman-teacher, who had an A B C school, taught me the letters, to spell, and "to read right," as it was called. She used to have her seat in a high-backed arm-chair near the clock, from which at every full stroke some little automata came out. She made use of a big rod, which she always carried with her. The school consisted mostly of girls. It was the custom of the school for all to spell loudly and in as high a key as possible. The mistress dared not beat me, as my mother had made it a condition of my going that I should not be touched. One day having got a hit of the rod, I rose immediately, took my book, and without further ceremony went home to my mother, asked that I might go to another school, and that was granted me. My mother sent me to Carsten's school for boys; there was also one girl there, a little one somewhat older than I; we became very good friends;

she used to speak of the advantage it was to be to her in going into service, and that she went to school especially to learn arithmetic, for, as her mother told her, she could then become dairy-maid in some great manor.

"That you can become in my castle when I am a nobleman!" said I, and she laughed at me and told me that I was only a poor boy. One day I had drawn something which I called my castle, and I told her that I was a changed child of high birth, and that the angels of God came down and spoke to me. I wanted to make her stare as I did with the old women in the hospital, but she would not be caught. She looked queerly at me, and said to one of the other boys standing near, "He is a fool like his grandpapa," and I shivered at the words. I had said it to give me an air of importance in their eyes, but I failed and only made them think that I was insane like my grandfather.

I never spoke to her again about these things, but we were no longer the same playmates as before. I was the smallest in the school, and my teacher, Mr. Carsten, always took me by the hand while the other boys played, that I might not be run over; he loved me much, gave me cakes and flowers, and tapped me on the cheeks. One of the older boys did not know his lesson and was punished by being placed, book in hand, upon the school-table, around which we were seated, but seeing me quite inconsolable at this punishment, he pardoued the culprit.

The poor old teacher became, later in life telegraph-director at Thorseng, where he still lived until a few years since. It is said that the old man, when showing the visitors around, told them with a pleasant smile: "Well, well, you will perhaps not believe that such a poor old man as I was the first teacher of one of our most renowned poets! H. C. Andersen was one of my scholars!"

Sometimes, during the harvest, my mother went into the field to glean. I accompanied her, and we went, like Ruth in the Bible, to glean in the rich fields of Boaz. One day we went to a place the bailiff of which was well known for being a man of a rude and savage disposition. We saw him coming with a huge whip in his hand, and my mother and all the others ran away. I had wooden shoes on my bare feet, and in my haste I lost these, and then the thorns pricked me so that I could not run, and thus I was left behind and alone. The man came up and lifted his whip to strike me, when I looked him in the face and involuntarily exclaimed,—"How dare you strike me, when God can see it?"

The strong, stern man looked at me, and at once became mild; he patted me on my cheeks, asked me my name, and gave me money.

When I brought this to my mother and showed it her, she said to the others, "He is a strange child, my Hans Christian; everybody is kind to him: this bad fellow even has given him money."

I grew up pious and superstitious; I had not the least idea of what it was to be in want; my father lived, as the saying is, from hand to mouth, but what we had was more than enough for me. As to my dress I was rather spruce; an old woman altered my father's clothes for me; my mother would fasten three or four large pieces of silk with pins on my breast, and that had to do for vests; a large kerchief was tied round my neck with a mighty bow; my head was washed with soap and my hair curled, and then I was in all my glory.

In that attire I went with my parents for the first time to the theater. Odense at that time had already a substantial play-house built, I believe, for the company of Count Trampe or that of Count Hahn; the first representations I saw were given in the German language. Mr. Franck was the director; he gave operas and comedies. "Das Donauweibchen" was the favorite piece; the first representation, however, that I saw was Holberg's "Village Politicians."

The first impressions which a theater and the crowd assembled there made upon me was, at all events, no sign of anything poetical slumbering in me; for my first exclamation on seeing so many people was, "Now, if we only had as many casks of butter as there are people here, then I would eat lots of butter!" The theater, however, soon became my favorite place, but, as I could only very seldom go there, I acquired the friendship of the man who carried out the play-bills, and he gave me one every day. With this I seated myself in a corner and imagined an entire play, according to the

name of the piece and the characters in it. That was my •
first, unconscious poetizing.

My father's favorite reading was plays and stories, although
he also read works of history and the Scriptures. He pondered in silent thought afterward upon that which he had read;
but my mother did not understand him when he talked with
her about it, and therefore he grew more and more silent.
One day he closed the Bible with the words, ''Christ was a
man like us, but an extraordinary man!'' These words horrified my mother and she burst into tears. In my distress I
prayed to God that he would forgive this fearful blasphemy in
my father. ''There is no other devil than that which we have
in our own hearts,'' I heard my father say one day, and I
made myself miserable about him and his soul; I was therefore entirely of the opinion of my mother and the neighbors,
when my father, one morning, found three scratches on his
arm, probably occasioned by a nail, that the devil had been
to visit him in the night, in order to prove to him that he
really existed.

My father had not many friends; in his leisure hours he
used to take me with him out into the woods. He had a great
desire for country life, and it happened just at this time that a
shoemaker was required at a manor house who would set up
his bench in the neighboring village, and there have a house
free of rent, a little garden, and pasture for a cow; by permanent work from the manor and these additional helps one
could manage nicely. My mother and father were very eager
to have the place, and my father got a trial job to sew a pair
of dancing-shoes; a piece of silk was sent him, the leather he
was to furnish himself. All our talk for a couple of days
turned upon these shoes; I longed so much for the little
garden where we could have flowers and shrubs, and I would
sit in the sunshine and listen to the cuckoo. I prayed very
, fervently to God that he would grant us our wishes, and I
thought that no greater happiness could be bestowed upon us.
The shoes were at last finished; we looked on them with a
solemn feeling, for they were to decide our future. My father
wrapped them in his handkerchief and went off, and we waited
for him with faces beaming with joy. He came home pale
and angry; the gracious lady, he said, had not even tried the

shoes on,—only looked at them sourly, and said that the silk was spoiled and that he could not get the place. "If you have spoiled your silk," said my father, "I can be reconciled to spoiling my leather too," so he took a knife and cut off the soles.

There was no more hope of our getting into the country. We mingled our tears together, and I thought that God could easily have granted our wish. If he had done so, I had no doubt been a peasant all my life; my whole future would have been different from what it has been. I have often since thought and said to myself: Do you think that our Lord for your sake and for your future has let your parents lose their days of happiness?

My father's rambles in the wood became more frequent; he had no rest. The events of the war in Germany, which he read in the newspapers with eager curiosity, occupied him completely. Napoleon was his hero: his rise from obscurity was the most beautiful example to him. At that time Denmark was in league with France; nothing was talked of but war; my father entered the service as a soldier, in hope of returning home a lieutenant. My mother wept, the neighbors shrugged their shoulders, and said that it was folly to go out to be shot when there was no occasion for it.

The morning on which the corps were to march I heard my father singing and talking merrily, but his heart was deeply agitated; I observed that by the passionate manner in which he kissed me when he took his leave. I lay sick of the measles and alone in the room, when the drums beat, and my mother accompanied my father, weeping, to the city gate. As soon as they were gone my old grandmother came in; she looked at me with her mild eyes and said it would be a good thing if I died; but that God's will was always the best.

That was the first day of real sorrow which I remember.

The regiment advanced no further than Holstein; peace was concluded, and the voluntary soldier returned to his work-stool. Everything fell into its old course. I played again with my dolls, acted comedies, always in German, because I had only seen them in this language; but my German was a sort of gibberish which I made up, and in which there oc-curred only one real German word, and that was *"Besen,"* a word which I had picked up out of the various dialects which my father brought home from Holstein.

"Thou hast indeed some benefit from my travels," said he in joke. "God knows whether thou wilt get as far; but that must be thy care. Think about it, Hans Christian!" But it was my mother's intention that, as long as she had any voice in the matter, I should remain at home, and not lose my health as he had done.

That was the case with him: his health had suffered. One morning he woke in a state of the wildest excitement, and talked only of campaigns and Napoleon. He fancied that he had received orders from him to take the command. My mother immediately sent me, not to the physician but to a so-called wise woman some miles from Odense. I went to her. She questioned me, measured my arm with a woolen thread, made extraordinary signs, and at last laid a green twig upon my breast. It was, she said, a piece of the same kind of tree upon which the Savior was crucified.

"Go now," said she, "by the river side toward home. If your father is to die this time, then you will meet his ghost."

My anxiety and distress may be imagined,—I, who was so full of superstition, and whose imagination was so easily excited.

"And thou hast not met anything, hast thou?" inquired my mother when I got home. I assured her, with beating heart, that I had not.

My father died the third day after that. His corpse lay on the bed; I therefore slept with my mother. A cricket chirped the whole night through.

"He is dead," said my mother, addressing it; "thou needest not call him. The ice maiden has fetched him."

I understood what she meant. I recollected that, in the winter before, when our window-panes were frozen, my father pointed to them and showed us a figure like that of a maiden with outstretched arms. "She is come to fetch me," said he, in jest. And now, when he lay dead on the bed, my mother remembered this, and it occupied my thoughts also.

He was buried in St. Knud's church-yard, by the door on the left-hand side coming from the altar. My grandmother planted roses upon his grave. There are now in the self-same place two strangers' graves, and the grass grows green upon them also.

After my father's death I was entirely left to myself. My mother went out washing. I sat alone at home with my little theater, made dolls' clothes, and read plays. It has been told me that I was always clean and nicely dressed. I had grown tall; my hair was long, bright, and almost yellow, and I always went bareheaded. There dwelt in our neighborhood the widow of a clergyman, Madame Bunkeflod, with the sister of her deceased husband. This lady opened to me her door, and hers was the first house belonging to the educated class into which I was kindly received. The deceased clergyman had written poems, and had gained a reputation in Danish literature. His spinning songs were at that time in the mouths of the people. In my vignettes to the Danish poets I thus sang of him whom my contemporaries had forgotten,—

> Spindles rattle, wheels turn round,
> Spinning songs depart;
> Songs which youth sings soon become
> Music of the heart.

Here it was that I heard for the first time the word *poet* spoken, and that with so much reverence, as proved it to be something sacred. It is true that my father had read Holberg's plays to me; but here it was not of these that they spoke, but of verses and poetry. "My brother the poet," said Bunkeflod's sister, and her eyes sparkled as she said it. From her I learned that it was a something glorious, a something fortunate, to be a poet. Here, too, for the first time, I read Shakespeare,—in a bad translation, to be sure; but the bold descriptions, the heroic incidents, witches, and ghosts were exactly to my taste. I immediately acted Shakespeare's plays on my little puppet theater. I saw Hamlet's ghost, and lived upon the heath with Lear. The more persons died in a play, the more interesting I thought it. At this time I wrote my first piece: it was nothing less than a tragedy wherein, as a matter of course, everybody died. The subject of it I borrowed from an old song about Pyramus and Thisbe; but I had increased the incidents through a hermit and his son, who both loved Thisbe, and who both killed themselves when she died. Many speeches of the hermit were passages from the Bible, taken out of the Little Catechism, especially from our duty to our neighbors. To the piece I gave the title "Abor and Elvira."

"It ought to be called 'Perch (Aborre) and Stockfish,'" said one of our neighbors wittily to me as I came with it to her after having read it with great satisfaction and joy to all the people in our street. This entirely depressed me, because I felt that she was turning both me and my poem into ridicule. With a troubled heart, I told it to my mother.

"She only said so," replied my mother, "because her son had not done it." I was comforted, and began a new piece, in which a king and queen were among the *dramatis personæ*. I thought it was not quite right that these dignified personages, as in Shakespeare, should speak like other men and women. I asked my mother and different people how a king ought properly to speak, but no one knew exactly. They said that it was so many years since a king had been in Odense, but that he certainly spoke in a foreign language. I procured myself, therefore, a sort of lexicon, in which were German, French, and English words with Danish meanings, and this helped me. I took a word out of each language, and inserted them into the speeches of my king and queen. It was a regular Babel-like language, which I considered only suitable for such elevated personages.

I desired now that everybody should hear my piece. It was a real felicity to me to read it aloud, and it never occurred to me that others should not have the same pleasure in listening to it.

The son of one of our neighbors worked in a cloth manufactory, and every week brought home a sum of money. I was at loose ends, people said, and got nothing. I was also now to go to the manufactory, "not for the sake of the money," my mother said, "but that she might know where I was, and what I was doing."

My old grandmother took me to the place, therefore, and was very much affected, because, said she, she had not expected to live to see the time when I should consort with the poor ragged lads that worked there.

Many of the journeymen who were employed in the manufactory were Germans; they sang and were merry fellows, and many a coarse joke of theirs filled the place with loud laughter. I heard them, and I there learned that, to the innocent ears of a child, the impure remains very unintelligible. It took no hold upon my heart. I was possessed at that time of a remarkably beautiful and high soprano voice, and I knew it; because when I sang in my parents' little garden, the people in the street stood and listened, and the fine folks in the garden of the states-councilor, which adjoined ours, listened at the fence. When, therefore, the people at the manufactory asked me whether I could sing, I immediately began, and all the looms stood still: all the journeymen listened to me. I had to sing again and again, whilst the other boys had my work given them to do. I now told them that I also could act plays, and that I knew whole scenes of Holberg and Shakespeare. Everybody liked me; and in this way the first days in the manufactory passed on very merrily. One day, however, when I was in my best singing vein, and everybody spoke of the extraordinary brilliancy of my voice, one of the journeymen said that I was a girl, and not a boy. He seized hold of me. I cried and screamed. The other journeymen thought it very amusing, and held me fast by my arms and legs. I screamed aloud, and was as much ashamed as a girl; and then, darting from them, rushed home to my mother, who promised me that I should never go there again.

I again visited Madame Bunkeflod, for whose birthday I invented and made a white silk pincushion. I also made an acquaintance with another old clergyman's widow in the neighborhood. She permitted me to read aloud to her the works which she had from the circulating library. One of them began with these words: "It was a tempestuous night; the rain beat against the window-panes."

"That is an extraordinary book," said the old lady; and I quite innocently asked her how she knew that it was. "I can tell from the beginning," said she, "that it will turn out extraordinary."

I regarded her penetration with a sort of reverence.

Once in the harvest time my mother took me with her many miles from Odense to a nobleman's seat in the neighborhood of Bogense, her native place. The lady who lived there, and with whose parents my mother had lived, had said that some time she might come and see her. That was a great journey for me: we went most of the way on foot, and required, I believe, two days for the journey. The country here made such a strong impression upon me, that my most earnest wish was to remain in it, and become a countryman. It was just in the hop-picking season; my mother and I sat in the barn with a great many country people round a great bin, and helped to pick the hops. They told tales as they sat at their work, and every one related what wonderful things he had seen or experienced. One afternoon I heard an old man among them say that God knew everything, both what had happened, and what would happen. That idea occupied my whole mind, and toward evening, as I went alone from the court, where there was a deep pond, and stood upon some stones which were just within the water, the thought passed through my head, whether God actually knew everything which was to happen there. Yes, he has now determined that I should live and be so many years old, thought I; but, if I now were to jump into the water here and drown myself, then it would not be as he wished; and all at once I was firmly and resolutely determined to drown myself. I ran to where the water was deepest, and then a new thought passed through my soul. "It is the devil who wishes to have power over me!" I uttered a loud cry, and, running away from the place as if I were pursued, fell weeping into my mother's arms. But neither she nor any one else could wring from me what was amiss with me.

"He has certainly seen a ghost," said one of the women, and I almost believed so myself.

My mother married a second time, a young handicraftsman; but his family, who also belonged to the handicraft class, thought that he had married below himself, and neither my mother nor myself were permitted to visit them. My step-father was a young, grave man, who would have nothing to do with my education. I spent my time, therefore, over my peep-show and my puppet theater, and my greatest happiness consisted in collecting bright colored pieces of cloth and silk, which I cut out myself, and sewed. My mother regarded it as good exercise preparatory to my becoming a tailor, and took up the idea that I certainly was born for it. I, on the contrary, said that I would go to the theater and be an actor, a wish which my mother most sedulously opposed, because she knew of no other theater than those of the strolling players and the rope-dancers. "Be sure, you will then get good whippings," said she; "they will starve you to death to make you supple, and they will give you oil to eat to make your limbs soft!" No, a tailor I must and should be. "You see how well Mr. Dickmann, the tailor, is getting on!" Mr. Dickmann, was the first tailor in the town. "He lives in Cross Street, has large windows and journeymen on the table; yes, if you could only be such a one!" The only thing which in some measure reconciled me to this prospect was, that I should then get so many fragments to make up for my theater.

My parents moved to a street out of the Monk-Mill's gate, and there we had a garden; it was a very little and narrow one, containing only one long garden-bed with currant and gooseberry bushes, and the path that led down to the river behind the Monk-Mill. Three great water-wheels were turning round from the falling water, and stopped when the water-gates were closed; then all the water ran out from the river, the bed dried up, the fishes plashed and jumped in its hollows so that I could catch them with my hands, and under the great water-wheels fat water-rats came forth to drink; suddenly the water-gates were opened and the water rushed roaring and foaming down: no rats were now to be seen, the river-bed was again filled, and I ran plashing through the water, as frightened as the amber-gatherers on the coasts of the western sea, when they happen to be far out and the flood sets in. I stood upon one of the big stones my mother used for washboard and sang with all my might the songs I knew, and sometimes there was neither meaning nor melody in them, but still I sang my own self-made tunes as well as I could. The neighboring garden belonged to Mr. Falbe, whose wife Oehlenschläger mentions in his autobiography; she had formerly been an actress, and was beautiful as *Ida Münster* in the drama "Herman von Unna;" she was then Miss Beck.

When they had company in the garden they were always listening to my singing, and I knew it. All told me that I had a beautiful voice, which would bring me luck in the world. I often meditated how this luck should come, and as the wonderful has always been truth for me, so I expected the most marvelous things would happen.

An old woman who rinsed clothes in the river, told me that the Empire of China was situated straight under the very river of Odense, and I did not find it impossible at all that a Chinese prince, some moonlight night when I was sitting there, might dig himself through the earth up to us, hear me sing, and so take me down with him to his kingdom, make me rich and noble, and then let me again visit Odense, where I would live and build me a castle. Many evenings I was occupied with tracing and making ground-plans for it.

I was quite a child, and long afterwards when declaiming and reading my poems in Copenhagen, I still expected and hoped for such a prince among my auditors, who would hear me, understand me, and help me.

My passion for reading, the many dramatic scenes which I knew by heart, and my remarkably fine voice, had turned upon me in some sort the attention of several of the more influential families of Odense. I was sent for to their houses, and the peculiar characteristics of my mind excited their interest. Among others who noticed me was the Colonel Hoegh-Guldberg, who with his family showed me the kindest sympathy; so much so, indeed, that he introduced me to Prince Christian, afterward King Christian the Eighth.

"If the prince should ask you what you have a liking for," said he, "answer him that your highest desire is to enter the grammar school." So I said this to the prince when he really asked me this question, and he answered me, that my singing and declamation of poetry were really good and beautiful, but for all that was no mark of genius, and that I must keep in mind that studying was a long and expensive course! in the meantime he would take care of me if I would learn a handy trade, for instance that of a turner. I had no inclination at all for it, and I went away very much disappointed, although this noble prince had spoken very naturally and was quite in the right. Since that, when my abilities were more clearly shown, he was, as we shall see, very kind and good toward me until his death, and he is held in my memory with the most tender feelings.

I grew rapidly, and was a tall lad, of whom my mother said that she could not let him any longer go about without any object in life. I was sent, therefore, to the charity school, but learned only religion, writing, and arithmetic, and the last badly enough; I could also scarcely spell a word correctly. I never studied my lessons at home; I used to learn them on the way to school and my mother boasting of my good memory at the expense of our neighbor's son, said, "He reads till it hums, but Hans Christian does not need to open his book and yet he knows his lesson." On the master's birthday I always wove him a garland and wrote him a poem; he received them half with smiles and half as a joke: the last time, however, he scolded me. His name was Velhaven and he was from Norway; he was no doubt a good man, but was of a violent nature, and seemed to be very unhappy. He spoke in earnest about religion, and when he went through our lessons in Biblical history he did it in such a vivid fashion that, listening to him, all the painted pictures on the wall-hangings representing scenes from the Old Testament, became full of life and had for me the same beauty, truth, and freshness that I afterwards found in the magnificent pictures of Raphael and Titian. Often I sat dreaming and gazing on the variegated wall, and he gave me a little reprimand because I was absent-minded. I told the boys curious stories in which I was always the chief person, but was sometimes rallied for that. The street lads had also heard from their parents of my peculiar turn of mind, and that I was in the habit of going to the houses of the gentry. I was therefore one day pursued by a wild crowd of them, who shouted after me derisively, "There runs the play-writer!" I hid myself at home in a corner, wept, and prayed to God.

My mother said that I must be confirmed, in order that I might be apprenticed to the tailor trade, and thus do something rational. She loved me with her whole heart, but she did not understand my impulses and my endeavors, nor indeed at that time did I myself. The people about her always spoke against my odd ways, and turned me to ridicule.

We belonged to the parish of St. Knud, and the candidates for Confirmation could either enter their names with the provost or the chaplain. The children of the so-called superior families and the scholars of the grammar school went to the first, and the children of the poor to the second. I, however, announced myself as a candidate to the provost, who was obliged to receive me, although he discovered vanity in my placing myself among his catechists, where, although taking the lowest place, I was still above those who were under the care of the chaplain. I would, however, hope that it was not alone vanity which impelled me. I had a sort of fear of the poor boys, who had laughed at me, and I always felt, as it were, an inward drawing towards the scholars of the grammar school, whom I regarded as far better than other boys. When I saw them playing in the church-yard, I would stand outside the railings, and wish that I were but among the fortunate ones—not for the sake of play, but for the sake of the many books they had, and for what they might be able to become in the world. At the provost's, therefore, I should be able to associate with them, and be as they were; but I do not remember a single one of them now, so little intercourse would they hold with me. I had daily the feeling of having thrust myself in where people thought that I did not belong. One young girl, however, there was, and one who was considered, too, of the highest rank, whom I shall afterwards have occasion to mention; she always looked gently and kindly at me, and even once gave me a rose. I returned home full of happiness, because there was one being who did not overlook and repel me.

An old female tailor altered my deceased father's great coat into a confirmation suit for me; never before had I worn so good a coat. I had also, for the first time in my life, a pair of boots. My delight was extremely great; my only fear was that everybody would not see them, and therefore I drew them up over my trousers, and thus marched through the church. The boots creaked, and that inwardly pleased me, for thus the congregation would hear that they were new. My whole devotion was disturbed; I was aware of it, and it caused me a horrible pang of conscience that my thoughts should be as much with my new boots as with God. I prayed him earnestly from my heart to forgive me, and then again I thought about my new boots.

During the last year I had saved together a little sum of

money. When I counted it over I found it to be thirteen rix dollars banco (about thirty shillings). I was quite overjoyed at the possession of so much wealth, and as my mother now most resolutely required that I should be apprenticed to a tailor, I prayed and besought her that I might make a journey to Copenhagen, that I might see the greatest city in the world.

"What wilt thou do there?" asked my mother.

"I will be famous," returned I; and I then told her all that I had read about extraordinary men. "People have," said I, "at first an immense deal of adversity to go through, and then they will be famous."

It was a wholly unintelligible impulse that guided me. I wept, I prayed, and at last my mother consented, after having first sent for a so-called wise woman out of the hospital, that she might read my future fortune by the coffee-grounds and cards.

"Your son will become a great man," said the old woman, "and in honor of him Odense will one day be illuminated."

My mother wept when she heard that, and I obtained permission to travel. All the neighbors told my mother that it was a dreadful thing to let me, at only fourteen years of age, go to Copenhagen, which was such a long way off, and such a great and intricate city, and where I knew nobody.

"Yes," replied my mother, "but he lets me have no peace; I have therefore given my consent, but I am sure that he will go no further than Nyborg: when he gets sight of the rough sea, he will be frightened and turn back again."

During the summer before my Confirmation, a part of the singers and performers of the Theater Royal had been in Odense, and had given a series of operas and tragedies there. The whole city was taken with them. I, who was on good terms with the man who delivered the play-bills, saw the performances behind the scenes, and had even acted a part as page, shepherd, etc., and had spoken a few words. My zeal was so great on such occasions, that I stood there fully appareled when the actors arrived to dress. By these means their attention was turned to me; my childlike manners and my enthusiasm amused them; they talked kindly with me, and I looked up to them as to earthly divinities. Everything which I had formerly heard about my musical voice, and my recitation of poetry, became intelligible to me. It was the theater for which I was born; it was there that I should become a famous man, and for that reason Copenhagen was the goal of my endeavors. I heard a deal said about the large theater in Copenhagen, and that there was to be seen what was called the ballet, a something which surpassed both the opera and the play; more especially did I hear the danseuse, Madame Schall, spoken of as the first of all. She therefore appeared to me as the queen of everything, and in my imagination I regarded her as the one who would be able to do everything for me, if I could only obtain her support. Filled with these thoughts, I went to the old printer Iversen, one of the most respectable citizens of Odense, and who, as I heard, had had considerable intercourse with the actors when they were in the town. He, I thought, must of necessity be acquainted with the famous dancer; him I would request to give me a letter of introduction to her, and then I would commit the rest to God.

The old man saw me for the first time, and heard my petition with much kindness; but he dissuaded me most earnestly from it, and said that I might learn a trade.

"That would actually be a great sin," returned I.

He was startled at the manner in which I said that, and it prepossessed him in my favor; he confessed that he was not personally acquainted with the dancer, but still that he would give me a letter to her. I received one from him, and now believed the goal to be nearly won.

My mother packed up my clothes in a small bundle, and made a bargain with the driver of a post carriage to take me back with him to Copenhagen for three rix dollars banco. The afternoon on which we were to set out came, and my mother accompanied me to the city gate. Here stood my old grandmother; in the last few years her beautiful hair had become gray; she fell upon my neck and wept, without being able to speak a word. I was myself deeply affected. And thus we parted. I saw her no more; she died in the following year. I do not even know her grave; she sleeps in the poor-house burial-ground.

The postilion blew his horn; it was a glorious sunny afternoon, and the sunshine soon entered into my gay, child-like mind. I delighted in every novel object which met my eye, and I was journeying toward the goal of my soul's desires. When, however, I arrived at Nyborg on the great Belt, and was borne in the ship away from my native island, I then truly felt how alone and forlorn I was, and that I had no one else except God in heaven to depend upon.

As soon as I set foot on Zéaland, I stepped behind a shed which stood on the shore, and falling upon my knees, besought of God to help and guide me aright; I felt myself comforted by so doing, and I firmly trusted in God and my own good fortune. The whole day and the following night I traveled through cities and villages; I stood solitarily by the carriage, and ate my bread while it was repacked. I thought I was far away in the wide world.

II

On Monday morning, September 5th, 1819, I saw from the heights of Fredericksberg, Copenhagen for the first time. At this place I alighted from the carriage, and with my little bundle in my hand, entered the city through the castle garden, the long alley, and the suburb.

The evening before my arrival had been made memorable by the breaking out of the so-called Jews' quarrel, which spread through many European countries. The whole city was in commotion; everybody was in the streets; the noise and tumult of Copenhagen far exceeded, therefore, any idea which my imagination had formed of this, at that time, to me great city.

With scarcely ten dollars in my pocket, I turned into a small public-house. My first ramble was to the theater. I went round it many times: I looked up to its walls, and regarded them almost as a home. One of the bill-sellers, who wandered about here each day, observed me, and asked me if I would have a bill. I was so wholly ignorant of the world, that I thought the man wished to give me one; I therefore accepted his offer with thankfulness. He fancied I was making fun of him, and was angry; so that I was frightened, and hastened from the place which was to me the dearest in the city. Little did I then imagine that ten years afterwards my first dramatic piece would be represented there, and that in this manner I should make my appearance before the Danish public.

On the following day I dressed myself in my confirmation suit, nor were the boots forgotten, although, this time, they were worn naturally, under my trousers; and thus in my best attire, with a hat on, which fell half over my eyes, I hastened to present my letter of introduction to the dancer, Madame Schall. Before I rung at the bell, I fell on my knees before the door and prayed God that I here might find help and support. A maid-servant came down the steps with her basket in her hand; she smiled kindly at me, gave me a skilling (Danish), and tripped on. Astonished, I looked at her and the money. I had on my confirmation suit, and thought I must look very smart. How then could she think that I wanted to beg? I called after her.

"Keep it, keep it!" said she to me, in return, and was gone.

At length I was admitted to the dancer; she looked at me in great amazement, and then heard what I had to say. She had not the slightest knowledge of him from whom the letter came, and my whole appearance and behavior seemed very strange to her. I confessed to her my heartfelt inclination for the theater; and upon her asking me what characters I thought I could represent, I replied, *Cinderella*. This piece had been performed in Odense by the royal company, and the principal characters had so greatly taken my fancy, that I could play the part perfectly from memory. In the meantime I asked her permission to take off my boots, otherwise I was not light enough for this character; and then taking up my broad hat for a tambourine, I began to dance and sing,—

"Here below, nor rank nor riches
Are exempt from pain and woe."

My strange gestures and my great activity caused the lady to think me out of my mind, and she lost no time in getting rid of me.

From her I went to the manager of the theater, to ask for an engagement. He looked at me, and said that I was "too thin for the theater."

"O," replied I, "if you will only engage me with one hun-

dred rix-dollars banco salary, then I shall soon get fat!''
The manager bade me gravely go my way, adding, that they
only engaged people of education.

I stood there deeply wounded. I knew no one in all
Copenhagen who could give me either counsel or consolation.
I thought of death as being the only thing, and the best thing
for me; but even then my thoughts rose upward to God, and
with all the undoubting confidence of a child in his father,
they riveted themselves upon Him. I wept bitterly, and then
I said to myself, ''When everything happens quite miserably,
then He sends help. I have always read so. People must
first of all suffer a great deal before they can bring anything
to accomplishment.''

I now went and bought myself a gallery ticket for the opera
of ''Paul and Virginia.'' The separation of the lovers affected
me to such a degree, that I burst into violent weeping. A few
women, who sat near me, consoled me by saying that it was
only a play, and nothing to trouble one's self about; and then
they gave me a sausage sandwich. I had the greatest confidence in everybody, and therefore I told them, with the utmost openness, that I did not really weep about Paul and
Virginia, but because I regarded the theater as my Virginia,
and that if I must be separated from it, I should be just as
wretched as Paul. They looked at me, and seemed not to
understand my meaning. I then told them why I had come
to Copenhagen, and how forlorn I was there. One of the
women, therefore, gave me more bread and butter, with fruit
and cakes.

On the following morning I paid my bill, and to my infinite
trouble I saw that my whole wealth consisted in one rix-dollar
banco. It was necessary, therefore, either that I should find
some vessel to take me home, or put myself to work with
some handicraftsman. I considered that the last was the
wiser of the two, because if I returned to Odense, I must
there also put myself to work of a similar kind; besides
which, I knew very well that the people there would laugh at
me if I came back again. It was to me a matter of indifference what handicraft trade I learned,—I only should make
use of it to keep life within me in Copenhagen. I bought a
newspaper, therefore, and found among the advertisements

that a cabinet-maker was in want of an apprentice. The man received me kindly, but said that before I was bound to him he must have an attestation, and my baptismal register from Odense; and that till these came I could remove to his house, and try how the business pleased me. At six o'clock the next morning I went to the workshop: several journeymen were there, and two or three apprentices; but the master was not come. They fell into merry and idle discourse. I was as bashful as a girl, and as they soon perceived this, I was unmercifully rallied upon it. Later in the day the rude jests of the young fellows went so far, that, in remembrance of the scene at the manufactory, I took the resolute determination not to remain a single day longer in the workshop. I went down to the master, therefore, and told him that I could not stand it; he tried to console me, but in vain: I was too much affected, and hastened away.

I now went through the streets; nobody knew me; I was quite forlorn. I then bethought myself of having read in a newspaper in Odense the name of an Italian, Siboni, who was the director of the Academy of Music in Copenhagen. Everybody had praised my voice; perhaps he would assist me for its sake; if not, then that very evening I must seek out the master of some vessel who would take me home again. At the thoughts of the journey home I became still more violently excited, and in this state of suffering I hastened to Siboni's house.

It happened that very day that he had a large party to dinner; our celebrated composer Weyse was there, the poet Baggesen, and other guests. The housekeeper opened the door to me, and to her I not only related my wish to be engaged as a singer, but also the whole history of my life. She listened to me with the greatest sympathy and then she left me. I waited a long time, and she must have been repeating to the company the greater part of what I had said, for, in a while, the door opened, and all the guests came out and looked at me. They would have me to sing, and Siboni heard me attentively. I gave some scenes out of Holberg, and repeated a few poems; and then, all at once, the sense of my unhappy condition so overcame me that I burst into tears; the whole company applauded.

"I prophesy," said Baggesen, "that one day something will come out of him; but do not be vain when, some day, the whole public shall applaud thee!" and then he added something about pure, true nature, and that this is too often destroyed by years and by intercourse with mankind. I did not understand it all. I believed implicitly every man's word and that all wished me well; I did not keep a thought to myself, but always spoke it right out.

Siboni promised to cultivate my voice, and that I therefore should succeed as singer at the Theater Royal. It made me very happy; I laughed and wept; and as the housekeeper led me out and saw the excitement under which I labored, she stroked my cheeks, and said that on the following day I should go to Professer Weyse, who meant to do something for me, and upon whom I could depend.

I went to Weyse, who himself had risen from poverty; he had deeply felt and fully comprehended my unhappy situation, and had raised by a subscription seventy rix-dollars banco for me. I then wrote my first letter to my mother, a letter full of rejoicing, for the good fortune of the whole world seemed poured upon me. My mother in her joy showed my letter to all her friends; many heard of it with astonishment; others laughed at it, for what was to be the end of it? In order to understand Siboni it was necessary for me to learn something of German. A woman of Copenhagen, with whom I traveled from Odense to this city, and who gladly would have supported me, had her means permitted, obtained, through one of her acquaintance, a language-master, who gratuitously gave me some German lessons, and thus I learned a few phrases in that language. Siboni received me into his house, and gave me food and instruction. He had an Italian cook and two smart servant-girls; one of them had been in Mr. Casorti's service and spoke Italian; I spent the day with them, willingly ran their errands and listened to their stories; but one day having been sent by them to the dinner-table with one of the dishes, Mr. Siboni arose, went out in the kitchen, and said to the servants that I was no "cameriére;" and from that time I came oftener into the parlor, where his niece Marietta, a girl of talent, was occupied in drawing Siboni's picture as *Achilles* in Paer's opera; I acted as model, dressed in a large tunic or toga, fit for the tall and strong Siboni, but not for me, a poor, lean, overgrown boy; this contrast, however, amused the lively Italian lady, who laughed heartily and drew with great rapidity.

The opera singers came daily for practice, and sometimes I was allowed to be present.

Half a year afterward my voice broke, or was injured, in consequence of my being compelled to wear bad shoes through the winter, and having besides no warm under-clothing. There was no longer any prospect that I should become a fine singer. Siboni told me that candidly, and counseled me to go to Odense, and there learn a trade.

I who in the rich colors of fancy had described to my mother the happiness which I actually felt, must now return home and become an object of derision! Agonized with this thought, I stood as if crushed to the earth. Yet, precisely amid this apparently great unhappiness lay the stepping-stones of a better fortune.

As I found myself again abandoned, and was pondering by myself upon what was best for me next to do, it occurred to me that the Poet Guldberg, a brother of the Colonel of that name in Odense, who had shown me so much kindness, lived in Copenhagen. He lived at that time near the new church-yard outside the city, of which he has so beautifully sung in his poems. I wrote to him, and related to him everything; afterward I went to him myself, and found him surrounded with books and tobacco pipes. The strong, warm-hearted man received me kindly; and as he saw by my letter how incorrectly I wrote, he promised to give me instruction in the Danish tongue; he examined me a little in German, and thought that it would be well if he could improve me in this respect also. More than this, he made me a present of the profits of a little work which he had just then published; it became known, and I believe they exceeded one hundred rix-dollars banco; the excellent Weyse and others also supported me. He and other good people subscribed a little sum for me, and the two servant-girls who lived at Siboni's also offered me kindly of their wages nine Danish marks quarterly; they only paid the first quarter, but still it proved their good-will toward me. I have never since seen these girls.

The composer, Mr. Kuhlau, with whom I never had spoken, was also among the subscribers; Kuhlau himself had known what it was to be a poor child; he was brought up in poverty, and it is told me, that he ran errands in the cold winter, and one evening, having gone for a bottle of beer, he fell and broke the bottle, and thus lost the sight of one of his eyes.

It was too expensive for me to lodge at a public-house; I was therefore obliged to seek for private lodgings. My ignorance of the world led me to a widow who lived in one of the most disreputable streets of Copenhagen; she was inclined to receive me into her house, and I never suspected what kind of world it was which moved around me. She was a stern but active dame; she described to me the other people of the city in such horrible colors as made me suppose that I was in the only safe haven there. I was to pay twenty rix-dollars monthly for one room, which was nothing but an empty store-room, without window or light, but I had permission to sit in her parlor. I was to make trial of it at first for two days; meantime, on the following day she told me that I could decide to stay or immediately go. I, who so easily attach myself to people, already liked her, and felt myself at home with her; but more than sixteen dollars per month Weyse had told me I must not pay, and this was the sum which I had received from him and Guldberg, so that no surplus remained to me for my other expenses. This troubled me very much; when she was gone out of the room, I seated myself on the sofa, and contemplated the portrait of her deceased husband. I was so wholly a child, that as the tears rolled down my own cheeks, I wetted the eyes of the portrait with my tears, in order that the dead man might feel how troubled I was, and influence the heart of his wife. She must have seen that nothing more was to be drained out of me, for when she returned to the room she said that she would receive me into her house for the sixteen rix-dollars. I thanked God and the dead man.

The following day I brought her all the money, very happy now at finding a home, but not leaving for myself a single skilling to buy me shoes, clothes, or other necessities, of which I was in great want.

I found myself in the midst of the mysteries of Copenhagen, but I did not understand how to interpret them. There was in the house in which I lived a friendly young lady, who lived alone, and often wept; every evening her old father came and paid her a visit. I opened the door to him frequently; he wore a plain sort of coat, had his throat very much tied up, and his hat pulled over his eyes. He always drank his tea with her, and nobody dared to be present, because he was not fond of company: she never seemed very glad at his coming. Many years afterward, when I had reached another step on the ladder of life, when the refined world of fashionable life was opened before me, I saw one evening, in the midst of a brilliantly lighted hall, a polite old gentleman covered with orders: that was the old father in the shabby coat,—he whom I had let in. He had little idea that I had opened the door to him when he played his part as guest, but I, on my side, then had also no thought but for my own comedy-playing; that is to say, I was at that time so much of a child that I played with my puppet theater and made my dolls' clothes; and in order that I might obtain gayly colored fragments for this purpose, I used to go to the shops and ask for patterns of different kinds of stuffs and ribbons. I myself did not possess a single skilling; my landlady received all the money each month in advance; only now and then, when I did any errands for her, she gave me something, and that went in the purchase of paper or for old play-books. I got many good and amusing books from the University Library. One day I went up to the University Dean, old Mr. Rasmus Nyrup, who was son of a peasant and had studied at Odense grammar school, and told him that I also was from Odense; he was struck by my peculiarities, took me into his favor, and allowed me to go and look over the books in the library at the Round Church. He only commanded me to put them again in their right place, and that I did very conscientiously. He let me also take home with me many picture-books.

I was now very happy, and was doubly so because Professor Guldberg had induced Lindgrön, the first comic actor at the theater, to give me instructions. He gave me several parts in Holberg to learn,—such as *Hendrik* and the *Silly Boy,* for which I had shown some talent. My desire, however, was to play the "Correggio." I obtained permission to learn this piece in my own way, although Lindgrön asked, with comic gravity, whether I expected to resemble the great painter? I, however, repeated to him the soliloquy in the picture gallery with so much feeling, that the old man clapped me on the shoulder, and said, "Feeling you have; but you must not be an actor, though God knows what else. Speak to Guldberg about your learning Latin: that always opens the way for a student."

I a student! That was a thought which had never come before into my head. The theater lay nearer to me, and was dearer too; yet Latin I had also always wished to learn. But before I spoke on the subject to Guldberg, I mentioned it to the lady who obtained for me gratuitous instruction in German; she told me that Latin was the most expensive language in the world, and that it was not possible to gain free instruction in it. Guldberg, however, managed it so that one of his friends, Provost Bentzien out of kindness, gave me two lessons a week.

The dancer, Dahlen, whose wife at that time was one of the first artistes on the Danish boards, opened his house to me. I passed many an evening there, and the gentle, warm-hearted lady was kind to me. The husband took me with him to the dancing-school, and that was to me one step nearer to the theater. There stood I for whole mornings, with a long staff, and stretched my legs; but notwithstanding all my good-will, it was Dahlen's opinion that I should never get beyond a figurante. One advantage, however, I had gained; I might in an evening make my appearance behind the scenes of the theater; nay, even sit upon the farthest bench in the box of figurantes. It seemed to me as if I had got my foot just within the theater, although I had never yet been upon the stage itself.

One night the operetta of the "Two Little Savoyards" was given; in the market scene, every one, even the supernumeraries, might go up to help in filling the stage; I heard them say so, and rouging myself a little, I went happily up with the others. I was in my ordinary dress,—the confirmation coat, which still held together, although, with regard to brushing and repairs, it looked but miserably, and the great hat which fell down over my face. I was very conscious of the ill condition of my attire, and would have been glad to have concealed it; but, through the endeavor to do so, my movements became still more angular. I did not dare to hold myself upright, because, by so doing, I exhibited all the more plainly the shortness of my waistcoat, which I had outgrown. I had the feeling very plainly that people would make themselves merry about me; yet, at this moment, I felt nothing but the happiness of stepping for the first time before the foot-lamps. My heart beat; I stepped forward; there came up one of the singers, who at that time was much thought of, but now is forgotten; he took me by the hand, and jeeringly wished me happiness on my début. "Allow me to introduce you to the Danish public," said he, and drew me forward to the lamps. The people would laugh at me—I felt it; the tears rolled down my cheeks; I tore myself loose, and left the stage full of anguish.

Shortly after this, Dahlen arranged a ballet of "Armida," in which I received a little part: I was a spirit. In this ballet I became acquainted with the lady of Professor Heiberg, the wife of the poet, and now a highly esteemed actress on the Danish stage; she, then a little girl, had also a part in it, and our names stood printed in the bill. That was a moment in my life, when my name was printed! I fancied I could see in it a nimbus of immortality. I was continually looking at the printed paper. I carried the program of the ballet with me at night to bed, lay and read my name by candle-light—in short, I was happy!

The widow of the celebrated Danish statesman, Christian Colbjörnsen, and her daughter, were the first ladies of high rank who cordially befriended the poor lad; who listened to me with sympathy, and saw me frequently. Mrs. von Colbjörnsen resided, during the summer, at Bakkehus, where also lived the poet Rahbek and his interesting wife. Rahbek never spoke to me; but his lively and kind-hearted wife often amused herself with me. I had at that time again begun to write a tragedy, which I read aloud to her. Immediately on hearing the first scenes, she exclaimed, "But you have actually taken whole passages out of Oehlenschläger and Ingemann."

"Yes, but they are so beautiful!" replied I in my simplicity, and read on.

One day, when I was going from her to Mrs. von Colbjörnsen, she gave me a handful of roses, and said, "Will you take them up to her? It will certainly give her pleasure to receive them from the hand of a poet."

These words were said half in jest; but it was the first time that anybody had connected my name with that of poet. It went through me, body and soul, and tears filled my eyes. I know that, from this very moment, my mind was awake to writing and poetry. Formerly it had been merely an amusement by way of variety from my puppet theater.

One day I went out to Bakkehus believing myself very nicely dressed; Edward Colbjörnsen had given me a very good blue dress-coat, better than I ever before had worn, but it was too large and wide for me, especially across the breast; I could not afford to get it altered, and so I buttoned it close up to the neck; the cloth looked quite new and the buttons were shining, but across the breast it was far too wide; in order to remedy this want, I filled out the empty room with a heap of old theater hand-bills; they were loosely laid one upon another between the coat and the breast, and looked like a hump. In this attire I presented myself to Madame Colbjörnsen and Madame Rahbek; they asked me if I would not unbutton my coat, it was so warm, but I took pretty good care not to for fear of dropping the hand-bills.

At Bakkehus lived also Professor Thiele, a young student at that time, but even then the editor of the Danish popular legends, and known to the public as the solver of Baggesen's riddle and as the writer of beautiful poetry. He was possessed of sentiment, true inspiration, and heart. He had calmly and attentively watched the unfolding of my mind, until we now became friends. He was one of the few who, at that time, spoke the truth of me, when other people were making themselves merry at my expense, and having only eyes for that which was ludicrous in me. People had called me, in jest, the little orator, and, as such, I was an object of curiosity. They found amusement in me, and I mistook every smile for a smile of applause. One of my later friends has told me that it probably was about this period that he saw me for the first time. It was in the drawing-room of a rich tradesman, where people were making themselves very merry over me. They desired me to repeat one of my poems, and, as I did this with great feeling, the merriment was changed into sympathy with me.

I must not forget to mention that I found a retreat, if I may call it so,—a cozy little room, where the voices of earlier days sounded in my heart; it was in the house of a worthy old lady, the mother of our renowned, now deceased, Urban Jürgensen; she had a very clear judgment and was well educated, but belonged to the last generation, in which she still lived. Her father had formerly been castellan of the castle of Antvorskov, and Holberg used to come there on Sundays from Sorö; he and her father would walk up and down the floor talking together about politics; one day the mother sitting at the spinning-wheel undertook to share in the conversation: "I believe the distaff is talking," said Holberg, and her mother could never forgive the witty, coarse gentleman these words! The one who was then a little child, now sitting an old, old woman by me, told me all these things.

How attractive that old woman's company was to me! I listened to all she had seen, thought, and read, and I was in her house as a dear child whom she loved to have near her. I read her my first verses, and my tragedy, "Skovkapellet" ("The Chapel in the Wood"), and she said one day, with an earnestness that made me humble: "You are a poet, perhaps as good as Oehlenschläger! in ten years—yes, when I am no longer here—please to remember me!" I remember that tears rushed to my eyes, I was so solemnly and wonderfully touched by these words; but I know also that I thought it impossible for me to reach so high as to be an acknowledged poet, and far less to be named with Oehlenschläger. "What a good thing it would be for you to study," said she; "but many ways lead toward Rome! your way will no doubt also bring you there."

It was just at the close of the theatrical season, in May, 1822, that I received a letter from the directors, by which I was dismissed from the singing and dancing school, the letter adding also, that my participation in the school teaching could lead to no advantage for me, but that they wished some of my many friends would enable me to receive an education, without which talent availed nothing. I felt myself again, as it were, cast out into the wide world, without help and without support. It was absolutely necessary that I should write a piece for the theater, and that it *must* be accepted; there was no other salvation for me. I wrote, therefore, a tragedy founded on a passage in history, and I called it "Alfsol." I was delighted with the first act, and with this I immediately went to the Danish translator of Shakespeare, Admiral Wulff, now deceased, who good-naturedly heard me read it. In Admiral Wulff's house and in his family circle I found a true home. Speaking of our first acquaintance, he told me many years afterward in joke, and exaggerating a little, that I said entering the room: "You have translated Shakespeare; I admire him greatly, but I have also written a tragedy: shall I read it to you?"

Wulff invited me to breakfast with him, but I would not take anything, but read and read all the time, and having finished my reading I said: "Do you think I shall amount to anything,—I wish it so much?" I put my papers into my pocket, and when he asked me to call again soon, I answered, "Yes, I will, when I have written a new tragedy."—"But that will be a long time," said he. "I think," said I, "that in a fortnight I may have another one ready," and with these words I was out of the door. In after years I met with the most cordial reception in his family. At that time I also introduced myself to our celebrated physicist Örsted, and his house has remained to me to this day an affectionate home, to which my heart has firmly attached itself, and where I find my oldest and most unchangeable friends.

A favorite preacher, the rural dean Gutfeldt, was living at that time, and he it was who exerted himself most earnestly for my tragedy, which was now finished; and having written a letter of recommendation, he sent it to the managers of the theater. I was suspended between hope and fear. In the course of the summer I endured bitter want, but I told it to no one, else many a one, whose sympathy I had experienced, would have helped me to the utmost of their means. A false shame prevented me from confessing what I endured. Still happiness filled my heart. I read then for the first time the works of Walter Scott. A new world was opened to me: I forgot the reality, and gave to the circulating library that which should have provided me with a dinner.

The present conference councilor, Collin, one of the most distinguished men of Denmark, who unites with the greatest ability the noblest and best heart, to whom I looked up with confidence in all things, who had been a second father to me, and in whose children I have found brothers and sisters,— this excellent man I saw now for the first time. He was at that time director of the Theater Royal, and people universally told me that it would be the best thing for me if he would interest himself on my behalf: it was either Örsted or Gutfeldt who first mentioned me to him; and now for the first time I went to that house which was to become so dear to me. Carl Bernhard has in his novel, "Chronicles of the Time of Christian II.," given a description of that old house, from its first days until its last celebrity as Collin's home. Before the ramparts of Copenhagen were extended, this house lay outside the gate, and served as a summer residence to the Spanish Ambassador; now, however, it stands a crooked, angular framework building, in a respectable street; an old-fashioned wooden balcony leads to the entrance, and a great tree spreads its green branches over the court and its pointed gables. It was to become a paternal house to me. Who does not willingly linger over the description of home?

I discovered only the man of business in Collin; his conversation was grave and in few words. I went away, without expecting any sympathy from this man; and yet it was precisely Collin who, in all sincerity, thought for my advantage, and who worked for it silently, as he had done for others, through the whole course of his active life. But at that time I did not understand the apparent calmness with which he listened, whilst his heart bled for the afflicted, and he always labored for them with zeal and success, and knew how to help them. He touched so lightly upon my tragedy, which had been sent to him, and on account of which many people had overwhelmed me with flattering speeches, that I regarded him rather as an enemy than a protector.

In a few days I was sent for by the directors of the theater, when Rahbek gave me back my play as useless for the stage;

adding, however, that there were so many grains of corn scattered in it, they hoped that perhaps, by earnest study, after going to school and the previous knowledge of all that is requisite, I might, some time, be able to write a work which should be worthy of being acted on the Danish stage.

In order therefore to obtain the means for my support and the necessary instruction, Collin recommended me to King Frederick VI., who granted to me a certain sum annually for some years; and, by means of Collins also, the directors of the high schools allowed me to receive free instruction in the grammar school at Slagelse, where just then a new, and, as was said, an active rector was appointed. I was almost dumb with astonishment: never had I thought that my life would take this direction, although I had no correct idea of the path which I had now to tread. I was to go with the earliest mail to Slagelse, which lay twelve Danish miles from Copenhagen, to the place where also the poets Baggesen and Ingemann had gone to school. I was to receive money quarterly from Collin; I was to apply to him in all cases, and he it was who was to ascertain my industry and my progress.

I went to him the second time to express to him my thanks. Mildly and kindly he said to me, "Write to me without restraint about everything which you require, and tell me how it goes with you." From this hour I struck root in his heart; no father could have been more to me than he was, and is; none could have more heartily rejoiced in my happiness, and my after reception with the public; none have shared my sorrow more kindly; and I am proud to say that one of the most excellent men which Denmark possesses feels toward me as toward his own child. His beneficence was conferred without his making me feel it painful either by word or look. That was not the case with every one to whom, in this change of my fortunes, I had to offer my thanks; I was told to think of my inconceivable happiness and my poverty; in Collin's words was expressed the warm-heartedness of a father, and to him it was that properly I was indebted for everything.

The journey was hastily determined upon, and I had yet for myself some business to arrange. I had spoken to an acquaintance from Odense who had the management of a small printing concern for a widow, to get "Alfsol" printed, that I might, by the sale of the work, make a little money. Before, however, the piece was printed, it was necessary that I should obtain a certain number of subscribers; but these were not obtained, and the manuscript lay in the printing-office, which, at the time I went to fetch it away, was shut up. Some years afterward, however, it suddenly made its appearance in print without my knowledge or my desire, in its unaltered shape, but without my name.

The fictitious name which I took seems at first sight a great piece of vanity, and yet it was not so, but really an expression of love,—a childish love, such as the child has when it calls its doll by the name it likes best. I loved William Shakespeare and Walter Scott, and of course I loved also myself. I took therefore my name Christian, and so I assumed the fictitious name "William Christian Walter." The book exists still, and contains the tragedy "Alfsol," and a tale, "The Spectre at Palnatoke's Grave," in which neither the specter nor Palnatoke play any part; it is a very rough imitation of Walter Scott. *Dana,* the speaker in the prologue, says that I am "only seventeen years old," and that I bring

—"a wreath of beech-roots and Danish flowers."

It is a very miserable production throughout.

On a beautiful autumn day I set off with the mail from Copenhagen to begin my school-life in Slagelse. A young student, who a month before had passed his first examination, and now was traveling home to Jutland to exhibit himself there as a student, and to see once more his parents and his friends, sat by my side, and exulted for joy over the new life which now lay before him; he assured me that he should be the most unhappy of human beings if he were in my place, and were again beginning to go to the grammar school. But I traveled with a good heart toward the little city of Zealand. My mother received a joyful letter from me. I only wished that my father and the old grandmother yet lived, and could hear that I now went to the grammar school.

III

WHEN, late in the evening, I arrived at the inn in Slagelse, I asked the hostess if there was anything remarkable there.

"Yes," said she, "a new English fire-engine and Pastor Bastholm's library,"—and those probably were all the lions in the city. A few officers of the Lancers composed the fine-gentleman world. Everybody knew what was done in everybody's house, whether a scholar was elevated or degraded in his class, and the like. A private theater, to which, at general rehearsal, the scholars of the grammar school and the maid-servants of the town had free entrance, furnished rich material for conversation. In my "Picture Book without Pictures," the fourth night, I have given a sketch of it.

I boarded with a respectable widow of the educated class, and had a little chamber looking out into the garden and field. My place in the school was in the lowest class, among little boys: I knew indeed nothing at all.

I was actually like a wild bird which is confined in a cage; I had the greatest desire to learn, but for the moment I floundered about, as if I had been thrown into the sea; one wave followed another; grammar, geography, mathematics; I felt myself overpowered by them, and feared that I should never be able to acquire all these. The Rector, who took a peculiar delight in turning everything to ridicule, did not, of course, make an exception in my case. To me he stood there as a divinity; I believed unconditionally every word which he spoke. One day, when I had replied incorrectly to his question, and he said that I was stupid, I mentioned it to Collin, and told him my anxiety, lest I did not deserve all that people had done for me; but he consoled me. Occasionally, however, on some subjects of instruction, I began to receive a good certificate, and the teachers were heartily kind to me; yet, notwithstanding that I advanced, I still lost confidence in myself more and more. On one of the first examinations, however, I obtained the praise of the Rector. He wrote the same in my character-book; and, happy in this, I went a few days afterward to Copenhagen. Guldberg, who saw the progress I had made, received me kindly, and commended my zeal.

"I advise you as a friend not to make any more verses," said he, and the same advice was repeated on all sides. I did not write more verses, but reflected on my duties, and on the very uncertain hope I had of becoming a student.

I had not been in my native town since I left it to seek my fortune; in that interval my old grandmother had died and also my grandfather.

My mother often told me, when I was a little boy, that I had a fortune in prospect: that I should be heir of my grandfather, who owned a house; it was a little, poor wooden house, which was sold after his death and immediately pulled down; most of the old man's money was applied to pay the taxes in arrear, and the authorities had seized "the big stove with brass drum," a piece worth owning, they said, and it was taken up to the town-hall. There was so much money that they could have made a cart-load of the coins, but they were the old reduced coins, which the government no longer received. In 1813, when these coins were reduced, the old insane man was told that they were good for nothing. "No man can reject the King's money!" said he, "and the King won't reject his own:" that was his whole answer. "The big inheritance" I had heard so much about was reduced to some twenty rix-dollars and passed over to me. I must however candidly confess that I did not care much about those riches; my thoughts were only lingering on my visit to my home. I felt rich and happy, and my mind was excited with expectation.

I crossed the Belt, and went on foot to Odense. When I came near enough to see the lofty old church tower, my heart was more and more affected; I felt deeply the care of God for me, and I burst into tears. My mother rejoiced over me. The families of Iversen and Guldberg received me cordially; and in the little streets I saw the people open their windows to look at me, for everybody knew how remarkably well things had fared with me; nay, I fancied I actually stood upon the pinnacle of fortune, when one of the principal citizens, who had built a high tower to his house, led me up there, and I looked out thence over the city and the surrounding country, and some old women in the hospital below, who had known me from childhood, pointed up to me. One afternoon, in company with the families of Guldberg and the Bishop, I sailed in a boat on the stream, and my mother shed tears of joy; "for," as she said, "I was honored like the child of a count."

As soon, however, as I returned to Slagelse, this halo of glory vanished, as well as every thought of it. I may freely confess that I was industrious, and I rose, as soon as it was possible, into a higher class; but in proportion as I rose did I feel the pressure upon me more strongly, and that my endeavors were not sufficiently productive. Many an evening, when sleep overcame me, I would wash my head with cold water, or run about the lonely little garden, till I was again wakeful, and could comprehend the book anew. The Rector filled up a portion of his hours of teaching with jest, nicknames, and not the happiest of witticisms. I was as if paralyzed with anxiety when he entered the room, and from that cause my replies often expressed the opposite of that which I wished to say, and thereby my anxiety was all the more increased. What was to become of me?

Among the pupils in the academy of nobles, there were two who made verses; they knew that I did the same, and they attached themselves to me. The one was Petit, who afterwards, certainly with the best intention, but not faithfully, translated several of my books. He has also written a strange, fantastical biography of me, in which, among other things, he gives a description of my paternal home that seems to have a great resemblance to that in "The Ugly Duckling." He makes my mother a Madonna, lets me run with rosy feet in the evening sun, and more of the same kind. Petit was nevertheless not without talent, and possessed of a warm, noble heart; life brought him many sorrowful days. Now he is among the dead, and his vivacious spirit may have attained more serenity and repose. The other was the poet Carl Bagger, one of the most gifted of men who has come forward in Danish literature, but who has been unjustly judged. His poems are full of freshness and originality; his story, "The Life of my Brother," is a clever book, by the critique on which the "Danish Monthly Review of Literature" has proved that it does not understand how to give judgment. These two academicians were very different from me: life rushed rejoicingly through their veins; I was sensitive and childlike, while I was the most grown of us three. The quiet Sorö, with its woody solitude, became thus for me a home of poetry and friendship.

An event that agitated much our little town was the execution of three criminals down at Skjelskjör. A rich young daughter of a farmer had induced her suitor to kill her father, who opposed their match; an accessory to the crime was the man-servant, who intended to marry the widow. Every one was going to see the execution, and the day was like a holiday. The Rector dismissed the upper class from school, and we were to go and see the execution, for it would be a good thing for us to be acquainted with it, he said.

The whole night we drove in open carriages, and at sunrise we reached Skjelskjör. It made a very strong impression upon me. I never shall forget seeing the criminals driven to the place of execution: the young girl, deadly pale, leaning her head against the breast of her robust sweetheart; behind them the man-servant, livid, his black hair in disorder, and nodding with a squinting look at a few acquaintances, who shouted out to him "Farewell!" Standing at the side of their coffins, they sang a hymn together with the minister; the girl's voice was heard above all the others. My limbs could scarcely carry me! these moments were more horrible for me than the very moment of death. I saw a poor sick man, whose superstitious parents, in order to cure him of a fit, had given him to drink a cup of blood from the persons executed; he ran away in wild flight till he sank exhausted on the ground. A ballad-maker was vending his "melancholy airs;" the words were put in the mouth of the malefactors, and sounded comically to a well-known melody. The whole tragedy made such an impression upon my fancy that for a long time after I was persecuted by the memory of it; and though many years have passed away, it is still as fresh to me as if it happened yesterday.

Events like this or other important incidents did not continue to happen; one day after another glided away, but the less there is going on and the more quiet and monotonous one's life is the sooner one thinks of preserving what passes,— of keeping a diary, as it is called. At that time I also kept such a one, of which I have retained a couple of leaves, in which the whole of my strange, childish nature at that time is faithfully reflected. I insert here some passages from it, copying them literally.

I was then in the upper class but one, and my whole existence and happiness depended on being promoted to the highest class at the approaching examination. I wrote:

"*Wednesday.*—Depressed in spirit I took up the Bible, which lay before me, for an oracle, opened it, pointed blindly at a place and read: 'O Israel, thou hast destroyed thyself! but in me is thine help!' (Hosea.) Yes, Father, I am weak, but thou lookest into my heart and wilt be my help so that I can be promoted to the fourth class. Have answered well in Hebrew.

"*Thursday.*—Happened to pull off the leg of a spider; went nicely through in mathematics. O God, God, to thee my heart's entire thanks.

"*Friday.*—O God, help me! The night is so wintry clear. The examination is well over—to-morrow comes the result. O Moon! to-morrow thou wilt behold either a pale, desperate being or one of the happiest. Read Schiller's 'Kabale und Liebe.'

"*Saturday.*—O God, now my fate is decided, but still hidden from me: what may it be? God, my God! do not forsake me! my blood runs so fast through my veins, my nerves tremble with fear. O God, Almighty God, help me—I do not deserve it, but be merciful O God, God!—(Later.) I am promoted—Is it not strange? My joy is not so violent as I supposed it would be. At eleven o'clock I wrote to Guldberg and to my mother."

At that time I made a vow to the Lord in my silent thoughts that if He would let me be promoted to the fourth class, I would go to Communion the following Sunday, and that I also did.

You can see by this what trouble I had in my pious mind, and what degree of development I had reached, although at that time I was already twenty years old. How much better other young men at that age would have written in their diary!

The Rector grew weary of his residence in Slagelse; he applied for the vacant post of Rector in the grammar school of Helsingör, and obtained it. He told me of it, and added kindly, that I might write to Collin and ask leave to accompany him thither; that I might live in his house, and could even now remove to his family; I should then in half a year become a student, which could not be the case if I remained behind, and that then he would himself give me some private lessons in Latin and Greek. I, of course, immediately received Collin's permission, and removed to the house of the Rector.

I was now to take leave of Slagelse: it was very hard for me to say good-by to my comrades and the few families whose acquaintance I had made: of course, I also on that occasion got an album, in which, amongst others, my old teacher Mr. Snitker wrote something: he had been Ingemann and Poul Möller's teacher when they were scholars there.

Carl Bagger wrote a poem addressed to me, which was more like a dedication to a young poet, than a poem to a boy going away to take his seat on a school-bench. And so I went thither, and approached heavy, wearisome days.

I accompanied the Rector to Helsingör; the journey, the first view of the Sound with its many sailing ships, the Kullen Mountains, and the beautiful country, all filled my mind with transport; I described it in a letter to Rasmus Nyrup, and as I thought it very well written, I sent the same letter to others, addressing it to each of them. Unfortunately it pleased Nyrup so well that he inserted it in the "Copenhagen Pietorial," so that each of them who had got the letter, or rather the copy of it, believed that he saw his letter printed in the newspaper.

The Rector's spirits were refreshed by the variety, the new company, and new activity, but only for a short time, and I soon felt myself forsaken; I became depressed and suffered much in mind. The Rector had sent Mr. Collin at that time an account of me, which I now have, in which he judges me and my abilities quite differently from what I and others had heard or could have believed him to say. If I had had any knowledge of it, I should have been strengthened: it would have made me healthier in mind, and would have acted beneficially upon my whole being.

I heard him every day condemn almost every intellectual faculty in me; he spoke to me as to an idiot,—to a perfectly brutish, stupid boy,—and at the same time he wrote earnestly about me to my patron Collin, who, on account of my frequent reports of the Rector's dissatisfaction with me and my poor abilities, had asked him for a statement.

"H. C. Andersen was, at the close of the year 1822, admitted to Slagelse grammar school, and being in want of the most necessary preliminary knowledge, in spite of his pretty advanced age, was put into the lowest class but one.

"Endowed by nature with a lively imagination and warm feelings, he attempted and acquired more or less completely the different branches of instruction, and in general made such progress, that it entitled him to be promoted successively from the lower classes to the highest, to which he at present belongs, only with the difference that he has removed with the undersigned from Slagelse to Helsingör.

"The kindness of others has until now maintained him in his course of study, and I cannot refrain from saying that he is perfectly worthy. His talents are good, and in one direction even excellent; his constant diligence, and his conduct, which springs from an affectionate disposition, are such that he might serve as a model for the pupils of any school. It may be stated further, that, by continuing his praiseworthy assiduity, he will, in October, 1828, be able to be promoted to the Academy.

"Three qualities which a preceptor wishes for, but rarely finds combined in the same pupil, namely, ability, diligence, and excellent conduct, are assuredly to be found in H. C. Andersen.

"In consideration of this, I must recommend him as very worthy of any support which may be given to him to enable him to continue his course, from which his advanced age will not well allow him to retire. Not only the disposition of mind, but also his faithful assiduity and undoubted talent, give sufficient warrant that what may be bestowed upon him for his welfare will never be lost.

S. MEISLING,
"*Ph. Dr., and Rector of Helsingör's grammar school.*
"HELSINGÖR, *July* 18, 1826."

Of this testimony which breathes so much goodness toward me and which ought to be known, I had no sort of knowledge. I was entirely depressed, and had neither belief nor confidence in myself. Collin sent me a few kind lines:—

"Don't lose courage, my dear Andersen! Compose your mind and be quiet and reasonable; you will see that all will go well; the Rector bears good-will to you. He takes perhaps another way of showing it from what others would, but still it leads to the same end.

"I may write more another time, to-day I am prevented.

"God bless you! Yours,

"COLLIN."

The scenery here made a lively impression upon me, but I dared only to cast stolen glances at it. When the school hours were over, the house-door was commonly locked; I was obliged to remain in the heated school-room and learn my Latin, or else play with the children, or sit in my little room; I never went out to visit anybody. My life in this family furnishes the most evil dreams to my remembrance. I was almost overcome by it, and my prayer to God every evening was, He would remove this cup from me and let me die. I possessed not an atom of confidence in myself. I never mentioned in my letters how hard it went with me, because the Rector found his pleasure in making a jest of me, and turning my feelings to ridicule.

Just then one of the masters went to Copenhagen, and related to Collin exactly what I had to bear, and immediately he removed me from the school and from the Rector's house. When, in taking leave of him, I thanked him for the kindness which I had received from him, the passionate man cursed me, and ended by saying that I should never become a student, that my verses would grow moldy on the floor of the bookseller's shop, and that I myself should end my days in a madhouse. I trembled to my innermost being, and left him.

Several years afterward, when my writings were read, when the "Improvisatore" first came out, I met him in Copenhagen; he offered me his hand in a conciliatory manner, and said that he had erred respecting me and had treated me wrong; but it now was all the same to me. The heavy, dark days had also produced their blessing in my life.

A young man, who afterward became celebrated in Denmark for his zeal in the Northern languages and in history, became my teacher. I hired a little garret; it is described in the "Fiddler;" and in "The Picture Book without Pictures" people may see that I often received there visits from the moon.

At this time, also, a fresh current of life was sent through the Danish literature; for this the people had an interest, and politics played no part in it.

Heiberg, who had gained the acknowledged reputation of a poet by his excellent works, "Psyche" and "Walter the Potter," had introduced the vaudeville upon the Danish stage; it was a Danish vaudeville, blood of our blood, and was therefore received with acclamation, and supplanted almost everything else. Thalia kept carnival on the Danish stage, and Heiberg was her secretary. I made his acquaintance first at Örsted's. Refined, eloquent, and the hero of the day, he pleased me in a high degree: he was most kind to me, and I visited him; he considered one of my humorous poems worthy of a place in his most excellent weekly paper, "The Flying Post." Shortly before I had, after a deal of trouble, got my poem of "The Dying Child" printed in a paper; none of the many publishers of journals, who otherwise accept of the most lamentable trash, had the courage to print a poem by a school-boy. My best known poem they printed at that time, accompanied by an excuse for it. Heiberg saw it, and gave it in his paper an honorable place. Two humorous poems signed "H." were truly my début with him.

I remember the first evening when the "Flying Post" appeared with my verses in it. I was with a family who wished me well, but who regarded my poetical talent as quite insignificant, and who found something to censure in every line. The master of the house entered with the "Flying Post" in his hand.

"This evening," said he, "there are two excellent poems: they are by Heiberg; nobody else could write anything like them." And now my poems were received with rapture. The daughter, who was in my secret, exclaimed, in her delight, that I was the author. They were all struck into silence, and were vexed. That wounded me deeply.

One of our least esteemed writers, but a man of rank, who was very hospitable, gave me one day a seat at his table. He told me that a new year's gift would come out, and that he was applied to for a contribution. I said that a little poem of mine, at the wish of the publisher, would appear in the same new year's gift.

"What, then: everybody and anybody are to contribute to this book!" said the man in vexation: "then he will need nothing from me; I certainly can hardly give him anything."

My teacher dwelt at a considerable distance from me. I went to him twice each day, and on the way there my thoughts were occupied with my lessons. On my return, however, I breathed more freely, and then bright poetical ideas passed through my brain, but they were never committed to paper; only five or six humorous poems were written in the course of the year, and these disturbed me less when they were laid to rest on paper than if they had remained in my mind.

In September, 1828, I was a student. Oehlenschläger, who was Dean at that time, pressed my hand and bid me welcome as *civis academicus:* that was an act of great importance for me. I was already twenty-three years old, but still much a child in my whole nature and my manner of speaking. A little incident of these days will perhaps give you an idea of it. Shortly before the examination day I saw a young man at the dinner-table of H. C. Örsted: he looked very embarrassed and retiring. I had not seen him there before, and thought that he had but just arrived from the country. I asked him without ceremony,—

"Are you going up to the examination this year?"

"Yes," he said with a smile, "I am going up there."

"I also," said I, and spoke now with him as a comrade a good deal about this great event. He was the professor who was to examine me in mathematics, the richly gifted and excellent Von Schmidten, who in his external appearance was so much like Napoleon, that in Paris he was taken for him. When we met at the examination-table we were both very much embarrassed; he was as kind as he was learned, and wished to encourage me, but did not know how to do it; he leaned over to me and whispered,—

"What is to be the first poetical work you will give us, when you have finished your examination?"

I gazed with astonishment on him and answered anxiously,—

"I don't know, sir, but be so kind as not to give me too difficult questions in mathematics!"

"You know, then, something?" said he, in a low voice.

"Yes, sir, I know mathematics tolerably; in the Helsingör school I often read 'the supplements' with the other scholars, and I got the certificate 'remarkably good,' but now I am afraid." In that style the professor and the pupil conversed, and during the examination, in which he tore all his pens to pieces, he did not say anything, but only put one of the pens aside to write down the result with.

When the examination (*Examen Artium*) was over, the ideas and thoughts, by which I was pursued on the way to my teacher, flew like a swarm of bees out into the world, and indeed, into my first work, "A Journey on Foot from the Holm Canal to the East Point of Amack,"—a peculiar, humorous book, a kind of fantastic arabesque, but one which fully exhibited my own individual character at that time, my disposition to sport with everything, and to jest in tears over my own feelings—a fantastic, gayly colored tapestry work was this poetical improvisation.

No publisher had the courage to bring out that juvenile work. I ventured therefore to do it myself, and in a few days after its appearance, the publisher Reitzel bought from me the copyright of the second edition, and after a while he had a third. In Fahlun, in Sweden, the work was reprinted in Danish, a thing which had happened only to the chief works of Oehlenschläger. A German translation was some years later published in Hamburg.

Everybody in Copenhagen read my book; I heard nothing but praise, only a protector of rank gave me a severe lecture, but it struck me as rather comical. The man found in the "Journey on Foot" a satire of the Royal Theater, which he not only considered as unseemly but also as ungrateful: unseemly because it was a royal theater, or, as he said, the king's house; and ungrateful because I had free admission to it.

This reproof of an otherwise reasonable man, was put out of mind by the triumph and praise the book received. I was a "student," a poet. I had attained the highest goal of my wishes. Heiberg noticed the book in a very kind and beautiful manner in the "Monthly Journal of Literature," and had earlier given extracts from it in his "Flying Post." The book was very much read in Norway, and that vexed Poul Möller, so that he criticized it without indulgence.

I did not know anything of it, and could not believe that anybody should not rejoice in the "Journey on Foot to Amack."

I was received with great consideration by my fellow-students, and I was in a youthful poetical intoxication, in a whirl of joy, sporting and searching for the wrong side in everything. In this state I wrote in rime my first dramatic work, the vaudeville, "Love on the Nicholas Tower; or, What says the Pit?" which had one essential fault, noticed also in the "Monthly Journal," "that of satirizing what no longer existed amongst us, namely, the Fate tragedies of the Middle Ages."

My fellow-students received the piece with acclamation and shouted "Long live the author!" I was overwhelmed with joy, and thought it to be of more importance than it deserved. I could not contain myself. I rushed out from the theater into the street, and then to Collin's house, where his wife was alone at home. I threw myself down upon a chair almost exhausted and wept in convulsions. The sympathizing lady did not know what to think, and trying to console me, said,— "Don't let it grieve you so much. Oehlenschläger has also been hissed, and many other great poets."—"They have not hissed at all," exclaimed I sobbing; "they have applauded and cried *Vivat!*"

I was now a happy human being, thinking well of all mankind; I possessed the courage of a poet and the heart of a youth.

All houses began to be open to me; I flew from circle to circle in happy self-contentment. Under all these external and internal affections, I still however devoted myself industriously to study, so that without any teacher I passed my second academical examination, *Examen philologicum et philosophicum,* with highest marks.

IV

UNTIL now I had only seen a small part of my native land,— that is to say, a few points in Funen and Zealand, as well as Möen's Klint, which last is truly one of our most beautiful places; the beech-woods there hang like a garland over the white chalk cliffs, from which a view is obtained far over the Baltic. I wished, therefore, in the summer of 1830, to devote my first literary proceeds to seeing Jutland, and making myself more thoroughly acquainted with my own Funen. I had no idea how much solidity of mind I should derive from this summer excursion, or what a change was about to take place in my inner life.

Poems sprung forth upon paper, but on the comic fewer and fewer. Sentiment, which I had so often derided, would now be avenged. I arrived, in the course of my journey, at the house of a rich family in a small city; and here suddenly a new world opened before me,—an immense world, which yet could be contained in four lines, which I wrote at that time:—

> A pair of dark eyes fixed my sight;
> They were my world, my home, my delight;
> The soul beamed in them, and childlike peace,
> And never on earth will their memory cease.

New plans of life occupied me. I would give up writing poetry,—to what could it lead? I would study theology, and become a preacher; I had only one thought, and that was *she*. But it was self-delusion: she loved another; she married him. It was not till several years later that I felt and acknowledged that it was best, both for her and for myself, that things had fallen out as they had. She had no idea, perhaps, how deep my feeling for her had been, or what an influence it produced in me. She had become the excellent wife of a good man, and a happy mother. God bless her!

In my "Journey on Foot," and in most of my writings, satire had been the prevailing characteristic. This displeased many people, who thought that this bent of mind could lead to no good purpose. The critics now blamed me precisely for that which a far deeper feeling had expelled from my breast. A new collection of poetry, "Fancies and Sketches," which was published for the new year, showed satisfactorily what my heart suffered. A paraphrase of the history of my own heart appeared in a serious vaudeville, "Parting and Meeting," with this difference only, that here the love was mutual: the piece was not presented on the stage till five years later.

I betrayed more and more in my writings an unhealthy turn of mind. I felt an inclination to seek for the melancholy in life, and to linger on the dark side of things; I became sensitive, and thought rather of the blame than of the praise which was lavished on me. My late school education, which was forced, and my impulse to become an author whilst I was yet a student, make it evident that my first work, the "Journey on Foot," was not without grammatical errors. Had I only paid some one to correct the proofs, which was a work I was unaccustomed to, then no charge of this kind could have been brought against me. Now, on the contrary, people laughed at these errors, and dwelt upon them, passing over carelessly that in the book which had merit. I know people who only read my poems to find out errors; they noted down, for instance, how often I used the word *beautiful,* or some similar word. A gentleman, now a clergyman, at that time a writer of vaudevilles and a critic, was not ashamed, in a company where I was, to go through several of my poems in this style; so that a little girl of six years old, who heard with amazement that he discovered everything to be wrong, took the book, and pointing out the conjunction *and,* said, "There is yet a little word about which you have not scolded.'" He felt what a reproof lay in the remark of the child; he looked ashamed and kissed the little one. All this wounded me; but I had, since my school-days, become somewhat timid, and that caused me to take it all quietly: I was morbidly sensitive, and I was good-natured to a fault. Everybody knew it, and some were on that account almost cruel to me. Everybody wished to teach me; almost everybody said that I was spoiled by praise, and therefore *they* would speak the truth to me. Thus I heard continually of my faults, the real and the ideal weaknesses. In the meantime, however, my feelings burst forth; and then I said that I would become a poet whom they should see honored. But this was regarded only as the crowning mark of the most unbearable vanity; and from house to house it was repeated. I was a good man, they said, but one of the vainest in existence; and in that very time I was often ready wholly to despair of my abilities, and had, as in the darkest days of my school-life, a feeling as if my whole talents were a self-deception. I almost believed so; but it was more than I could bear, to hear the same thing said, sternly and jeeringly, by others; and if I then uttered a proud, an inconsiderate word, it was addressed to the scourge with which I was smitten; and when those who smite are those we love, then do the scourges become scorpions.

For this reason Collin thought that I should make a little journey, in order to divert my mind and furnish me with new ideas. I had by industry and frugality laid aside a little sum of money, so that I resolved to spend a couple of weeks in North Germany.

In the spring of 1831, I left Denmark for the first time. I saw Lübeck and Hamburg. Everything astonished me and occupied my mind. There were as yet no railways here; the broad, deep, and sandy route passed over the heaths of Lunenburg, which looked as I had read of them in the admired "Labyrinth" of Baggesen.

I arrived at Braunchweig. I saw mountains for the first time,—the Hartzgebirge—and went on foot from Goslar over the Brocken to Halle.

The world expanded so astonishingly before me my good humor returned to me as to the bird of passage, but sorrow is the flock of sparrows, which remains behind and builds in the nests of the birds of passage.

In the book at the summit of the Brocken, where so many travelers write down their names, thoughts, and sentiments, I also wrote down mine in a little verse:—

> Above the clouds I stand here,
>   Yet must my heart confess
> That nearer far to heaven I was
>   When I *her* hand could press.

Next year a friend told me that he had seen my verse, when he visited the Brocken, and a countryman had written below, "Poor little Andersen, save your verses for Elmquist's 'Reading book,' and trouble us not with them abroad, where they never find their way except when you come and write them down."

The little journey in Germany had great influence upon me, as my Copenhagen friends acknowledged. The impressions of the journey were immediately written down, and I gave them forth under the title of "Shadow Pictures." Whether I were actually improved or not, there still prevailed at home the same petty pleasure in dragging out my faults, the same perpetual schooling of me; and I was weak enough to endure it from those who were officious meddlers. I seldom made a joke of it; but if I did so, it was called arrogance and vanity, and it was asserted that I never would listen to rational people. Such an instructor once asked me whether I wrote *Dog* with a little *d;*—he had found such an error of the press in my last work. I replied, jestingly, "Yes, because I here spoke of a little dog."

But these are small troubles, people will say. Yes, but they are drops which wear hollows in the rock. I speak of it here; I feel a necessity to do so; here to protest against the accusation of vanity, which, since no other error can be discovered in my private life, is seized upon, and even now is thrown at me like an old medal.

I willingly read for everybody whom I visited what I lately had written that pleased me. I had not yet learned by experience how seldom an author ought to do this, at least in this country. Any gentleman or lady who can hammer on a piano or sing a few songs, has no hesitation, in whatever company they may enter, to carry their music-book with them and place themselves before the piano; it is but very seldom that any remark is made on that; an author may read aloud others' poetical works but not his own—that is vanity.

That has been said many times about Oehlenschläger, who was always willing to read his works in the different circles where he went, and read them very beautifully too. How many remarks I have heard about it from people who seemed to think that they made themselves interesting thereby, or showed their superiority to the poet: if they allowed themselves to do thus toward Oehlenschläger, how much further could they not then go toward Andersen?

Sometimes my good humor lifted me above the bitterness that surrounded me; I discovered weakness in others as well as in myself. In such a moment I brought forth my little

---

[1] A popular expression for senseless gabble and chatter.

poem, "Snik-snak,"[1] which was printed, and I was made the subject of many verses and poems in papers and periodicals. A lady whom I used to visit sent for me, and catechized me to know "if I ever visited houses where this poem had any appropriateness; she did not believe that it had anything to do with the company that met at her house, but as I was a guest there, people would imagine that her house was the place I had aimed at," and then she gave me a good lecture.

In the vestibule of the theater one evening a well-dressed lady, unknown to me, came up very near me, and with an expression of indignation looked me in the face and said, "Snik-snak." I bowed: politeness does for an answer!

Through the writings of Hoffmann my attention had been turned to the masked comedies of Gozzi, and finding among these "Il Corvo" to be an excellent subject for an opera text, I read Meisling's translation of it, became quite enraptured, and in a few weeks I wrote my opera text of "The Raven."

I gave it to a young composer, almost unknown at that time, but a man of talent and spirit, a grandson of him who composed the Danish folk's-song of "King Christian stood by the tall, tall mast." My young composer was the present Professor J. P. E. Hartmann.

It will sound strange to the ears of many, when I say that I at that time, in my letter to the theatrical directors, recommended him and gave my word for his being a man of talent, who would produce something good. He now takes rank among the first of living Danish composers.

My text to "The Raven" is without freshness and melody, and I have not inserted it in my collected writings; only a chorus and a song are introduced among the poems.

I worked up also Walter Scott's "Bride of Lammermoor," for another young composer, Bredal. Both operas appeared on the stage; but I was subjected to the most merciless criticism, as one who had stultified the labors of foreign poets. I have a reminiscence of Oehlenschläger at that time which not only displays his irritability, but also, in a high degree, his thoroughly noble nature.

The "Bride of Lammermoor" had appeared on the stage and was received with acclamation. I took the printed text to Oehlenschläger, who smiled and congratulated me on the great applause I had received, but said that it was easy for me to obtain it, as I had taken from Walter Scott, and had been assisted by the composer. It grieved me much to hear him say so, and tears came into my eyes; when he saw that he embraced and kissed me, and said: "Other people are making me cross too!" and now he was heartiness itself, presented me with one of his books, and wrote his and my name in it.

The composer Weyse, my earliest benefactor, whom I have already mentioned, was, on the contrary, satisfied in the highest degree with my treatment of these subjects. He told me that he had wished for a long time to compose an opera from Walter Scott's "Kenilworth." He now requested me to commence the joint work, and write the text. I had no idea of the summary justice which would be dealt to me. I needed money to live, and, what still more determined me to it, I felt flattered to have to work with Weyse, our most celebrated composer. It delighted me that he, who had first spoken in my favor at Siboni's house, now, as artist, sought a noble connection with me. I had scarcely half finished the text, when I was already blamed for having made use of a well-known romance. I wished to give it up; but Weyse consoled me, and encouraged me to proceed. Afterward, before he had finished the music, when I was about to travel abroad, I committed my fate, as regarded the text, entirely to his hands. He wrote whole verses of it, and the altered conclusion is wholly his own. It was a peculiarity of that singular man that he liked no book which ended sorrowfully. Amy Robsart, in "Kenilworth," must marry Leicester. "Why make them unhappy, when one with only a few pen-strokes can make them happy!" said he. "But it is not historical," replied I. "What shall we then do with Queen Elizabeth?"—"She may say: 'Proud England, I am thine!'" answered he. I yielded, and let him finish the opera with these words.

My affairs were now in their worst condition; and precisely in that same year in which a stipend for traveling had been conferred upon Hertz, I also had presented a petition for the same purpose. I looked up to King Frederic VI. with true reverence and heartfelt gratitude. I had grown up with these feelings, and I felt a strong desire to give them expression. I could not do it in any other way than by presenting him a book, which he had allowed me to dedicate to him, "The Twelve Months of the Year."

A man, who meant well by me and was acquainted with what needed to be done, told me that I ought, in order to take proper measures to receive a stipend for traveling, to tell the King when I presented him my book, shortly and clearly who I was; that since becoming a student I had made my way without any support; and that travel would, more than anything else, serve to complete my education; then the King would probably answer, that I could bring him a petition, which I was to have by me and thereupon hand to him. I thought it monstrous that at the same moment when I presented him my book I should ask him a favor! "That is the way," said he; "the King is very well aware that you give him the book in order to ask for something!" This made me almost desperate, but he said, "That is the only way to do it," and I did it. My audience must have been very comical indeed; my heart was beating with fear, and when the King, in his peculiar manner, stepped abruptly toward me and asked what book I brought him, I answered,—"A cycle of poems!"

"A cycle, cycle—what do you mean?" Then I became quite disconcerted and said,—

"It is some verses to Denmark!" He smiled:—

"Well, well, it is very good, thank you!" and so he nodded and dismissed me. But as I had not yet begun on my real errand, I told him that I had still something more to say to him; and now, without hesitation, I told him about my studies and how I had gone through them. "That is very praiseworthy," said the King; and when I reached the point of a stipend for traveling, he answered, as I had been told he would: "Well, send me your petition!"

"Yes, sire!" exclaimed I in all simplicity. "I have it with me! but it seems to me so dreadful, that I should bring it along with the book; they have told me that I ought to do so, that it was the right way, but I find it so dreadful: it is not like me!"—and tears rushed from my eyes. The good King laughed heartily, nodded in a friendly fashion, and took the petition. I made a **bow and ran away** at full speed.

The universal opinion was that I had reached the point of culmination, and if I was to succeed in traveling, it must be at this present time. I felt, what since then has become an acknowledged fact, that traveling would be the best school for me. I received a stipend for traveling—Hertz a larger and I a smaller one: and that also was quite in the order of things.

I left Copenhagen Monday, 22d April, 1833. I saw the steeples of the city dissolving from my view—we approached the promontory of Möen; then the Captain brought me a letter and said jokingly: "It came just now down through the air." It was a few words more, an affectionate farewell from Edward Collin. Off Falster another letter from another friend. At bed-time a third, and early in the morning near Travemünde a fourth—all "through the air!" said the Captain. My friends had kindly and sympathetically filled his pockets with letters for me.

v̄

I saw the Rhine! Its banks appear least favorable at spring-time, the vines looking meanly, as they rise toward the castle ruins. I had imagined it all much more grand. What I saw was below my expectation, and I think that I am not alone in that opinion; the most beautiful point is undeniably Loreley, near St. Goar. The banks of the river Danube are more romantic, even the Rhone has points which surpass those of the Rhine. The traditions are the chief attractions of the Rhine. Tales and songs—those charming songs, which the German poets have sung to the honor of that mighty sea-green stream—are its highest beauty.

From the Rhine we continued our journey for three nights and days over Saarbrück, through the chalk district of Champagne, to Paris. I looked eagerly toward this "city of cities," as I then called it, and asked so many times if we should not soon be there that at last I stopped asking, and so we passed the very Boulevards even before I knew that we had reached that mighty city.

All my traveling impressions on my way from Copenhagen

to Paris are presented in what I have here written, and but very little was I able to get hold of on this rapid passage. Still there were people at home who already expected to see something from me; they did not consider that if even the curtain is raised the play is not immediately seen or clearly conceived.

I was now in Paris, fatigued and sleepy. I descended at the Hôtel de Lille, Rue Thomas, near the Palais Royal. To go to bed and get a good sleep was the best thing for me, but I had not slept long before I was awakened by a dreadful noise; it was light all around. I started to the window; opposite, in the narrow street, was a large building. I looked through the windows: a crowd of people rushed down the stairs, crying and bellowing; there was a great rush and rumble and flashing, and I, being still half asleep, thought of course that all Paris was in a revolution. I rang the bell and asked the waiter what the matter was. "C'est le tonnerre!" said he; "Le tonnerre!" said the maid; and seeing that I did not understand them, they rolled with the tongue, "Tonnerre-re-rrre!" showing me how the thunderbolt beats down, and meanwhile it lightened and rumbled. It was the thunder, and the house opposite was the Vaudeville Theater, where the play was just finished and people were rushing downstairs; that was my first awakening in Paris.

One day I entered "Europe Litteraire," a kind of Parisian "Athenæum," where Paul Duport had introduced me. A little man of Jewish cast came toward me. "I hear you are a Dane," said he; "I am a German: Danes and Germans are brothers, therefore I offer you my hand!"

I asked for his name, and he said: "Heinrich Heine!" the poet whom, in my recent young erotic period of life, I had admired so much, and who had so entirely expressed my thoughts and feelings in his songs. There was no man I could have wished more to see and meet with than he, and so I told him.

"Only phrases!" said he smiling; "if I had interested you as much as you tell me, you should have sought me out before!"

"I could not," replied I; "you have so much sense of the ludicrous, that you might have thought it absurd in me, who

am a Danish poet entirely unknown to you, to seek you. I
know also that I should have behaved very awkwardly toward
you, and if you had then laughed at me, or perhaps quizzed
me, I should have been deeply wounded, for the very reason
that I estimate you so highly; so I should rather have missed
seeing you at all."

My words made a good impression on him, and he was very
kind and amiable. The next day he returned my visit in
Hôtel Vivienne, where I lived. We met each other often,
and sometimes we promenaded together on the Boulevard,
but I did not then place full confidence in him, and I did
not feel that hearty attraction which several years afterward
I felt when we met again in Paris, and he had read my
"Improvisatore" and some of my small stories. On my
departure from Paris to Italy he wrote to me:—

"I should have wished, my dear colleague, to scribble some
verses to you, but to-day I can hardly write tolerably in prose.
Farewell! I wish you a pleasant sojourn in Italy. Learn
German well in Germany, and when you return to Denmark
write down in German what you have seen and felt in Italy.
That would make me very happy.

"H. HEINE.

"PARIS, *August* 10, 1833."

The first French book I tried to read in Paris was Victor
Hugo's novel, "Notre Dame." I used daily to visit the
cathedral and look upon the scenes depicted in that poetical work. I was captivated by those stirring pictures and
dramatic characters, and what could I do better than go
and see the poet, who lived in a corner-house in the Place
Royale. They were old-fashioned rooms, hung with engrav-
ings, wood-cuts, and paintings of Notre Dame. He received
me in his bed-gown, drawers, and elegant morning boots.
Taking leave of him, I asked him for his name on a piece of
paper; he complied with my wishes, and wrote his name close
up to the edge of the paper. I felt very badly, for it came
immediately to my mind that he did this because he did not
know me, and was cautious that no place should be left for
me to write above his name. At a later stay in Paris I came
to know the poet better.

During my journey to Paris, and the whole of the first month I spent there, I heard not a single word from home. I asked for letters at the post-office, but in vain. Could my friends, perhaps, have nothing agreeable to tell me? Could it be that I still was envied the traveling stipend which the recommendations of so many had procured me? I was much depressed. At length, however, a letter arrived,—a large unpaid one, which cost a large sum in postage, but then it was such a splendid great one. My heart beat with joy and yearning impatience to read it; it was, indeed, my first letter from home. I opened it, but I discovered not a single written word, nothing but a printed newspaper,—"The Copenhagen Post," of Monday, May 13, 1833, containing a lampoon upon me; and that was sent to me all that distance with postage unpaid, probably by the anonymous writer himself.

That was to be my first greeting from home. This abominable malice wounded me deeply. I have never discovered who the author was; the verses betrayed a practiced pen; perhaps he was one of those who afterwards called me "friend" and pressed my hand. Men have base thoughts; I also have mine.

I remained in Paris till the July festivals were over; they were then in their first freshness, and I saw on one of the days the unveiling of Napoleon's pillar at the Place Vendôme.

The evening before, while the workmen were at work, the statue still covered, and people gathered in crowds on the place, a strange-looking, lean old woman came toward me, and with laughter and an expression of insanity said to me, "There they have placed him; to-morrow, perhaps, they take him down again. Ha, ha, ha! I know the French people!" I went away with sad thoughts.

The following day I had a seat upon a high scaffold at the corner of the place. I gazed on Louis Philippe, with his sons and generals. The "garde nationale" passed with music and with bouquets of flowers stuck in the gun-barrels; people shouted Hurra! but also "À bas les forts" was heard.

In the Hôtel de Ville was a people's ball in splendid style; all classes came together, from the royal family to the fishwomen. The crowd was so dense that Louis Philippe and his queen reached the seats arranged for them with considerable difficulty. It made a sad impression on me to hear the orchestra play the dance-music of the opera "Gustavus the Third," when the royal family entered. I looked to see in the face of Queen Amelie an impression similar to what I felt: she was deadly pale and clung tightly to Louis Philippe, who with a jovial smile saluted all and shook hands with several persons.

I saw the Duc d'Orleans, young and full of vigor, dancing with a poorly dressed young girl,—probably one of the lowest classes.

This feast and gayety continued through several days; in the evenings funereal flambeaux burned upon the graves of the fallen citizens, which were adorned with wreaths of everlastings; tournaments in boats were held in the Seine; Danish sports in fine style were seen in Champs d'Elysées. All the theaters in Paris were open to the public, even in the middle of the day, and representations were given with open doors; everybody could come and go as they liked. Sometimes the people interrupted the performance of tragedies and operas, and began to sing "La Parisienne" and "Allons Enfants." In the evenings rockets and fire-works flashed and cracked in the air, and there were brilliant illuminations of churches and public buildings.

Thus ended my first visit to Paris, and the finale could not have been more grand and festive.

We had left the flat plains of France and reached the Jura Mountains; here in a little village, late in the evening, the conductor helped two young farmer's daughters to get into the diligence, where I was the only passenger.

"If we do not let them drive with us they will be obliged to walk two hours on a desert road," said the conductor; they whispered and tittered together; they knew that a gentleman was in the coach, but could not see me; at last they took courage and asked me if I was a Frenchman, and learning that I was from Denmark, they made me believe that they knew that country. They recollected from the geography that Denmark was the same as Norway. Copenhagen they could not pronounce, but always said "Corporal," and so forth.

They asked me whether I was young, and married, and how I looked. I kept quiet in a dark corner, and gave them as ideal a description as I could; they understood the sport, and when in turn I asked them of their appearance, they made themselves out to me real beauties.

They urged me to show my face when we arrived at the next station; I would not yield to their wishes, and so they covered their faces with their handkerchiefs and alighted, and, laughing merrily, held out their hands to me; they were young and had very beautiful figures. Those two unknown, invisible, gay girls represented a laughing image of my traveling life.

VI

ON the 5th of September, 1833, I crossed the Simplon on my way to Italy. On the very day on which, fourteen years before, I had arrived poor and helpless in Copenhagen, did I set foot in this country of my longing and of my poetical happiness.

The day at last came when we were to see Rome. We drove in rain and mud; we passed by "Monte Soracte," celebrated by Horace's song, through the Campagna of Rome; but none of us felt its grandeur, nor were captivated by the colors and beautiful outlines of the mountains; we only thought how soon we were to get there, and of the repose we should then have. I must confess that when we came to the hill of La Storta, where those coming from the north get the first sight of Rome, I felt indeed happy; but the impression was not that of a poet: at the first sight of Rome and St. Peter's I exclaimed: "God be praised! now we can soon get something to eat!"

ROME!

It was the 18th of October, in the middle of the day, when I arrived at Rome, the city of cities, where I soon was to feel as if I had been born there and was in my own house. I reached the city in time to witness a most rare event—the second funeral of Raphael. The Academia St. Luca had kept for many years a skull which was asserted to be the head of Raphael; but in later years, its genuineness being called in question, Pope Gregory XVI. gave permission to have the grave opened in the Pantheon, or as the place is now called,

Santa Maria della Rotunda. The dead man was found safe and sound, and the corpse was again to be deposited in the church.

When the grave was opened and the bones brought forth, the painter Camuccini had sole permission to paint the whole scene. Horace Vernet, who lived in the French Academy at Rome and knew nothing about it, took his pencil and made a sketch. The papal police present forbade it; he looked surprised at them, and said very quietly: "But at home I can do it from memory?" Nobody could say anything against that, and in the time from twelve o'clock at noon until six o'clock in the evening he painted a beautiful and very truthful picture, and had it engraved afterward; but the plate was immediately seized by the police and confiscated. Thereupon Vernet wrote a violent letter and demanded that they should deliver him the plate within twenty-four hours; that art was not a monopoly, like salt and tobacco. They sent it back, and he broke it in pieces and dispatched them with a letter to Camuccini, written in a very fiery style, telling him that he might know by this that he was not going to make use of it to Camuccini's detriment. Camuccini had the plate put together again and sent it, accompanied with a very friendly letter, to Horace Vernet, declaring that he had entirely given up publishing his drawing. After that everybody was allowed to take a drawing of the grave, and in consequence there was a host of pictures.

We reached the Austrian frontier. My passport from Copenhagen was in French, the frontier guard looked at it, and asked for my name. I answered, "Hans Christian Andersen!"

"That name is not in your passport, your name is Jean Chrétien Andersen; so you travel under another name than your own?"

Now commenced an examination, which became very amusing. I, who never carried either cigars or other prohibited articles with me, had my trunk searched through and through, and I myself was scrupulously examined; all my letters from home were looked through; they made me declare on oath whether they contained anything beside family affairs; after that they asked me what my "chapeau bras" was. I answered, "A hat for society."—"What kind of society?" asked they,—"a secret society?" My ivy wreath from the Christmas Feast in Rome seemed very suspicious to them. "Have you been in Paris?" they again asked. "Yes!" And now they let me know that all was as it ought to be in Austria, that they were not going to have revolutions, and were very well contented with their Emperor Franz. I assured them that I was of the same mind, and that they might be entirely at rest; I hated revolutions, and was a tiptop kind of subject. That all went for nothing; I was more severely searched than all the others, and the only reason was that the officer in Copenhagen had translated the Danish name Hans Christian by Jean Chrétien.

After spending a month in Vienna I commenced my journey homeward by way of Prague, enjoying "the poetry of traveling life" as people call it. A crowd of people were squeezed together, the coach jerked and rattled, but this brought out some droll characters that helped to keep up the good humor in the coach. Among others we had an old gentleman who was displeased with everything; he had been the victim of extortion, and was continually calculating how much money he had spent, and he found that it was always too much; first it was for a cup of coffee that was not worth the money, then he was vexed by the degeneracy of the young people nowadays, who had too much to do with everything, even with the fate of the world. A dirty Jew who was seated at his side, prattled all the time and told ten times over his journey to Ragusa in Dalmatia! he would not, he said, be a king,—that was too much; but he would like to be a king's valet, like one he had known, who had grown so fleshy that he could not walk, and was obliged to have a valet for himself. He was nasty from head to foot, and yet he was continually talking of cleanliness. He was indignant at hearing that in Hungary they used to heat the ovens with cow's dung! he served up old anecdotes to us. Suddenly he became absorbed in thought, drew a paper out of his pocket, rolled his eyes about, and wrote. He had ideas! he said, and asked me to read what he had written down.

There were no reserved seats in the coach, and we had to

agree the best way we could; but the two best places were after all taken away from us by two new travelers, who stepped in at Iglau while we, weary and hungry, went to the supper-table. They were a young woman with her husband; he was already asleep when we reëntered the coach; she was awake enough for both of them, and loquacity itself; she spoke of art and literature, of refined education, of reading a poet and comprehending him, of music and plastic art, of Calderon and Mendelssohn. Sometimes she stopped, and sighed, at her husband, who leaned his head upon her: "Raise your angelic head, it crushes my bosom!" said she. And now she talked about her father's library, and of the meeting she was again to have with him; and when I asked her of the Bohemian literature, she was intimately acquainted with all the authors of note in the country,—they came to her father's house, who had in his library a complete collection of books belonging to modern literature, etc. When day broke I perceived that she and her husband were a fair Jewish couple; he awoke, drank a cup of coffee, and fell asleep again, leaned his head against his wife, opened his mouth only once to utter a wornout witticism, and so slept again—that angel!

She wanted to know about us all, what our positions and conditions were, and learning that I was an author, she took much interest in me. When we gave our names at the gates of Prague, an old deaf gentleman said that his name was "Professor Zimmermann!" "Zimmermann!" she cried out; "Zimmermann's 'Solitude!' Are you Zimmermann?" She did not know that the author she meant had been dead a long time. The deaf gentleman repeated his name, and now she burst out into lamentations that only at the hour of separation she had learned with whom she had been traveling.

I had told her that I meant to go early next morning to Dresden; she said that she was very sorry for it, because she would have invited me to see her father and his library, and, perhaps, meet with people of sympathetic mind! "We live in the largest house in the place!" She pointed it out to me, and I saw that both she and her husband entered it. When they took leave, the husband gave me his card. The next morning I decided to stay two days in Prague, so I could pay my traveling companions a visit, and take a view of the library with its Bohemian literature.

I went to the large house where I had seen the couple enter. In the first story nobody knew anything of the family, nor in the second story; mounting the third, I mentioned the great library that was said to be there! no, nobody knew of it. I reached the fourth story, but neither here was any information to be had, and they said that no other families lived in the house except those I had seen; there lived, to be sure, an old Jew in a couple of garrets in the top of the house, but they were sure that I could not mean him. Nevertheless I mounted the stairs,—the walls to the staircase consisting of rough boards; there was a low door at which I knocked. An old man dressed in a dirty night-gown opened it, and I stepped into a low-studded room; in the middle of the floor stood a large clothes-basket filled with books. "It is not possible that family lives here!" said I.

"My God!" cried a female voice from a little side-chamber. I looked in that direction and beheld my traveling lady in *negligée*, balancing her fine, black silk traveling gown over her head in order to get it on, and in the opposite chamber her husband gaped in a sleepy fashion, drowsily nodding his "angel head." I stood amazed: the lady stepped in, the dress open in the back, an untied bonnet on the head, and her cheeks blushing with surprise. "Von Andersen!" said she, and uttered an excuse. All was out of order here, and her father's library—she pointed at the clothes-basket. All the boasting in the traveling coach was reduced to a garret and a bag filled with books!

Already for many years there had existed, under Frederick VI., an institution which does the highest honor to the Danish government, namely, that beside the considerable sum expended yearly for the traveling expenses of young literary men and artists, a small pension shall be awarded to such of them as enjoy no office emoluments. All our most important poets have had a share of this assistance,—Oehlenschläger, Ingemann, Heiberg, C. Winther, and others. Hertz had just then received such a pension, and his future subsistence was made thus the more secure. It was my hope and my wish that the same good fortune might be mine—and it was. Frederick VI. granted me two hundred rix-dollars banco yearly. I was filled with gratitude and joy. I was no longer *forced* to write in order to live; I had a sure support in the possible event of sickness; I was less dependent upon the people about me.

A new chapter of my life began.

VII

In Constantinople I passed eleven interesting days; and according to my good fortune in travel, the birthday of Mohammed itself fell exactly during my stay there. I saw the grand illumination, which completely transported me into the "Thousand and One Nights."

Our Danish ambassador lived several miles from Constantinople, and I had therefore no opportunity of seeing him; but I found a cordial reception with the Austrian internuncius, Baron Stürmer. With him I had a German home and friends. I contemplated making my return by the Black Sea and up the Danube; but the country was disturbed; it was said there had been several thousand Christians murdered. My companions of the voyage, in the hotel where I resided, gave up this route of the Danube, for which I had the greatest desire, and collectively counseled me against it. But in this case I must return again by Greece and Italy— it was a severe conflict.

I do not belong to the courageous; I feel fear, especially in little dangers; but in great ones, and when an advantage is to be won, then I have a will, and it has grown firmer with years. I may tremble, I may fear; but I still do that which I consider the most proper to be done. I am not ashamed to confess my weakness; I hold that when out of our own true conviction we run counter to our inborn fear, we have done our duty. I had a strong desire to become acquainted with the interior of the country, and to traverse the Danube in its greatest expansion. I battled with myself; my imagination pointed to me the most horrible circumstances; it was an anxious night. In the morning I took counsel with Baron Stürmer, and as he was of opinion that I might undertake the voyage, I determined upon it. From the moment that I had taken my determination I had the most immovable reliance on Providence, and flung myself calmly on my fate. The fourth of May I went on board the ship, which lay by the garden of the Seraglio.

Early in the morning, when we weighed anchor, we heard the sad news that the large Austrian steamship, which we had expected to meet us, had struck upon a rock the night before in the fog in the Black Sea, and was totally wrecked. We passed through the strange-looking Bosphorus, suffered heavy seas and foggy weather, stopped one day at the city of Kostendsche, near the decayed rampart of Trajan, and rode in big carriages of basket-work, drawn by white oxen, along the desolate country, where wild dogs were strolling about. Only the tumbled down tombstones of two cemeteries showed us that here had been towns, which were burnt by the Russians in the War of 1809. It was the city of Dobrudscha. We spent two days in passing over the whole remarkable seat of war of the Russians and Turks. I have thus in my head the best map I could obtain of the Danube territory,—the clearest idea of the miserable small towns and ruined fortresses; I saw whole ruins of fortifications, built of earth and basket-work. We did not hear anything of the disturbances in the country until we reached Rustschuk, with its many minarets. The shore was crowded with people: two Frankish-dressed young men were thrown into the Danube; they swam toward land; one of them reached it, but the other, who was stoned, swam out toward us and cried out: "Help! they are killing me!" We stopped in the middle of the river, got him up, and made signals by a cannon-shot. The pasha of the city came on board and took the poor Frank under his protection.

From the ship we saw next day the Balkan Mountains, covered with snow; between them and us the revolt was raging. In the night we heard that an armed Tartar, who carried letters and dispatches from Widdin to Constantinople, was attacked and killed; another, I believe, had the same fate. The third got his escort scattered, escaped from it himself, and came down to the Danube, where, hidden among the reeds, he had awaited the arrival of our steamship. The man, in his sheepskin clothes, just coming out of the mire, and armed to the teeth, as we call it, looked horrible when we at lamp-light beheld him coming on board; he traveled with us a whole day up the Danube.

On my arrival at Hamburg there was a great musical festival. I met many countrymen at the table d'hôte, and while speaking to my friends of the beautiful Greece, of the rich Orient, an old Copenhagen lady addressed me with the words:—

"Mr. Andersen, have you on your many and long travels ever seen anything abroad so beautiful as our little Denmark?"

"Indeed I have!" answered I: "I have seen many things far more beautiful!"

"Fie!" exclaimed she, "you are no patriot!"

I passed through Odense, just at the time of St. Knud's Fair. "I am very glad," said a respectable lady of Funen, "that you have arranged your great journey so as to come to the fair. I see that you keep to Odense: that I have always said!" So there I passed for a patriot!

It was a time when the newspapers in my native city, Odense, always called me "Our city's child," and gave information about me which could not be of any interest to the public. Extracts were given from my private letters when I was abroad, which became ridiculous when given in the newspaper: thus, for instance, when I once wrote home from Rome that I had seen Queen Christina in the chapel of Pope Sixtus, and added that she put me in mind of the wife of the composer Hartmann, it was reported in the Funen newspaper that "Queen Christina resembled a certain lady in Copenhagen." Of course they laughed at that. How often have I experienced the awkward friendship that vexes us. From that time until now I have always feared to speak of such things to a thoughtless news-writer, and yet I have not escaped. I was afterward again ridiculed when it was no fault of mine. I was on a journey, and stopped for half an hour at the Odense post-office, where a news-writer asked me,—

"Are you going abroad now?"

"No," I answered.

"Do you not expect to?"

"It depends on whether I can get money. I am writing a

piece for the theater; if it proves successful I presume I shall go away.''

''Where will you then go?''

''I do not yet know; either to Spain or to Greece, I think.''

The same evening I read in the newspaper a paragraph to the effect that—''H. C. Andersen is writing a piece for the theater: should it prove to be successful he is going abroad, either to Spain or to Greece.''

Of course I was ridiculed, and a Copenhagen newspaper was right in saying that my journey was rather a distant prospect. The piece was to be written, played, and have its success, and then one could not be sure whether my journey would be to Spain or Greece. People laughed, and one who is laughed at has lost his cause. I became depressed and took no pains to conceal it. When boys throw stones at a poor dog which is swimming against the stream, it is not because they are wicked but because they think it fun, and people had similar sport with me. I had no defenders, I did not belong to any party, I had no newspaper-writing friends, and therefore I was compelled to do as I did. In the meantime it was said and written and frequently repeated, that I lived only in the company of my admirers! How little they knew about it. What I here must present is no complaint; I will not cast a particle of shade over the many whom I really love; I am sure that if I had fallen into great need and trouble, they would have put forth all their endeavor not to let me go under, but a poetic nature needs sympathy of another kind, and of that I have been very much in want. My dearest friends have as severely and loudly as any critic expressed their surprise at the appreciation my works have received abroad. Fredrika Bremer discerned it and was very much astonished. We were in company together in Copenhagen at a house where it was said that I was a spoiled child. She thought she was telling something agreeable when she said: ''It is almost incredible how Andersen is loved in Sweden from south to north; in almost every house we see his books!''

''Don't make him believe such things!'' was the answer, and said in real earnest. Much has been said about the fact that to be noble or of high birth has no longer any significance: that is only nonsense. The able but poor student is not received in what we call good houses with the same kindness as the well-dressed child of nobility, or the son of a public functionary. I could illustrate it by many examples, but I will only give one, which may stand for all,—one out of my own life. The guilty is or was—I will not say which—a person highly honored, whose name I will omit.

When Christian VIII., for the first time as king, visited the theater, "The Mulatto" was played. I was seated in the parquette by the side of Thorwaldsen, who, when the curtain fell, whispered to me: "The King is bowing to you!"

"It must be for you!" I answered; "it cannot concern me!" I looked up to the royal box: the King again bowed, and plainly it was intended for me; but I felt that a possible misunderstanding on my part would lead to my being laughed at by the public, and therefore I sat quietly, and the next day I went to the king to give him my thanks for that unusual favor, and he teased me for not returning his greeting on the spot. A few days after there was a grand *bal parée* at the castle of Christiansborg for all classes of the community. I had received a card of invitation.

"What shall you do there?" asked one of our elder men of learning, when I spoke of the festival to him. "What do you have to do with such places!" repeated he.

I answered in joke,—"Well, it is because I am always so well received in that circle!"

"But it is not your place there!" said he angrily.

There was nothing for me but to answer freely and laughingly, as if I did not feel the sting,—

"The king himself has in the theater saluted me from his box, so I think I may also go to his *bal parée!*"

"Saluted you from his box, you say!" exclaimed he: "but that does not prove that you have any right to intrude!"

"But people of the same class that I belong to will be at the ball!" added I more earnestly; "students will be there!"

"Yes, but what students?" he asked. I named a young student of the gentleman's own family.

"Yes, but that is different!" replied he then: "he is the son of a Counselor of State! What was your father?"

My blood boiled at that. "My father was a tradesman!"

said I. "I have, by the help of God and by my own work, acquired the position I now have, and which you think honorable enough I make no doubt!" He never apologized to me for his rudeness.

It is very difficult to tell in a roundabout way of wrong that one has suffered, when the wrong has not been malicious, and I have throughout my book felt this difficulty, and therefore I have refused to show the full cup of bitterness: I have only let fall some drops from it. The journey had strengthened me and I began to show indications of a firmer purpose, a more certain judgment. Many heavy seas still followed, but from that time I steadily advanced through smooth water toward the recognition I could wish for and claim of my own country,—such also as Örsted had predicted in his comforting words.

VIII

POLITICAL life in Denmark had, at that time, arrived at a higher development, producing both good and evil fruits. The eloquence which had formerly accustomed itself to the Demosthenic mode,—that of putting little pebbles in the mouth, the little pebbles of every-day life,—now exercised itself more freely on subjects of greater interest. I felt no call thereto, and no necessity to mix myself up in such matters; for I then believed that the politics of our times were a great misfortune to many a poet. Madame Politics is like Venus: they whom she decoys into her castle perish. It fares with the writings of these poets as with the newspapers: they are seized upon, read, praised, and forgotten. In our days every one wishes to rule; the subjective makes its power of value; people forget that that which is thought of cannot always be carried out, and that many things look very different when contemplated from the top of the tree, to what they did when seen from its roots. I will bow myself before him who is influenced by a noble conviction, and who only desires that which is conducive to good, be he prince or man of the people. Politics are no affair of mine. God has imparted to me another mission: that I felt, and that I feel still.

I met in the so-called first families of the country a number of friendly, kind-hearted men, who valued the good that was in me, received me into their circles, and permitted me to participate in the happiness of their opulent summer residences; so that, still feeling independent, I could thoroughly give myself up to the pleasures of nature, the solitude of woods, and country life. There for the first time I lived wholly among the scenery of Denmark, and there I wrote the greater number of my fairy tales. On the banks of quiet lakes, amid the woods, on the green grassy pastures, where the game sprang past me, and the stork paced along on his red legs, I heard nothing of politics, nothing of polemics; I heard no one practicing himself in Hegel's phraseology. Nature, which was around me, and within me, preached to me of my calling. I spent many happy days at the old house of Gisselfeld, formerly a monastery, which stands in the deepest solitude of the woods, surrounded by lakes and hills. The possessor of this fine place, the old Countess Danneskjold, mother of the Duchess of Augustenburg, was an agreeable and excellent lady. I was there not as a poor child of the people, but as a cordially received guest. The beeches now overshadow her grave in the midst of that pleasant scenery to which her heart was allied.

In honor of Thorwaldsen a musical-poetic academy was established, and the poets, who were invited to do so by Heiberg, wrote and read each one a poem in praise of him who had returned home. I wrote of Jason who fetched the golden fleece—that is to say, Jason-Thorwaldsen, who went forth to win golden art. A great dinner and a ball closed the festival, in which, for the first time in Denmark, popular life and a subject of great interest in the realms of art were made public.

One morning at Nysö—at the time when he was working at his own statue—I entered his work-room and bade him good morning; he appeared as if he did not wish to notice me, and I stole softly away again. At breakfast he was very parsimonious in the use of words, and when somebody asked him to say something at all events, he replied in his dry way :—

"I have said more during this morning than in many whole days, but nobody heard me. There I stood, and fancied that Andersen was behind me, for he came and said Good-morning! so I told him a long story about myself and Byron. I thought that he might give me one word in reply, and turned myself round; and there had I been standing a whole hour and chattering aloud to the bare walls.''

We all of us besought him to let us hear the whole story yet once more; but we had it now very short.

"O, that was in Rome," said he, "when I was about to make Byron's statue; he placed himself just opposite to me, and began immediately to assume quite another countenance to what was customary to him. 'Will not you sit still?' said I; 'but you must not make these faces.'—'It is my expression,' said Byron. 'Indeed?' said I, and then I made him as I wished, and everybody said, when it was finished, that I had hit the likeness. When Byron, however, saw it, he said, 'It does not resemble me at all; I look more unhappy.'

"He was, above all things, so desirous of looking extremely unhappy," added Thorwaldsen, with a comic expression.

In his company I wrote several of my tales for children—for example, "Ole Lucköie" ("Old Shut Eye"), to which he listened with pleasure and interest. Often in the twilight, when the family circle sat in the open garden parlor, Thorwaldsen would come softly behind me, and, clapping me on the shoulder, would ask, "Shall we little ones hear any tales to-night?"

In his own peculiarly natural manner he bestowed the most bountiful praise on my fictions, for their truth; it delighted him to hear the same stories over and over again. Often, during his most glorious works, would he stand with laughing countenance, and listen to the stories of "The Top and the Ball," and the "Ugly Duckling."

One morning, when he had just modeled in clay his great bas-relief of the "Procession to Golgotha," I entered his study.

"Tell me," said he, "does it seem to you that I have dressed Pilate properly?"

"You must not say anything to him," said the Baroness, who was always with him: "it is right; it is excellent; go away with you!"

Thorwaldsen repeated his question.

"Well then," said I, "as you ask me, I must confess that it

really does appear to me as if Pilate were dressed rather as an Egyptian than as a Roman.''

''It seems to me so too,'' said Thorwaldsen, seizing the clay with his hand, and destroying the figure.

''Now you are guilty of his having annihilated an immortal work!'' exclaimed the Baroness to me with warmth.

''Then we can make a new immortal work,'' said he, in a cheerful humor, and modeled Pilate as he now remains in the bas-reliefs in Our Lady's Church in Copenhagen.

Balzac, with whom I made acquaintance in the saloon of the Countess Bocarme, was an elegant and neatly dressed gentleman, whose teeth shone white between his red lips; he seemed to be very merry, but a man of few words, at least in society. A lady, who wrote verses, took hold of us, drew us to a sofa, and placed herself between us; she told us how small she seemed to be when seated between us. I turned my head and met behind her back Balzac's satirical and laughing face, with his mouth half open and pursed up in a queer manner; that was properly our first meeting.

One day I was going through the Louvre, and met a man who was the very image of Balzac in figure, gait, and features, but the man was dressed in miserable tattered clothes, which were even quite dirty; his boots were not brushed, his pantaloons were spattered with mud, and the hat was crushed and worn out. I stopped in surprise; the man smiled at me: I passed him, but the resemblance was too strong; I turned, ran after him, and said: ''Are you not M. Balzac?'' He laughed, showed his white teeth, and only said, ''To-morrow Monsieur Balzac starts for St. Petersburg!'' He pressed my hand,—his was soft and delicate,—nodded, and went away. It could not be other than Balzac: perhaps in that attire he had been out on an author's investigation into the mysteries of Paris; or, was the man perhaps quite another person, who knew that he resembled Balzac strongly, and wished to mystify a stranger? A few days after I talked with Countess Bocarme, who gave me a message from Balzac—he had left for St. Petersburg.

I also again met with Heine. He had married since I was last here. I found him in indifferent health, but full of energy, and so friendly and natural in his behavior toward me, that I felt no timidity in exhibiting myself to him as I was. One day he had been telling his wife in French my story of "The Constant Tin Soldier," and, whilst he said that I was the author of this story, he introduced me to her.

"First, are you going to publish your travels?" he asked; and when I said No, he proceeded, "Well then I will show you my wife." She was a lively, pretty young lady. A troop of children—"Some we've borrowed of a neighbor, not having any of our own," said Heine—played about in their room. We two played with them whilst Heine copied out one of his last poems for me.

IX

I now turn back to the year 1840. One day in the hotel in which I lived in Copenhagen, I saw the name of Jenny Lind among those of the strangers from Sweden. I was aware at that time that she was the first singer in Stockholm. I had been that same year in this neighbor country, and had there met with honor and kindness: I thought, therefore, that it would not be unbecoming in me to pay a visit to the young artist. She was, at this time, entirely unknown out of Sweden, so that I was convinced that, even in Copenhagen, her name was known only by few.

There is not anything which can lessen the impression which Jenny Lind's greatness on the stage makes, except her own personal character at home. An intelligent and child-like disposition exercises here its astonishing power; she is happy,—belonging, as it were, no longer to the world; a peaceful, quiet home, is the object of her thoughts; and yet she loves art with her whole soul, and feels her vocation in it. A noble, pious disposition like hers cannot be spoiled by homage. On one occasion only did I hear her express her joy in her talent and her self-consciousness. It was during her last residence in Copenhagen. Almost every evening she appeared either in the opera or at concerts; every hour was in requisition. She heard of a society, the object of which was to assist unfortunate children, and to take them out of the hands of their parents by whom they were misused, and compelled either to beg or steal, and to place them in other and better circumstances. Benevolent people subscribed annually a small sum each for their support, nevertheless the means for this excellent purpose were small.

"But have I not still a disengaged evening?" said she; "let me give a night's performance for the benefit of these poor children; but we will have double prices!"

Such a performance was given, and returned large proceeds; when she was informed of this, and that, by this means, a number of poor children would be benefited for several years, her countenance beamed, and the tears filled her eyes.

"Is it not beautiful," said she, "that I can sing so!"

I value her with the feeling of a brother, and I regard myself as happy that I know and understand such a spirit. God give to her that peace, that quiet happiness which she wishes for herself!

Through Jenny Lind I first became sensible of the holiness there is in art; through her I learned that one must forget oneself in the service of the Supreme. No books, no men have had a better or a more ennobling influence on me as the poet, than Jenny Lind, and I therefore have spoken of her so long and so warmly here.

To return from such a scene as this to a royal table, a charming court concert, and a little ball in the bath-saloon, as well as to the promenade by moonlight, thronged with guests, a little Boulevard, had something in it like a fairy tale,—it was a singular contrast.

As I sat on the above-mentioned five-and-twentieth anniversary, on the 5th of September, at the royal dinner-table, the whole of my former life passed in review before my mind. I was obliged to summon all my strength to prevent myself from bursting into tears. There are moments of thankfulness in which, as it were, we feel a desire to press God to our hearts. How deeply I felt, at this time, my own nothingness; how all, all, had come from him. Rantzau knew what an interesting day this was to me. After dinner the King and the Queen wished me happiness, and that so—graciously, is a poor word—so cordially, so sympathizingly! The King wished me happiness in that which I had endured and won. He asked me about my first entrance into the world, and I related to him some characteristic incidents.

In the course of conversation he inquired if I had not some certain yearly income: I named the sum to him.

"That is not much," said the King.

"But I do not require much," replied I, "and my writings procure me something."

The King, in the kindest manner, inquired further into my circumstances, and closed by saying,—

"If I can, in any way, be serviceable to your literary labors, then come to me."

In the evening, during the concert, the conversation was renewed, and some of those who stood near me reproached me for not having made use of my opportunity.

"The King," said they, "put the very words into your mouth."

But I could not, I would not have done it. "If the King," I said, "found that I required something more, he could give it to me of his own will."

And I was not mistaken. In the following year King Christian VIII. increased my annual stipend, so that with this and that which my writings bring in, I can live honorably and free from care. My King gave it to me out of the pure good-will of his own heart. King Christian is enlightened, clear-sighted, with a mind enlarged by science; the gracious sympathy, therefore, which he has felt in my fate is to me doubly cheering and ennobling.

X

THERE was a time when I suffered so very bitterly from a too severe and almost personal criticism, that I was often at the point of giving up, but then there came moments where humor, if I dare call it so, raised me from the sadness and misery into which I had sunk; I saw clearly my own weakness and wants, but also what was foolish and absurd in the insipid rebukes and learned gabble of the critics.

Once in such a moment I wrote a critique upon H. C. Andersen as an author; it was very sharp, and finished by recommending study and gratitude toward those who had educated him. I took the conceit with me one day to H. C. Örsted's, where a company was gathered for dinner. I told them that I had brought with me a copy of a shameless and harsh criticism, and read it aloud. They could not imagine why I should copy such a thing, but they also condemned it as harsh.

"It is really so," said Örsted, "they are severe against Andersen, but yet it seems to me that there is something in it, some arguments which are really striking and give us an insight into you!"

"Yes," I answered, "for it is from myself!" and now there was surprise, and laughter and joking; most of the company wondered that I could have been able to write such a thing myself.

{'He is a true humorist!" said Örsted, and that was the first time that I discovered for myself that I was in possession of such a gift.

I wished one evening to go to the theater: it was scarcely a quarter of an hour before the commencement of the opera: Speckter accompanied me, and on our way we came up to an elegant house.

"We must first go in here, dear friend," said he; "a wealthy family lives here, friends of mine, and friends of your stories; the children will be happy."

"But the opera," said I.

"Only for two minutes," returned he; and drew me into the house, mentioned my name, and the circle of children collected around me.

"And now tell us a tale," said he; "only one."

I told one, and then hastened away to the theater.

"That was an extraordinary visit," said I.

"An excellent one; one entirely out of the common way!" said he exultingly. "Only think: the children are full of Andersen and his stories; he suddenly makes his appearance amongst them, tells one of them himself, and then is gone! vanished! That is of itself like a fairy tale to the children, that will remain vividly in their remembrance."

I had already, on a former occasion, visited the brothers Grimm, but I had not at that time made much progress with the acquaintance. I had not brought any letters of introduction to them with me, because people had told me, and I myself believed it, that if I were known by anybody in Berlin, it must be the brothers Grimm. I therefore sought out their residence. The servant-maid asked me with which of the brothers I wished to speak.

"With the one who has written the most," said I, because I did not know, at that time, which of them had most interested himself in the "Märchen."

"Jacob is the most learned," said the maid-servant.

"Well, then, take me to him."

I entered the room, and Jacob Grimm, with his knowing and strongly marked countenance, stood before me.

"I come to you," said I, "without letters of introduction, because I hope that my name is not wholly unknown to you."

"Who are you?" asked he.

I told him; and Jacob Grimm said, in a half-embarrassed voice, "I do not remember to have heard this name: what have you written?"

It was now my turn to be embarrassed in a high degree; but I now mentioned my little stories.

"I do not know them," said he; "but mention to me some other of your writings, because I certainly must have heard them spoken of."

I named the titles of several; but he shook his head. I felt myself quite unlucky.

"But what must you think of me," said I, "that I come to you as a total stranger, and enumerate myself what I have written: You must know me! There has been published in Denmark a collection of the 'Märchen' of all nations, which is dedicated to you, and in it there is at least one story of mine."

"No,'" said he good-humoredly, but as much embarrassed as myself; "I have not read even that, but it delights me to make your acquaintance. Allow me to conduct you to my brother Wilhelm?"

"No, I thank you," said I, only wishing now to get away; I had fared badly enough with one brother. I pressed his hand, and hurried from the house.

That same month Jacob Grimm went to Copenhagen; immediately on his arrival, and while yet in his traveling dress, did the amiable, kind man hasten up to me. He now knew me, and he came to me with cordiality. I was just then standing and packing my clothes in a trunk for a journey to the country; I had only a few minutes' time: by this means my reception of him was just as laconic as had been his of me in Berlin.

Now, however, we met in Berlin as old acquaintance. Jacob Grimm is one of those characters whom one must love and attach oneself to.

One evening, as I was reading one of my little stories at the Countess Bismark-Bohlen's, there was in the little circle one person in particular who listened with evident fellowship of feeling, and who expressed himself in a peculiar and sensible manner on the subject. This was Jacob's brother, Wilhelm Grimm.

"I should have known you very well, if you had come to me," said he, "the last time you were here."

I saw these two highly gifted and amiable brothers almost daily. The circles into which I was invited, seemed also to be theirs; and it was my desire and pleasure that they should listen to my little stories, that they should participate in them,— they whose names will be always spoken as long as the German "Volks Märchen" are read.

The fact of my not being known to Jacob Grimm on my first visit to Berlin had so disconcerted me, that when any one asked me whether I had been well received in this city, I shook my head doubtfully and said, "But Grimm did not know me."

XI

In the course of the year 1846 several of my writings, such as "The Bazaar," "Wonder Stories," and "The Picture-book without Pictures," were published in England, and were there received by the public and the critics in the same kind way as "The Improvisatore" before. I received letters from many unknown friends of both sexes, whom I there had won. King Christian VIII. received my works, richly bound, from the well-known London book-seller, Richard Bentley. One of our men of note told me that the King on that occasion expressed his joy at the reception I was getting, but also his astonishment at my being so often attacked and depreciated at home while abroad I was fully acknowledged. The kindness the King felt for me became greater when he read my Life.

"Now for the first time I know you!" said he kindly to me, as I entered the presence-chamber in order to bring him my latest book. "I see you very seldom!" continued he; "we must oftener have a little talk together!"

"That depends on your Majesty!" answered I.

"Yes, yes, you are right!" answered he, and now he expressed his joy at my reception in Germany, and especially in England; spoke of the story of my life, which he had understood clearly, and before we separated he asked me. "Where do you dine to-morrow?"

"At a restaurant!" answered I.

"Then come rather to us! dine with me and my wife: we dine at four o'clock!"

I had, to my very great pleasure, received from the Princess of Prussia a beautiful album, in which were several interesting autographs; their Majesties looked through it, and when I received it back again King Christian VIII. had written with his own hand the significant words: "To have acquired an honorable place by means of well-applied talent is better than favor and gift. Let these lines recall to you your affectionate   CHRISTIAN R."

It was dated the second of April; the King knew that that was my birthday. Queen Caroline Amelie also had written honorable and dear words; no gifts could have rejoiced me more than such a treasure in spirit and word.

One day the King asked whether I should not also see England. I answered yes, that I intended to go there the coming summer. "You must have some money from me!" said his Majesty. I thanked him and said,—

"I have no need of it! I have eight hundred rix-dollars from the German edition of my writings, and this money I shall spend!"

"But," said the King with a smile, "you represent now the Danish literature in England, and you should therefore live a little more comfortably!"

"That I also expect to do, and when I have spent my money I shall return home!"

"You must write directly to me what you want!" said the King.

"O no, your Majesty, I have no need for it now; another time I should perhaps be more in want of your Majesty's favor; now I must not make use of it; it is not right always to be importunate,—it is so unpleasant for me to speak about money. But if I might dare write to your Majesty without asking for anything; write, not as to the King—for then it would only be a letter of ceremony; if I might dare write to one who is truly dear to me!" The King granted my wish and seemed to be pleased with the manner in which I met his favor.

It was in 1860 I was in an old country-house. I was going in broad daylight through one of the great halls, and suddenly I heard a loud ringing as of a dinner-bell; the sound came from the opposite wing of the house where I knew the apartments were not occupied. I asked the mistress of the house what bell it was that I heard. She looked earnestly at me.

"You have heard it too?" said she, "and heard it now in broad day;" and she told me that was often heard, especially late in the evening when they were going to sleep; yes, that the sound then was so loud that it could be heard by folks down in the cellar.

"Let us then look into it," said I. We went through the hall where I had heard the mysterious bell and met the master of the house and the clergyman of the place. I told about the sounding of the bell and protested as I went up to the window that "it was no ghost;" and while the words were spoken, the bell rang again still louder. At that I felt a shiver down my back, and said not quite so loud, "I don't deny it, but I don't believe in it."

Before we left the hall the bell rang once again, but at the same moment my eye fell accidentally on the great chandelier under the ceiling. I saw that the many small glass pendants were in motion: I seized a stool, stood upon it with my head against the chandelier.

"Go quickly and heavily over the floor here," I bade them; they did so, and now we heard all the loud bell sounds that had been ringing as if far away, and so the ghost was found out. An old clergyman's widow who heard about it, said afterward to me:—

"That bell was so interesting. How could you, who are a poet, bear to destroy it, and for nothing at all?"

Still another ghost story—the last. I was at Copenhagen. I woke up in the middle of the night and saw before me at the foot of the bed placed on the stove a chalk-white bust which I had not before noticed. "Surely it is a present," thought I. "Who could have given it?" I rose up in bed, and stared at the white shape, which at the same moment vanished. I shuddered, but got up, lighted the candle and saw by the clock that the hour was just one. At the same moment I heard the watchman call out the hour.

I wrote out the little incident and lay down again, but I could not get any rest, when it entered my head: "It must be the light of the moon that shines through the window upon the white wall." I again got up and looked out; the air was clear, the new moon must also have been long gone, all the street lamps were extinguished, nor could the light from one of them possibly have been seen.

The next morning I made search in the room and looked out over the street; over at the opposite neighbor's was a lamp. The light from it could, with the half-raised curtain and a sail in a vessel on the canal, form on the wall the shape of a human head. I went therefore when it was evening into the street and asked the watchman at what time he put out the lamp.

"At one o'clock," said he; "just before I call the hour." It was the reflection on the wall that I had seen and stared at; the watchman had at the same moment put out the light and the ghost.

After a couple of days' stay here in the grand wild nature that with its screaming flock of birds suggested scenery for Aristophanes' "Birds," I turned again southward on my way home. One of my Jutland friends and the minister's sister-in-law accompanied me. The waves darting up were too heavy to permit us to drive on the shingle; we were obliged to drive through the deep sand in the dunes, and go forward very slowly. I talked and told about foreign lands I had seen, told of Italy and Greece, of Sweden and Switzerland. The old post-boy listened, and said with a kind of astonishment: "But how can such an old man as you be content to roll round so?" I answered with quite as much surprise,—

"Do you think me so old?"

"You are indeed an old man," said he.

"How old do you think?" I asked.

"Well on to eighty."

"Eighty!" exclaimed I. "Traveling has certainly aged me; do I look sickly?"

"Yes, you do look dreadfully lean," said he. To be fleshy was his idea of good condition.

I spoke of the new beautiful light-house at Skagen.

"The king ought to see it;" and I added,—

"I shall tell the king about it when I talk with him." At that the old fellow smiled to my fellow-passengers.

"When *he* talks with the king!"

"Yes, I have talked with the king," I answered, "and I have eaten with the king." Then the old fellow laid his hand on his forehead, shook his head, and smiled knowingly.

"He has eaten with the king!" He thought I was a little cracked.

In Geneva I wished to spend some time: the way thither from Le Locle lay by St. Croix to Yverdun, through the loveliest part of the Jura Mountains, and where one from the heights has the most magnificent view of the Alpine range and the lakes of Neufchatel and Geneva. I saw the view in the wonderful evening light with the Alpine glow and the harmonious stillness. A good *pension* at Madame Achard's in Geneva was recommended to me: I had a room looking out on the lake. I made excursions out on the lake, had a delightful company of French and Americans about me, and I soon found friends and acquaintances in town: I was introduced to the Swiss poet Petit-Senn, a most excellent old man, —a Swiss Béranger. He had a pretty country-house outside the town. I dined with him, and found him very youthful and merry and full of spirits. Dinner over and the coffee drunk, he took his guitar, and like a Northern minstrel sang several of his songs.

One of the first days after I had moved to Madame Achard's I wished to visit one of the families I was introduced to, and I took a drosky at my door and showed the driver the address on the letter, the street and house I wanted to go to. I sat in the carriage and we drove and drove: it was a long way up street and down street, beyond the old abandoned rampart; at length I was at the place. I got out of the carriage, looked about me and found myself in a street hard by the square from which I had driven all this long way. I saw Madame Achard's house from which I had set out.

"Are you a Swiss?" I asked the driver. He answered "Yes."

"That cannot be true," said I. "I came from a long way off, from far up in the North, and there we have read of Switzerland and heard of William Tell, and the noble, brave Swiss people stand in high honor with us; and now I come down here, so that I may tell people at home truly about these brave people, and then I take my seat in a carriage over there the other side of the square, show the address where I want to go,—it is only a few steps to drive, and I am carried all over town on a half-hour tour. It is a cheat, and no Swiss will cheat. You are not a Swiss!"

The man at this was quite abashed: he was a young fellow, and burst out, "You shall not pay at all, or only pay what you please. The Swiss *are* brave folk." His words and voice touched me and we parted good friends.

Mr. Story took me to see the English poetess, Elizabeth Barrett Browning; she was ill and suffering greatly, but she looked upon me with her lustrous gentle eyes, pressed my hand, and thanked me for my writings. Two years afterward I heard from Lytton Bulwer's son how kindly and tenderly Mrs. Browning thought of me; her last poem, too, "The North and the South," written in Rome in May, 1861, on the day of my visit, closes the volume of her writings called "Last Poems," that appeared after her death. I lay the fragrant flowers between these leaves.

THE NORTH AND THE SOUTH

"Now give us lands where the olives grow,"
  Cried the North to the South,
"Where the sun with a golden mouth can blow
  Blue bubbles of grapes down a vineyard row!"
  Cried the North to the South.

A. V. 13—19

"Now give us men from the sunless plain,"
  Cried the South to the North,
"By need of work in the snow and the rain
 Made strong and brave by familiar pain l"
  Cried the South to the North.

"Give lucider hills and intenser seas,"
  Said the North to the South,
"Since ever by symbols and bright degrees
 Art, child-like, climbs to the dear Lord's knees,"
  Said the North to the South.

"Give strenuous souls for belief and prayer,"
  Said the South to the North,
"That stand in the dark on the lowest stair
 While affirming of God, 'He is certainly there,'"
  Said the South to the North.

"Yet O, for the skies that are softer and higher,"
  Sighed the North to the South;
"For the flowers that blaze and the trees that **aspire**
 And the insects made of a song or a fire!"
  Sighed the North to the South.

"And O for a seer to discern the same!"
  Sighed the South to the North;
"For a poet's tongue of baptismal flame
 To call the tree or flower by its name!"
  Sighed the South to the North.

The North sent therefore a man of men
  As a grace to the South;
And thus to Rome came Andersen:
"Alas! but must you take him again?"
  Said the South to the North.

XII

My journey home in 1867 was a hasty one, and it **was** only in Odense that I took a day and night for rest. The Dannebrog waved from the houses, new soldiers were to arrive. In the Riding-house there were preparations making for their reception. I was invited. The tables were loaded down with meat and drink. The ladies and their daughters in the town, all appeared there as ready to serve. The soldiers came, gave a hurra, and sang songs, and made speeches. How changed for the better! how bright and pleasant a time as compared with the old time which I knew. I spoke of this, and remarked that when I was last here, in the Riding-house, a long time ago indeed, I was quite a little boy, and I saw a soldier run the gauntlet; now I came and saw the soldiers, our defenders and guardians, greeted with song and speeches, and sit beneath the waving of flags. Blessed be our time!

A few of my friends said to me that I must come back here at least once a year, and not always go flying through my birthplace; that it would make a celebration for me, and that I should certainly get an invitation in November. I had no inkling how great it was to be, to what a summit of fortune in my life I was to be raised. I answered that I was truly glad at their kind expressions, but added,—"Forget it then till 1869, on the fourth of September, when it will be half a century since I left Odense for Copenhagen. The sixth of September I was there, and that is the great day of my life, but it is not likely that any one would think of that. Rather let me come over here to Odense upon the semi-centennial of my departure."

"It is all of two years till then," they answered. "One ought not to put off any good pleasure. We will see in November."

And so it came about. The old prophecy, made when I was a poor boy, going out from Odense, that the town would one day be illuminated for me, was fulfilled in the most beautiful shape. Late in November I received in Copenhagen a communication from the Common Council in Odense.

"In the Odense Common Council: We herewith have the honor to announce to your Excellency that we have elected you an honorary burgher in your native town; permit us to invite you to meet with us here in Odense on Friday, the sixth of December next ensuing, upon which day we desire to deliver to you the certificate of citizenship." Then followed the signature. I replied:—

"Last night I received the communication of the honorable Common Council, and hasten to present my sincere thanks. My birthplace proffers me, through you, gentlemen, a mark of esteem greater than I ever dared dream of receiving.

"It is this year forty-eight years since I, a poor boy, left my native place; and now, rich in happy memories, I am received in it as a dear child is received in his father's house. You will understand my feelings. I am lifted up, not in vanity, but in thankfulness to God for the heavy hours of trial and the many days of blessing He has granted me. Accept the thanks of my whole heart.

"It will give me great pleasure on the day appointed, the six December, if God grant me health, to meet with my noble friends in my beloved native town.

"Your grateful and humble

"H. C. ANDERSEN."

On the fourth of December I went to Odense. The weather had been cold and stormy; I had a cold and suffered from toothache, but now the sun shone and it was quiet, pleasant weather. Bishop Engelstöft met me at the station, and took me to my home at the Bishop's house by Odense River, which I have described in my story of "The Bell's Hollow." Several of the town officers were invited to dinner, which went off pleasantly and with great liveliness.

Now came the important sixth of December, my life's most beautiful feast. I could not sleep at night. I was oppressed in body and soul. I felt pains in my breast and my teeth ached, as if to remind me,—In all your honor, you are yet a child of mortality, a worm of the dust; and I felt it not only in my body's aches, but in the humility of my soul. How should, how ought I to enjoy my incredible fortune! I knew not. I was all in a tremble.

I heard in the morning of the sixth of December that the town was beautifully decorated, that all the schools had a holiday, because it was my festival. I felt cast down, humble, and poor, as if I were standing before my God. There was a revelation to me of every evil thing within me, every fault and simple thought, word, and deed. Everything sprang forth strangely clear in my soul, as if it were the Day of Judgment, —and it was the day of my honor. God knows how mean I felt myself to be, when men so exalted and honored me.

In the forenoon came the Chief of the Police, State Councilor Koch, and Burgomaster Mourier, and escorted me to the Guild Hall, that I might receive my diploma of honorary citizenship. From almost all the houses in the streets through which we drove the Dannebrog waved. There was a great concourse of people from the town, and from the country, citizens and farmers. I heard the shouts of hurra, and before the Guild Hall I heard music; the citizens' chorus was drawn up, and they sang melodies to my songs, "Gurre" and "I love thee, Denmark, father-land!" I was overcome, and one can understand that I said as I must say to my two escorts, "What must it be to be carried to the place of execution! I believe I understand the sensation now."

I was to fulfill the prophecy which the old woman made when as a boy I left my birthplace,—Odense should be illuminated for me. I stepped to the open window; there was a blaze of light from the torches, the place was quite full of people. They sang, and I was overcome in my soul. I was physically overcome indeed, and could not enjoy this summit of fortune in my life. The toothache was intolerable; the icy air which rushed in at the window made it blaze up into a terrible pain, and in place of fully enjoying the good fortune of these minutes, which never would be repeated, I looked at the printed song to see how many verses there were to be sung before I could slip away from the torture which the cold air sent through my teeth. It was the pitch of suffering; when the flames of the torches piled together sank down, then my pain decreased. How thankful was I to God. Gentle eyes looked upon me from all sides, every one wished to speak to me, to press my hand. Wearied out, I reached the Bishop's house and sought rest, but I did not get it until the morning hour, so filled to overflowing was I.

I wrote at once to his majesty the King and expressed my deeply felt thanks; I wrote to the Students' Association and to the Workingmen's Union, and now I received many visits. Especially must I mention an old widow who as a child had been a boarder for a short time with my parents; she wept for gladness over my life's career, and told how she had stood in the evening with the torch-light procession on the square and seen the parade: "It was just as it was for the King and Queen when they were here." Then she had thought of my parents, and upon me as a little boy; she had talked about it with several old people who stood by her: she had wept and they had wept, that the poor boy should so turn out and be honored like a king.

Now came the day of departure, the eleventh of December. People come crowding into the railway station, so that it was filled with them. My lady friends brought me flowers. The train came which I was to take, and it stopped only for a few minutes. The Burgomaster, Herr Mourier, bade me good-by. I uttered my farewell; the loud, repeated hurras rang forth, they were lost in the air as we moved away, but still from single groups of people in the town and near by the shouts continued to be sent up. Now first as I sat quite alone, did there seem to rise into one great account all the honor, gladness, and glory which had been given me by God in my native town.

The greatest, the highest blessing I could attain was now mine. Now for the first time could I fully and devoutly thank my God and pray,—

"Leave me not when the days of trial come."

COPENHAGEN, *March* 29, 1869.

THE END

EUGENIE DE GUERIN

A PURE AND GENTLE FRENCH CATHOLIC DEVOTEE

1805-1848

(INTRODUCTORY NOTE)

When the Journal of Eugenie de Guerin was published some years after her death, it aroused a world-wide interest. Women of such type as she, so gentle, so retired, and yet so keenly alive and intellectual, have but seldom left a record of their feelings. She was a devout Catholic, and the Catholic world pointed with pride to the beauty of this self-revealed pure soul, as showing what their faith could really do for its devotees. Readers of other faiths as well, in brief, every literary student of human nature turned with almost equal interest to this book of this cultured, esthetic, rapturous and yet simple hearted modern saint. Few books have won such honored rank in so short a time. The universal judgment of modern critics has already placed this brief and broken narrative among the classics of the world.

Eugenie de Guerin was a sister of the poet Maurice de Guerin, and being his elder by some five years she was partly mother to him also. They belonged to an ancient Catholic family of southern France and Maurice was educated to be a priest. Religious scruples, however, turned him to the Protestant faith, a defection which agonized his sister, but did not break the close bond which held them together. Her Journal was written to him in little note-books, each of the earlier books being sent to him when filled. Maurice married a wealthy Creole young lady and shortly afterward died of consumption. His devoted sister survived him only a few years. Her Journal had already, during the life of her brother, attracted the warm interest of his intimate friends; and at their urgence she continued it after his death, but only intermittently. The last entries are scattered and fragmentary. The entire Journal covers only a few years, but reaches repeatedly back into the past to tell of earlier days, so that it, to some extent, reviews her entire life. Would that such lives were more common to our age—or rather that their existence were more often recognized!

JOURNAL OF EUGENIE DE GUERIN

TO MY BELOVED BROTHER MAURICE

"Je me dépose dans votre âme."
(*Hildegarde to St. Bernard.*)
Nov. 15, 1834.

SINCE then you wish it, my dear Maurice, I am going to continue the little Journal you so much like.[1] But as I have no paper at hand, I shall make use of a stitched copy-book, intended for poetry, of which I only remove the title;[2] the rest, thread and leaves, are all left as they were; and bulky though it be, you shall have it by the first opportunity.

I date from the 15th of November, exactly eight days since your last letter came. Just at this present hour I was carrying it in my bag from Cahuzac hither, together with an announcement of a death, that of M. d'Huteau, which his family wished us to be informed of. How often joy and sorrow arrive hand in hand!

Thy letter gave me great delight, but this death saddened us, made us regret a worthy and amiable man who had at all times shown himself our friend. The whole of Gaillac mourned him, great and small. Poor women kept saying, while on their way to his death-bed, "Such a one as he should never have died," and they wept while praying for his peaceful end. This it is that renders one hopeful about his soul: virtues that make us loved by men must make us loved of God. Monsieur the Curé saw him every day, and doubtless he will have done more than merely see him. It is from *the Illustrious*[3] that we have heard these tidings with others current in the Gaillac circle, and I for my part by way of amusement read them and think of her.

17th.—Three letters since yesterday, three very great pleasures, for I am so fond of letters and of those who have

---

[1] We learn from the opening of the next book that this present Journal was the second, the first has not been found.

[2] The half-effaced word *Poems* is still to be deciphered at the head of the page.

[3] A name by which she refers to her sister, *Mimi, Mimin,* or *Mary.*

written them to me: Louise, Mimi, and Félicité. That dear Mimi says such sweet charming things about our separation, her return, her weariness, for she gets weary of being far from me, as I of being without her. Each moment I see and feel that I want her, at night more especially, when I am so accustomed to hear her breathe close to my ear. That slight sound sets me to sleep; and not to hear it inspires me with melancholy reflections. I think of death, which also silences everything around us, which also will be an absence. These night thoughts depend somewhat on those I have had during the day. Nothing gets talked of but sickness and death; the Andillac bell has done nothing but toll these last days. It is typhus fever that is now raging, as it does every year. We are all lamenting a young woman of your age, the prettiest and most respectable in the parish, carried off in a few days! She leaves a young infant that she was still nursing. Poor little thing! the mother was Marianne de Gaillard. Last Sunday I went to bid farewell to a dying girl of eighteen. She knew me, poor young creature, spoke just a word and fell back to her praying. I wished to say something to her, but I did not know what to say; the dying speak better than we. They buried her on the Monday. How many reflections these new graves suggest! Oh my God, how quickly we go out of this world! At night when I am alone, all these dead faces come before me. I am not afraid, but all my thoughts put on mourning, and the world appears to me sad as a tomb; and yet I told you that those letters gave me pleasure. Oh, yes, it is very true, in the midst of this mortality my heart is not dumb, and, indeed, only feels the more keenly what brings it life. Accordingly your letter gave me a flash of joy, or rather of true happiness, by all the good news of which it is full. At length your future begins to dawn; I see before you a profession, a social position, some certainty as to material existence. God be praised! this is the thing in the world that I most desired for thee and for me too, for my future is linked with thine, they are brothers. I have had beautiful dreams on this head, and may perhaps tell them thee. But for the present good-by, I must write to Mimi.

18*th*.—I am furious with the gray cat. The wicked creature has just robbed me of a young pigeon that I was warming by the fire. The poor little thing was beginning to revive, I had meant to tame it, it would have got fond of me, and now all this ends in its getting crunched up by a cat! What disappointments there are in life! This event, and indeed all those of the day, have occurred in the kitchen; it is there that I have spent the whole morning and part of the evening since I have been without Mimi. It is necessary to overlook the cook. Papa too comes down sometimes, and I read to him beside the stove or in the chimney corner, out of the "Antiquities of the Anglo-Saxon Church." This great book struck Peterkin with amazement, *Qué de monts aqui dedins!* [*] That child is quite a character; one evening he asked me if the soul was immortal, and afterwards what a philosopher meant. You see we had got upon lofty questions. When I replied that it was some one who was wise and learned: "Then, Mademoiselle, you are a philosopher!" This was said with a simplicity and sincerity that might have flattered Socrates, but which made me laugh so much that my solemn catechizer took himself off for the evening. This child left us one of these last days to his great regret, his term was up on the festival of St. Brice, and there he is now hunting for truffles with his little pig. If he comes this way I shall go and find him out, to ask if he still thinks I look like a philosopher.

With whom do you suppose I was spending this morning by the kitchen fire? With Plato: I did not dare to say so, but he chanced to come under my eyes, and I determined to make his acquaintance. I am only at the first pages as yet. He seems to me most admirable, this Plato; but one of his notions strikes me as singular, that of ranking health before beauty in the catalogue of God's gifts? If he had consulted a woman, Plato would not have written thus: you feel sure of that, don't you. So do I, and yet, remembering that I am a *philosopher,* I rather incline to his opinion. When one is in bed and really ill, one would gladly sacrifice one's complexion or one's bright eyes to regain health and enjoy the sunshine. And besides, a small degree of piety in the heart, a little love of God, is enough to make one speedily renounce such idolatries; for a pretty woman adores herself. When I was a child

[*] In the patois of the district, "How many words inside it!"

I thought nothing equal to beauty, because I said to myself, it would have made Mamma love me better. Thank God this childishness has passed away, and the beauty of the soul is the only one I covet. Perhaps even in this I am still childish as of yore, I should like to resemble the angels, this may displease God; the motive is still the same: to be loved better by Him. How many things occur to me, only I must leave thee! I have got to say my rosary, night is at hand, and I like to end the day in prayer.

20th.—I delight in snow, there is something heavenly about this white expanse. Mud, bare earth displeases and depresses me; to-day I see nothing but the tracks on the road, and the footprints of little birds. However lightly they settle, they leave their small traces, which make all sorts of patterns in the snow. It is pretty to watch those tiny red feet, like coral pencils drawing themselves. Thus winter too has its charms and prettinesses. *Everywhere God sheds grace and beauty.* I must go now and see what there is of pleasant to be found by the kitchen fire, sparks at all events. This is a mere good morning that I say to the snow and to thee on jumping out of bed.

27th.—I close St. Augustine, my soul full of those soothing words, "Throw yourself into the bosom of God, as upon a bed of rest." What a beautiful idea! and what refreshment we should find in life, if, like the saints, we knew how to rest in God. They go to Him as children to their mother, and on His breast they sleep, pray, weep, abide. God is the home of the saints; but we earthly-minded ones know no other than this earth—this poor earth—dry, black, and mournful, as a dwelling under a curse. Nothing came to-day, not even the sun; this evening only a few crows have flown by. No walk, no going out, except in thought; but my thought does not wander, it soars. This evening our reading will be the report of the famous Carrat case, which occupies the whole country; but I am not fond of such affairs, and criminal celebrity has nothing about it interesting according to me. However, I am going to give myself up to it. The wretched man has written from his prison to Mademoiselle Vialar, to ask her for an *"Imitation."* Such an idea in this active spirit might lead us to hope for a conversion; but it is to be feared that it only shows hypocrisy, since he continues to be a wretch, they say. Erembert is gone to Alby to hear the trial, which draws crowds. Whence can we get this curiosity of ours about monsters?

28th.—This morning, before daylight, my fingers were in the ashes looking for fire enough to light a candle. I could not find any, and was just going back to bed when a little bit of charcoal that I happened to touch showed a spark, and there was my lamp lit. Dressing got over quickly, prayer said, and we were with Mimi in the Cahuzac road. That unfortunate road, I so long took it alone, and how glad I was to take it with four feet to-day! The weather was not fine, and I could not see the mountain; that dear district I look at so much when it is clear. The chapel was engaged, which was a pleasure to me. I like not to be hurried, and to have time before I enter in there to raise my whole soul before God. This often takes long, because my thoughts find themselves scattered like leaves. At two o'clock I was on my knees, listening to the finest teaching imaginable; and I came out feeling that I was better. The effect of every burden laid down is to leave us relieved; and when the soul has laid down that of its faults at the feet of God, it feels as though it had wings. I admire the excellency of confession. What ease, what light, what strength I feel conscious of every time that I have said "It is my fault!"

29th.—Cloaks, clogs, umbrellas—all the apparatus of winter —followed us this morning to Andillac, where we stayed till evening between the parsonage and the church. This Sunday life, so stirring, so active, how much I like it! We come upon each other in passing, and then chatter while walking on together about the poultry, the flocks, the husband, the children. My great pleasure is to caress these last, and to see them hide themselves, red as fire, in their mother's petticoats. They are afraid of *las doumaiselos,* as of everything unfamiliar. One of these urchins said to his grandmother, who was speaking of coming here, "*Minino,* don't go to that castle; there is a black dungeon there." Why is it that castles have at all times inspired terror? Is it because of the horrors that were committed in them of yore? I think so. Oh! how sweet it is, when the rain is heard pattering, to be by the corner of one's fire, tongs in one's hand, making sparks! This was my amusement just now. I am very fond of it; sparks are so pretty! they are the flowers of the chimney. Really, there are charming things going on amongst the embers, and when I am not occupied I like to watch the phantasmagoria of the hearth. There are a thousand little fairy shapes coming, going, dilating, changing, disappearing; now angels, now horned demons, children, old women, butterflies, dogs, sparrows. One sees a little of everything in the embers. I remember one face, with an expression of heavenly suffering, which reminded me of a soul in purgatory. I was struck by it, and should like to have had a painter by my side. Never was there a more perfect vision. Remark the logs burning, and thou wilt agree that, unless we are blind, we ought not to find time tedious beside a fire. Listen, above all, to that little whistle which sometimes comes from below the burning half of the wood, like a singing voice. Nothing can be more exquisite or pure; one would say it was some very diminutive spirit of fire that was chanting. There, my friend, are my evenings and their amusements; to which add sleep, which is by no means the least of them.

30th.—I have been told a striking story of a sick woman at Andillac. After having swooned away, and remained, as it were, dead for sixteen hours, this woman suddenly opened her eyes and called out, "Who has brought me back from the other world? I was between heaven and hell; the angels were drawing me one way, the devils the other. Oh God! how I suffered, and how awful is the sight of the abyss!" And, turning round, she began to repeat in a supplicatory voice litanies of the Divine mercy that had never been read anywhere; then took again to speaking of hell that she had seen and been close to, in her swoon. And when she was told that she should not keep thinking of such frightful subjects, "Hell is not for dogs," she said, "I have seen it, I have seen it!" Is not this a dramatic scene? and it is quite true. It was Françoise, the sister of the Curé, who told it to me, and who had herself watched beside the sick woman that very night. The sufferer was none of the most pious before, and now she is full of faith, fervor, and resignation. The Curé is the only physician she wants; she says nothing to the other.

May we not believe that God has had a hand in this? Who knows all that a dying soul may see—

When the next world appears before its gaze.

But I won't write poetry.

Listen to a striking miracle that I have just been reading. It is one of Saint Nicaise, who, when evangelizing in Gaul, found himself in a country ravaged by an enormous dragon. The saint, taking advantage of this event to make known to the people the power of the God he proclaimed, gave his stole to one of his disciples and sent him to meet the monster, which the disciple bound with this stole, and brought into the presence of the whole people, before whom he burst. I admire the simplicity of the narrative, and the grand prodigy in which I believe. Good night, with St. Nicaise!

1st December.—It is with the same ink that I have just written my letter to thee that I go on writing here; the same drop, falling half of it in Paris, half on this page, will jot down for thee all manner of things—here tender words, there scoldings, for I always send thee whatever passes through my mind. I am sorry to have only written thee two or three words. I might have sent thee this, and the idea did occur to me of detaching these few sheets; but suppose they were to be lost in the public-houses where Master Delaruc is sure to go and drink! Better keep our chit-chat for a safe opportunity. It will be with the pie, then, that I shall send it, if I can without risk put papers into the case.

2nd.—I am vexed with myself for being weak enough to suppose thee indifferent to us and to me. And yet, absurd as this idea is, it occupied and saddened me yesterday the whole day. Accordingly you see how little I said to thee. Sadness makes me dumb; forgive it me; I prefer to be silent rather than to complain. It is thy letter to Mimi that has caused it all. I will tell thee why. When you read this, my friend, recollect that it is written on the 1st of December—a day of rain, gloom, and vexation—on which the sun has not shown itself, when I have seen nothing besides crows, and had only a very short letter of yours to read.

7th.—Yesterday the evening was spent in talking about Gaillac, of these, and those, and a thousand things going on in the little town. I do not care much for news; but news of friends always gives·pleasure, and one listens to it with more interest than to news of the world and of tiresome politics. Nothing makes me yawn so soon as a newspaper. It was not so formerly, but tastes change, and the heart detaches itself from something or other every day we live. Time and experience too disabuse; as we advance in life we at length gain the proper position whence to judge ·of our affections and know them in their true light. I have all mine now present before me. First I see dolls, toys, birds, butterflies, that I loved—sweet and innocent childish affections. Then comes reading, conversation, dress in a slight degree, and dreams, beautiful dreams! . . . But I am not going to confess. It is Sunday. I have returned alone from the first mass at Lentin, and I am enjoying in my little room the sweetest calm in the world, in union with God. The happiness of the morning penetrates me, flows into my soul, and transforms me into something that I cannot express. I leave thee. I must be silent.

9th.—I have just been warming myself by every fireside in the village. This is a round that we make with Mimin from time to time, and which is by no means without its attractions. To-day it was a visiting of the sick; accordingly we discussed medicines and infusions. "Take this;" "do that;" and we are listened to as attentively as any doctor. We prescribed clogs to a little child that had made itself ill by walking barefoot, and a pillow to its brother, who with a violent headache was lying quite flat; the pillow relieved him, but will not cure him, I think. He seems to be suffering from an affection of the chest, and these poor people in their hovels are like cattle in their stalls; the bad air poisons them. Returning to Cayla, I find myself in a palace compared to their cottages. Thus it is that, having habitually to look beneath me, I always find myself fortunately placed.

10th.—Hoar-frost, fog, icy prospect; this is all I see to-day. Accordingly I shall not stir out, and am going to curl myself up in the. chimney-corner with my work and my book; now one, now the other—the alternation amuses me; and yet I should like to read all day long, but I have other things that must be done, and duty goes before pleasure. I call pleasure

all reading that is in no way essential to me. There is a flea!
—a flea in winter; it is a present from "Trilby." Indeed it
seems that in every season insects are devouring us, whether
dead or alive; the least numerous of them being those we see;
for our teeth, our skin, our whole body, is, they say, full of
them! Poor human body! to think of our soul having to
dwell in such an abode! No wonder it finds little pleasure
therein, so soon as it takes to reflecting about where it is!
Oh! the glorious moment when it issues thence, when it enjoys
life—heaven—God—the other world! Its amazement, I think,
would resemble that of the chicken coming out of its shell,
if only the chick had a soul.

Last day of December.—A fortnight has passed without
my adding anything here. Do not ask me why? There are
times when one does not want to speak, things one does not
desire to tell. Christmas is over, beautiful festival, my favorite of all, which brings me as much joy as to the shepherds of
Bethlehem. Truly the whole soul sings aloud at this glad
advent of God, which is announced on all sides by carols and
the pretty *nadalet.*[5] Now in Paris nothing gives one the idea
of its being Christmas. You have not even the midnight
mass. We all went to it, with Papa at our head, by an en-
chantingly fine night. Never was there a more beautiful sky
than that midnight one, so that Papa kept putting his head out
from his cloak from time to time to look up. The ground was
white with hoar-frost, but we were not cold, and, besides, the
air was warmed before us as we went, by the bundles of fag-
gots that our servants carried to light us. It was charming,
I assure you, and I wished I could have seen you walking
along, as we did, towards the church, through roads bordered
with little white bushes, that looked in full blossom. The
frost makes beautiful flowers. We saw one sprig so pretty
that we wanted to make a nosegay of it for the Blessed Sacrament, but it melted in our hands. All flowers are short-lived.
I much regretted my bouquet; it was sad to see it melt and
shrink drop by drop. I slept at the parsonage. The good
sister of the Curé kept me there, and prepared me an excel-

---

[5] Name given to a particular way of ringing the bells during the fortnight preceding Christmas Day; which, in the dialect of Languedoc is
called *Nadal.*

lent *réveillon*[6] of hot milk. Papa and Mimi returned to warm themselves at home by the great fire of the *Souc de Nadal.*[7] Since, there has come cold, fog, everything that darkens the sky and the soul. To-day, that the sun shines again, I revive; I expand like the pimpernel, that pretty flower which only opens to the sun.

Here, then, are my last thoughts, for I shall write nothing more this year. In a few hours it will be all over; we shall have begun the new year. Oh how fast the time flies! Alas! alas! would one not say that I am regretting it? My God, no; I do not regret either time, or what it takes from us. It is not worth while to throw one's affections into the torrent. But the empty careless days, lost as regards Heaven, these are what make one cast a regretful glance on life. Dear brother, where shall I be on this same day, at this same time, same instant, next year? Shall I be here or elsewhere? Here below, or in heaven above? God knows; and here I stand at the gate of the future, resigning myself to whatever may issue thence. To-morrow I shall pray that thou mayest be happy; pray for Mimi, for Papa, for all I love. It is the day of gifts: I shall take mine to heaven. It is thence that I derive all my blessings; for, truth to tell, on earth I find but few things to my taste. The longer I live in it the less I enjoy it; and accordingly I see, without any regret, the approach of years, which are so many steps towards the other world. It is neither pain nor sorrow which makes me feel thus, do not suppose it. I should tell thee if it were; it is only the home-sickness which lays hold of every soul that sets itself to thinking of heaven. The hour strikes, the last that I shall hear while writing to thee. I would have it interminable, like all that gives pleasure. How many hours have sounded from that old clock, that dear piece of furniture that has seen so many of us pass, without ever going away; as it were a kind of eternity! I am fond of it, because it has struck all the hours of my life, the fairest ones when I did not listen to them. I can remember that my crib stood at its foot, and I used to amuse myself in watching the hands

[6] Meal taken by Catholics after returning from the midnight mass on Christmas eve.

[7] Yule-log.

move. Time amuses us then; I was four years old. They are reading pretty things in the parlor. My lamp is going out; I leave thee. Thus ends my year beside a dying lamp.

3rd January, 1835.—A letter from Brittany reached me this morning, like a sweet New Year's gift. I have spent the whole day in thinking of Madame de La Morvonnais, and in deciphering the handwriting of her husband, which is by no means a plain one. Now, however, I have made it out, and perfectly understand his idea, but I cannot respond to it. The poetess he takes me for is an ideal being, quite apart from the life that I lead, a life of occupation, of housekeeping, which absorbs all my time. How can it possibly be otherwise? I know not; and, moreover, this is my duty, and I will not depart from it. Would to God that my thoughts, my soul, had never winged their way beyond the narrow sphere in which I am forced to live. It is in vain to talk to me thus; I cannot rise above my needle or my distaff without going too far. I feel, I believe this. I shall therefore remain where I am placed, whatever may be said about it. My soul will inhabit high places only in heaven.

1st March.—It is a long time now that my journal has been neglected. I came upon it in opening my desk, and the idea of leaving a word or two in it recurred to me. Shall I tell thee why I gave it up? It was because I looked upon the time spent in writing as wasted. We owe an account of our moments to God; and is it not spending them ill to trace down here days that go by? And yet I find a charm in it, and afterwards like to look over the path of my life through my solitude. On reopening this book, and reading some pages of it, it occurred to me that in twenty years, if I lived as long, it would be an exquisite pleasure to me to re-read it, to find myself once more here, as in a mirror that should retain my youthful features. I am not young, however, but at fifty I shall consider that I was young now. Therefore I will give myself this pleasure; if a scruple returns I will put the book by at once. But the good God may, perhaps, be less strict than my conscience, and forgive me this small pastime. To-morrow, then, I will resume my journal. I must record my happiness of yesterday, a very sweet, very pure happiness, a kiss from a poor creature to whom I was giving alms. That kiss seemed to my heart like a kiss given by God.

3rd.—Everything was singing this morning while I was at my prayers—thrushes, finches, and my little linnet. It was just like spring; and this evening here we have clouds, cold, gloom, winter again—melancholy winter. I don't much like it; but each season must be good, since God has made them all. Therefore, let frost, wind, snow, fogs, clouds, weather of every description, be welcome! Is it not sinful to complain when one is warm and comfortable beside the fire, while so many poor people are shivering out of doors? At twelve o'clock a beggar found great delight in a plateful of hot soup that was given to him at the door, and did perfectly well without sunshine. Surely, then, so may I. The fact is, one longs for something pleasant this day of general amusement, and we wanted to keep our Shrove-Tuesday in the sun out of doors and in taking long walks; whereas we have been obliged to limit ourselves to the hamlet, where every one wanted to feast us. We thanked, without taking anything, as we had had dinner. The little children came about us like chickens. I made them prick some nuts that I had put into my pocket to give them. Twenty years hence they will remember our visit, because we gave them something good, and the memory will be pleasant. Those were well employed nuts. I did not write yesterday, because I thought it was not worth while to write down nothings. It is the same, however, to-day. All our days are pretty nearly alike, but only as to what is external. The life of the soul is different; nothing more varied, changing constantly. Don't let us speak of it; there would be no end of it, if it were only about one single hour. I am going to write to Louise: this by way of fixing myself in a happy mood.

7th.—To-day a new hearthstone has been placed in the kitchen. I have just been standing upon it, and I note down here this sort of consecration of the stone of which the stone will retain no trace. It is an event here, this stone, somewhat like a new altar in a church. Every one goes to see it, and hopes to pass pleasant hours and a long life before this hearth of the house (for all gather there, masters and servants). But who can tell? . . . I myself shall perhaps be the first to leave. ' My mother departed early, and they say that I am like her.

8th.—Last night I had a grand dream. The ocean came up under our windows. I saw it; I heard its billows rolling like thunder, for it was of a sea in storm that I had this vision, and I was terrified.

A young elm springing up, with a bird singing on it, dispelled this terror. I listened to the bird: no more ocean and no more dreams.

9th.—The day broke mild and beautiful; no rain or wind. My bird was singing all morning long, and I too, for I felt cheerful, and had a presage of some happiness for to-day. Here it is, my friend: it is a letter from thee! Oh, if I only got such every day! I must now write to Louise.

While I was writing the clouds and wind all returned. Nothing more variable than the sky and one's own soul. Good night!

10th.—Oh, the beautiful moonbeam that has just fallen on the Gospel that I was reading!

11th.—To-day, at five o'clock in the morning, fifty-seven years had elapsed since my father came into the world. We all went—he, Mimi, and I—to church as soon as we were up, to celebrate this anniversary and to hear mass. To pray God is indeed the only way to celebrate anything here below. Accordingly, I have prayed a great deal on this day, when the most tender, most loving, best of fathers was born. May God preserve him to us, and add to his years so many more that I shall not see them end! My God! no, I would not be the last to die; to go to heaven before all the rest would be my delight. But why speak of death on a birthday? It is because life and death are sisters, and born together like twins.

To-morrow I shall not be here. I shall have left thee, my dear little room! Papa takes me with him to Caylus. This journey gives me little satisfaction; I do not like going away, changing place, or sky, or life; and all these change when we travel. Adieu, then, my confidant! thou must wait for me in my desk. Who knows when we shall meet again? I say in a week; but who can reckon upon anything in this world? Nine years ago I spent a month at Caylus. It will not be without pleasure that I shall see the place again, as well as my cousin, her daughter, and the good chevalier who used to be so fond of me. They will have it that he is still so; I am going to find out. It is possible that he may be the same, but he will find me much changed since ten years ago. Ten years are a whole age for a woman; so we shall be about contemporaries, for the worthy man is over fourscore.

12th.—It was a real distress to me to go away; Papa discovered it and left me behind. He said to me last night, "Do as you like." I wanted to stay, and felt quite sad, thinking that to-night I should be far away from here, far from Mimi, from my fire, my little room, my books; far from Trilby, far from my bird; everything, down to the merest trifle, presents itself when you are about to leave, and so twines itself around you that there is no breaking loose. This is my experience, whenever there is any talk of a journey. Like the dove, I like to return every evening to my nest. No other spot attracts me.

30th.—Two letters have come; the one of joy, an announcement of the marriage of Sophie Decazes; the other of mourning to tell us of death. This last is from M. de La Morvonnais, who writes to me weeping, quite full of his dear Marie. How he loved her, and loves her still! They were two souls that could not bear to leave each other. Accordingly they will remain united in spite of death, and separated from the body where no life is. This is Christian union, a union spiritual, immortal; a divine tie formed by the love, the charity that never dieth. Hippolyte in his widower-state is not alone, he sees Marie, Marie everywhere, Marie always. "Speak to me of her, always of her," he says, and again, "Write to me often, you have certain modes of expression that vividly recall her to me." I was not the least aware of this; it is God's doing, who has infused into my soul some things akin to that other soul, that is why she loved me and I her: sympathy springs from relation of souls; and then moreover I found in Marie something infinitely gentle that I so delight in, that can only emanate from a pure spirit. "The true mark of innocence," says Bossuet, "is gentleness." How many charms, what advantages I should have enjoyed in this celestial friendship! God decided otherwise, and has taken it away just one year after it was first granted me. Why so soon? No complaining. God does not allow it on account of what He removes from us, or of a few days of separation. Those who die do not go so far away after all, for heaven is quite close to every one of us. We have but to raise our eyes and we see their dwelling. Let us console ourselves by that sweet prospect; let us become resigned on earth, which is but a step to the gate of Paradise.

1st April.—So then a month has passed, half sad, half beautiful, much like the whole of life. This month of March has some gleams of spring, which are very sweet; it is the first to see any flowers, a few pimpernels that open a little to the sun, some violets in the woods under the dead leaves that screen them from the hoar frost. The little children amuse themselves with them and call them *March flowers*, a very appropriate name. We dry them too to make "tea" of them. This flower is good and soothing for colds, and, like hidden virtue, its perfume betrays it. Swallows have been seen to-day, glad harbingers of spring.

2nd.—To-day my whole soul turns from the sky to a tomb, for on it sixteen years ago my mother died at midnight. This sad anniversary is sacred to mourning and prayer. I have spent it before God in regret and hope; even while I weep I look up and see the heavens where my mother is doubtless happy, for she suffered so much—the illness was long and her spirit patient. I do not remember a single complaint escaping her, nor that she cried out ever so slightly in spite of the pain that tore her; no Christian ever bore suffering better. One saw that she had learned it before the cross. She would smile upon her bed like a martyr on the rack. Her face never lost its serenity, and even in her dying moments she seemed to be thinking of a festival. This surprised me who saw her suffer so much, and myself cried at the least thing, and did not know what resignation under pain meant. And when they told me that she was going to die, I looked at her, and her cheerful aspect made me disbelieve them. She did die, however, at midnight on the 2nd of April, while I had fallen asleep at the foot of her bed. Her gentle death did not waken me, never did any soul leave the world more quietly. It was my father. . . .

Oh God! I hear the priest, I see lighted tapers, a pale face in tears! I was led away into another room.

3rd.—At nine o'clock in the morning my mother was laid in the tomb.

4th.—I am going to Cahuzac with the sun straight above my head. If this tires me I shall think of the Saint of the day, St. Macarius, toiling along in the desert beneath a basket of sand to get rid of a temptation. He afflicted his body in order to save his soul.

8th.—I don't know why I have put down nothing for four days; I return to it now that I find myself alone in my room. Solitude leads to writing, because it leads to thought. One enters into conversation with one's own soul. I ask mine what it has seen to-day, what it has learnt, what it has loved, for every day it loves something. This morning I saw a beautiful sky, and the budding chestnut-tree, and heard little birds singing. I was listening to them beneath the great oak, near Téoulé, whose basin was being cleaned out. These pretty songs and this washing of the fountain suggested different trains of thought; the birds delighted me, and when I saw the escape of the muddy water, so clear a short time before, I could not but regret that it had been troubled, and pictured to myself one's soul when something stirs it up; for even the most beautiful loses its charm when you stir the bottom, there being a little mud at the bottom of every human soul. But is it worth while to take ink out of the inkstand to write thee all these inutilities? It would be better to speak of Jean Tamisier, who, seated near the porch, related to me some of his adventures in his rounds. I thanked him for it by a glass of wine which will give him a fresh flow of words, as well as legs to reach his sleeping-place to-night. Then I read a sermon; not being able to go and hear one, I make my little room a church, where methinks I can find God, and without any disturbing causes. When I have prayed I reflect, when I have meditated I read, then sometimes I write, and all this goes on before a little cross on the table as before an altar—below is the drawer which holds my letters, my relics.

9th.—This morning I meditated upon the tears of the Magdalen. What sweet tears, and how beautiful a history that of this woman who loved so much! Here is Papa, I leave everything.

13th.—Since Papa's return I have laid by my journal, my books, and many things. There come these days of exhaustion when the soul retires from all its affections, and sinks back upon itself in utter weariness. This weariness without fatigue, what else is it but weakness? We must conquer it, like so many other weaknesses that attack this poor soul of ours. If we did not kill them one by one, they would end by fretting us away, as worms do cloth. I pass so suddenly from sadness to joy; when I say *joy* I mean that sweet calm happiness of the soul which only shows externally as serenity. A letter, a thought of God or of those I love, will have this effect upon me, and yet sometimes too a quite contrary one. It is when I take things ill that they sadden me. God knows the fears and the raptures He gives; you, my friends, do not know how sweet and bitter both you are to me. Do you remember, Maurice, that little short letter which tormented me for a fortnight? how cold, how indifferent, how little kind you seemed to me!

I have just been suspending the sacred branch to my "bénitier." Yesterday was Palm Sunday, the festival of children, who are so happy with these consecrated branches, dressed up with cakes in the church. This joyous entrance of theirs is no doubt granted them in memory of the Hosannas sung by children to Jesus in the temple. God leaves nothing unrewarded. Here is my copybook come to an end! Shall I begin another? I know not. Good-by to this one and to thee!

II

14th April, 1835.

WHY should I not go on writing to thee, my dear Maurice? This book will please thee as much as the two others; I go on therefore. Will you not be very glad to know that I have just been spending a pleasant quarter of an hour on the terrace-steps, seated by the side of an old woman, who was singing me a lamentable ballad on an event that occurred long ago at Cahuzac? This came about à propos of a gold cross that has been stolen from the neck of the blessed Virgin. · The old woman remembered her grand-mother telling her that she had heard in olden times of this same church being the scene of a still more sacrilegious rob-bery, since it was then the blessed sacrament that was carried off one day when it was left exposed in the empty church. A young girl came to the altar while everybody was busy in the harvest, and, mounting upon it, put the pyx into her aprón, and went and placed it under a rose-tree in a wood. The shepherds who discovered it told where it was, and nine priests came in procession to adore the blessed sacrament under the rose-tree, and to carry it back to the church. But for all that, the poor shepherdess was arrested, tried, and condemned to be burned. Just when about to die, she re-quested to confess, and owned the fact to a priest; but it was· not, she said, because of any thievish propensities she took it, but that she wanted to have the blessed sacrament in the forest. "I thought that the good God would be as satisfied under a rose-tree as on an altar." At these words an angel descended from heaven to announce her pardon, and to comfort the pious criminal, who was burnt on a stake of which the rose-tree formed the first faggot. This is what the beggar-woman said to me, while I listened to her as to a nightingale.

I heartily thanked her, and then offered her something as payment for her ballad; but she would only take flowers. "Give me a bit of that beautiful lilac." I gave her four bunches, big as plumes, and the poor old woman went off, her stick in one hand, her nosegay in another; and I back into the house with her ballad.

15th.—On waking I heard the nightingale, but only a sigh, a mere hint of his voice. I listened a long while, and heard nothing more. The charming musician had only just arrived, and was merely announcing himself. It was like the first sweep of the bow of a great concert. Everything sings or is about to sing now.

I have not read the life of the saint of to-day. I am going to do so; it is my custom before dinner. I find that while one is eating, while one is at the *manger*, it is well to have something spiritual in one's mind, like the life of a saint.

Easter Thursday.—Here are several days that I have written neither to thee nor any one else. The services have occupied all my time, and I have lived, so to speak, in the church. Sweet and sacred life that I regret to see come to an end; but I find it again here whenever I will. I open the door of my little room, and there I enjoy calm meditative solitude. I know not why I ever leave it.

There is just now on my window-sill a bird, who has come to visit mine. He is frightened—he is off—and the poor caged one is saddened, and flutters as if he wanted to make his escape. I should do the same were I in his place, and yet I keep him prisoner. Shall I open his cage? He would fly away, would sing, build his nest, be happy; but he would be mine no longer, and I am fond of him and like having him. I shall keep him. Poor little linnet, thou wilt always be a prisoner; I enjoy thee at the cost of thy liberty; I pity, and yet detain thee! So it is that pleasure triumphs over justice. But what wouldst thou do, if I gave thee thy liberty? Dost know that thy wings, which have never been spread, could not carry thee far into that wide expanse thou seest through the wires of thy cage? Then thy food—thou wouldst not know where to find it. Thou hast never tasted what thy brothers eat, and indeed, they would probably banish thee like a stranger from their family feast. Better stay with me, who care for thee. By night the dew would wet thy feathers, and the cold of early morning would prevent thee from singing.

In digging the field a stone has been turned up which covered a large hole; I am going to see it. Jack, furnished with a rope, has been down into the cave and explored it on all sides. It is nothing but an excavation, incrusted with pretty little stones, rough, like sugared almonds; I kept some as a memento of our discovery. Some day I will go down into the grotto, and perhaps I shall see something more there than Jack did.

28th.—When everybody is busy, and I am not wanted, I go into retreat, and come here at all hours to write, read, or pray. I note down here, too, what goes on, either in my mind or in the house, and in this way we shall be able to find again day by day the whole past. For me what passes is of little worth, and I should not write it down, but that I say, "Maurice will be very glad to see what we were doing while he was away, and to reënter thus into the family life;" and so I note it for thee.

But I observe that I hardly make any mention of others, and that my egotism always occupies the stage. I keep saying, "I do this; I have seen that, have thought so and so;" leaving the public in the background, after the manner of self-love; but mine is that of the heart, which knows only how to speak of itself. The inferior painter can but give his own portrait to his friend; the great painter has pictures to offer. So I go on with the portrait. But for the rain we had this morning, I should be now at Gaillac. Much obliged to the rain; I would rather be here. What drawing-room can be so pleasant as my bed-room? what companionship should I have had equal to what surrounds me now? Bossuet, St. Augustine, and other holy books, that speak to me when I will, enlighten, console, strengthen me, correspond to all my needs. To leave them grieves me, to take them with me is difficult; the best plan is not to leave them.

In my leisure moments I am reading a work of Leibnitz, which charms me by its catholicity and the admirable pious passages it contains, as, for instance, this on confession: "I look upon a pious, earnest, and discreet confessor as a great instrument in the hands of God for the salvation of souls; for his counsels serve to direct our affections, to enlighten us as to our faults, to help us to avoid occasions of sin, to dis- sipate doubts, to raise the downcast spirit; in short, to re- move or mitigate all diseases of the soul; and if we can hardly find anything on earth more excellent than a faithful friend, what happiness to find one who shall be bound by the inviolable religion of a divine Sacrament to preserve the faith and to succor souls!"

Now, this heavenly friend I have in M. Bories: hence the tidings of his departure profoundly afflict me. I am sad with a sadness which makes the soul weep. I should not say this elsewhere: it would be taken ill, and, perhaps, would not be understood. The world does not know what a confessor is to one: the man who is the friend of the soul, its most inti- mate confidant, its physician, its master, its light; he who binds us and looses, who gives us peace, who opens the gates of heaven; to whom we speak upon our knees, calling him, as we do God, our Father; nay, faith makes him in very deed God and Father to us. When I am at his feet, I see in him only Jesus listening to the Magdalen, and forgiving her much because she has loved much. Confession is but the expansion of repentance into love.

[*No date.*]—Here I am at this dear Cayla, and have been several days without telling thee. The fact is, in taking my copybook out of my portmanteau I placed it under a carpet, and there it has lain ever since. In rummaging about my hand fell upon it, the book opened, and I continue the writing. It was a sweet moment when I saw my family again— Papa, Mimi, Erembert, who all embraced me so tenderly, and made me feel how deep the happiness of being loved.

Yesterday was a fortunate day; four letters and two friends arrived, M. Bories and the Abbé F——, the brother of Cécile. I do not know which of the two gave us most pleasure or was most agreeable, the one by his mind, the other by his heart. We had a great deal of chat; we laughed, drank healths, and, as a wind-up, set to playing childish games, and cheating each other. No solemnity at all; it was a day of relaxation, when the soul takes its ease while retaining its bent; it was the mirthfulness of priests and Christian friends.

18th May.—Who could ever have guessed what has happened to me to-day? I am surprised, engrossed, and much pleased by it. I think and contemplate my present constantly, my Creole poems, addressed to me by a poet of the Isle of France. I shall speak of them to-morrow, it is now too late; but I could not sleep without noting down here this event of my day and my life.

19th.—Here I am at the window, listening to a chorus of nightingales, which sing in the Moulinasse in a ravishing way. Oh the beautiful picture, the beautiful concert which I have to quit, to go and take some relief to poor lame Annette!

22nd.—Mimi has left me for a fortnight; she is at ——, and I pity her in the midst of that paganism; she so holy and good a Christian! As Louise once said to me, she makes upon one the effect of a righteous soul in hell, but we shall get her away as soon as the time allowed to the proprieties is over. I, on my part, think it long; I get tired of my solitude, so much have I the habit of being two together. Papa is in the fields almost all the day, Eran out shooting; for sole society I have Trilby and my chickens, which are as noisy as imps, and occupy without amusing me, for *ennui* is at the very core and basis of my soul to-day. What I like best has little power to divert me. I have tried to read, write, pray, but each and all only lasted a moment; even prayer wearied me. 'Tis sad, oh my God! Fortunately I recalled those words of Fénélon, "If God wearies you, tell Him that He wearies you." Oh! indeed, I did tell Him this folly!

4th August.—I have wanted to speak to thee of thy birth, of my joy when I heard of it, and how I made haste to open that portmanteau where Papa told me he had got thee. I wanted to tell thee all that and many other things, about the baptism and thy early life; but I was sad, afflicted, tearful, and when I weep I do not write, I only pray; it is all I can do; but now a degree of serenity is returning to me. God has been with me; then came books, and a letter from Louise, three things that make me happy. When I began to write I was quite sad, and afterwards I felt almost joy, and that I had God within my heart. O, my friend, did you but know how sweetly the soul in affliction consoles itself in God! what strength it draws from divine power!

The book—I mean the work which gives me such delight —is Fénélon, that Papa has bought me. All my life long I had wished to have these Spiritual Letters, so sweet, so heavenly, so adapted to every condition and attitude of the soul. I shall make them my consolation and support now that I am about to lose M. Bories, and that my soul feels itself as it were orphaned. I had asked some substitute from God, and these letters have come to me; accordingly, I look upon them as a gift from Heaven. Thanks to God and to my father.

20th.—I have just been hanging around my neck a medal of the blessed Virgin that Louise has sent me as a preservative from the cholera. It is the medal that has worked so many miracles, they say. This is not an article of faith, but it does no harm to believe it. I do therefore believe in the holy medal as in the sacred image of a mother the sight of whom may do one good. I shall throughout life wear on my heart this holy relic of the Virgin and of my friend, and will have faith in it if the cholera comes, a disease for which there is no human remedy. Let us then have recourse to the miraculous. People do not sufficiently trust to Heaven, and so they tremble. I don't know why, but this advance of the cholera does not affect me. I should not think about it were it not for the prayers ordered by the Archbishop, Why is this, I wonder? Can it be through indifference? I should be sorry for that. I would be insensible to nothing, not even the plague. Whence comes my security?

21st.—Here is another ornament for my little room, St. Theresa, that I have been at length able to get framed. I was longing to have this beautiful saint before my eyes, above the table where I say my prayers, where I write, where I read. It will be an inspiration, helping me to pray, love, and suffer well. I shall raise my heart and eyes to her in my prayers and my sadnesses. I begin at once and say, "Look down on me from Heaven, blessed Saint Theresa; see me on my knees before your picture contemplating the features of a lover of Jesus with an earnest desire to have them engraved in me. Obtain for me this holy resemblance, obtain for me something of yourself; lend me your glance to seek for God, your mouth to pray to Him, your heart to love Him. May I obtain your courage in adversity, your meekness in suffering, your constancy in temptation." St. Theresa suffered for twenty years from disinclination to prayer without letting herself be disheartened. This is of all her triumphs the one that surprises me most. I am far from such constancy, but I like to remember that when I lost my mother I went, like St. Theresa, to throw myself at the feet of the Holy Virgin, and pray her to take me for her daughter. This occurred before the Chapel of the Rosary, in the church of St. Peter's, at Gaillac. I was then thirteen.

1st September.—Here I am at Cahuzac in another little room, leaning on my elbow on the small table where I write. Everywhere I must have tables and paper, because everywhere my thoughts follow me, and want to pour themselves out for thee, my friend. I have sometimes the idea that thou wilt find a certain charm in them, and this idea encourages and leads me on; but for this, my heart would very often remain closed, through indolence or indifference, to whatever is mine.

I have sometimes childlike pleasures, as, for instance, that of coming for a few days here. You could not imagine how cheerfully I came to take possession of this deserted house. The fact is, you see, that I find myself alone—quite alone— in a place that favors meditation. I hear the passers-by without even disturbing myself; I am at the foot of the church; I can catch the very last vibration of the bell which rings in noon, or the Angelus, and I listen to it as to a harp. Then I can go and pray, can confess when I will; this is enough for a few days of happiness, of a happiness *my very own*. Papa will come and see me this afternoon. I enjoy this visit as though we had been separated for a long time.

The devil tempted me just now in a little closet, where I stumbled upon some romances. Read a word or two, I said to myself; let's just look at this, look at that; but the titles were very displeasing to me. There were "Love Letters of a Nun," "The General Confession of a Rake," and other histories of that character. Fie upon the very idea of my reading such trash! I am no longer tempted now, and am only going to remove those books from the closet, or rather to throw them into the fire.

22nd.—Ever since I returned from Cahuzac, my confidant has been sleeping in a corner, and would sleep there still, were this not the 22nd of September, the day of St. Maurice, and thy name-day, which has afforded me a degree of joy, and re-opened my heart to the pleasure of writing to thee and leaving some memorials here. I remember that on the same day last year I also wrote to thee, and spoke about thy festival. I was happy, I saw *to-day*, and thee; hoping then to embrace thee on St. Maurice's, and there thou are a hundred leagues off! My God! how ill we reckon, and how little ought we to reckon upon anything in life!

Monsieur the Curé and his sister have come to keep thy

festival, and drink thy health. But what is better is that Monsieur the Curé remembered thee at mass, and that Françoise also prayed for you. May St. Maurice protect thee, and make thee strong in the conflicts of life! Will you bring me back his image that I gave you!

[19th Nov.]—To-day, November 19, I have taken up my poor forsaken book, already gnawed by rats, and the idea has occurred to me of returning to it and continuing to write. This writing gives me pleasure, diverts me in my solitude; but I have often neglected it, and I shall neglect it again. Nevertheless, I will fill my page to-day, and to-morrow we shall see. I find myself changed. My books, my poems, my birds, that I was so fond of, all these used to occupy my heart and head, and now. . . . No, I am not doing right, and I am not happy since the renunciation of the affections of my life; are not they sufficiently innocent for me to permit myself the whole of them? My God, the recluses of the Thebaid occupied themselves in the same way. I see them work, read, pray, write; some of them singing, others making mats and baskets, all working for God, who blessed the labor of each. In like manner I will offer Him my days and everything that is to fill them, whether work or prayers, whether writing or thoughts, not excepting this little manuscript book that I also desire to see blest.

[No date.]—I have passed the day in complete solitude, alone, quite alone; Papa is at the Cordes fair, Eran dining at the priest's house, Mimi at Gaillac. They are all dispersed, and I for my part have thought much, and realized what a longer dispersion would be; and that, alas! will come one day. But I am wrong in dwelling upon gloomy thoughts that do me so much harm. These things are to the soul what clouds are to the eyes.

30th.—Oh, my God, more tears! In vain we determine not to afflict ourselves, every day brings some affliction, some loss. Here we are now mourning that poor cousin De Thézac, who was so fond of us. Oh! no doubt he is better off now than we; he must be in heaven, for he suffered much. His patience was admirable, both throughout his life of pain and just now in his last trials. Mimi, whom I was expecting, was not able to come; she remained with the sufferer, helping him, exhorting him in his last moments, speaking to him of heaven.

Oh, how well Mimi knows to speak on these subjects, and how I should wish to have her by my side when I was dying! Papa is gone to see the bereaved family, and I am alone in my room with my thoughts in mourning, and the thousand voices of the wind that, like an organ, moans for the dead. One should find this accompaniment good for praying, for writing; but what should I write? A little sleep will be better. The repose of the body passes over into the soul. I am therefore going to bed, after a *De profundis* for the dead, and a remembrance of thee before God. May He grant thee a good night! I never go to sleep without occupying myself about thy rest. Who knows, I say to myself, if Maurice is as comfortable as he would be here, where I should see to the making of his bed? Who knows whether he may not be cold? Who knows? . . . and a thousand other too tender tendernesses.

Wilt thou accept it, my friend, this book, written during the last two years? It is old indeed, but the things of the heart are eternal. Time, methinks, in no way affects them; I therefore give thee up these, after a few corrections, a few lines erased. When we go back over the past, we must needs efface; we find so many errors in it! We used even to talk nonsense with thee once upon a time as we walked together.

III

1836.

I CHANGE the form of my Journal, to make it more convenient for my pocket, into which I mean to put it when I go from home. In this way we shall find in it whatever chances to strike me when I go out, whether into the world or into the country. Upon such occasions I see, hear, feel, think, a thousand things that please, displease, surprise me, and that I should like to fix somewhere or other. This would be useful, showing me in some degree what I am when away from home, when mixing with the world, its conversations and amusements, and all else to which I am unaccustomed. I am conscious of something unwonted going on within me at these times; thoughts and feelings before unknown occur to me, and I feel that I am not like others, nor like what I am here. When thus in this unusual mood I am aware of it, indeed, but fail to take any particular note of it, and yet it would be well to see whither it leads me. I shall revert to this subject; but now I have something even better to do than to write, I am going to pray. Oh, how I love prayer!

I would that all the world knew how to pray; I would that children, and those who are old; that the poor, the afflicted, the diseased in body and mind; that all who live and suffer could feel the balm of prayer! But I cannot speak of these things. What should be said of them is ineffable.

Our new Curé came to see us to-day. He is a mild, cheerful man, wearing on his countenance the impress of a beautiful soul. I should think he was clever, but he does not let it appear. His conversation is most ordinary, without any characteristic features, any bright sallies, merely going on in a plain way from one thing to another. But, however, I observe that he answers correctly, and speaks à propos. He is a simple pastor of simple souls; quite full of God, and nothing more.

11*th March.*—I have a very happy heart to-day. Eran is gone to confess. I hope much from this confession to the gentle Curé, who knows so well how to speak of God's mercy. And then to-day is Papa's birthday too.

12*th.*—I was admiring just now a little landscape, presented by my room, as it was being illuminated with the rising sun. How pretty it was! Never did I see a more beautiful effect of light on the paper, thrown through painted trees. It was diaphanous, transparent. It was almost wasted on my eyes; it ought to have been seen by a painter. And yet does not God create the *beautiful* for everybody? All our birds were singing this morning while I was at my prayers. This accompaniment pleases me, though it distracts me a little. I stop to listen; then I begin again, thinking that the birds and I are alike singing a hymn to God, and that, perhaps, those little creatures sing better than I. But the charm of prayer, the charm of communion with God, they cannot enjoy that; one must have a soul to feel it. This happiness that the birds have not is mine. It is only nine o'clock, and I have already known joy and sorrow. How little time is needed for that! The joy comes from the sun, the mild air, the song of birds, all delights to me.

IV

1st May, 1837.

It is here, my friend, that I intend to return to that intimate correspondence which pleases and is necessary to us: to thee in the world, to me in my solitude. I am sorry not to have continued it, now that I have read your letter, in which you tell me why it was you did not reply. I was afraid of wearying you by the details of my life, and I see that it was quite otherwise. No more anxiety, then, on that head, no more doubts about thy affection or anything else in thy truly fraternal heart. It was I that was wrong: so much the better; I was afraid it was you. Let us, then, in all joy and freedom, resume our conversation—that secret, confidential, strictly private intercourse, which stops short at the least sound, the least glance. The heart does not approve of being overheard in its confidences. You are right to say that I have to plot and contrive a little in writing my books; I have indeed read some parts of them to Papa, but not all. The good father might, perhaps, be made a little anxious by what I say, by what sometimes crosses my soul; an air of sadness would seem to him a sorrow. Let us hide these little clouds from him: it is not well that he should see them, or know anthing of me but my calm, serene side. A daughter should be so sweet a thing to a father! We ought to be with regard to parents much what the angels are to God. It is different between brothers and sisters: here there is less respect and more freedom. For thee, then, the course of my heart and life just as it occurs.

7th.—I don't know what came to turn me away yesterday, when I wanted to tell thee of my little library, of the books I have, and those I should like to have. I want St. Theresa, those most spiritual of pious letters. I saw them in the possession of a servant, poor girl! But who knows? perhaps she can comprehend them better than I. Holy things come within the reach of the heart and of every pious intellect. I have very often observed this, and that a person who seems simple and ignorant in the eyes of the world is marvelously well versed in intellectual matters and in the things of God. I know many clever people who are stupid here: two gentlemen, for instance, who would not allow that God was good, because He gave us restraining laws, because there was a hell. They considered the observance of fasting and the belief in original sin absurd, and the veneration of images thoroughly ridiculous. Poor people! how many such there are who pretend to be wise on sacred subjects, holy hieroglyphics that they read without understanding and then call follies!

Our country people are actually getting as bad: one of them quoted the Council of Trent to our Curé, in a case where his learning ill became him. To venture to interpret the Councils, and not say the *Pater*, how lamentable! This is to what science leads in our country districts—the science of the alphabet; for it is because it knows how to read that the people believes itself learned. Mounted on its pedestal of pride, it meddles with the highest matters, and considers as within its reach what it ought to contemplate on its knees. It is bent on seeing, comprehending, grasping, and walks boldly on to unbelief. It requires to have its faith proved to it now-a-days; whereas formerly it believed everything. Our peasants have lost much by coming into contact with books; and what have they gained but an additional ignorance—that of their duty? One cannot but grieve over these poor people. It would be better that they should not know how to read, unless they were at the same time taught what reading was profitable. In the mountains at Rayssac they all read; but then it is the catechism, missals, or devotional books. That is the proper end of schools, and the thing that should be taught in them is religion, the making good Christians.

22nd.—No writing yesterday. The whole of Sunday gets spent in church or on the road; in the evening I am tired, it was with difficulty that I read after supper a little of the "History of the Church"; but for all that I thought much of thee, God knows. I have asked Rose to pray for thee. She has promised to do so. This has comforted me; and ever since I am more tranquil, because I believe prayer to be all

powerful. I know a proof of it in the case of a little child
suddenly restored from total blindness. It is a pretty story,
and I must tell it thee. There was at Ouillas, in one of our
mountain convents, a young girl as pupil, who was so pious,
so sweet, so innocent, that every one loved and revered her
like. an angel. They say that her confessor, M. Chabbert,
whom we had once for curé, found her so pure that he admitted her to her first communion without giving her absolution. She died at the age of fourteen, held in such love and
veneration by her former companions that they daily went
one after the other to visit her grave, which is kept quite
white with lilies in the season of flowers, and to ask her
whatever they would; and more than once the saint granted
their prayers. For two years people had been flocking to
the cemetery, when a poor woman, coming to pick up wood
close by, with her little blind boy, happening to call to mind
the wonders related of Marie, bethought her of taking her
child to the grave and imploring his cure. This was pretty
nearly her prayer:—

"Little St. Mary, you whom I have seen so good and compassionate, hear me now out of Paradise where you are; restore my son's sight; may God grant me this mercy through
you!"

Hardly were the words uttered when the poor mother, still
on her knees, hears her child exclaim that he sees! *Ay,
mama, té bési!* Scales that closed up his eyes fell off: the
same disease had covered his head, so that not a hair was to
be seen, and, eight days after, the poor mother was showing everybody her child with beautiful eyes and pretty flaxen
curls.

I heard this from Mademoiselle Carayon d'Alby, who had
seen the child both in its blind state and after its miraculous
cure. It is a charming story, in which I fully believe, and
which almost makes me long to go to Ouillas to implore also
a something that I should pray for with the whole fervor of
my soul.

June.—Two visitors, both persons that I like and who will
give us pleasure so long as they will stay here. One cannot
say as much for all guests, but Eliza R—— is good and clever,
her cousin A—— is very sweet, and without being beautiful

has a youthful charm which makes me admire her. My little room is given up to them, so that I shall come to it less often. However, from time to time, I do escape and make my way here, as I am doing now, to write, read, and pray—three things that are of use to me. Every now and then the soul needs to find itself alone, and to recollect itself undisturbed. This is what I come here to do. I have written to Félicité, and answered Gabrielle, who eagerly asked after you so soon as she knew that you were ill. These proofs of friendship touch me and make me bless God for being loved. Affection is so sweet a thing, it blends with joy and softens affliction. Marie de Thézac, too, has shown the same interest. At all events thou hast true friends.

26th of January, 1838.

I REËNTER for the first time the little room in which you still were this very morning. How sad the room of an absent friend is! One sees him everywhere, without finding him anywhere. Here are thy shoes under the bed, thy table all dressed out, the looking-glass suspended on the nail, the books thou wert reading last night before going to sleep; and here am I, who then embraced thee, touched thee, beheld thee! What is this world in which everything disappears? Maurice, my dear Maurice, oh, how I want thee and God! Accordingly, as soon as we had parted, I went to church, where one can weep and pray at one's ease. What do you do—you, who do not pray—when you are sad, when your heart is broken? For my part, I feel that I require a superhuman consolation; that one must needs have God for friend, when what one loves makes one suffer.

What has happened to-day that can be written down? Nothing but thy departure; I have seen only thee going away, only that cross where we parted. Had the King come here, I should not have cared; but I have seen no one but Jeannot bringing back your horses. I was at the window at the time, but drew my head in; it seemed as though I were looking at the return of a hearse.

It is evening now; the end of a very long, very sad day. Good night; thou mightest still almost hear me, thou art not far away yet; but to-morrow—the day after—ever further, further off!

27th.—Where art thou this morning? After this cry I am going hence as if to look for thee, here and there, where we have been together so lately.

I have done nothing but sew and iron. I have read but little, only the good old St. Francis de Sales, at his chapter on the affections. That was the very one for me! the heart ever seeks out appropriate food. For my part, I could live upon loving; whether father, brothers, sisters, something I must always have.

What is there to be said on Sundays, when the pastor does not preach? It is the manna of our desert—this word from Heaven—which drops down gentle and stainless, and has a pure and simple taste that I love. I came back fasting from Andillac; but since, I have been reading Bossuet, those fine sermons so scored by thy hand. I left them with my mark often above thine. So it is, everywhere we meet, like a pair of eyes; what you see to be beautiful, I see beautiful too. The Almighty has made a part of the soul very much alike in us two.

31st.—I have discovered in myself a droll affection indeed. Foolish heart of mine, that takes to everything! Shall I tell it? I am fond of the three leeches that are on the mantel-piece. I should not like either to give them away, or to see them die; I change their water every day, taking great care that none of them drop out. If I do not see them all, I take up the phial and look what is going on inside it, with other unequivocal signs of affection; and this because these leeches were brought here for Charles—that Charles came with Caroline—and that Caroline came for thee! Droll sequence this, which makes me laugh at what the heart can string together. What a variety of things! It is amusing to reflect on this, and to be able to see you, amidst leeches! Impossible even to separate you as yet; these creatures indicate hot or cold weather, rain, sunshine, and I have been continually consulting them since you went away. Fortunately the phial has always stood at fair. We say, over and over again, "Maurice will have arrived without catching cold, without severe weather, without rain."

Thus it is, my friend, that we keep thinking of thee—that everything makes us so think.

1st February.—A dark cloudy day, dismal inside and out. I am more dejected than usual, and, as I do not choose to yield to dejection, I have taken up my sewing to kill it with the point of my needle; but the ugly serpent still writhes, though I have cut off head and tail both, that is to say, idleness and enervating thoughts. The heart gets debilitated by these mournful impressions, and that does harm. Oh, if I but knew music! They say it is so good, so soothing for disorders of the soul.

2nd (Friday).—This day week, at this very hour, you went away. I am about to pass along the road where we parted. It is Candlemas; I am going to church with my taper.

We have come back from Andillac with a letter from Félicité; there was one for thee from Caroline, which I returned, slipping into it a word for the dear sister. I may well call her so at the point we have got to; it is but anticipating a few months, I hope. And yet who knows? I am always in anxiety about this affair, and about you, bad artisan of happiness that you are! I am afraid that you will not perfect this happiness; that you will leave unfastened the last link of the chain that would unite you forever. . . . *Forever* seems to me alarming for thee, independent, wandering eagle! How fix thee in thy aëry! . . .

Nor is this the only particular. God knows what others I find in thee that distress and sadden me. If from the heart we pass on to the soul, oh it is there, it is there! . . . But what is the use of talking, and observing, and complaining? I do not feel myself holy enough to convert, or strong enough to influence thee. God alone can do this. I pray much that He may, for my own happiness depends on it. You may not perhaps conceive how. You, with your philosophical eye, do not discern the tears of a Christian eye over a soul in danger, a soul so much loved, the soul of a brother, a sister soul. All this makes one lament like Jeremiah.

Here is this day ending with snow. I am glad to think of you at your journey's end, now that the cold has returned. Provided only that you do not suffer from your long walks —that your chest keep well—that M. d'A—— do not make you sit up too late while relating his troubles. A thousand anxieties suggest themselves and sadden me; a thousand thoughts rise in me, and fall in flakes over Paris.

I found my first poem among some scraps of paper, and put it by. I put by everything I find that I should have shown thee, hadst thou been here. That you should no longer be here sometimes seems impossible; I keep saying to myself that you will soon return, and yet you are very far away; and your shoes, those two empty feet that still stand in your room, do not stir. I look at them, I love them almost as much as that little pink shoe you were reading about to me the other day in Hugo. The heart can thrust itself in everywhere, into a shoe, into a phial; one would say it was a very silly thing. Do you not say so?

19th.—Waited till evening, to see what I should have to say. Nothing. Do you like that? If you preferred words, I could find some in my heart, even when they did not spring from anything without. A woman's heart is talkative, and does not require much; it is able of itself to extend to infinity, and to play the eloquent out of that little chest where it dwells, as out of an orator's tribune. My friend, how many times I have harangued thee thus! but when I do not believe either that I can give thee pleasure, or be of use to thee, why, then I am silent. I take up my distaff, and, instead of *the woman of the seventeenth century,* I am the simple country-girl, and this pleases me, diverts me, relaxes my mind. There is one side of my character which comes into close contact with the simplest classes, and infinitely enjoys them. Accordingly I have never been given to dream of greatness or fortune, but how often of a little home far from cities, very neat, with its deal furniture, its shining household utensils, its trellised door, hens! and myself there, with I know not whom, for I would not have a peasant such as ours, who are boors, and who beat their wives. Do you remember . . . ?

VI

Continuation of the 19th *February* (1838).

HERE is a new book. What shall I put into it? what shall I say, shall I think, shall I see, before I get to the end of it! Will it contain happiness or unhappiness? But what matters it! I shall take whatever comes, just as the brook does down yonder. These inquiries into the future only serve to torment one, because we generally foresee in it more pains than pleasures. The sick, the dead, the afflicted, how know I what phantoms are to be met with in this obscurity?

Yesterday it struck me that Papa might be going to have a stroke, because he complained of a numbness of the right side; his father having died of one much at the same age. Poor Father! what should I do on earth without him? I have never looked upon myself as placed in the world for anything else than his happiness; God knows this, and that I have devoted my life to him. The idea of leaving him never occurred to me, except to enter a convent; and even this thought is wearing out, so impossible do I feel it to tear myself hence, to go away from home even to go with thee. Paris has little attraction for me, I assure you; I should never take two steps in its direction if you came here as a family man to be with us, to live with us. Impossible delight! Present sadness and bitterness; this is all that comes of meddling with the future! It would have been better to have taken up the thread of the other book; to have continued my tale like Scheherazade.

I was about then to ask you whether you remembered that man we met once upon the Gaillac road, who by his way of entering his home like a thunderclap gave me a sort of terror; and how much talk you and I had about conjugal happiness and unhappiness. Then, turning to the subject of your marriage, pleasant thoughts came into our minds. I told thee that the good God had surely made Caroline for thee as He did Eve for Adam, and you asked me to pray that He might also grant you a little angel of a daughter. As soon as you are married I shall not fail to do so. Night calls me hence.

24th.—A day that begins with rain and the cawing of crows. We shall see what will happen between this and evening. I have not written for some days, owing to certain visits we have had; to I know not what besides that prevented my writing. It is not the heart that keeps silence.

How well I did to wait until evening! Could I have put in anything more charming than what I see, what I hold, what I feel,—than the pleasure thy letter has given me, the second thou hast written since thy return to Paris? Oh! how full of happiness it is, and how delighted I am to know thou art at length as I have long wished thee to be! You do not go out, you do not endanger your health, you do not see company; in the midst of Babylon your letters might be dated from some solitude. Unexpected wisdom this, which enchants me, makes me bless God, makes me hopeful, consoles me, fills my heart with a nameless feeling that leads me to rejoice on your account. O! brothers, brothers, we love you so much! If you but knew it, if you but understood how precious your welfare is to us, and by what sacrifices we would purchase it! O my God, may they indeed understand it, and not so readily expose their dear healths and their dear souls!

16th March.—The *Vialarette* will never more bring you chestnuts and *échaudés* from Cordes; poor girl! she died last night. I regret her on account of her good qualities, her fidelity, her attachment to us. If we were ill, there she was at once; if we wanted any little service rendered, she was ready; and then she was so discreet, so much to be trusted, one of the small number of persons to whom one might safely confide a secret. This was the sublime feature of her condition as it seems to me, this religion of secret-keeping which she had not learnt from education. I would have trusted her with anything.

Not one of the Andillac women approaches this poor Marie in elevation of feeling, or strong and living faith. You should have heard her speak out, clearly and straightforwardly to the village philosophers, to those who spoke lightly of God, of confession, of all the holy things at which it is too much the custom to laugh in village gatherings. Oh! she loved them all! She used to confess, to fast, to keep Lent with five pennyworth of oil, to believe in heaven; and she must be there, I hope. God will have accepted this pure and simple soul. Her faults were merely inequalities of temper; oddities of character which sometimes made her disagree with her neighbors. But they were soon forgotten; some service rendered would rub out hasty words, and now they are all sounding her praises.

I went to see her yesterday evening, she did not know me. I took her hand, it was cold and pulseless; when I went away I was quite aware that I had seen her for the last time. That cold hand, that smothered pulsation, it was death that I had been touching! How sad, how gloomy, how awful it is, this passage into the other life! What would become of us, my God, if faith did not throw its light, its hopes athwart it! Happy they who can hope, who can say with La Vialarette, "I have known God and have served Him!" Her knowledge did not go beyond the Catechism, nor her prayers beyond the *Pater Noster;* but everything is included therein for Christians, great and small. Would to God that M. de Lamennais had never gone further!

Mimi acted as sister of charity to our poor friend, and by her exhortations helped her to endure. It was to her the sufferer confided her secrets connected with the next life, told what masses she desired for the repose of her soul, and for this purpose made over to her sixty francs that she had kept deposited in a faggot, a faggot collected branch by branch as was the money penny by penny. Holy idea this of the poor! What merit this deposit will have in God's sight! Of how much cold and heat, of how many steps, efforts, privations, has it been composed! Who knows how many bits of bread she bought from her hunger to devote their price to her soul? Simple and admirable faith!

17th.—I have just returned from the funeral of this poor girl, the first person I ever saw committed to the grave. It was a painful sight; but I wished to accompany to the last her who had neither brother nor sister of her own, her who had followed to that same church-yard all those members of her family whom she had seen die, her who had taken so many steps for us, alas! on this very day, *Saturday.* In short, I determined to show her this mark of affection, and to accompany her by my prayers to the borders of the next world. I heard mass by the side of her coffin.

There was a time when this would have terrified me; but now, I know not how it is, I find it quite natural to die; coffins, deaths, tombs, churchyards, only inspire me with feelings of faith, only raise my soul on high. The thing that struck me most was hearing the coffin drop into the grave: hollow, lugubrious sound, man's last! Oh! how penetrating it is, how far it enters into the soul that listens to it! But all do not listen; the grave-diggers seemed to look on as at a falling tree; little Cotive, and other children, kept peeping in as into a ditch where there were flowers, with inquisitive, wondering faces. My God! my God! what indifference surrounds the tomb!

How wise the saints are to die beforehand, to perform their own obsequies by retiring from the world! Is it worth while to remain in it? No, it is not worth while, were it not for a few beloved souls with whom God wills us to keep company in this life. There is Papa, who has just been to pay me a visit in my room, and in going away left two kisses on my brow. How can one leave these tender fathers?

31st.—I do not know who or what made me fling my copy-book under the counterpane of thy bed; I break off and hide the moment any one enters the room. I only write for thee; and in order to do this avail myself of the first excuse that I hit upon: now it is a letter to be written, now some notes that I am taking; but what always answers the purpose is the copy-book filled with poems, that Papa has asked me for. I write out three or four verses a day, and when Papa comes into my room and says, "What are you about?" I reply, "The copy-book." This is not an untruth, only I am writing two copy-books, and I take more delight in the one than the other. However, I shall finish Papa's, since he wishes it; the dear father well deserves that I should please him too, he who would give me the moon.

6th April.—Nineteen years ago to-day, was born on the bank of the Ganges a fragile little child, who was called Caroline. She comes, she grows up, gets beautiful, and the sweet young girl is now thy betrothed. I admire thy happiness, my friend, and how careful God has been of it in giving thee such a companion, giving thee this Eve come out of the East with so many graces and charms! And then I see in her such admirable moral qualities, so much sweetness, goodness, devotedness, candor; everything about her is so beautiful and so good that I look upon her as a heavenly treasure for thee. May you be united, be happy! We have just been hearing mass to your intention and according to the expression of Mademoiselle Martin, asking God for Caroline's happiness and for the graces necessary to the new life that is about to open out to her. Let us, oh! do let us have Heaven on our side; let us ask God for what we need, we poor and impotent creatures. The good pastor will say another mass for you to-morrow, he proposed this himself. "One must pray, too, for M. Maurice." Consequence this of the idea of the nose-gay, presentiment of your union.

VII

[*30th* JULY].—Here I am again, after a space of eight days, after a fall, after death having clutched me, and let me go as God willed. Oh, it is indeed God who has saved me! who wills that I should remain yet a while on earth, here, beside Papa; in my little room just now, that I may write to thee and many others; that I may make of my life—I know not what that is good, gentle, useful, so far as lies in my power. I told thee of my adventure in my letter of this morning; and now I want to tell thee my delight at being able to come at length to Paris; no, not to Paris, to the wedding: it is that I am coming to see.

What a man Victor Hugo is! I have just been reading some of him: he is divine, infernal, wise, mad; he is the people, the king; he is man, woman, painter, poet, sculptor; he is everything; he has seen all, done all, felt all; he amazes, repels, and enchants me! and yet I hardly know him, except in "Cromwell," some prefaces, "Marie Tudor," and a little, of "Notre Dame." I shall go and see this Notre Dame in Paris. How many things to be seen for me when I emerge from my desert!

The *8th (August).*—Françoise, the sister of M. Limer, is come to see me in my solitude, which is more than ever solitary since Mimi is not here; she is at Gaillac, the dear sister! Meanwhile, awaiting her return, I am charmed that Françoise should have come to fill up the blank somewhat; she used, you know, to be our Sunday companion, so kind, lively, and gay! I find her somewhat changed. Time! oh, Time! She left us two years ago; since then she has lost her brother, who was drowned, and a cousin, a tall, handsome young man, whom she had to see reduced to nothing, consumed by suffering, and whom for three months she watched night and day. Poor good girl! this is what has aged her. Now she is going to offer her life to a convent—her tried, disenchanted life—without pleasure in the world. It is thus that women console themselves, happy, very happy, in that God has provided for them happiness in Himself. I have just been writing her a long letter about her affairs. Thus it happens, that, in occupying myself about these retreats for others, I return to thinking of them, to saying to myself that they will go God-wards, and I into the world, as St. Bernard's little brother used to say to his brothers setting out for Citeaux. Already a good number of my acquaintance have gone off in this direction. And now I am going to write down, in order not to forget it, an inspiration of night that I have approved by day.

In entering my little room this evening, at ten o'clock, I am met by the white light of the moon, which rises round and full, behind a group of oaks, at the Mérix; there she is, higher, higher, ever higher, each time I look up. She travels faster over the sky than my pen over this paper; but I can follow her with my eyes, wondrous faculty of *seeing*, so elevated, extended, and enrapturing. We may enjoy the heavens whenever we will; even at night from my bed I perceive through a chink in the shutter a little star that frames itself there about eleven o'clock, and shines on me long enough for me to fall asleep before it passes on; hence I call it the star of sleep, and love it. Shall I be able to see it in Paris? I fancy my days and nights will be changed, and I cannot think of this without regret. To take me hence is to drag Paula out of her grotto; it must be for thee that I leave my desert, thee for whom, God knows, I would go to the end of the world. Farewell to the moonshine, the cricket's chirp, the *glouglou* of the brook. I had the nightingale in addition a short time ago; but some charm is ever wanting to our charming things. And now, nothing but God, prayer, and sleep.

9th.—Could you guess what is now causing me positive suffering? It is thinking of that little queen, Jane Grey, beheaded when so young, so sweet, so charming.

13th.—Joy upon joy! another letter from Caroline; more kindness: all sorts of love to Papa, Eran, Mimi, and all; a box of things for us: good, good, good sister that she is; may God return her in blessings all that she does for us; all that I feel in my heart towards her! My friend, how I shall love this charming sister; how I do love her! how I long to hold her in my arms!

14th.—Only one word, because I am tired; because I ought to sleep, and should not sleep if I were to write; and that body and soul are alike exhausted. Letters from Caroline, Louise, Irène, Mimi. My heart is full: good night!

15th.—I thought I should have died last night: a faintness, a numbness, a palpitation of the heart roused me from my first sleep. I shook myself, ran to the window, the air, the fresh night, which restored me. This attack procured me a moment's enjoyment of the beautiful sky, the beautiful stars that I had been on the point of going to see up there; then I returned to my bed with serious thoughts of death, that death which comes we know not when. Let us be ready.

16th.—What a pretty benediction this! (no ink.)

17th.—Come! ink at length! I can write; ink! happiness and life. I was dead for three days that the circulation of this blood had been arrested; dead to my Journal, to thee, to intimacy. My friend, my heart is full of thee, of Caro, of your happiness, of this box, these gowns, these bonnets trimmed with flowers, these white gloves, these little shoes, these open-work stockings, this embroidered petticoat. Oh, I have looked at, touched, worn, dressed my heart out in all these a hundred times since they came, an hour ago. Oh, kind, kind and charming sister; India had indeed a sweet treasure there, that God bestows on thee! What a genial nature! What pleasure in giving pleasure! Never was wedding present bestowed with more delight, nor received with more gratitude; mine overflows my powers of expression; it is one of the things that God sees and knows. From Him, the giver of all good, I ask for her all blessings and eternal happiness. I shall take great delight in my pretty dresses, though dress, in general, gives me little pleasure; but in these there is something sweeter and more beautiful than mere outward appearance; something more than vanity; they are the gift of thy betrothed; it is a sister's robe that she is giving me. I wrote to her the moment I had seen the things; my heart goes out towards her; I want her to know at once the pleasure she has given me, and gives us all, with her altar-flowers, her tablecloth, her Virgin, her dresses, and so many beautiful, graceful things. How I love her! May God bless her; God, who does not let a cup of cold water given remain without reward!

This is what came to us from Gaillac with ink, a letter from Mimi, pepper and oil; this is telling thee everything. I may also add that Eran has killed a hare and a partridge, and has brought me back two quails alive and suffering. Whatever suffers belongs to me, and has always done so. As a child I used to take possession of all the lame chickens; to do good, to relieve, is such an intimate delight, the very marrow of a woman's heart.

I end where I began, with that benediction of animals on the day of St. Roch, so impressive, so religious a ceremony to those who discern in it God surrounding man with so many creatures consecrated to his service; true image of creation, this gathering of animals, of them all, even down to the pig. I kept thinking of Bijou, whom I should certainly have had blessed.

29th.—Farewell, my little room; farewell, my Cayla; farewell, my book, although, indeed, I take it with me, but it will travel in my trunk.

I have just returned from a mass that the kind pastor has said for my prosperous journey. I have received all the good-bys and hand-shaking of Andillac.[1]

VIII

You are my witness, Lord, that I find consolation nowhere;
rest in no creature.—THOMAS À KEMPIS.

10th April (1839), *at Nevers.*

EIGHT days, eight months, eight centuries, I don't know what length of time, of endless tedium, since I left thee, my friend,

[1] This seventh book ends the 29th of September, 1838, when Mademoiselle E. de Guérin was leaving the Cayla to attend her brother Maurice's wedding.

my poor invalid! Is he well, is he better, is he worse? Questions that go on forever and ever without any reply. Distressing ignorance, hard to endure; heart ignorance, the only one that causes suffering, or at least that causes us most suffering. It is fine weather, everywhere sunshine, and a flower-scented air which will do thee good. Spring warmth will cure you better than any medicines. I tell thee this out of a hopeful heart, alone in a hermit's chamber, with a chair, a cross, and a little table under a little window where I write. From time to time I see the sky and hear the bells, and some passers-by in the streets of Nevers, the dull. Is it Paris that has spoiled me, and made me think everything small and gloomy? Never was there a more deserted, dark, tiresome town than this, spite of the *charms that inhabit it,* Marie and her amiable family. There is no charm, however, strong enough to resist certain influences. Oh! despondency! the most malignant, most pertinacious, most at home of all, which when one has driven it out by one door comes back by another, which costs us so much labor to prevent its remaining mistress of the abode. I have tried everything, even bringing out my distaff from the recesses of its case, where it had been since I left the Cayla. This reminded me of the shepherd who, when he got to court, kept the chest in which his crook lay, and was wont, by way of enjoyment, to open it sometimes. I also found some pleasure in seeing my distaff once more and spinning a little. But I was spinning so many things besides!

A letter at length! A letter in which you are reported better, a letter from thy friend who has seen and talked with thee, and found thee almost cheerful. *O res mirabilis,* cheerfulness! provided only it be not put on, that you are not trying to deceive us! Invalids do sometimes play these tricks. But yet why not believe that it really is so? Doubt is good for nothing in any case. What makes me so much esteem your friend is that I do not doubt him, that I believe him unchangeable in friendship and a true man of his word. What makes me love him and want more of his letters is that he stands nearest to thee in heart and mind, and that I see thee in him.

16*th.*—An *émeute,* bloodshed, roar of cannon, rumors of

death! Tidings that fall like a thunderclap in our solitude and calm way of life. Maurice, Caro, my Paris friends, I am anxious; I seem to see you on a volcano. My God! I have just written to Caro, and begun a few words to M. d'Aurevilly, my other brother in interest.

18*th*.—No letter yesterday, nor any writing here. I did nothing but wait, wait for a disappointment. Sad ending this for a day of hope, which comes back to-day: there is no estranging her from the heart, deceiver that she is!

I am going to read, but what shall I read? The choice of books is as perplexing as that of men; there are few that are true and agreeable.

19*th*.—A letter from Louise, full of interest in thee; nothing but heart, intellect, and charm from one end to the other. She has a way of saying things which is to be met with only among those Rayssac rocks. It is solitude that does it; ideas spring up therein, unlike anything in the world; fresh, attractive as flowers or mosses. Charming Louise, how much I love her! This time I find in her a degree of calm and an absence of illusions that surprises me, she who is so full of them in general. I am going to join the other Louise, who so much resembles this one, do you not think so? and who also prays and gets others to pray for your recovery. "The other day," she writes me word (Louise of Rayssac), "that I was at the Platée, my aunt's parish, I went up to a holy maiden lady who lives in that church from morning to evening, and who has a great reputation for sanctity. I raised a corner of her black veil and said in a very low voice, 'Your pardon, Mademoiselle; I wanted to request your prayers for a young man who is ill, the brother of the person I love best on earth.' 'Well then, I will pray,' she replied with an air of modesty which gave still greater confidence to my request. I have not seen her since."

Was not this a pretty instance of piety, my friend, this young girl going about soliciting prayers for thee, with a look of heavenly interest? She is charming. Angels would give her all she wished.

21*st*.—My happiness, my enjoyment, my delight, to write in the sunshine, listening to the birds.

It was not to last very long, the beauty of this morning.

Alas! my friend, a letter from Caro has come, speaking in
so sad a tone of thy health that I am quite overwhelmed
by it. He coughs, he coughs still! Since then these words
echo round go where I will; a heartbreaking thought pursues
me, passes and repasses, within, without, and then drops
down on a churchyard; I cannot look at a green leaf without
thinking how soon it will fall, and that it is then the con-
sumptive die. My God! remove these forebodings from me;
cure me this poor brother! What ought I to do for him? Impotent affection! All that I can do is to suffer for thee.

22nd.—If ever you read this, my friend, you will have an
idea of a permanent affection; that something for some one
which occupies you when you go to bed, when you rise,
throughout the day and always; which makes sadness or
joy, the motive power and center of the soul.—In reading a
work on geology, I came upon a fossil elephant in Lapland, and a canoe disinterred in l'Ile des Cygnes, in digging
for the foundations of the Pont des Invalides. There I am
on the elephant, in the canoe, making the circuit of the
Northern Seas, and of the Swan Island; seeing those places
as they were in the time of these things. Lapland warm,
green, and peopled not with dwarfs, but with tall handsome
men, with women riding about on elephants through those
forests and hills, all petrified now-a-days; and then the
Swan Island, white with flowers and down; oh! how beautiful I think it! And its inhabitants, who are they? What
are they doing in this corner of the globe? Descended like
me from the exile of Eden, do they know his birth, life,
fall, his lamentable and marvelous history, that Eve for
whom he lost heaven, so much happiness and unhappiness
both, so much hope in their faith, such tears shed over their
children, so many and many things that we know, and that
perhaps were known before by this people of whom nothing
but a plank remains? Wrecks of humanity of which God
alone takes cognizance, the very fragments of which He
has hid away in the depths of the earth, as though to guard
them from our curiosity! If He permits something of them
to emerge, it is to teach us that this globe is an abyss of
misery, and that all we gain by stirring its depths is the
discovery of funereal inscriptions, and burying-places. Death

is at the bottom of everything, and we keep continually digging as though we were seeking for immortality.

A letter from Félicité, which gives no better account of thee. When will they write, they who know more about the matter? If they could see a woman's heart beat, they would have more compassion for it. Why are we so made that a desire consumes us, a fear shatters, an expectation haunts, a thought engrosses, and all that touches makes us shudder? Remembrance of letters, post-time, the sight of a paper, God knows how much I go through from them all! The solitude of the Coques will have witnessed much connected with thee. My sweet friend, my sister in grief and affection, is there, on one hand for my comfort, on the other to sadden me, when I see her suffer, and have to hide my sufferings to spare her sensitiveness.

24th.—Growing uneasiness and terror; a letter from M. de Frégeville, who thought thee worse. My God! must I thus learn, as it were accidentally, that I may lose thee? Will no one nearer than a stranger speak to me about thee, tell me that he has seen thee for me? When thus at a distance nothing is so killing as silence. It is death anticipated. My friend, my brother, my dear Maurice, I know not what to think, to say, to feel. After God, it is only in thee that I live, like a martyr, live in suffering. But what would that signify if I could offer it up to redeem thee, if I could plunge into a sea of sorrow to save thee from shipwreck? All redemption is effected by suffering: accept mine then, O God! unite it with that of the sisters of Lazarus, unite it with that of Mary, with that sword that pierced through her soul beside her expiring son; accept it, my God! strike, cut away what Thou wilt in me, but let there be a resurrection!

25th.—The postman has passed without leaving anything for me. The same doubts and uncertainties, the same encroaching terrors. To know and not to know! State of indescribable anguish. And here is the end of this book: my God! who will read it?[1]

[1] Who was to read it? As Eugenie de Guérin foresaw, it was not to be Maurice, who, brought back by her with great difficulty to the Cayla, faded away there in less than two months from the date of this page, on the 19th of July, 1839.

IX

Still to Him.
To Maurice dead, to Maurice in heaven!
He was the pride and the joy of my heart.
O how sweet a name and how full of tenderness is that
of brother!

Friday, 19th of July, at half-past eleven, eternal date!

21st of July (1839).

No, my friend, death will not separate us, will not take thee out of my thoughts; death only separates from the body; the soul, instead of being there, is in heaven; and this change of place in no way impairs its affections.—Far otherwise, I hope; one must love better in Heaven, where everything becomes divine. O, my friend, Maurice, Maurice! art thou far from me? dost thou hear me? What are they, those abodes that hold thee now? What that God, so glorious, mighty, and good, who, by the ineffable vision of Himself, makes thee happy while unveiling for thee eternity? Thou seest what I expect; possessest what I hope for; knowest what I believe. Mysteries of another life, how profound, how terrible ye are! —sometimes, how sweet! Yes, very sweet, when I reflect that Heaven is the place of happiness. Poor friend, thou hadst scarcely any of it here below; thy short life had no time for rest. Oh, God, sustain me! establish my heart in faith.

Alas! I have not had enough of this support. How we watched, and caressed, and kissed thee, thy wife, and we thy sisters, dead in thy bed, thy head lying on a pillow, as though thou wast sleeping! Then we followed thee to the Cemetery, to the grave, thy last bed: wept and prayed; and here we are, I writing to thee as if during an absence, as when thou wert in Paris! My friend, is it true? shall we never see each other again anywhere on earth? Oh, as for me, I will not leave thee! A sweet something appertaining to thee seems present with me still, calms me, prevents me from weeping. Sometimes tears come in torrents; then the soul gets parched. Is it that I do not regret him? All my life will be one of mourning; mine a widowed heart, without any intimate union. I am very fond of Marie and of my remaining brother, but not with the same sympathy as between us. Received a letter of thy friend d'Aurevilly for thee. Heartrending letter which arrived to reach thy coffin! How this made me realize thy absence! I must leave off; my head will not bear it; sometimes I feel my brain reel. Why will not tears come? I would drown everything in them.

22nd.—St. Magdalen's to-day; she to whom much was forgiven, because she loved much. How this thought, which occurred to me while we were hearing mass said for thee, consoled me as to thy soul! Oh, that soul will surely have been pardoned! Oh, my God! I can recall a whole period of faith and love which will not have been lost before thee!

> "Where Eternity abides
> Even the Past may be recovered."

A virtuous past, more especially, which must cover present weaknesses and errors. Oh, how that world, that other world, where thou art, occupies me now! My friend, thou liftest me on high; my soul detaches itself more and more from earth; death, I believe, would be welcome to me.

Oh, what indeed should we do with eternity in this world! Visits from my aunt Fontenelles, Eliza, M. Limer, Hippolyte, Thérèse; all persons, alas! who were to have come for a joyous wedding party, and who are here for a funeral. Good night, my friend. Oh, how we all prayed this morning on thy tomb—thy wife, thy father, and thy sisters!

Visitors; always visitors! Oh, how sad to see the living, to enter into conversation, to return to the ordinary course of things, when for the heart everything is changed! My poor friend, what a blank you have left me! Everywhere to see thy place, and not to find thee there! These girls, these young men, our relations, our neighbors, who at this moment fill the drawing-room, gathered around the dead, they would have surrounded thee living and joyous; for you used to take pleasure in them, and their youthful mirth enlivened you.

A touching letter from the Abbé de Rivières, who mourns thee as a friend; and a similar letter from his mother to me, containing the tenderest expressions of regret—a mother's sorrow blent with mine. Oh, she knew that thou wert **the son of** my heart!

No date.—I do not know what I was going to say yesterday when I broke off. Always tears and regrets. This does **not** pass away; on the contrary, profound sorrows are like the in-flowing sea, ever advancing, scooping out the ground more and more. Eight nights this evening that thou hast rested, down yonder at Andillac, in thy bed of earth. O God, my God! console me! Help me to look and hope far beyond the tomb, higher than where the body has fallen. Heaven, heaven! Oh, that my soul may rise to heaven!

4th August.—On this day came into the world a brother that I was to love much, and weep much. Alas! these often go together. I saw his coffin in the very spot in the very room where I can remember as a child to have seen his cradle, when they brought me back from Gaillac, where I was staying, for his baptism. That baptism was a gay one, a perfect festival, much more than that of any of the rest of us: markedly different, indeed—I amused myself a great deal, and went back the next day, very fond of the little new-born infant. I was then five, and two years later I returned, bringing him a frock that I had made him. I put it on him, and led him by the hand along the northern enclosure, where he took a few steps alone, his first, which I ran off very joyously to announce to my mother—"Maurice has walked alone!" Remembrances which come to me now all steeped in tears.

6th.—A day of prayer and pious consolation: a pilgrimage of thy friend, the holy Abbé de Rivières, to Andillac, where he said mass, and came to pray with thy sisters beside thy tomb. Oh! how this touched me, how in my inmost heart I blessed this pious friend kneeling on thy remains, whose soul far beyond this world soothed thine in suffering, if indeed it suffers! Maurice, I believe thee in heaven. Oh, yes, I have this confidence, given me by thy religious senti-ments, inspired by the mercy of God. God who is so good, so compassionate, so loving, so fatherly; will He not have had pity and tenderness for a son returned to Him? Oh, there are three years that afflict me; I would efface them with my tears. My God, so many supplications have been made! My God, Thou hast heard, Thou hast granted them. Why art thou sorrowful, oh, my soul; and why art thou so disquieted within me?

13*th.*—I feel a want to write, to think; a want to be alone, and not alone, with God and thee. I find myself isolated in the midst of all the rest. Oh, living solitude, how long thou wilt be!

17*th.*—Began to read "Holy Desires of Death," a book that suits my taste. My soul lives in a coffin. Oh, yes, buried —interred in thee, my friend; just as I used to live in thy life, I am dead in thy death—dead to all happiness, all hope here below. I had staked everything as a mother does on her son; I was less sister, indeed, than mother. Dost thou remember that I used to compare myself to Monica weeping over her dear Augustine, when we spoke of my distress about thy soul, that dear soul in error? How I had asked thy salvation of God, how I had prayed, implored! A holy priest once said to me, "Your brother will come back." Oh, he did come back, and then he left me for heaven—for heaven I hope. There were evident signs of grace, of mercy in this death. My God, I have more cause to bless Thee than to complain. Thou madest him one of the elect by sufferings that redeem; by acceptation and resignation that merit; by faith that sanctifies. Oh! yes, faith had revived in him fervent and profound; this was evident in his religious acts, his prayers, his readings, and in that kiss to the Cross given by him with so much love and emotion a short time before he died. Oh, I who saw him do this, I who watched him so closely in his last actions, I said, my God, I said that he was going to Paradise. Thus end all those who depart to the better life.

Maurice, my friend, what is heaven, that home of love? Wilt thou never give me a sign from thence? Shall I never hear thee, as they say the dead are sometimes heard? Oh! if thou wast able, if there exist any way of communication between this world and the next, return! I should not be afraid if some evening I saw an apparition, something from thee to me, we who were so united. Thou in heaven and I on earth. Oh, how death separates us! I write this in the little room, that little room so beloved, where we have talked together so much, we two alone. There is thy place, and beside it mine. Here lay thy portfolio, so full of secrets of the intellect and the affections—so full of thee and of things which decided thy life. I believe it; I believe that circumstances have had an influence over thy existence. If thou hadst remained here, thou wouldst not be dead. *Dead!* dreadful and only thought of thy sister.

20*th*.—Yesterday I went to Cahuzac to hear a mass for thee in unison with the one that the Prince of Hohenlohe was offering up in Germany to request thy recovery from God; requested, alas! too late. A fortnight after thy death, the answer has come to bring me grief instead of hope. How I regret not to have thought before of this means of deliverance which has saved so many others! It was on the authority of well-authenticated facts, that I had recourse to the holy wonder-worker, and I had such full faith in the miraculous. My God, I believe in it still; I believe in it weeping. Maurice! a flood of sadness has swept over my soul to-day. Every day increases thy loss, increases my heart's capacity for regret. Alone in the wood with my father, we sat down in the shade speaking of thee. I was looking at the place where you came to sit two years ago, the first day, I think, that you went out at all. Oh, what recollections of illness and recovery! I am sorrowful unto death. I want so to see thee. I am continually praying God to grant me this grace. Is the sky, the heaven of souls, so far from us, the heaven of time from that of eternity? O, profundity! oh, mysteries of that other life that separates us! I who was always so anxious about him, who wanted so much to know everything, wherever he may be now there is an end to that. I follow him into the three abodes; I stop at that of bliss; I pass on to the place of suffering, the gulf of fire. My God, my God, not so! Let not my brother be there, let him not! He is not there. What, his soul, the soul of Maurice, among the reprobates! Horrible dread, no! But in purgatory, perhaps, where one suffers, where one expiates the weaknesses of the heart, the doubts of the soul, the half-inclinations to evil. Perhaps my brother is there, suffering and calling to us in his pangs as he used to do in bodily pain: "Relieve me, you who love me." Yes, my friend, by prayer.

I am going to pray. I have prayed so much, and always shall. Prayer! oh, yes, prayers for the dead; they are the dew of purgatory.

4th October.—I wanted to send his friend two pomegranates from the tree about the roots of which he dug a few days before his death. That was his last effort on earth.

6th.—At this very hour, twelve o'clock, the first Sunday in October, I was in Paris, I was in his arms, Place Notre Dame des Victoires. A year ago, my God! How struck I was with his thinness, his cough; I who had dreamed of him as dead on my journey! We went together to Saint Sulpice, to the one o'clock mass. To-day to Lentin, in rain; to-day poignant memories and solitude. . . . But, my soul, be thou satisfied with thy God, whom thou hast received in that little church. He is thy brother, thy friend, the beloved Sovereign whom thou wilt never see die; who will never fail thee either in this life or the next. Let us comfort ourselves by this hope and by the knowledge that in God we find again all that we have lost. If I could go hence on high; if I felt heave within my breast that sigh which is the last, that breath of the dying which carries the soul to heaven, oh! I should not much regret life. But then life is a probation, and is mine long enough; have I suffered enough? When we betake ourselves to Calvary, we see what it costs to reach heaven. Oh! many tears, agonies, thorns, the vinegar and the gall. Have I tasted of all these? My God, take away from me all complaining; sustain me in silence and resignation at the foot of the Cross with Mary and the women who loved Thee.

19th.—Three months to-day since that death, that separation! Oh! the sorrowful date, which, nevertheless, I will note down each time it comes round. There is for me so tender and attaching a sadness in this return of the 19th, that I cannot see it without marking it in my life—since I do take note of my life. Oh! what indeed should I have to record now, did I not record my tears, my memories, my regrets for what I have best loved? This is all you will get, oh you who wish me to go on with this Journal, these books, *my every day* at Cayla. I was going to give them up, there was too much bitterness in speaking to him in his grave; but since you are there, my living brother, and take pleasure in hearing me, I continue my intimate communications; I link again with you what death had snapped. *I will write for you as I wrote for him.* You are my brother by adoption, the brother of my heart. In this there is illusion and reality, consolation and sadness, Maurice everywhere. It is then on this day, the 19th of October, that first I date for you, and that I mark this day as an epoch in my life, my isolated, solitary, unknown life, which goes out toward some one in the world, toward you in Paris, pretty much, as I believe I told you, as if Eustochia, from her Bethlehemite desert, had written to some gay Roman noble. The contrast between us is remarkable, but does not surprise me. Some one, a woman, told me that in my place she should find herself very much embarrassed in writing to you. As for me, I cannot see why I should be so. Nothing hampers me with you—in fact, no more than with Maurice; to me you are he, both to the heart and the intellect. That is the stand-point of our intimacy.

20*th*.—What a beautiful autumn morning! A transparent atmosphere, a radiantly calm sunrise, masses of clouds from north to south, clouds of such brilliancy, of a color at once soft and vivid, gilded fleece on a blue sky. It was beautiful, beautiful! I regretted to be the only one to see it. I thought of our painter and friend M. Augier, he who feels so keenly, and so readily admits the beautiful into his artist-soul. And then Maurice, and then you, I would fain have seen you all under my Cayla sky; but are we ever to meet again on earth?

In going to Posadou I wanted to gather a very pretty flower, but left it for my return, and then took another way! So adieu to my flower. If I were to return now, where would it be? Another time I will not leave my flowers on the road. And yet how often we do this in life!

This is Sunday. Again saw at Andillac that tomb quite green with grass already: How fast it has sprouted! How soon life seizes upon death, and how sad this seems to our sight! How heartbreaking would it be without that faith which tells us that we are to live again, to come forth from those cemeteries in which we seem to disappear!

The 1st of November.—What an anniversary! I was in Paris, sitting alone in the drawing-room at a table, thinking, as now, on this festival of All Saints. He, Maurice, came to find me, to chat a little heart to heart, soul to soul, and gave me a quire of paper, saying, "I want you to write me down there your *every day* in Paris." Oh, poor friend! I did indeed write it, but he never read it.[1] He was carried away so suddenly, so rapidly, before he had time to do anything,—that young man, born, as it seemed, to do so much. But God disposed of him differently to our expectations. There are beautiful souls, of which we are only here below to see the promise, and whose entire realization takes place elsewhere, in the other life. This world is but a place of transition, as the saints have believed it, as the soul which presages *a somewhere else* also believes. Oh, what happiness that this is not our all! Impossible, impossible! If we ended at the grave, the good God would be wicked, yes, wicked, to create unhappy creatures for a few days: horrible to think of. Tears alone are enough to make us believe in immortality. Maurice has finished his period of suffering, I hope, and to-day I seem continually to see him amongst the blessed. I say to myself that he must be there, that he pities those he sees upon earth, that he wishes for me where he is, as he wished for me in Paris. Oh, my God, this reminds me that on this very day last year we were together; that I had a brother, a friend, whom I can no longer see or hear. After so much intimacy, no intercourse whatever! It is this which makes death so painful. In order to meet him again, that beloved being so knit with one's heart, one must plunge into death and eternity. Those who have not God with them in this terror, what can they do? What becomes of you,— you, friend so much crushed by his loss, when your sorrow does not turn towards the other world? Oh, doubtless you do not lack faith, but have you a consoling, a pious faith? Believing that you have not much of this, I find myself pitying you bitterly. The anxiety that I had on this head regarding his brother-soul is now transferred to yours, almost as dear. I cannot say to what a degree I loved him, and still love him; it is something that rises toward the infinite,

[1] This book also has escaped all search.

towards God. Here I stop; with this thought are linked a million thoughts, dead and living; but above all dead; my journal, begun for him, continued for you on the same date, last year in some degree of happiness, and now all made up of tears. *My poor Maurice, I have been left behind in a land where there are continual tears and constant anguish.*

10th December.—At length shall I be able to write? How many times I have taken up my pen this last week, and the pen has fallen from my fingers unused! There has been such sadness in my soul, such shocks in my being, O God! it seemed as though I were nearing to my end, to a kind of moral annihilation. How terrible this state is! Nothing soothes, nothing sustains; occupation, repose, books, men, everything nauseates. One would die if one could. In such a struggle the soul without faith would be lost, oh! lost, if God did not reveal Himself; but He never fails to do so, something unexpected ever comes from on high.

I have found in the words of a priest (another friend of Maurice's) unhoped-for aid; soothing, calming, a religious balm which has made me realize faith in what it has of sweetest and strongest, its power of consolation. Very often I cannot of myself attain to this; my efforts fatigue and break me down. We are too small for heavenly things, we feel in ourselves the need of a mediator. Between God and man, Jesus Christ. Between Jesus Christ and us, the priest; he who brings the Gospel within the reach of each one of us. Some require threats, others hopes, for me love is needed, the love of God, the only true love. So soon as I am brought back to that, that I am able fully to realize it, I cease to suffer desperate sufferings. Blessed be the holy priest, the brother's friend who has consoled the sister! It is because he knew Maurice that I went to seek him out, that I thought he would understand me better than any other. I was not mistaken, he did indeed understand me. He has full knowledge of the heart, and of the agonies of the soul, and of that sorrowfulness unto death, and he sustains you, this angel.

Who could have guessed, ten years ago, when they were both at college, that that child would know my griefs, that I should confide them to him, and that he would soothe them by words such as I have not heard; divine words which I shall go from time to time to listen to, though it be rather far from home? When I suffer too much I shall make this pilgrimage. Brother of my heart, you see me here entirely as I am, you see down to the depths of my soul, as Maurice used to do. Perhaps you will only read this after my death, and then you will find what used to pass within that poor anchorite during her life; what she used to relate to you about her soul, less incomprehensible, less strange to you.

13th.—Before I go away from my room, I want to tell this dear Journal that you pray me to continue, that I have just been reading one of your letters, a brotherly, friendly letter, quite open in its affection and confidence, in which these words more especially touched me: *I want you to have the clew to my soul, I want you to be able to call yourself my sister by predestination as well as by voluntary and deliberate reflection. . . .* I grasp at this, and out of this *clew to your soul* form between you and me a tie that will never be loosened.

Prayed for Paula. Poor young girl's soul! where is it? This death that has deprived you of her, whither will it have borne her? There are many mansions in the other world, and for my part I tremble for those who go hence, who die in so passionate and faulty a youth. I did not know Paula, but a chance word of yours has made me fear; and then who knows how she was bound to you, that child who was more attached to you than to any living soul? But I stop short there; and indeed it is right not to judge harshly of any one.

14th.—A letter to Marie about what you ask me from her. I have neither read, nor done anything but write. Thought springs again and flows, a stream checked by a coffin, but the waters have risen above it. I shall return to my course here, sometimes a torrent, sometimes a mere thread of water, according to what happens in the soul. Night takes me hence, and from my little room where I have spent a whole day in calm and solitude. It is strange how much I enjoy this being apart from everything.

15th.—Returning from mass (it is Sunday), I walked with a woman who related her sorrows to me. Poor miller's wife! Surrounded by eight children, perfectly consumed by affections, and nevertheless going on weeping for one, continually mourning the mother she has lost. "I look for her everywhere," she said to me, "and at night I dream of her and feel that she caresses me." There is in this sorrow and this way of feeling an infinite tenderness, an expression of a feminine heart which pleases so much thus unsophisticated, and which perhaps is not so well seen in the world as in these poor country-women. Here they are as God has made them; elsewhere as we make ourselves under the fashioning of education, custom, and vanity. Everything is surface in the world. It is so indeed; and in a very short time I witnessed many a drawing-room comedy. I had been told of this, but yet I should not have believed Paris quite what it is,—for it is in Paris only that one sees society on a large scale, as a body. Here in the provinces we have only fragments and finger-ends of it, which can give no complete idea. My poor woman of the mill revealed to me what I hold to be the sweetest thing of all, a woman's heart in its natural sensibility.

16*th.*—Marie, Marie, you write me too many things, you have excited me too much. No one has had the same influence over my life as this woman during the two years since our friendship began. Everything that disturbs her agitates me.

31*st December.*—This last day of the year must not pass away like any other; it is too important, too solemn and touching, as is everything that comes to an end, too near eternity not to affect my soul, ah! most profoundly. What a day indeed, what a year, which bequeaths me, in departing, so many events, so many separations, so many losses, so many tears, and on my heart a coffin! One less amongst us, a blank in the family circle, in that of my affections. This is what time shows us. *Thus ends a year!* Alas! alas! life flows on like water, like that brook that I hear running under my window which widens in proportion as its banks fall. How many banks have fallen in my prolonged life! My first loss was my mother, whose death came upon me between childhood and youth, and thus put tears between the two ages. From being very lively and mirthful, I became pensive, reflective, my life changed all at once, it was a flower thrown into a coffin. From that epoch dates an increase of faith, a religious tendency, a love of God which used to transport me above everything, and which has left behind what sustains me now, a hope in God which early consoled me. Then I saw a cousin die, a tenderly-loved friend, the charm of my childhood, who used to take me upon his knees to teach me to read without making me cry, and to tell me stories. When I was older I made an elder brother of him. I confided Maurice to his care when he went away to Paris. My cousin was one of the body-guard. It is ordained that I should always have brothers in Paris, and that always they shall die there. This one went to the Versailles cemetery in 1829. I was then no longer a child; I got deeper and deeper among tombs; for two or three years I thought of nothing but death, and almost of dying. My poor Victor, whom Maurice resembled! Oh, I was always afraid that they would resemble each other throughout. Both so young, both dead, both killed in Paris. My God, these are terrible things and cutting memories; three deaths one upon another! This is what floods my memory to-day. I see only the departed; my mother, Victor, Philibert of the Isle of France, Marie of Brittany, Lili d'Alby, Laura de Boisset, all affections more or less close to my heart; and now the one that overlaid them all, the heart of my heart, Maurice, dead too! What swift passengers we are, my God! Oh! how short this world is! Earth is a mere transition step. They wait for me above. It is in the midst of these funerals that I end my day, my last writing, my last thoughts bequeathed to you, as on the same day, at the same hour, I bequeathed them last year to that poor brother. I wrote to him from Nevers, still pretty near to Paris and to him. Oh, how death separates us! What can I address to him where he is but prayers? It is to these that I turn now. Prayer is the dew of purgatory. If his poor (soul) were suffering there! Good night to you who replace him upon earth. I can say nothing more affectionate than that. I say so to you before God, and before him whom methinks I see at my side smiling at my adoption of his brother.

The 1st January, 1840.—What will happen to me, oh, my God, this year? I know not, and even if I could, I would not lift the curtain of the future. What is concealed beneath it might perhaps be too terrifying; to sustain the vision of things to come, one should be saint or prophet. I consider it a blessing to see no further than a day, than the next moment. If we were not thus limited by the present, where would the soul stop in apprehension, in grief both for itself and for what it loves? How much even a presentiment, that shadow of the future, can make us feel and suffer when it passes across the mind! At this moment I am without anxiety or emotion about any one; my year begins in confidence respecting those I love. My father is in good health, Erembert is improving, Marie has still her rosy apple-like cheeks, and the other Marie, the friend of my tears, the woman of sorrows, bears up with somewhat more strength. For all this, thanks be to God, whom I pray to bless and preserve all my dear ones. Christians look for their new year's gifts to heaven, and I turn thither on your behalf, while you are going into society, into the gay salons of Paris, to offer compliments and bonbons. If I were there perhaps I should have some too; as it is, perhaps I shall have a thought, a remembrance from that brother to whom Maurice has bequeathed me for sister. How beautiful the sky is, this winter sky!

A letter from Louise, sweet new year's gift of the heart, but nothing any longer gives me much pleasure; nothing that comes can console me for what is missing. This morning, in embracing my father—this poor father who for the first time in the first year did not embrace all his children—I was very sad. I seemed to see Jacob when he had lost Joseph.

Here are my first written thoughts, my first date of 1840, which is bound by a tie of crape to 1839 and to you.

2nd.—I make my escape here from the new year's letters that I have to get through. What a tiresome custom it is to be bandying compliments for a whole day long, and sending them to a distance! My lazy mind, which prefers dreaming to working, is not very ready to set about these flattering compositions. As to that, one does it because it has to be done, but briefly, with only a few phrases of the season and good wishes at the beginning and end. The world and those of the world excel in this; in speaking prettily and flatteringly. Not so I; I have no fluency in this gilded, brilliant talk, this lip-tinsel that one meets with in the world. *In the desert one only learns to think.* I used to say to Maurice, when he talked to me about Paris, that I should not understand its language. And yet there are some there that I did understand. Certain souls in all places comprehend each other. This helps me to believe what is said of the saints who communicate with the angels, although of different natures. The one looks up, the other bends down, and thus it is they meet, thus that the Son of God came down among us. This reminds me of a passage of the Abbé Gerbet, in one of his books that I like much: *One would say that the whole creation rested on an inclined plane, so that all beings whatever bend down to those below them to love and to be beloved by them.* Maurice pointed out this thought to me, and we thought it charming. Dear friend! who knows whether he may not be bending down towards me now, towards you, towards those he loved, to draw them up to the high sphere in which he is, to raise us from earth to heaven! May we not believe that those who precede us into the splendors of life take compassion upon us, and in their love communicate to us some attraction to the other world, some gleam of faith, some burst of light which before had not illumined the soul! If I dwelt near a king, and you were in prison, most assuredly I should send you all I could from the court. Thus, in the celestial sphere, whither our affections doubtless follow us, and become divinized and participate in God's love for man.

4th February.—I might, indeed, write a letter, but I prefer to turn my pen here; here by inclination, elsewhere by conventionality, and conventionality is very cold. The heart does not like it; turns aside, draws back from it as much as it can. With the exception of duties, I let it alone. As to the letter, I shall do it; it is but a slight thing, and it is no mighty effort to overcome a short *ennui.* There are certain long ones which we must bear to the end, and the one accustoms us to the other. Small conflicts lead to and fit us for great. These disagreeables are good for us, like bitters. They first require an effort of will to get swallowed, and then they strengthen. If everything came to us in the shape of sweetness and pleasure, what would become of us at the end, at the terrible shock of death? It is good to anticipate this. Hence it is that hermits and all saints—those who understand the soul of man so well—vow themselves to renunciation, voluntarily strip themselves, die daily in the prospect of that death that we all must undergo. Accordingly they depart very gently out of this world. I have been told of a young girl, a nun at Alby, who burst out crying with joy when she heard the doctors saying amongst themselves that all hope was over.

I don't know why, but in the time of the cholera, I, too, felt a sort of transport in the prospect of death. I envied all the dying. This made such an impression upon me that I spoke of it to my confessor. Was it the vague languor of youth? was it the longing for heaven? I do not know. One thing certain is, that the feeling is over or nearly so. I find myself, when contemplating death, in an attitude of submission, sometimes of fear, rarely of desire. Time changes us. It is not in this alone that I am conscious of age. When my hair is white, I shall again be quite different. O, these human metamorphoses, to grow ugly, to grow old! To console oneself under them we need to believe in the resurrection. How faith serves every purpose! Yes; this thought of the resurrection to many women who make their body an object of love, their beauty a happiness, might be a comfort when their charms were over, and very probably more than one fair Christian avails herself of it, those to whom some terrible change of appearance is sent. She, for instance, who said, "To die is nothing, but to die disfigured!" That was the insupportable in her eyes. Poor woman! I laughed heartily at this once, now I compassionate the feeling; it pains me to see that the soul does not get raised higher than the body. Who knows? If I were pretty, perhaps I should feel the same.

[*No date.*]—What can I say; what can I reply? What is this you announce to me as preparing for Maurice! Poor ray of glory which is to fall upon his tomb! How I should have loved it on his brow, during his life, when we could have seen it without tears! It is too late now for the joy to be complete, and yet I experience a certain sorrowful happiness from this funereal note of fame which is to connect itself with the name I have so much loved, and to tell me that this dear memory will not die. Oh! how fain would the heart immortalize what it loves! I had heard this said, I feel it, and the desire extends from heaven to earth. Whether through love or faith, for this world or the next, the soul rejects annihilation. Maurice, my friend, still lives; he has been extinguished, has disappeared from us here below, only as a star dies in one place to live again in another. How this thought consoles, supports me in this separation; how much of hope I link with it! This ray which is to shine on Maurice; I seem to see it come down from heaven, it is the reflection of his aureole, of that crown which shines on the brow of the elect, of saved spirits. Those who lose themselves have nothing before God which marks them out, which remains theirs—whatever distinctions men may confer upon them—for all human glory passes quickly away. I should not rejoice if I saw only this last for my brother, but his was a holy death, and I accept with delight this glorification of his intellect which may associate itself with the canonization of his soul.

I shall say no more to you on this infinite subject, having written to you and expressed my feelings and my profound acknowledgments to you, to M. Sainte-Beuve, and to Madame Sand, for the part that you are each of you to take in the publication of the "Centaur," this beautiful unknown work of my brother's; in the bringing his life and his talents to light.

Oh, how you touch me when you say that my thoughts, my expressions, my images, often remind you of Maurice; that he and I were twin brother and sister in mind! This is the most beautiful likeness that you can find for me, and the sweetest to myself.

Easter Eve.—Oh, what a difference last year, at Paris! A return of deep memories! That evening there had been a consultation of doctors; I was much affected. We were at Valentino, it was there that a packet sealed with black was delivered; there, too, that poor Maurice chanced to be; singular meeting on a last evening; that concert wound up my stay in Paris; it was the knell of my death to the world, that I heard ring with I know not what sweet and sad emotion, somewhat like what I now feel in recalling these things, these persons, who return to me like shadows in my little room, at the same hour and less harmoniously than at Valentino. My concert now is the rain beating on my window, and so many regrets that beat on my soul. I have felt, I have seen what then I only dreaded; death, separation forever. How much I need to dwell upon to-morrow's festival! What a blessed thing this resurrection! My God, since we must see die, how sweet to believe that we shall also see rise again! May these thoughts of faith, to which I am about to devote myself, banish others which crowd thick and oppress my soul.

The Evening of Easter Day.—O Easter, flowery Easter, day of revival, refreshment, celestial jubilee! I know not what to say, how to express this feast of the Passover so magnificently beautiful in ancient and modern times, which has prompted the music of *In Exitu* and *O Filii,* and in me so many internal hymns, when I saw Erembert this morning at the communion table. Another brother saved! One must be a Christian sister to feel this and the peculiar happiness which springs from the hope of heaven for a soul one loves, from seeing it united to God and Sovereign good.

20th April.—Oh, it was indeed a nightingale that I heard this morning. It was about daybreak, and just as I woke, so that afterwards I thought I had been dreaming; but I have just heard him again; my minstrel is arrived. I note two things every year—the arrival of the nightingale and of the first flower. These are epochs in the country and in my life. The beginning of spring, which is so exquisitely beautiful, is thus chronicled, and the lateness or earliness of the season. My charming calendars do not mislead; they correctly announce fine days, the sun, the green leaves. When I hear the nightingale, or see a swallow, I say to myself, "The winter is over," with inexpressible pleasure. For me it is a new birth out of cold, fog, a dull sky, out of a whole dead nature. Thought reappears with all its flowers. Never was epic poem written in winter.

1st June.—A rare visitor; superior conversation. Every now and then some charming passer-by drops in at the Cayla, that great empty desert, a valley peopled pretty much as the earth was before man made his appearance in it. One spends days sometimes without seeing anything but sheep, or hearing anything but birds. A solitude this not without its charms for a soul disconnected and disenchanted with the world.

5th.—Oh, this must be dated this day, this "Revue" just arrived, this moment when at last I am about to read the "Centaur." I have it then, I hold it, I look at it, I hesitate to open it, this posthumous collection for which I would have given my eyes a minute ago. My God, how full of contraries this heart of ours!

9th.—For four days past I have remained without stirring under the impression made by this "Centaur," these letters, these revelations so lofty or so intimate, these heart-words so deep and so sad, these presentiments of an approaching end so unhappily realized, these numerous precious and painful things of Maurice's, which the "Revue des Deux Mondes" has brought me. Nothing ever touched me so much as its perusal; not even what I had already read of Maurice's. Is it because these writings of his, which I did not know, renew and increase the feeling of his loss, or that, put forth with a charm that enhances their value, I am more touched by them than with what I had seen without this? Be that as it may, mine is an enjoyment steeped in tears, a happiness of two tastes, a more full, more highly estimated, and consequently more sad possession of Maurice than ever, in this beautiful "Centaur" and these private fragments. How penetrating he is in his heart-sayings; in that gentle, delicate, and subtle way of talking sadness that I have only known in him! Oh! Madame Sand is right in saying that these are words to be set like costly diamonds at the summit of the diadem. Or rather, he was all diamond, was Maurice.

Blessed be those who estimate him as he deserves; blessed be the voice that praises him, that lifts him up so high with so much respect and intelligent enthusiasm! But this voice is mistaken on one point, mistaken when it says that faith was wanting to this soul. No! faith was not wanting to it; this I declare and attest by what I have seen and heard, by prayer, by religious reading, by the sacraments, by all Christian acts, by a death that unveiled the life, a death upon a crucifix. I have a great mind to write to George Sand, to send her something that I have in idea about Maurice, like a crown to hide this stain that she has placed on his brow. I cannot bear that the very slightest feature should be taken away or added to that face, so beautiful in its reality; and this irreligious and pagan light disfigures it.

15th.—What is this that has come to me from Paris for Maurice? for him who never thought about fame; who did not wish for it? But I accept it, in and for his memory. A Comte de Beaufort has just offered me the publication of a notice in the "Revue de Paris," which will counterbalance that in the "Revue des Deux Mondes," by all the honesty and purity of a Christian portrait. Madame Sand makes of Maurice a skeptic, a great poet after the manner of Byron, and it grieved me to see the name of my brother brought forward under this false light, a name pure of those deplorable errors. I wanted to write to render homage to truth, and now here is a voice that makes itself heard. God be praised! I have but to give our approbation which is requested. We shall gladly give it.

[*No date.*]—For some time past I neglect my Journal a good deal; I had almost entirely done with it, but I return to it to-day; not that I have anything interesting to note down in it, but simply to go back to a thing beloved, for I do love this poor record in spite of my forsaking it. It is linked with a chain of joys, with a past too dear to my heart not to value whatever is a result of it. These pages, then, shall be continned. I leave off and then resume this dear writing, continuous like the pulsation in the heart, though sometimes suspended a while by oppression.

The little course of my days is then about to flow on here as before. For the moment, I note down a visit, or one of those I should occasionally like as an agreeable diversion. Although he is a very young man, one can converse with him because he has read, seen the world, and has a gentleness and decision in his opinions which I like in general conversation. We have not the same way of viewing things, and, my age permitting me to express myself freely and to support mine, I find myself contradicting him, from conviction as well as inclination, for whatever I say I think.

If there be anything sweet, delicious, inexpressibly calm and beautiful, most certainly it is one of our fine nights, this, for instance, that I have just been looking at out of my window; which is going on beneath the full-moon, in the transparency of a balmy air, in which everything is defined as under a crystal globe.

21*st November*.—Châteauroux, where I am alone in a dark room, walled round within two feet of the window, as in the

Spielberg; like Pellico, I am writing at a deal table; that is, if I am writing. What can one write to the noise of an alien wind, and under a weight of depression? On arriving here, on losing sight of those familiar faces of the diligence, I flung myself into my room and on my bed, in a state of desperate dejection. The expression is a strong one, perhaps, but it was something, in short, which flew to the head and oppressed the heart. To find oneself *alone* in a hotel, in a crowd, is so novel, so strangely sad, that I cannot make up my mind to it. Oh, if it were for long! But to-morrow I am setting out; to-morrow I shall be with my friend; a delight of which I have not even the wish to speak. Formerly I should have expressed it all—that formerly is dead.

Sleep, and a short time in the church, have calmed me. I have written to the Cayla, my dear, sweet home, where they are thinking of the traveler as I think of them.

7th December.—I have received a sealed packet from a friend. Sad and precious relic, deposited in my heart with tears. This was a day of deposits. I, on my side, and without any idea of imitation, since I was not expecting what happened, gave into the hands of a holy priest certain papers of my own. I wanted a doubt decided for me. Oh, my poor thoughts, that I dare no longer judge! May God judge them!

My poor friend! She has talked of receiving the Sacrament, and other things connected with death. The little cross that I passed round her neck has pleased her; I have often seen her kiss it. Alas! another departing one glued his lips to it!

10th.—A tolerably calm day; conversation; almost cheerfulness and animation. It is a good sign when the soul reappears.

11th.—I am set at ease; the priest to whom I had given certain writings, or rather my thoughts, my heart, to judge, has returned them to me, not condemned, but approved, enjoyed, understood better than I had understood them myself. Do we need that another should reveal us to ourselves? Yes, when one's mind is ignorant and one's heart timid.

At Saint Martin.—Shall I read or write, or what shall I do now in my room, so well arranged for all my favorite pursuits?—A good fire, books, a table with ink, pens, and paper, appliances and inducements. Let us write; but what? Why, this little Journal, which will contain my thoughts and my life; this life out of its ordinary course at present, as if our brook should find itself transported to the banks of the Loire; that Loire, that country that I ought naturally never to have seen, so far away from it was I born. But God has led me here. I cannot help seeing Providence clear as noonday in certain events of my life; not that it is not in all of them, but more or less manifest.

With somewhat more taste for writing, I might have left here a long memorandum of my stay at St. Martin, with its beautiful, grandiose park and water. I have seen few places so striking, so remarkable by nature and art. One sees that Lenôtre has had to do with it. I am leaving with the most sweet and agreeable recollections, both of within and without: this charming family into which I am adopted, where I have received the most touching evidences of affection; true affection, because disinterested. What do they gain by loving me? Nothing but to be loved in their turn and blessed by me before God! Oh, how sweet all this would be to me if I did not think of Maurice, to whom I owe this happiness that I enjoy after his death! I asked to see his room; I do not take a step, to the chapel, in the garden, the saloon, that he has not taken too. Alas! we do nothing but tread in the footsteps of the dead!

Last day of December.—My God! how time has a something sad about it, whether it comes or goes! and how right the saint is who says, "Let us anchor our hearts in eternity!"

16th.—Date only.

17th September, 1841.—There are things which I should have said yesterday, but which I cannot say to-day. I have seen *you,* we have spoken, and that is enough to relieve my heart, to set free my mind again, to lift off that oppressive weight of thought and feeling which only you could take from me. So I am comforted; but though my burden is gone from me, the ache remains.

Oh, end of all! end of all things, and always the dearest things! an end that comes from no cause that the heart knows, but some hidden element of dissolution which mingles with them all! In the moment of union the seed of separation is sown. Cruel illusion for such as had believed in friendships that might be eternal. Let me learn the lesson. Let me—but the knowledge is bitter.

Who will remain to me? You, unshaken friend. I always desired a strong friendship, such as death only could overthrow; a joy and a grief, alas! that I had in Maurice. No woman ever could, or ever can, take his place; no woman, however distinguished from the rest, could bring to me the same similarity of intelligence and of tastes; a relation so large, so whole, so firmly fixed. There seems nothing fixed, nothing lasting, nothing vital in the feelings of women for each other; their mutual attachments are only pretty little bands of ribbon. I observe these slightly-built attachments among all circles of female friends; but must I conclude that women are incapable of loving each other in another way? I do not know any instance of it now, or even in history. Orestes and Pylades are sisterless. It makes me indignant to think of it. Can I bear to reflect that you men carry something about in your breasts which we women have not? But then, we have the capacity of self-sacrifice.

A beautiful voice in the street! The only agreeable voice I have ever heard in the streets of Paris, where the voices seem thick and harsh. Degradation of soul makes itself heard in them all.

It appears to me that we women are very ill-educated, and in a way quite contrary to the indications of our natural destiny. We have to suffer much, and they take away our energy; they cultivate our nerves, and our sensibilities, and our vanity; religion and morality, of course, but as matters external, without seeking to fill our souls with them, for our true guidance. Sad to think of, ye poor little maidens all!

22nd.—Nothing pains me more deeply than injustice, no matter who endures it, myself or another. It grieves me beyond belief to see somebody make excuses to a child who is in the wrong, and *vice versâ*. The smallest deflection from the truth displeases me. Is this susceptibility a fault? I know not—nobody has ever told me it is. My father loves me too dearly to criticize me, to find any fault in me. To judge another mind fairly, and see its faults, the eye must neither be too near nor too far off. You, Jules, are just at the right distance for looking at me justly, and seeing what I lack. I think I must lack a great many things. Before you leave us I will take your opinion. I wish to have your comments to keep by me as a proof of your affection. It is a duty to oneself to try and make perfect what one loves. We always *will* it so much that we cannot help speaking out our thoughts, even though we speak ill, or at ill times.

2nd October.—Upon our return from the Palais-Royal I lie down in my room and think over our conversation. A woman said that, for her, friendship was a velvet couch in a boudoir. Very nice; but let me be outside of the boudoir, sitting on a lofty peak, high above the world. To sit apart from all in this way delights me in the same manner.

3rd.—Disturbed yesterday upon my mountain-top. I resume this journal only to close it, because I find I cannot write in peace. To-day is Sunday; happily, I breathed in strength and calmness at church, enough to enable me to withstand a vigorous assault from the world without.

[1842. *Rivières.*] 'Tis long since I have written, but there are days that one does not like to lose, and I must not let this day pass unrecorded, so full as it has been of emotions, of tears. Strange power of places, of memory! It was to this place, to R——, that he used frequently to come in vacation time—a glad student, playing in the fields, and leaping the waterfalls with the children from the château. We have been recalling these times, and speaking of him—talking familiarly, and at length, with this good, kind, perfect Madame de R——. She wept. How impatient I was to see her, in order that we might do this—might speak of Maurice! I found, in doing so, a joy in the very heart of grief, an unutterable sweetness in tears. . . . And I, my God, am living, with the living, this day! What touched me very much was to see a college box of his, in which he went halves with little G——, for keeping his books. It has been carefully kept, and now I have been asked to give it away as a souvenir. Some of these simple things go to the very heart.

Opened by accident an album, in which I found recorded the death of Maurice—death everywhere! I was very much.

affected to find it there, in those private pages, the journal of a young girl who had kept it, as it were, in her very heart. Surely this unexpected tribute to the memory of Maurice is the tenderest of any. How true that is: *he was the life of us all!* No one who knows us could help saying it. There are beings, there are hearts, of an order that furnish forth so much for other hearts that the others seem to live by that borrowed life. Maurice was to me as a source of being: from him to me flowed friendship, sympathy, counsel, sweet possibilities of life springing from the sweetness of my converse with him; he was the leaven of my thought, the sustenance of my soul. Lost friend divine! it is God alone can fill the void in my heart.

To hope or to fear for another is the sole thing which can give to humanity the fulfilled consciousness of its own being.

[31*st December. Cayla.*] 'Twas my habit once to end the year, in thought, with somebody—with Maurice. Now he is dead my thought is unshared, dumb; and I keep that to myself which over these decays and falls of time climbs back to eternity. *A last day,* how sad, how awful it is!

THE END

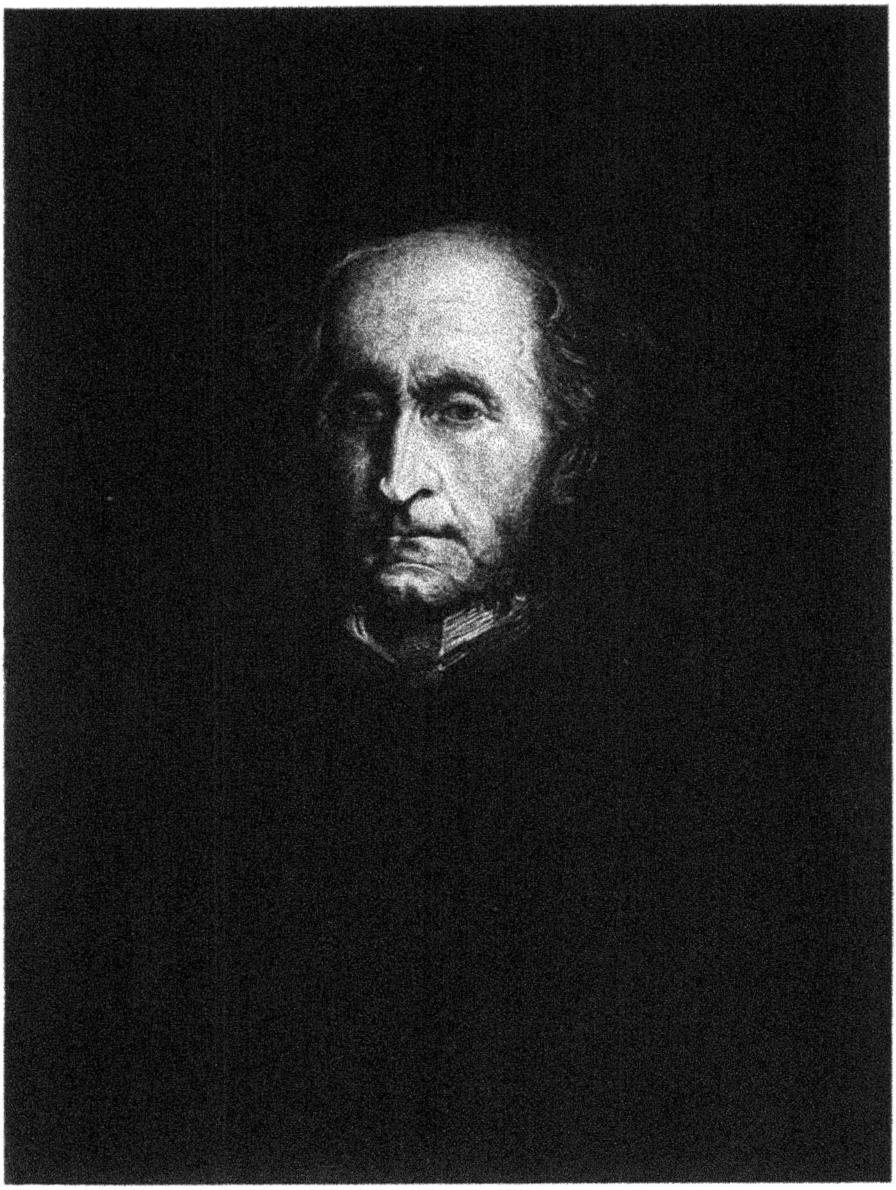

LOGIC
POLITICAL ECONOMY
ESSAY ON LIBERTY

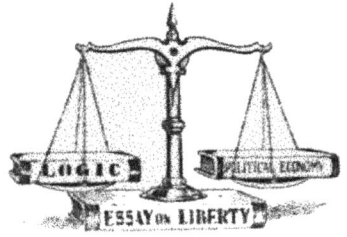

John Stuart Mill gives us the earliest of those remarkable educational studies of self by strictly scientific men, for which the nineteenth century was so noteworthy. It was the misfortune of John Stuart Mill to have a father with most exacting views of education. When James Mill discovered that his eldest son was possessed of mental capabilities that might in time make him a certain scholar, his education was immediately begun. At an early age the learning process was introduced, and begun far beyond the usual

JOHN STUART MILL

lad and afterwards critically discussed between father and son. His father, a writer and a man of brilliant intellect, is described by his son as "the most impatient of men," and under the goad of personal supervision, the young scholar advanced in his studies by leaps and bounds.

But many elements were neglected. While the logical method produced a certain hardness of mental fiber, the compensating elements, such as love of poetry, literature, and art, were thrust aside as unworthy. It was inevitable that, in time, the pendulum should swing to the other extreme, for we find the younger Mill confessing, with an undercurrent of apology, to a delight in natural scenery. Poetry, too, came to his aid during the dark days of a mental crisis and lent its uplifting aid.

It is a curious fact that in the autobiography of John Stuart Mill we find no allusion whatever to his mother, and the only mention of the eight younger brothers and sisters is when he states that for teaching he was allowed to teach them, he was obliged to review in part to them.

Dominated by the father of whom every one stood in dread, the home life of John Stuart Mill was most unfortunate. Little wonder then his affections were called when, at the age of twenty-five, he met a married woman, Mrs. Taylor, so gifted that Carlyle admired her for her beauty and "vivacement." Though this association gave rise to much adverse comment, yet for many years Mill's friendship for Mrs. Taylor was earnest, and

JOHN STUART MILL

LEADER OF THE NINETEENTH CENTURY "UTILITARIAN" PHILOSOPHERS

1806-1873

(INTRODUCTORY NOTE)

John Stuart Mill gives us the earliest of those remarkable scientific studies of self by strictly scientific men, for which the nineteenth century was so noteworthy. It was the misfortune of John Stuart Mill to have a father with most exacting views of education. When James Mill discovered that his eldest son was possessed of certain capabilities that might in time make him a notable scholar, his education was strenuously begun. At an early age the forcing process was instituted, and lessons far beyond the standards of to-day were learned by the docile little lad and afterwards critically discussed between father and son. This father, a writer and a man of brilliant intellect, is described by his son as "the most impatient of men," and under the goad of parental ambition, the young scholar advanced in his studies by leaps and bounds.

But many elements were neglected. While the logical method produced a certain hardness of mental fiber, the compensating elements, such as love of poetry, literature, and art, were thrust aside as unworthy. It was inevitable that, in time, the pendulum should swing to the other extreme, for we find the younger Mill confessing, with an undercurrent of apology, to a delight in natural scenery. Poetry, too, came to his aid during the dark days of a mental crisis and lent its uplifting aid.

It is a curious fact that in the autobiography of John Stuart Mill we find no allusion whatever to his mother, and the only mention of his eight younger brothers and sisters is when he states that the learning, so early forced upon him, he was obliged to communicate in part to them.

Dominated by the father of whom every one stood in dread, the home life of John Stuart Mill was most unfortunate. Little wonder that his affections went astray when, at the age of twenty-five, he met a married woman, Mrs. Taylor, so gifted that Carlyle alludes to her as "vivid" and "iridescent." Though this association gave rise to injurious gossip, yet for many years Mill's friendship for Mrs. Taylor was constant, and on the death of her husband she became his wife. For nearly thirty years she was the lodestar of his life, and when she died we find Mill and his step-daughter making their home near her last resting-place.

Of religion, Mill had none whatever. The Christian faith he looked upon as dispassionately and as unconcernedly as he looked upon the rites of the ancient Romans. But we to-day are indebted to John Stuart Mill, and indirectly to his irascible but scholarly father, for three works that bid fair to stand the test of time,—"Logic," "Political Economy," and the "Essay on Liberty."

MY AUTOBIOGRAPHY

CHAPTER I

CHILDHOOD AND EARLY EDUCATION

It seems proper that I should prefix to the following biographical sketch, some mention of the reasons which have made me think it desirable that I should leave behind me such a memorial of so uneventful a life as mine. I do not for a moment imagine that any part of what I have to relate, can be interesting to the public as a narrative, or as being connected with myself. But I have thought that in an age in which education, and its improvement, are the subject of more, if not of profounder study than at any former period of English history, it may be useful that there should be some record of an education which was unusual and remarkable, and which, whatever else it may have done, has proved how much more than is commonly supposed may be taught, and well taught, in those early years which, in the common modes of what is called instruction, are little better than wasted. It has also seemed to me that in an age of transition in opinions, there may be somewhat both of interest and of benefit in noting the successive phases of any mind which was always pressing forward, equally ready to learn and to unlearn either from its own thoughts or from those of others. But a motive which weighs more with me than either of these, is a desire to make acknowledgment of the debts which my intellectual and moral development owes to other persons; some of them of recognized eminence, others less known than they deserve to be, and the one to whom most of all is due, one whom the world had no opportunity of knowing. The reader whom these things do not interest, has only himself to blame if he reads farther, and I do not desire any other indulgence from him than that of bearing in mind, that for him these pages were not written.

I was born in London, on the 20th of May, 1806, and was the eldest son of James Mill, the author of the History of British India. My father, the son of a petty tradesman and (I believe) small farmer, at Northwater Bridge, in the county of Angus, was, when a boy, recommended by his abilities to the notice of Sir John Stuart, of Fettercairn, one of the Barons of the Exchequer in Scotland, and was, in consequence, sent to the University of Edinburgh, at the expense of a fund established by Lady Jane Stuart (the wife of Sir John Stuart) and some other ladies for educating young men for the Scottish Church. He there went through the usual course of study, and was licensed as a Preacher, but never followed the profession; having satisfied himself that he could not believe the doctrines of that or any other Church. For a few years he was a private tutor in various families in Scotland, among others that of the Marquis of Tweeddale, but ended by taking up his residence in London, and devoting himself to authorship. Nor had he any other means of support until 1819, when he obtained an appointment in the India House.

In this period of my father's life there are two things which it is impossible not to be struck with: one of them unfortunately a very common circumstance, the other a most uncommon one. The first is, that in his position, with no resource but the precarious one of writing in periodicals, he married and had a large family; conduct than which nothing could be more opposed, both as a matter of good sense and of duty, to the opinions which, at least at a later period of life, he strenuously upheld. The other circumstance, is the extraordinary energy which was required to lead the life he led, with the disadvantages under which he labored from the first, and with those which he brought upon himself by his marriage. It would have been no small thing, had he done no more than to support himself and his family during so many years by writing, without ever being in debt, or in any pecuniary difficulty; holding, as he did, opinions, both in politics and in religion, which were more odious to all persons of influence, and to the common run of prosperous Englishmen in that generation than either before or since; and being not only a man whom nothing would have induced to write against his convictions, but one who invariably threw into everything he wrote, as much of his convictions as he thought the circumstances would in any way permit: being, it must also be said, one who never did anything negligently. But he, with these burdens on him, planned, commenced, and completed, the History of India; and this in the course of about ten years, a shorter time than has been occupied (even by writers who had no other employment) in the production of almost any other historical work of equal bulk, and of anything approaching to the same amount of reading and research. And to this is to be added, that during the whole period, a considerable part of almost every day was employed in the instruction of his children; in the case of one of whom, myself, he exerted an amount of labor, care, and perseverance rarely, if ever, employed for a similar purpose, in endeavoring to give, according to his own conception, the highest order of intellectual education.

I have no remembrance of the time when I began to learn Greek, I have been told that it was when I was three years old. My earliest recollection on the subject, is that of committing to memory what my father termed vocables, being lists of common Greek words, with their signification in English, which he wrote out for me on cards. Of grammar, until some years later, I learned no more than the inflexions of the nouns and verbs, but, after a course of vocables, proceeded at once to translation; and I faintly remember going through Æsop's Fables, the first Greek book which I read. The Anabasis, which I remember better, was the second. I learned no Latin until my eighth year. At that time I had read, under my father's tuition, a number of Greek prose authors, among whom I remember the whole of Herodotus, and of Xenophon's Cyropædia and Memorials of Socrates; some of the lives of the philosophers by Diogenes Laertius; part of Lucian, and Isocrates ad Demonicum and Ad Nicoclem. I also read, in 1813, the first six dialogues (in the common arrangement) of Plato, from the Euthyphron to the

Theoctetus inclusive: which last dialogue, I venture to think, would have been better omitted, as it was totally impossible I should understand it. But my father, in all his teaching, demanded of me not only the utmost that I could do, but much that I could by no possibility have done. What he was himself willing to undergo for the sake of my instruction, may be judged from the fact, that I went through the whole process of preparing my Greek lessons in the same room and at the same table at which he was writing: and as in those days Greek and English lexicons were not, and I could make no more use of a Greek and Latin lexicon than could be made without having yet begun to learn Latin, I was forced to have recourse to him for the meaning of every word which I did not know. This incessant interruption, he, one of the most impatient of men, submitted to, and wrote under that interruption several volumes of his History and all else that he had to write during those years.

The only thing besides Greek, that I learned as a lesson in this part of my childhood, was arithmetic: this also my father taught me: it was the task of the evenings, and I well remember its disagreeableness. But the lessons were only a part of the daily instruction I received. Much of it consisted in the books I read by myself, and my father's discourses to me, chiefly during our walks. From 1810 to the end of 1813 we were living in Newington Green, then an almost rustic neighborhood. My father's health required considerable and constant exercise, and he walked habitually before breakfast, generally in the green lanes towards Hornsey. In these walks I always accompanied him, and with my earliest recollections of green fields and wild flowers, is mingled that of the account I gave him daily of what I had read the day before. To the best of my remembrance, this was a voluntary rather than a prescribed exercise. I made notes on slips of paper while reading, and from these in the morning walks, I told the story to him; for the books were chiefly histories, of which I read in this manner a great number. In these frequent talks about the books I read, he used, as opportunity offered, to give me explanations and ideas respecting civilization, government, morality, mental cultivation, which he required me afterwards to restate to him in my own words. He was fond of putting into my hands books which exhibited men of energy and resource in unusual circumstances, struggling against difficulties and overcoming them. Of children's books, any more than of playthings, I had scarcely any, except an occasioual gift from a relation or acquaintance: among those I had, Robinson Crusoe was preëminent, and continued to delight me through all my boyhood. It was no part, however, of my father's system to exclude books of amusement, though he allowed them very sparingly.

In my eighth year I commenced learning Latin, in conjunction with a younger sister, to whom I taught it as I went on, and who afterwards repeated the lessons to my father: and from this time, other sisters and brothers being successively added as pupils, a considerable part of my day's work consisted of this preparatory teaching. It was a part which I greatly disliked; the more so, as I was held responsible for the lessons of my pupils, in almost as full a sense as for my own: I, however, derived from this discipline the great advantage, of learning more thoroughly and retaining more lastingly the things which I was set to teach: perhaps, too, the practice it afforded in explaining difficulties to others, may even at that age have been useful. I went in this manner through the Latin grammar, and a considerable part of Cornelius Nepos and Cæsar's Commentaries, but afterwards added to the superintendence of these lessons, much longer ones of my own.

In the same year in which I began Latin, I made my first commencement in the Greek poets with the Iliad. After I had made some progress in this, my father put Pope's translation into my hands. It was the first English verse I had cared to read, and it became one of the books in which for many years I most delighted: I think I must have read it from twenty to thirty times through. Soon after this time I commenced Euclid, and somewhat later, Algebra, still under my father's tuition.

From my eighth to my twelfth year, the Latin books which I remember reading were, the Bucolics of Virgil, and the first six books of the Æneid; all Horace, except the Epodes; the Fables of Phædrus; the first five books of Livy (to which from my love of the subject I voluntarily added, in my hours of leisure, the remainder of the first decade); all Sallust; a considerable part of Ovid's Metamorphoses; some plays of Terence; two or three books of Lucretius; several of the Orations of Cicero, and of his writings on oratory; also his letters to Atticus, my father taking the trouble to translate to me from the French the historical explanations in Mingault's notes. In Greek I read the Iliad and Odyssey through; one or two plays of Sophocles, Euripides, and Aristophanes, though by these I profited little; all Thucydides; the Hellenics of Xenophon; a great part of Demosthenes, Æschines, and Lysias; Theocritus; Anacreon; part of the Anthology; a little of Dionysius; several books of Polybius; and lastly Aristotle's Rhetoric, which, as the first expressly scientific treatise on any moral or psychological subject which I had read, and containing many of the best observations of the ancients on human nature and life, my father made me study with peculiar care, and throw the matter of it into synoptic tables. During the same years, I learned elementary geometry and algebra thoroughly, the differential calculus, and other portions of the higher mathematics far from thoroughly: for my father, not having kept up this part of his early acquired knowledge, could not spare time to qualify himself for removing my difficulties, and left me to deal with them, with little other aid than that of books: while I was continually incurring his displeasure by my inability to solve difficult problems for which he did not see that I had not the necessary previous knowledge.

As to my private reading, I can only speak of what I remember. History continued to be my strongest predilection, and most of all ancient history. Mitford's Greece I read continually. Roman history, both in my old favorite, Hooke, and in Ferguson, continued to delight me. A book which, in spite of what is called the dryness of its style, I took great pleasure in, was the Ancient Universal History, through the incessant reading of which, I had my head full of historical details concerning the obscurest ancient people, while about modern history, except detached passages, such as the Dutch War of Independence, I knew and cared comparatively little. A voluntary exercise, to which throughout my boyhood I was much addicted, was what I called writing histories. I successively composed a Roman History, picked out of Hooke; an Abridgment of the Ancient Universal History; a History of Holland, from my favorite Watson and from an anonymous compilation; and in my eleventh and twelfth year I occupied myself with writing what I flattered myself was something serious. This was no less than a History of the Roman Government, compiled (with the assistance of Hooke) from Livy and Dionysius: of which I wrote as much as would have made an octavo volume, extending to the epoch of the Licinian Laws. It was, in fact, an account of the struggles between the patricians and plebeians, which now engrossed all the interest in my mind which I had previously felt in the mere wars and conquests of the Romans. I discussed all the constitutional points as they arose: though quite ignorant of Niebuhr's researches, I, by such lights as my father had given me, vindicated the Agrarian Laws on the evidence of Livy, and upheld, to the best of my ability, the Roman Democratic party. A few years later, in my contempt of my childish efforts, I destroyed all these papers, not then anticipating that I could ever feel any curiosity about my first attempts at writing and reasoning. My father encouraged me in this useful amusement, though, as I think judiciously, he never asked to see what I wrote; so that I did not feel that in writing it I was accountable to any one, nor had the chilling sensation of being under a critical eye.

But though these exercises in history were never a compulsory lesson, there was another kind of composition which was so, namely, writing verses, and it was one of the most disagreeable of my tasks. Greek and Latin verses I did not write, nor learned the prosody of those languages. My father, thinking this not worth the time it required, contented himself with making me read aloud to him, and correcting false quantities. The verses I was required to write were English. When I first read Pope's Homer, I ambitiously attempted to compose something of the same kind, and achieved as much as one book of a continuation of the Iliad. I had read, up to this time, very little English poetry. Shakespeare my father had put into my hands, chiefly for the sake of the historical plays, from which, however, I went on to the others. My father never was a great admirer of Shakespeare, the English idolatry of whom he used to attack with some severity. He cared little for any English poetry except Milton (for whom he had the highest admiration), Goldsmith, Burns, and Gray's Bard, which he preferred to his Elegy: perhaps I may add Cowper and Beattie. He had some value for Spenser, and I remember his reading to me (unlike his usual practice of making me read to him), the first book of the Faerie Queene; but I took little pleasure in it. The poetry of the present century he saw scarcely any merit in, and I hardly became acquainted with any of it till I was grown up to manhood, except the metrical romances of Walter Scott, which I read at his recommendation and was intensely delighted with; as I always was with animated narrative. Dryden's Poems were among my father's books, and many of these he made me read, but I never cared for any of them except Alexander's Feast, which, as well as many of the songs in Walter Scott, I used to sing internally, to a music of my own: to some of the latter, indeed, I went so far as to compose airs, which I still remember. Cowper's short poems I read with some pleasure, but never got far into the longer ones; and nothing in the two volumes interested me like the prose account of his three hares. In my thirteenth year I met with Campbell's poems, among which Lochiel, Hohenlinden, The Exile of Erin, and some others, gave me sensations I had never before experienced from poetry. Here, too, I made nothing of the longer poems, except the striking opening of Gertrude of Wyoming, which long kept its place in my feelings as the perfection of pathos.

From about the age of twelve, I entered into another and more advanced stage in my course of instruction; in which the main object was no longer the aids and appliances of thought, but the thoughts themselves. This commenced with Logic, in which I began at once with the Organon, and read it to the Analytics inclusive, but profited little by the Posterior Analytics, which belong to a branch of speculation I was not yet ripe for. Contemporaneously with the Organon, my father made me read the whole or parts of several of the Latin treatises on the scholastic logic; giving each day to him, in our walks, a minute account of what I had read, and answering his numerous and searching questions. My own consciousness and experience ultimately led me to appreciate quite as highly as he did, the value of an early practical familiarity with the school logic. I know of nothing, in my education, to which I think myself more indebted for whatever capacity of thinking I have attained. The first intellectual operation in which I arrived at any proficiency, was dissecting a bad argument, and finding in what part the fallacy lay: and though whatever capacity of this sort I attained, was due to the fact that it was an intellectual exercise in which I was most perseveringly drilled by my father, yet it is also true that the school logic, and the mental habits acquired in studying it, were among the principal instruments of this drilling.

During this time, the Latin and Greek books which I continned to read with my father were chiefly such as were worth studying, not for the language merely, but also for the thoughts. This included much of the orators, and especially Demosthenes, some of whose principal orations I read several times over, and wrote out, by way of exercise, a full analysis of them. My father's comments on these orations when I read them to him were very instructive to me. He not only drew my attention to the insight they afforded into Athenian institutions, and the principles of legislation and government which they often illustrated, but pointed out the skill and art of the orator—how everything important to his purpose was said at the exact moment when he had brought the minds of his audience into the state most fitted to receive it; how he made steal into their minds, gradually and by insinuation, thoughts which, if expressed in a more direct manner would have roused their opposition. At this time I also read the whole of Tacitus, Juvenal, and Quintilian. The latter, owing to his obscure style and to the scholastic details of which many parts of his treatise are made up, is little read, and seldom sufficiently appreciated. His book is a kind of encyclopædia of the thoughts of the ancients on the whole field of education and culture; and I have retained through life many valuable ideas which I can distinctly trace to my reading of him, even at that early age. It was at this period that I read, for the first time, some of the most important dialogues of Plato, in particular the Gorgias, the Protagoras, and the

Republic. There is no author to whom my father thought himself more indebted for his own mental culture, than Plato, or whom he more frequently recommended to young students. I can bear similar testimony in regard to myself. I have felt ever since that the title of Platonist belongs by far better right to those who have been nourished in, and have endeavored to practice Plato's mode of investigation, than to those who are distinguished only by the adoption of certain dogmatical conclusions, drawn mostly from the least intelligible of his works, and which the character of his mind and writings makes it uncertain whether he himself regarded as anything more than poetic fancies, or philosophic conjectures.

In going through Plato and Demosthenes, since I could now read these authors, as far as the language was concerned, with perfect ease, I was not required to construe them sentence by sentence, but to read them aloud to my father, answering questions when asked: but the particular attention which he paid to elocution (in which his own excellence was remarkable) made this reading aloud to him a most painful task. Of all things which he required me to do, there was none which I did so constantly ill, or in which he so perpetually lost his temper with me. It was at a much later period of my youth, when practicing elocution by myself, or with companions of my own age, that I for the first time understood the object of his rules, and saw the psychological grounds of them.

A book which contributed largely to my education, in the best sense of the term, was my father's History of India. It was published in the beginning of 1818. During the year previous, while it was passing through the press, I used to read the proof sheets to him; or rather, I read the manuscript to him while he corrected the proofs. The number of new ideas which I received from this remarkable book, and the impulse and stimulus as well as guidance given to my thoughts by its criticisms and disquisitions on society and civilization in the Hindoo part, on institutions and the acts of governments in the English part, made my early familiarity with it eminently useful to my subsequent progress. And though I can perceive deficiencies in it now as compared with a perfect standard, I still think it, if not the most, one of the most instructive histories ever written, and one of the books from which most benefit may be derived by a mind in the course of making up its opinions.

On learning, in the spring of 1819, about a year after the publication of the History, that the East India Directors desired to strengthen the part of their home establishment which was employed in carrying on the correspondence with India, my father declared himself a candidate for that employment, and, to the credit of the Directors, successfully.

This new employment of his time caused no relaxation in his attention to my education. It was in this same year, 1819, that he took me through a complete course of political economy. His loved and intimate friend, Ricardo, had shortly before published the book which formed so great an epoch in political economy: a book which never would have been published or written, but for the entreaty and strong encouragement of my father. The same friendly encouragement induced Ricardo, a year or two later, to become a member of the House of Commons; where, during the few remaining years of his life, unhappily cut short in the full vigor of his intellect, he rendered so much service to his and my father's opinions both on political economy and on other subjects.

Though Ricardo's great work was already in print, no didactic treatise embodying its doctrines, in a manner fit for learners, had yet appeared. My father, therefore, commenced instructing me in the science by a sort of lectures, which he delivered to me in our walks. He expounded each day a portion of the subject, and I gave him next day a written account of it, which he made me rewrite over and over again until it was clear, precise, and tolerably complete.

The path was a thorny one, even to him, and I am sure it was so to me, notwithstanding the strong interest I took in the subject. He was often, and much beyond reason, provoked by my failures in cases where success could not have been expected; but in the main his method was right, and it succeeded. I do not believe that any scientific teaching ever was more thorough, or better fitted for training the faculties, than the mode in which logic and political economy were taught to me by my father.

At this point concluded what can properly be called my

lessons: when I was about fourteen I left England for more than a year; and after my return, though my studies went on under my father's general direction, he was no longer my schoolmaster. I shall therefore pause here, and turn back to matters of a more general nature connected with the part of my life and education included in the preceding reminiscences.

In the course of instruction which I have partially retraced, the point most superficially apparent is the great effort to give, during the years of childhood an amount of knowledge in what are considered the higher branches of education, which is seldom acquired (if acquired at all) until the age of manhood. The result of the experiment shows the ease with which this may be done, and places in a strong light the wretched waste of so many precious years as are spent in acquiring the modicum of Latin and Greek commonly taught to schoolboys; a waste which has led so many educational reformers to entertain the ill-judged proposal of discarding these languages altogether from general education. If I had been by nature extremely quick of apprehension, or had possessed a very accurate and retentive memory, or were of a remarkably active and energetic character, the trial would not be conclusive; but in all these natural gifts I am rather below than above par; what I could do, could assuredly be done by any boy or girl of average capacity and healthy physical constitution: and if I have accomplished anything, I owe it, among other fortunate circumstances, to the fact that through the early training bestowed on me by my father, I started, I may fairly say, with an advantage of a quarter of a century over my contemporaries.

There was one cardinal point in this training, of which I have already given some indication, and which, more than anything else, was the cause of whatever good it effected. Most boys or youths who have had much knowledge drilled into them, have their mental capacities not strengthened, but overlaid by it. They are crammed with mere facts, and with the opinions or phrases of other people, and these are accepted as a substitute for the power to form opinions of their own: and thus the sons of eminent fathers, who have spared no pains in their education, so often grow up mere parroters of what they have learned, incapable of using their minds except in the furrows traced for them. Mine, however, was not an education of cram. My father never permitted anything which I learned to degenerate into a mere exercise of memory. He strove to make the understanding not only go along with every step of the teaching, but, if possible, precede it. Anything which could be found out by thinking I never was told, until I had exhausted my efforts to find it out for myself. As far as I can trust my remembrance, I acquitted myself very lamely in this department; my recollection of such matters is almost wholly of failures, hardly ever of success. It is true the failures were often in things in which success in so early a stage of my progress, was almost impossible. I remember at some time in my thirteenth year, on my happening to use the word idea, he asked me what an idea was; and expressed some displeasure at my ineffectual efforts to define the word: I recollect also his indignation at my using the common expression that something was true in theory but required correction in practice; and how, after making me vainly strive to define the word theory, he explained its meaning, and showed the fallacy of the vulgar form of speech which I had used; leaving me fully persuaded that in being unable to give a correct definition of Theory, and in speaking of it as something which might be at variance with practice, I had shown unparalleled ignorance. In this he seems, and perhaps was, very unreasonable; but I think, only in being angry at my failure. A pupil from whom nothing is ever demanded which he cannot do, never does all he can.

One of the evils most liable to attend on any sort of early proficiency, and which often fatally blights its promise, my father most anxiously guarded against. This was self-conceit. He kept me, with extreme vigilance, out of the way of hearing myself praised, or of being led to make self-flattering comparisons between myself and others. From his own intercourse with me I could derive none but a very humble opinion of myself; and the standard of comparison he always held up to me, was not what other people did, but what a man could and ought to do. He completely succeeded in preserving me from the sort of influences he so much dreaded. I was not at all aware that my attainments were anything unusual at my age. If I accidentally had my attention drawn to the fact that some other boy knew less than myself—which happened less often than might be imagined—I concluded, not that I knew much, but that he, for some reason or other, knew little, or that his knowledge was of a different kind from mine. My state of mind was not humility, but neither was it arrogance. I never thought of saying to myself, I am, or I can do, so and so. I neither estimated myself highly nor lowly: I did not estimate myself at all. If I thought anything about myself, it was that I was rather backward in my studies, since I always found myself so, in comparison with what my father expected from me. I assert this with confidence, though it was not the impression of various persons who saw me in my childhood. They, as I have since found, thought me greatly and disagreeably self-conceited; probably because I was disputatious, and did not scruple to give direct contradictions to things which I heard said. I suppose I acquired this bad habit from having been encouraged in an unusual degree to talk on matters beyond my age, and with grown persons, while I never had inculcated on me the usual respect for them. My father did not correct this ill-breeding and impertinence, probably from not being aware of it, for I was always too much in awe of him to be otherwise than extremely subdued and quiet in his presence. Yet with all this I had no notion of any superiority in myself; and well was it for me that I had not. I remember the very place in Hyde Park where, in my fourteenth year, on the eve of leaving my father's house for a long absence, he told me that I should find, as I got acquainted with new people, that I had been taught many things which youths of my age did not commonly know; and that many persons would be disposed to talk to me of this, and to compliment me upon it. What other things he said on this topic I remember very imperfectly; but he wound up by saying, that whatever I knew more than others, could not be ascribed to any merit in me, but to the very unusual advantage which had fallen to my lot, of having a father who was able to teach me, and willing to give the necessary trouble and time; that it was no matter of praise to me, if I knew more than those who had not had a similar advantage, but the deepest disgrace to me if I did not. I have a distinct remembrance, that the suggestion thus for the first time made to me, that I knew more than other youths who were considered well educated, was to me a piece of information, to which, as to all other things which my father told me, I gave implicit credence, but which did not at all impress me as a personal matter. I felt no disposition to glorify myself upon the circumstance that there were other persons who did not know what I knew; nor had I ever flattered myself that my acquirements, whatever they might be, were any merit of mine: but, now when my attention was called to the subject, I felt that what my father had said respecting my peculiar advantages was exactly the truth and common sense of the matter, and it fixed my opinion and feeling from that time forward.

It is evident that this, among many other of the purposes of my father's scheme of education, could not have been accomplished if he had not carefully kept me from having any great amount of intercourse with other boys. He was earnestly bent upon my escaping not only the corrupting influence which boys exercise over boys, but the contagion of vulgar modes of thought and feeling; and for this he was willing that I should pay the price of inferiority in the accomplishments which schoolboys in all countries chiefly cultivate. The deficiencies in my education were principally in the things which boys learn from being turned out to shift for themselves, and from being brought together in large numbers. From temperance and much walking, I grew up healthy and hardy, though not muscular; but I could do no feats of skill or physical strength, and knew none of the ordinary bodily exercises. It was not that play, or time for it, was refused me. Though no holidays were allowed, lest the habit of work should be broken, and a taste for idleness acquired, I had ample leisure in every day to amuse myself; but as I had no boy companions, and the animal need of physical activity was satisfied by walking, my amusements, which were mostly solitary, were in general, of a quiet, if not a bookish turn, and gave little stimulus to any other kind even of mental activity than that which was already called forth by my studies: I consequently remained long, and in a less degree have always remained, inexpert in anything requiring manual dexterity; my mind, as well as my hands, did its work very lamely when it was applied, or ought to have been applied, to the practical details which, as they are the chief interest of life to the majority of men, are also the things in which whatever mental capacity they have, chiefly shows itself.

I was constantly meriting reproof by my inattention, inobservance, and general slackness of mind in matters of daily life. My father was the extreme opposite in these particulars: his senses and mental faculties were always on the alert; he carried decision and energy of character in his whole manner and into every action of life: and this, as much as his talents, contributed to the strong impression which he always made upon those with whom he came into personal contact. But the children of energetic parents, frequently grow up unenergetic, because they lean on their parents, and the parents are energetic for them. The education which my father gave me, was in itself much more fitted for training me to *know* than to *do*. Not that he was unaware of my deficiencies; both as a boy and as a youth I was incessantly smarting under his severe admonitions on the subject. There was anything but insensibility or tolerance on his part towards such shortcomings: but, while he saved me from the demoralizing effects of school life, he made no effort to provide me with any sufficient substitute for its practicalizing influences. Whatever qualities he himself, probably, had acquired without difficulty or special training, he seems to have supposed that I ought to acquire as easily. He had not, I think, bestowed the same amount of thought and attention on this, as on most other branches of education; and here, as well in some other points of my tuition, he seems to have expected effects without causes.

CHAPTER II

MORAL INFLUENCES IN EARLY YOUTH. MY FATHER'S CHARACTER AND OPINIONS

IN my education, as in that of every one, the moral influences, which are so much more important than all others, are also the most complicated, and the most difficult to specify with any approach to completeness. Without attempting the hopeless task of detailing the circumstances by which, in this respect, my early character may have been shaped, I shall confine myself to a few leading points, which form an indispensable part of any true account of my education.

I was brought up from the first without any religious belief, in the ordinary acceptation of the term. My father, educated in the creed of Scotch Presbyterianism, had by his own studies and reflections been early led to reject not only the belief in Revelation, but the foundations of what is commonly called Natural Religion. I have heard him say, that the turning point of his mind on the subject was reading Butler's Analogy. That work, of which he always continued to speak with respect, kept him, as he said, for some considerable time, a believer in the divine authority of Christianity; by proving to him, that whatever are the difficulties in believing that the Old and New Testaments proceed from, or record the acts of, a perfectly wise and good being, the same and still greater difficulties stand in the way of the belief, that a being of such a character can have been the Maker of the universe. He considered Butler's argument as conclusive against the only opponents for whom it was intended. Those who admit an omnipotent as well as perfectly just and benevolent maker and ruler of such a world as this, can say little against Christianity but what can, with at least equal force, be retorted against themselves. Finding, therefore, no halting place in Deism, he remained in a state of perplexity, until, doubtless after many struggles, he yielded to the conviction, that, concerning the origin of things nothing whatever can be known. This is the only correct statement of his opinion; for dogmatic atheism he looked upon as absurd; as most of those, whom the world has considered Atheists, have always done. These particulars are important, because they show that my father's rejection of all that is called religious belief, was not, as many might suppose, primarily a matter of logic and evidence: the grounds of it were moral, still more than intellectual.

I am thus one of the very few examples, in this country, of one who has, not thrown off religious belief, but never had it: I grew up in a negative state with regard to it. I looked upon the modern exactly as I did upon the ancient religion, as something which in no way concerned me. It did not seem to me more strange that English people should believe what I did not, than that the men I read of in Herodotus should have done so. History had made the variety of opinions among mankind a fact familiar to me, and this was but a prolongation of that fact. This point in my early education had, however, incidentally one bad consequence deserving notice. In giving me an opinion contrary to that of the world, my father thought it necessary to give it as one which could not prudently be avowed to the world. This lesson of keeping my thoughts to myself, at that early age, was attended with some moral disadvantages; though my limited intercourse with strangers, especially such as were likely to speak to me on religion, prevented me from being placed in the alternative of avowal or hypocrisy. I remember two occasions in my boyhood, on which I felt myself in this alternative, and in both cases I avowed my disbelief and defended it. My opponents were boys, considerably older than myself: one of them I certainly staggered at the time, but the subject was never renewed between us: the other who was surprised and somewhat shocked, did his best to convince me for some time, without effect.

My father's moral convictions, wholly dissevered from religion, were very much of the character of those of the Greek philosophers; and were delivered with the force and decision which characterized all that came from him. Even at the very early age at which I read with him the Memorabilia of Xenophon, I imbibed from that work and from his comments a deep respect for the character of Socrates; who stood in my mind as a model of ideal excellence: and I well remember how my father at that time impressed upon me the lesson of the "Choice of Hercules." At a somewhat later period the lofty moral standard exhibited in the writings of Plato operated upon me with great force.

But though direct moral teaching does much, indirect does more; and the effect my father produced on my character, did not depend solely on what he said or did with that direct object, but also, and still more, on what manner of man he was.

It will be admitted, that a man of the opinions, and the character, above described, was likely to leave a strong moral impression on any mind principally formed by him, and that his moral teaching was not likely to err on the side of laxity or indulgence. The element which was chiefly deficient in his moral relation to his children was that of tenderness. I do not believe that this deficiency lay in his own nature. I believe him to have had much more feeling than he habitually showed, and much greater capacities of feeling than were ever developed. He resembled most Englishmen in being ashamed of the signs of feeling, and by the absence of demonstration, starving the feelings themselves. If we consider further that he was in the trying position of sole teacher, and add to this that his temper was constitutionally irritable, it is impossible not to feel true pity for a father who did, and strove to do, so much for his children, who would have so valued their affection, yet who must have been constantly feeling that fear of him was drying it up at its source. This was no longer the case later in life, and with his younger children. They loved him tenderly: and if I cannot say so much of myself, I was always loyally devoted to him. As regards my own education, I hesitate to pronounce whether I was more a loser or gainer by his severity. It was not such as to prevent me from having a happy childhood. And I do not believe that boys can be induced to apply themselves with vigor, and what is so much more difficult, perseverance, to dry and irksome studies, by the sole force of persuasion and soft words.

During this first period of my life, the habitual frequenters of my father's house were limited to a very few persons, most of them little known to the world, but whom personal worth, and more or less of congeniality with at least his political opinions (not so frequently to be met with then as since) inclined him to cultivate; and his conversations with them I listened to with interest and instruction. My being an habitual inmate of my father's study made me acquainted with the dearest of his friends, David Ricardo, who by his benevolent countenance, and kindliness of manner, was very attractive to young persons, and who after I became a student of political economy, invited me to his house and to walk with him in order to converse on the subject. I was a more frequent visitor (from about 1817 or 1818) to Mr. Hume, who, born in the same part of Scotland as my father, and having been, I rather think, a younger schoolfellow or college companion of his, had on returning from India renewed their youthful acquaintance, and who coming like many others greatly under the influence of my father's intellect and energy of character, was induced partly by that influence to go into Parliament, and there adopt the line of conduct which has given him an honorable place in the history of his country. Of Mr. Bentham I saw much more, owing to the close intimacy which existed between him and my father. In 1813 Mr. Bentham, my father, and I made an excursion, which included Oxford, Bath and Bristol, Exeter, Plymouth, and Portsmouth. In this journey I saw many things which were instructive to me, and acquired my first taste for natural scenery, in the elementary form of fondness for a "view."

I owed another of the fortunate circumstances in my education, a year's residence in France, to Mr. Bentham's brother, General Sir Samuel Bentham. I had seen Sir Samuel Bentham and his family at their house near Gosport in the course of the tour already mentioned (he being then Superintendent of the Dockyard at Portsmouth), and during a stay of a few days which they made at Ford Abbey shortly after the peace, before going to live on the Continent. In 1820 they invited me for a six months' visit to them in the South of France, which their kindness ultimately prolonged to nearly a twelvemonth. Sir Samuel Bentham, though of a character of mind different from that of his illustrious brother, was a man of very considerable attainments and general powers, with a decided genius for mechanical art. His wife, a daughter of the celebrated chemist, Dr. Fordyce, was a woman of strong will and decided character, much general knowledge, and great practical good sense of the Edgeworth kind: she was the ruling spirit of the household, as she deserved, and was well qualified, to be. Their family consisted of one son (the eminent botanist) and three daughters, the youngest about two years my senior. I am indebted to them for much and various instruction, and for an almost parental interest in my welfare. When I first joined them, in May, 1820, they occupied the Château of Pompignan (still belonging to a descendant of Voltaire's enemy) on the heights overlooking the plain of the Garonne between Montauban and Toulouse. I accompanied them in an excursion to the Pyrenees, including a stay of some duration at Bagnères de Bigorre, a journey to Pau, Bayonne, and Bagnères de Luchon, and an ascent of the Pic du Midi de Bigorre. This first introduction to the highest order of mountain scenery made the deepest impression on me, and gave a color to my tastes through life. During this residence in France I acquired a familiar knowledge of the French language, and acquaintance with the ordinary French literature; I took lessons in various bodily exercises, in none of which, however, I made any proficiency; and at Montpellier I attended the excellent winter courses of lectures at the Faculté des Sciences, those of M. Anglada on chemistry, of M. Provençal on zoölogy, and of a very accomplished representative of the eighteenth century metaphysics, M. Gergonne, on logic, under the name of Philosophy of the Sciences. I also went through a course of the higher mathematics under the private tuition of M. Lenthéric, a professor at the Lycée of Montpellier. But the greatest, perhaps, of the many advantages which I owed to this episode in my education, was that of having breathed for a whole year, the free and genial atmosphere of Continental life.

In my way through Paris, both going and returning, I passed some time in the house M. Say, the eminent political economist, who was a friend and correspondent of my father, having become acquainted with him on a visit to England a year or two after the peace. He was a man of the later period of the French Revolution, a fine specimen of the best kind of French Republican, one of those who had never bent the knee to Bonaparte though courted by him to do so; a truly upright, brave, and enlightened man. He lived a quiet and studious life, made happy by warm affections, public and private. He was acquainted with many of the chiefs of the Liberal party, and I saw various noteworthy persons while staying at his house; among whom I have pleasure in the recollection of having once seen Saint-Simon, not yet the founder either of a philosophy or a religion, and considered only as a clever *original*. The chief fruit which I carried away from the society I saw, was a strong and permanent interest in Continental Liberalism, of which I ever afterwards kept myself *au courant*, as much as of English politics: a thing not at all usual in those days with Englishmen, and which had a very salutary influence on my development, keeping me free from the error always prevalent in England, and from which even my father with all his superiority to prejudice was not exempt, of judging universal questions by a merely English standard. After passing a few weeks at Caen with an old friend of my father's, I returned to England in July, 1821, and my education resumed its ordinary course.

CHAPTER III

LAST STAGE OF EDUCATION, AND FIRST OF SELF-EDUCATION

FOR the first year or two after my visit to France, I continued my old studies, with the addition of some new ones. When I returned, my father was just finishing for the press his Elements of Political Economy, and he made me perform an exercise on the manuscript, which Mr. Bentham practiced on all his own writings, making what he called "marginal contents"; a short abstract of every paragraph, to enable the writer more easily to judge of, and improve, the order of the ideas, and the general character of the exposition. I am not sure whether it was in this winter or the next that I first read a history of the French Revolution. I learnt with astonishment that the principles of democracy, then apparently in so insignificant and hopeless a minority everywhere in Europe, had borne all before them in France thirty years earlier, and had been the creed of the nation. As may be supposed from this, I had previously a very vague idea of that great commotion. I knew only that the French had thrown off the absolute monarchy of Louis XIV. and XV., had put the King and Queen to death, guillotined many persons, one of whom was Lavoisier, and had ultimately fallen under the despotism of Bonaparte. From this time, as was natural, the subject took an immense hold of my feelings. It allied itself with all my juvenile aspirations to the character of a democratic champion. What had happened so lately, seemed as if it might easily happen again: and the most transcendent glory I was capable of conceiving, was that of figuring, successful or unsuccessful, as a Girondist in an English Convention.

During the winter of 1821-2, Mr. John Austin, with whom at the time of my visit to France my father had but lately become acquainted, kindly allowed me to read Roman law with him. My father, notwithstanding his abhorrence of the chaos of barbarism called English Law, had turned his thoughts towards the bar as on the whole less ineligible for me than any other profession: and these readings with Mr. Austin, who had made Bentham's best ideas his own, and added much to them from other sources and from his own mind, were not only a valuable introduction to legal studies, but an important portion of general education. It was at the commencement of these studies that my father, as a needful accompaniment to them, put into my hands Bentham's principal speculations, as interpreted to the Continent, and indeed to all the world, by Dumont, in the Traité de Législation. The reading of this book was an epoch in my life; one of the turning points in my mental history.

After this I read, from time to time, the most important of the other works of Bentham which had then seen the light, either as written by himself or as edited by Dumont. This was my private reading: while, under my father's direction, my studies were carried into the higher branches of analytic psychology. I now read Locke's Essay, and wrote out an account of it, consisting of a complete abstract of every chapter, with such remarks as occurred to me, which was read by, or (I think) to, my father, and discussed throughout. I performed the same process with Helvetius de l'Esprit, which I read of my own choice. This preparation of abstracts, subject to my father's censorship, was of great service to me, by compelling precision in conceiving and expressing psychological doctrines, whether accepted as truths or only regarded as the opinion of others. After Helvetius, my father made me study what he deemed the real master-production in the philosophy of mind, Hartley's Observations on Man. The other principal English writers on mental philosophy I read as I felt inclined, particularly Berkeley, Hume's Essays, Reid, Dugald Stewart and Brown on Cause and Effect.

I have now, I believe, mentioned all the books which ·had any considerable effect on my early mental development. From this point I began to carry on my intellectual cultivation by writing still more than by reading. In the summer of 1822 I wrote my first argumentative essay. I remember very little about it, except that it was an attack on what I regarded as the aristocratic prejudice, that the rich were, or were likely to be, superior in moral qualities to the poor. My performance was entirely argumentative, without any of the declamation which the subject would admit of, and might be expected to suggest to a young writer. In that department, however, I was, and remained, very inapt. Dry argument was the only thing I could manage, or willingly attempted; though passively I was very susceptible to the effect of all composition, whether in the form of poetry or oratory, which appealed to the feelings on any basis of reason. My father, who knew nothing of this essay until it was finished, was well satisfied, and as I learnt from others, even pleased with it; but, perhaps from a desire to promote the exercise of other mental faculties than the purely logical, he advised me to make my next exercise in composition one of the oratorical kind: on which suggestion, availing myself of my familiarity with Greek history and ideas and with the Athenian orators, I wrote two speeches, one an accusation, the other a defense of Pericles, on a supposed impeachment for not marching out to fight the Lacedæmonians on their invasion of Attica. After this I continued to write papers on subjects often very much beyond my capacity, but with great benefit both from the exercise itself, and from the discussions which it led to with my father.

I had now also begun to converse, on general subjects, with the instructed men with whom I came in contact: and the opportunities of such contact naturally became more numerous. The two friends of my father from whom I derived most, and with whom I most associated, were Mr. Grote and Mr. John Austin. The acquaintance of both with my father was recent, but had ripened rapidly into intimacy. Mr. Grote was introduced to my father by Mr. Ricardo, I think in 1819 (being then about twenty-five years old), and sought assiduously his society and conversation.

Mr. Austin, who was four or five years older than Mr. Grote, was the eldest son of a retired miller in Suffolk, who had made money by contracts during the war, and who must have been a man of remarkable qualities, as I infer from the fact that all his sons were of more than common ability and all eminently gentlemen. The one with whom we are now concerned, and whose writings on jurisprudence have made him celebrated, was for some time in the army, and served in Sicily under Lord William Bentinck. After the peace he sold his commission and studied for the bar, to which he had been called for some time before my father knew him. He was not, like Mr. Grote, to any extent, a pupil of my father, but he had attained, by reading and thought, a considerable number of the same opinions, modified by his own very decided individuality of character. On me his influence was most salutary. It was moral in the best sense. He took a sincere and kind interest in me, far beyond what could have been expected towards a mere youth from a man of his age, standing, and what seemed austerity of character. There was in his conversation and demeanor a tone of highmindedness which did not show itself so much, if the quality existed as much, in any of the other persons with whom at that time I associated.

His younger brother, Charles Austin, of whom at this time and for the next year or two I saw much, had also a great effect on me, though of a very different description. He was but a few years older than myself, and had then just left the University, where he had shone with great *éclat* as a man of intellect and a brilliant orator and converser. Through him I became acquainted with Macaulay, Hyde and Charles Villiers, Strutt (now Lord Belper), Romilly (now Lord Romilly and Master of the Rolls), and various others who subsequently figured in literature or politics, and among whom I heard discussions on many topics, as yet to a certain degree new to me. The influence of Charles Austin over me differed from that of the persons I have hitherto mentioned, in being not the influence of a man over a boy, but that of an elder contemporary. It was through him that I first felt myself, not a pupil under teachers, but a man among men.

. It was in the winter of 1822-3 that I formed the plan of a little society, to be composed of young men agreeing in fundamental principles—acknowledging Utility as their standard in ethics and politics, and a certain number of the principal corollaries drawn from it in the philosophy I had accepted—and meeting once a fortnight to read essays and discuss questions conformably to the premises thus agreed on. The fact would hardly be worth mentioning, but for the circumstance, that the name I gave to the society I had planned was the Utilitarian Society. It was the first time that any one had taken the title of Utilitarian; and the term made its way into the language, from this humble source. I did not invent the word, but found it in one of Galt's novels, the "Annals of the Parish," in which the Scotch clergyman, of whom the book is a supposed autobiography, is represented as warning his parishioners not to leave the Gospel and become utilitarians. With a boy's fondness for a name and a banner I seized on the word, and for some years called myself and others by it as a sectarian appellation; and it came to be occasionally used by some others holding the opinions which it was intended to designate. The Society so called consisted at first of no more than three members, one of whom, being Mr. Bentham's amanuensis, obtained for us permission to hold our meetings in his house. The number never, I think, reached ten, and the society was broken up in 1826. It had thus an existence of about three years and a half. The chief effect of it as regards myself, over and above the benefit of practice in oral discussion, was that of bringing me in contact with several young men at that time less advanced than myself, among whom, as they professed the same opinions, I was for some time a sort of leader, and had considerable influence on their mental progress.

In May, 1823, my professional occupation and status for the next thirty-five years of my life were decided by my father's obtaining for me an appointment from the East

India Company, in the office of the Examiner of India Correspondence, immediately under himself. I was appointed in the usual manner, at the bottom of the list of clerks, to rise, at least in the first instance, by seniority; but with the understanding that I should be employed from the beginning in preparing drafts of dispatches, and be thus trained up as a successor to those who then filled the higher departments of the office. My drafts of course required, for some time, much revision from my immediate superiors, but I soon became well acquainted with the business, and by my father's instructions and the general growth of my own powers, I was in a few years qualified to be, and practically was, the chief conductor of the correspondence with India in one of the leading departments, that of the Native States. This continued to be my official duty until I was appointed Examiner, only two years before the time when the abolition of the East India Company as a political body determined my retirement. ·I do not know any one of the occupations by which a subsistence can now be gained, more suitable than such as this to any one who, not being in independent circumstances, desires to devote a part of the twenty-four hours to private intellectual pursuits. Those who have to support themselves by their pen must depend on literary drudgery, or at best on writings addressed to the multitude; and can employ in the pursuits of their own choice only such time as they can spare from those of necessity; which is generally less than the leisure allowed by office occupations, while the effect on the mind is far more enervating and fatiguing. For my own part, I have, through life, found office duties an actual rest from the other mental occupations which I have carried on simultaneously with them. I cared little for the loss of the chances of riches and honors held out by some of the professions, particularly the bar, which had been, as I have already said, the profession thought of for me. But I was not indifferent to exclusion from Parliament, and public life: and I felt very sensibly the more immediate unpleasantness of confinement to London; the holiday allowed by India-House practice not exceeding a month in the year, while my taste was strong for a country life, and my sojourn in France had left behind it an ardent desire of traveling. But though these tastes could not be freely indulged, they were at no time entirely sacrificed. I passed most Sundays, throughout the year, in the country, taking long rural walks on that day even when residing in London. The month's holiday was, for a few years, passed at my father's house in the country: afterwards a part or the whole was spent in tours, chiefly pedestrian, with some one or more of the young men who were my chosen companions; and, at a later period, in longer journeys or excursions, alone or with other friends. France, Belgium, and Rhenish Germany were within easy reach of the annual holiday: and two longer absences, one of three, the other of six months, under medical advice, added Switzerland, the Tyrol, and Italy to my list. Fortunately, also, both these journeys occurred rather early, so as to give the benefit and charm of the remembrance to a large portion of life.

CHAPTER IV

YOUTHFUL PROPAGANDISM. THE WESTMINSTER REVIEW

THE occupation of so much of my time by office work did not relax my attention to my own pursuits, which were never carried on more vigorously. It was about this time that I began to write in newspapers. The first writings of mine which got into print were two letters published towards the end of 1822, in the Traveller evening newspaper. I soon after attempted something considerably more ambitious. The prosecutions of Richard Carlile and his wife and sister for publications hostile to Christianity were then exciting much attention, and nowhere more than among the people I frequented. Freedom of discussion even in politics, much more in religion, was at that time far from being, even in theory, the conceded point which it at least seems to be now; and the holders of obnoxious opinions had to be always ready to argue and re-argue for the liberty of expressing them. I wrote a series of five letters, under the signature of Wickliffe, going over the whole length and breadth of the question of free publication of all opinions on religion, and offered them to the Morning Chronicle. Three of them were published in January and February, 1823; the other two, con-

taining things too outspoken for that journal, never appeared
at all.   But a paper which I wrote soon after on the same
subject, *à propos* of a debate in the House of Commons, was
inserted as a leading article; and during the whole of this
year, 1823, a considerable number of my contributions were
printed in the Chronicle and Traveller: sometimes notices
of books but oftener letters, commenting on some nonsense
talk in Parliament, or some defect of the law, or misdoings
of the magistracy or the courts of justice.   In this last
department the Chronicle was now rendering signal service.
After the death of Mr. Perry, the editorship and management of the paper had devolved on Mr. John Black.   Black
was a frequent visitor of my father, and Mr. Grote used
to say that he always knew by the Monday morning's article,
whether Black had been with my father on the Sunday.

Contrary to what may have been supposed, my father was
in no degree a party to setting up the Westminster Review.
The need of a Radical organ to make head against the Edinburgh and Quarterly (then in the period of their greatest
reputation and influence), had been a topic of conversation
between him and Mr. Bentham many years earlier, and it
had been a part of their *Château en Espagne* that my father
should be the editor; but the idea had never assumed any
practical shape.   In 1823, however, Mr. Bentham determined
to establish the Review at his own cost, and offered the editorship to my father, who declined it as incompatible with his
India House appointment.   It was then entrusted to Mr.
(now Sir John) Bowring, at that time a merchant in the
City.   Mr. Bowring had been for two or three years previous
an assiduous frequenter of Mr. Bentham, to whom he was
recommended by many personal good qualities, by an ardent
admiration for Bentham, a zealous adoption of many, though
not all of his opinions, and, not least, by an extensive acquaintanceship and correspondence with Liberals of all countries, which seemed to qualify him for being a powerful
agent in spreading Bentham's fame and doctrines through
all quarters of the world.   My father had seen little of
Bowring, but knew enough of him to have formed a strong
opinion, that he was a man of an entirely different type
from what my father considered suitable for conducting a

political and philosophical Review: and he augured so ill of the enterprise that he regretted it altogether, feeling persuaded not only that Mr. Bentham would lose his money, but that discredit would probably be brought upon Radical principles. He could not, however, desert Mr. Bentham, and he consented to write an article for the first number. As it had been a favorite portion of the scheme formerly talked of, that part of the work should be devoted to reviewing the other Reviews, this article of my father's was to be a general criticism of the Edinburgh Review from its commencement. Before writing it he made me read through all the volumes of the Review, or as much of each as seemed of any importance (which was not so arduous a task in 1823 as it would be now), and make notes for him of the articles which I thought he would wish to examine, either on account of their good or their bad qualities. This paper of my father's was the chief cause of the sensation which the Westminster Review produced at its first appearance, and is, both in conception and in execution, one of the most striking of all his writings.

In the meantime the nascent Review had formed a junction with another project, of a purely literary periodical, to be edited by Mr. Henry Southern, afterwards a diplomatist, then a literary man by profession. The two editors agreed to unite their corps, and divide the editorship, Bowring taking the political, Southern the literary department. Southern's Review was to have been published by Longman, and that firm, though part proprietors of the Edinburgh, were willing to be the publishers of the new journal. But when all the arrangements had been made, and the prospectuses sent out, the Longmans saw my father's attack on the Edinburgh, and drew back. My father was now appealed to for his interest with his own publisher, Baldwin, which was exerted with a successful result. And so, in April, 1824, amidst anything but hope on my father's part, and that of most of those who afterwards aided in carrying on the Review, the first number made its appearance.

That number was an agreeable surprise to most of us. The average of the articles was of much better quality than had been expected. The literary and artistic department had rested chiefly on Mr. Bingham, a barrister (subsequently a police magistrate), who had been for some years a frequeuter of Bentham, was a friend of both the Austins, and had adopted with great ardor Mr. Bentham's philosophical opinions. Partly from accident, there were in the first number as many as five articles by Bingham; and we were extremely pleased with them. I well remember the mixed feeling I myself had about the Review; the joy at finding, what we did not at all expect, that it was sufficiently good to be capable of being made a creditable organ of those who held the opinions it professed; and extreme vexation, since it was so good on the whole, at what we thought the blemishes of it. When, however, in addition to our generally favorable opinion of it, we learned that it had an extraordinary large sale for a first number, and found that the appearance of a Radical Review, with pretensions equal to those of the established organs of parties, had excited much attention, there could be no room for hesitation, and we all became eager in doing everything we could to strengthen and improve it.

My father continued to write occasional articles. The Quarterly Review received its exposure, as a sequel to that of the Edinburgh. Of his other contributions, the most important were an attack on Southey's Book of the Church, in the fifth number, and a political article in the twelfth. I was myself the most frequent writer of all, having contributed, from the second number to the eighteenth, thirteen articles; reviews of books on history and political economy, or discussions on special political topics, as corn laws, game laws, law of libel. Occasional articles of merit came in from other acquaintances of my father's, and, in time, of mine; and some of Mr. Bowring's writers turned out well. On the whole, however, the conduct of the Review was never satisfactory to any of the persons strongly interested in its principles, with whom I came in contact. Hardly ever did a number come out without containing several things extremely offensive to us, either in point of opinion, of taste, or by mere want of ability. The unfavorable judgments passed by my father, Grote, the two Austins, and others, were reëchoed with exaggeration by us younger people; and as our youthful zeal rendered us by no means backward in making complaints, we led the two editors a sad life.

Meanwhile, however, the Review made considerable noise in the world, and gave an recognized *status,* in the arena of opinion and discussion, to the Benthamic type of Radicalism, out of all proportion to the number of its adherents, and to the personal merits and abilities, at that time, of most of those who could be reckoned among them.

I conceive that the description so often given of a Benthamite, as a mere reasoning machine, though extremely inapplicable to most of those who have been designated by that title, was during two or three years of my life not altogether untrue of me. It was perhaps as applicable to me as it can well be to any one just entering into life, to whom the common objects of desire must in general have at least the attraction of novelty. There is nothing very extraordinary in this fact: no youth of the age I then was, can be expected to be more than one thing, and this was the thing I happened to be. Ambition and desire of distinction, I had in abundance; and zeal for what I thought the good of mankind was my strongest sentiment, mixing with and coloring all others. But my zeal was as yet little else, at that period of my life, than zeal for speculative opinions. It had not its root in genuine benevolence, or sympathy with mankind; though these qualities held their due place in my ethical standard. Nor was it connected with any high enthusiasm for ideal nobleness. Yet of this feeling I was imaginatively very susceptible; but there was at that time an intermission of its natural aliment, poetical culture, while there was a superabundance of the discipline antagonistic to it, that of mere logic and analysis.

From this neglect both in theory and in practice of the cultivation of feeling, naturally resulted, among other things, an undervaluing of poetry, and of Imagination generally, as an element of human nature. An article of Bingham's in the first number of the Westminster Review, in which he offered as an explanation of something which he disliked in Moore, that "Mr. Moore *is* a poet, and therefore is *not* a reasoner," did a good deal to attach the notion of hating poetry to the writers in the Review. But the truth was that many of us were great readers of poetry; Bingham himself had been a writer of it, while as regards me (and the same thing might be said of my father), the correct statement would be, not that I disliked poetry, but that I was theoretically indifferent to it. I disliked any sentiments in poetry which I should have disliked in prose; and that included a great deal. And I was wholly blind to its place in human culture, as a means of educating the feelings. But I was always personally very susceptible to some kinds of it. In the most sectarian period of my Benthamism, I happened to look into Pope's Essay on Man, and though every opinion in it was contrary to mine, I well remember how powerfully it acted on my imagination.

About the end of 1824, or beginning of 1825, Mr. Bentham, having lately got back his papers on Evidence from M. Dumont (whose Traité des Preuves Judiciaires, grounded on them, was then first completed and published) resolved to have them printed in the original, and bethought himself of me as capable of preparing them for the press; in the same manner as his Book of Fallacies had been recently edited by Bingham. I gladly undertook this task, and it occupied nearly all my leisure for about a year, exclusive of the time afterwards spent in seeing the five large volumes through the press. My name as editor was put to the book after it was printed, at Mr. Bentham's positive desire, which I in vain attempted to persuade him to forego.

This occupation did for me what might seem less to be expected; it gave a great start to my powers of composition. Everything which I wrote subsequently to this editorial employment, was markedly superior to anything that I had written before it.

It was at this time that I learnt German; beginning it on the Hamiltonian method, for which purpose I and several of my companions formed a class. For several years from this period, our social studies assumed a shape which contributed very much to my mental progress. The idea occurred to us of carrying on, by reading and conversation, a joint study of several of the branches of science which we wished to be masters of. We assembled to the number of a dozen or more. Mr. Grote lent a room of his house in Thread-needle Street for the purpose, and his partner, Prescott, one of the three original members of the Utilitarian Society, made one among us. We met two mornings in every week, from half-past eight till ten, at which hour most of us were called off to our daily occupations. Our first subject was Political Economy. We chose some systematic treatise as our text-book; my father's "Elements" being our first choice. One of us read aloud a chapter, or some smaller portion of the book. The discussion was then opened, and any one who had an objection, or other remark to make, made it. Our rule was to discuss thoroughly every point raised, whether great or small, prolonging the discussion until all who took part were satisfied with the conclusion they had individually arrived at; and to follow up every topic of collateral speculation which the chapter or the conversation suggested, never leaving it until we had untied every knot which we found.

When we had enough of political economy, we took up the syllogistic logic in the same manner, Grote now joining us. From this time I formed the project of writing a book on Logic, though on a much humbler scale than the one I ultimately executed.

Having done with Logic, we launched into Analytic Psychology, and having chosen Hartley for our text-book, we raised Priestley's edition to an extravagant price by searching through London to furnish each of us with a copy. When we had finished Hartley, we suspended our meetings; but my father's Analysis of the Mind being published soon after, we reassembled for the purpose of reading it. With this our exercises ended. I have always dated from these conversations my own real inauguration as an original and independent thinker.

Our doings from 1825 to 1830 in the way of public speaking, filled a considerable place in my life during those years, and as they had important effects on my development, something ought to be said of them.

There was for some time in existence a society of Owenites, called the Coöperation Society, which met for weekly public discussions in Chancery Lane. In the early part of 1825, accident brought Roebuck in contact with several of its members, and led to his attending one or two of the meetings and taking part in the debate in opposition to Owenism. Some one of us started the notion of going there in a body and having a general battle: and Charles Austin and some of his friends who did not usually take part in our joint exercises, entered into the project. It was carried out by concert with the principal members of the Society, themselves nothing loth, as they naturally preferred a controversy with opponents to a tame discussion among their own body. The question of population was proposed as the subject of debate: Charles Austin led the case on our side with a brilliant speech, and the fight was kept up by adjournment through five or six weekly meetings before crowded auditories, including along with the members of the Society and their friends, many hearers and some speakers from the Inns of Court. When this debate was ended, another was commenced on the general merits of Owen's system: and the contest altogether lasted about three months.

The great interest of these debates predisposed some of those who took part in them, to catch at a suggestion thrown out by M'Culloch, the political economist, that a Society was wanted in London similar to the Speculative Society at Edinburgh, in which Brougham, Horner, and others first cultivated public speaking. Our experience at the Coöperative Society seemed to give cause for being sanguine as to the sort of men who might be brought together in London for such a purpose. M'Culloch mentioned the matter to several young men of influence, to whom he was then giving private lessons in political economy. Some of these entered warmly into the project, particularly George Villiers, afterwards Earl of Clarendon. He and his brothers, Hyde and Charles, Romilly, Charles Austin and I, with some others, met and agreed on a plan. We determined to meet once a fortnight from November to June, at the Freemasons' Tavern, and we had soon a fine list of members, containing, along with several members of Parliament, nearly all the most noted speakers of the Cambridge Union and of the Oxford United Debating Society. Nothing could seem more promising. But when the time for action drew near, and it was necessary to fix on a President, and find somebody to open the first debate, none of our celebrities would consent to perform either office. Of the many who were pressed on the subject, the only one who could be prevailed on was a man of whom I knew very little, but who had taken high honors at Oxford and was said to have acquired a great oratorical reputation there; who some time afterwards became a Tory member of Parliament. He accordingly was fixed on, both for filling the President's chair and for making the first speech. The important day arrived; the benches were crowded; all our great speakers were present, to judge of, but not to help our efforts. The Oxford orator's speech was a complete failure. This threw a damp on the whole concern: the speakers who followed were few, and none of them did their best: the affair was a complete *fiasco;* and the oratorical celebrities we had counted on went away never to return, giving to me at least a lesson in knowledge of the world. This unexpected breakdown altered my whole relation to the project. I had not anticipated taking a prominent part, or speaking much or often, particularly at first, but I now saw that the success of the scheme depended on the new men, and I put my shoulder to the wheel. I opened the second question, and from that time spoke in nearly every debate. It was very uphill work for some time. In the season following, 1826-7, things began to mend. Our debates were very different from those of common debating societies, for they habitually consisted of the strongest arguments and most philosophic principles which either side was able to produce, thrown often into close and *serré* confutations of one another. The practice was necessarily very useful to us, and eminently so to me. I never, indeed, acquired real fluency, and had always a bad and ungraceful delivery; but I could make myself listened to: and as I always wrote my speeches when, from the feelings involved, or the nature of the ideas to be developed, expression seemed important, I greatly increased my power of effective writing; acquiring not only an ear for smoothness and rhythm, but a practical sense for *telling* sentences, and an immediate criterion of their telling property, by their effect on a mixed audience.

The Society, and the preparation for it, together with the

preparation for the morning conversations which were going on simultaneously, occupied the greater part of my leisure; and made me feel it a relief when, in the spring of 1828, I ceased to write for the Westminster. The Review had fallen into difficulties. Though the sale of the first number had been very encouraging, the permanent sale had never, I believe, been sufficient to pay the expenses, on the scale on which the Review was carried on. Those expenses had been considerably, but not sufficiently, reduced. One of the editors, Southern, had resigned; and several of the writers, including my father and me, who had been paid like other contributors for our earlier articles, had latterly written without payment. Nevertheless, the original funds were nearly or quite exhausted, and if the Review was to be continued some new arrangement of its affairs had become indispensable. My father and I had several conferences with Bowring on the subject. We were willing to do our utmost for maintaining the Review as an organ of our opinions, but not under Bowring's editorship: while the impossibility of its any longer supporting a paid editor, afforded a ground on which, without affront to him, we could propose to dispense with his services. We and some of our friends were prepared to carry on the Review as unpaid writers, either finding among ourselves an unpaid editor, or sharing the editorship among us. But while this negotiation was proceeding with Bowring's apparent acquiescence, he was carrying on another in a different quarter (with Colonel Perronet Thompson), of which we received the first intimation in a letter from Bowring as editor, informing us merely that an arrangement had been made, and proposing to us to write for the next number, with promise of payment. We did not dispute Bowring's right to bring about, if he could, an arrangement more favorable to himself than the one we had proposed; but we thought the concealment which he had practiced towards us, while seemingly entering into our own project, an affront: and even had we not thought so, we were indisposed to expend any more of our time and trouble in attempting to write up the Review under his management. Accordingly my father excused himself from writing; though two or three years later, on great pressure, he did write one more political article. As for me, I positively refused. And thus ended my connection with the original Westminster.

CHAPTER V

A CRISIS IN MY MENTAL HISTORY. ONE STAGE ONWARD

FOR some years after this time I wrote very little, and nothing regularly, for publication: and great were the advantages which I derived from the intermission. It was of no common importance to me, at this period, to be able to digest and mature my thoughts for my own mind only, without any immediate call for giving them out in print. Had I gone on writing, it would have much disturbed the important transformation in my opinions and character, which took place during those years. The origin of this transformation, or at least the process by which I was prepared for it, can only be explained by turning some distance back.

From the winter of 1821, when I first read Bentham, and especially from the commencement of the Westminster Review, I had what might truly be called an object in life; to be a reformer of the world. My conception of my own happiness was entirely identified with this object. The personal sympathies I wished for were those of fellow laborers in this enterprise. This did very well for several years, during which the general improvement going on in the world and the idea of myself as engaged with others in struggling to promote it, seemed enough to fill up an interesting and animated existence. But the time came when I awakened from this as from a dream. It was in the autumn of 1826. I was in a dull state of nerves, such as everybody is occasionally liable to; unsusceptible to enjoyment or pleasurable excitement; one of those moods when what is pleasure at other times, becomes insipid or indifferent; the state, I should think, in which converts to Methodism usually are, when smitten by their first "conviction of sin."

At first I hoped that the cloud would pass away of itself; but it did not. A night's sleep, the sovereign remedy for the smaller vexations of life, had no effect on it. I awoke to a renewed consciousness of the woeful fact. I carried it with me into all companies, into all occupations. Hardly anything had power to cause me even a few minutes' oblivion of it. For some months the cloud seemed to grow thicker and thicker. The lines in Coleridge's "Dejection"—I was not then acquainted with them—exactly describe my case:

> "A grief without a pang, void, dark and drear,
> A drowsy, stifled, unimpassioned grief,
> Which finds no natural outlet or relief
> In word, or sigh, or tear."

In vain I sought relief from my favorite books; those memorials of past nobleness and greatness from which I had always hitherto drawn strength and animation. I read them now without feeling, or with the accustomed feeling *minus* all its charm; and I became persuaded, that my love of mankind, and of excellence for its own sake, had worn itself out. I sought no comfort by speaking to others of what I felt. If I had loved any one sufficiently to make confiding my griefs a necessity, I should not have been in the condition I was. My father, to whom it would have been natural to me to have recourse in any practical difficulties, was the last person to whom, in such a case as this, I looked for help. Everything convinced me that he had no knowledge of any such mental state as I was suffering from, and that even if he could be made to understand it, he was not the physician who could heal it. My education, which was wholly his work, had been conducted without any regard to the possibility of its ending in this result; and I saw no use in giving him the pain of thinking that his plans had failed, when the failure was probably irremediable, and, at all events, beyond the power of *his* remedies. Of other friends, I had at that time none to whom I had any hope of making my condition intelligible. It was however abundantly intelligible to myself; and the more I dwelt upon it, the more hopeless it appeared.

I was thus, as I said to myself, left stranded at the commencement of my voyage, with a well-equipped ship and a rudder, but no sail; without any real desire for the ends which I had been so carefully fitted out to work for: no delight in virtue, or the general good, but also just as little in anything else. The fountains of vanity and ambition seemed to have dried up within me, as completely as those of benevolence. I had had (as I reflected) some gratification of vanity at too early an age: I had obtained some distinction, and felt myself of some importance, before the desire of distinction and of importance had grown into a passion: and little as it was which I had attained, yet having been attained too early, like all pleasures enjoyed too soon, it had made me *blasé* and indifferent to the pursuit. Thus neither selfish nor unselfish pleasures were pleasures to me.

These were the thoughts which mingled with the dry heavy dejection of the melancholy winter of 1826-7. During this time I was not incapable of my usual occupations. I went on with them mechanically, by the mere force of habit. I had been so drilled in a certain sort of mental exercise, that I could still carry it on when all the spirit had gone out of it. I even composed and spoke several speeches at the debating society, how, or with what degree of success, I know not. Of four years continual speaking at that society, this is the only year of which I remember next to nothing. Two lines of Coleridge, in whom alone of all writers I have found a true description of what I felt, were often in my thoughts, not at this time (for I had never read them), but in a later period of the same mental malady:

> "Work without hope draws nectar in a sieve,
> And hope without an object cannot live."

I frequently asked myself, if I could, or if I was bound to go on living, when life must be passed in this manner. I generally answered to myself, that I did not think I could possibly bear it beyond a year. When, however, not more than half that duration of time had elapsed, a small ray of light broke in upon my gloom. I was reading, accidentally, Marmontel's "Memoires," and came to the passage which relates his father's death, the distressed position of the family, and the sudden inspiration by which he, then a mere boy, felt and made them feel that he would be everything to them—would supply the place of all that they had lost. A vivid conception of the scene and its feelings came over me, and I was moved to tears. From this moment my burden grew lighter. The oppression of the thought that all feeling was dead within me, was gone. I was no longer hopeless: I was not a stock or a stone. I had still, it seemed, some of the material out of which all worth of character, and all capacity for happiness, are made. Relieved from my ever present sense of irremediable wretchedness, I gradually found that the ordinary incidents of life could again give me some pleasure; that I could again find enjoyment, not intense, but sufficient for cheerfulness, in sunshine and sky, in books, in conversation, in public affairs; and that there was, once more, excitement, though of a moderate kind, in exerting myself for my opinions, and for the public good. Thus the cloud gradually drew off, and I again enjoyed life: and though I had several relapses, some of which lasted many months, I never again was as miserable as I had been.

The experiences of this period had two very marked effects on my opinions and character. In the first place, they led me to adopt a theory of life, very unlike that on which I had before acted, and having much in common with what at that time I certainly had never heard of, the anti-self-consciousness theory of Carlyle. I never, indeed, wavered in the conviction that happiness is the test of all rules of conduct, and the end of life. But I now thought that this end was only to be attained by not making it the direct end. The enjoyments of life (such was now my theory) are sufficient to make it a pleasant thing, when they are taken *en passant*, without being made a principal object. Once make them so, and they are immediately felt to be insufficient. They will not bear a scrutinizing examination. Ask yourself whether you are happy, and you cease to be so. The only chance is to treat, not happiness, but some end external to it, as the purpose of life. This theory now became the basis of my philosophy of life. And I still hold to it as the best theory for all those who have but a moderate degree of sensibility and of capacity for enjoyment, that is, for the great majority of mankind.

The other important change which my opinions at this time underwent, was that I, for the first time, gave its proper place, among the prime necessities of human well-being, to the internal culture of the individual. I ceased to attach almost exclusive importance to the ordering of outward circumstances, and the training of the human being for speculation and for action.

I now began to find meaning in the things which I had read or heard about the importance of poetry and art as instruments of human culture. But it was some time longer before I began to know this by personal experience. The only one of the imaginative arts in which I had from childhood taken great pleasure, was music; the best effect of which (and in this it surpasses perhaps every other art) consists in exciting enthusiasm; in winding up to a high pitch those feelings of an elevated kind which are already in the character, but to which this excitement gives a glow and a fervor, which, though transitory at its utmost height, is precious for sustaining them at other times. This effect of music I had often experienced; but like all my pleasurable susceptibilities it was suspended during the gloomy period. I had sought relief again and again from this quarter, but found none. After the tide had turned, and I was in process of recovery, I had been helped forward by music, but in a much less elevated manner. I at this time first became acquainted with Weber's Oberon, and the extreme pleasure which I drew from its delicious melodies did me good, by showing me a source of pleasure to which I was as susceptible as ever. The good, however, was much impaired by the thought, that the pleasure of music (as is quite true of such pleasure as this was, that of mere tune) fades with familiarity, and requires either to be revived by intermittence, or fed by continual novelty.

This state of my thoughts and feelings made the fact of my reading Wordsworth for the first time (in the autumn of 1828), an important event in my life. I took up the collection of his poems from curiosity, with no expectation of mental relief from it, though I had before resorted to poetry with that hope. In the worst period of my depression, I had read through the whole of Byron (then new to me), to try whether a poet, whose peculiar department was supposed to be that of the intenser feelings, could rouse any feeling in me. As might be expected, I got no good from this reading, but the reverse. The poet's state of mind was too like my own. His was the lament of a man who had worn out all pleasures, and who seemed to think that life, to all who possess the good things of it, must necessarily be the vapid, uninteresting thing which I found it. His Harold and Manfred had the same burden on them which I had; and I was not in a frame of mind to desire any comfort from the vehement sensual passion of his Giaours, or the sullenness of his Laras. But while Byron was exactly what did not suit my condition, Wordsworth was exactly what did. I had looked into the Excursion two or three years before, and found little in it; and I should probably have found as little, had I read it at this time. But the miscellaneous poems, in the two-volume editor of 1815 (to which little of value was added in the latter part of the author's life), proved to be the precise thing for my mental wants at that particular juncture.

In the first place, these poems addressed themselves powerfully to one of the strongest of my pleasurable susceptibilities, the love of rural objects and natural scenery; to which I had been indebted not only for much of the pleasure of my life, but quite recently for relief from one of my longest relapses into depression. In this power of rural beauty over me, there was a foundation laid for taking pleasure in Wordsworth's poetry; the more so, as his scenery lies mostly among mountains, which, owing to my early Pyrenean excursion, were my idea of natural beauty. But Wordsworth would never have had any great effect on me, if he had merely placed before me beautiful pictures of natural scenery. What made Wordsworth's poems a medicine for my state of mind, was that they expressed, not mere outward beauty, but states of feeling, and of thought colored by feeling, under the excitement of beauty. They seemed to be the very culture of the feelings, which I was in quest of. In them I seemed to draw from a source of inward joy, of sympathetic and imaginative pleasure, which could be shared in by all human beings; which had no connection with struggle or imperfection, but would be made richer by every improvement in the physical or social condition of mankind. From them I seemed to learn what would be the perennial sources of happiness, when all the greater evils of life shall have been removed. And I felt myself at once better and happier as I came under their influence. There have certainly been, even in our own age, greater poets than Wordsworth; but poetry of deeper and loftier feeling could not have done for me at that time what his did. I needed to be made to feel that there was real, permanent happiness in tranquil contemplation. Wordsworth taught me this, not only without turning away from, but with a greatly increased interest in the common feelings and common destiny of human beings. And the delight which these poems gave me, proved that with culture of this sort, there was nothing to dread from the most confirmed habit of analysis.

After 1829 I withdrew from attendance on the Debating Society. I had had enough of speech-making, and was glad to carry on my private studies and meditations without any immediate call for outward assertion of their results. I found the fabric of my old and taught opinions giving way in many fresh places, and I never allowed it to fall to pieces, but was incessantly occupied in weaving it anew. I never, in the course of my transition, was content to remain, for ever so short a time, confused and unsettled. When I had taken in any new idea, I could not rest till I had adjusted its relation to my old opinions, and ascertained exactly how far its effect ought to extend in modifying or superseding them.

The writers by whom, more than by any others, a new mode of political thinking was brought home to me, were those of the St. Simonian school in France. In 1829 and 1830 I became acquainted with some of their writings. They were then only in the earlier stages of their speculations. They had not yet dressed out their philosophy as a religion, nor had they organized their scheme of Socialism. They were just beginning to question the principle of hereditary property. I was by no means prepared to go with them even this length; but I was greatly struck with the connected view which they for the first time presented to me, of the natural order of human progress; and especially with their division of all history into organic periods and critical periods. Among their publications, too, there was one which seemed to me far superior to the rest; in which the general idea was matured into something much more definite and instructive. This was an early work of Auguste Comte, who then called himself, and even announced himself in the title-page as, a pupil of Saint Simon. In this tract M. Comte first put forth the doctrine, which he afterwards so copiously illustrated, of the natural succession of three stages in every department of human knowledge: first, the theological, next the metaphysical, and lastly, the positive stage; and contended, that social science must be subject to the same law; that the feudal and Catholic system was the concluding phasis of the theological state of the social science, Protestautism the commencement, and the doctrines of the French Revolution the consummation, of the metaphysical; and that its positive state was yet to come.

M. Comte soon left the St. Simonians, and I lost sight of him and his writings for a number of years. But the St. Simonians I continued to cultivate. I was kept *au courant* of their progress by one of their most enthusiastic disciples, M. Gustave d'Eichthal, who about that time passed a considerable interval in England. I was introduced to their chiefs, Bazard and Enfantin, in 1830; and as long as their public teachings and proselytism continued, I read nearly everything they wrote. Their criticisms on the common doctrines of Liberalism seemed to me full of important truth; and it was partly by their writings that my eyes were opened to the very limited and temporary value of the old political economy, which assumes private property and inheritance as indefeasible facts, and freedom of production and exchange as the *dernier mot* of social improvement. The scheme gradually unfolded by the St. Simonians, under which the labor and capital of society would be managed for the general account of the community, every individual being required to take a share of labor, either as thinker, teacher, artist, or producer, all being classed according to their capacity, and remunerated according to their work, appeared to me a far superior description of Socialism to Owen's. Their aim seemed to me desirable and rational, however their means might be inefficacious; and though I neither believed in the practicability, nor in the beneficial operation of their social machinery, I felt that the proclamation of such an ideal of human society could not but tend to give a beneficial direction to the efforts of others to bring society, as at present constituted, nearer to some ideal standard.

In giving an account of this period of my life, I have only specified such of my new impressions as appeared to me, both at the time and since, to be a kind of turning points, marking a definite progress in my mode of thought. But these few selected points give a very insufficient idea of the quantity of thinking which I carried on respecting a host of subjects during these years of transition. I saw that though our character is formed by circumstances, our own desires can do much to shape those circumstances; and that what is really inspiriting and ennobling in the doctrine of freewill, is the conviction that we have real power over the formation of our own character; that our will, by influencing some of our circumstances, can modify our future habits or capabilities of willing.

In this frame of mind the French Revolution of July found me. It roused my utmost enthusiasm, and gave me, as it were, a new existence. I went at once to Paris, was introduced to Lafayette, and laid the groundwork of the intercourse I afterwards kept up with several of the active chiefs of the extreme popular party. After my return I entered warmly, as a writer, into the political discussions of the time; which soon became still more exciting, by the coming in of Lord Grey's Ministry, and the proposing of the Reform Bill. For the next few years I wrote copiously in newspapers. It was about this time that Fonblanque, who had for some time written the political articles in the Examiner, became the proprietor and editor of the paper. It is not forgotten with what verve and talent, as well as fine wit, he carried it on, during the whole period of Lord Grey's Ministry, and what importance it assumed as the principal representative, in the newspaper press, of Radical opinions. The distinguishing character of the paper was given to it entirely by his own articles, which formed at least three-fourths of all the original writing contained in it: but of the remaining fourth I contributed during those years a much larger share than any one else. I wrote nearly all the articles on French subjects, including a weekly summary of French politics, often extending to considerable length; together with many leading articles on general politics, commercial and financial legislation, and any miscellaneous subjects in which I felt interested, and which were suitable to the paper, including occasional reviews of books.

It remains to speak of what I wrote during these years, which, independently of my contributions to newspapers, was considerable. In 1830 and 1831 I wrote the five Essays since published under the title of "Essays on some Unsettled Questions of Political Economy," almost as they now stand, except that in 1833 I partially rewrote the fifth Essay. They were written with no immediate purpose of publication; and when, some years later, I offered them to a publisher, he declined them. They were only printed in 1844, after the success of the "System of Logic."

In 1832 I wrote several papers for the first series of Tait's Magazine, and one for a quarterly periodical called the Jurist, which had been founded, and for a short time carried on, by a set of friends, all lawyers and law reformers, with several of whom I was acquainted. The paper in the Jurist, which I still think a very complete discussion of the rights of the State over Foundations, showed both sides of my opinions, asserting as firmly as I should have done at any time, the doctrine that all endowments are national property, which the government may and ought to control; but not, as I should once have done, condemning endowments in themselves, and proposing that they should be taken to pay off the national debt. On the contrary, I urged strenuously the importance of having a provision for education, not dependent on the mere demand of the market, that is, on the knowledge and discernment of average parents, but calculated to establish and keep up a higher standard of instruction than is likely to be spontaneously demanded by the buyers of the article. All these opinions have been confirmed and strengthened by the whole course of my subsequent reflections.

CHAPTER VI

COMMENCEMENT OF THE MOST VALUABLE FRIENDSHIP OF MY LIFE. MY FATHER'S DEATH. WRITINGS AND OTHER PROCEEDINGS UP TO 1840

IT was at the period of my mental progress which I have now reached that I formed the friendship which has been the honor and chief blessing of my existence, as well as the source of a great part of all that I have attempted to do, or hope to effect hereafter, for human improvement. My first introduction to the lady who, after a friendship of twenty years, consented to become my wife, was in 1830, when I was in my twenty-fifth and she in her twenty-third year. With her husband's family it was the renewal of an old acquaintanceship. His grandfather lived in the next house to my father's in Newington Green, and I had, sometimes when a boy, been invited to play in the old gentleman's garden. He was a fine specimen of the old Scotch Puritan; stern, severe, and powerful, but very kind to children, on whom such men make a lasting impression. Although it was years after my introduction to Mrs. Taylor before my acquaintance with her became at all intimate or confidential, I very soon felt her to be the most admirable person I had ever known. It is not to be supposed that she was, or that any one, at the age at which I first saw her, could be, all that she afterwards became. Least of all could this be true of her, with whom self-improvement, progress in the highest and in all senses, was a law of her nature; a necessity equally from the ardor with which she sought it, and from the spontaneous tendency of faculties which could not receive an impression or an experience without making it the source or the occasion of an accession of wisdom. Up to the time when I first saw her, her rich and powerful nature had chiefly unfolded itself according to the received type of feminine genius. To her outer circle she was a beauty and a wit, with an air of natural distinction, felt by all who approached her: to the inner, a woman of deep and strong feeling, of penetrating and intuitive intelligence, and of an eminently meditative and poetic nature.

Married at an early age, to a most upright, brave, and honorable man, of liberal opinions and good education, but without the intellectual or artistic tastes which would have made him a companion for her, though a steady and affectionate friend, for whom she had true esteem and the strongest affection through life, and whom she most deeply lamented when dead; shut out by the social disabilities of women from any adequate exercise of her highest faculties in action on the world without; her life was one of inward meditation, varied by familiar intercourse with a small circle of friends, of whom one only (long since deceased) was a person of genius, or of capacities of feeling or intellect kindred with her own, but all had more or less of alliance with her in sentiments and opinions. Into this circle I had the good fortune to be admitted, and I soon perceived that she possessed in combination, the qualities which in all other persons whom I had known I had been only too happy to find singly. In her, complete emancipation from every kind of superstition (including that which attributes a pretended perfection to the order of nature and the universe), and an earnest protest against many things which are still part of the established constitution of society, resulted not from the hard intellect, but from strength of noble and elevated feeling, and co-existed with a highly reverential nature. In general spiritual characteristics, as well as in temperament and organization, I have often compared her, as she was at this time, to Shelley: but in thought and intellect, Shelley, so far as his powers were developed in his short life, was but a child compared with what she ultimately became. Alike in the highest regions of speculation and in the smaller practical concerns of daily life, her mind was the same perfect instrument, piercing to the very heart and marrow of the matter; always seizing the essential idea or principle. The same exactness and rapidity of operation, pervading as it did her sensitive as well as her mental faculties, would, with her gifts of feeling and imagination, have fitted her to be a consummate artist, as her fiery and tender soul and her vigorous eloquence would certainly have made her a great orator, and her profound knowledge of human nature and discernment and sagacity in practical life, would, in the times when such a *carrière* was open to women, have made her eminent among the rulers of mankind.

Her intellectual gifts ministered to a moral character at once the noblest and the best balanced which I have ever met with in life. Her unselfishness was not that of a taught system of duties, but of a heart which thoroughly identified itself with the feelings of others, and often went to excess in consideration for them by imaginatively investing their feelings with the intensity of its own. The passion of justice might have been thought to be her strongest feeling, but for her boundless generosity, and a lovingness ever ready to pour itself forth upon any or all human beings who were capable of giving the smallest feeling in return. The rest of her moral characteristics were such as naturally accompany these qualities of mind and heart: the most genuine modesty combined with the loftiest pride; a simplicity and sincerity which were absolute, towards all who were fit to receive them; the utmost scorn of whatever was mean and cowardly, and a burning indignation at everything brutal or tyrannical, faithless or dishonorable in conduct and character, while making the broadest distinction between *mala in se* and mere *mala prohibita*—between acts giving evidence of intrinsic badness in feeling and character, and those which are only violations of conventions either good or bad, violations which whether in themselves right or wrong, are capable of being committed by persons in every other respect lovable or admirable.

To be admitted into any degree of mental intercourse with a being of these qualities, could not but have a most beneficial influence on my development; though the effect was only gradual, and many years elapsed before her mental progress and mine went forward in the complete companionship they at last attained. The benefit I received was far greater than any which I could hope to give; though to her, who had at first reached her opinions by the moral intuition of a character of strong feeling, there was doubtless help as well as encouragement to be derived from one who had arrived at many of the same results by study and reasoning: and in the rapidity of her intellectual growth, her mental activity, which converted everything into knowledge, doubtless drew from me, as it did from other sources, many of its materials. I have often received praise, which in my own right I only partially deserve, for the greater practicality which is supposed to be found in my writings, compared with those of most thinkers who have been equally addicted to large generalizations. The writings in which this quality has been observed, were not the work of one mind, but of the fusion of two, one of them as preëminently practical in its judgments and perceptions of things present, as it was high and bold in its anticipations for a remote futurity.

One of the projects occasionally talked of between my father and me, and some of the parliamentary and other Radicals who frequented his house, was the foundation of a periodical organ of philosophic radicalism, to take the place which the Westminster Review had been intended to fill: and the scheme had gone so far as to bring under discussion the pecuniary contributions which could be looked for, and the choice of an editor. Nothing, however, came of it for some time: but in the summer of 1834 Sir William Molesworth, himself a laborious student, and a precise and metaphysical thinker, capable of aiding the cause by his pen as well as by his purse, spontaneously proposed to establish a Review, provided I would consent to be the real, if I could not be the ostensible, editor. Such a proposal was not to be refused; and the Review was founded, at first under the title of the London Review, and afterwards under that of the London and Westminster, Molesworth having bought the Westminster from its proprietor, General Thompson, and merged the two into one. In the years between 1834 and 1840 the conduct of this Review occupied the greater part of my spare time. In the beginning, it did not, as a whole, by any means represent my opinions. I was under the necessity of conceding much to my inevitable associates. The Review was established to be the representative of the "philosophic Radicals," with most of whom I was now at issue on many essential points, and among whom I could not even claim to be the most important individual. My father's coöperation as a writer we all deemed indispensable, and he wrote largely in it until prevented by his last illness. The subjects of his articles, and the strength and decision with which his opinions were expressed in them, made the Review at first derive its tone and coloring from him much more than from any of the other writers. I could not exercise editorial control over his articles, and I was sometimes obliged to sacrifice to him portions of my own.

All speculation, however, on the possible future developments of my father's opinions, and on the probabilities of permanent coöperation between him and me in the promulgation of our thoughts, was doomed to be cut short. During the whole of 1835 his health had been declining: his symptoms became unequivocally those of pulmonary consumption, and after lingering to the last stage of debility, he died on the 23rd of June, 1836. Until the last few days of his life there was no apparent abatement of intellectual vigor; his interest in all things and persons that had interested him through life was undiminished, nor did the approach of death cause the smallest wavering (as in so strong and firm a mind it was impossible that it should) in his convictions on the subject of religion. His principal satisfaction, after he knew that his end was near, seemed to be the thought of what he had done to make the world better than he found it; and his chief regret in not living longer, that he had not had time to do more.

In the power of influencing by mere force of mind and character, the convictions and purposes of others, and in the strenuous exertion of that power to promote freedom and progress, he left, as my knowledge extends, no equal among men and but one among women.

In the year 1837, I resumed the Logic. I had not touched my pen on the subject for five years, having been stopped and brought to a halt on the threshold of Induction. I had gradually discovered that what was mainly wanting, to overcome the difficulties of that branch of the subject, was a comprehensive, and, at the same time, accurate view of the whole circle of physical science, which I feared it would take me a long course of study to acquire; since I knew not of any book, or other guide, that would spread out before me the generalities and processes of the sciences, and I apprehended that I should have no choice but to extract them for myself, as I best could, from the details. Happily for me, Dr. Whewell, early in this year, published his History of the Inductive Sciences. I read it with eagerness, and found in it a considerable approximation to what I wanted. I now set myself vigorously to work out the subject in thought and in writing. The time I bestowed on this had to be stolen from occupations more urgent. I had just two months to spare, at this period, in the intervals of·writing for the Review. In these two months I completed the first draft of about a third, the most difficult third, of the book. What I had before written, I estimate at another third, so that only one-third remained. What I wrote at this time consisted of the remainder of the doctrine of Reasoning (the theory of Trains of Reasoning, and Demonstrative Science), and the greater part of the Book on Induction. When this was done, I had, as it seemed to me, untied all the really hard knots, and the completion of the book had become only a question of time. Having got thus far, I had to leave off in order to write two articles for the next number of the Review. When these were written, I returned to the subject, and now for the first time fell in with Comte's Cour de Philosophie Positive, or rather with the two volumes of it which were all that had at that time been published.

My theory of Induction was substantially completed before I knew of Comte's book; and it is perhaps well that I came to it by a different road from his, since the consequence has been that my treatise contains, what his certainly does not, a reduction of the inductive process to strict rules and to a scientific test, such as the syllogism is for ratiocination. Comte is always precise and profound on the method of investigation, but he does not even attempt any exact definition of the conditions of proof: and his writings show that he never attained a just conception of them. This, however, was specifically the problem which, in treating of Induction, I had proposed to myself. Nevertheless, I gained much from Comte, with which to enrich my chapters in the subsequent rewriting: and his book was of essential service to me in some of the parts which still remained to be thought out.

I had been long an ardent admirer of Comte's writings before I had any communication with himself; nor did I ever, to the last, see him in the body. But for some years we were frequent correspondents, until our correspondence became controversial, and our zeal cooled. I was the first to slacken correspondence; he was the first to drop it. I found, and he probably found likewise, that I could do no good to his mind, and that all the good he could do to mine, he did by his books.

To return to myself. The Review engrossed, for some time longer, nearly all the time I could devote to authorship, or to thinking with authorship in view. The articles from the London and Westminster Review which are reprinted in the

"Dissertations," are scarcely a fourth part of those I wrote.

In the spring of 1840 I made over the Review to Mr. Hickson, who had been a frequent and very useful unpaid contributor under my management: only stipulating that the change should be marked by a resumption of the old name, that of Westminster Review. Under that name Mr. Hickson conducted it for ten years, on the plan of dividing among contributors only the net proceeds of the Review, giving his own labor as writer and editor gratuitously. I did not cease altogether to write for the Review, but continued to send it occasional contributions, not, however, exclusively; for the greater circulation of the Edinburgh Review induced me from this time to offer articles to it also when I had anything to say for which it appeared to be a suitable vehicle.

CHAPTER VII

GENERAL VIEW OF THE REMAINDER OF MY LIFE

FROM this time, what is worth relating of my life will come into a very small compass; for I have no further mental changes to tell of, but only, as I hope, a continued mental progress; which does not admit of a consecutive history, and the results of which, if real, will be best found in my writings. I shall, therefore, greatly abridge the chronicle of my subsequent years.

The first use I made of the leisure which I gained by disconnecting myself from the Review, was to finish the Logic. In July and August, 1838, I had found an interval in which to execute what was still undone of the original draft of the Third Book. The Book on Language and Classification, and the chapter on the Classification of Fallacies, were drafted in the autumn of the same year; the remainder of the work, in the summer and autumn of 1840. From April following, to the end of 1841, my spare time was devoted to a complete rewriting of the book from its commencement. It is in this way that all my books have been composed. In my own case, moreover, I have found that the patience necessary for a careful elaboration of the details of composition and expression, costs much less effort after the entire subject has been once gone through, and the substance of all that I find to say has in some manner, however imperfect, been got upon paper. The only thing which I am careful, in the first draft, to make as perfect as I am able, is the arrangement.

During the re-writing of the Logic, Dr. Whewell's Philosophy of the Inductive Sciences made its appearance; a circumstance fortunate for me, as it gave me what I greatly desired, a full treatment of the subject by an antagonist, and enabled me to present my ideas with greater clearness and emphasis as well as fuller and more varied development, in defending them against definite objections, or confronting them distinctly with an opposite theory. The controversies with Dr. Whewell, as well as much matter derived from Comte, were first introduced into the book in the course of the re-writing.

At the end of 1841, the book being ready for the press, I offered it to Murray, who kept it until too late for publication that season, and then refused it, for reasons which could just as well have been given at first. But I have had no cause to regret a rejection which led to my offering it to Mr. Parker, by whom it was published in the spring of 1843. My original expectations of success were extremely limited. What hopes I had of exciting any immediate attention, were mainly grounded on the polemical propensities of Dr. Whewell; who, I thought, from observation of his conduct in other cases, would probably do something to bring the book into notice, by replying, and that promptly, to the attack on his opinions. He did reply, but not till 1850, just in time for me to answer him in the third edition. How the book came to have, for a work of the kind, so much success, and what sort of persons compose the bulk of those who have bought, I will not venture to say read, it, I have never thoroughly understood. But taken in conjunction with the many proofs which have since been given of a revival of speculation, speculation too of a free kind, in many quarters, and above all (where at one time I should have least expected it) in the Universities, the fact becomes partially intelligible.

Being now released from any active concern in temporary politics, and from any literary occupation involving personal communication with contributors and others, I was enabled to indulge the inclination, natural to thinking persons when the age of boyish vanity is once past, for limiting my own society to a very few persons. A person of high intellect should never go into unintellectual society unless he can enter it as an apostle; yet he is the only person with high objects who can safely enter it at all. Persons even of intellectual aspirations had much better, if they can, make their habitual associates of at least their equals, and, as far as possible, their superiors, in knowledge, intellect, and elevation of sentiment. All these circumstances united, made the number very small of those whose society, and still more whose intimacy, I now voluntarily sought.

Among these, the principal was the incomparable friend of whom I have already spoken. At this period she lived mostly with one young daughter, in a quiet part of the country, and only occasionally in town, with her first husband, Mr. Taylor. I visited her equally in both places; and was greatly indebted to the strength of character which enabled her to disregard the false interpretations liable to be put on the frequency of my visits to her while living generally apart from Mr. Taylor, and on our occasionally traveling together, though in all other respects our conduct during those years gave not the slightest ground for any other supposition than the true one, that our relation to each other at that time was one of strong affection and confidential intimacy only. For though we did not consider the ordinances of society binding on a subject so entirely personal, we did feel bound that our conduct should be such as in no degree to bring discredit on her husband, nor therefore on herself.

The Political Economy was far more rapidly executed than the Logic, or indeed than anything of importance which I had previously written. It was commenced in the autumn of 1845, and was ready for the press before the end of 1847. In this period of little more than two years there was an interval of six months during which the work was laid aside, while I was writing articles in the Morning Chronicle (which unexpectedly entered warmly into my purpose) urging the formation of peasant properties on the waste lands of Ireland. This was during the period of the Famine, the winter of 1846-47, when the stern necessities of the time seemed to afford a chance of gaining attention for what appeared to me the only mode of combining relief to immediate destitution with permanent improvement of the social and economical condition of the Irish people. But the idea was new and strange; there was no English precedent for such a proceeding: and the profound ignorance of English politicians and the English public concerning all social phenomena not generally met with in England (however common elsewhere), made my endeavors an entire failure.

The rapid success of the Political Economy showed that the public wanted, and were prepared for such a book. Published early in 1848, an edition of a thousand copies was sold in less than a year. Another similar edition was published in the spring of 1849; and a third, of 1250 copies, early in 1852. It was, from the first, continually cited and referred to as an authority, because it was not a book merely of abstract science, but also of application, and treated Political Economy not as a thing by itself, but as a fragment of a greater whole; a branch of Social Philosophy, so interlinked with all the other branches, that its conclusions, even in its own peculiar province, are only true conditionally, subject to interference and counteraction from causes not directly within its scope: while to the character of a practical guide it has no pretension, apart from other classes of considerations. The amount of its worth as an exposition of the science, and the value of the different applications which it suggests, others of course must judge.

For a considerable time after this, I published no work of magnitude; though I still occasionally wrote in periodicals, and my correspondence (much of it with persons quite unknown to me), on subjects of public interest, swelled to a considerable bulk. I continued to watch with keen interest the progress of public events. But it was not, on the whole, very encouraging to me. The European reaction after 1848, and the success of an unprincipled usurper in December, 1851, put an end, as it seemed, to all present hope of freedom or social improvement in France and the Continent. In England, I had seen and continued to see many of the opinions of my youth obtain general recognition, and many of the reforms in institutions, for which I had through life contended, either effected or in course of being so. But these changes had been attended with much less benefit to human well-being than I should formerly have anticipated, because they had produced very little improvement in that which all real amelioration in the lot of mankind depends on, their intellectual and moral state: and it might even be questioned if the various causes of deterioration which had been at work in the meanwhile, had not more than counterbalanced the tendencies to improvement.

Between the time of which I have now spoken, and the present, took place the most important events of my private life. The first of these was my marriage, in April, 1851, to the lady whose incomparable worth had made her friendship the greatest source to me both of happiness and of improvement, during many years in which we never expected to be in any closer relation to one another. Ardently as I should have aspired to this complete union of our lives at any time in the course of my existence at which it had been practicable, I, as much as my wife, would far rather have foregone that privilege forever, than have owed it to the premature death of one for whom I had the sincerest respect, and she the strongest affection. That event, however, having taken place in July, 1849, it was granted to me to derive from that evil my own greatest good, by adding to the partnership of thought, feeling, and writing which had long existed, a partnership of our entire existence. For seven and a-half years that blessing was mine; for seven and a-half only! I can say nothing which could describe, even in the faintest manner, what that loss was and is. But because I know that she would have wished it, I endeavor to make the best of what life I have left, and to work on for her purposes with such diminished strength as can be derived from thoughts of her, and communion with her memory.

[The remaining sections of the autobiography deal chiefly with the writer's parliamentary career and contain but little personal matter.]

THE END

HENRY WADSWORTH LONGFELLOW

THE FOREMOST OF AMERICAN POETS

1807-1882

(INTRODUCTORY NOTE)

Longfellow's life is too well known to need introduction. He wrote no autobiography, but his letters, his diary and even his poems themselves have frequent autobiographical touches. Most valuable in this respect is the manly letter which he wrote to his father at the age of seventeen, mapping out for himself his future career. Of interest also are his comments on his work of teaching and translating, and on the coming of old age. Longfellow was so wholly and earnestly a poet that every other class of work stirred him to something like impatience.

His private life, so far as a knowledge of it is needed to understand the letters and the man, included a well-to-do childhood home in Maine, and an excellent college education in which he so distinguished himself in literary studies that the trustees of his college sent him abroad to study in Europe and qualify himself for the professorship of Foreign Languages and Literature. He traveled much and wrote both prose and poetry suggested by his journeying. Two of his prose works of travel, "Outre Mer" and "Hyperion," have a distinct autobiographical flavor. In 1836 he was made professor of Modern Languages and Literature at Harvard, and passed there the greater portion of his life, the recognized poet-laureate of the American people.

LETTER FROM LONGFELLOW TO HIS FATHER AS TO A FUTURE CAREER

December 5, 1824.

I TAKE this early opportunity to write to you, because I wish to know fully your inclination with regard to the profession I am to pursue when I leave college.

For my part, I have already hinted to you what would best please me. I want to spend one year at Cambridge for the purpose of reading history, and of becoming familiar with the best authors in polite literature; whilst at the same time I can be acquiring a knowledge of the Italian language, without an acquaintance with which I shall be shut out from one of the most beautiful departments of letters. The French I mean to understand pretty thoroughly before I leave college. After leaving Cambridge I would attach myself to some literary periodical publication, by which I could maintain myself and still enjoy the advantages of reading. Now, I do not think that there is anything visionary or chimerical in my plan thus far. The fact is—and I will not disguise it in the least, for I ought not—I most eagerly aspire after future eminence in literature; my whole soul burns most ardently for it, and every earthly thought centers in it. There may be something visionary in *this,* but I flatter myself that I have prudence enough to keep my enthusiasm from defeating its own object by too great haste. Surely, there never was a better opportunity offered for the exertion of literary talent in our own country than is now offered. To be sure, most of our literary men thus far have not been professedly so, until they have studied and entered the practice of Theology, Law, or Medicine. But this is evidently lost time. I do believe that we ought to pay more attention to the opinion of philosophers, that "nothing but Nature can qualify a man for knowledge."

Whether Nature has given me any capacity for knowledge or not, she has at any rate given me a very strong predilection for literary pursuits, and I am almost confident in believing, that, if I can ever rise in the world, it must be by the exercise of my talent in the wide field of literature. With such a belief, I must say that I am unwilling to engage in the study of the law.

Here, then, seems to be the starting point: and I think it best to float out into the world upon that tide and in that channel which will the soonest bring me to my destined port, and not to struggle against both wind and tide and by attempting what is impossible lose everything.

A COMMENT ON THE LABOR OF TEACHING, FROM LONGFELLOW'S DIARY

APRIL 3, 1848.—It seems like folly to record the college days —the working in the crypts of life, the underground labor.

Pardon me, O ye souls, who seeing education only from afar, speak of it in such glowing words! You see only the great pictures hanging in the light; not the grinding of the paint and oil, nor the pulling of hair from the camel's back for the brushes.

A LETTER TO MR. NEAL, WHO HAD PRAISED LONGFELLOW'S TRANSLATION OF DANTE

August 2, 1867.

I HAD the pleasure of receiving your letter yesterday, and am very happy to get your hearty approval of my attempt to tell the exact truth of Dante. A great many people think that a translation ought not to be too faithful; that the writer should put *himself* into it as well as his original; that it should be Homer and Co., or Dante and Co.; and that what the foreign author really says should be falsified or modified, if thereby the smoothness of the verse can be improved. On the contrary I maintain—and am delighted that you agree with me—that a translator, like a witness on the stand, should hold up his right hand and swear to "tell the truth, the whole truth, and nothing but the truth." You, who all your life long have been fighting for the truth in all things, without fear or favor, could not, I am sure, think otherwise.

A LETTER TO MR. GREENE, ON RETURNING TO COLLEGE WORK

September, 16, 1870.

WE returned yesterday from Nahant all in good condition, sailing up the harbor in a yacht in the lovely September day. Entering the old house again was like coming back from Europe. I had a kind of dazed feeling, a kind of familiar unfamiliar sense of place. But in the evening one of my most intimate bores came in, saying, "I did not know that you had got back, but thought I would come up and see." So he came up and saw, and—I knew that I was in Cambridge.

This fact was still further confirmed to-day; for immediately after breakfast came one of my crazy women, and I had no sooner disposed of her than there appeared another bore, who occasionally frequents these forests—huge, Hyrcanian, hopeless! There can be no doubt of the fact, I am certainly in Cambridge.

While I **was** writing the last line an Irishwoman called with a petition to the Governor to pardon her son, in prison for theft, "that he may become what he is capable of being,— an honor to his family and the community."

A LETTER TO GEORGE W. CHILDS, ON REACHING THE AGE OF SEVENTY YEARS

March 13, 1877.

You do not know yet what it is to be seventy years old. I will tell you, so that you may not be taken by surprise when your turn comes. It is like climbing the Alps. You reach a snow-crowned summit, and see behind you the deep valley stretching miles and miles away, and before you other summits higher and whiter, which you may have strength to climb, or may not. Then you sit down and meditate and wonder which it will be. That is the whole story, amplify it as you may. All that one can say is that life is opportunity.

THE END

AUTOBIOGRAPHIES IN THE UNIVERSITY LIBRARY

AUTOBIOGRAPHIES IN THE LIBRARY

Lightning Source UK Ltd.
Milton Keynes UK
UKHW010937180119
335792UK00009B/470/P